PRAISE FOR T
ALCHEMIST MYSTERIES

"Pandian launches a supernatural cozy series that hits high marks for a modern twist on an ancient practice. Amusing supporting characters and historical details solidify this engaging mystery."
—*Library Journal*

"Pandian sets this series apart from other paranormal mysteries with Zoe's cute nonhuman sidekick and some mouthwatering vegan recipes." —*Publishers Weekly*

"This new series is off to an excellent start with an intriguing, eccentric amateur detective... This reviewer is eagerly anticipating more from this series, and a return of a cast more fun than an episode of Portlandia." —*RT Book Reviews*

"Zoe and Dorian are my new favorite amateur-sleuth duo!"
—Victoria Laurie, *New York Times* bestselling author

"*The Accidental Alchemist* is a recipe for a great read. Gigi Pandian's pen never disappoints." —Juliet Blackwell, *New York Times* bestselling author of the Witchcraft Mystery Series

"Mysterious, captivating, and infused with the rich history of the Northwest... fantastic." —*Portland Book Review*

"Readers won't want to put this book down." —*Vegetarian Journal*

THE ACCIDENTAL ALCHEMIST MYSTERIES

BOOKS 1-3

GIGI PANDIAN

GARGOYLE GIRL PRODUCTIONS

CONTENTS

THE ACCIDENTAL ALCHEMIST

BOOK 1

CHAPTER 1

The once-beautiful Craftsman house was falling apart. Sloppily applied sections of wood covered several windows. A chunk of the roof was missing, a plastic tarp in its place to keep out the frequent Pacific Northwest rains. More exposed wall than lavender paint showed on the outer walls. And on the inside? Well, let's just say that the plumbing had seen better days—and I'm pretty sure those better days weren't any time during the previous century.

In other words: *perfect.*

At least, it was perfect for what I had in mind. I smiled as I looked at the rundown structure through the window of my trailer. Finding this house in the artsy Hawthorne neighborhood of Portland, Oregon hadn't been easy. Real estate agents had a difficult time grasping the fact that I wanted a house in complete disrepair.

It was probably my own fault, because I didn't lie to them. I told them I wasn't a professional home renovator. Nor was I a house flipper. No, I wasn't a masochist either. But I left it at that, letting them think I was a single young woman with trendy dyed-white hair and a limited budget who loved a challenge. I didn't tell them I was someone who needed a residence where doing substantial construction wouldn't raise eyebrows—that I was someone who wanted to hide in plain sight.

As soon as I'd seen the listing that a peppy young real estate agent emailed me with a healthy dose of skepticism and at least a dozen exclamation points, I knew this was the perfect house for me. I'd even found the perfect contractor, who'd come highly recommended by the real estate agent for being discreet.

The contractor wanted me on-site to make sure he was correctly executing my unique instructions, which is how I found myself moving into my new home during a furious winter storm, the day before he promised to begin work. I love the rain, but I love it most when I'm inside the warm, cozy trailer where I've lived for years, listening to the rhythmic sound of the rain tapping on the roof.

Inside the silver Airstream trailer, I bundled my coat around me and scooped up a bag of a few essentials before running the few yards to the house. Not that there was much more to move inside. I was born and raised in Massachusetts, but I'd been living out of that old trailer for a long time. Half the space in the trailer was taken up with the trinkets I sold at flea markets across the country. Most of the antique wares I'd accumulated over the years were in storage. I was waiting for a shipping company to deliver them that afternoon.

I hung my silver raincoat on a rusty hook next to the front door, then carried the bag to the kitchen. It contained my blender, a kettle and mug, a few jars of dried herbs, raw chocolate, and a bag of produce and nuts from a hearty farmer who braved the rains at the farmers market. Like I said: essentials.

The water from the kitchen's mid-century faucet ran a yellowish-brown color, but I wasn't deterred. A small sip of the water assured me it was only rust. A little extra iron would do me good. Still, I let the water run for a few minutes while I poked around the kitchen. Though it was in desperate need of cosmetic upgrades, its bones were solid. The vintage porcelain stove was functional, and it would be beautiful after a little cleaning. The pink fridge was one of the models popular in the 1950s that looked like it could have withstood a bomb blast. The best part was the window box above the sink, perfect for growing delicate herbs. My blender didn't explode when I plugged it into a socket, which was a good sign. I made a green smoothie with fresh leafy greens, an apple, avocado, mint, chocolate, and ginger.

Energizing drink in hand, I was ready to explore my new house. I'd toured it already, but that was different. Now it was *real*. A home I could make my own. I couldn't remember the last time I'd allowed myself to feel so optimistic. I was almost hopeful. Almost.

I shook out the faded curtains that covered the tall living room windows. Branches of unpruned cherry trees scraped against the windows like claws.

The trees would need to be trimmed, but not too much—I liked the privacy they granted.

Floorboards creaked underfoot as I made my way up the stairs. Before I reached the second floor, a honk that played the opening notes of Beethoven's Fifth Symphony alerted me to the movers' presence. You've gotta love movers who enjoy the little things in life—and who don't ask questions about the items they're delivering. In addition to the furniture for the house and the antiques I sold online, the crates contained glass jars I didn't want anyone looking at too closely.

Within an hour, the efficient father-son team had carried the heavy furniture and crates inside, and I'd made us all a pot of mint tea with a hint of licorice. I had to scrounge up two additional mugs from my trailer; I'm not used to entertaining.

After the movers departed, I sank into the green velvet couch that had been in storage for years, enjoying the sound of the rain. The respite didn't last long. As soon as I pried open one of the crates, I knew something was wrong. *Someone had tampered with my shipping crates.*

It was the smell that hit me first. A metallic scent assaulted my senses. With the crowbar still in my hand, I examined the mess. The glass and copper antiques that had been carefully wrapped in old newspapers were now exposed. This wasn't the type of chaos that could have been created by a turbulent flight, or even damage that would have resulted from the crate being tipped on its side or placed upside down. Taking a closer look, I saw that not only had the contents been unwrapped, but the lids from several glass jars had been sloppily resealed. That's where the metallic fragrance was coming from. There could be no doubt that someone had rifled through the contents.

The strange thing was, nothing seemed to be missing. Even the jar containing a small amount of gold was there. Instead, as I removed the glassware and pushed aside the tangle of newspaper padding, I saw that something had been *added.*

A three-foot stone gargoyle stared up at me from the wreckage that used to be carefully organized antique alchemy artifacts.

Instinctively, I stepped backward. How had this statue been added to my sealed crate? And why on earth would someone do so?

I ran out the front door, but the movers had already departed. The porch sagged beneath my feet and the rickety front door banged shut behind me in the strong wind. When I turned the door handle to let myself back inside, the brass knob came off in my hand. *Be careful what you wish for, Zoe Faust.*

Thankfully, a strong shove was all the door needed to open. Back inside my new home, I returned to the crate for a closer look. The gargoyle reminded me of the stone carvings on Notre Dame in Paris. The gray creature looked similar to the famous "thinker" gargoyle, with short horns and folded wings. The main difference was that this gargoyle held an old, leather-bound book in his arms. That was odd. I would have expected any added detail to be made of stone, not this real book with leather binding. I couldn't place the type of stone used to carve the gargoyle. Granite? Sandstone? Or perhaps softer soapstone? It wasn't like any stone I'd seen. I leaned in for a closer look. There was something...

The gargoyle blinked.

My fist tensed around the crowbar. I stumbled backward, falling into the large couch.

Sprawled out on the couch, I laughed at myself. I'd seen a fair share of magic shows in my time. I knew what this gargoyle was. He was something that had been a popular attraction over a century ago: an automaton.

"You're the best-looking automaton I've ever seen," I said.

The gargoyle's shoulders moved, as if it was stretching. It was a wonderfully constructed piece. It must have been programmed to awaken when light shone on him. A good trick for the stage.

"I am no automaton," a deep voice emanating from the automaton said. He —for his voice assured me he was male—climbed out of the crate onto the hardwood floor.

I gasped and fell off the edge of the couch. *Ouch.*

I'd seen ingenious automatons created by stage magicians. None were as advanced as this one. If I were to believe my eyes, I would have sworn he was alive. But then again, technology had progressed since automatons were popular in stage shows of the 1800s. A famous example of an early automaton was The Turk, a chess-playing machine that drew huge crowds to watch him play chess against famous chess players. Automatons were a combination of technical wizardry and stage showmanship, and the most famous automatons were aided by human helpers. There was no way a person was inside the crate with this creature, so he had to be completely mechanized.

"Where are my manners?" the creature said, bowing before me. "I did not mean to startle you. Allow me to introduce myself. I am Dorian Robert-Houdin." He spoke in English with a thick French accent.

I pulled myself together and stood up. "Either I'm going crazy, or your creator had a mischievous sense of humor. Incorporating a recording of his voice—"

I broke off when the gargoyle who called himself Dorian Robert-Houdin blinked at me again. The effect was quite disconcerting. His eyelids looked like granite, but the eyes themselves were a liquidy black substance.

"I assure you," he said, "I am not a robotic automaton, nor are you going crazy."

Most people would have run screaming from the room if they saw a walking, talking gargoyle emerge from their storage crate. I admit I was surprised, but I've seen many things in my lifetime. I stood my ground and took a closer look at the creature, trying to find evidence he was an incredibly advanced robot. I didn't see any. All I saw before me was a creature that looked every bit as alive as I was. It wasn't only the wrinkles in his gray skin and the absence of visible mechanized parts—it was the spirit that showed in his eyes.

Through my shock and confusion, another emotion poked through: disappointment. It was a feeling I knew well. Portland was supposed to be my chance at a normal life. I'd been traveling for far too long. Running. I was tired. Ready to settle down. My trailer had been my sanctuary for years as I crisscrossed the country, never staying in one place for too long. But when I'd passed through Portland the previous year, the city spoke to me. It had all the elements I cared about. Plentiful greenery, an ancient river, vibrant weather, and most of all, welcoming people—many of whom I felt might be kindred spirits. Feeling instantly at home in Portland had struck me as too good to be true. Maybe it was. This was the last place on earth I expected to find a creature that wasn't supposed to exist.

"Surely you know what I am," the gargoyle continued,

"*Alchemist.*"

The word hit me more forcefully than a slap.

Did I mention that when I was born in Massachusetts, it was 1676? I've been around for a while. But even my many years hadn't prepared me for what I'd find in Portland.

CHAPTER 2

Being an alchemist isn't as glamorous as it sounds. Turning lead into gold? It's a laborious, utterly draining process that's incredibly difficult to replicate. Living a longer life? Not without unpleasant consequences, such as outliving everyone you love and feeling the effects of years of unhealthy living.

Alchemy means different things to different people, but at its core it's about transformation that strives to achieve perfection. It's a personal journey that involves transforming yourself as you transform plants or metals. Finding the philosopher's stone to create gold and the Elixir of Life to live forever are the most famous goals of alchemists, but those are only two parts of a much greater whole.

It's a lonely life. Because there are so few of us who have succeeded in realizing alchemy's true potential, and because we've seen what has befallen alchemists over the centuries, we're forced to keep the extent of our alchemical transformations a secret.

It's not as bad as it was during the Salem Witch Trials, when misunderstandings had consequences much worse than hateful comments on Facebook. Society has come a long way since then, but people are still afraid of what they don't understand. The people I've met in my travels love that I can use herbs to create healthful elixirs that heal what ails them or sell them a decorative alchemical relic. But tell them about my deeper connection to plants, my ability to detect poisons, and the fact that I first did so over three hundred years ago? They'll get as far away from me as possible and probably call a psychiatrist. I've learned not to tell people the whole truth. It's better for everyone. That's why I was doubly disconcerted to have a living gargoyle standing in my new home announcing who I really was.

The creature's eyes followed me as I took a few slow steps backward and leaned against the wall, steadying my trembling legs.

"How do you know me?" I asked. "Why do you say I'm an alchemist?"

Dorian bowed again. This time his wings widened as he did so. They, too, looked visually like stone, but moved like the wings of a bird or a bat.

The rain had stopped, at least for the moment, but a strong breeze outside rustled the branches of the trees in the front yard and they again brushed against the living room windows. Standing in the shadow of the crate, Dorian cocked his head and looked at the windows, his eyes narrowed.

"You will draw the curtains," Dorian said. "Then we may speak more freely."

I kept the creature in view as I stood up to close the musty curtains. Part of me thought he'd disappear if I let him out of my sight.

"There is no need to pretend with me," he said. "Besides, you give yourself away, Alchemist. You seem rather unsurprised to find a living gargoyle in your luggage."

"You don't call falling off the couch surprised?"

"You are sitting here speaking with me," he said. "That is more than most people would do if they saw me."

"You lucked out and hid in the crate of an open-minded person."

The gargoyle rolled his eyes. Apparently it was a universal way to express exasperation. Or maybe I really was going crazy.

"Zoe," he said. "I knew your apothecary shop, Elixir, in Paris."

"My grandmother's shop?" Maybe that explained things. Well, as much as things could be explained with a talking gargoyle in one's living room. "I've got a great collection of historical alchemical supplies she left me, as you must have seen from rooting through my shipping crate. I sell things like these antiques to make a living."

"*Mon dieu*," Dorian said. "I know that you are the same person as the young woman from a century ago you claim was your grandmother."

"That's ridiculous," I said, hoping my shaking voice didn't betray me.

"If you are not going to trust that your secret is safe with me, at least you can feed me. Do you have any food? *J'ai faim.* That crate was in transit for much longer than I imagined it would be. I apologize that this is why I searched through your belongings. I was hoping to find something to eat."

"You *eat food?*"

"But of course."

Something about the gargoyle saying how hungry he was made me realize the absurdity of the situation. I glanced around the expansive living and dining room, empty except for shipping crates, a green velvet couch, a mango wood coffee table, and a oak dining table with chairs. I half-expected a Frenchman with a remote control to jump out from behind the couch and tell me this was a practical joke for a reality TV show.

"What are you?" I asked. The gargoyle was even larger that I'd originally thought. He stood three-and-a-half feet tall, two feet shorter than my five-foot-six frame, and looked every bit as real as I did.

"I would think that was evident," he said. "*Je suis un gargouille*—a gargoyle. As I said, my name is Dorian. I am no less alive than you."

The hilarity I felt a moment before drained from my body, replaced by fear.

"You're a homunculus," I whispered. I no longer cared about what I said in front of the creature, even if it meant admitting I was a practicing alchemist. Keeping my secret was now the least of my problems. Having such a creature in my home was far more dangerous than the most advanced robot—because he had a mind that was controlled from afar. A homunculus could not be deactivated or killed by anyone besides the person who created him.

There were rumors of alchemists who had succeeded in creating a homunculus—a living being created out of an inanimate object— but none of the rumors had ever been proven true. They were either stories told by men who wanted to appear more powerful than they really were, or legends created to make people fear alchemists. It couldn't be…

"My father did not think so," he said casually, as if this was a normal conversation.

"Your *father?*"

"The man who raised me and cared for me. That is what one calls a father, no?"

"Yes, but how—"

"There is much to tell, but I am hungry," he whined.

"But why are you here in the first place?" I asked. "What were you doing in my moving crate?"

"You visited Paris so briefly," Dorian Robert-Houdin answered, looking up at me. "You were there only to pack up your storage unit. That did not leave me time to speak with you about my book." He held up the antique book clutched in his clawed hands. "I assure you I am no homunculus. I have a mind of my own, you see. You have nothing to fear."

Though I wasn't sure how much better it made me feel to know that he had a mind of his own, I didn't have time to give the matter more thought. A crash sounded from the direction of the kitchen. The swinging door burst open and a scrawny boy fell to the floor.

Dorian's black liquid eyes bulged and he scampered back inside his crate.

Sprawled on the hardwood floor was a boy who looked about thirteen or fourteen years old. Curly black hair stuck to the sides of his face, messy from the earlier rain. He met my gaze as he pushed himself up. His hazel eyes resembled those of a cornered animal— defiance masking fear.

Instead of anger at the realization that he'd been spying on us from behind the swinging kitchen door, my first thought was concern. A large streak of blood covered the boy's forearm.

"You're hurt," I said.

"I'm fine," he stammered, his voice breaking as he held his bleeding arm.

"Let me get something to bandage that. Then you can tell me why you were *in my house* eavesdropping—"

"I'm fine," he repeated, "and I didn't see anything." He stood still for a second longer, then bolted back toward the swinging kitchen door.

He was fast, but Dorian was faster. The gargoyle jumped out of his crate and grabbed the boy's leg.

"Don't hurt me!" The boy tried to shake free of Dorian's grasp, but the little creature was strong.

"*Mon dieu*," Dorian said. "We are not going to hurt you. But you must give us your word of honor you will not speak of what you saw."

"I swear I won't say anything." The boy kept squirming, but Dorian's grip was unrelenting.

"What's your name?" I asked.

The boy glared at me.

"What do you think you saw?" I asked. "I was unpacking my robot—"

"Nothing," he said quickly. "I didn't see anything."

"The boy is not stupid," Dorian said. "It is evident I am no robot."

"I'm not a boy," he said, jerking his arm away. This time Dorian let go. "I'm fourteen. And I'm just leaving—"

"Let me clean your cut," I said.

"I told you, I'm fine."

"No, you're not," I said. "You're also breaking and entering."

His face paled. "You can't call the cops. This place is abandoned. I'm not doing anything wrong."

"As you can see," I said, spreading my arms and looking over the room from the velvet couch to the crates, "I'm the new owner. How did you get in?"

He looked at the floor.

"Watch him," I said to Dorian.

I poked my head into the kitchen. One of the windows had been forced open. A smear of blood covered the rusty latch.

"There's no way that window latch is sanitary," I said to the boy. "Let me clean that cut."

He crossed his arms and glowered at me, but didn't attempt to run.

"I'll be right back," I said.

I went to my trailer to find an antiseptic salve and a bandage. It took me a few minutes, and when I returned, Dorian and the boy were sitting cross-legged in front of the brick fireplace. They watched each other skeptically, apparently having reached a détente.

"Let me see your arm." I took his hand in mine.

He wore a black hoodie that was pushed up to his elbows. The blood from his cut had soaked the cuff. He winced as I cleaned the cut and applied an herbal salve of yarrow and aloe. Though the boy was scrawny, his hands were strong. His fingertips were calloused, like he played a stringed instrument. I wondered which one. I couldn't see him playing in a school orchestra, but one thing I've learned over the years is that people never fail to surprise me.

"Why did you break in?" I asked.

"I told you," he said. "This place was supposed to be abandoned. We saw the trailer in the driveway." He shrugged. "We wanted to know who would be staying in a haunted house."

Dorian rolled his little black eyes.

"Your friends are with you?" I asked. This situation kept getting worse and worse.

"They stayed down the street. None of them were brave enough..."

"You're here on a dare?"

He glared at me again. The kid seemed to have a lot of practice.

"They won't believe you, you know," I said.

A brisk knock sounded at the door.

"*Mon dieu!*" Dorian exclaimed. "What is this, *une fête?*"

"Maybe you should—"

"*Oui,*" Dorian said. But instead of getting back inside the crate, he stood next to the fireplace. After stretching his shoulders for a moment, he stood so still that I would have sworn he was a stone gargoyle, just as solid and unmoving as a garden decoration.

"Could it be your friends?" I asked the boy.

He shook his head, confusion showing on his face. "They wouldn't—"

"Police," a deep voice called out from beyond the door. "May I speak with you?"

What were the police doing at my door? I felt my pulse quicken as memories flooded back to me. I wasn't alone in my reaction. My young intruder's eyes grew wide.

The boy hovered nervously behind me as I opened the door to find a handsome man with deep brown eyes standing on my rickety porch. Instead of a police uniform, he wore dark blue jeans, a slim-fitting black sweater, and a jacket. Two kids, a boy and a girl, stood next to him.

"What can I do for you?" I asked, hoping I didn't sound as nervous as I felt.

My injured intruder groaned, slinking further behind me.

"I'm Detective Liu," the man said. "Max Liu. These two were worried about their friend Brixton. They said they saw him—" He broke off and cleared his throat.

"Let me guess," I said. "You were going to say they saw him disappear into the neighborhood haunted house." The house had been uninhabited for several years, due to a legal battle among the family of the elderly woman who'd lived here. That's how it had fallen into its current state of disrepair. I knew about the history from the real estate agent, but for everyone else in the neighborhood who saw the biggest house on the block sitting empty for unknown reasons, rumors about ghosts made perfect sense.

"Bingo." The detective raised an eyebrow at Brixton's friends.

The girl shrugged awkwardly. "Brixton said he'd be *right* back. He didn't show, so I texted him and still didn't hear back..."

"He fell and hurt his arm," I said. "He got a nasty cut and I was helping him clean it."

"He wasn't disturbing you?" Detective Liu asked as a cold wind pushed up the collar of his jacket. "Trespassing?"

"Not at all. He was simply saying hello to his new neighbor. I'm Zoe." I paused to shake his hand. In spite of the chilly air, his hand was warm. And there was something else... A faint scent of lavender wafted up from his hand, along with another plant essence I couldn't place. The overall effect was familiar and comforting. "Do you want to come in? It's getting cold out there."

"This is nothing," he said, stepping inside. "I take it you're not originally from Portland."

"I've lived in much colder places, but I always appreciate the warmth." I paused as it hit me that I hadn't seen any identification from Detective Liu. He didn't look like a typical police officer. It wasn't just the fact that he wasn't dressed like one. I've known detectives in many eras and countries. There was something different about Max Liu. He was guarded and open at the same time. Looking into his eyes as I'd shaken his hand, I had the strongest sense that he was both genuinely friendly and hiding a burdensome secret.

"You introduced yourself as 'detective,'" I added. "Isn't it a bit much to send a detective because a fourteen-year-old decided to turn off his cell phone for a few minutes?"

"I live in the neighborhood," he said. He reached into his pocket and brought out his badge. "They found me at the teashop down the street."

"I bought this place last month," I said, "and moved in today."

"Why?" the girl next to Detective Liu asked. She gaped at me, ignoring her friend who was jabbing her with his elbow. Even in ballet flats, she was several inches taller than either boy. She was beautiful, but from the way she held herself I could tell she couldn't see it. She hadn't yet figured out how to hold her long limbs gracefully.

Her friend remained silent. With a white t-shirt, leather jacket, and I'm-the-cool-silent-type expression on his face, he looked right out of a 1950s movie. But he wasn't fooling me. His inquisitive eyes betrayed a curiosity even greater than the girl's.

"I love a challenge," I said—but the words were drowned out by a crash from overhead. My body tensed. I stole a glance at Dorian, stock still as his stone self next to the fireplace. It wasn't Dorian who was upstairs.

The girl screamed. Brixton jumped. The other boy's body jerked in surprise, followed by a cringe at the fact that he hadn't played it cool.

"Should you check on whoever that is?" Max Liu asked.

"There's nobody else here," I said.

Before I'd finished speaking, the detective was already bounding up the stairs.

"Stay there," he called down to us.

"Another friend?" I asked the kids.

They shook their heads in unison.

I followed the detective up the stairs. What was going on? Was there another stowaway in my boxes?

"Miss," Detective Liu said, rushing out of the master bedroom and nearly giving me a heart attack. "You shouldn't be up here while I—"

"I know what's going on," I said, pushing past him.

He followed me as I knelt down and picked up a sheet of plywood.

"This," I said, "used to be attached to the frame of this broken window. The wind must have dislodged it."

The detective groaned.

"Sorry to have worried you, Detective," I said.

"Max," he said. "Since we've caught a rogue piece of plywood together, I think you can call me Max."

"Sorry, Max." I tried to ignore the effect Max's voice was having on me as I wrestled the piece of wood back into the window frame. The thin wood had warped and refused to stay in place.

"You're *living here* already?"

"I've got a repairman coming first thing in the morning to fix up the place."

Brixton and his friends appeared in the doorway.

"False alarm," I said.

"The house moved on its own?" the girl asked. "Spooky."

"Not really." I held up the warped piece of wood.

"Come on, Veronica," Max said. "We should leave our new neighbor in peace to fix up her house."

"Good luck," Veronica said, a timid smile on her face.

I smiled back at her. My smile was genuine, but I was also wondering what to do about Brixton. I couldn't have him telling Max Liu about Dorian after they left. Brixton knew he could get in trouble if I told the detective he'd broken in. I had the bloody latch to prove it. Was that enough? I wasn't into taking chances.

"I know the place needs a lot of work," I said. "That's why I was so grateful that Brixton offered to help me weed the yard. Isn't that right, Brixton?"

Brixton had a sudden coughing fit.

"Tomorrow after school?" I said, patting him on the back.

Brixton looked from me to the detective and nodded. How had a fourteen-year-old cultivated such a wary look?

A gargoyle, a hoodlum, and a detective. And I'd been in my new home for less than a day.

CHAPTER 3

"They're gone," I said. I ran my hands through my short white hair, wondering what I'd gotten myself into. I needed to keep an eye on Brixton to make sure he didn't start talking about things nobody would believe. When I turned to face Dorian, he had already uncurled himself from his stiff perch at the fireplace.

"You have good instincts, Alchemist," he said. "The boy does not wish you to press charges, so he will help you and not tell anyone what he saw of me."

"I hope so."

"Do you always worry this much?"

"You aren't worried?"

He gave a Gallic shrug. "I have hidden from people since the day I was brought to life by my father. It was a mistake, you see. He did not know what he was doing."

"What do you mean he—"

"I have learned," he continued, ignoring my half-formed question, "that people discount what they do not wish to believe. We can run, Zoe Faust, but we cannot truly hide. You are only fooling yourself if you believe you can control those around you. The boy may tell his friends. There is nothing you can do about that. But rest assured, they will not believe him. They will think he has an overactive imagination."

And here I was thinking that the day couldn't get any weirder. The gargoyle's words reminded me of my mentor, the alchemist Nicolas Flamel. Nicolas and his wife Perenelle discovered the secret of eternal life in the fifteenth century, as well as how to turn lead into gold, but they were wise enough to know the world wasn't ready for their secrets. They donated huge sums of gold to charity before "dying" of old age in Paris. In truth, they faked their deaths to avoid scrutiny, living their lives in the shadows after their official deaths, only revealing their true identities to alchemists like me. I wished I hadn't run from them during a difficult period of my life. I had never been able to find them again.

"I have but one question," Dorian said. "Why is everyone speaking English?"

"Why wouldn't we be speaking English? You're speaking English."

"You spoke to me first. You were speaking English. It was only polite that I reply in the language you spoke."

"You know you're in Portland, Oregon."

Dorian's snout twitched. His granite mouth opened but no sound came out. "Oregon?" he said finally. "You left *France?*"

"Where did you think my shipping crates were going?"

"I did not have time to find out! I wanted your assistance, but I could not approach you when you were with others. Your assistant turned her back for but a moment when packing. That is when I climbed into this crate. I could not ask her where it was being sent. *Mon dieu*, this explains why the journey took so many days!"

His wings flapped in a single violent motion. Though the movement was fluid, as if the gray wings were thick feathers, the tip of his wing clipped the edge of the fireplace, sending a chunk of brick crumbling to the floor. He closed his eyes and squared his shoulders, folding his wings back to their resting place.

"*Je suis désolé*," he said. "I am sorry. I have control of myself now. I simply do not understand why anyone would leave France! But you are a grown woman who can do as she pleases."

"A grown woman who didn't expect to find a gargoyle in her living room in the town she thought was finally going to give her a normal life." I crossed my arms and looked down at the little Francophile.

"If you are done being maudlin," Dorian said, "we can have a more civilized conversation after we eat. What are you cooking for dinner?"

"Dinner? I was going to make myself a simple vegetable soup."

The gargoyle's black eyes darkened and widened. "*Mais non!* You cannot be serious!"

"Sorry to disappoint you. But you were also going to tell me why you're a castaway in my crate."

Dorian sighed and stretched his neck and shoulders from side to side. His movements were more controlled now. I suppose it must have been rather cramped in my shipping crate. "If I finish explaining about my book," he said, "you will feed me a real meal?"

"That's rather presumptuous for a castaway."

He stopped stretching and locked intensely on my gaze. "Please?"

How could one say no to a polite gargoyle? Especially if that was the only way to get this curious creature to tell me how he knew I was an alchemist and why he had traveled across the world to show me the worn book he clutched.

"All right," I agreed. "We'll make dinner, then you'll tell me all about this book of yours as well as how you found me."

"You drive a hard bargain, Alchemist," he said, narrowing his eyes at me. The pupils of his eyes looked more like glass than stone. A fluid, moving glass. He extended his clawed right hand.

I reached out to shake it. His hand was cool, but didn't feel like stone. It was a little bit rougher than human skin, but malleable in the same way.

"You have ham?" he asked.

"Ham?"

"Yes, the cured meat. Made from a pig—"

"I know what *ham* is," I said. "No, I don't have any ham."

"Bacon, then," Dorian said.

"No bacon."

"*Mon dieu!*"

"You only eat pork products?" I asked. This gargoyle was making me more and more curious.

"Of course I eat more than ham and bacon." Dorian sniffled, his little snout moving side to side. "But with a ham hock or a slice of bacon as a base starter, and a few herbs, I can create a masterpiece, regardless of the other ingredients you have available."

"I see," I said, unsure of what else one could say to that. A talking gargoyle was standing in my living room lecturing me about cooking. Even for me, this was pretty weird. "I'm a vegan."

"*Pardon?*"

"I eat a wide range of plant-based foods, but I don't eat animal products."

Dorian swore in French and shook his head. "You at least have basic supplies?"

"Fresh winter vegetables and a few herbs are in the kitchen already, and cooking pans, oils, and more herbs and spices are in my trailer outside."

I went to my trailer to retrieve a portion of my kitchen bounty, from a hanging bunch of dried cayenne peppers to newly ground garlic powder in a glass jar, which I carried inside using a copper saucepan. I've always been aware of the link between food and health, but didn't always treat my own body as well as I treated the people I healed. It wasn't until recently—a little over a hundred years ago—that I felt worthy of taking care of myself. I kept my cooking simple, but used pure, healthful ingredients.

Dorian conceded the high quality of my home-prepared dried herbs and infused oils, after which he banished me from the kitchen. I sat down on the couch with his book on my lap, hoping my instincts were right to trust him in the kitchen. I wondered if the smoke detectors had batteries.

Looking at the book more closely for the first time, the title gave me pause. This was an alchemy book. Translated from Latin, *Non Degenera Alchemia* would be *Not Untrue Alchemy*. What a strange title. What was the point of the double negative? Why wasn't it simply *True Alchemy*?

It took me a few minutes before I could bring myself to open the book. I hadn't practiced alchemy in years. I hadn't been ready. Not after what had happened.

I breathed in a scent I knew well as I opened the book. I work with lots of old books, but in spite of the familiar scent of its binding—seventeenth-century calf-skin, I guessed—this one held unfamiliar secrets. I carefully flipped through a few pages. The title was in Latin, as was some of the text inside, but it didn't look like the alchemy I'd studied. It also included something similar to the coded images used by alchemists, but these symbols weren't quite like any I'd seen before. In the many woodcut illustrations in the book, the necks of the birds twisted to the left to an unnatural degree that reminded me of something seen in a horror movie. I shivered and shut the book. A woody scent wafted up to my nostrils as I did so.

I had excelled in spagyrics, also known as plant alchemy, which uses alchemical techniques to extract the healing properties of herbs rather than the precious properties of metals. The general idea behind all types of alchemy is the same: transforming a substance into something greater than its original whole by making the corruptible into something pure.

I feared I was beyond my depth here. I closed my eyes and clutched the gold locket I wore around my neck. The locket I always kept close to me yet hadn't opened in many years. I hadn't even wanted to *think* about practicing alchemy for decades. Not since Ambrose.

Stop it, Zoe. It wasn't your fault.

I repeated my mantra of that past century a few times before opening the book again. Pushing all thoughts of Ambrose to the back of my mind, I tried to focus on the handwritten calligraphy of the title page. I wasn't sure where to start. Many of my old alchemy books were packed in the shipping crates. It would take some time to locate what I needed. For the time being, I took a cursory look at how the book was organized and snapped a few photos of interesting pages with my cell phone. As I did so, I became more certain than ever that this wasn't alchemy. The illustrations resembled alchemical symbolism only superficially, as if the person making the illustrations had never studied it. Perhaps that explained the convoluted title.

I wasn't sure how long I'd been absorbed in *Not Untrue Alchemy* when a heavenly aroma wafted out from the kitchen. Sage, rosemary, and onions. Dorian carried a hot casserole dish from the kitchen and set it down on a cork mat on the solid oak table. He ran back to the kitchen for the plates and utensils I'd brought inside earlier.

"You made this with what I had in the house?" I asked, my eyes wide and my mouth watering.

He grinned proudly. "Butternut squash roasted in olive oil with onions, sage, and a hint of rosemary. The sauce is lemon tahini, with cayenne-infused salt and toasted pumpkin seeds sprinkled on top. The fat from the sesame seeds used to make the tahini fools the senses into thinking there is a ham base."

"This is amazing," I said.

Dorian ate quickly but with refinement, serving himself a second helping before I was halfway through eating my first. I ate slowly, savoring the exquisite flavors. With the same ingredients I was planning on using to create a simple meal, Dorian had created a feast.

"*Pardon,*" he said after a small burp.

"That meal was incredible," I said.

"*C'est rien,*" he said. "It was nothing. I would have made something better if I was not so hungry."

"I haven't eaten such a gourmet meal in ages," I said.

"You will help me with my book?" he said, looking across the table expectantly.

"You haven't told me exactly what you need done with it, remember? If you're looking for a translator, I'm not the best person."

"*Mais oui!*" he said. "Now that we have satisfied our earthly needs, we may discuss practical business." He scrambled off his chair and returned a moment later with the book I'd left on the couch.

"You are an alchemist. You can help me not only translate my book, but *decipher* it."

"I'm sorry to disappoint you," I said. "Especially after you traveled all this way. But this isn't an alchemy book."

"You are correct it is not a normal one," Dorian said, "but there are alchemy tenets inside. The philosopher's stone, Alkahest, recipes with the three essential ingredients of mercury, sulfur, and salt. It is all here. It is the same principles for creating an Elixir of Life, no?"

"Yes, but that doesn't mean—"

"I," Dorian said, cutting me off, "was once stone. This book is what brought me to life."

I stared across the table at the gargoyle. "That's not possible."

The philosopher's stone was the alchemical creation that enabled both the transformation of eternal life and the creation of gold. But it wasn't something that could be used to bring an inanimate object to life. There was a natural order to things. Steps that had to be taken both outwardly and inwardly—planetary alignments, clockwise rotations, separating and rejoining elements in the proper order, connecting yourself to the processes.

"The secret to immortality is personal," I continued, "not something that can be granted to inanimate objects. Even if stories of the homunculus were true, it's a transformation that doesn't give a personality, a soul, or a mind of your own—meaning it can't possibly be what happened to you. I'm glad you're alive"—and I really was; the little creature was growing on me, especially after that meal—"but books can't achieve that kind of transformation."

"Yet here I am before you," Dorian said. "*Regardez.* I am telling you, this is no normal book. I know about you. I know you can do this."

"What do you mean you *know about me?*"

"There is something strange about this book. A secret that you, of all people, would wish to know."

"Why me?"

He sighed. It was a slow, sad, movement. "I saw what you were doing nearly eighty years ago, after you closed your shop, Elixir." "How could you?" But as I spoke the words, I knew.

"I was there," Dorian said, "when you were nearly discovered. You, as the woman you claim to be your grandmother, were called in by *un Commandant* to help with a strange occurrence at a manor outside of the city."

I nodded slowly. I remembered it well. I was in bad shape, emotionally, at the time. It's why I shut the shop for good and returned home to the U.S., buying a brand-new 1942 Chevy pickup truck, followed a few years later by an Airstream trailer. The truck and trailer allowed me to keep running.

"You may recall," he said, "that the estate had gargoyles. I had been brought to life some years before, and had come to know Paris and its surrounding areas well. I would often hide as stone, as I was that day."

"You were there," I whispered. "Watching."

"I see it as clearly on your face now as I could see it then. You do not feel as if you belong. You never have."

It was so close to the truth that sadness overcame me. Dorian must have known that feeling, too. He was a gargoyle. In the shadows. Always watching, but never able to join in.

"It was *you* who saved me from being discovered that day," I said, staring at the little creature and seeing him in a new light. "You created the distraction by throwing pebbles off the roof, stopping me from telling the French police the truth about how I solved the puzzling crime, giving me time to think it through." On that day eighty years before, I was recovering from an experience that had left me shaken and prone to acting without thinking. I would have been discovered had it not been for my anonymous savior who created a commotion on the roof.

He shrugged. "We are alike, you and I. I have suffered the same fate. Of course I would do what I could once I realized what you were. I do not believe you understand more about why you are alive than I do. Alchemy is about one true thing, no? Yet it is not that simple. This book can help explain it. *To both of us.*"

We stared at each other for several seconds before my phone chirped the soothing sound of a sandpiper.

Dorian shook his head. "Americans," he mumbled. "Never silencing their phones during meals." He tossed his napkin on the table and began to clear the plates.

I saw my contractor's name on the phone's screen and picked up. "Mr. Macraith."

"Eight in the morning work for you to get started? I like to get an early start on the day." His voice was gravely, as I remembered, but even rougher than in our previous conversations. I hoped the jack-of-all-trades handyman was up for the large job I'd given him.

"That works," I said. "Thanks again for scheduling something on such short notice. I'm eager to get started fixing up this place."

"Until then." He clicked off.

Dorian cleaned the dishes while I spread out on the dining table with his book and a cup of chamomile tea. Dorian wouldn't tell me more about the strange tenets in the book. "Simply have a look," he said.

Now that I knew how we'd crossed paths before, how could I say no?

The fact that this wasn't a straightforward alchemy book made it easier to focus. It allowed me to avoid dwelling on the old memories of alchemy that were trying to push their way to the front of my mind. I thought it had been long enough that I was ready for anything. I didn't want to be wrong.

I spent a short time searching for information online, before realizing that was a dead end. I then turned to unpacking my crates in search of alchemy books that might be helpful, but I wasn't hopeful. I already knew what was in those books, and I doubted they could help me. But it had been a long time since I'd opened those books. I wondered what I would find if I reacquainted myself with their secrets.

I fell asleep at the table with one of my alchemy books resting under my head. Not a good position to sleep in if you happen to like moving your neck without searing pain.

I woke up at dawn. My body is so attuned to planetary shifts that I wake up with the sun, even when it's a cloud-covered day and I've slept for only a few hours in an upright position. Since it was wintertime, shortly after the start of the new year, it was a few minutes after seven o'clock.

I saw no sign of Dorian, even after a thorough search of the house.

After taking an alternatively freezing cold and scorching shower that made me glad Charles Macraith would be arriving soon, I made myself a breakfast smoothie of blended fruits and vegetables. There was still no sign of Dorian. I hadn't asked him where he slept—or even *if* he slept—so I wasn't sure where else to look. He'd taken care of himself without being discovered before he met me, so I told myself not to worry. Perhaps he hadn't liked my suggestion that he return to the shipping crate while the contractor worked on the house, and had hidden elsewhere.

I had a little time before our scheduled meeting time, so I set out on a walk. Dorian's meal and my morning juice had used up most of what I'd bought the day before, so I stopped at a small market to buy fresh produce.

Though I'm attuned to plants and planets, I don't have an inner compass. I got turned around rather badly and didn't arrive back at my new house until shortly after eight o'clock.

I walked up the narrow path overgrown with weeds, feeling the stillness of the day. I loved how the house was centrally located but at the same time set back from the street, giving me the privacy I liked. I didn't see anyone waiting for me on the raised porch in front of the house. I was wondering when Charles Macraith would show up, when I realized he wouldn't.

Not alive.

Lying on the ground in front of the rickety porch was the prostrate body of my contractor. The acrid scent of poison overwhelmed the fragrant oranges that dropped from my hand as I knelt over his dead body.

CHAPTER 4

In the hours following the death of Charles Macraith, I was back in 1692. Between the whiff of poison and the suspicion directed at me by well-dressed men in positions of power, I was transported back to my first experience with death, when I was sixteen years old and the Salem Witch Trials were going strong.

I felt an irrational sense of panic rise within me. Though I had no connection to the murder, I knew firsthand how easy it was for innocent people to get caught up in hysteria. A false answer is often easier than a complicated truth. Even if it destroys the innocent.

The uniforms were different today, as were the formal attitudes about innocence before guilt proven beyond a reasonable doubt. But people were still fallible, victims of their own minds trying to make sense of things. And death was the same. A tiny amount of the right poisonous plant extract could fell a healthy man in his prime.

I knew little of Charles Macraith beyond the facts that he was a man of few words, a skilled home renovator who charged a rate I could afford, and that he had only recently returned to work after an injury sustained on the job. How had he come to die on my front porch?

As soon as I was certain he was dead, I didn't touch anything else. I also stopped myself from entering the house to look for Dorian. After a few frantic moments of calling Dorian's name and getting no response, I gave up and called the police from my cell phone.

That was how I came to be waiting at the police station to talk to a detective while my new home was roped off as a crime scene.

Three people, with expressions ranging from curt to eager-to-please, told me I was welcome to help myself to coffee. All of them registered shock or confusion when I said I didn't drink coffee. This was apparently the wrong town for such admissions.

"Sorry to keep you waiting," a friendly voice said. It wasn't the tone of the voice itself that was friendly, I realized, but my positive association with it. How odd for me to have had that reaction. It was the detective who had visited my house the previous night.

"Hello again," he continued. Unlike the night before, he was now dressed in a charcoal gray suit and tie. Both were cut narrowly, matching his frame.

"Detective Liu."

"And you're Zoe Faust. Interesting last name."

"It's an old family name," I said, answering with a partial truth. Unlike Zoe, the name Faust wasn't one I had been born with, but it was a name I felt a connection to on many levels. Johann Faust was an alchemist who lived in the early sixteenth century and died during an alchemical experiment. The Faust most people think of when they hear the name is the character in the play by Goethe— the man who sells his soul to the Devil. The Puritan preachers of my childhood in Salem Village spoke unrelentingly of the Devil, and as a child, he was as real to me as anything in this world. Once I realized what I had become, Faust felt a fitting name to assume.

"You okay?" Detective Liu grimaced at his own question. "Sorry, dumb question after what you saw today. Did anyone offer you coffee?"

"I'm not a coffee person."

He took a moment to look at me before answering. "You and I may be the only two people in Portland who feel that way." He stopped speaking as he glanced at a commotion taking place at the other side of the floor. "C'mon, let's talk somewhere quieter."

"Small world," I said as we walked through the large station.

"I'm here because I'd already been over to your house—" He paused as we reached a door, which he held open for me.

We entered what I assumed was an interrogation room. He hadn't read me my Miranda rights, so I wasn't going to jump to the conclusion that I was a suspect. *Breathe, Zoe.*

"You've had quite a day." He set a bottle of water in front of me.

"This wasn't what I was expecting the second day at my new home."

"Where'd you move here from?"

"You saw the trailer in my driveway? I've been living out of it for a few years. Traveling around. I wanted to see the country."

"Taking some time to see the world after college?"

"Something like that," I said. "But I didn't go to college." It was true. I had never earned a formal degree. I'd studied with some brilliant scholars in the United States, Europe, and Asia, but couldn't risk the records that would be created if I had applied for a formal degree. It was easier to stay out of sight as much as possible.

Modern technology and the internet were a mixed blessing. At first it seemed like it would make it impossible to keep one's identity a secret. But with a little bit of effort, one could be even more anonymous online than in real life. That was true of my shop Elixir, now an online store where I didn't have to stand behind a counter to greet customers.

I had shown the police my Massachusetts drivers license that listed my age as twenty-eight years old. According to official documents, I was the child of an American mother who looked remarkably like me and also bore a strong resemblance to my French grandmother. People often commented on the uncanny resemblance, but nobody ever suspected that we were the same person.

"So." Max rested his elbows on the table. "How did you know Charles Macraith?"

I looked at the ceiling. Low and confining. "The real estate agent recommended him to me. I only had money to buy a fixer-upper, but I really wanted a house. I've been traveling so long..." Longer than I could say. "Sorry. I'm tired. I haven't finished unpacking yet. I didn't sleep well in the new place. I'm usually on my second cup of tea by now."

"I won't keep you long."

"I don't know what else I can tell you. I have no idea who would poison him."

Max Liu's body jerked back. "Who said anything about poison?"

"The smell. It was obvious." I thought back on the awful sight of Charles Macraith's still form on my porch. I hadn't detected anything that anyone familiar with herbalism wouldn't have sensed, had I? I tried to think about that moment. The scent was fleeting. Familiar fragrances mingled with unfamiliar essences. What exactly *had I* detected?

The intensity of his eyes grew as he sat back and studied me in silence. "It was obvious?" he repeated with an intonation that said it was anything but that. His strong reaction faded as quickly as it had surfaced, and he was once again calm in the seat across from me.

"Maybe it wasn't as strong by the time the authorities arrived," I suggested.

He nodded slowly, but the skepticism in his expression was apparent.

"I've studied some herbalism," I said. "I've always been a natural with plants. I grow herbs, dry them, and cook with them. I have a good sense of smell." God, why wouldn't I shut up? I wanted him to believe me. I knew my innocence would be proven, but it was more than that. I hated the way he was now looking at me.

"You want to start over? Tell me what happened at your house this morning?"

My mouth was dry, but before my hand touched the bottle of water, I stopped. Fingerprints. He wanted my fingerprints. I breathed deeply and swallowed.

"I went on a walk," I said, "and got turned around on my way home. Charles Macraith had already arrived when I came through the gate. He must have been waiting for me on the porch when someone found him and poisoned—"

I closed my eyes and thought back on what I remembered. I hadn't imagined the scent of poison. But I should have seen signs in addition to the smell. Many poisons would have resulted in the victim vomiting, but not all poisons had that effect. I tried to think back...

"You didn't find him robbing your house?" Detective Liu asked.

My eyes popped open. Many of the items I'd taken out of storage were valuable antiques that were my livelihood.

"I didn't give him a key," I said. "He was meeting me on the porch." I groaned and put my face in my hands. "The door knob," I said. "It broke off yesterday. What was stolen?"

Max Liu's expression shifted from detached to confused.

"You didn't go inside?"

"Why would I have done that? A man was dead and I had no idea anyone had been inside my house." My house with my living gargoyle. "Wait. I've been unpacking. It's a mess. How do you know anything was stolen?"

"Broken glass and an antique book with ripped pages. Didn't look like something you would have done yourself. Uh, you don't look very well. I'll be right back."

I nodded, my head spinning. The faint voices coming from outside the room weren't the voices of rational police officers but the voices of an angry mob. I wasn't inside a rather pleasant modern-day police station, but in a grimy cell awaiting trial.

When the door opened, I snapped back to the present. Detective Liu set a steaming mug of tea down in front of me.

"Chinese privet," I said as the steam reached my nostrils. "For calming the nerves of someone who's stressed out. That's the scent you had on your hands, along with lavender, last night."

He sighed. "You weren't lying about smelling a poison, were you?"

"You didn't bring me this tea to help my nerves, did you? It was a test."

"Can't it be both?"

"Why would I have made up that I smelled poison?"

He ran a hand through his black hair. "Could you tell what it was?"

I shook my head. "It wasn't something I could identify. It was harsh. Toxic. I'm trying to think what would help narrow it down."

"We'll run a tox screen."

I knew that toxicology wasn't magic. It wasn't as simple as testing blood for "poison." You had to know what you were looking for and run a specific test to find it. When it was a new science about a century ago, it did seem rather like magic, working backward to detect a particular poison inside the complex human body.

"You don't want the tea?" he said.

"I'm all right. It smells wonderful though."

He watched me for a moment before speaking. "We already have your fingerprints from your house, you know," he said. "It had been cleaned before you moved in and it looks like only you and Brixton touched the doors and windows without gloves since then. Computer databases are a wonderful thing for expediency. I know you're not in the system."

I laughed nervously. "Guess I watch too much television." As part of being careful with my identity, I'd never held a job that required fingerprinting. I took a sip of the tea.

"Where did you get this?" I asked. "It's incredible."

"I grow it in my backyard."

"You made this yourself?"

"Yeah, I learned about it from my grandmother." It wasn't exactly a smile on his face when he spoke, but his face softened when he spoke of her. "She and my grandfather were apothecaries in China. That's what they were called back then."

I wished we'd met under other circumstances. I wanted to ask him about his garden, about this tea, and about his grandmother, but it was a ridiculous thought at that moment. A man was dead, I had possibly been robbed of all of my possessions, and my new, unbelievable friend was nowhere to be found.

"Have I given you enough information to narrow down the poison?"

"We don't need more information about what you thought you smelled."

"What do you mean *thought* I smelled?"

"We don't need to run a tox screen to know what happened."

"You're saying you already know what poisoned him? Then why ask me all these questions? To gauge my reaction?" I mentally kicked myself. He wasn't a genuinely nice guy. He'd been playing "good cop" to get at what I knew.

"That's not what I'm saying," Detective Liu said. "Charles Macraith didn't die of poisoning."

My hand clamped over my mouth. "He's not dead?" How could I have been wrong? No, there was no way I had been mistaken. I'd seen more dead bodies in my lifetime than I liked to think about.

"You misunderstand me," he said. "I don't know what you're trying to do by misleading us with talk of poisons, but we'll find out. Charles Macraith wasn't poisoned. He was stabbed. That's what killed him."

CHAPTER 5

I was free to leave the police station. After I was dismissed by Detective Liu, a uniformed officer drove me home to look around the house to see what had been stolen.

On the short drive, I thought more about what the detective had said. Charles Macraith *hadn't been poisoned.* How was that possible? I was sure I'd smelled poison and that it was coming from his body. I was rusty, though. I hadn't honed in on the poison as precisely as I should have.

But I wasn't wrong.

Not only was I letting down a dead man who deserved justice, but the most interesting man I'd met in ages thought I was both crazy and a suspect who was lying about something. Zoe Faust, crazy murder suspect. *Ugh.*

"You okay?" the officer asked, glancing at me as he merged onto the Hawthorne Bridge.

Whoops, I must have said "ugh" out loud.

"I'm fine. Just rattled."

He nodded and turned his attention back to the road.

Portland was a city of bridges. My new house was on the east side of the Willamette River. Downtown Portland, where my district's police station was located, was west of the river. The Hawthorne Bridge was one of many bridges that connected the city. As we drove across the river, I looked over the water and the bridges to the north. Cars, bikes, and people made their way across the city as if nothing had happened.

When we stepped out of the police car in my driveway, the wind whipping around us was so strong that it rattled the front windows, making me jumpy as we walked up to the house.

"You're *living here?*" the officer asked.

I followed his gaze to the tarp that covered half the roof.

"It's a fixer-upper."

"I'll say."

I wasn't permitted to retrieve anything inside the house, but in order to determine whether theft was a motive, I was able to walk through it to inventory what was missing.

I had unpacked only a few of the items in the crates. Most were valuable books and items related to alchemy that I sold online. After I'd closed the bricks-and-mortar location of my shop in Paris nearly a century ago, I catalogued the antiques that I left in a storage unit in Paris. Once the internet created an online marketplace, I hired an assistant living in Paris who could ship items to buyers when an online purchase was made. My website's inventory was small because it consisted of collectors' items rather than a high volume of low-price trinkets.

Now that I had a house, I was planning on converting the attic into a business office and storing items myself, which was why I'd brought the contents of my storage unit here to Portland. High on Charles's to-do list for my new house was making sure it was secure. Keeping everything on site was supposed to make my life *simple*. Now it looked like I'd achieved the opposite effect, my carefully preserved items ransacked and drawing the attention of the authorities.

Many years ago, I used to make a living selling dried herbs and herbal remedies, before I gave up practicing alchemy. Herbalism wasn't the same thing as alchemy, but the processes overlapped enough that creating herbal remedies reminded me too much of my old life. My life with Ambrose.

In the modern age of regulations, it was also simpler to sell secondhand items. It was easy to accumulate desirable objects, which I began to do when I realized that many of the utilitarian items I'd once used were considered "antiques." I didn't think of it as a career. I didn't have to sell much. Compound interest is a wonderful thing. Even though I was awful at turning lead into gold, I knew how to open a bank account. A small amount of money over a hundred years adds up. Still, I hadn't ever cared much about money, spending more of it on others in need than on myself. While I'd been living in Albuquerque the previous year, I gave an anonymous donation to a family who had befriended me when I was new to town, after they were badly injured in a car accident. Most of my remaining savings had gone into buying the house and moving. The little bit I had left over was meant to pay for fixing up the house. Maybe it wasn't such a bad idea to try to get better at turning lead into gold. I sighed and turned my attention back to the task of inventorying the items at the house.

The thief hadn't spent much time rooting through the crates, but most of the items I had already removed were gone. Five original alchemical manuscripts, two alembics used in the Court of Rudolph II, and a portrait of Isaac Newton, an alchemist better known for his more mainstream scientific discoveries. A few items remained, but it looked like that was because they had broken. Shattered glass covered the floor, along with the brittle, torn pages of a fifteenth-century book on alchemy.

Two items that weren't mine were also missing. Dorian was gone. And so was his book.

Had Dorian gone in search of his missing book? Or had he been taken himself? The shiver I felt creep up my spine wasn't from the drafty front door.

I gave the officer a list of the missing items—except for the last two. I couldn't very well tell the police about a half-living half-stone gargoyle, and I didn't know the provenance of Dorian's book. For all I knew it could have been stolen, either by Dorian or at some point in the past. I had taken a few photos of it with my phone, but I was hesitant to give the police the full details about the book. I first had to find out what had happened to Dorian. *Where was he?*

I assured the officer I could stay in my trailer until they were done with the crime scene. He left me in the overgrown front yard, the wind swirling around me.

I'd been living out of my trailer for long enough that I'd made it a home. A tiny home, but one that was free of the prying eyes of the outside world. I unlocked the door of my sanctuary, the 150-square-foot Airstream trailer. I'd spent years slowly customizing it. In spite of the madness going on around me, stepping into the trailer lifted my spirits.

Along the back window, I kept a small herb garden. The potted plants lived in trays that I could move between the inside of the trailer and the outside world—I even had a sill on the side of the trailer to set the planter box. The only danger was remembering to bring it inside if I was going to move the trailer. I had only made that mistake twice. Well, maybe three times.

My current winter mix consisted of cottage rosemary, lemon thyme, sage, shiso, chervil, Mediterranean oregano, and aloe, all growing out of clay pots in the long wooden planter. Rounding out the mix were two larger containers of mint varieties that needed more space. Spearmint and lemon balm flanked the rack of fresh herb pots, their tendrils wrapped around the wooden planter box. The mint would have easily overtaken the other plants if I hadn't used some leaves daily. A sweet, minty scent filled the trailer.

The plants were arm's length from a tiny kitchenette. I kept my cooking simple, so building out the kitchen wasn't necessary. It was the plant ingredients themselves I cared about, which is what I made space for. In a nook next to the kitchen was an area I kept dark with an added curtain. That's where I hung dried herbs next to a custom-carved wooden shelf full of herb-infused oils, tinctures, and salts.

Underneath a narrow couch that converted into a bed, drawers slid out to reveal the less expensive alchemical items I sold at flea markets in my travels across the U.S., including a full drawer of vintage European and Americana postcards—a reliable bestseller. Finishing out the trailer interior was a modern, though minute, bathroom. I had grown up without indoor plumbing, so in spite of its size and lack of water pressure, it felt luxurious.

Conspicuously absent was space for alchemical transformations. That was the point. I hadn't wanted any reminder of practicing alchemy. Getting involved in it had been an accident to begin with. And discovering the Elixir of Life? The biggest accident of all. I hadn't done it for myself. I had been trying to help my brother and I hadn't understood what I'd done. But it didn't matter. It was too late.

"Zoe?" a young voice called out, pulling me back to the present. "You in there?"

I opened the door of the trailer. Brixton stood in the tall grass, a backpack on his back. Of course. I had told him to come over after school to weed the garden, which now seemed completely unimportant. Not twenty feet behind him stood the crime scene tape.

"I don't know if you've heard," I said, jumping down from the trailer's front door.

"The murder," he said with a shrug. "Yeah, I heard. Everyone heard."

"I'm not going to press charges for you letting yourself into my house," I said. "You don't have to do any weeding. But what you *think* you saw—"

"The gargoyle," he said matter-of-factly. "Where is he?"

I opened my mouth to protest, but thought better of it. "Why aren't your friends here?" I asked instead. "Surely they'd want to see a walking, talking gargoyle."

He glared at me.

"They didn't believe you, huh?" I said. So Dorian had been right about that.

"I looked up alchemy. Is that how you brought a piece of stone to life?"

What had I gotten myself into? "Brixton, I don't think it's a good idea for you to be here."

"We could go inside. So nobody overhears us. That's what you're worried about, right?"

"No. Well, yes. But mainly it's that you shouldn't be at a crime scene. I'm sure your mom wouldn't want you here."

"She knows I'm coming over. Can we go inside or what?"

"You may have noticed the crime scene tape. I can't even go inside myself."

"I meant your trailer. You live here, right? I used to live in one with my mom. Ours wasn't nearly this nice. It's starting to rain. You going to let me in?"

"A little rain never hurt anyone."

"I want to see the gargoyle."

"He's not inside."

"Where is he?"

"He's not my pet. I don't have him on a leash—"

"You mean he's gone?"

Two women walking past slowed down as they passed the front gate. With the large yard, they were far enough away they couldn't hear what we were saying, but Brixton was right. This was a conversation that would be better without prying eyes.

"Come on in," I said.

"Wicked," he said as he stepped inside, apparently forgetting about Dorian. "Can I see the philosopher's stone? Is it over here in the corner?" he pulled back the curtain keeping my dried herbs and infused oils in the dark.

"You did some research."

"Can I see it?"

"What do you think it does?"

"Makes gold. And makes you immortal."

"You think I'm immortal?"

He gave me a look that only a teenager can. The equivalent of rolling the eyes but without moving a muscle.

I could have told him that although I'd lived for centuries, I could die almost as easily as anyone else. I had mostly stopped aging, so I wasn't likely to die of an old-age-related condition, but I could be killed by anything else that would kill a person, such as disease or violence. Therefore I wasn't exactly immortal. I hadn't even entirely stopped aging. The white hair that everyone thought was so stylishly dyed was my true hair color.

Instead of explaining all that to Brixton, I gave him the simple version: "I'm not immortal."

"If you don't have the philosopher's stone, what about Alkahest?" He looked around the trailer.

"The universal solvent? Why do you ask about that?" Asking about the famous philosopher's stone, I understood. But Alkahest? It wasn't an element popularized in books or movies.

"It's the part of alchemy I looked up online that didn't make any sense at all. If it dissolves *everything*, then how would you keep it? I mean, wouldn't it, like burn through anything you tried to keep it in? Wouldn't it even burn through the earth, destroying the world?"

"Good point. Maybe that's why I've never encountered it." The theories asserted about how to make Alkahest were dubious. I'd seen recipes that called for ingredients including blood, sweat, and worms. "Not everything you read online is true, you know."

Again with the eye roll.

"I'm good with plants like these herbs," I said, pointing at my beloved herb garden. "I can transform them into a lot of things, like the salve I used on your arm. That's what makes me an alchemist. I don't make gold. And I don't bring stone gargoyles to life."

"So," Brixton said, making himself comfortable on the long seat in the living area. "You think the gargoyle did it?"

"Feet," I said automatically, knocking his sneakers off the cushions. "Did what?"

"Killed Charles. Because he didn't want to be discovered."

I stared at Brixton. The kid was right. Dorian took not being discovered seriously. *Very* seriously. My pulse quickened as Brixton's words sunk in. I felt my heartbeat so strongly in my ears that I could barely hear what Brixton was saying. It was like that damn story by Poe. Though I wasn't guilty of murder myself, it might have been done because of me.

Why hadn't I thought of it before? I knew why. Because I liked the little creature. A misfit, like me. And he'd helped me in Paris years ago... hadn't he? How would he have known about that if he hadn't been there? And he couldn't go around killing anyone who saw him. He was the one who'd pointed out that nobody would believe Brixton. The gargoyle wouldn't have turned violent... would he?

"Earth to Zoe," Brixton said.

"It doesn't fit," I said, shaking my head.

Brixton shrugged. "At least you didn't say *oh he's such a nice guy, he would never have done it.* I hate it when they say that on TV."

"This isn't TV."

"Are you always this much of a downer?"

"A man was killed."

"Yeah, I liked him."

"You knew Charles Macraith?"

"He came around the teashop. He didn't talk much, but he used to help me with my homework sometimes."

"Teashop?" I wondered if it could be the same place I'd visited when I'd fallen in love with this neighborhood. The welcoming café was one of the main reasons I'd felt so at home here.

"Yeah, Blue's teashop. That's where I know Detective Liu from, too. Hey, are those chili peppers floating in that bottle?" He jumped up and pulled back the half-closed curtain that shaded my nook of herbs. He lifted a glass jar of sesame oil infused with peppers. "Wicked. I love spicy food. Did you make all this stuff? Is that lemon balm and pineapple sage floating in these other bottles?"

"How on earth did you recognize those?"

He shrugged. "Blue loves wildcrafting. She taught me about what that meant and about finding plants in their natural habitats. She harvests herbs for her teas and other stuff."

I hadn't met many wildcrafters. Under other circumstances I would have asked him more about it. But now, I had more pressing matters to deal with. "You were telling me about Charles Macraith visiting the teashop."

"Yeah, nobody had anything against him." Brixton set the bottle back on the shelf and looked right at me. "That gargoyle of yours is the only logical explanation for why he's dead."

CHAPTER 6

Brixton offered to live up to his end of the bargain and weed the yard, but the rain pelting on the roof of the trailer assured me there wouldn't be any gardening that day. Brixton had heard the rain too. I wondered if he'd have made such a generous offer if there was any chance I would have taken him up on it. He was a smart kid. I sent him home with a clear conscience, but as I watched him ride off on his bike, I wondered if I had been too trusting.

I could see the crime scene tape on my porch from the window of the trailer. Also in view was the tarp covering a huge section of my roof. It swayed in the strong winds but looked like it was holding firm. I had no idea where Dorian could be. I didn't know if I'd lost his alchemy-that-wasn't-alchemy book or if he'd taken it with him. Brixton's assumption about Dorian couldn't be right. It couldn't be.

In spite of the rain, I needed to walk and clear my head. I grabbed my silver raincoat and headed out.

Portlanders weren't afraid of a little rain. Or even a lot of it. Hawthorne Boulevard was packed. Locals poured out of organic restaurants, coffee shops, and an annex of Powell's Books. I stopped in a café and ordered an orange and pomegranate salad. It was good but didn't compete with Dorian's cooking. I looked out into the nighttime downpour. *Where was he?*

That night, I feel asleep to the sound of the wind whispering to the rain, but woke up a few hours later with an irate gargoyle standing over me.

"*Où est mon livre!?*" Dorian screamed. "Where is my book!?"

The trailer was nearly pitch black. Dorian hadn't turned on a light, but I knew his voice and smelled his fruity breath close to my face. Could he see in the dark? I sat up abruptly at the thought, accidentally head-butting his snout. I hadn't realized he was *that* close to me.

"*Merde*," he mumbled, hopping down from the edge of the bed as I flipped on a light.

"Where have you been?" I asked as Dorian's claw snagged the blanket and pulled it to the floor along with him. Luckily I was fully covered by my white cotton nightgown. I'd had it handmade by a seamstress in North Carolina several years ago, based on a pattern from the previous century. Seventeenth-century women had to wear scratchy, heavy, and overall burdensome clothing, but the night clothes from the Victorian era were the most comfortable I'd ever encountered.

"This city," Dorian said, rubbing his snout, "she has a different lunar cycle than Paris. I did not realize the sun would rise an hour earlier. I was not yet close to the house when day began."

"You had to hide."

He nodded and sniffed. "I could not return without being seen."

"I've been worried. I'm glad you're safe." I thought about what Brixton had suggested about Dorian, but pushed it from my mind. Besides the fact that I had already grown quite fond of Dorian, I wasn't lying to myself that it didn't make any sense for him to have killed the handyman.

"I hid in one of the forests. There were many to choose from. I chose one that had wild blueberries and blackberries."

"I don't think they're technically forests—" I began. I don't know why I said such an inane thing, except that I wasn't at my best after being woken up after midnight by a furious creature who smelled like wild berries and could see in the dark.

"What has happened?" Dorian asked. "When night returned, I found my way back. *Mais*... there is blood at the door and the bright strips of plastic that say 'police line do not cross.' When I went inside—"

"You *crossed the police line?*"

"I thought my book was inside."

I groaned and rubbed my eyes.

"Yet my book was not there," Dorian continued. "Last night you fell asleep at the table with your head on the pages. I did not wish to disturb you. Dorian Robert-Houdin is a gentleman."

I stood up and looked around the trailer. The bedside lamp cast stark shadows, but illuminated the whole interior. The door was closed, as I'd left it.

Locked.

"Dorian... How did you get in here?"

His throat rumbled. I couldn't tell if he was growling or attempting to imitate an awkward cough. He held up his clawed fingers.

"Better than lock picks."

"You *broke in?*"

"My father was a great magician. He taught me many things."

I groaned again and sat back down on the bed. I'm no good at being awake in the middle of the night. When the sun disappears and the plants sleep, I feel myself drawn to sleep as well.

"Robert-Houdin," I said in my foggy state. "Wait. That name. Your father was Jean Eugène Robert-Houdin, the famous French stage magician!"

"*Oui,* I told you this."

"You told me *your* first name, not his."

"There is no other Robert-Houdin. He joined his surname with his wife's. Quite unheard-of at the time."

"He was an alchemist?"

I knew of the French stage magician who was a huge sensation in the mid-1800s. I had once seen him perform on stage. He was talented, performing feats that seemed like magic to sold-out theater audiences. I had believed, then, that he was simply a skilled stage magician. He was, after all, such a master magician that he was asked by the French government to avert a military crisis in Algeria by showing French magic to be more powerful than that of local tribal leaders. The history books had recorded Jean Eugène Robert-Houdin's feats as illusions, skillful tricks performed by a master showman. But now I had to wonder—had he used real magic?

"He was no alchemist," Dorian said. "Yet he was the one who brought me to life."

"That doesn't make sense."

"He did not understand what the book was capable of." He shook his head. "I was meant to be a prop in a stage show. The book is filled with lyrical passages of text. He found them quite theatrical. But he never considered the power in the pages from which he read. I will show you. Where is the book?"

"Dorian, we need to talk. About a lot of things."

"Yes, I agree. I do not see my book. You have put it away?"

His little black eyes looked at me so expectantly that I hated to tell him what had transpired.

"I'm sorry," I began. "The book is gone."

"*Pardon?* I must not understand your English; I am nearly fluent, yet—"

"The man who was going to fix and secure the house was killed this morning. That was the blood you saw."

"*Je suis desolé.* But what does his death have to do with my book?"

"When he was killed," I said slowly, "the house was also burglarized. Your book was one of the things stolen."

Dorian's eyes grew wide. His stony shoulders tensed and his wings flew out from his sides, knocking over my pot of chervil with one wing and scraping a gash into a wood panel with the other. The pot shattered as it hit the floor.

"You let someone steal *my* book?" His body shook, adding additional gashes to the wooden wall paneling surrounding him. Even after seeing how his wing had chipped the fireplace, I hadn't realized just how strong and heavy they were.

"We'll get it back. The police are investigating."

"You told *the police* about my alchemy book?"

"Not about your book in particular. And of course not about you. Or me, for that matter. Many of my rare books were stolen." My head felt heavy at the reminder of everything that had been lost in the past day. In addition to losing much of my livelihood, I'd lost a book that didn't belong to me, and a man had lost his life.

"You knew how valuable my book was. How could you have let this happen?"

"There was no reason for it to happen!" I said, struggling to keep the heavy feeling in my head from turning into a massive headache. I got myself a small glass of water and added a few drops of peppermint oil to stimulate my senses and wake me up; Dorian glared at me as I did so. "It must have been a crime of opportunity. Charles Macraith was killed, and the person who killed him saw items that looked valuable and grabbed them. The police think they were in a hurry."

"You were not there? How could you not be there?" Dorian stamped his clawed feet like a toddler throwing a tantrum. I would have offered him some tea to calm his nerves except that my kettle was inside the house beyond the crime scene tape.

"*Nobody knew* we had valuable books inside the house. There was no reason to think I couldn't go on a short walk to buy some food before Charles was due at the house. But you're right. When I couldn't find you, I shouldn't have left your valuable book alone. I'm so very sorry, Dorian."

Dorian's wings collapsed back to their usual resting place at his sides. "I understand your desire to buy food," he said, "yet leaving the book unattended was unwise. Someone had to have known about it."

"*Someone?*" Was there more going on here than he'd told me? "Do you have a particular person in mind?"

"I do not know! This is why I came to you!" His wings vibrated, but didn't fly out.

"Does anyone know you came here to see me and get my help?" I asked.

"No. It is not possible."

"Then how—"

"I do not know!"

"Then why do you think this is about your book?" Now that I was a little more awake and coherent, I was beginning to realize that there may have been more going on than a crime of opportunity. "Tell me more about this book."

Dorian's snout flared, but he remained mute.

"What," I said, "aren't you telling me?"

Dorian's shoulders slumped. He sat down next to me on the edge of the bed. "I did not lie to you."

"I didn't say you did. But you didn't tell me everything either."

"I did not think you would believe me."

"You're a living gargoyle and I'm an alchemist who was born over three hundred years ago, but you didn't think I'd believe you about a book?"

"It is for that exact reason that you could not know," he said. "I thought it would be easier for you to solve the riddle of my book without already having a particular outcome in mind. If a scientist thinks he knows what the result will be, it prejudices the study."

"I understand," I said. "But I'm so far from understanding what's going on that you need to tell me everything you can."

"Now that the book is gone, it does not matter." His wings crumpled like a wilting flower as he shook his head.

"The book isn't entirely gone." I lifted my cell phone from the side table, tapped a couple keys, and handed it to Dorian. "Take a look. I took photos of some of the more interesting pages of the book."

"Zoe Faust, I take back what I was thinking about you."

I thought it wise not to ask what he was thinking about me. "Thank you," I said. "I think."

"I might have a chance yet."

"A chance at what?"

"I am dying," Dorian said. "This book is the only way to save me."

CHAPTER 7

"My body," Dorian said, "is slowly turning back into stone. You might say this is the natural state of things, for us all to die. But this is not a natural death. When I turn to stone, I do not sleep. I will be awake but forever trapped in this stone shell."

"Oh, Dorian—"

He held up a clawed hand. "I did not wish to speak of it. It makes it more the truth. Now that the book has been stolen—" He broke off and shook his head.

"Why is this happening now? What changed?"

"I do not know. If I had known this would happen, I would have sought you out before now. Now that I am here, you can help me by deciphering the remaining pages of the book. Perhaps there are answers in the pages you found interesting enough to photograph."

"Maybe, but I need to understand more—"

"Yet I know very little." His words were clipped. "This is why I have come to you."

I felt the weight of his words sink in. He was putting so much faith in me, and I didn't know if I would be able to help. But I had to try.

"You know more than you think you do," I said. "Tell me about the trans-formation. The day Jean Eugène Robert-Houdin brought you to life."

"I do not remember the moment," he said, his voice softening. "It is a blur, as they say. I will tell you the story told to me by my father. He had been given a great gift from his friend, the architect Eugène Viollet-le-Duc, who was restoring the cathedral of Notre Dame de Paris. Father's friend had fanciful plans for the cathedral, including a balcony of stone chimeras. Unlike the water spout gargoyles along the sides of the cathedral, his stone carvings had personality. I was one of his prototypes. I was not large enough, though. Because my father collected many items for his stage performances, Viollet-le-Duc thought he would appreciate this carving—and he was correct."

"That's amazing," I said, thinking of the gallery of gargoyles at Notre Dame I had climbed many times. When I had first seen Dorian, he reminded me of one of the gargoyles there. Now I knew why.

"My father created mechanized automatons. He was planning on building an automaton based on my stone carving. He had already retired to Saint-Gervais and was working on his memoirs, but his mind was restless. He wished to continue innovating for the stage. The idea for his new illusion was to read from an ancient alchemy book, at which point the automaton would begin to move— the illusion of coming to life." Dorian closed his eyes and paused.

"I know it must be difficult to talk about this, but it will help me understand what happened to you."

Dorian nodded. "As my father built his clockwork automaton, he placed the stone prototype—me—on stage, to practice. He was not very good at reading Latin. He practiced again and again so the words would sound dramatic for his audience. One day, he pronounced the words properly. This is the day I came to life."

"If I'd known what was happening to you, I could have read the Latin out loud to rejuvenate you."

Dorian shook his head. "I have already tried this. *Tristement*, it is not that simple. That is why I need you."

"Where did your father get the book?"

"This," Dorian said sadly, "I do not know."

"You must know something."

"What I know is that my father found stage magic accidentally. He had ordered two books on his vocation, clockmaking. In their place, he received books on magic. It is for this reason that he always collected an assortment of books. The more happenstance, the better. Friends and well-wishers knew this of him. Many people gave him strange books. There is no way to trace the origins of *Non Degenera Alchemia*."

"He didn't remember who gave it to him?"

"If he did, he did not tell me. I did not give the book much thought for many years. Only when my body began to change did I realize my life continued to be tied to the book. I can read and write in many languages, but have never studied alchemy. This secret language of alchemists is a mystery to me. You, Zoe Faust, are the one person I knew of who could help me."

In spite of my desire to know more, that was all he could tell me. I was also about to fall over. I needed sleep. I wasn't built to be awake in the middle of the night. I'm so attuned to the sun that simply staying awake at night is challenging.

Dorian cleaned up the broken pot of chervil and told me to get some sleep, saying I looked like I needed it. He assured me he would pay more attention to Portland's sunrise, then disappeared into the darkness. The sadness on his face before he headed out into the night lingered in my mind. Was he really dying? Could I help? Even if we had the book back, I didn't know what I could do as an out-of-practice alchemist who didn't speak whatever coded language the book was written in. But he had been right the night before. He and I were two outcasts who didn't understand what had happened to us. I didn't want to let him down—or to lose him.

As always, I awoke with the sun. In spite of my fatigue, I had tossed and turned for several hours. Yawning, I pulled open the trailer curtains, thin muslin from Egypt that assured privacy on the inside but let in natural light from the outside.

With my blender stuck in the roped-off house, I couldn't start the day with a smoothie of fruits and vegetables. As the sun rose, I ate dried heirloom apples and wild blueberries with a handful of walnuts, and drank a large glass of water with lemon essence. The familiar flavors and hydrating water helped calm my nerves after Dorian's upsetting revelation.

I tucked my legs under me and sat in the window in the direction of the sunrise, thinking over the strange events of the last two days. If it hadn't been for the scratches running across the panels near my bed and the broken pot in my herb garden, I might have been able to believe Dorian's presence the previous night had been a dream.

Was Charles Macraith's death a result of his own life catching up with him at my front door? He was, after all, known for being "discreet," a word with an added meaning that hadn't occurred to me when the real estate agent gave me his card. Or was his death a consequence of someone in search of Dorian's book, an unintended casualty because he was in the wrong place at the wrong time? Whatever was going on, Dorian and I were right in the middle of it.

I scrolled through the photographs of Dorian's book I had on my phone. I stopped on an image of the earth being engulfed in flames. That pretty much summed up how I was feeling about my life.

After my night, I needed a calming cup of tea to think straight and decide what to do about Dorian's dilemma. Since I couldn't make tea without my kettle, I went in search of the teashop Brixton had mentioned. Brixton hadn't referred to it by name, but if it was the same teashop I'd visited, it would be easy to find. I remembered it had a large weeping fig tree growing in the midst of the tables.

After a quick shower using my trailer's nearly depleted water supplies, I slipped on custom-made gray wool slacks and cream cashmere sweater, and grabbed my silver raincoat. I've never gotten the hang of wearing off-the-rack clothes. How do people wear clothes that aren't made specifically to fit their unique shape? Tailored clothes weren't always considered the luxury item they are today. It was simply how things were done. Once mass-produced clothes were a reality, that's what felt like a luxury to people. There's certainly the instant gratification from seeing something you like and taking it home with you, but it doesn't compare.

I found Blue Sky Teas on Hawthorne Boulevard, several blocks from my house. From the sidewalk, I could see it was the same teashop I remembered. Beyond the tall glass windows, the familiar weeping fig tree filled the welcoming space without dominating it. The plaque above the teashop's bright orange door read: "'There is no trouble so great or grave that cannot be diminished by a nice cup of tea.' —Bernard-Paul Heroux."

It was a few minutes before 7:30 and a woman with wild gray hair was turning a hand-painted wooden sign from "closed" to "open." She caught my eye and smiled.

The storefront was narrow, but as I stepped inside, I felt as if I'd set foot in an expansive forest. The ceiling was taller than the width of the shop. Mosaic tiles covered the floor except for a spot in the center of the shop where a live weeping fig tree with gnarled roots grew out of a three-foot circle. The branches stretched up to the curved ceiling, which was painted the color of a deep blue sky with wispy white clouds. As long as I didn't stare directly at it, it felt like real sky hanging above me—minus the fickle Pacific Northwest weather. Eight tables lined the walls, their tops made of solid redwood with the tree rings showing. The walls were unadorned, as I remembered, except now one corner held a framed photo of a young red-haired woman. The picture was surrounded by cards and dried flowers, including fragrant lavender.

Walking through to the counter, located at the back, a cacophony of scents washed over me, but in a pleasing rather than overwhelming way. I could pick out many of the scents—mint, jasmine, honeysuckle, cinnamon—while many of the herbs blended together. Breathing in the fragrance of the teashop had an immediate effect on calming my nerves. I wasn't exactly relaxed, but poking through my apprehension was the same feeling of hope I'd had when I first visited Portland. I wanted desperately to grab hold of the feeling and not let it go.

"I'm glad I opened early today," the gray-haired woman said. "Zoe, right? Brixton mentioned you."

"You must be Blue," I said. "He mentioned you too." I hadn't recognized her until the scent of jasmine triggered my memory. It was the same woman who'd been here the previous year when I bought the best cup of lemon ginger tea I'd ever tasted. If I recalled, her secret ingredients were fresh turmeric and a hint of cayenne.

Though not classically beautiful, here in her element she was radiant. She wore no makeup, but her round cheeks had a natural glow. Curly hair more gray than brown swept halfway down her back, falling on the simple white blouse she wore over faded jeans. She stood behind the counter, a steaming cup of jasmine green tea in her hands.

"Blue Sky," she said, setting down her cup of tea and offering me her hand. "And yes, that's really my name."

"I wasn't going to ask. It suits you."

"Thanks for not pressing charges against Brixton. His mom lets him run wild, but he's a good kid. Anything you'd like, it's on the house."

"That's not necessary. He didn't do any harm. I was going to have him help weed my yard, but then…"

"Charles," Blue finished for me. "Such a shame."

"You knew him?"

"Not well. But this neighborhood is like a small town in many ways. Charles came into the shop, especially while he was off work recovering from a construction accident. He was a man of few words. I always got the feeling he was more comfortable whittling on wood than talking to people. You know —" she paused and frowned. "I don't even know where he's from. Portland is a place that gives fresh starts for a lot of people. It's what the city did for me. I didn't try to get to know him better. I wish now that I had…" I never knew what to say surrounding death. You'd think it would get easier, but it never does. Maybe that's a good thing. I remained silent, letting Blue have the time she needed. No platitude would help.

"I'm sorry that was your introduction to your new home," Blue continued, then snapped her fingers. "You look like a fan of cinnamon. I bet you'll like my homemade spicy chai."

"I don't do dairy," I said. "I follow a plant-based diet."

"Even better. There's no milk in my chai. People often complain about that —until they taste it."

With a wink, she turned away from me to brew my chai. It gave me more time to look around the teashop. I placed my hand on the rough bark of the tree. It was old. The building must have been built around it. There was so much to love here, but now I knew there was also something to fear.

"See if you like this," Blue said, startling me from my thoughts.

The intermingling scents of cinnamon, ginger, cloves, fennel, and cardamom wafted up from the clay mug. Unlike many teashops and coffee-houses across the country, the liquid in this mug wasn't close to boiling. It was hot enough to be steaming, but cool enough to drink. Just as tea was meant to be served.

"Real Ceylon cinnamon," I said.

"I can tell you're going to keep me on my toes."

I felt an immediate sense of warmth spread through my body. "This is exactly what I needed after yesterday."

Blue smiled, the wrinkles around her friendly eyes crinkling. "You shouldn't let Brixton off the hook."

I breathed in the aromatic scent of the tea, hoping it would help me decide what to do about a lot of things. "I don't know."

"Cleaning up your yard after he broke your window is exactly what he needs." She saw the hesitation on my face. "You don't need to protect him from anything. It's unfortunate Charles's life caught up with him outside your house, but life is about moving forward. And that boy needs structure. He's been in trouble before."

"What kind of trouble?"

Blue waved off the question. "Nothing serious. Just kid stuff. But I worry."

"You sound like you know him well."

"His mom, Heather, had him when she was sixteen. I moved here when Heather was twenty and Brixton was four. What a precocious boy he was —still is."

"I noticed."

Blue smiled wryly. "For the last ten years, she's often left him at the teashop, letting me babysit. Until he was old enough to be on his own after school, he'd often sit at that table by the window and do his homework." She pointed at one of the smaller tree-ringed tabletops. "The regulars loved to help him with his homework."

"You said that in the past tense."

"He's in high school now. Old enough that he can do what he wants. Which doesn't seem to involve doing homework."

A bell chimed and an exceptionally tall young man walked in. He wasn't especially young, though he looked it to me. He must have been in his late twenties, around the same age people thought I was, which I'd never stop thinking of as young.

"Morning, Blue," he said, giving her a sad smile. "The usual."

"Coming right up."

I brought my chai to a table near the tree while Blue helped the customer, who got a tea to go in a personal travel mug. Now that my attention wasn't focused on Blue, I noticed the vast array of teas in metal jars lining several narrow shelves behind the counter.

The man smiled at me as he left with his tea. Blue came out from behind the counter and joined me at my table.

"I'm an early bird," Blue said, "so I like to get started early, even though I don't usually get many customers this early. Tea isn't the usual choice of commuters looking for a quick caffeine fix on their way to work. A lot of my teas are actually decoctions that take a while to brew."

"How long have you run this place?" I asked.

"It's why I stayed in Portland. This tree was here on the corner and was about to be cut down to build more storefronts. I was able to save it."

"I love it," I said. I wasn't just being polite. The old tree brought so much life to the shop.

"I can tell you're going to like it here. Brixton told me you moved into that haunt—I mean the house that's been sitting empty for years."

"You don't have to censor yourself. I've already heard it's known as the local haunted house."

"We're a tight-knit community. It's all well-meaning. So don't you worry about what they're saying about you."

"Wait, *what?*"

"Looks like the rush is starting," Blue said, standing up and turning her attention to four people who were walking up to the counter. "Stay and enjoy the chai."

CHAPTER 8

I was in no hurry to get back to my trailer overlooking the crime scene. I didn't yet know how I could help Dorian, no matter how much I wanted to. I didn't have any faith I could decipher his book, especially when I was left with only the few pages I'd photographed. Furthermore, was it possible a murderer had followed him from Paris? Someone who wanted this book badly enough that they wanted to make doubly sure the person standing in their way was dead? A tingling fear crept over me as I thought about what that might mean.

I breathed in the aroma of the chai to calm my nerves. As I did so, another chilling idea occurred to me: Could the murder have something to do with *me*? Dorian wasn't the only one who had things of value in his possession.

Neither scenario made sense. Both Dorian and I lived off the grid, and we hadn't been in Portland long enough for anyone to know what we were. The murder had to be about Charles Macraith himself. It had to be. Didn't it?

With shaking hands, I looked at the photos of Dorian's book that were saved on my phone. On the screen, the images were too small to see the details, but zooming obscured the bigger picture. I preferred tangible photographs to computer screens. The only two modern inventions I adopted early were automobiles and blenders, both of which were perfected in the 1940s, as far as I was concerned. My vintage blender now sat behind the crime scene tape. Crime scene tape! I'd been so careful over the years. In two days I'd drawn more attention to myself than I had in the last two decades.

Having a nervous breakdown wasn't going to help anyone. I had to relax if I was going to make sense of any of this. Placing the phone facedown on the table, I took a beaten-up paperback from my coat pocket. One of the things I had learned the hard way was that when faced with a stressful task, it's important to take a few deep breaths before beginning. Books served as a psychological deep breath. Before I tackled the task of deciphering the pages of Dorian's book, I could give myself these few minutes to enjoy a cup of tea and a few of my favorite passages.

Living out of my trailer, I didn't have space for many books, so I owned only a few dozen favorite paperbacks. If I wanted to keep a new book, something old had to go. It was a small cost for living on the road, but a difficult one.

One of the very few purely positive things about living so long was getting to read so many books. While styles of prose changed over time and varied across different cultures, storytelling remained fundamentally the same. People have changed how they express themselves, but the human condition doesn't change, and neither does how we relate to it. Instead of making new stories unnecessary, each successful storyteller puts their own twist on a familiar tale and finds a way to connect with the readers of their time. Especially successful writers reach across time, ending up as classics.

It was fascinating to see how history created false images of famous authors after their deaths. Even the author whose book I now held in my hand, Sir Arthur Conan Doyle, was far different than popular culture would have people believe. Casual fans of Sherlock Holmes assume his creator was a scientific-minded man like his famous detective. People who study his life in more depth believe he gave up rationalism for spiritualism. Neither was the whole story. He was grieving for deceased loved ones—his wife and son, among others. It was a feeling I knew all too well. One part of his life was blown out of proportion as he sought to reconnect with those he missed dearly.

Regardless of how history documented the man, there's no arguing that his stories stood the test of time. I opened my battered copy of *The Hound of the Baskervilles*.

The teashop didn't sell coffee, but that didn't prevent it from doing a bustling business. From the moment Blue went back to the counter, people funneled into the teashop, keeping her busy. Though an assortment of pastries was available, most customers only ordered tea.

"Did you hear about the murder?" a woman whispered loudly to her friend as they stood in line.

My shoulders tensed and I felt an instinctive desire to flee. I shoved the book back into my pocket and stood up to leave.

"Oh, don't go." The voice came from the table next to mine. The older woman sat alone. She sat with her back to the wall, giving her a full view of her surroundings. "You're the one who bought the house on the hill, aren't you?"

So much for settling in quietly.

"I need to get going," I said, forcing a smile.

"Nonsense. What an awful introduction to our neighborhood you've had. Let me buy you another cup of tea."

"Thank you, but—"

"I won't take no for an answer."

She stood and swooped in on the counter. That was really the only way to describe it. She wore a blood-red shawl and timed her approach to the counter perfectly to correspond to a lull in customers. I had a moment to study her unobserved as she ordered two teas. She knew who I was, knew about Charles and his murder the previous day, and nodded at several of the people in the teashop. I guessed she spent a fair amount of her time here. Though it was difficult to discern because of her perfect makeup and rich brown hair that was pulled back into a bun, I guessed she was old enough to be retired, giving her plenty of time to spend at the teashop. She couldn't have been much taller than five feet, and I doubted she weighed a hundred pounds.

She returned a minute later with a pot of tea and two small mugs. The aroma told me it was a simple black tea, but smelled high quality and delicious.

"Olivia Strum," she said.

"Zoe Faust. And thank you for the tea." I wondered how quickly I could drink it and extricate myself. I should have known people would know who I was. With the murder fresh in everyone's minds, this wasn't how I wanted to meet people. Especially before the police had solved the crime.

Olivia leaned in. "You mustn't order the food here. Blue knows how to make the most superb tea that tastes sublime and makes you feel alive, but she couldn't cook a decent pastry if her life depended on it. She insists on making everything herself, so she can make them *healthy*." She shuddered. "Can you believe that her desserts are mostly *vegan*? Life is too short to eat inedible food because it's healthy. My nephew Sam is the one who convinced me to try the teas here. One of the few sensible suggestions he has ever made. I should also warn you Blue only accepts cash. She doesn't trust credit cards. Ah, Ivan! Come sit with us."

An unshaven middle-aged man with a newspaper tucked under his arm approached our table. I wondered how long Olivia would have gone on talking if it hadn't been for the interruption.

"This is Zoe, the woman who bought the house on the hill," Olivia said to him. "Zoe Faust, this is Ivan Danko."

He nodded politely but without smiling, then headed for the counter, pausing first at the sole photograph on the wall. Other people had done so as well, but Ivan's gaze lingered.

"Don't mind him," Olivia said. "He hates retirement. He's still getting used to it."

"What's the interest in the photograph of the young woman on the wall?" I asked. "Is she Blue's daughter?"

"Anna passed away several months ago," Olivia said. "She wasn't Blue's daughter, but she was a regular here."

"She's so young." No wonder the photograph interested customers who must have known her. I could see, now, that it was a shrine that had been set up for the poor girl. Though the death of Charles Macraith was tragic, the death of someone so young was especially devastating.

In the midst of unfamiliar faces, a familiar one came through the door. Max Liu breezed by us and headed straight for the counter. For a detective, he wasn't very observant that morning. Though he passed by quickly, I noticed the dark circles under his eyes. Only when he turned around with a cup of tea to go did he notice me.

His body gave a jerk as he stopped abruptly.

"Will you excuse us a moment?" he said to Olivia.

Being pulled aside by the police in gossip-central? Not good.

I stood and followed him outside, feeling Olivia watching me.

Max's hand brushed against my elbow as he opened the door for me. I felt a little jolt of electricity. It was a feeling I hadn't felt in years. *Get a grip, Zoe. This guy is investigating a murder—a murder he thinks I might be involved in.* What was the matter with me?

"Were you looking for me?" I asked. We stood just outside the teashop, under the blue awning that matched the painted blue sky inside.

"Stopping in on my way back to the station, but I'm glad I found you."

"You are?"

"How did you know?" he asked. Up close, I saw further evidence of sleep deprivation beyond the dark circles under his eyes. He hadn't shaved, his eyes were bloodshot, and his collar wasn't folded properly, as if he'd dressed in a hurry, or perhaps slept in his clothes.

"Know what?"

"About the poison."

"So Charles Macraith *was* poisoned in addition to being stabbed?"

He held my gaze, ignoring his tea. I could smell the faint scent of jasmine from the hole in the lid of his traveling mug.

"Do you believe what I told you or not?" I asked.

"I want to know why you thought it was poison."

"I already told you," I said. "I smelled it."

"But how did you know what you smelled was poison if you couldn't identify it?"

I took a moment before responding. How could I answer that question? The real answer was complicated—more complicated than could be explained to a detective on a Portland street corner. More complicated than could be explained in any way Max would understand, for that matter.

Ever since I was a small child, I've had more of an affinity to plants than most people. People with my gift were called "simplers." I've always been sensitive to the elements that make up plants. Their smell, texture, taste, healing properties—and their poisonous properties, too. It never seemed magical to me as a child. I still don't think of it as magic. *Natural* magic, perhaps, but not a sorcery type of magic. I wasn't born with unexplained knowledge. I merely let myself be open to my natural sensitivities, then studied to learn what the sensations I was experiencing meant.

When I was forced to flee my home with my little brother because my talents were equated with witchcraft, it was the alchemists who took me in. They were the ones who shaped my knowledge of plants, turning my natural aptitude into a skill to practice alchemy. I hadn't even heard of alchemy before an alchemist found me—or, I should say, before the alchemist found my brother Thomas. We were selling the healing tinctures I made, and the strange man assumed it was Thomas who had the aptitude for transforming plants. Thomas was more amused than I was.

"The foul smell," I said, choosing my words carefully. I was tempted to say more, but I knew it wasn't a good idea. Saying less was almost always better. I'd learned that the hard way.

"Why did your mind jump to poison, though? Did you recognize it as something specific?"

"No, not really."

"Then why didn't you think it was garbage nearby? Why did your mind jump to poison if it wasn't something you could identify."

It was a good question. But it wasn't odd that I hadn't identified the exact poison. There are many different ways plant essences can be manipulated, causing toxicity in different ways.

I glanced into the teashop. Olivia wasn't attempting to hide her interest in watching us. When she saw me look at her, she gave a little wave. The sleeve of her blouse fell to her elbow, revealing scars on her forearm. Ivan's face was hidden behind a newspaper.

"As I told you before," I said, "I work with plants. Scents fall into different general categories. I didn't know with absolute certainty it was a poisoning, but I thought I smelled a foul herbal odor. The type of thing that's suggestive of poison. Since there was a man lying at an unnatural angle who wasn't breathing, I jumped to that conclusion. Since you're asking me about it, I'm guessing I was right that he was poisoned in addition to being stabbed."

"I can't comment on an ongoing investigation."

"Then what exactly are you asking me?"

"If you happened to have ideas about the type of poison we might be dealing with…"

"Is the lab having trouble identifying the specific poison?" Though modern toxicology had come a long way, I knew it was far easier to detect damage to internal organs than it was to determine the cause.

He took a sip of his tea but didn't speak. Instead his face contorted into a pained expression.

"Are you all right?" I asked.

"It's nothing." He rubbed his lower back with his free hand, again wincing in pain. "I got hurt chasing a suspect last month. It's the stupidest thing, really. I fell through a trap door. They say you never see it coming, but *that* I truly couldn't have seen coming."

Max's cell phone beeped. He read something on the screen and put it back in his pocket. "We're done with your house. You're free to go back inside."

"Before you go, there's something I forgot." I held up my cell phone showing a picture of the cover of Dorian's book. "I have a photograph of one of the books missing from my house."

Was it just my imagination, or did Max Liu's breath catch when I showed him the photograph of *Not Untrue Alchemy?*

CHAPTER 9

Even if my imagination was overactive, there was *something* going on with Dorian's book. I found the local library, but I needn't have bothered with the library card. None of the alchemy books at the library could tell me more than my own collection. These were books about alchemy, not original alchemy manuscripts. The earliest published alchemy book at the library was far too modern, from 1888. I gave up and went to the market.

When I returned home with a bag of groceries and printed photos from *Not Untrue Alchemy*, a gargoyle poked his head around the kitchen door.

"Those men," Dorian said, "I thought they would never leave."

"You hid, right?"

"*Mon dieu.* You would do me the courtesy of giving me some credit. I have been surrounded by humans for over a century. I know how to hide."

"I'm sorry. Of course you know how to take care of yourself." I set the groceries down and turned back to Dorian. "Something strange is going on here. My contractor was both poisoned *and* stabbed. And now the detective seemed to recognize your book. It's so obscure there's nothing about it on the internet. How could he recognize it?"

"The book was never in danger until I came here! France is a much more civilized country."

"It has its charms," I agreed. "But Portland does too. As soon as I came here, I—" I stopped myself, unsure of what I wanted to say next. It would have been so easy to open up to Dorian, with his concerned eyes looking up at me. I knew he wouldn't run screaming from whatever I told him, because he was a fellow freak of nature. But I wasn't ready to tell *anyone* about my hopes for this place. Hope was a dangerous thing. If I shared it with anyone, I feared I might make it too real to take back.

Dorian didn't seem to notice that I'd stopped speaking mid-sentence. He stood on his toes on the stepping stool and tipped the bag of vegetables onto the counter. He looked up at me, holding an acorn squash in his hand. "You said you have spoken to *les flics*. What have you learned about the retrieval of my book?"

"They're looking into it."

"And before they get it back, you will translate the pages you photographed?"

"I'm working on it." I removed the short stack of 8x10 photos from my bag and set them on the counter next to the food.

Abandoning the squash, Dorian rooted through the photographs.

"I don't want you to get your hopes up," I said.

"American idioms are odd," Dorian mumbled as he looked through the photos. He stopped and looked up at me. "I have faith in you, Zoe Faust."

I smiled. Nobody had said that to me in a long time.

"I have faith you are a good alchemist," he continued. "As for a cook... What are you making for lunch?"

"I thought I'd make roasted winter vegetables with steamed greens and pecans. I have enough ingredients for both of us."

Dorian returned his attention to the bag of food, nodding to himself. "I will cook, giving you time to begin translating. This will work for now, but I will give you a shopping list of a few more ingredients for dinner—all plant-based. I respect your wishes. I am a good houseguest."

I crossed my arms. This was getting ridiculous. "I've got plenty of herbs and spices in the trailer—"

"Yes, yes," he said, scribbling on a notepad I'd left on the counter. He tore off the paper and handed it to me.

"You certainly are a little gourmet," I said.

"You will buy these, yes?"

"I wish your tastes were a little less expensive."

He stared at me with a confused expression. "You are an *alchemist*," he said. "Can you not simply make more gold?"

"The thing is..." I looked away for a moment, embarrassed. "I never really got the hang of that part of alchemy." I watched as his eyes widened in horror.

"But then we could buy good wine and truffles!"

~

While Dorian cooked, I took a quick look at my email. Someone had ordered one of the rare antiques I listed for sale on Elixir's website. I knew the embossed brass medicinal container had to be *somewhere* in the crates. Until my assistant and I had packed up my inventory, the antiques had sat on shelves in a small Paris storage unit, which my assistant Agnès had visited once a week to mail items that had been purchased. One of the reasons I liked this house was that it had a large attic that would be perfect for storing my small inventory—at least it would be once I got the roof fixed. In the meantime, I would have to keep the items in crates stacked at the side of the living room. I sighed as I thought about the volume of wares I would have to root through.

I briefly contemplated ignoring the order in favor of the more pressing matter of deciphering the pages of Dorian's book, but knew I should first attend to practical tasks. Every alchemist knows that a distracted mind leads to disaster. In the back of my mind I knew that if my business failed, I'd have zero income. It wouldn't matter that I saved Dorian's life if we starved to death or were crushed beneath a crumbling house.

While I searched for the brass container, an antique from China, I kept my phone to my ear, calling locksmiths. I was hoping to find someone who could come that day. The first two I called were disorganized, realizing they couldn't make it only after I'd taken time to give them details about what I needed and told them my address. That was odd. On my third try, I found one who said he could be there later that day to change the locks and secure the broken ones.

"What are you doing?" Dorian's voice startled me. "Why are you not looking at the pages from my book?" He stood behind me, clutching a baking dish.

"One of us has to make a living and keep a roof above us."

"If you learned how to transmute gold like a proper alchemist..." Dorian mumbled under his breath as he scampered to the dining table.

The sweet scent of sugar hit my nostrils as I sat down at the table. "Where did you find the sugar?" I asked. "It can't be maple I smell."

He smiled with satisfaction. "The acorn squash is baked in caramelized onions, with a pecan puree stuffing, and lightly braised kale with garlic."

I don't know how he did it with the simple ingredients I had on hand. After another of the best meals I'd eaten in years, Dorian was clearing the dishes when there was a knock at the door.

"I wish," he said, "you were not so popular."

"The locksmith must be early."

Dorian left the remains of the stuffed acorn squash on the table and went to the fireplace, where he stood still and turned to stone. It was a disconcerting sight.

I showed the locksmith the doors where I wanted new locks along with added deadbolts. He eyed the baked squash dish with hungry eyes as we walked by the table on the way to the back door. It was easy to see what his eyes were doing—the thick black eyeliner circling his pale eyes made every expression dramatic. I'd hired a Goth locksmith. He also had a handlebar mustache with perfectly curled edges. The mustache didn't seem very Goth to me, but hey, this was Portland. Maybe he was a Goth-hipster, a new trend I hadn't yet heard about. Or was the proper term hipster-Goth?

Just as I was coming to understand one new trend, a new one would inevitably emerge. I had long since abandoned trying to keep up. I liked to think I wore classic clothes that never went out of style—tailored dress pants in neutral colors with simple cotton blouses in warm weather, and knitted sweaters with my beloved silver raincoat in cold climates—but I noticed that sometimes I was considered more trendy than at other times. It was language that I was better at keeping up with. Because I was forced to move around so much, I had become accustomed to picking up local languages, including a language's changing vernacular and speech patterns.

"There's plenty of food," I said. "Shall I get you a plate?"

An hour later, I felt a lot safer and I had a Goth-hipster friend for life. The locksmith was just starting out, he told me, so he lived on canned food and the occasional food truck meal. He said he hadn't eaten a meal that tasty and satisfying in ages, and was shocked to learn the meaty-textured nut stuffing didn't contain meat. I sent him home with leftovers.

As soon as he left, another visitor arrived at the door, leaving me no time to work on the pages of Dorian's book. I sighed and opened the door for Brixton.

"Where should I start?" he asked.

"I let you off the hook, remember?"

"I feel bad about breaking in. Veronica and Ethan wanted to hang out, but my mom said I should do like I promised."

There was no defiance in his expression. Where had this polite version of Brixton come from? I hesitated for a moment while I contemplated what to do about him.

"Thanks," I said. "You can get started weeding the backyard. Everything along the edges of the fence. I'll grab gloves from the trailer and show you what to do."

"The *whole fence?*"

"I thought you wanted to help."

"Yeah, I do. It's just... Nothing. It's cool. I just thought maybe you'd want to tell me more about alchemy, so I don't, like, go asking other people about it. You wouldn't want that, right?"

I doubt I had been that intelligent—or manipulative—at fourteen.

"All right," I said. "Here's your first lesson. The heart of alchemy is transformation. Something new is created based on how you transform existing elements. A perfect example is this garden. Right now it's full of weeds, but through your efforts you're going to transform it into something new."

"I've got a better example. Turning lead into gold. You said you don't, but that's what you guys do, right?"

"Some alchemists have tried to turn lead into gold, but I'm a plant alchemist."

"How did you buy this house, then?"

"I have a job, like everyone else."

"Why aren't you at work?"

"What kind of question is that? I run an online business."

"Can I see the website?"

"Maybe after you practice some alchemy in the yard." I dreaded what a fourteen-year-old would think of my outdated website.

He mumbled something under his breath, but donned the gloves I handed him and watched as I showed him how to pull weeds from the root. He had a lot to do, which would give me time to research the pages of Dorian's book.

I spread the photographs on the dining table, again struck by the fact that the images and text weren't like anything in my own alchemy books. I wished I hadn't lost touch with the alchemists I'd known. Without personal contacts, it would be close to impossible to find a real alchemist. Though there were many people who considered themselves alchemists, most were either scholars or spiritual alchemists. Neither category would understand what had happened to Dorian. And I didn't know how much time I had.

Before I could decide if I should join an internet discussion group of alchemists, a frantic pounding sounded at the front door.

"Zoe!" Brixton yelled. "Let me in!" My newly secured doorknob shook but didn't open.

I jumped up and opened the door for him.

"I didn't mean to pry," he said, rushing past me into the house. "Really, I didn't. I was just looking for a snack."

"What's going on, Brixton?" I felt his fear. He wasn't joking around.

"Poison! I found poison in your trailer." He thrust the bottle into my hand.

I gasped, then I saw what he'd handed me. "This," I said, laughing as I let go of my tension, "isn't poison. It's asafoetida. A spice."

"No way. It smells like—"

"I know. One of its nicknames is 'Devil's Dung.'"

"It's *food?*"

"Sure is," I said, getting my laughter under control.

"Why would anyone eat this?"

"As soon as it's heated in a dish, it transforms itself and brings out the flavors of other spices. It also helps digestion."

Brixton swore. "I, uh, kind of messed up your trailer. Some bottles fell and broke when I ran out of there. Sorry."

~

While Brixton cleaned up the mess he'd made in the trailer and got back to weeding, I walked to the market to buy the items on Dorian's list. I chuckled when I got to the bottom. He'd added bacon to the list, as if I wouldn't notice. I didn't object to other people—or gargoyles, for that matter—eating whatever they wanted to. But I was a single vegan woman living alone. I had enough secrets to cover up. I wasn't going to buy suspicious products for my secret guest.

When I got back, a few weeds were gone, but there was no sign of Brixton in the yard or the trailer. I found him in the kitchen. Dorian was showing him how to safely light an old gas stove with a match, and Brixton was rolling his eyes as if the gargoyle was treating him like a child.

"Did you find everything on my list?" Dorian asked in an innocent voice.

"Nice try."

The two of them seemed content, chopping food for dinner, so I left the kitchen, taking the photographs from *Not Untrue Alchemy* to the dining table. The disturbing bird images again made me want to look away, but I forced myself to examine the woodcuts. The twisted, broken necks stirred a feeling of apprehension deep within me. Along with my revulsion was a flicker of recognition, but the flame quickly faded and I was left with nothing.

Coded symbols such as these allowed for secret alchemical teachings to be passed down from one generation to the next. The pelican, for example, symbolizes self-sacrifice, which is a code for distillation. But the birds in this book weren't familiar to me. Instead of elegant pelicans, crows, peacocks, and phoenixes, these birds had twisted shapes and looked more like dodos and pterodactyls.

In the past, coded messages were often publicly displayed, carved onto buildings during alchemy's heyday in the Middle Ages. The markings could describe alchemical operations, such as a dove representing the purifying transformation turning from the Black Phase to the White Phase and the phoenix representing the final alchemical operation resulting in the philosopher's stone.

But here in *Not Untrue Alchemy*, I couldn't easily identify the significance of any of the illustrations. I made out an ouroboros—a dragon eating its own tail —on one page, but the dragon's body wasn't curled in a circle to symbolize eternal re-creation as one would expect. Instead, the creature was contorted and looked as if it was writhing in pain.

Distressed shouts interrupted my thoughts.

I ran into the kitchen. Brixton clutched his hand and Dorian held a cell phone.

"He was recording me!" Dorian screamed.

I took a deep breath. And another. I now understood Brixton's apparent change of heart.

Dorian held the phone in his clawed hand. The image displayed on the screen showed a gargoyle cooking in my kitchen.

CHAPTER 10

"Make the video play, Zoe." Dorian was close to shouting as he held the phone in an unsteady hand. "The touch screen of the phone does not respond to my fingers."

"It would help if you handed me the phone."

"*Non*." The grip of his clawed hand tightened around the phone.

"You can make it play with the phone safely in my hand."

I glanced at Brixton, sulking in the corner of the kitchen with his arms folded, then tapped the screen of his phone in Dorian's hand. The video on the cell phone screen clearly showed the gargoyle chopping vegetables as he explained to Brixton how to use acidulated water to stop chopped vegetables from turning brown.

"Brixton," I snapped. "What did you do?"

"He scratched my hand!"

"You would not give me your phone!" Dorian said. "What could I do?"

"I'll tend to your hand, Brixton," I said, grabbing the salve I'd applied just two days before on the cut he received while breaking into the house. "But *what did you do?*"

"Nobody believed me! What was I supposed to do?"

"You don't realize what you've done." I was past anger. I was disappointed. *And scared.*

Brixton heard the change in my voice. "It's not even posted yet," he said quietly, looking down at the 1950s linoleum floor.

"You're telling the truth?"

He nodded, still not looking up at me.

My shoulders relaxed and Dorian recited a prayer of thanks in French. I had forgotten I was holding the aloe salve to treat Brixton's scratch.

Brixton watched me as I treated the wound made by Dorian's claw. "Why doesn't it sting?"

"Not everything good for you hurts."

"Thanks," he mumbled so quietly it was barely audible.

"You don't even need a bandage this time," I added.

"He would have killed me if you hadn't come in."

"He knows not what he says," Dorian said, flapping his wings in what could only be described as a huff. "I would never hurt a child."

"Only an adult who was here to fix the house," Brixton said, his voice defiant.

Dorian gasped. "You cannot think—" His head whipped between the two of us. "Zoe, you do not think I was responsible for that poor man's murder, do you? You cannot think I would do such a thing."

Before I could decide what to do about either of them, a burst of knocking sounded at the front door. *Wonderful.*

"Stay here," I said. "Both of you."

Looking out the peephole in the front door, I saw a young woman with long blond hair, several strands in messy braids woven with flowers at the ends. She held a plate of cookies in her hands. Friendly new neighbor?

"I bet it's my mom," Brixton said from behind me. "She said she wanted to thank you for not pressing charges against me. I never know if she's going to follow through on anything, so I didn't know if she'd really show up."

She knocked again. Brixton stepped past me and looked through the peephole.

"Yeah," he said. "That's her."

A quick survey of the room assured me Dorian was gone, so I opened the door. Brixton's mom's smile was powerful enough that under normal circumstances it would have brightened up a room, but at that moment it was only strong enough to make the tension bearable.

"Zoe!" Instead of handing me the platter of cookies in her hand, she set it on the floor and enveloped me in a warm hug. "Thank you for looking out for my pumpkin."

"Mom," Brixton said.

Brixton's mom let go of me and gave her son an even bigger hug. Even on the chilly overcast day, she was barefoot. She stood on her tiptoes as she hugged her son. Before letting go, she kissed his forehead, causing him to turn bright red. Even if what Blue had said was true about Brixton's mom not always being there for her son, Brixton certainly wasn't lacking in physical affection.

"I'm Heather," she said. "And these—" she paused and picked up the tray of cookies, "are my famous vegan oatmeal cookies."

"You told your mom about my being vegan?" I asked Brixton. I hadn't realized he'd paid attention to that fact. And, more importantly, I wondered what else he'd told his mom and others about me. Had he told the truth that he hadn't uploaded the video of Dorian on his phone?

Heather gave me an even bigger grin. "Brix, you didn't tell me that!"

"Um, yeah," Brixton said. "Now you two can be BFFs or something. So, can we go now?"

"I'm not a strict vegan," Heather said. "That would be tough, seeing as I don't cook much. These cookies are the one thing I do well. The dinner you're cooking smells delicious."

The scent of the food Dorian had been cooking did smell mouthwatering. He was using a common herb pairing of marjoram, rosemary, and thyme to bring out the flavors of the winter vegetables. I also recognized the scent of other herbs that were transforming the dish into something greater than the sum of its parts. If I hadn't been worried about that video, I would have been a lot more curious about the meal.

When I hesitated, Brixton gave me a strange look. "Yeah, Mom," he said. "Zoe is a great cook. Isn't that right, Zoe? Because *who else* could be cooking in your kitchen?"

"That's sweet of you to say," I said through clenched teeth.

"I hope my baby isn't causing you too much trouble," Heather said.

"He's really taken to gardening, even though some stinging nettles scratched his hand. Isn't that right, Brixton?"

"Can we go, Mom? I just need to get my phone. I left it in the kitchen."

"I'll come with you," I said. "I need to check the stove. Heather, please make yourself at home in the living room. I'm still unpacking, so don't mind the mess."

Dorian wasn't hiding. Not exactly. He stood in the corner of the kitchen, unmoving. He looked exactly as he had when I first opened the crate: a sleeping stone statue. The only difference was that instead of an alchemy book in his hands, he held Brixton's cell phone.

"What the—" Brixton said with a start.

"We're alone, Dorian," I said quietly. "Brixton's mom is in the other room."

Gray stone shifted. The movement was subtle and fascinating. I hadn't been this close when his transformation from stone to life had taken place before. It was like watching an avalanche at a quarry. Granite-colored sand granules shifted in a cascading effect until stone had morphed into thick gray skin.

"No way," Brixton whispered.

Dorian rolled his head from side to side and stretched his wings. "You must delete it," he said, handing me Brixton's phone. "I cannot use the screen of the phone with my fingers. Mobile phones were much better when they had real buttons."

I found the video file and deleted it before handing the phone back to Brixton. He was still staring at Dorian. I had to push him out the kitchen door.

Once Brixton and his mom were gone, I made sure all the curtains were drawn and the doors and windows locked. I tried one of Heather's cookies. She wasn't exaggerating about how good they were. She'd used a sweet and savory combination of dried cherries and salted walnuts. I followed my nose back to the kitchen, where Dorian had resumed cooking. He stood on the stepping stool, stirring the contents of a Dutch Oven pot with a wooden spoon.

How could he be so calm after the close call?

"Dorian, what—"

"*Un moment, s'il vous plaît,*" he said, holding up his clawed index finger. He lifted a spoonful to his snout, nodded to himself, then added a shake of sea salt. He placed the lid on the pot, rested the spoon on the counter, and hopped down from the stool to face me.

"I will require," he said, "an apron and a spoon rest." ·

"An apron?"

"Yes, you did not appear to have one. Quite uncivilized."

"About Brixton—" I began, caught between being somber about the near-disaster of a video of Dorian going viral and the absurdity of imagining a gargoyle in my kitchen wearing a frilly apron.

"Zoe, it is done. Crisis averted. There is no sense dwelling on the unfortunate occurrence. That would only distract you from discovering the secrets of my book. I will be your personal gargoyle chef while you translate the pages from my book. That way you will have sufficient time to devote to it."

I burst out laughing. Once I started, I couldn't stop. My very own personal chef. I was laughing so hard a tear trickled down my cheek.

"*Mon amie,* you are hysterical."

"Dorian, what's going on?" I leaned back against the counter, my shoulders still shaking but getting hold of myself. "Nothing makes sense."

Dorian jumped up to sit on a free section of the counter next to me. "I do not think things make much sense once one has left France."

"Maybe that's it. The last few decades traveling across America have been a blur."

"This meal will make you feel better. It is an old recipe from the French countryside. Adapted, of course, for your preferences. But I am nothing if not a gentleman. I had no idea a cassoulet could be so decadent without pig fat."

"How did you learn how to cook?"

"From a chef."

"Who was open to teaching a gargoyle?"

"It is complicated to explain..."

"If you hadn't noticed, I have a complicated life."

"I think the cassoulet needs more seasoning." He left his spot next to me and resumed his position on the stepping stool in front of the stove.

"You're avoiding my question."

"Give the alchemist a prize."

"I can better help you with the alchemy book if I understand your history."

He sighed. "He was blind."

"A blind chef?"

"He was not always blind."

I waited a few moments, but he didn't continue.

"The blind chef," I prompted.

"Fine, yes, all right," he said impatiently, still fussing with spices instead of looking at me. "There was a kitchen fire. This is what blinded him. He saved his staff, but was badly burned and lost his vision. He had been a successful chef who once had much power. He lived alone in a large house, where he was both lonely and angry for losing the adoration he once had. He was a friend of my father's. My father knew of fame, and he felt sorry for his friend's predicament. Since the man could not see, I was able to visit him with my father. In spite of the chef's reputation for being difficult, we got along well. Father was nearing the end of his life and did not know what would become of me. He told his friend I was 'unemployed' and that I was wary of people seeing me because I was disfigured. The lonely former chef hired me to be his live-in assistant. He previously had people delivering prepared meals to him. Upon hiring me, he ordered uncooked food to be delivered, and taught me how to cook. I took to it quite well. Before he passed away, he wrote me a reference. I became a chef for other blind people who wanted good food and companion-ship at home. That is what I have been doing."

"That's lovely," I said, imagining the gargoyle happily at work in the kitchens of people who had no idea of his visage. "Why didn't you want to tell me?"

He turned to face me with a wooden spoon in his hand. "You of all people, Zoe Faust, know that speaking of the past brings up unintentional memories we do not wish to remember."

CHAPTER 11

I woke up to the scent of coffee. *Coffee?* Why was there coffee in my house? I shot out of bed and promptly shivered. I'd sealed off the broken window as best I could, but painter's tape wasn't as robust as the fitted piece of wood. I found my thickest pair of woolen socks and crept downstairs.

"Where did you get that?" I asked, indicating the large contraption on the kitchen counter.

"I took the liberty of ordering an espresso maker. It is uncivilized that you do not have one."

"How did it get here?"

"One of the benefits of American impatience is the rapidity of express delivery. *C'est très vite.*"

"You have a credit card?"

"I am cooking for you," he said, blinking at me, "should I not receive payment of some kind?"

I sighed and rubbed my temples. "No more taking my credit card without asking, okay?"

"I did not wish to interrupt you while you studied the pages of my book. I understand alchemists do not like to be interrupted."

"Well, yes, that's true—" I broke off when I saw a French-language newspaper spread out on the table. "You also ordered *Le Monde?*"

"Yes, is it not agreeable that they offer this service outside of France?"

"Was it really urgent enough that you couldn't ask? Is this how you treated the previous people you cooked for?"

Dorian sniffed and sipped his mug of espresso. "I was homesick."

My mood softened. "Have you ever been outside France before?"

He shook his head.

"Well," I said, feeling my anger dissipating, "just be sure to ask me in the future if you want to charge anything."

"I have *l'espresso et le journal*, what else could I possibly want?"

~

After making myself my usual morning smoothie and watering the portable herb garden I'd moved into the kitchen window box, I set out for a brisk walk to clear my head before working on the pages of Dorian's book. I walked in the direction of Blue Sky Teas, thinking I'd get a cup of tea to go.

Bells chimed when I walked through the door, and Blue's voice called from the back: "Be out in a minute!"

I walked around the weeping fig tree and looked up at the painted sky. I didn't feel as comfortable in the teashop as I had before. It wasn't because of the gossip I knew would be taking place there shortly. It was something else. Something was... off.

The comforting teashop from the day before had changed. I whipped my head around, searching for the difference. I sniffed the air, wondering if Blue had accidentally burned something she was cooking. That wasn't it either. I couldn't place the source of my discomfort. All I knew was that I had to get out of there. I turned and ran out the door. I didn't stop running until I'd reached my street.

The exertion made my chest hurt. I stopped to catch my breath. What had happened back there? There was too much going on for me to think. I desperately needed to unravel the secrets of *Not Untrue Alchemy* to keep Dorian from the awful fate of being trapped in a dead stone body while his mind lived on, yet I hesitated before walking up to the house. My mind was troubled with too many thoughts that would get in the way. *What was going on at Blue's teashop? Had her words about Portland meant she was running from something? What had happened to Charles Macraith? What was Max Liu hiding? Why had someone stolen Dorian's book? Was the gargoyle capable of more than I thought?*

I turned on my heel and headed the other direction. What I needed was a long walk, far away from the distractions of my house and the teashop. Only then would I be in the right mindset to decipher the riddles of Dorian's book. I had so few of the pages that I needed all the help I could get.

In all the places I've lived, I've found the nearby places where I could walk in nature. Forests, deserts, swamps. It didn't matter where it was. What mattered was that the natural plant life surrounding me made me feel at ease. I was in my element smelling the scents of fragrant trees of the forest like pine, maple, and hickory. I could watch the plants of swamps interact with the water for hours, from wispy cattails rising from the dark waters to the duckweed floating on the surface. Even the desert begat life. Creation could come from anywhere.

I hadn't had much time to explore Portland's greenery yet. Even when I'd purchased the house, I hadn't done much exploring. That was the whole point of buying the house! To have time to settle in and explore the area's many parks, forests, arboretums, gardens, and other hidden places I didn't yet know about. I didn't know where I was going, but I was hoping that in this city of trees I'd hit a park or something similar before too long.

Sure enough, after walking a few blocks, I came to a beautiful park blanketed in trees. It turned out to be the Lone Fir Cemetery, which a plaque informed me was the oldest cemetery in Portland, dating back to 1846. What a young city this was. I walked through the serene grounds, letting my mind wander to the trees and the Gothic mausoleum I passed. The gardens and trees didn't appear to be part of a central plan, which made it all the more charming.

With my mind clear, I allowed myself to turn back to the events of the present. Only now was I able to identify what I had sensed at Blue's teashop. It was such an unexpected thing that my conscious mind hadn't put it together: the odd scent I had detected over Charles Macraith's dead body was similar to what I'd smelled at Blue Sky Teas.

I wasn't being dense or forgetful. The odor had mingled with the scents of the numerous teas in a way that made it difficult to distinguish. But here in a cemetery park full of an assortment of plants, I'd been unconsciously picking apart the mingled fragrances of the trees and winter flowers.

I had to get back to the teashop.

The sun was high overhead. I must have been walking for hours, which explained why I'd passed the same trees again and again.

When I reached Blue Sky Teas, it wasn't Blue who was behind the counter. Instead, a stunning red-headed woman greeted me with a smile that didn't reach her eyes. The deep lines and puffiness around her light green eyes didn't match the rest of her polished appearance.

"Blue had to leave early today to prepare for a houseguest," she explained. "Can I help you?"

Could she? The poisonous scent that I thought I had detected earlier was no longer there. Had Blue taken it with her? For her houseguest?

I bit back my shock and confusion, instead giving the woman behind the counter a wide smile. "I was supposed to be here earlier to bring her something for her guest," I said. "I lost track of the day. Do you have her address so I can bring it to her?"

"Oh, of course. That's very sweet of you to go out of your way."

~

I went home to get my truck, not venturing inside the house. I'd deal with Dorian's wrath later. This was more important.

Twenty minutes later, I stood outside Blue's house. The cottage was on the outskirts of Portland, in a less crowded part of the city where houses had acres of land. Blue's yard, if you could call it that, was an overgrown plot of land that might look like weeds to most people. Technically these were indeed weeds, but these were *useful* weeds. Even with a brief glance, I identified field mustard, sorrel, and wild onions. I understood why she lived here. It was a wildcrafter's dream here in her own yard.

Standing in the wild yard, I hesitated. If I gave myself time to think, I'd convince myself this was a stupid idea. If I thought Blue was going to poison someone, I should call the police. But what could I tell them? *I think I maybe smelled something strange, which I can't identify, and you'll never be able to detect it yourself, and now it's gone?* No, I had to see if I could find it on my own.

I took a deep breath and knocked on the door. The knock was met with silence. I tried the doorbell, followed by another knock. Still, nothing.

An old VW Bug was parked outside, but for all I knew she might have multiple cars. I walked to the closest window and looked inside.

The first thing I spotted beyond the half-drawn curtains made my body jolt with a mix of relief and anger. On a side table next to the window, nestled in an ornamental woven bowl, sat two of my antique alembics that had been stolen. That had to mean Dorian's book was nearby too. I was giddy with relief before the anger hit me. I was vexed not only with Blue for taking a life and my possessions, but also with myself for letting my emotions get in the way of thinking she was capable of such things.

The second thing I saw drained the anger from me, a wave of numbing cold washing over me in its place. Beyond the side table, Blue's body lay on the floor.

72

CHAPTER 12

Hospitals and medicine have come a long way in the last few centuries. Plague doctors once wore beaked masks filled with straw and fragrant mint, cloves, myrrh, and rose petals thought to protect the doctor from miasmatic bad air, and used a pointed cane to examine patients without touching them. Their frightening costume has been immortalized in woodcuts from the seventeenth century, but in person they were even more terrifying. Imagine lying listless with fever, unable to keep down food or water, your body covered in painful boils, only to be visited not by an angelic sympathetic doctor, but by a demonic, faceless figure who poked you with a stick and told you to repent your sins. It was an image I would never forget.

I hadn't been one of the unfortunate souls on the other end of the plague doctor's stick, but I had seen their work when I used to practice plant alchemy and was more actively engaged in making herbal remedies to heal people. Just as doctors couldn't stop the plague, healers like me were helpless to save everyone. My work wasn't enough to save the people I loved.

That was a long time ago, but hospitals still made me uncomfortable. Contagious people crammed into sickbeds with countless others had given way to the sterile hospitals of the present century. The details didn't matter. The very fact that sickness and death were such a part of life was something I'd been running from for a long time.

After seeing Blue sprawled on the floor, I had dialed 911. The fire department was the first to arrive. They discovered Blue had a pulse, and the ambulance that arrived minutes later took her to the hospital. As the gurney transported her from the house to the ambulance, I knew what had happened. Wafting up from her body was a mix of scents similar to what I'd sensed earlier. Similar, but not the same. I frowned to myself, wondering what was going on.

Blue hadn't regained consciousness and was now in a coma. After the police arrived, Blue's hospital room was placed under guard. They must have thought the person who tried to kill her might try again.

I shivered in the sterile atmosphere of the hospital. I knew I should have trusted my instincts. Blue *wasn't* responsible for the murder of Charles Macraith. She was a victim herself. Why would she leave stolen items in plain sight in her house? It was as if they were meant to be found—placed there to frame her, by the same person who tried to kill her. Would Dorian's book be among the items recovered?

The tea from the hospital's café consisted of pre-bagged cardboard boxes of black and green teas, plus one herbal mint blend. I took the scalding paper cup from the café to the waiting room. The scent of modern abrasive chemicals was making me feel sick. I was hoping the mint tea would help calm my stomach.

A light rain gave the view from the waiting room windows a hazy appearance. It wasn't falling hard enough to see the raindrops, yet the mist gave the trees outside a surreal sheen, as if I was watching an old movie instead of experiencing it as reality.

I was caught up in my thoughts and didn't notice when Max sat down opposite me.

"You most likely saved her life," he said, "by finding her when you did."

I glanced around. Aside from me and Max, the only other people in the waiting room were two elderly women in the opposite corner. "Have you gotten any sleep?"

"I look that bad, huh?" He ran his hand through his disheveled black hair as his lips ticked up into a faint smile.

He didn't look bad at all. In fact, in his rumpled suit, a barely visible spot of tea spilled on his white dress shirt, and despite his unshaven face, I felt stirrings in me I hadn't felt in years. His sallow skin, however, suggested that he needed a good meal and a solid chunk of sleep more than what I was thinking about.

"How is she?" I asked.

"Stable. I don't know much myself, but I can tell you that much."

"What's going on, Max?"

"It's an ongoing investigation."

"Which involves me—"

"I wasn't finished. It's ongoing, and because Blue is in a coma we can't question her yet. But we found more of your stolen possessions, hidden at her house."

"You found my books?"

"Books?"

"Books were among the antiques that were stolen."

Max scrolled through the screen on his phone. "Damn."

"What is it?"

"The crew found several of the items you reported, but none of the books."

I groaned. I'd been holding out hope that it would be simple to recover Dorian's book.

"It's early in the investigation," Max said.

"What's the guard for? You really think someone is going to try to finish the job?"

Max studied my face for a moment.

"What?" I said, hoping I didn't have a chunk of kale caught between my teeth.

"Why would you think that?"

"You answer a lot of questions with another question, Detective Liu."

He sighed. "You ask a lot of questions, Ms. Faust."

"This couldn't have been an accident, if that's what you're getting at. The poison I smelled wasn't something she would have mixed by accident. Someone gave it to her."

"The poison that *only you* somehow detected."

"This again?" Now I was annoyed. "I told you, I've studied herbs enough that I'm more sensitive to this type of scent than other people."

"I don't think she ingested it accidentally either."

"Oh. You agree with me. Then what are we arguing about?"

"You're forgetting something."

"What?" I snapped. I was tired of riddles.

"Blue is a good person." He paused but held my gaze. "I don't think she took the poison accidentally—because there's a good chance she took it on purpose."

I was speechless for a few moments. "You think she was trying to kill herself? Why?"

"I've seen good people be driven to murder before. It eats them up inside."

"Wait, you mean you think *Blue* may have had something to do with the murder?" I thought back on my conversation with Blue. I remembered a kindred spirit, not a guilt-stricken woman.

Max started to say something else, but his words were drowned out by someone shouting as they ran down the hallway.

"Is this the right way? Blue!"

Max jumped up and stopped Brixton before he got close to the room with the guard.

"Hold on, kiddo."

"Where is she?" Brixton asked. His face was streaked with tears he hadn't bothered to wipe away.

A lanky man followed a few steps behind Brixton. He looked familiar, though it took me a moment to place the tall, sandy-haired young man. I'd seen him at the teashop, Blue's second customer of the day who'd gotten his tea to go.

"You can't see her right now," Max said.

Brixton tried to push past Max, who grabbed his wrist.

"Ow!" Brixton said. Max didn't release his grip.

"You drove him, Sam?" Max asked.

"I knew he'd ride his bike here if I didn't. I wanted to see her, too."

"I'll stay here," Brixton said. "I promise. Just let go of your death grip. Isn't this, like, police brutality?"

"You're fine," Max said, but at the same time he released Brixton.

"I'm Zoe," I said to the newcomer.

"Sam Strum. I'm one of Brixton's teachers."

"Who *cares?*" Brixton said, tossing his backpack to the floor and flinging himself into a chair. "Blue is lying there dying—"

"She's not really dying, is she?" Sam asked, scratching his neck. The skin was already raw. I understood the feeling of being uncomfortable in hospitals.

"She's stable," Max said. His expression was unreadable.

"Thank God." Sam rubbed his neck nervously again. "God, I hate hospitals. I spent far too much time in this place with Aunt Olivia last year."

At the mention of Olivia's name, I realized this was the nephew she said recommended the teashop to her. It had taken me a moment to make the connection, because the difference between the two was striking. While Olivia was a tiny figure, Sam stood well over six feet tall. Yet where Olivia's personality made her seem larger than her slight body, the impact of Sam's exceptional height was lessened by his slumped shoulders.

Brixton tapped his foot and glared at us. "Why can't we see Blue?"

"She's asleep, Brix," Max said, omitting the facts that Blue was in a coma and there was a police guard at her door.

Brixton glared at Max. "She'd want to see me."

"I'm sure she needs her rest," Sam said. "Let me take you home."

"I'm staying here."

"You can't stay here," Sam began.

"Why not? My mom isn't home. She's at an artist retreat. And my stepdad is away on business."

"She leaves you at home alone?" I asked.

"I was supposed to go over to Blue's house after school today. I was going to stay with her for a few days."

Max and Sam glanced at each other. So it was Brixton who was going to be Blue's houseguest.

"Can you call your mom?" Sam asked. "She'd want to come home to be with you now."

Brixton started to type a text message, but Sam elbowed him. "*Call* her," he said.

Brixton grumbled but did as he was told. He spoke quietly into the phone. I didn't hear what he was saying until he handed the phone to me. "She wants to talk to you," he said.

"Me?"

Brixton rolled his eyes and handed me the phone.

"Would it be too much trouble for Brix to stay with you for a couple of days?" Heather asked.

I walked with the phone to the other end of the waiting room. To make sure my voice wouldn't carry back to Brixton and the others, I turned to face the window. The misty rain had turned into a heavier downpour.

"Brixton is really upset," I said softly. "I think he'd like you to come home."

"Oh, Brix is a resilient kid. He said Blue's okay. He'll be fine."

"She was poisoned."

"But she's not dead or anything."

I stared at the phone. Heather was so very young. I put the phone back to my ear. "Blue has been a big part of his life since he was little, right? He's really upset. If you could come back—"

"If it's too much trouble for him to stay with you—"

"Wouldn't he feel more comfortable staying with one of his friends?"

"Have you *met* Ethan's parents? No, I don't want him staying there. And

Veronica's parents don't have an extra room—and now that the kids are four-teen... If you don't want to have him stay with you, don't worry. He knows how to take care of himself. He'll be fine on his own. I'll be back in three days—"

"Hold on."

"You mean you'll do it, Zoe?"

CHAPTER 13

I added an extra scoop of unsweetened cocoa powder to the mixture in the blender.

"I'm not drinking that," Brixton said.

"One sip," I said, "is all I ask."

"Whatever." He skulked to the other side of the kitchen and stuffed his hands in the pockets of his jeans, then took them out and crossed his arms. Without a cell phone, he didn't seem to know what to do with his hands.

I'd driven Brixton back to my house from the hospital. Of course I wasn't letting a grieving kid stay in his house by himself. I wasn't sure how Dorian was going to react to Brixton's staying at the house for a few days, or to the new information that his book wasn't among the items recovered at Blue's house. Upon seeing us come into the house, Dorian hadn't yelled or hidden. Instead, he held up a clawed hand and simply said, "Phone." Brixton complied, handing over the device. "I will return it to you when you leave the house," Dorian told him. Brixton wouldn't be getting any more videos of the gargoyle.

I hadn't yet told Dorian that his book wasn't one of the items recovered. I knew how important it was, so I couldn't bring myself to break it to him. Brixton didn't know Dorian was dying, so I had to wait until he wouldn't hear us talking. I wasn't looking forward to that conversation.

I turned my attention back to the blender. The trick to creating a kid-friendly green smoothie is all in the chocolate. Fruits have natural sugars that sweeten a smoothie, but without chocolate, the flavor of vegetables can over-power the fruit.

In addition to the subtler flavors of cucumber and avocado, the sweetness of a large pear, and the spicy kick of a knob of ginger, I added a few leaves of light green curly kale. Kale is a winter vegetable, making it abundant at local farmers markets. As it was, it would have been a perfect smoothie for me, but I was making this for Brixton. Since meeting him earlier that week, I had seen him eat cookies and peanut butter sandwiches he had in his backpack, but I hadn't seen him eat a single vegetable. That was going to change. And he was going to like it.

To make sure it would be palatable for his taste, I added a scoop of peanut butter and instead of plain water I opted for coconut water, which was sweeter. After blending it well, I poured half of the creamy mixture into a mug and handed it to Brixton.

He took a sip and scowled at me. "What's in it?"

"You saw everything I did."

"Yeah, but this actually tastes *good*."

I smiled. "Come on, I'll show you where you can sleep."

Even with my old furniture the movers had delivered, the house was sparsely furnished. Brixton would have to settle for the small mattress I'd brought inside from my Airstream trailer, which I'd placed in the upstairs bedroom with the least leaky windows.

When we reached the top of the creaking stairs, Brixton lagged behind.

"When do we get to check on Blue?" he asked.

"I'll call and check on her. I promise I'll let you know as soon as I hear anything."

In addition to a small backpack, Brixton had a guitar with him. Maybe that would help get him out of his funk. The scuffs and stickers on the case suggested the instrument was well-loved. I'd tried out several instruments over the years, but it was the piano that spoke to me most. Not the most prac-tical thing for someone who lived on the road. But now that I had a house... If I could solve the madness surrounding me, was I fooling myself thinking I could stay a while? From the top of the stairs, I turned to look down at the living room. It was still filled with moving crates, but I could imagine a grand piano in the corner. Such an instrument might be worth the depleting task of transmuting lead into gold.

"Why don't you bring your guitar downstairs after you get settled," I said.

"I'm not playing for you," he said.

"You don't have to."

"Whatever."

I left Brixton to unpack his small bag and found Dorian attending to the fireplace. "Both you and the boy are wearing heavy sweaters," he said, "so it must be cold inside."

"You don't feel it?"

"I feel the difference in temperature, but I do not mind it. I checked the chimney last night. It is sound. I thought we would have a fire."

"That's a great idea."

"Zoe Faust," Dorian said, "for someone who has had time to learn to lie, your face is an open book, as they say. You are keeping something from me. Is it about the woman who was found nearly dead? Is her condition more serious than you are allowing the boy to think?"

"It's about her, but not in the way that you think." I hesitated. I hated being the bearer of bad news. "Some of the items stolen from the house were found at her house."

"*Mon livre!*"

"I'm sorry," I said, "your book wasn't among the items recovered."

Dorian fired a million questions at me—or at least a dozen— none of which I knew the answer to. I was more than ready for a break from the gargoyle's interrogation when Brixton came downstairs and found us sitting in front of a blazing fire. He brought his guitar with him but wore a skeptical look on his face.

"*Est ce que tu connais 'Dame Tartine,' Zoe?*" Dorian said to me.

"Of course you'd think of that folk song. It's all about butter."

"Not only butter," Dorian said. "Also anise and raisins."

Brixton looked at us like we were crazy. But he also looked like he was itching to play the beaten-up acoustic guitar he held with a confident hand.

"If you play these chords," Dorian told Brixton, "we will sing."

Dorian and I sang the French-language verses about sweet pralines, fried croquettes, and baked biscuits, with Dorian prompting Brixton when to play different chords.

"It's about a woman, Dame Tartine, who lives in a house of food," I explained. "A tartine is a French style of open-faced sandwich."

"I'm fourteen, you know," Brixton said. "Not eight."

"But the song is in French," Dorian said. "It has a very nice sound. If you learn the words, you do not have to tell your girlfriend what they mean."

"Veronica is *not* my girlfriend," Brixton said. He didn't blush when he said it, but it was interesting that he immediately thought of her when Dorian used the word. I remembered the tall, awkward girl standing on my porch earlier that week who was going to be a knockout once she grew into her own skin.

"How long have the three of you been friends?" I asked.

"Me and VCM have been best friends since we were little."

"VCM?"

"Veronica Chen-Mendoza. V or VCM for short. Anyway, Ethan moved here two years ago. Everybody wanted to be friends with him except us."

"I must have misunderstood your English," Dorian said. "Is he not your friend?"

"Me and V hated him at first. His parents are, like, uber-rich. He has everything. But then we learned he doesn't care about that stuff. He's cool."

"Why does he dress like James Dean?" I asked.

"Yeah, kinda weird, huh? He had us over to his house and showed us this movie *Rebel Without a Cause*. That's when we knew he was cool." His face clouded over. "Do you think Blue tried to kill herself? That's what people are saying."

"I honestly don't know."

"She's like a mom to me, you know? You met my mom. She acts more like Veronica's little sister than a mom sometimes. I don't know what I'd do if Blue doesn't—" He broke off and stood up, walking away from us. He wiped his face with his sleeve.

Dorian stood up. I put my hand on his arm to hold him back, giving Brixton space.

"When do we eat around here?" Brixton said after a minute. "I'm starving."

"That is the best suggestion I have heard all day," Dorian said. "Let us cook."

I followed them into the kitchen to get a glass of water.

"We begin with *mise en place*," Dorian said to Brixton. "This means putting everything you wish to use in a meal in its proper place, before you begin cooking. What shall we cook for dinner?"

While they prepared dinner in the kitchen, I sat in front of the fireplace and stared into the richly colored flames. What was I going to do about the two of them? I couldn't let either of them down.

Since the police hadn't recovered Dorian's book with the other items found at Blue's house, there was renewed urgency in deciphering the few pages I had.

I spread out the photographed pages, stopping on the one with an unsettling image of a basilisk, the creature that symbolizes the destructive fire necessary to perform transformations. As you'd normally find in an alchemical woodcut, the creature had the head of a bird and the body of a serpent. That's where the similarities ended. The tail of this serpent was contorted and wrapped in such an unexpected and disconcerting way that I was sure it had to mean something. But what that was, I had no idea. Perhaps the background setting had significance. The contorted basilisk was perched at the top of crumbled castle ruins, clinging to the one turret that remained.

My own books hadn't yet proven helpful to decipher any of the pages, so I again opened my laptop, delving deeper on the internet for anything that might be remotely relevant. Nothing like this image seemed to exist. I typed sections of the convoluted Latin into a search, again coming up empty-handed. Read literally, the text explained how one needed to walk in the direction where one cannot see. Riddles! The alchemists always had their riddles. I had never appreciated that part of alchemy. I liked my mysteries solved, which is probably why I loved the detective fiction that came of age in the nineteenth century. Yet there was something about the riddle of these pages that tickled at my brain—as if I'd been searching in the wrong places and the answers were within me.

"Ignore the color of the soup," Dorian said, carrying a tray of three steaming bowls from the kitchen.

"What's wrong with the... oh." The creamed soup was certain shade of brown that should be reserved for a room of the house that wasn't the dining room.

"He didn't warn me," Brixton said, following Dorian out of the kitchen carrying a Dutch oven with two pot holders. "I thought using the purple carrots would be cool."

"Don't worry," I said. "I've done it myself. It's simple chemistry. Purple blended with the other vegetables gives you brown."

"The risotto is a much more palatable color," Dorian said.

As we ate, I couldn't pull my mind from *Not Untrue Alchemy.* I was missing a crucial element of deciphering the pages, making me simultaneously far away and close to unlocking the secrets in those pages.

I knew what I had to do.

There was one thing I hadn't yet tried. The more I thought about it, the more sure I was that it was the key. I could immerse myself in alchemy, doing something I hadn't done in nearly a century. I could set up my alchemy laboratory. I didn't know if I was ready, but that didn't matter. I had to be.

CHAPTER 14

The empty concrete basement smelled of mildew and beer. The scents alone would be distracting to the point of causing failure. I looked at the harsh light bulb suspended from the ceiling and considered my options.

Becoming an alchemist takes years of study. Learning the foundations is essential to be successful at your transformations. I was an impatient young woman when I began my alchemical studies. Nicolas Flamel had taken me in, with my brother in tow, when he received word from an acquaintance about my aptitude with plant transformations. Since alchemy, at its core, is about transformation, he had high hopes of training me to be an alchemist like him and his wife Perenelle. But my alchemical training was incomplete. I had given it up after my brother Thomas died. I was his big sister. I was supposed to take care of him, but I failed.

I shook my head at the memory, and my hand automatically flew to my gold locket. I pushed the painful thoughts from my mind and forced my hand to let go of the locket. I couldn't let myself get distracted by misfortunes that had caused me to act rashly. Though I had never completed my training, there was still a great deal I knew about alchemy. But so much time had passed. I was sure that was a big part of the reason I was having difficulty under-standing Dorian's strange alchemy book. Getting back into hands-on practice would help me see what I was missing.

That was the idea, anyway.

When I'd had the foolish notion that I might have a normal life for a little while here in Portland, I thought I might be ready to practice alchemy again. Not right away, but I wanted to give myself the space I needed to see if I was ready. It's why I had wanted a house with a basement in need of renovation.

This basement was the reason I had hired Charles Macraith. Working with a contractor with a versatile set of skills who was known for keeping his mouth shut, it would have been possible for me to build the type of alchemy lab I thought I might want again. Not merely a room, but a carefully organized laboratory including a tower furnace.

Even before Dorian came into my life with his peculiar book, the reason I was drawn to practicing alchemy again was because I wanted to feel whole. Alchemy had dominated so much of my life that even though I had run from it, I couldn't escape it. But while I was running, I was also running from myself. I wondered if I needed to practice alchemy to find myself again.

My plan, when I bought this house, had been to ease myself into it. Finding a place to call home, working the land to create an edible garden of herbs and vegetables, and fixing up a working laboratory to practice alchemy. The *last* step would be creating spagyric plant transformations to heal myself both physically and psychologically. Now that fate had forced my hand, that final step had to jump to the forefront.

I had already found the Elixir of Life, but the elixir is only a small part of alchemy. As I had explained to Brixton, alchemy is about the transformation of the impure into the pure. Transforming lead into gold. Transforming the body to free it from its bonds of mortality. Transforming the spirit into mental well-being.

I had lost sight of myself over the last century. I had been taking care of myself physically, because I could make simple healing foods without thinking. But I wasn't really living. Ever since Ambrose.

Besides my brother, Ambrose was the only person I had ever loved. After Thomas died, it was Ambrose who taught me how to live again. For a while, at least. But that, too, ended in a tragedy I didn't anticipate. Because of me, they had both died painful deaths, alone. How could I have known what Ambrose would do?

But that was all in centuries past. I had been running without looking back for long enough. I felt my gold locket again. The metal was warm from where I wore it close to my heart. The only two people I had ever loved with all my heart were gone. There was nothing I could do about that now. But I could save those I cared about in the present.

I had to have a clean workspace free from distractions before beginning an alchemical transformation. I had never shied away from hard work, so even though I couldn't build a proper lab, I could clean the basement and set up the old alchemy laboratory supplies I'd shipped from Paris. I needed to buy some new materials, but I would be able to do some simple transformations right away.

I hoped.

~

After I saw Brixton off to school the next morning—listening to him grumble about water torture from the malfunctioning shower— I got to work.

With a combination of vinegar and strength of will, four hours later my basement no longer smelled like a dank moldy brewery. Now it smelled like a fresh-scented brewery. A previous owner must have brewed his own beer down here. I was going to do my own brewing, but not of beer.

Now that the floor was clean, I noticed a scrape running across the center of the large room. Had someone previously built the basement into separate rooms? I thought again of the plans I had wanted Charles Macraith to execute, immediately followed by a pang of guilt. The man was dead. And I didn't know if his death was related to me.

The idea would have been easier to dismiss as paranoia if not for the reaction of other contractors I tried to hire. I was willing to settle for a handyman who could do basic repairs to the roof, broken windows, and pipes. I'd deal with real fixes later. If there was a later.

But as soon as I mentioned the address of the house, everyone I contacted gave excuses for why they couldn't come. They were booked. For how long? For the foreseeable future. They hung up without saying goodbye. One person even had a bout of shingles come on while they were talking on the phone. I knew the economy was doing better, but were they all so worried about the possibility that I was a lunatic murderer that they didn't want such a big job? *Oh.* When I thought of it like that, maybe they were being prudent. It had made the papers that Blue was under suspicion. But Blue Sky Teas was a Portland institution. I, on the other hand, was new in town. The day after I arrived, a man was not only poisoned but stabbed right outside my front door. If I didn't know me, I'd probably run away screaming.

I sighed and took a look at what I'd been able to accomplish on my own in the basement. At least it was no longer a moldy room that reeked of hops so strongly as to overwhelm the senses, I reminded myself.

I had a few more hours before Brixton was due back from school. Enough time to get started.

I've never liked the expression that something you used to do but haven't done in years is "like riding a bike." I didn't learn to ride a bike until I was over one hundred years old, shortly after the miserable contraption was invented. It was called a *velocipede* at the time. And it never came easily to me. Maybe it was because of the discomfort of those first bicycles that didn't have air-pressurized tires, giving them the nickname "bone shakers." Give me a motorcar any day. Now *that* was an invention I related to. I took to driving almost as naturally as I did to plants. I was quite disappointed when speed limits were introduced.

Setting up my alchemy lab turned out to be *exactly* like riding a bike—meaning I completely failed at picking it up again.

Though I didn't have everything I would need for a full laboratory, in theory I had enough to get started. Several glass retorts—long-necked containers that could be heated over a flame and sealed with a stopper—and other glass containers that had survived the journey, including a hermetic vase, skull cup, angel tube, spirit holder, and tomb of the dead. I never said alchemists weren't creative. I was missing an athanor—the furnace Charles Macraith was going to build into the wall below the living room fireplace—and I'd need to restock several ingredients.

When Dorian crept down the stairs to bring me a sandwich, he nearly dropped the plate when he saw me. I didn't blame him. My arms were covered in green sludge. Perhaps the consistency would have been better described as slime. If I thought my creaking old house was actually haunted, I would have sworn a ghost had vomited ectoplasm on me.

"Take a break," Dorian said. "Brixton will return from school soon. I'll keep this sandwich warm in the oven for you. "

After taking a quick, icy shower in the upstairs bathroom that needed plumbing help, I joined Dorian at the dining table. Brixton was already there, inhaling a sandwich.

"Thith ith tho good," Brixton said through a mouthful. "What ith thith?" He swallowed. "I thought Zoe didn't eat meat or cheese."

Dorian grinned and removed my roasted mushroom sandwich with truffle cream from the oven. The cream sauce was made from blended cashews, not dairy, with the mushrooms giving the sandwich its hearty "meaty" texture. It was the same thing Brixton was eating, and it was every bit as good as he said. I hadn't realized how famished I was until I took a bite of the heavenly toasted baguette sandwich.

"Can we go see Blue?" Brixton asked.

Dorian raised an eyebrow at me, then lifted another two untoasted open-faced sandwich slices into the oven.

"Why don't you give your mom a call," I said, "while I call and see about Blue."

Brixton sat back in his chair and crossed his arms. "The gargoyle has my phone."

"*Mon dieu*," Dorian said. "You may have the phone to call your mother, but I will be watching. *N'est-ce pas?*"

Two minutes later, we all returned to the table, disheartened. Brixton's mom hadn't asked him about Blue during their brief text message conversation. On my end, I was told that the hospital wasn't allowing visitors.

As we ate in moody silence, Dorian threw his hands into the air.

"I cannot stand this!" he said. "If you wish to eat without speaking to savor the flavors I have created, that is one thing. But this? I cannot tolerate such a maudlin mood while eating. I will at least tell you of some interesting news stories I have been reading in *Le Monde*."

"What's *Le Monde*?" Brixton asked.

"You may never have seen one of these before," Dorian said, scampering off his chair and picking up one of the folded newspapers from the far side of the table. "It is called a *newspaper*. A very civilized invention that has neither pop-up ads nor viruses."

Brixton rolled his eyes.

"Listen to this," Dorian said. "Three museums on the continent are reporting that gold pieces from their museums have been switched for fakes! None of them know how the switch was made, but the fakes are crumbling."

"What's 'the continent'?" Brixton asked.

"*Mon dieu*. The European continent. France, Spain, Italy, Portugal, Germany, Luxembourg—"

Brixton grunted a laugh. "You made up that last one."

Dorian sputtered.

"I don't think he's had geography or world history yet," I said.

"Yeah we did."

"You're not helping yourself, Brixton."

"What? I know all about local history. That what's important, isn't it? Did you know there's a wicked series of tunnels that runs under Portland? Mr. Strum took us on a field trip to the Shanghai Tunnels in his class last fall. It was pretty funny, because he had to walk hunched over the whole time; otherwise he'd smack his head on the low beams in the ceiling. He showed us all sorts of hidden areas—that was before the tunnels were boarded up even more and he couldn't take anyone back. We learned all about the history of this place. In the old days, guys who went to bars would be kidnapped and sold to ship captains. It was called Shanghaiing, since they were put on ships headed to Asia. Pretty wicked, huh?"

Dorian gave up at that point. We were done eating anyway.

It was raining again that afternoon, so instead of fitting in weeding first, I sent Brixton upstairs to do his homework, asking him to let me know if he needed any help.

"I know what we must do," Dorian said, speaking quietly so as not to be overheard.

"Brixton is only in ninth grade. It's okay that he hasn't been paying attention in class."

"Not that. I know what we must do as a next step in our investigation."

"What do you mean *our investigation*? There is no *our investigation*."

"Things are moving too slowly."

"I know. That's why I set up my lab. I think it's the last step I need to figure out the riddles of your book. I'm already beginning to remember more."

"And the specific pages from the book? You have had more success translating the pages you have?"

"It's tough without greater context, but I'm getting closer to an overall understanding—"

"It was difficult," Dorian said, "for me to shift from stone to life today." He gave one firm shake of his head. "We can no longer wait for you to see what you can accomplish with only those few pages. *We must find the book.*"

"I can't stand seeing this happen to you, but how do you propose we get it?"

"Blue Sky possessed your other stolen items. Is it not possible the police missed something? They did not know what they were looking for. We must go to Blue's house."

"It's a crime scene, Dorian."

He tapped his claws on the table. "Then we must break in."

CHAPTER 15

Getting a closer look at Blue's house was a tempting thought. Tempting, but dangerous. I wasn't into danger these days. I'd had enough of it for many lifetimes.

"I'm not breaking into someone's house," I said.

"Why not?" Dorian asked.

"It being *illegal* is the first thing that springs to mind."

The gargoyle rolled his eyes. "For someone who lives outside of normal society, you have a strange concept of justice."

"I'm not talking about it being *wrong* to break in." I'd lived through the execution of enough unjust laws that "the law" wasn't high on my list of things I respected. "I'm talking about it being risky. I'm trying to stay under the radar." He squinted at me.

"Oh," I said, "'under the radar' is an idiom that means I don't wish to be detected."

"Ah yes, I understand now. But this is not the time for an English lesson. If we wish to learn what has become of my book, there is much more we must learn of Blue, no?"

"There are other ways."

"Such as?"

"I haven't thought of them yet," I admitted.

"You know why this is so important to me." His eyes bore into me.

"I know, Dorian," I said. "I know."

~

That's how a few hours later I found myself making an energizing chocolate elixir to stay alert in the middle of the night.

"Brixton is getting ready for bed," I said as I came through the kitchen door with a coconut. After dinner I'd made a quick stop at the market for the coconut and checked on Brixton.

Dorian was finishing cleaning up the kitchen after the three-course dinner he'd cooked us—a potato mushroom soup starter, a pumpkin loaf crusted with poppy seeds as the main dish, and a bed of arugula with fennel and orange for the third course. Brixton had eaten everything except the fennel, which he refused to taste. I thought the licorice flavor of fennel would appeal to him, but not so much. He'd accepted a lot that week. I wasn't going to push.

During dinner that night, Brixton had continued to ask intelligent questions about alchemy. He was understandably confused about what was real and what wasn't, due to pop culture's treatment of alchemy that gave it magical properties. The more answers I gave him, the more questions he had. That was alchemy.

Once Dorian finished washing the dishes, he untied the apron from around his waist and hung it on the door hook. "I do not understand why we cannot make the boy a dessert and add something to it that will *help* him sleep while we are out tonight."

"I'm *not* drugging Brixton," I said emphatically.

"It would be safer."

"I draw the line at drugging a kid." I slammed a butcher's knife into the fresh young coconut, splitting the thick white husk on the first try. Two more firm pounds with the edge of the knife and I had a triangular hole in the coconut.

Cutting into a coconut is daunting if you're not used to it, but coconut was an important part of the energizing elixir that helped keep me awake when I had to be up well past dark. Being alert during the middle of the night was nearly impossible for me. My only chance at being coherent was natural sugars and fats with a little bit of caffeine.

"Now that you have successfully massacred the coconut," Dorian said, "you should place it in the fridge."

"I need to drink this before we go."

"How long does it last? We should not venture out until after midnight."

"After *midnight*?" I set down the knife. "Can't we go earlier?"

He shook his head resolutely.

~

I stayed awake by again looking through the pages of Dorian's book, this time hoping the mental preparation of setting up an alchemy lab was enough to spark further understanding.

I paused on a woodcut showing a menagerie of animals. At the bottom of the illustration, the land was covered with toads, symbolizing the First Matter. Yet even in the still illustration, the toads were clearly dead. In the sky above, bees swarmed, symbolizing purification and rebirth. The carving alluded to motion, showing the wind pushing the bees in a counterclockwise direction, pushing them toward the earth.

The stress of not understanding, while knowing what was at stake, did a decent job keeping me awake. Still, I felt myself fading. Midnight might not be a bewitching hour, but it effectively turns me into a pumpkin.

At a few minutes to midnight, I grabbed a jar of unsweetened cocoa powder from the cabinet and scooped a few tablespoons into the blender, scraped vanilla paste from a vanilla pod I kept in a glass jar, added the coconut meat and liquid from the fruit I'd split open earlier, and blended the mixture. I offered half to Dorian. He politely declined.

Before we left, I walked by Brixton's room, trying not to make too much noise on the creaking floor. I could see through the one-inch space between the door and the floor that his light was off.

We drove my truck to an isolated field near Blue's house. Dorian took my hand to lead me through the field. His eyes were able to see in the dark much better than mine, so it allowed us to move without a flashlight.

"Is that it?" I asked, pointing to a house blanketed in shadows.

"Yes," Dorian agreed, "I can see the police tape."

We had reached the edge of a growth of trees but were still at least fifty yards from the storybook cottage. I hadn't had much time to study the yard the first time I'd visited. Now that my eyes had adjusted to the moonlight, I couldn't help noticing some of the more interesting plants. Caught up in the bounty surrounding me, I lost sight of Dorian.

I whipped my head around. I didn't see him. Some of the weeds grew higher than three feet, so he could have been anywhere in the field.

"Dorian," I whispered.

He didn't answer, but I heard a click. I followed the sound. He had just opened the front door.

I hurried to the door, following Dorian inside and closing it behind us.

Unlike the wild nature of the outside of the house, the inside of the cottage was well maintained. In the kitchen, colorful handcrafted dishes filled open cabinets. The remnants of dried herbs hung from hooks on the ceiling. The police must have taken the rest as evidence.

One thing was lacking from the house: photographs. I wondered at first if it was the police who had taken the photos as evidence, until I saw that there were a few photos on a bookshelf. One was a photo of Blue with a younger Brixton. I didn't recognize the people in the other photos, but they all had Portland backdrop. There was no evidence of Blue's life before she moved here. *The life she'd been running from.*

I took a step from the dining room bookshelf into the living room. This was the room I'd seen from the window. The room where Blue's unconscious body had been. As my foot touched the carpet, the sensation hit me like a gust of cold air. Only there were no doors or windows open.

"What is it?" Dorian asked.

"There's poison here," I murmured. I crouched down. "The glass has been removed, but some of the contents spilled onto the rug here."

"What are you doing?" Dorian exclaimed. "We are not looking for poison. We are looking for my book!"

Ignoring Dorian, I touched the moist rug and smelled my fingertips. I felt a shiver spread from my fingers to the rest of my body. Something was wrong. This wasn't a concoction infused with Blue's personal touch. More than that, *it was something reminiscent of alchemy.*

I stood up hastily, knocking over a small wooden table.

"Are you well?" Dorian asked.

"We need to get out of here."

"What is wrong?"

"This isn't something Blue created," I said. "I'm sensitive to the energies put into extracting plant essences, and Blue's energy isn't here."

"What does that mean?"

"This was no accident. And no suicide attempt."

"Who made it?"

"All I can tell from this small amount is that it was deliberate poisoning. Someone tried to kill her." I didn't say the question hanging on my lips. The question that sent a lightning-bolt shiver through me. *Was this the work of an alchemist?*

Dorian's head darted around. His eyes locked on a box of tissue across the room. He moved quickly. A few seconds later, he took my hand in his, wiping away the drops of poison with half of the tissues in the box.

I smiled at the gesture. "I can feel it through my skin because I'm attuned to it, but it's not going to poison me this way." I hesitated. "At least I don't think so." I could handle toxins, as all alchemists must if they wish to perform laboratory experiments beyond theoretical exercises. But this was different. There was something both strange and familiar about it. I tried to think what it could be, but there wasn't enough of the substance remaining.

"*Mon dieu.*"

"We need to leave so I can tell Max that Blue is innocent."

Dorian crossed his arms and glared at me. "You cannot think you are getting involved in a *police* investigation. *Les flics* cannot help us."

"It's all connected, Dorian. If we find out what happened to Blue, we find your book. Max seems like a good guy."

"You propose," Dorian said stiffly, "waking him up at two o'clock in the morning, telling him you broke into a crime scene, and explaining how you detected that Blue herself did not create the poison she ingested. You are not that careless."

My body began to shake. What was going on?

"You are ill!" Dorian said. "Do you know what poison it was you touched? Is there an antidote?"

I shook my head as I sat down on the couch and pulled a small purple blanket over me. "I'm only shivering because it's cold and it's hours past when I should be sound asleep." I silently cursed myself. Of course a poison would have a greater effect on me in the middle of the night! Like plants unfurling, I get my strength from the light. I had never before touched a poisonous substance after dark.

"But the poison?"

I shook my head again. "I can't tell what it is. There isn't enough here in the rug for me to determine what it is or who made it." There was another possibility that I hoped wasn't true. I had pushed my memories of alchemy so far to the back of my mind. Was it possible I could no longer access the knowledge?

"Your skin is pale."

"I'm fine."

"Can you walk?"

"Yes. Just give me a minute."

"*Merde.* You sit here while I search the yard for anywhere my book could be hidden."

"I told you—"

"Yes, yes. You are fine. *Mais non.* Take a nap here on the couch while I search outside. I will return shortly."

Shortly after Dorian slipped out the door, I felt myself falling asleep. I hopped up. If I went to sleep now, I wouldn't want to wake up. Instead, I pulled the blanket around me and continued searching Blue's house for anything the police might have missed. I didn't have high hopes. Now that I was certain Blue hadn't poisoned herself on purpose, it was clear she was being framed. The person framing her would have left the stolen items where they would be easily discovered. Meaning Charles Macraith's murderer must still have Dorian's book. What did they want with it? And was that all they wanted?

Dorian returned while I was finishing leafing through the books on Blue's bookshelf, which was full of books on tea, wildcrafting, meditation, plus several dozen romance novels. Dorian's expression was somber.

"I didn't find anything either," I said.

We walked back to the car in silence. The cold chilled me to the point where I began to shake again.

"What you need is a bisque to warm you up," Dorian said. "I have a container of broth in your fridge, so it will take no time to cook."

I was too cold and tired to argue. I blasted the heat on our drive back to the house. There was no rain, but the wind was whipping up leaves and bending tree branches.

At first, that's what I thought I was seeing as I approached the house. As we grew closer, I realized I was mistaken. It wasn't swaying tree branches in my yard.

Two shadowy figures were creeping up to the house.

CHAPTER 16

I killed the engine before we reached the driveway.

"You saw the shadows too," Dorian said.

"We never should have left Brixton there alone," I said, hastily throwing off my seatbelt and reaching for the door handle. "At the very least I should have insisted you give him back his cell phone you confiscated!"

Dorian's firm hand gripped my arm. "Go. I will hide, but I will be near in case you and the boy need me."

My earlier feelings of exhaustion and cold disappeared, replaced with adrenaline as I crept up the side of the yard. What was going on? Charles Macraith was dead and Dorian's book was gone. What could the thief and murderer want with my house?

The two figures were dressed in black. Hooded sweatshirts covered the backs of their heads. One was tall and thin, the other short with an average build. Neither was very large. I had learned different schools of self-defense moves over the years, but hadn't put any into practice in decades. If I had to use any now, I might be rusty but at least I had a fighting chance.

The figures had almost reached the porch.

I followed at a distance, walking up to the house along the side of the fence rather than the main path. There was nothing shielding me from their line of sight. If they turned, they would see me. It was a risk, but I had no choice.

The porch light clicked on. I cursed under my breath. Brixton was exactly the type of kid who'd take it upon himself to investigate if he heard strange noises. That didn't surprise me. But his next move did. The front door eased open. *What was Brixton doing?*

Brixton motioned the figures inside. When the taller figure stepped forward, I caught a glimpse of the face beneath the hooded sweatshirt. It was Brixton's friend Veronica.

I couldn't see the face of the other figure, but he was the right stature to be their friend Ethan.

Confusion replaced my apprehension. I briefly considered joining them before the front door closed behind them but thought better of it. Whatever they were doing, they were unlikely to tell me about it if I asked them directly.

"Dorian," I whispered. "Are you here?"

He wasn't.

A light clicked on inside the living room. I crept to one of the large windows. The curtains were drawn, as I'd been careful to do because of Dorian. I couldn't see or hear anything.

I hurried to the back door that led to the kitchen. I opened it as quickly as I could, but it gave a shrill squeak. I stopped and waited. I heard young voices trying to whisper but failing and speaking animatedly instead. They hadn't heard me. I closed the door behind me and went to the swinging kitchen door, the exact place from which Brixton had eavesdropped on me and Dorian. Between the swinging door and the door frame, there was a half-inch gap through which I could see a section of the dining and living rooms.

"You begin with *mise en place*," a voice said.

I froze. It was *Dorian's* voice.

I peeked through the door. Dorian was nowhere in sight. Brixton was holding up a cell phone—a different model from the one Dorian had confiscated. The voice was coming from the phone.

Foiled from getting a video recording of the gargoyle, Brixton had recorded Dorian's voice.

It all made sense now. It had been far too easy to get Brixton to accept that Dorian's existence needed to be a secret. He hadn't accepted it at all. He was pretending to befriend the gargoyle so he could prove to his friends that Dorian existed.

Anger bubbled up inside me. Brixton was old enough that he should have thought about the consequences of his actions. Watching him and his friends through my hiding place, I had to stop myself from bursting through the door. Before confronting Brixton, I needed a plan.

Brixton stopped the recording. "I told you," he said to his friends.

"So what?" Ethan said. "You've got an audio recording of a guy with a French accent."

"That's why I invited you here," Brixton said. "I thought he'd be here, near the fireplace. That's where he was earlier. But he's a creature of the night. He must have gone out."

"A creature of the night?" Veronica said. "Like a vampire?"

"Yeah, except vampires aren't real. The gargoyle is real."

"So we wait," Ethan said. "I brought snacks." He spread out on the couch and tossed a bag of pretzels in gourmet packaging onto the coffee table.

Veronica tore into the bag. "No chocolate?"

"Keep it down, you guys," Brixton said. "I don't know how soundly Zoe sleeps."

My anger barely contained, I slipped out the back door and circled to the front of the house. Giving up any pretense of being quiet, I shoved my key into the door and opened it.

Veronica screamed and dropped the bag of pretzels.

"Slumber party?" I asked.

"Zoe?" Brixton croaked. "What are you—I mean, I thought you were asleep."

"I stepped out to visit a friend. Sorry, if I'd known you were going to be up, I would have left you a note."

"Sorry about your floor, Ms. Faust," Veronica said, picking up broken pretzel fragments.

"Please, call me Zoe. Don't you guys have school tomorrow?"

"Group research project, Zoe," Ethan said. He was the only one still sitting calmly. He'd made himself comfortable on the couch. He leaned forward with his elbows resting on his knees, an easy smile on his face.

"Research, huh? Anything I can help with?" I looked pointedly at Brixton.

"Uh, yeah, we're just about done."

"Since you've been working so hard, let me get you all a proper snack."

I led them to the kitchen and removed a chocolate cake from the fridge. Dorian had made it the day before while I was working in my makeshift alchemy lab. He was cooking more food than the two of us could eat and had used up most of the food in my pantry. The last of the cashews had gone into making the creamy frosting for the cake.

Veronica's eyes grew wide.

"You like dark chocolate?" I asked.

She nodded, hungrily eyeing the frosted cake. I took plates from the cabinet and let the kids cut whatever size pieces they wanted. Veronica took the largest piece, which made me smile.

"Omigod," she said, closing her eyes and savoring the mouthful.

"I think this is like the best cake I've ever eaten, Ms. Faust."

Brixton took a bite of cake while sulking silently in the corner.

"So, Zoe," Ethan said, eyeing me and leaving his cake untouched, "you were out visiting a 'friend' in the middle of the night."

Veronica kicked him.

"He's a Frenchman," I said, following through on my idea to disabuse them of the notion that I had a French gargoyle in my house. "The French enjoy late dinners. I drank wine, so I had to wait a while before it was safe for me to drive home."

"You have a French boyfriend?" Veronica said. "That's so romantic! I've always wanted to go to Paris. Is he from Paris?"

"He's from Paris," I said, thinking about the other stone gargoyles carved by Eugène Viollet-le-Duc. "But he's just a friend."

"A *gargoyle*, huh?" Ethan said to Brixton.

"What's that, Ethan?" I said in my most innocent voice.

Brixton glared at me.

"Brixton," Ethan said, "was telling us all about your French friend. Weren't you, Brix?"

"Shut up and try the cake, Ethan," Brixton said.

With a smirk on his face, Ethan took a bite of cake. His expression changed. "Wow, that *is* good. Is this from Petunia's?"

"It's homemade," I said.

"Nice," Ethan said.

A creaking noise sounded.

"I'll be right back," I said. "I don't remember if I locked the front door."

I looked around and didn't see Dorian. It was probably the wind trying to get through one of the broken windows or drafty doors. I double-checked that I'd locked up. Everything seemed in place.

I paused before returning to the kitchen. I could hear Veronica speaking to the boys.

"You're such a jerk!" she said. "Calling Zoe's boyfriend a gargoyle. Is he disfigured, or just ugly? No, he couldn't be ugly. He's French."

I smiled to myself and pushed open the kitchen door.

"I love your dyed white hair," Veronica said. "The short, slanted bob is very Parisian."

"Like you'd know," Brixton said.

"This has been fun, Zoe," Ethan said. "But like you said, it's a school night. We should go."

"Thanks, Ms. Faust," Veronica said. She smiled awkwardly at me before shooting Brixton a dirty look, presumably still upset that she thought he'd come up with a nasty nickname for my romantic French boyfriend.

"Maybe we could meet your *friend* some other time," Ethan said.

Think, Zoe. "He's shy. He's self-conscious about a nasty scar. People in America are less accepting than they are in France." *Ugh.* It was an awkward lie, but something had to be done.

"You are *such* a jerk," Veronica whispered to Brixton. He glared at me.

I held open the kitchen door. "Let me drive you home."

"They've got their bikes," Brixton said.

"They'll fit in the back of the truck."

"Um," Veronica said, "I'm not really supposed to be out this late."

"I won't wake up your parents," I promised. "We won't all fit in the cab of the truck, so Brixton, you can clean the dishes while I'm gone. We're not done. I'll be right back."

I shivered as I walked back out into the night. Now that my adrenaline had worn off, I could feel an unwelcome substance coursing through my veins.

~

After dropping off Veronica and Ethan, I found a sulking teenager and a gargoyle waiting for me in the living room. My body shook more from anger than the residual effects of the poison.

"He wouldn't let me go to bed," Brixton said. "That's child abuse."

"I thought you said you weren't a child," I said.

He glared at me.

"You betrayed us, Brixton," I said, glaring back at him. "To say I'm disappointed in you doesn't convey the gravity of what you've done. Don't you realize what could happen to Dorian if anyone found out he existed?"

Brixton didn't answer. He turned his glare from me to his feet.

"People might lock him up, caging him like an animal to study him," I continued. "Is that what you want?"

"They can't do that, can they?" Brixton asked, looking from me to Dorian. "He's, like, a real person. That's not what I—You know I don't want that."

"Do I?"

"I didn't mean anything by it! V and Ethan didn't believe me. I just wanted them to believe me."

"Do not be too hard on the boy," Dorian said. "His wish to be understood is only natural. No harm was done. I thank you for your quick-thinking explanation about a French friend."

"Can I go upstairs now?" Brixton mumbled.

"This is serious!" I ran my hands through my hair and tried to calm down. A small clump came out in my hands. It must have been the poison. Fear gripped me. Had I been affected more than I thought? I couldn't seem to shake the chill that was now covering every inch of my body. This was no place for Brixton. Why had I agreed to let him stay with me?

"I get it!" he said. "You won. Now V thinks I'm a loser who makes fun of disabled people. You can stop yelling."

"This isn't about winning! And this isn't just about Dorian. We're on your side, trying to help you."

He stopped glaring for a fraction of a second, but the expression returned a moment later. "By having my friends think I'm a jerk?"

"By finding out what happened to Blue."

"What are you talking about?"

"Why do you think I was out in the middle of the night? Do you know how hard it is for an alchemist to be awake when the sun isn't? We were investigating at Blue's house. That's what we were doing tonight."

"Really? You went to Blue's cottage?"

"Past the crime scene tape," Dorian said.

"You found something the police missed? Something that will help Blue?"

"I think so," I said. "We're working on it."

"Did you tell Detective Liu?"

I glanced at Dorian. "It's complicated."

"Everything is always complicated! Why can't people just say what they mean?"

"I wish it was that simple."

"Whatever." He stomped up the rickety stairs so hard that I half-expected one of them to break.

"Let him go," Dorian said. "He will feel calmer in the morning. Those friends of his are a good influence."

"I'm guessing you heard them say they liked your cake."

"*Oui.* If you would be so kind as to obtain oat flour, almonds, cashews, and fine quality cocoa powder, I shall fix a new chocolate dessert for Veronica tomorrow."

I eyed the gargoyle.

"We failed at locating my book," he said. "While you work in your alchemy lab and on the pages you photographed, I wish to stay busy so I do not disturb you. I know you will do what you can."

I looked from my crates stacked in the corner to the bowed stairs before turning back to Dorian's resigned eyes. I'd come to care for the creature. I didn't want him to die—or to suffer the fate worse than death that awaited him, being awake but trapped inside a body of unmoving stone.

If I was being truthful with myself, my selfish side liked having someone around with whom I could be my true self. My moral compass also didn't like the idea of someone getting away with murder and framing Blue.

All those thoughts flitted through my brain without a lot of coherency. My teeth continued to chatter in the drafty house. Between my anger, fear, chill, being awake in the middle of the night, and the poison, I was in bad shape. I was certain I would wake up with the sun, but at least I could get a few hours of sleep before then. That would help my body heal itself.

To come and go as he pleased during the night, Dorian had discovered he could use the hole in the roof that was covered with a tarp. The hole wasn't big enough for a person to get through, but the small gargoyle could easily maneuver through it and tie the tarp back into place.

I wrapped a blanket around me and went into the kitchen. To cleanse the toxins from my body after touching the unknown poison, I made myself a dandelion root tea. With the warm mug in one hand, I walked through the drafty house, making sure the doors and windows were locked. I clicked off the porch light and the other lights downstairs, pausing in front of the living room bay windows to straighten the curtains. The lights were now off inside, so nobody could see in. But I could see out.

A streetlight halfway down the block cast faint light on the front part of my yard near the street. A moving shadow caught my eye. Not only because it was the middle of the night, but because of where the figure was. It didn't appear on the sidewalk or the street; the shadow flitted across the fence inside my yard.

I gripped the edge of the curtain as my eyes followed the figure. Dorian was already outside, but this figure was the wrong shape to be Dorian. It was the shape of a human. Should I venture outside? If I did, I could see who it was, but they might be dangerous and then I'd be leaving Brixton exposed.

Before I could act, the decision was made for me. As my fingers closed more tightly over the curtain, the figure vanished. I shook my head. People don't just vanish. The person must have disappeared from my line of sight. That was all. Most of the yard was bathed in darkness.

Veronica and Ethan were safely at home, so it couldn't have been either of them. *So who—or what—was it?*

CHAPTER 17

I woke up not with a start but with a groan. I'd slept on the living room couch. After seeing the shadow lurking around the house the previous night, I'd added an extra layer of protection to the house. I fished through my crates for a string of bells from Morocco. I separated the bells and placed them in front of the front and back doors. Several windows were effectively locked by virtue of being rusted shut, so I only tied bells to the latches of the ground floor windows that could be opened.

"What is the purpose of the bells?" a deep voice asked. "And for you sleeping on the couch?" Dorian sat in front of the fireplace a few feet away from me.

"It's creepy to find you hovering while I sleep," I said, stretching. My body ached more than I expected from the couch. It was the poison I'd touched.

"You are the one who is not in your proper bed."

"I don't like how we don't know what's going on. With Brixton staying with us, I wanted to add an extra layer of security." I omitted the fact that I'd seen someone lurking outside the house. Part of me wasn't sure I'd seen anything. The poison had affected me more than I wanted to admit.

"Why do you not call a security company?"

"I tried that already. They all said the house needs to be fixed up first. It has too many loose parts, so I'd get too many false alarms."

"*Mon dieu.*"

"Agreed. And none of the home renovators will call me back after what happened to Charles Macraith."

"How odd."

"Not really," I said. "They probably think I'm a murderer."

"*C'est vrai?*"

"Yes, unfortunately I think it's true." Though as I spoke the words, I realized it *was* strange that the people I'd called got skittish as soon as I said the address, but not for the reason I'd originally considered. Even if people didn't like the idea of working for a possible murderess, *how did they know?* It wasn't as if I was only calling contractors who frequented Blue Sky Teas or who lived in my neighborhood.

I shook off the disconcerting feeling. The murder had taken place only days ago. The address could have been reported on the news. That must have been it. Still, I couldn't shake the feeling I was missing something.

I hadn't heard any of my makeshift alarm bells during the night. Dorian followed me through the house as I checked that all of them were in place and the house was secure. I picked up the bells and put them in a basket on the mantle. Now the decorative tin bells looked like a piece of home decor, not a burglar alarm. No need to unnecessarily worry Brixton. Even though I was still mad about what he'd done, I wanted to protect him from what was going on, both physically and emotionally.

In spite of only sleeping for a few hours, my mind was alert. I watered my herb garden in the kitchen window box. The two mint varieties had grown a few inches in as many days. They liked their new home. In spite of the pressures weighing on me, so did I. After drinking a cup of lemon tea, I hopped into the shower, cursing as the water alternated between glacially cold and blisteringly hot, as usual. It did nothing for my aching muscles.

Being in the sun would help, but Brixton would be up for school shortly, so I couldn't go far. I took my laptop to the back porch to look up a few more ideas about Dorian's book. When I sat down on the rickety back steps, the sun was poking through the clouds at the same time that a light mist fell from the sky. As I hit another dead end in my research, the light rain turned into a full-blown downpour. It was time to go inside anyway. I found Dorian and Brixton sitting at the dining table, which was covered with enough food to feed half a dozen people.

"The boy has apologized," Dorian said.

"Yeah," Brixton mumbled, speaking to the table. "It was stupid. I see that now."

"You understand you can't ever let anyone know about Dorian," I said.

Brixton's hazel eyes met mine. Instead of the defiance I had so often seen in his eyes, I saw humility. "I promise."

"*Bon*," Dorian said. "Help yourself to food, Zoe."

"Crepes?" I asked, looking at the spread of thin folded pancakes.

"*Galettes*, to be precise," Dorian said, looking up from *Le Monde*, "because they are made of buckwheat. These are a specialty from the Brittany region of France."

"You should try one, Zoe," Brixton said. "They're wicked. The filling is mushroom. I used to hate mushrooms, so I think Dorian is magic. I mean, he *is* kind of magic, right? There's no other way these would taste so good."

"I didn't think it was possible to get these so thin without an egg batter," I said, scooping one of the buckwheat crepes onto my plate.

"Silken tofu is an amazing invention," Dorian said, a pleased look on his face.

"There's tofu in here?" Brixton said, stopping mid-bite and eyeing the gooey crepe suspiciously.

"*Pardon*, I misspoke. It was not tofu used for the *galettes*. For these buck-wheat crepes, I soaked freshly ground flax seeds in a warm water to replicate the properties of the egg. The tofu was used in my chocolate cake."

"There's *tofu* in the cake?" Brixton repeated.

"*Mon dieu*. Here, let me read you news for the day. The European gold thefts are spreading. There are no leads. The thieves are clever. They also have a flair for the dramatic. They continue to leave crumbling imitation-gold statues and gold dust in place of the gold items they are stealing."

The way Dorian spoke of the crumbled gold made the thefts sound much more ominous than they must have been. The little gargoyle had a flair for the dramatic himself. A sense of unease crept up my spine as he recounted the news.

"You're going to be late for school, Brixton," I said. "It's raining too hard for you to take your bike. I'll drive you to school."

On the way home after dropping Brixton off at the high school, I passed the teashop. I had expected it to be closed. Not only was it open, but people poured out into the street. Blue was in a coma, so of course people would flock to the store. I should have expected it. Morbid curiosity no longer surprised me.

People would say the right things—that they were there to support the shop and to come together to offer each other a shoulder to cry on—but I knew the truth. I'd seen the crowds that flocked to the town square back when there were public executions. When murder and mayhem could be observed at a safe distance, people wouldn't miss an opportunity to be there.

But who had opened the teashop?

Instead of driving on, I found myself pulling over and walking through the melee into the shop. I was human, too. I was curious. I suppose it was human nature drawing us all to the teashop.

It was crowded enough that nobody noticed me. Stepping into the line that was six people long, I caught a glimpse of Olivia. Though she was tiny, it was impossible to miss her in the deep red shawl draped around her shoulders. The gossip who had brought me tea now stood behind the counter, taking orders herself.

I caught snatches of conversation from various people, most of whom were talking about Blue, but a few seemed not to know who owned the teashop. They were drawn in by the presence of a crowd, and I heard them asking their friends what it was about this shop that made it so popular.

When I reached the counter, Olivia took my order before waving to a woman sitting at a table near the counter. It was the redhead I'd spoken to when she manned the counter two days before. The woman excused herself from her conversation and stepped behind the counter while Olivia made my ginger tea. Again I was struck by the fact that the woman looked like she had been crying. She covered it up well, but the signs were there.

"This place is claustrophobic," Olivia said, handing me the tea in a to-go cup. "Cora can cover while we go to the hospital to see Blue."

"Are they allowing visitors now?"

"Not that I've heard. That doesn't mean she won't feel our presence nearby. I've spent more time than I'd care to think about in the hospital. It's not the visit as much as it is knowing that someone was there to see you. I thought we could pick up some flowers for her."

"That's a lovely idea," I said, thinking I'd misjudged Olivia. "I'm surprised this place is open. I didn't know anyone else worked here."

"Sam works here part-time during the peak afternoon tea-time hours, after he's done teaching for the day." Olivia took her coat and purse from behind the counter. "It's charity, of course."

I gave her a questioning look.

"Blue doesn't really need help most of the time." She led us through the shop, maneuvering through the crowd. "When Sam and I were having trouble paying our bills, after my illness made me too sick to work, Blue offered him the job, even though it was a stretch for Blue to pay him as generously as she did."

We reached the sidewalk and Olivia kept right on talking without missing a beat. "Sam teaches during the day, so he can't be here now. It's the least I can do to help the teashop make money while Blue can't be here. Who knows what kind of medical bills she'll have. Health care costs are exorbitant these days. We can stop at the corner shop to pick out flowers. Over-priced, but quite skillfully prepared. They'd better be, at those prices! And where is your car parked?"

It took me a moment to realize she'd stopped talking.

"My car is right over here." I pointed at my truck.

Olivia frowned disapprovingly at my lovingly up-kept truck. I reminded myself to feel more charitable toward her. Underneath her faults, she was a good person, helping keep open the teashop to help Blue. Or had she opened it because she wanted everyone to gather there and gossip? I tried not to be cynical.

We picked out an assortment of white flowers that Olivia insisted upon, but let me pay for, before getting into the car.

Olivia frowned again as I revved the engine. It was in perfect condition, but wasn't as silent as modern engines. She pointed me in the direction I should drive, then shook her head as I pulled into traffic. If Olivia wasn't going to hide her feelings, I might as well take advantage of the opportunity to learn something useful.

"The police aren't telling me anything," I said. "You seem to know everyone here. You must have had people open up to you about it. What do you think is going on?" A little flattery never hurt.

Out of my peripheral vision I saw her frown change to a sly smile.

"I thought it was *you* who would know more, my dear. The Taylor boy is staying at your house, is he not?"

"Brixton?"

"And what kind of a name is that? Heather has damaged that boy in so many ways. It's too late for him."

"He's only fourteen."

"He's already been arrested for assault."

My hands tensed on the steering wheel. Blue had said he'd been in trouble before. But in trouble with the law? Assault?

"Oh, you didn't know?" Olivia's smile widened.

I was almost afraid to ask. "What happened?"

"I'll spare you the details, but he's a violent child. I thought it wise you should be warned, since you're vulnerable alone with him in that big house of yours."

"Why did you think Brixton would know what's going on? You don't seriously think he had anything to do with Charles Macraith's death?" Brixton may have been making my life difficult by trying to show the world Dorian existed, but I couldn't imagine him hurting anyone.

"I wouldn't put it past him. But that's not what I meant. That boy is always sticking his nose where it doesn't belong." Olivia paused and pointed. "Turn here."

"You were saying?" I prompted, hoping we had a little more time before we reached the hospital.

"Wisdom comes with age. You wouldn't understand this yet, dear. I've tried to counsel Brixton's mother Heather to improve herself and the life of her boy. And I tried to stop her from marrying her deadbeat husband."

"I haven't met him."

"You wouldn't have. He's never here. Some people, there's no reasoning with."

"What do you mean he's never here?"

"He disappears for long periods of time."

"And you don't know why?"

"I'm not one to gossip."

"Of course not."

"Now *Charles*," Olivia said, "he was a better father figure to Brixton. I would often see him helping the boy with his studies. He was the most sensible of the lot of them. Brixton's mother thinks my nephew Sam is a good influence, but I don't buy it. Sam was too lazy to finish a PhD. Instead of being a true historian, he's teaching history to children at the high school! That's why he can't afford a place of his own and has to live with me. What kind of message does that send? Turn again here, dear."

"Mmm hmm," I murmured, following her directions.

"I wish my friend Ivan were a better role model. Did I introduce you to him? Oh yes, the other day at the teashop. That's a man who was a scholar during his time. A prominent chemistry professor. But he doesn't take care of himself. He has health issues but won't look into finding a cure. I don't understand that man. I tell you, I don't understand any of them. *Men.*"

CHAPTER 18

At the hospital, we weren't allowed to see Blue, or even leave her flowers. We were told her condition hadn't changed; she was still in a coma but stable. Olivia insisted on taking the flowers home with her, so the beautiful bouquet "wouldn't go to waste."

Olivia asked to be dropped off at her house, a Craftsman in an East Portland neighborhood not far from mine. Though a similar style to mine, her house was half the size, but in much better condition. Barren rose bushes lined the small yard in front of the porch. I imagined that in the springtime they would match the pink shutters. It was walking distance to Blue Sky Teas, and Olivia said she wanted to eat lunch before returning to the teashop.

"Blue's healthy pastries will be good for another day or so," she said, "but I don't enjoy the taste of sawdust."

"They can't be that bad."

"I gave you fair warning."

I was again curious about how bad Blue's cooking could possibly be, but I didn't have time to find out. Brixton would be home from school in a few hours, which gave me enough time to try another experiment in the basement. I was still holding out hope that by going through the motions my subconscious would kick in and I'd remember the important subtleties of alchemy I learned long ago, helping me see what I was missing in the coded illustrations and text of Dorian's book.

As soon as I came through the front door, planning on heading straight to the basement, I was accosted by a frantic gargoyle.

"Where were you? I was worried."

"I went to see Blue at the hospital."

"You left only to take Brixton to school. I thought you would be returning home presently."

I'd been on my own for so long that it hadn't occurred to me anyone would be worried about me. "I'm so sorry," I said. I'd been pushing people away for so long that this was a big adjustment. Attachments were too painful. But along with the pain, I'd lost sight of the joy they could bring.

He sniffed. "I used up the last of the fresh vegetables cooking us lunch. You will need to buy more food before you resume work in your alchemy lab."

"Ah," I said. "That's why you missed me."

"The provider of food is a very important role." He sniffed. "As is the chef."

With that, he returned to the kitchen. I followed behind to see what he was making. He'd cooked a fresh loaf of bread to accompany a roasted beet soup. I often made a pureed beet soup in the blender, but Dorian's stove-top version was a combination of chunks of seasoned beets and other root vegetables floating in a creamy broth. The attention to detail in the small touches in the meal assured me that Dorian's transformation back into stone wasn't progressing more quickly. We had at least a little bit of time. I hoped.

After lunch and a quick trip to the market, I took a few deep breaths and walked down the stairs to the basement.

The French cooking idea of *mise en place*, where you set up all your ingredients and tools before starting to cook a meal, also applies to alchemy. Even without a proper lab set up, it was important to locate the tools and measure the ingredients. Glass vessels, a stone mortar and pestle, herbs I'd dried myself, and pure alcohol. It wasn't much, but it would do for now.

Dorian poked his head in the door. "We are out of coconut sugar again," he said.

"Already?"

"I know you are busy. You can buy more at your earliest convenience."

That gargoyle was going to send us to the poor house. If it wasn't such a draining process, there was no question that I would have worked on turning metal into gold as my foray back into alchemy.

For now, I returned to a basic plant alchemy transformation. I used a mortar and pestle to grind the dried herb, mixing in a rhythmic, clockwise circle. As soon as I mixed the herbs and alcohol together, the concoction began to steam. That *wasn't* what was supposed to happen. I knew what must have happened. In all my efforts to clean up the basement itself, I hadn't cleaned the mortar and pestle. It was a stupid mistake. One I never would have made before. I couldn't remember what I had last ground with it. The contents of the steaming jar began to bubble.

This couldn't be good.

The mixture exploded from its glass jar, showering me with *gray* slime this time.

"*Mais non!*" a voice called out from the stairs. "What has happened?"

I wiped gray slime from my lips. "I told you not to disturb me until it was time for me to pick up Brixton from school."

"It is time. You are going to be late."

I could have sworn only thirty minutes had passed, not three hours.

"This is part of alchemy?" Dorian asked skeptically. "Turning yourself gray is correct?"

~

Half an hour later, Brixton voiced a similar question.

"What happened to you?" he asked as he climbed into the truck.

I hadn't had time to shower to get rid of all the slime. I thought I'd gotten most of it with a wet washcloth. Apparently not.

"I forgot to put the lid on the blender," I said.

"You're making *gray* smoothies now? There's no way I'm trying one of those."

Brixton knew I was using my skills in an attempt to figure out the poison used on Blue, so we could save her and clear her. But I was shielding him from the reason I was setting up a complete alchemy lab. I didn't want to burden Brixton with the knowledge that someone else was dying, and that I needed to solve the riddle of *Not Untrue Alchemy* to save Dorian's life. Worrying about Blue was enough for him.

Brixton had convinced Dorian to let him use his phone for short interludes while the gargoyle watched him, and Brixton had started calling the hospital to check on Blue's condition. That made it clear how important it was to him, because the thought of speaking to someone on the phone, rather than texting them, horrified him. He knew she was still in critical condition, still in a coma.

While Brixton devoured the desserts Dorian had been baking, I headed to the bathroom to get rid of the remaining gray slime. I was nearly as good as new when I joined Brixton and Dorian downstairs. I smiled at the sight of the two of them at the dining table.

The thick wooden table was something I'd found in the south of France in the late 1860s. It wasn't practical by any stretch of the imagination, even at the time. I knew I would only be in the village for a few years, until it was obvious I wasn't aging. I'd learned that it was easiest to live as simply as possible. The less baggage—both emotional and physical—made it easier to move on. But living without attachments also took its toll.

The local man who built the table was a true artist and also a struggling widower with four small children. I didn't have the money to pay what the table was worth, so for more than a month I went through the draining process of creating gold. By the time two full moons had come and gone, I hadn't yet transmuted enough lead into gold. I must have looked as tired as I felt, because the town took up a collection to send for a doctor to attend to me. I was so touched that I paid everyone back twofold with gold. With the renewed energy their generosity had given me, I was able to transform the largest amount of lead I'd ever turned to gold. I paid the craftsman more than he was asking for the table. It's one of the most beautiful pieces of furniture I've ever owned. I kept in touch with his daughter for many years. After I had to leave, we kept up a correspondence of letters until she passed away from old age. I would have liked to have seen her again, but there was no way I could have let her see me. The table was one of the special items I kept in my storage collection.

Brixton had an algebra textbook in front of him on the hundred-year-old table.

"Can we go visit Blue?" he asked.

"The last time I checked, they weren't allowing visitors."

"It doesn't hurt to try, right?"

"Are you done with your homework?"

"It's *math*," he said, slamming the book shut. "I suck at math."

"Um…" I began. I knew mathematics as it applied to calculating measurements and documenting chemical interactions, and also in its older and broader usage that included astronomy and physics. But I wasn't sure any of that would come in handy with algebra homework.

"Do not look at me," Dorian said, not looking up from the paperback book he was reading. "I can assist with French literature, linguistics, and the sciences, not mathematics."

"We can check on Blue," I said. "We'll figure out the math later."

"While you are out," Dorian said, "please stop by the library to get me more detective fiction novels." He gave a contented sigh and closed the Agatha Christie novel in his hands.

"I've got a whole shelf of them in the trailer," I said.

"I know. I have finished them."

"There are dozens of books."

"Yes, I never knew how entertaining such books could be. British 'penny dreadfuls' were looked down upon when I was a child."

"You," Brixton said, "were a child?"

"Of course," Dorian said. "Were you born knowing everything you know today?"

"A little baby gargoyle?" Brixton shook his head. "My life is too weird."

"I was never smaller than I am now," Dorian said, "yet I did not possess the knowledge I now have."

"I hadn't considered that," I said. "What *did* happen right after you were brought to life? Could you speak, or were you as helpless as a newborn?"

"You have not obtained another recording device?" Dorian asked Brixton.

"No way. You're helping clear Blue. You don't have to worry about me."

"I was not," Dorian said, "an infant in the traditional sense. I was neither tiny nor helpless. I spoke only Latin."

"*Only*," Brixton muttered.

I agreed with the sentiment. Nicolas Flamel had insisted I learn Latin for my alchemical studies. I hadn't taken to it nearly as well as I had to plants. But after learning the basics of Latin, other languages followed much more easily.

"You spoke Latin," I said, "because that was the language of the text that brought you to life." It made sense in an alchemical way— transformations rearrange existing elements. I wished that knowledge of the strange visual symbols included in the book had been transferred to the gargoyle as well.

"What are you two talking about?" Brixton asked.

Damn. I had spoken before thinking. I was used to keeping my own secrets, but having a gargoyle in my life was something new. But Dorian didn't seem to mind. He chuckled.

"My father's Latin was not so good," Dorian said. "It took time for us to learn to communicate and for him to teach me French."

"Your *father*," Brixton repeated.

"You have heard, of course, of the great Jean Eugène Robert-Houdin?"

Brixton stared at him blankly. "That name sounds French. I live in Oregon. So your dad's like an actor or something in France?"

Dorian's complexion didn't turn red when he was angry, but dark gray granules gathered in his cheeks when he became agitated. His face was now visibly darkening.

"He was a very famous stage magician," I said before Dorian could explode. "This was in the 1800s. He used to create mechanized illusions that were technologically much more advanced than the times."

"That's wicked," Brixton said.

Dorian's coloring returned to normal.

"I'll pick up some books for you," I said. "Come on, Brixton. Let's go check on Blue."

I hadn't expected the trip to the hospital to be successful, but visitors were allowed in to see her. Though Brixton was happy about this development, I wasn't so sure I was. There was still a murderer out there who had already tried to kill her once.

Blue's condition remained the same. Brixton sat with her for the twenty minutes until visiting hours were over.

"Can't you, like, *do something?*" Brixton whispered at one point. "With your alchemy? Do you have any of that Elixir of Life stuff? That should save her, right?"

"I wish it worked like that," I said. "The Elixir of Life can't be transferred between people."

I spoke the truth about the Elixir, but at the same time Brixton's words were more true than he knew. I used to be thought of as a healer. But that was centuries ago. I'd pushed those skills aside along with the painful memories I tried to keep at bay. There was no longer anything I could do for her.

Neither of us spoke on the drive to the library. Brixton stayed in the car while I selected the maximum number of books I could check out. I was only half paying attention to what I'd selected for him. I grabbed anything that fit the description of being from the Golden Age of Detective Fiction.

I handed Brixton the books to look through in the car, but he simply set the stack down at his feet. When we reached the house, he went straight up to his room and slammed the door.

"*Qu'est que sait?*" Dorian asked.

"He's worried about Blue."

I set down the stack of books on the dining table. Dorian hopped up on a chair and looked through them, nodding with approval.

"These will work," he said.

"You mean you'll enjoy them?"

He set down the book in his hand and faced me. "I did not wish to speak in front of the boy. It is my body. If I allow myself to be completely still, I begin to turn to stone. This did not used to be a problem. *Maintenant*, it is more and more difficult for me to resume my normal moving form. Even small movements, such as reading, keep my body awake. This is why I have asked for books. While you and the world sleep, I must stay awake—or I fear I may remain trapped in my stone body forever, never to return."

CHAPTER 19

At dawn the next morning, the house was silent. I'd like to say I knew something was wrong right away. That the house was "too still." But I didn't.

On my way downstairs, I noticed that Brixton's door was ajar. I poked my head in. The bed was empty.

"Dorian!" I called out, rushing down the stairs. "Brixton!" I opened every squealing door in the house, one of which fell off its hinge when I yanked too firmly. I even checked under the beds, holding out a false hope that they were playing a joke on me. I circled the house, thinking maybe they couldn't sleep and had gone outside to eat an early breakfast. I checked inside the trailer. They weren't there, but a strong odor was. The confusing scent rattled me until I remembered that Brixton had broken several bottles. I continued my search. My truck was parked in the driveway behind the trailer as usual. There was only one thing out of place. Brixton's bike, normally resting in a spot next to the back door, was missing.

I had once known a Native American tracker, but I had no idea how the skill was executed. I couldn't even detect a bike track leading out of my yard. I had no way to know where they'd gone. Could I have slept through the two of them being abducted? I'm a sound sleeper to start with, and I'd been exhausted.

The sound of wheels skidding echoed in the early morning stillness. I sprinted to the front door. An out-of-breath Brixton ran through the open door a second later, Dorian right behind.

"What's going on?" I asked. "Are you all right?"

Brixton bent over and breathed deeply, his gloved hands on his knees. "I think we lost him."

Dorian nodded, clicking off the living room light and peeking out the windows. "You have it?"

"What are you two talking about?" I looked between them but neither of them looked back at me. "What's happening?"

Brixton stuck his hand into the pocket of his bomber jacket and removed a small glass vial.

This couldn't be good.

"What is that?" I said.

"The poison that hurt Blue." Brixton handed the vial to Dorian. "Don't worry, it's not blood or anything. It's the liquid remains they found of whatever she drank."

"I will hide this with Zoe's other alchemy supplies," Dorian said.

"You didn't," I said. "The *police lab*? You broke into the police lab?" I sat down, not feeling so well.

"Dorian said you could learn more about the poison than the police," Brixton said. "You said you were trying to help her." When he spoke of Blue, his eyes weren't those of a jaded teenager but of a worried child.

"Brixton, this isn't a movie. You can't go around breaking into places you don't belong—especially police labs—no matter what Dorian says."

Dorian coughed indignantly. "I resent the assumption it was my idea."

"Wasn't it?"

"*Mais oui.* Of course this was my idea. But I did not wish the child to come with me."

"I'm not a child!" The outburst made him sound more like a child than usual.

"He followed me," Dorian continued, "on his bicycle."

"What?" Brixton said when I gave him a pointed look. "He told me what he was doing. Did he really think I wouldn't follow?"

"It is not my fault that he followed!" Dorian said.

This must be what it felt like to have children. I took two deep breaths to moderate my voice when I spoke. "Just tell me," I said, pausing to take another calming breath, "what happened."

"The boy could not sleep during the night," Dorian said. "I was here reading, and I made him a snack. He asked about what you and I were doing to help Blue. You did not have a large enough sample of the poison from Blue's house. He told me the police lab would have it. He knows much about this city. He knew where the lab was."

"How did you get inside?"

"It was not difficult," Dorian said, tapping his claws together.

"But there was an alarm," Brixton added.

I put my head in my hands. "Of course."

"It was a silent alarm. We didn't know—" Brixton broke off and looked to the gargoyle.

"Until the police arrived," Dorian finished.

I groaned. "How did you get away? Did they see you?"

Brixton flipped up the hood of the black hoodie he was wearing under his jacket and held up his hands. Between his shadowed face and gloved hands, even in close proximity it was difficult to identify him.

"This isn't the first time I've broken in somewhere," Brixton said. "I know what I'm doing. I'm the reason we got out of there."

"He is a very intelligent boy," Dorian chimed in.

"You're not helping, Dorian," I snapped. "How could you let him go into the lab with you?"

"He was already there! Would it not have been worse to leave him outside?"

"No," I said. "It would have been a million times better if he hadn't *broken into* a police lab."

"We're back," Brixton said. "And we got the poison. No reason to be so upset."

"*No reason?*" I said. "Do you realize you've broken the whole chain of evidence? Anything we learn from this can't be used as evidence."

I took measured breaths, trying to calm myself. I really shouldn't leave those two alone.

"Who cares about evidence?" Brixton said. "I just want you to fix Blue."

It was difficult to be blindingly angry when I knew why they were each doing it. Desperate times called for desperate measures. My exasperation faded. But only a little. "What happened when the police arrived?"

"I'd hidden my bike a little ways away," Brixton said. "We ran there and I put Dorian on the handle bars."

"The police didn't follow?"

"It was weird," Brixton said. "I didn't think they had seen us, but then one guy caught up. I took us through the Shanghai Tunnels to get away. My bike got beaten up going down the stairs, but Dorian was able to fix it in the dark.

We stayed down there for a little while, to make sure nobody was following us. That's why we're back so late."

I hadn't noticed until now that they were both dusty. The underground tunnels explained it.

"Get cleaned up," I said. "I'll drive you to school."

"It's Saturday."

"Oh, well, then... take a shower to clean that tunnel dirt off."

"Your shower is either freezing or boiling. It's torture."

"Then let the cold and hot water run together and take a bath." He grumbled on his way upstairs.

"Is this enough?" Dorian asked, holding up the vial.

"This is a bad idea," I said.

"Do you have a better one?"

～

Dorian cooked breakfast—brown bread fresh from the oven with wild blackberry preserves from wild blackberries he found in the woods during one of his recent nights out exploring.

"I have not yet perfected a vegan butter," he lamented. "Nut butters are not the same. I will master it yet. Dorian Robert-Houdin does not walk away from a challenge."

I had a challenge of my own to tackle. I waited until Brixton climbed into bed before getting to work on the poison.

With fear as a motivator, I was more effective in the laboratory than I'd been the day before. In a strange way, I was also happy. I had experienced some of the happiest moments of my life when Ambrose and I worked side by side.

We each worked differently—he with metals and me with plants—but we complemented each other. They talk about couples completing each other's sentences. Ambrose and I completed each other's thoughts about our alchemical transformations. If I needed a glass retort for the next phase of a process, Ambrose would hand it to me moments before I moved to get one myself. If he needed a crucible to move his creation into the fire of the athanor, I knew when he was ready for it. In alchemy, a practitioner's energy is transferred to the vessels they work with. Therefore most alchemists didn't let other alchemists touch any of the items in their labs. But with two of us, it was as if those rules didn't apply. We were so in synch that our alchemy transformed us into one. I had never felt so connected to life as I was when I was in the laboratory with Ambrose.

Remembering those moments, I found my rhythm. Like many alchemists before me, I was so caught up in the moment, so focused on the process, that I forgot I was dealing with an unknown substance. I should have been working more carefully, but I was giddy with getting back into the rhythm of alchemy. Through the distillation process, some of the liquid from the vial had turned to steam. It was too late to stop the process, or to leave the room. I breathed in the noxious fumes.

I felt myself falling. I must have been physically falling to the hard concrete at my feet, but that's not what it felt like. I was falling in slow motion, through the sky.

I knew, then, what I was feeling. The toxin in the air was the most essential metal in all of alchemy: *mercury.*

The last thought I had was that I was being killed by an alchemist.

Then everything went dark.

CHAPTER 20

I awoke to the sharp smell of ammonia overwhelming my senses. I shot up from the cold, concrete floor, feeling like I was going to vomit. My head throbbed. The room spun around me. The light was so bright it felt like the sun was in the room with me. I pressed my eyes shut. The scent of ammonia dissipated, but the bright room kept spinning.

"Drink," a deep voice said. Cold hands pushed a glass jar to my lips.

I sipped the water. The sensation washing over me triggered a sense of familiarity. I remembered what I had been doing before passing out. *Mercury.*

"It is better?" Dorian asked.

"The air!" I said, realizing the fumes might have remained. "We need to get out of the basement."

"There is nothing in the air."

"Mercury doesn't have a scent."

"Mercury?"

"I'm sure of it."

Along with sulfur and salt, mercury is one of the three essential elements of alchemy. The dangerous one. I knew it well, having conducted many alchemical transformations using the enigmatic metal. It has a dual nature, both therapeutic and poisonous, both liquid and solid, which is why it's called the *rebis*. It's an essential ingredient for creating the philosopher's stone, but one that has also poisoned countless alchemists.

"Do you need further care?" Dorian asked.

"With the amount I ingested, I should be fine. But we need to air out the basement."

"I will take care of it."

"Be careful, Dorian."

"*Mais oui.*"

Dorian helped me up the stairs. I lay down on the couch, awake but reeling. I closed my eyes. A raw ache radiated from my shoulder and spread through my arm. I must have hurt it when I passed out.

A sharp claw poked my side. I opened my eyes. The little creature stood bending over me, his eyes wide. "I do not think you should be lying down."

"Doesn't matter," I mumbled.

He poked me again, harder this time.

"Fine." I let him pull me to a sitting position. "This is better."

"How did you know?" I croaked.

"I heard the sound of a crash. When I came to investigate, I found you unconscious on the floor. You did not have smelling salts that I could see, therefore I took a jar of ammonia to wake you."

I smiled weakly. My body trembled.

"*D'accord,*" Dorian said. "You may rest. I will watch you."

Though my body pleaded for rest, my mind raced. Now that I had ingested a stronger dose, I had a better understanding of what the poison was. But it raised even more questions. The strangest thing was, what I had told Dorian was true. Mercury didn't have the noxious scent of other poisons. It was odorless. *Then what had I smelled on Charles Macraith and Blue Sky?*

I'd let myself be confused because it wasn't poison. Not exactly.

I recognized some of the herbs from an old Chinese herbal remedy, which included mercury—but this blend had been tainted with additional substances I couldn't identify. It wasn't poison for poison's sake. And it wasn't the same mixture that had been used on Charles Macraith. It was as if someone hadn't checked for toxic contaminants in formulas that otherwise would have been harmless or even healing. I had no way of knowing if it was purposeful, or if someone had been cutting corners. Either way, coupled with mercury, it was a dangerous mix.

Front and center was mercury, but not in a high enough dose to kill anyone. In spite of my initial reaction when I realized there was mercury present, an alchemist wasn't the only explanation. There was something I was missing.

I must have dozed off. I hadn't meant to, but my body needed the rest to recover. Being attuned to natural substances makes me both stronger and weaker than the average person. Stronger when it comes to natural substances, because of my connection to plants. But weaker when it comes to unnatural additives, such as some of the toxins I'd ingested.

When I woke up, I was back in the basement. How had that happened? No, that wasn't right. This wasn't my basement. I was back in the old alchemy lab I'd shared with Ambrose. He was there, working at my side. The underground stone walls were covered with rich green ivy, so bright it was nearly fluorescent. The plant's tendrils covered not only the walls but the floor as well. As I watched, the ivy grew. The tendrils reached out like octopus arms, enveloping our glass and copper materials, even wrapping itself around Ambrose. Why wasn't he reacting? This must have been a dream, though it didn't feel like one. I was awake and sleeping at the same time. The ivy wrapped itself around my ankles. I screamed. Just before I was swallowed up by the plant, a stick poked me.

I opened my eyes. Dorian was seated cross-legged a few feet away from me. He held a hardcover book from the library in one hand and a stick in the other.

"Quit it with the poking," I said, my voice hoarse.

"You were making odd noises. Whenever a look of distress appeared on your face, I poked you. It calmed you."

"Odd noises?" The dream came back to me. It had to have been a dream, but it felt *so real*. Because it wasn't a normal dream. It was a hallucination.

"Your complexion did not change," he said, "nor your temperature. I thought it was best to let you sleep instead of dialing 9-1-1."

"Good choice," I said, stretching. Pain shot through my shoulder, but it was a surface pain, not the bone. "Oh God, what time is it?"

"Do not worry. The boy still sleeps."

I sighed. "I should call Max."

"You cannot go to the detective with the information you learned from the stolen vial. Especially since you said it was an unscented poison. How would you explain your information? This is information for us to find Blue's killer and retrieve my book."

He was right. I couldn't tell Max how I'd learned it was Chinese herbal remedies tainted with mercury and God knows what else. I wasn't even sure what that meant. I was somewhat familiar with Chinese herbs, but not enough to identify the exact mixture. But I had to do something. On shaky legs, I stood up.

"You are going to the police station?" Dorian asked as I bundled in my thick wool sweater and jacket.

"I haven't figured out what I'm doing."

"Then where are you going?"

"I need to walk off the effects. You'll stay here with Brixton?"

I walked to Blue Sky Teas, taking the long way around the neighborhood. The rain was holding off, for which my roof was thankful, though clouds blanketed the sky. When I reached the main drag, the sidewalks were crowded with people going to restaurants, coffee houses, bookstores, specialty shops, or simply walking their dogs.

Olivia's friend Cora was behind the counter at the teashop when I arrived. I was unsurprised that Olivia passed off her good deed to the frazzled woman. The shop was only half-full now, a stark contrast to what I'd seen the day before. I supposed there was nothing more for people to learn. Still, even with only a few customers to deal with, Cora looked at least as distressed as she had the day before. Her red curls were pulled into a messy knot, which had fallen onto the side of her head.

Before I reached the short line, I was startled by who I saw sitting at a back table: Max Liu.

I held my locket between my fingers, took a deep breath, and walked over to him. He looked up at me but didn't offer me a seat. Two newspapers and an eBook reader filled the table, along with a teapot and teacup.

"Shouldn't you be off catching bad guys?"

"I'm on leave."

"You're *what*? Why?"

"It doesn't matter why," he said. "What matters is that right when we might have a breakthrough in the case, I'm off it."

"A breakthrough?"

"I can't talk about an ongoing investigation."

"But you said you were off the case."

"I'm sure Detective Dylan would greatly appreciate me telling the details of the case to one of the suspects."

"I'm still a suspect? I thought you said there was a breakthrough."

Max's facial features relaxed a little. He didn't smile, but his deep brown eyes softened as he looked at me. "I think he'd be wasting his time if he focuses on you."

"Thanks."

"Don't thank me." The warmth in his eyes was gone, if it had even been there to begin with. "I can't do anything about what happens from here."

The poison was in my basement. Oh, God. What if they got a search warrant?

"What's the matter?" he asked.

I shook my head. "I don't like any of this. A man was killed outside my new home and meaningful objects were stolen. I don't believe Blue did it."

"Neither do I." He sighed. "You might as well sit down." He folded the newspapers, making room on the table.

I sat across from him, not entirely sure why I'd walked up to him in the first place. I wanted to tell him what I'd learned about the poison, but hadn't yet figured out a way to do it. I also couldn't deny that I was drawn to the man. But there was something different about him today. He held himself at an emotional distance that I hadn't felt before.

"I feel like I should be asking you what's the matter, too. For a guy on leave, you don't look very relaxed."

He looked over my face for a moment before speaking. I felt suddenly self-conscious. I hadn't looked in a mirror since being knocked out from the tainted herbs.

"Remember how I told you how I was injured," he said, "when I fell through a trapdoor while chasing a suspect?" I nodded.

"That wasn't all there was to the story."

"What happened?"

"That night, I discharged my weapon." My breath caught.

"I didn't kill anyone," he said. "I've never killed anyone. But that night... It was down in the old tunnels that run beneath the city. They were built to transport supplies from ships to merchants without clogging up the streets, but many of them were used for unsavory purposes."

"The Shanghai Tunnels."

"You're learning your local history. Kidnapping able-bodied men and forcing them into indentured servitude on ships is a big part of this city's history." He paused to take a sip of his tea, wincing as he raised the cup.

"You're hurt."

"It's nothing. I've had much worse." He shifted in his chair and I noticed he was trying to keep one of his legs straight. "Last month, in those tunnels, I fell through a trapdoor—which I learned is technically a 'deadfall' when it's made for the express purpose of capturing an unsuspecting man. I wasn't careful because I didn't think it was possible—I was already below ground *in* a tunnel, but it turns out there's another level of tunnels I didn't know about."

"Didn't you have backup?"

"I hadn't waited for it. Stupid, I know. But the case was important. A girl had died." He indicated the lone photo hanging on the wall.

"You knew her?"

"We all did. Blue has created a great sense of community at the teashop. All of us who are drawn to the healing properties of tea find each other here."

"The girl who died was one of them—one of you?"

Max lowered his voice before continuing. "Anna West. A real shame. She was supposed to start college this fall. Her mother likes to spend time here now, to feel close to her. I don't see that it helps her, though." He looked toward the counter.

"The woman working the counter is her mother?" Of course. Now that I looked at the framed photo on the teashop wall, I saw the resemblance, most strikingly with the lush red hair they shared.

Max nodded.

"Anna was killed in the tunnels?" I asked quietly.

"No, it was a suicide at her home, but I suspected it was connected to the people who I was chasing in the tunnels."

"Since you were on your own when you got hurt down there, how did you get out?"

"I was lucky not to have broken any bones. I was able to get out of there myself. But I saw some strange things."

"Strange?"

"I don't know what I saw. In the darkness in those tunnels, I saw shadows... Shadows that I was convinced were monsters. That's what I shot at."

I remained silent. He must have taken my silence for skepticism.

"I know what you're thinking. The psychologist who examined me after the shooting agrees it was trauma brought on by the acute pain caused by the fall. That I had a mental break. She was loath to put me back on duty. She reluctantly agreed to it. But after what happened last night, she put me back on leave."

Oh no. Last night? I was afraid to ask. "What happened?"

"There was a break-in at the lab where we sent the poison found at Blue's house."

"You were there?" I swallowed, feeling guilt and bile rise in my throat.

"Since it was my case, I got a call. The perpetrator had already gotten away, and the first responders had lost sight of him. But from the direction I came from, I caught sight of a suspect fleeing."

My heart was beating so furiously that I was sure he would hear it. "And?"

He laughed, but it was a mirthful laugh. "I think that psychologist was right. I'm going crazy. I've had an overactive imagination ever since I was a kid. My grandmother told me the most amazing stories about what apothecaries could do. It took me way too long to stop believing in her magical stories. I don't know why I said anything in the first place. Only, doing things by the book is important to me. I know it might sound stupid to someone who's not a cop—"

"It doesn't sound stupid. It doesn't sound stupid at all."

"I've never lied on a police report," Max said. "Never."

"What did you see?"

"It was a damn monster."

I didn't know what to say. None of this made sense. He must have seen Dorian last night, without realizing what he'd seen, or even believing his own eyes. But how was it possible he'd also seen Dorian *last month*?

"What did it look like?" I asked. "The monster, I mean."

He gave me a sharp look. Did he think I was mocking him?

"I should go." He stood up, favoring his right knee.

I was too stunned on many levels to do anything as he brushed past me and headed for the door. It had to have been Dorian he saw last night. At least he hadn't seen Brixton. But what had Max seen the previous month? Dorian had only arrived in Portland this week, with my shipping crates.

Hadn't he?

CHAPTER 21

I was startled from my thoughts by two people sitting down at the table next to me. Olivia placed two steaming mugs on the tree ring table top and tossed her red shawl over her shoulder as she sat down. Ivan sat down next to her, gave me a friendly nod, and buried his scruffy, haggard face in a book that looked to be in a Slavic language.

"That poor boy," Olivia said, shaking her head as she watched Max depart.

"I don't think his injury is too bad," I said. "He'll be fine."

Olivia barked a laugh. "You are quite dense for a smart young woman."

"What do you mean?" I was fairly certain I knew what she was going to say: that Max believed I was a suspect.

"He knows."

"Knows what? I didn't have anything to do with the crimes—"

She laughed again. "Not *that*. I'm talking about your French boyfriend."

"I don't—" I began, but realized I had to keep up the lie. One little lie to protect Dorian… I should have known people beyond Brixton and his friends would hear about what I told them.

"Why would Max care if I happen to have a French friend?"

Ivan sighed and shook his head. His tired eyes and unkempt beard and hair didn't match his tailored wool suit.

"You should go after him," Olivia said with the first genuinely warm smile I'd seen.

She was right. I stood up and went after Max. When I reached the sidewalk, there was no sign of him. I closed my eyes for a moment. Running after him had been a stupid idea anyway. What would I have said to him if I'd caught up with him? Told him I wanted to push all thoughts of poison and murder from my mind and sit down with him and talk about his apothecary grandparents and the tea he grew? That was only a fantasy.

Back to reality, I hurried home. I needed to hide the stolen vial. Now that Max was on leave and a new detective on the case, there was no way I could entertain the notion of telling anyone what I'd learned. I hadn't even figured out how I was going to tell Max. Instead of knowing more, I knew *less* than I had before. I hadn't learned more about Charles Macraith. I hadn't identified the exact makeup of the poison. I hadn't gotten any closer to figuring out who had killed Charles Macraith, stolen Dorian's book, and was trying to frame Blue Sky.

The only thing I'd learned was that one of the key components of the poison was the most important element to an alchemist.

I had more questions than I knew what to do with. Had Dorian hidden out in my crate as he'd told me, only emerging when I opened the box? I believed him to be trustworthy from what I'd seen of him and from what he did for me years ago in Paris. But what other explanation was there for what Max saw? Could there be more creatures like Dorian out there? If *Not Untrue Alchemy* brought one stone carving to life, could it do the same to others?

~

It was Brixton's last day staying with me before his mom returned from her artist retreat. I was going to miss the kid, but at this point I was wondering if he would have been better off on his own these last few days.

I needed to wash away all the evidence that he and Dorian had stolen the poison. I wasn't going to destroy the liquid remaining in the vial, but it would need to be hidden somewhere safe, away from the house, until I could figure out what to do with it.

Before reaching the basement door, I was waylaid by smoke curling from underneath the kitchen door. Or rather, the room formerly known as a kitchen. It looked as if a tornado had blown through the room. Dorian wore the apron I'd picked up for him on a recent trip to the store, but that hadn't prevented his entire body from being coated in flour, which also coated large swaths of the walls and window blinds. Wisps of smoke escaped from the old oven. Nuts crunched under my shoes as I stepped into the room. And was that sweet potato on the ceiling?

"Um, Dorian?"

He turned from the stool he stood on as he mixed a bowl of frothy batter. His black eyes stood out against the white powder on his face.

"The boy is playing his guitar upstairs," he said.

"What happened here?"

"Do you know how difficult it is to make a soufflé without eggs? Who does not eat *eggs*? You know there is a family a few houses over who have chickens in their backyard. It would be so simple to take the eggs during the night. You are lucky I respect your wishes."

"By destroying my kitchen?"

"You need a new oven regardless."

"What did you do to my oven?"

"I told you, I am trying to make a vegan soufflé. I almost have it!"

I couldn't imagine this gargoyle gourmet having a sinister plan and lying to me about when he arrived in Portland. Unfortunately, I didn't like the alternative any better: that there was another creature out there—and one that might not be as goodhearted as Dorian.

"I need to ask you something," I said.

"Sweet potato."

"What?"

"That is the ingredient I was hoping would make the soufflé work without eggs. Sadly, I was mistaken, thus the potato on the ceiling. I have learned that similar to what worked for the *galettes*, ground golden flax seeds in warm water or nut milk works well as an egg replacement."

"Oh. That's great. That's not what I was going to ask you."

"No?" He resumed whipping the batter with a whisk.

"When you hid out in my shipping crates, you didn't open the crate and come out before I opened the crates in my living room, did you?"

"How would I have done that?"

"You use your claws to get into all sorts of places. Like police labs."

"Yes," he said. "But not when heavy wooden boxes are stacked on top of each other in those metal containers that go on lorries. Why do you ask?"

"Just curious," I said.

He stopped mixing, setting the bowl down and jumping off his cooking stool. "You," he said, walking up to me, "should be a better liar for someone who has lived for so long."

"I didn't want to worry you unnecessarily," I said.

"I respect your privacy, but if this involves me—"

"Someone saw you last night."

"*Zut. Je suis desolé*. I did not think anyone had seen us!"

"Just you, not Brixton. It was Max. But he thinks he imagined it."

"This is good."

"No," I said. "It's not. He saw something similar last month, here in Portland."

"Last month? But I was not here."

"Exactly. So *who was?*"

"But this is impossible! I have had the book in my possession all these years. How else could there be someone like me? Especially here in Portland."

"I don't know, Dorian," I said. "I don't know."

"I shall investigate tonight."

"No. You've done enough investigating. Speaking of which, I need you to take the vial you stole far away from here. Max is off the case and there's a new detective working it. I don't know if he'll consider me a serious suspect. We need to make sure there's nothing linking us to the break-in. I'm going to clean up the vessels I used to test it, and I'll give you the vial to hide tonight."

"You are done with it?" he asked.

"It doesn't matter," I said. "But it can't stay here. You can climb somewhere that nobody will be able to get to it, but that we can get back if we need it."

"You do not yet know *who* is connected to the poison. You could try one more time."

"It doesn't work like that."

Dorian scowled. "You said the poison would help."

"It's sort of like a fingerprint," I said. "I can't detect the person who created a poison if I haven't already seen what they can do. Like how a fingerprint is meaningless unless you've got something to compare it to. The reason I could tell it wasn't Blue who mixed that particular concoction was that it didn't have her signature."

"You mean it is a process of elimination?"

"If I have already seen the way someone has put things together and the energy they have put into it, I can tell if a new substance was created by the same person. Their own unique signature. Only..."

"Only *what?*"

"If this mixture was created by someone other than the person who used it, I wouldn't be able to link it to the killer. And since it was a mix of mercury, herbs, and other substances, I don't know exactly what's going on with it."

"Why did you ask me to steal the vial, then, if it could not help?"

"I didn't ask you to!"

"You implied it. You wished me to take action where you could not."

"It wasn't for nothing," I admitted. "I'm more sure than ever that Blue is innocent and being framed. I know mercury is involved, meaning we need to be extra careful, because we don't know who we're dealing with. And now I know more about some of the ingredients that were given to Blue—" I broke off. I couldn't believe I'd been so stupid. There was a time when this type of poisoning was much more common. A time when I knew how to heal people.

"What is it?" Dorian asked.

"Wait here," I said.

"Where would I go?" He glanced around the disaster area that was my kitchen.

I ran down the basement stairs. I found the vial of poison Dorian and Brixton had stolen, still half full, and slipped it into my pocket. I rooted through my glass vessels. I knew it had to be somewhere... I'd seen the blue-tinted glass when I'd carried things downstairs. *Yes.* I found the tincture I was looking for and ran back up the stairs. It had been so long since I'd thought of it that I'd forgotten it was there.

"Here's the stolen vial," I said, handing Dorian the vial after wiping it off with a kitchen rag.

"Where are you going?"

"There's something I need to try. I'll be back soon."

I arrived at the hospital with a few minutes left during visiting hours. Though I was relieved that the only police officer in sight was chatting with a nurse at the far end of the hallway, I again wondered how safe Blue was. If I could get to her so easily, who else could? I was there to give her something I hoped might save her, but someone else might come with different intentions.

Blue looked so peaceful that I could have easily believed her to be asleep, if it hadn't been for the tubes and machines surrounding her. Though I knew the plastic tubes were doing her good, the sight of them still made me shudder. Doctors of the past who prescribed bloodletting and other cures always thought they were doing good. They did the best they could with what they knew.

"I don't know if you can hear me, Blue," I whispered, "but I'm sorry someone did this to you. I want to help."

I glanced over my shoulder to make sure nobody was watching, then removed the small glass jar I'd brought with me. I removed its dropper lid and put three drops through her parted lips.

It was a spagyric tincture I'd created a century ago—a mixture of plant essences in alcohol with calcinated plant ash to strengthen the effect of what would otherwise be a simple healing tonic. Tinctures last many years, but I had no idea if they lasted *that* long. I no longer knew how to create this concoction, and it was the last of the batch I'd transformed all those years ago. I had made it back when I was practicing alchemy with Ambrose, before I gave it up. Back then, I had often created healing tincture and tonics. They helped people, but they weren't miracle cures. I hadn't thought about this tincture for Blue's coma until I realized the nature of what had poisoned her body. It was something I created to help the body detoxify from a mercurial poison that was making industrial workers sick, before the effects were known to be poisonous.

A knock sounded at the door, startling me. The dropper fell from my hand and into the folds of the bedding. I couldn't see where it had gone.

Cupping the container in my hand and slipping it into my pocket, I turned to the person who'd knocked.

"Visiting hours are ending," the nurse said.

"I'll just be a minute."

"I can wait. I'm here to check her vitals."

Behind her, a police officer appeared. He frowned as he looked past the nurse into the room.

Time for a new plan. "Take care, Blue," I said, leaning over to squeeze her arm, hoping it looked like a natural affectionate gesture as I attempted to see where the dropper had fallen.

I didn't see it.

The nurse and officer stood in the doorway and watched me as I left, empty-handed.

CHAPTER 22

By the time I reached the house, I had thought up a long list of the many horrible things that could happen if the dropper was discovered on Blue. What if my fingerprints were found on the dropper? What if they thought it was poison? My tincture wouldn't hurt her, but it was possible it wouldn't have any effect. It was a harmless plant mixture, but would modern doctors or the police realize that? Or would they think I had poisoned Blue and was trying to finish what I'd started? I was the one who'd found her lying unconscious, after all. The person who calls in something like that is automatically suspected.

Dorian was almost finished cleaning the kitchen. He was a responsible little gargoyle, I'd give him that.

"You do not look well," he said, a scouring brush in his hand.

"I'm tempted to pack up and move to Paris."

"Truly?"

"No, not really. It's just been a bad day."

"Oh." His shoulders fell.

"I'm sorry, Dorian. I didn't mean to tease you. You miss it, don't you?"

"Why do you think I have been cooking soufflés today? If I merely wished to stay awake, I would read one of the many books you kindly brought me from the library."

"You're cooking comfort food the same reason you ordered *Le Monde*," I said. "You're homesick."

He gave a Gallic shrug. "This is a strange country."

"What's been going on here isn't normal."

"I am not speaking of the murder and the theft of my book. I realize it was I who brought this upon you. For that I am truly sorry."

"You couldn't have known."

"You are a kind woman, Zoe. This is why I wonder if perhaps I should leave you and return to Paris myself."

"Are you serious? You can't leave."

"Why not?"

"We need to find out what's happening to you. Find a way to reverse the effects of whatever is killing you."

"Maybe I am meant to die this cursed death. Perhaps," he said, "it is my fate."

"I know you're French, but you don't have to be so resigned."

"I do not hear Brixton playing his guitar," he said.

"Nice try. Don't change the subject."

"I am serious. We should hear him."

I rushed upstairs. The guitar rested on Brixton's unmade bed. There was no sign of Brixton.

After searching the house and yard, I sent him a text, only to hear the beeping of a phone—coming from Dorian. The phone was in the pocket of his apron, where Dorian was keeping it to prevent Brixton from filming another video.

"Why did I agree to let him stay here?" I said. "There was a murder here, and a murderer still out there. What was I thinking?"

"Do not forget that the boy and I were also seen last night by the detective. Someone else may have seen us too."

"You're not helping."

"*Fais l'autruche?*"

"No. You're right. I don't want to bury my head in the sand like an ostrich."

"You are worried. But you must keep a calm mind."

"A calm head."

"*Exactement.*"

"His mom is picking him up tonight. He knows that. He knows he should be here. What if something has happened to him?"

"It is too early to think that."

"I hate feeling helpless." I grabbed my keys. "It's sunny for the first time this week. Maybe he and his friends are out enjoying it."

Though my little neighborhood felt much like a small town, I quickly remembered how big a city Portland was. Over half a million people lived here. And I was looking for one kid.

He wasn't at the park across the street from the high school, where I knew he sometimes liked to hang out. Checking there had been my grand idea. I wasn't sure where else to look. Was downtown Portland a draw for teenagers who lived across the river? I drove through Old Town and ended up on the main drag with Powell's Books. I doubted they would be at the bookstore.

I returned to the house shortly after dark, empty-handed. I was frantically considering options when a very dirty Brixton opened the back door with the key I'd given him.

I ran up to him and gave him a hug, a huge wave of relief washing over me.

"Are you okay?" I held him at arm's length, looking him over. Dirt covered the lower half of his face and much of his clothing. He held an odd hard hat in his hand. "What happened?"

"I'm fine. You can chill."

"What happened?"

"Nothing. I was out with Veronica and Ethan."

"You should have told me you were going out."

"My mom never asks me."

Of course not. "What were you doing?"

Brixton grinned and held up the strange hat I'd noticed. "Spelunking."

The hard hat was clean but looked decades old. A light was affixed to the top. "Where on earth did you find that?"

"Ethan found it online. He gets bored. I think the school he went to before moving here was harder. He's always buying stuff online. He found this and thought it would be perfect for the tunnels. He knew I was bummed about Blue, so he ordered us all hats so we could go out and stay busy."

I softened a little. "That was nice of him."

"Ethan's generous like that. So, um, have you learned anything else about Blue? Like with the poison Dorian and I got for you?"

"Brixton, you know you can't tell *anyone* what you did, right? Not even Veronica and Ethan."

"I'm not stupid."

"It wasn't long ago that you were trying to convince them about Dorian."

"That was two whole days ago."

Right. What was the calculation of two days in teenage years? Definitely a lot longer than what two days meant to me.

"Things are different now," Brixton said. "I know Dorian is a secret, and obviously B&E is a secret. V is great and all, but she's sort of a gossip."

Which explained how everyone knew about my "French boyfriend."

"Good," I said. "Nobody besides us knows about the breaking and entering."

"You going to tell me what you learned?"

"I was right that Blue didn't poison herself."

"You told the police?"

"There's nothing I can tell them. I told you the evidence is worthless now."

"But it should lead you to the person who did it."

"It only told me Blue didn't create it herself."

"I thought you were supposed to be good at this stuff."

"Being good at something doesn't mean it's easy."

"Then what's the point?"

"I may have found a way to counteract some of the effects of the poison."

"Really? You can cure her?"

"I don't know if it worked or not. I went to visit her in the hospital today. Visiting hours were ending, so I couldn't stay longer to see if she would wake up."

Brixton slammed the hard hat into the arm of the couch.

"It could still work," I said.

"Right." He turned away from me and wiped his eyes with his sleeve, then brushed past me to pick up the hard hat from where he'd tossed it.

"Why did you need the hat for the tunnels?" I asked. "Don't they have lights?"

"Not the ones we go to."

I was about to suggest it was a bad idea to go exploring unlit city tunnels, but stopped myself. I wasn't his mother. His mother would be here shortly. She could deal with him. Besides, the tunnels were probably a lot safer than what was going on above ground.

"Why don't you get cleaned up before your mom gets here," I said instead.

"Is the shower fixed yet?"

"I've had other things to deal with."

I chose to ignore the language he used as he dragged his feet up the stairs. Brixton would be leaving shortly, so I returned his phone to him.

A few moments later, it began to ring. "Zoe!" he called from the top of the stairs. I rushed back into the living room, expecting to find that he'd fallen through a rickety stair.

"It's Blue!" he said. "You did it! She's awake!"

"It's her on the phone?"

"Yeah." He put the phone back to his ear. "Blue, I'm here with Zoe. We're coming right over. Wait, what? *What?* No, don't go. Blue? Blue?"

"What's going on?" I asked.

He stood mute, then sank down onto the top step.

"Brixton, what's happening?"

"She's awake," he said, "and they're arresting her for murder."

CHAPTER 23

"Hold on!" I said as Brixton rushed past me.

"We need to go!"

"No, we don't." I caught up with him before he reached the front door and put my hand on his dust-covered shoulder. "We know she's okay, which is what counts. If the police are arresting her, it's not a good idea for us to go to the hospital." I thought of the dropper of tincture left on her bed. That was one reason I wanted to stay far away from the hospital. I also didn't want Brixton to see Blue being hauled off by the police.

"I thought you cared about her too." He shrugged off my hand. "But that was a lie, wasn't it? You were just using her to help Dorian."

I stared at him.

"You thought I didn't know he's dying?" Brixton said.

"He told you?"

"He didn't have to." He glared at me. "I'm not stupid. I saw there was something wrong with him, so I asked him. You could have told me what was going on."

"I was—"

"What? Trying to *protect me*? You were trying to protect yourself. Are you going to the hospital or what?"

"We're not going," I said.

"Maybe you're not." He ran to the back door, grabbed his bike, and sped down the driveway.

I wasn't able to catch him, but I could follow. I knew where he was going. The tires of the truck screeched as I pulled out of the driveway and headed for the hospital. What I didn't count on was the fact that there was traffic. The start-and-stop traffic inched along, making me more anxious by the minute. It was Saturday evening and apparently everyone in the city of Portland had decided it was a nice night to go out.

I ran into Brixton's teacher Sam—literally—as the elevator doors opened on Blue's floor of the hospital. I nearly knocked down his tall frame in my rush to find Brixton.

"Blue is with the police," Sam said. "They won't let me see her."

"Have you seen Brixton?" I asked, catching my breath.

"He was here a few minutes ago. I assumed he was here with you. Were you parking the car while he came up?"

"He ran off without me."

He gave a sad chuckle. "He's like that."

"You said he *was* here. Does that mean he's gone?"

"I don't know where he went. He was really upset when they wouldn't let us see Blue."

"She's all right?"

"You could call it that. She seems to have made a miraculous recovery. But the police are questioning her. I heard a little bit of the conversation before they pushed us back. They're treating her like she's a suspect in her own attempted murder. I don't get it."

"Did you hear anything else?"

"Like what?"

Oh, I don't know, I thought, *like about a tincture dropper on her bed?*

"I need to look for Brixton," I said instead.

"If he left without you, I have a feeling I know where he might go."

"Where?"

"His mom is still out of town, right?"

"Until later tonight."

"Try Max Liu's house."

"The detective?"

"He's one of the few adults Brixton trusts." Sam consulted his phone and wrote down an address for me.

∾

Thirty minutes later, I knocked on a red door with a gold dragon knocker.

"Have you ever thought of being a detective?" Max Liu asked as he opened his front door for me.

"I take it I was right that Brixton is here?"

"Come on in," Max said.

"Go away!" a young voice called from somewhere beyond the threshold.

Max smiled at the admonition, quickly followed by a cough to cover it up.

The exterior of the single-story house was Spanish architecture with a red-tiled roof that matched the front door. Inside, Max's house was simplicity itself. The open floor plan revealed only the barest assortment of furniture. A single white couch with a pewter-topped coffee table filled the center of the hardwood living room floor. Two large canvas paintings of scenic forests, each at least six feet high, covered one wall. The only thing out of place was Brixton's bicycle, which was propped up in the entryway.

The main room looked over both the kitchen and, through sliding glass doors, the backyard. The only items visible in the kitchen were a cast iron tea kettle resting on the gas stove and two framed photos: a colorful image of a twenty-something south Asian woman in a field of tulips, and a black-and-white photo of an older Chinese woman in front of a row of metal jars.

Though it was a moonless evening, a soft light from an outdoor lamp illuminated the backyard. I could see that the small yard held a tree, an assortment of edible herbs and plants in a row of clay pots, and a wooden bench sheltered by an awning. The bench was in the perfect position for the person sitting on it to gaze at the tree, herb garden, and sky. Right now a cranky teenager sat on the bench.

"Your house is perfect," I said, not realizing I was speaking aloud until I'd already begun.

"A lot of people ask if I've just moved in and haven't bought any 'stuff' yet."

"I don't mean to intrude, but I need to get Brixton."

Max tilted his head toward the backyard. "What did you do to him? It looks like he bathed in mud."

"I have a new appreciation for mothers."

"He's a handful, but he's a good kid."

"I know. His mom is due to pick him up at my house any time now. I'd better let her know we're running late."

"I think Brixton already took care of that."

Brixton opened the sliding doors. "My mom texted me. She's outside."

"Your stuff is still at my house. Should I bring it by your place later?"

He looked at his mud-covered shoes. I cringed when I thought about what Heather would think of my child-care abilities. "Nah," he said. "Can Dor—I mean, can me and my mom go by your place on our way home? I still have the extra key you gave me. I'll bring it back to you tomorrow."

I hesitated for a moment. Even if he was at home, Dorian was good at hiding. And even though Brixton was upset, I didn't believe he was trying to reveal Dorian's existence any longer.

"Sure," I said. "See you tomorrow."

Brixton gave Max a fist bump before leaving.

"He doesn't want you to see where he lives," Max said.

"That's what that was about? Is it that bad?"

"Only the fact that the apartment is in a rundown building. I checked in on him there a few times after he got into trouble. It's a nice enough place. His mom is a painter, and keeps the house full of art and books. But most of his friends have houses. He's kind of touchy about it."

"You mentioned when he got in trouble—"

"You want some tea?"

"I'd love some."

Max went to the kitchen and put water in the kettle. It was both ornate and simple. And *old*. An embossed Chinese dragon wrapped around the iron kettle.

"Where did you find that?" I asked. "It's beautiful."

"It was my grandmother's kettle."

"It's your grandmother in this photo?" I indicated the black-and-white photograph in a simple bamboo frame. In the photo, the woman stood in front of a cabinet of brass jars. I remembered Max saying his grandparents had been apothecaries in China. Her lips were unsmiling, but the photograph captured a mischievous smile that could be seen in her eyes. I could tell why he liked the photo.

"It was taken in China," Max said, "before she came here with my mom. The other is of my wife."

"Your wife?" I croaked. He wasn't wearing a wedding ring, but not everyone did. I had already been feeling foolish about my feelings for the man, and now I had even more reason to do so.

"Chadna passed away shortly after we were married."

"I'm so sorry, Max."

"It was a long time ago. Shortly after she finished medical school. Chadna was the one who saved me from the immature ideas I had about magic as a child. It's because of her that I straightened my life around."

I gave him a moment, but he didn't seem to want to say more. "I wasn't kidding when I said this house is perfect," I said, changing the subject. "It's rare to find such an uncluttered space." I couldn't remember seeing anything so purposefully sparse in the last century.

Max turned off the kettle as it began to steam, then removed two handle-less porcelain teacups from the cupboard, along with a box of loose leaf tea.

"If you have one teapot," he said, pouring hot water over tea leaves, "that will do you quite well. How much does he lack himself who must have a lot of things?"

"You're quoting Sen Rikyū," I said. At that moment, I wished more than anything that I had been in Max's house under other circumstances.

Max tilted his head and looked up from the tea. "How did you know that?"

"One of the few books I've kept in my trailer over the years is a book of quotations about tea. It reminds me to live in the moment and appreciate what I have in front of me." I didn't add how many years I'd had to read about tea and learn that lesson, but here in this house I found myself wanting to tell Max everything. It was a dangerous impulse, especially after hearing him talk about his scientific wife and dismissing the teachings of his grandmother. It was foolish of me to hope we could share something. Yet in this sanctuary he'd created for himself, I was more drawn to him than ever. I pulled myself back from that dangerous ledge and changed the subject. "You were going to tell me about Brixton."

"I wasn't, actually."

"It sounded like you were."

"You're too damn easy to open up to, Zoe. Do you know that?"

"I feel the same way." Our eyes locked and I lost all sense of time and place.

Max cleared his throat. "Breaking and entering, and assault. That's what Brixton did."

That startled me back to the present. "He's just a kid. How can whatever he did count as assault?"

"He beat up a guy who was harassing his mom. His stepdad was out of town for a while and this guy was hitting on his mom—close to harassment, but not enough for a restraining order." Max sighed and looked out the window. "Brixton was only twelve at the time, smaller than he is now. He knew he was too little to do anything to the guy if the guy could see it coming, so he broke into his house one night and beat him up, telling him never to touch his mom again."

"That sounds more heroic than criminal."

"The guy ended up in the hospital with several broken bones."

"Oh."

"Nobody liked it, but the guy wanted to press charges."

"Did he go to juvenile jail, or whatever it's called?"

Max shook his head. "Community service, but he's got a juvenile record now."

"You felt sorry for him, like he got a bad deal."

"I saw myself in him." He paused as he finished making the tea and handed me a cup. "I could see what was coming. I thought getting caught up in the system might push him into doing *more* bad things, because he saw that what he thought was a good deed was met with getting arrested."

"Were you right?"

"Yes and no. His mom isn't much of a disciplinarian. That friend of his, Veronica, keeps him in line more than his mom."

"I thought he said he had a stepfather."

"He's not around much."

"You said you saw yourself in him," I said, wondering what he'd meant a minute before.

"So," Max said, suddenly very interested in his tea leaves, "Brixton told me Blue woke up. I'm glad to hear it."

"Yeah, except that now she's being arrested."

"At this point, she's only being questioned. But that's why Brixton came over. He didn't know I was off the case. He was upset and thought it was my fault."

"So she's not under arrest?"

"I told you I'm off the case."

"Surely you know what's going on, though."

"I'm on leave, Zoe. I told you I play things by the book. I'm here in my sanctuary, not following up on cases that aren't my own."

Max's cell phone rang.

"Liu," he said. He listened for a few moments, his face stoic. "Sure. I know where she is. I'll bring her." He clicked off.

"What was that about?"

"Blue is asking for you," he said. "She says she'll talk, but only if you're the one she talks to. She says you saved her life."

I gripped the teacup. How did Blue know? And what had she told people?

"Why would she say that?" Max asked.

"I visited her. I've always wondered if people in comas can hear what people say to them. Maybe she heard me." I was used to leaving out details that would make people think I was crazy, but I hated lying to Max. Maybe I really should leave Portland before it was too late.

Max nodded, but his expression remained skeptical. "She's still at the hospital under observation, with a guard checking on her regularly. They're waiting for us."

I wanted to take my own car to the hospital to be alone with my thoughts, but Max said he had something to tell me before we got there. He insisted we ride together. I slid into the passenger side of a sleek black sedan. It suited him.

"What was it you wanted to tell me?" I asked.

"Blue Sky isn't her real name."

"Yeah, I kinda figured that."

"It's the real name on her identification," Max said.

"You mean she officially changed her name?"

"Not exactly. After we started looking into her, I discovered the truth. Since you're going to talk with her, you should know the truth going into this."

"I thought you didn't believe she was a killer either."

"Instincts aren't the same as facts, Zoe. You should know what you're agreeing to when you speak with her."

"What are you trying to tell me?"

"Blue's real name is Brenda Skyler. Ten years ago, she faked her own death."

CHAPTER 24

"You came," Blue said. Her voice was weak, but she was sitting up in the hospital bed. It had been adjusted so she could talk without getting out of bed.

I was being allowed to speak with Blue alone, on the condition that the conversation was being recorded. I wasn't sure why she would talk to me but not the police, but I was going to find out. "Of course I came. You know we're being recorded, right?"

"They told me." She held up her finger to her lips, then turned over her palm. There was something in her hand. It was the tincture dropper that had fallen into her bed after I'd given her a few drops. She handed it to me. "Thank you," she said, "for coming to visit me. The nurse told me you were the last person to come visit me before I woke up, even though the police think I'm the one who killed—" She broke off and gave me an earnest look. "I didn't do it."

"Why did you want to see me?"

"They told me Brixton was staying with you. That was the first thing I thought of when I woke up. He was supposed to stay with me. How is he?"

"Concerned about you."

"But he's all right?"

"He's good." Sure, he'd snuck out in the middle of the night and broken into a police lab... but he was well-fed and healthy.

"Does he think—he doesn't think I did this, does he?"

"No, he believes in you. You're the one thing he talks about more fondly than anything."

She blinked back tears. I started to get up, but she grabbed my hand. "I asked for you because life is too short to waste time doing things one doesn't want to do. I know, now, that the truth has to come out, but I'll be damned if it's going to be on someone else's terms. I want to tell it to someone who understands."

"You barely know me."

"I know what you're doing here," she said.

My pulse quickened. "I don't know what you mean."

"Portland is the perfect place to reinvent oneself."

"I'm not—"

She laughed, then cringed. "Owe, I've got the damnedest headache."

"Let me get a doctor. I don't think you're up for talking." I didn't like the direction this conversation was going. I needed an excuse to get out of there. I had the strongest impulse to hook up my trailer to my truck and never look back.

"Wait, I want to get this off my chest," Blue said. "I can see it in your eyes. You're a kindred spirit. Someone who's here to start fresh. Was it a bad breakup? No, you don't have to tell me. That's the whole point of starting fresh."

I let out a sigh of relief. "Something like that. I've been living out of my trailer for a long time. But when I got to Portland…"

"It feels like home, doesn't it?"

"It does."

"I'm glad my instincts were right about you. You seem like you're too young to understand what it's like to feel so desperate that you need to flee your entire life, never looking back but always wondering if it's right over your shoulder. But you're an old soul. I hope you'll understand."

I wished I could tell her how right she was. That I could tell her I understood running more than she thought.

"You look like you want to say something," Blue said.

I shook my head. "You should probably start telling me what the police want to know, before they decide I'm not a good interrogator and they should do it themselves."

"I don't know where to begin."

"I already know," I said, "about Brenda."

"Ah. I suppose you want to call me that now."

"Not if you prefer Blue."

I was in no position to judge. After all, Faust was the name I'd chosen for myself after realizing what I'd become.

"I was going to tell you myself, but I guess they beat me to it." She ran a hand through her wild gray hair. "If you can believe it, I used to have perfectly coifed hair and not a gray hair in sight. I paid obscene amounts of money to have my hair dyed, straightened, and styled."

"I can't picture you without your untamed curls. They suit you."

"I agree. My old life didn't suit me in any way imaginable."

"Lawyer?"

"Lawyers always get a bad rap, don't they? Don't people think of any other profession that would be a drag?"

"So you weren't a lawyer?"

"No, you were right." She laughed. "I was a lawyer. Sort of. I went to law school straight out of college because it's what was expected of me. It never occurred to me that I could do something different with my life. I met my husband during law school. He was the charming guy all the women in our class fell for—handsome but with a little bit of quirkiness that showed in his imperfect nose, smart enough to do well at school without having to study all the time, confident enough to be a good public speaker and to flatter women in just the right way. I should have known he was too perfect."

"Things like that usually are."

"He wasn't as smart as we all thought. He was cheating on tests. The worst part was, after I found out, I *helped him*. I thought I was in love. I, however, took the code of ethics seriously. I couldn't bring myself to take the bar exam, because I knew I was morally compromised. For him. He knew he had me. We got married right after law school. He did a clerkship for a judge, during which I helped him with a lot of the work without anyone knowing. After the clerkship, he started his own private practice. It was early in his career to do so, but he was charming enough to pull it off—with my help. I couldn't legally practice law, but I helped him with research and cases, as a legal assistant. I played the part. I know I was fooling myself, thinking I was being ethical by not being a practicing lawyer myself. He was a master at psychologically manipulating me. It took years for me to see it. Years during which I blindly followed his lead."

"What happened to change your mind?"

"He knew me. He knew I was a good lawyer who did everything ethically except for lying about the work I did for him. He knew he could only push me so far and that I'd never do anything I knew to be *morally* wrong. "

"But he would."

"There were some of his cases," she said, "where he didn't ask for my help. He didn't even tell me he was working on them. I could see why. They were worse than I could have imagined. When I found out, I kept the knowledge to myself. But I knew what I had to do."

"You left him?" I asked.

"If only it had been that simple. He kept meticulous records. One of his files was a fake record of everything illegal I had supposedly done—without his knowledge, of course. He'd been keeping the records as insurance, in case he ever did push me too far. A few years before I found out the extent of his crimes, I had a brief moment of clarity during which I thought about leaving him. It was induced by one too many martinis—an indulgence that used to get me through my days with him—so I stupidly told him I might leave him. That's when he showed me the file."

"What was in it?"

"Falsified records about things he claimed I had done that would send me to jail. He had the gall to pretend I'd actually done these things and that he was being a faithful husband by protecting me and not turning me in. Spousal privilege and all that." She scoffed. "If I left him or told any 'lies' about him, he would no longer feel obliged to cover up my crimes."

"That's awful." What was even worse was that after everything I'd seen in my life, I could imagine him getting away with it.

"I knew, then, that I could never leave him. Not safely. I started putting away money. We spent so lavishly that it was easy to save a hundred dollars here and there without him noticing. It added up. But I didn't yet have a plan. I was a broken woman then. I couldn't see any way out. I still believed his only crime was in what he was doing to me—manipulating me into doing his work for him. He'd never physically abused me, so I told myself I wasn't being abused, even though I was. It would have been easier if he'd hit me."

As screwed up as that sounded, it made sense. Her husband had known how to push her just to the brink but not over the edge.

"Once I found out he was breaking the law to help corrupt clients, that's when I had the idea to disappear."

"But you knew you couldn't leave him without repercussions."

"Even if I'd gone to jail myself," she said, "that would have been okay, as long as I brought him down with me. But knowing him, I'd have ended up serving a life sentence while he came off looking like a saint for caring for a deranged wife for so long. I wasn't left with many options. But by then, I had saved up a decent amount of money that he didn't know about. Not a great deal of money compared to what we were used to spending, but what did I care about that? I never cared about the clothes or the spa treatments. I'd always wanted to do something like I'm doing here in Portland."

She paused to take a sip of water. Her hand shook as she did so.

"Do you need a doctor?" I asked, helping her raise the glass to her parched lips and then set it back on the side table.

"Hell, no. I've been asleep for days. It's just taking me a little time to wake up. Where was I? Oh, right, taking charge of my life." She clapped her hands together. "I'd wasted too much of my life with that bastard. I wasn't going to let him ruin the rest. Without him knowing, I collected my own evidence— real evidence—that he was falsifying documents for crooked clients. Sent the evidence to the proper authorities, left a suicide note, then drove my car into Lake Michigan."

"You died that day."

"Brenda Skyler died that day. Blue Sky was born."

"Max said it was smart of you to take a name so similar to your own. That way you'd recognize it and respond when people addressed you."

"*Max*, huh." Her eyes twinkled. "I know that look."

"You were explaining how you faked your death," I said, feeling the color rise in my cheeks. "How did you pull it off? And please tell me your husband didn't get away with his crimes."

"I met a lot of interesting people while we practiced law together. I was able to get a fake ID pretty easily, then got a real one once I moved to Oregon. As for my husband—" She paused and gave me a conspiratorial grin. "The bugger got disbarred and served five years in jail. The last I heard, he was selling men's suits in Detroit. I, on the other hand, have been living exactly the life I wanted to. No more working fourteen-hour days. No more dieting. No more playing hostess to people I never liked. No more straightening and dying my hair. No more manicures."

She paused to pat her ample belly and show me her calloused hands with short fingernails.

"I eat without starving myself," she said. "I use my hands to garden and collect wildcrafted plants, and opened the teashop to make enough money to live simply while doing something I love."

"I suppose it's illegal to fake your own death," I said. "But why is that important now?"

"That's not why they want to arrest me," she said.

"I know." I suddenly felt very awkward, knowing I was the one who found the poison attributed to Blue, which I was now certain had been planted to frame her.

"They have this crazy idea," she said, "that Charles was *blackmailing* me about my past. They think that's why I killed him."

CHAPTER 25

"What, *what?*" I said. "Blackmail?"

Blue looked taken aback. "I thought you said you already knew why they were arresting me."

"I do. Because of the poison and stolen items at your house."

"What are you talking about?" Blue said, trying to get out of bed but realizing she was still attached to an IV. "There are stolen goods and poison at my house?"

"Don't try to stand," I said.

"Did anyone get hurt?" She gave up fiddling with the IV and stared at me. "Oh, God, Brixton. You said he was okay, right?"

"Brixton is just fine."

Blue rested her head against the pillow and crossed herself. "Thank God for that. Anyone else?"

"Just you."

"I drank something, didn't I? Things are still a bit fuzzy."

A nurse stepped into the room. "That's enough for today."

"I'm fine," Blue said. "I want to know what's happening."

A detective followed the nurse into the room.

"I agreed to tell you what you wanted to know to fill in the blanks of my past," Blue snapped at the detective. "But you're not telling me everything. I have a right to know the charges against me."

"Thank you, Ms. Faust," the detective said. "We've got what we need."

"What do you mean?" None of this made any sense.

"*Thank you*, Ms. Faust," the detective repeated. "Your service in the interest of justice is greatly appreciated."

I held Blue's gaze for a moment before walking out the door.

I found Max in the waiting room. "What's going on?" I asked.

"Not here."

We walked in silence to his car.

"Blackmail?" I said. "You think Charles Macraith was blackmailing Blue? Why would you think that?"

Max drew a deep breath, his hands taught on the steering wheel of the car, looking straight ahead at the concrete parking garage. "I shouldn't have anything to do with this case."

"I might know something," I said before I could stop myself.

His head snapped toward me. He was so close to me I could smell peppermint on his breath. "If you know something, you should tell Detective Dylan."

"He won't believe me."

"Why would *I* believe you?"

"Isn't poison a strange choice for a killer these days?" I asked.

It used to be a lot more common for people to poison each other. Before modern toxicology, it had been easy to get away with it. Many fatal poisons could easily be confused with diseases of the day. Arsenic was such a popular way to kill someone and disguise the death as being from natural causes that it acquired the nickname "inheritance powder." But these days, poison was a strange choice, especially when it was such a diluted form.

This didn't make sense on so many levels. If Dorian and Brixton hadn't stolen the vial, I was confident the lab would have come across the mercury and isolated the other toxins. The killer hadn't stabbed Blue, so the lab *would* have been looking for poison in her case, unlike with Charles Macraith. It wouldn't have gone undetected. Which didn't seem worth it, since there wasn't enough poison to kill.

"I can't figure you out," Max said. "Why can't you answer a simple question with a simple answer?"

"It wasn't a simple question."

"So you have to answer it with another question? Why don't you just tell me what you're getting at."

"If you tell me what's going on with the blackmail."

"Why do you care? Detective Dylan isn't pursuing you as a suspect. You can get on with your life."

"I suppose 'justice' isn't a good enough answer?" I asked. I couldn't tell him about Dorian, the dying gargoyle, for whom I needed to solve the case in order to retrieve the book that I hoped could save him.

"One of the reasons I'm good at being a cop is because I know human nature. Justice is a damn good reason, but *only* if it accompanies something more personal."

"Brixton cares about Blue," I said, "and I care about Brixton."

"He got to you, huh?"

"You're telling me he hasn't gotten to you?"

"That was different."

"Why?"

"Because I saw myself in him." Max looked away and started the car, but didn't make a move to back out of the parking space.

"You mentioned that before. What did you mean by it?"

He hesitated for a brief moment. "Only that you were never a fourteen-year-old boy."

"I had a brother. He was impetuous like Brixton. He—" I broke off. My hand flew to my locket. I hadn't meant to let it slip out, but it was too easy to let my guard down around Max.

"I'm so sorry, Zoe."

"Why?"

"You used the words *was* and *had.*"

"You picked up on that, huh?"

"Good cop skills, remember." He tried to smile but failed.

"It was years ago."

"I'm even sorrier to hear it, then. It's never easy to lose someone you love, but it's especially difficult when they're taken too young."

"We're supposed to be talking about Blue."

"*We're* not supposed to be talking about anything." He leaned back in the seat of the car and shook his head. "You're supposed to go talk to Detective Dylan about whatever it is you think you know about the case."

"It's only an observation."

"Your observations have been pretty good so far. Blue probably wouldn't have been found in time if you hadn't suspected something and gone to see her."

"A lot of good I did her."

"The evidence still would have pointed to her, regardless of when we found her. But because of you, she pulled through."

"Thanks for being a good liar. I doubt there was enough poison in her system to kill her."

"What do you mean?"

"That's what I wanted to tell you. Ever since you told me the poison was stolen from the lab, I've been trying to think more about what I smelled." It wasn't exactly a lie. Omitting facts he didn't need to know was hardly the same thing.

"You placed the scent?"

"I told you it reminded me of something I couldn't put my finger on. I realized what it was. It smelled like an old Chinese herbal remedy... that had been tainted." I tried to think of a way to mention the mercury, but there was no good way to do it. It was odorless.

Max shook his head. "I know a thing or two about Chinese herbs. You're off base."

"You learned from your grandmother."

"I did." His lips tightened as he said it.

"She wouldn't have exposed you to toxins. To anything dangerous."

He opened his mouth and took a breath to speak but decided against it.

"You admit I have a point," I said.

"Maybe. It's too bad you didn't think of this *before* the sample was stolen. This could have helped the lab guys narrow things down."

"I know," I murmured. I wondered if there was a way for the vial to be "found." It wouldn't be able to be used as evidence, but successfully prosecuting the culprit was less of a concern of mine than finding Dorian's book and making sure Blue wasn't unjustly convicted. Would the police even consider testing something that was lost and then found? Maybe there was a way we could plant the vial in the grass near the lab, making it look like the thief dropped it...

"Zoe?"

"Yes?"

"I lost you for a minute."

"Sorry. I'm distracted. I've got a lot on my mind."

"Tell me about it. Let me drive you home."

"There's something else I've been thinking about," I said as he maneuvered out of the parking garage.

"Tell it to Dylan."

"Let me run it by you first."

He sighed and kept his eyes on the road, flipping on the windshield wipers as a misty rain began to fall.

"You guys are looking into some blackmail angle about Blue's past—"

"I can't talk about it," Max cut in.

"I know. That's fine." It wasn't fine, but I could deal with that later. "What I mean is that you might be ignoring the real motive."

"Which is?"

"Those antiques of mine that were stolen. I've been spending a little bit of time cataloging, and some of the things might be even more valuable than I previously realized."

"Mmm hmm."

"Is that the cop sound for a noncommittal answer?"

"We've been looking into all the angles, Zoe. You don't have to play detective. We know what we're doing."

"But the alchemy book—" I broke off when I saw Max's hands tighten on the steering wheel. His expression had changed. A wall had gone up. This wasn't like the other information he was withholding. He was hiding something.

CHAPTER 26

The light rain had turned into a full-blown rainstorm by the time Max dropped me off at my house. Gusts of windswept rain crashed against the car, making it difficult to have a conversation, which was fine by me. I didn't trust myself to speak. Max *couldn't* be involved. Not only because he was a detective, but because of what my gut was telling me. The question was whether I should believe my instincts.

As I entered the house, I discovered the rain wasn't only falling outside. Hearing dripping water, I went straight to the attic room that I had been hoping to turn into my business workspace.

I found Dorian there, placing buckets and bowls under the leaks.

"*Il pleut des cordes,*" he said. "You caught up with the boy? Were you able to speak with Blue Sky?"

I filled Dorian in on what had happened that evening with Brenda Skyler, a.k.a Blue Sky.

"You have learned nothing helpful!" Dorian said, jumping up from where we sat on the hardwood floor in between the buckets of rainwater. A drop of water fell on his head. He swore.

"Moving into an old house during the wintertime might not have been a wise decision," he said, pushing one of the buckets under the new leak with his feet. "*Merde. Mon pied.*"

"Your foot?"

"It is nothing."

158

But as he spoke, I could see his foot rested at an awkward angle. It wasn't bending like the rest of his body. It was solid stone.

"Dorian—"

"I said it is nothing!" he snapped.

If he didn't want to talk about how quickly his body was turning to stone, I wouldn't force the issue. What I needed to do was figure out how to help him.

My eyes searched the beams of the sloping ceiling. "The tarp is secure. Where are all these leaks coming from?"

"Modern construction is not the same as the solid buildings from the old days."

"This house is about a hundred years old."

"*Exactement,*" Dorian said. "Modern."

We couldn't live like this. I needed to keep calling contractors until I found one who hadn't heard about the recent murder that was making people wary to work on the house. I didn't care about any of the cosmetic upgrades I had originally been interested in. For now, what we needed was someone who could make the house habitable.

I had to figure out what to do with Dorian while someone fixed the house. Because of his deteriorating life force, it wasn't a good idea for Dorian to turn himself to stone and pretend to be a decorative stone object in the house. I would have to lock the basement door and have Dorian stay there during the day while a handyman made stopgap fixes to the rest of the house.

But the house was the least of my problems. I was no closer to figuring out who was framing Blue and where Dorian's book was. I'd tackled memories from the past that I wasn't yet ready to face, all to help the little gargoyle, but I had little to show for it beyond the amorphous feeling that I might be close to understanding more about the book's coded illustrations.

"There is a haunted look in your eyes, *mon amie,*" Dorian said.

I looked up at the dripping beams. "Speaking with Blue brought up memories I didn't want to think about."

"Come. We have done as much as we can to protect the room from water. Have you eaten dinner?"

I shook my head.

"I will cook."

Despite the fact that it was Dorian who was dying, I was the one who couldn't remain calm through our dinner of roasted chickpeas in a cayenne spice mix with cabbage braised in mustard and cumin seeds. I hated feeling helpless. I had grown accustomed to being lonely, but I was good at taking care of everything that had to get done. I could grow my own food from seeds, turn plants into healing remedies for the ailing, fix the engine of a truck on a desolate country road, and learn new languages and adapt to local customs. What I *couldn't* do was unravel the mysteries I'd encountered that week: Who killed Charles Macraith and why? Where was Dorian's book? What did the pages I'd photographed mean?

My unrest became unbearable when Dorian brought out a beautiful apple tart he made for dessert. It reminded me of food I'd eaten as a child on special occasions.

"The food was not good?" he asked.

"It's what the apple tart made me think of. You don't know the story of where I'm from. Before you knew of me in Paris."

"From your accent, I know you are American."

"I was born in Salem, Massachusetts."

"The same city as the famous witch trials. Oh! You do not mean—"

"I do."

"*Mais non.* This is terrible." Beneath his horns, his forehead creased with concern. "I did not know."

"You had no way to know the foods you cooked tonight would remind me of it."

"They burned you?" His black eyes widened.

I shook my head. "It didn't come to that." I took a deep breath. Dorian had told me his story. I wanted to tell him mine.

"By the time I was sixteen years old," I said, "the witch trials were going strong. I wasn't a witch. Therefore I thought I had nothing to hide. It was a foolish assumption."

"You were already an alchemist?"

"I was known as a 'simpler'—someone who understands how to use plants more than most people. Because I understood the cycles of nature, people said the plants 'spoke to me.' They said it was witchcraft."

"*Mon dieu.*"

"By the time I realized what was happening, hysteria had taken over. I was going to be arrested and tried with those poor women."

"Were any of them witches?"

"I don't think so. But really, I knew so little at the time. I had led a sheltered life. Difficult, but sheltered. I came from a family of farmers in Salem Village, growing oats and rye in the rocky soil. It was a deeply religious community, one where you didn't dare speak out of line. If it hadn't been for Thomas..." I removed my locket necklace and held it in my hand for a moment before handing it to Dorian. "My brother was the one who saved me.

He was only fourteen at the time, the same age as Brixton, but things were different then. We were expected to grow up more quickly. That's a miniature portrait of Thomas on the left side of the locket."

"Such a serious boy."

I pushed past my urge to cry. "He helped me escape to London, by boat. I was so hesitant to leave my mother and sisters that Thomas insisted on coming with me. As the only son in the family, he was expected to take over the farm, but he was willing to give up his whole life to help me escape my fate."

Dorian returned the locket.

"The trip to London used all of our money. This was the 1690s. A fourteen-year-old boy and a sixteen-year-old girl with no family and no formal training didn't have many options for employment. With my skills, I was able to make simple plant mixtures that helped people. It was enough to survive. It was also enough that alchemists took notice of my abilities. An alchemist used a tincture we had sold to track us down. When he found out it was I, not Thomas, who had used plants in such a way, he was wary. Female alchemists were quite rare. His associate, Nicolas Flamel, was more open to the idea. Nicolas and his wife took us in and agreed to train me."

"The famous French scrivener and bookseller," Dorian said. "Yes, I know of him. He and his wife Perenelle turned lead into gold and gave much money to charities in Paris. When wandering the streets of Paris during the night, I would often walk by their graves. But wait—the dates on their headstones were before the Salem Witch Trials."

"They discovered the Elixir of Life. When their graves were exhumed, they were found to be empty. They faked their deaths because the world was not yet ready to know the secrets of alchemy."

"Something you believe as well."

"I do. For many reasons. It takes rigorous study to truly understand alchemy. There are no quick fixes, which is what people would want. The Flamels knew that well. After faking their deaths, Nicolas and Perenelle moved to an estate in the French countryside, assuming new identities. It was there that I studied with them for several years. Thomas came with me and became a gardener. Then the plague came.

"It was the early 1700s. The plague hadn't been entirely eradicated in Europe. Before the Black Death killed much of the population of Marseille in 1720, it swept through the countryside where we were living. Thomas fell ill.

"I had been studying alchemy for nearly ten years, but as the study of alchemy goes, ten years isn't a very long time. I hadn't yet been expected to transmute base metals into gold or extend life. But when Thomas fell ill, and my usual herbal remedies failed to cure him from the plague, I was desperate. I threw myself into finding the Elixir of Life, hoping I would be able to share it with Thomas because of our strong familial bond. The Flamels told me that transferring the immortality of the Elixir of Life from one person to another couldn't be done, and that even the most clever of alchemists had never understood why. They suggested I spend Thomas's last days keeping him company. I didn't listen. I didn't know if it would work, but I had to do *something*. Everyone had told me I had a gift. My connection to plants was considered alchemy, so I thought I could use my plant knowledge to create the philosopher's stone and in turn use it to create the Elixir of Life. I'm human like anyone else. I wanted that quick fix. I worked so hard and slept and ate so little that I was often delirious. I didn't know what I was doing by then. I thought I might have been getting close when Thomas died."

"*Je suis desolé, mon amie,*" Dorian said. "I am so sorry, Zoe."

"If I had listened to the Flamels, I would have spent my time trying to heal Thomas through the means I already knew, or at least to have spent more time with him before he died. You can understand why I abandoned alchemy for many years after that. I left the Flamels and wandered for years, barely surviving. I didn't realize that I had indeed discovered the Elixir of Life until my hair turned white but the rest of me didn't age."

"How could you not know you had discovered it?"

"Alchemists speak in riddles. There was no way for me to know what the philosopher's stone looked like. Some alchemists suggest that it's not even a stone, but a powder or a liquid. The Greek alchemist Zosimos described it as a 'stone that is not a stone.' The Flamels told me that no alchemist can know what it is until they find it for themselves."

"*Alchemists,*" Dorian said, his snout flaring.

"Because I hadn't taken any of my research with me, I wasn't sure which of my transformations was 'the one true thing.' It was only my love for Thomas that had made me focused enough to discover alchemy's deepest secrets. Once I realized what had happened to me, I returned to the Flamels. But where their house had been—" I broke off, the memory of the landscape as clear as if it had happened that day. I saw the blackened land. I smelled the sodden ash.

"I found only charred ashes," I said. "The house had burned to the ground. I couldn't tell if they had died in the fire or escaped. The nearby villagers couldn't tell me anything. The other alchemists I knew who also knew the Flamels had died by then, so I wasn't able to find out what happened to them."

"I thought you said they were immortal."

"The Elixir of Life doesn't stop violent or accidental death. It only stops the progression of aging. It's why I adopted the food habits I have now—if I was potentially going to live forever, I wanted to feel healthy."

"The Flamels might be out there somewhere."

"I don't know, Dorian. I tried to find them, but it was as if my whole life with them had been an illusion. I found no evidence of their existing after they faked their deaths in Paris."

"They were careful."

"Too careful. I never saw them again."

CHAPTER 27

The next morning, I willed my eyes to focus on the woodcut illustrations from Dorian's book. The longer I stared at them, the more they blurred together. The twisted birds, the desolate landscapes, the fragments of Latin text that spoke vaguely of alchemy but didn't include nearly enough steps.

I took a brief break to fix myself a bowl of date and cinnamon oatmeal, as much for warmth as energy. In addition to rainwater, the house was leaking enough cold air that I couldn't shake a chill. I was seriously considering moving back into my trailer until I got the house fixed up. As I held the bowl cupped in my hands for warmth, there was a knock at the door.

Brixton stood in the doorway, a small paper bag in his hand.

"Don't you have school?"

"It's Sunday. But it's cool. You've got enough going on that I don't think you're senile or anything."

"Thanks. I think."

"So can I come in or what? It's freezing out here."

The rain had stopped but a cold wind was blowing. Brixton was dressed in his usual jeans, t-shirt, and hoodie, but it was cold enough that he'd also bundled in a bomber jacket.

"Sure," I said, "but it's not much warmer inside the house. And I thought your mom would want to spend time with you, now that she's home."

He rolled his eyes as he came inside. "Where's Dorian? I bought him something."

"He's upstairs dumping out the buckets of rainwater we collected last night, courtesy of the leaking roof."

"Do you need help with the tarp? I'm a good climber."

"I've got a professional coming over later today, hopefully before the rain comes back."

"How'd you find someone to come to a haunted house?"

"I don't think superstition would keep rational adults from a good job."

"It's not just superstition. We *told you* the place was haunted. That's why I came to check it out the first day I met you."

"You really believe that? Why weren't you afraid to stay in a haunted house?"

He shrugged. "I think it would be cool to see a ghost."

"Sorry to disappoint you."

"It could still happen. I've only been hanging out with you for a few days. The strange lights didn't appear that often."

I froze. "*What* strange lights?"

"The people who sold you the house didn't tell you? I thought they had to, like, legally tell you that stuff."

"*What lights*, Brixton?"

"That's why the house was empty for so long. Because nobody wanted to move into a haunted house."

"It was empty because there was a legal disagreement between the heirs."

"That's not what I heard. But it doesn't matter what I heard. It's what I saw. What *everyone* saw. Weird lights coming from this place. At first people said there must be homeless people crashing here. But whenever they sent the cops out here, they could never find a soul. Pretty freaky, right?"

Pretty freaky indeed. So *that* explained why everyone I called already knew about the house I was talking about. *What was going on here?*

Even if I believed in ghosts—and I'd never seen one in over three hundred years—I hadn't seen anything strange at the house. Various creaking noises, sure, but that was to be expected in an old house.

Dorian appeared on the stairs. He stepped more slowly than usual, holding the railing. At the sight of the limping creature, I forgot about Brixton's ghost story.

"I brought you Stumptown beans," Brixton said. "These are the ones I told you about that are wicked good."

"*Très bien*," Dorian said, taking a bag of coffee beans from Brixton's hands when he reached the bottom of the stairs. "*Merci*, my young friend."

"Aren't you too young to be drinking coffee?" I said to Brixton.

He gave me a look that reminded me I was over three hundred years old. Come to think of it, Brixton had never asked me how old I was. He'd asked me about gold and transformations, about being immortal, and about food, but he hadn't specifically asked about my age. At fourteen, he must have felt like he'd live forever, so a formula to live forever wouldn't have been of much interest. But gold for a poor kid? And food for an eternally hungry kid? Those were things he could relate to.

"Brixton, how old do you think I am?"

"My mom told me I was never supposed to answer that question if I knew what was good for me."

Dorian laughed, then retreated into the kitchen with his coffee beans.

"It's okay," I said, "I promise I won't be upset."

Brixton studied me for a few moments. "I dunno. I know you're old."

"Thanks."

His face reddened. "You told me I should guess!"

"I was kidding! Make your guess."

"Not cool, Zoe. Not cool. Anyway, you're like, at least ten years older than me. Maybe... twenty-six?"

"Not bad." I had been twenty-eight when I accidentally discovered the Elixir of Life. If that hadn't occurred to Brixton, it was a conversation for another day. "Twenty-eight."

"I think Mr. Strum is around your age."

"Your teacher?"

"Yeah, maybe you two should be hang out. I mean, when all this is over. All he ever does is work, and you two are like the only cool old people I know. Max is all right, too, but he's a cop. And he's ancient—he's like forty."

It was oddly refreshing to be considered "old." Looking young did have its advantages, but it had almost as many disadvantages. It was difficult to be taken seriously as a young woman. The "woman" part of the equation had become easier over time, as society became more accepting of women being equal, but the "young" part had gotten worse. It used to be that someone was considered an adult at sixteen, the age that I fled from my home with my brother. It wasn't unusual for people like me and my brother to be on our own and have already learned a trade. By twenty-eight, it was expected that you had come far in mastering a skill. Nowadays, it was more likely that a twenty-eight-year-old would be finishing graduate school or trying out different professions.

"Blue isn't cool?" I asked.

"Nah. Blue is mom-cool. That's different."

"That was nice of you to bring Dorian coffee," I said, suppressing a smile. I didn't think he was working an angle like he was before, but I couldn't figure out where the gesture had come from.

"Yeah, well, he said he was having trouble staying awake, so, you know..." He shrugged and looked down at the floor.

"It was really thoughtful, Brixton."

"Whatever."

Dorian stuck his head out of the kitchen. "Espresso, Brixton?"

"Americano. Six sugars."

And that explained why he liked coffee. Diluted and with plenty of sweetness.

"I need to take care of a few things," I said. "Are you two okay on your own?"

They both gave me a look that *really* made me feel three hundred.

"Sheesh, I was just being nice!"

As I headed to the basement, I heard Brixton explaining to Dorian, "It's an expression that means she's annoyed."

"Ah, so."

I'd found a handyman who said he could be here later that morning. He couldn't hear very well, so I hoped he got the address right—and that he wouldn't leave after he realized what house it was. Now I had to get everything into the basement that I didn't want the handyman to see. I began by cleaning up the mess I'd made, so there would be space to move things into the room without having them covered in gray slime.

I didn't have time to properly unpack my crates. *Still.* One day at a time.

Instead of unpacking my crates and moving them into the basement, I decided it made the most sense to seal them back up so the handyman wouldn't go poking around. Most of the items inside were the objects I'd collected over the years that I sold online, but a few of them were more personal alchemy items I'd saved for myself. The items wouldn't reveal my secret to anyone who didn't already suspect anything, but I didn't want anyone raising questions.

I hadn't checked for online orders in a couple of days, so I went upstairs and opened my laptop. There wasn't yet any furniture in the room that would become my home office. I hadn't had a proper office before, only a small table in my trailer with my laptop computer plus the storage unit, so I hadn't ever acquired office furniture. Sitting on the water-spattered hardwood floor, I scrolled through a couple dozen emails, half of them spam.

Most people I'd met since the turn of the century would have been bombarded with many more emails and social media messages after staying offline for a couple of days. Though I was often tempted to stay in touch with many of the people I'd met on my travels, I had to be practical. The whole reason I moved on was because people couldn't learn who I was. I couldn't create an online presence. Though it was often painful at the time, it was for the best.

All I had was the email address I used for my shop, Elixir, which was a generic email that didn't contain my name. Even my email was lonely.

Since I only sold a small collection of high-end items online, I didn't have frequent sales to fulfill. The items I sold hadn't cost me much when I bought them, so along with the compound interest on my savings, selling a few items a month kept me afloat. But now that I'd plunked down most of my savings to buy and fix up this house, I had to step up my sales. Maybe even start *marketing*. I shuddered at the thought.

I hadn't had any new sales since the last time I'd checked, which was fortunate. It meant I didn't have to waste time rooting through crates and could devote my time to helping Dorian. I hoped the handyman would be able to stabilize the worst parts of the house quickly. I shut my laptop and went downstairs.

At the dining table, Dorian and Brixton sat across from each other, a crystal on a gold necklace chain in Dorian's hand. In an outstretched arm, he held the chain so the crystal swayed back and forth in a rhythmic cadence.

I knew where the crystal had come from. I sighed as I looked over at the crate I'd sealed up, now open with its contents spilling out on the living room floor.

"Dorian, what are you—"

"Do not interrupt us! He will forever think he is a chicken!"

"Um…" What did one say to that?

"I'm not hypnotized, Dorian," Brixton said.

Dorian frowned. "You are not?"

"No."

"Not even a little?"

"I don't think so."

I snatched the crystal from Dorian's hand. "What are you two doing?"

"You tell her," Brixton said. "It was your idea."

"It is a good idea," Dorian said. "Once she has thought it through, Zoe will agree."

"That means I'm not going to like it, doesn't it?"

"You said the detectives are keeping information from you," Dorian said. "Information that is vital for solving the case, clearing Blue's name, and retrieving the book that can save my life."

"I haven't even deciphered the pages I photographed yet," I said.

"Yes, but with the entire book it will be easier."

"I know. That's why I agreed to go to Blue's house with you, against my better judgment. What does that have to do with hypnotizing Brixton?"

"We wish to learn what the detectives know."

"By turning Brixton into a chicken?"

"I am teaching him to hypnotize people. I know of this skill from the magicians my father worked with. Once I impart my knowledge, Brixton can hypnotize the new detective and he will tell us many things."

"That's a terrible idea," I said, "for so many reasons." I knew of the varied skills of Jean-Eugène Robert-Houdin. When I had seen him perform, I had been impressed by the range of illusions he had perfected. In addition to his automated "orange tree," a mechanized tree that hid many wonders, he took advantage of modern ideas that interested the people of the mid-1800s. He used "ether" to make his son float into the air, hovering high above the stage. And using "second sight," he would read the minds of audience members. Jean-Eugène Robert-Houdin was such an accomplished man that it was no wonder Dorian had the confidence to think he could teach Brixton to hypnotize a detective.

"Even if you *could* teach Brixton to hypnotize someone on our timeframe," I said, "you realize there's no way you could get a detective to agree to sit there while Brixton mesmerizes him with a crystal."

"You think I have not thought of this?" Dorian said.

I crossed my arms.

Dorian crossed his own arms and stared me down. His black eyes could be unnerving. I was glad he was on my side.

"The crystal is only phase one," Brixton said. "It's the easiest way to hypnotize people. Once I master it, then he'll show me how to hypnotize people without them knowing I'm doing it."

"Nobody," I said, "is hypnotizing anyone. Dorian, put everything back into the crate and seal it up. Brixton, you're welcome to stay here, but a handyman will be here to patch up the roof and look at the pipes shortly, so Dorian will need to be down in the basement. I need to run a few errands—"

"I have made a shopping list," Dorian said.

"I expected nothing less."

"It is on the fridge. You cannot miss it."

"I'll stop by the market. I'm also getting a lock for the inside of the basement door, so you can lock yourself in there while there are strangers in the house. No hypnotizing. Agreed?"

"It wasn't working anyway," Brixton said.

Dorian pouted for another few seconds before giving in.

"Agreed."

I've never gotten used to modern supermarkets. I don't mind picking out my own items, as opposed to having a shop clerk select things from behind the counter, the way things used to be done. But small specialty shops have always made much more sense to me. Nobody can be an expert at everything. I liked that there was a revival of specialty shops going on in towns like Portland.

Today, however, I found myself at a sprawling supermarket with harsh fluorescent lighting. I'd be able to get all the items on Dorian's shopping list as well as a lock for the basement door. There was something to be said for convenience.

In the produce section, I saw a familiar face. His unshaven stubble remained unchecked and was growing into a scruffy beard.

"Ivan," I said, greeting Olivia's friend next to a pyramid of tangerines. "Nice to see you."

"*Dobrý den*," Ivan said. "It is Zoe, is it not? Lovely to see you."

I forced myself to keep smiling, even as I felt my blood turn cold. I gave an excuse about being late for an appointment and rushed off.

At the checkout counter, I felt myself shaking. I had never heard Ivan speak before, since he was always with the talkative Olivia. I'd seen him reading a book in a Slavic language, but hadn't wondered exactly where he was from. But his accent was unmistakable.

Ivan was Czech, from Prague. The center of alchemy.

The missing connection to alchemy had been in front of me this whole time.

CHAPTER 28

Prague had been the center of alchemy in the late 1500s and early 1600s. Alchemists flocked to Rudolph II's Court, establishing it as a center of alchemical innovation. The king of Hungary and Bohemia invited over two hundred alchemists to Prague, and the impact has lasted to this day.

Rudolph was before my time, but I had visited Prague many times. I knew it well, and I could identify a Prague accent. Ivan had one.

Being from Prague itself wasn't enough to make me worried. Olivia had given me the missing piece of information about Ivan, without realizing she'd done so. When she was bemoaning the fact that her own nephew had given up academic pursuits, she had told me that Ivan was a professor of chemistry who had retired early due to fading health and frequented the teashop promoting good health.

Olivia didn't know what that convergence meant. But I did. Alchemy was a precursor to modern chemistry. Ivan was a chemist from the center of alchemy who was ill and wanted to cure himself.

I felt certain I was onto something, but I was missing some piece of the puzzle. I tried to think back on when I'd first visited Portland and found Blue Sky Teas. Had Ivan seen me then? Even if he had, so many things still didn't make sense. Finding Dorian's book could have been a crime of opportunity, but how would he know I was an alchemist in the first place?

Nearly dropping my bag of groceries, I sprinted to my truck and drove like a mad woman on the way home.

Thankfully, Brixton had gotten bored and left, allowing me to speak freely with Dorian. I didn't want Brixton to get any ideas about dealing with a murderer himself. With how much he cared for Blue, I didn't doubt for a minute that he would act rashly.

"*Mon dieu!*" Dorian exclaimed upon hearing my theory. "This makes perfect sense!"

"We need to learn more about him."

"Google?"

"Google."

An internet search told us that Ivan Danko had been a well-regarded chemistry professor in Prague before he retired early for medical reasons.

"Listen to this," I said. "One of the courses he taught was a history of alchemy as a predecessor to modern chemistry."

"This is uncommon, no?"

"Very uncommon. Alchemists who were also scientists have almost always had to hide the alchemical side of their research. Isaac Newton was incredibly secretive about the alchemical experiments he conducted."

"*The* Isaac Newton?" Dorian asked.

"Oh yes. Newton carried out more alchemical experiments than anything else. He wrote all about them, too, but most of those works were never published. Newton himself felt the world wasn't ready for the power of alchemy."

"*Mon dieu.*"

"I wonder," I said, "if, like Newton, Ivan became ill while doing his own alchemy experiments."

"I must question him," Dorian said.

"Um, no. That's not going to happen."

"I am not a pet! I am Dorian Robert-Houdin!" His wings flew open, crashing into the wall and taking a large swath of plaster with it. His mouth hung open, shocked at what he'd done. He was losing control of his body.

"I didn't mean—"

The doorbell sounded. Wonderful. I hadn't had time to install the lock on the inside of the basement door. At least the handyman was half deaf, so hopefully he hadn't heard a French voice shouting.

Dorian folded his wings as best he could, glowering at me the whole time. "I will be in the basement," he whispered. He puffed up his chest, grabbed three paperback novels from the coffee table, and limped down the stairs.

I greeted the handyman and got him to work patching the roof. As soon as I was certain he'd be occupied for a short time, I installed the new lock on the inside of the basement door so Dorian wouldn't have any unexpected visitors. Home handiwork wasn't one of my talents, but the installation wasn't bad. It wasn't pretty, but it was functional.

While the handyman worked, I had a chance to do more research on Ivan, but there wasn't much more to learn. He didn't have an online presence after leaving his university several years before.

Two hours later, the handyman had finished patching the worst hole in the roof and taping the worst leaky pipes. He said the roof should hold for now, but he'd need to pick up supplies for further patches, and that I really needed to hire a proper roofer and plumber. I gave him a bag of ginger cookies to take along with his payment, and scheduled another appointment with him later in the week. It was the only dessert Dorian had cooked that Brixton hadn't liked, and there was no way I was going to eat three dozen cookies.

I knocked on the basement door. My knock was met with no response.

"It's me," I called out.

A few moments later, the lock slid open and Dorian peered out at me.

"We need a special knock," he said, "to be sure it is you."

"Can't you just listen for my voice?"

"Interesting point. Yet a knock is more dramatic. That must explain why it is employed in fiction."

"You're enjoying the detective novels, then?"

"They are most entertaining—and also enlightening."

"Enlightening?" That couldn't be good.

"I have had an inspired idea," he said. "I will tell you about it as I prepare lunch."

I followed Dorian into the kitchen as he began cooking. He banished me to the far corner of the kitchen, where I jumped up to sit on the pristine counter. The cleaning crew who had cleaned the house before my arrival hadn't been able to clear away the years of grime as well as Dorian had. I watched as he created a *roux* out of olive oil, flour, and broth, transforming an oily, clumpy mixture that looked like clay into a creamy sauce that made my mouth water.

"These books from the library," Dorian said as he whisked, "it is interesting how they are all unique and stand the test of time, yet, at the same time, there is a common type of resolution."

I eased down from the counter and poked my head out the kitchen door to look over at the assortment of books strewn across the room on the coffee table. Agatha Christie, Ellery Queen, Dorothy Sayers, Arthur Conan Doyle, Margery Allingham.

"In this resolution," Dorian continued, "the hero of the story has put together facts in his mind—using his *little gray cells* as Poirot would say—to reveal that the killer is someone we already know, and one of the least likely suspects."

"Dorian—"

"This person," he said, "we now know to be Ivan."

"This isn't fiction."

"*Mon dieu.* Art imitates life. Life imitates art. This is why we must do what they do in the books. We must bring all the suspects together for a dinner party at which all will be revealed."

"I don't think so."

"But you *must* think so."

"Why is that?"

"Because it is already done."

My skin prickled. "What do you mean it's already done."

"While I was trapped in that dank room, I shared my plan with Brixton, via text message."

"Wait, how? You don't have a phone. You can't even use a phone screen with your fingers."

He pulled a Blackberry out of the apron pocket. "Brixton got this for me from his friend Ethan. I can punch the keys with my fingers."

"You told Brixton you thought Ivan was a murderer?"

"It is not nice to keep secrets from the people we are working with."

"He's fourteen!"

"I explained the plan to ensure he would not run off and do anything stupid before the dinner party. What are you doing?"

"I'm calling Brixton to tell him to forget whatever you told him."

"It is too late, Zoe."

"Why?"

"He has already emailed all the guests. The teashop regulars were overjoyed to be invited over to a home-cooked housewarming meal tonight from 'great chef Zoe.'"

CHAPTER 29

I spent the afternoon preparing the house for the dinner party. There's nothing like the combined fear of knowing a murderer might be coming over for dinner—along with your new neighbors. Surrounded by moving crates in my leaky house, I wasn't sure which was scarier.

The party was to take place that night, just hours after Brixton invited everyone. Didn't these people have lives? I supposed it was the same human curiosity that made people crane their necks to get a better look at a car accident. Whatever plans people had, they had cancelled them so they could be here. I wasn't surprised. They were curious about me, had heard about my cooking, and had the natural human pull toward the macabre. And here I was throwing a housewarming party with gourmet food at the haunted house where a murder had taken place.

In addition to our suspect, Ivan, Brixton and Dorian had invited five other teashop regulars: Brixton's teacher Sam, Sam's aunt Olivia, Olivia's friend Cora, Brixton's mom Heather, and because the instigators claimed they were being responsible, Detective Max Liu was the final member of the guest list.

The plan was for Dorian to cook the meal ahead of time and for Brixton to serve the meal, leaving me free to sit with the guests and help steer the conversation where I wanted it to go. I would also be on high alert for any hint of poison. Between my keen ability to detect the poison and our quest for justice and a cure for Dorian, I was confident in the plan. Somewhat confident. Okay, at least I knew it wouldn't be a disaster that ended with someone dead. I admit I was desperate.

Brixton enlisted the help of Veronica and Ethan to clear the worst of the weeds from the front yard, promising them a tasty snack plus cake to take home. Though the dinner party guests would be arriving after dark, I wanted to at least have the tall, wild grass pulled away from the path leading to the front door.

I had to run a couple of errands, so Brixton's job was to make sure the kids stayed in the yard and didn't come into the kitchen without warning. I'd rigged curtains in the kitchen so it was impossible to see in from the outside, including a curtain that blocked the herb garden's glass window box, but couldn't do anything about the swinging door leading from the living room to the kitchen.

After cooking, Dorian was going to turn to stone, playing the part of the antique stone gargoyle he originally was. I would have felt more comfortable with him hiding, because returning to life from stone was becoming increasingly difficult for him, but he insisted he wanted to be present to see what was happening.

By four o'clock Sunday afternoon, when the kids came in from the yard for a much-deserved snack, the house was beginning to look like I envisioned it would when I bought it. Between the weeded front yard and the few boxes I'd unpacked, I allowed myself a moment to appreciate the transformation. I'd been so focused on my frantic search for a cure for Dorian that I hadn't had many moments to step back and enjoy what was in front of me.

"Wow," Brixton said, rubbing the soles of his sneakers on the welcome mat.

"Is this stuff from Paris?" Veronica asked.

"Some of it is. I lived there for a few years."

She ran past me to the mantle, where I'd set up a display of antique alchemical items I found deep in my storage crates: two hermetic vases, a spirit holder, matrix vase, and in the center, a philosopher's egg. Honestly, I sometimes think the secret language alchemists created had as much to do with trying to outdo each other with clever names than with conveying information. The pelican made sense, because the glass vessel resembled the bird's beak. A snake was self-explanatory too. But a matrix vase? I was pretty sure that the motivation behind names had at least as much to do with guy trying to be cool as it did a spiritual connection to laboratory supplies.

I stood back and looked at the display. Rooting through the crates, I selected two brass apothecary boxes that would go nicely.

The curated display was my contribution to the plan. Dorian had initially suggested that once I gathered everyone together, I should lock all the doors and declare that I knew who the killer was, somehow forcing Ivan to confess. I countered with the idea that we let things unfold more naturally by placing alchemical objects on display in the living room to provoke a reaction from Ivan. Much more sensible than kidnapping people and making unsubstantiated accusations. I hoped it would work.

The boys made a beeline for a different section of the room. They headed straight for the dining table. Two large loaves of homemade bread, one a nut loaf and one a simple Parisian-style baguette, dominated the center of the table on a wooden cutting board from Marseille. A Spanish platter of nut cheeses sat to one side of the bread, its twin platter loaded with a pile of savory scones. Poking out from the baby lettuce leaves in a wooden salad bowl from Lisbon were tangerine wedges, thinly sliced roasted beets, and toasted almonds. I smiled to myself, watching the boys eat. I was glad I'd been able to unpack the special serving items I'd had in storage for too long.

Veronica ran her fingers along the carvings on the mantel before joining us at the table. I was glad Dorian was hiding for the time being; otherwise I had no doubt Veronica would have run up to a Dorian statue and patted it on the head. Dorian didn't care about eavesdropping on the kids, so he was brushing up on his Poirot deductive skills in the basement before the kids departed and he could finish preparing the evening meal.

"Thank you, Ms. Faust," Veronica said as she sat down.

The boys grunted in between bites of food.

"I can't thank you enough for helping with the yard," I said, pouring them ice water with fresh mint leaves.

"No problem, Zoe," Ethan said. "I should be thanking you. Now Brixton owes *me* a favor."

Veronica kicked him under the table. "Can't you do anything out of the goodness of your heart?"

"That hurt! I totally came, didn't I?"

"Remember," Brixton said, "she's paying you in cake too."

Veronica and Ethan stopped glaring at each other, and they departed half an hour later with chocolate cake. Dorian would have been horrified at the brevity of the meal, but he had to finish cooking.

"Sorry, man," Ethan said to Brixton in a low voice as he left.

"What was that about?" I asked, closing the door behind Veronica and Ethan.

"He thinks I'm staying longer to help out so you won't press charges for that day I met you last week."

Had it only been a week? Before coming here, months could go by without much happening. I would tend to my small herb garden and go on long walks wherever I had parked my trailer. I'd stay for a short duration of time, ranging from a week to a year, careful to never put down roots. Occasionally I became immersed in something I didn't plan on, but this had been the longest week I'd experienced in decades.

"I couldn't tell him the truth," Brixton continued, "that I'm helping you catch the guy who framed Blue and is keeping Dorian from getting better."

"*You* aren't catching anyone. Remember what we talked about. Anything bad starts to happen and you run out the door and call for backup."

"I'll go get Dorian," Brixton grumbled, knocking on the basement door. "Hey, why isn't he answering. Do you think he's okay?"

"He doesn't respond to knocks on the door unless it's a coded knock you worked out in advance."

"Oh. So how are we supposed to get him?"

"Just call his name. He'll recognize your voice."

Brixton's summoning worked, and the gargoyle and his assistant spent the afternoon preparing dinner.

The guests began to arrive at five minutes after seven. At the sound of the doorbell, I nodded at Dorian.

He limped to the side of the fireplace and gave me a curt nod. He pulled back his shoulders, stretched his wings, and squatted into a pose resembling a watchful stance on a perch. Dark, cracked lines covered his soft gray skin. Dorian was once again stone. I shivered and pulled the door open.

CHAPTER 30

Heather held a bunch of long-stemmed snowdrops. The winter-blooming white flowers were held together with twine.

"Thanks for the invitation." She grinned and handed me the flowers. "And for looking after Brixton while I was painting." She had shoes on her feet tonight, but in spite of the cold she wore only a light shawl over her white cotton dress.

"He's a great kid."

"I think helping you around the house is really good for Brix. There's my baby!" She squealed and enveloped Brixton in a big hug.

"Hey, watch it!" Brixton extricated himself from his mom's hug and straightened his collar. "I should have stayed in the kitchen."

"Look at you. A tuxedo! We can't afford—"

"It's just a rental," I said, "and I'm taking care of it."

Dorian was enthusiastic about the idea of hosting a proper English manor house dinner party. That meant Brixton's role was that of the butler-slash-server, which of course required a tuxedo.

Finding one at the last minute had been one of my errands that afternoon. I hadn't expected Brixton to go for it, but he'd taken to the idea. So much so that he took a picture of himself in the tux and texted it to his friends.

"Such a handsome young man," Heather said, taking over for Brixton's clumsy attempts to straighten the collar.

"*Mom.*"

The doorbell rang a second time. Rather than opening the door, my butler retreated into the kitchen. I wasn't sure what Brixton thought a butler was supposed to do, but clearly opening doors wasn't one of his presumed duties. I opened the door and found Max standing on the porch. He smiled and handed me a mason jar filled with tea leaves. His face was unreadable, but he looked sexy as hell in black slacks, black and white wingtip shoes, a slim gray dress shirt, and black leather jacket.

Olivia, Sam, and Ivan arrived before I closed the door. Sam held a bottle of red wine and Ivan raised a bottle of Becherovka, a Czech liquor I was quite fond of that tasted of cinnamon and ginger. Sam had the same sad smile I remembered from the first time I'd seen him, and I wondered if his aunt had bullied him into attending when he'd had other plans.

"Cora sends her regrets," Sam said.

Olivia clicked her tongue. "That woman has been in mourning for her daughter for too long."

"People grieve differently," Max said.

Brixton saved us from an awkward conversation by backing out of the kitchen. He held a silver platter with seven crystal glasses of sherry. I hated the stuff, but Dorian insisted that it made the dinner party more authentic.

"Aperitif?" Brixton said.

Heather squealed, then whispered to me, "You're such a good influence on him, Zoe. I can never get him to study for vocab tests."

I wasn't entirely sure "good influence" was the best way to describe our relationship over the course of the past week. Especially since he was currently carrying a tray of alcohol.

"Brixton, my man," Sam said, "you clean up nicely. Looking quite dapper tonight."

"Thank you, Mr. Strum," he said, doing his best impression of a British accent and not failing too terribly.

Everyone laughed. Brixton joined along. He'd done a better job at breaking the ice than anything I could have planned.

"Where is this French boyfriend of yours?" Sam asked. "I expected he'd be here. Veronica told me after class that he's, quote, 'dreamy.'" He laughed. "I have no idea what counts as 'dreamy' these days, so I wanted to see for myself."

"He's only a friend," I said, feeling all eyes on me, "and he's not big on parties. Anyone need another drink?"

"I just handed out the first ones," Brixton said, squinting at me like I'd lost my mind.

"Right." Right. Why had I made up that stupid lie?

"Interesting gargoyle statue," Max said.

I would have been thankful for the change of subject except that I wondered if he recognized Dorian from the other night. ·

"He's a replica of one of the gargoyles of Notre Dame in Paris," I said. "In case you were wondering why you recognized him."

"Isn't it heavy?" Heather asked. "I thought I caught a glimpse of him in your kitchen before."

"I haven't yet found the right place for him."

"I know what you mean," Heather said. "I'm always moving my artwork around until I find the perfect spot where the light hits a painting just right. At least canvas isn't as heavy as stone."

"He's a handful," I said, "but I can handle him."

From there, I talked of Paris, which kept the group interested for some time. I had to stay on my toes not only because I was watching Ivan, but because most of my memories of Paris were from before everyone in the room was born. I'd occasionally slipped up over the years, but since people never believed I could have been alive centuries ago, they assumed I was "eccentric" when I covered up my mistakes by explaining I was an avid reader who got lost in the stories.

Once we finished our drinks, only Heather wanted a second glass of sherry. The rest of the group opted for wine or seltzer water.

I purposefully didn't bring up the alchemy display as we mingled before dinner. I wanted to gauge Ivan's natural reaction. Instead I tried to keep conversation light—until Olivia brought up the death of Charles Macraith.

"We should raise a glass to our departed comrade," she said.

We clinked glasses awkwardly, before an even more awkward hush fell over the group.

"Has anyone heard how Blue is doing?" Sam asked. "I can't believe it. Max, do you know more—"

"I'm not on the case. Besides, we're here to welcome our new neighbor. Let's not worry about all that tonight."

"Are you all ready for the first course?" Brixton asked.

Ivan laughed. "You have gone from an English to a Russian accent."

"Crap, I was thinking of the wrong movie character."

"Language," Sam snapped, then grimaced. "Sorry, a teacher's force of habit."

"Remember to carry the bowls one by one, Brixton," I said.

He rolled his eyes before disappearing into the kitchen. He came back carrying two bowls of pumpkin bisque, one in each hand. A splash of soup fell to the floor as he served Olivia and his mom. When he returned for the next round, he carried a single bowl.

By the time we moved on to the main course—ratatouille, which Dorian had selected because it was a dish that tasted even better when prepared in advance since it allowed time for the flavors to transform each other—Ivan still hadn't commented on the alchemical display in the living room. I'd even given him the seat with the most direct view of the items. Perhaps he wasn't feeling well. I noticed his hand shaking as he picked up his fork.

"Where did you learn to cook, Zoe?" Sam asked.

"For someone so young, this is quite impressive." Olivia smiled at her backhanded compliment.

"I've learned from people all over the place."

"She traveled all around the country in her trailer," Brixton said from his position standing next to the kitchen. He shuffled his feet back and forth. Being a proper butler must have been more difficult than he'd imagined.

"Really?" Olivia said. "Were you a college dropout?" Sam elbowed his aunt.

"I've always been someone who learns more from experience," I said. "I've traveled to most of the states in my trailer over the last few years. I'm a bit of a history buff. That's why I got into collecting all the antiques I've got in the living room."

"I recognize the brass medicine container," Max said. "That's got to be centuries old."

I smiled. "That's one of my favorites."

"Quite an expensive hobby," Olivia said.

"I sell them," I said. "Most of them, at least. Never my favorites." I caught Max's eye and my heart fluttered a little. I cleared my throat. "I've got a business selling these things. That's how I make a living. I find old things like alchemy laboratory supplies that some people find interesting." I looked at Ivan as I spoke.

"That's what brings you to Portland?" Sam asked.

"My online store is called Elixir. I can run it from anywhere, but when I got here, I—"

"Fell in love?" Olivia finished for me. It was an innocent enough statement, but her eyes darted between me and Max as she said it.

"So," Max said, clearing his throat. "The house is looking good."

"There's still a lot to be done."

"If I didn't already have two jobs," Sam said, "I'd offer to help."

I hadn't counted on them all being so polite. Even Olivia's normally snarky tongue wasn't especially bitter that night.

"Dessert?" Brixton asked, clearing the ratatouille plates.

While plates were cleared and the chocolate soufflé brought out, I excused myself. Maybe I wasn't evoking the right response from Ivan because I hadn't put the right kind of items on display.

It took me a few minutes to find the books I was looking for, two old alchemy texts that I'd unearthed from deep in my crates. By the time I came down the stairs, the group was finishing dessert.

"What do you say, Max," Ivan was saying. "Shall we break out the Becherovka?"

"Sounds good to me."

"Ivan," I said, returning to the table with the books. "I thought you might be interested in these books."

"The soufflé was delicious," Heather said. "But I thought you were a vegan."

"This is a vegan soufflé," I answered curtly. My focus remained on Ivan, watching to see his reaction to the books. The problem was, he didn't seem to have any reaction at all.

Heather and Olivia took their wine glasses to the living room while I cleared space on the table to set the two books.

"You're not supposed to leave the table," Brixton said, his eyebrows pressed together.

His mom gave him a questioning look.

"It's okay," I said. The sentiment was Dorian's doing, no doubt. To be a proper English manor house mystery, all the suspects had to remain sitting around the table, or sitting in a circle in the drawing room, or some such artificial circle.

"Ah!" Ivan said, as soon as he'd opened the first book to its title page. "I did not realize what this was. My eyesight is not as good as it once was."

"I thought I saw you looking interested when I mentioned alchemy," I lied. "Have you studied the subject?"

"My field of study is chemistry, but you must know from your love of history that alchemy was a precursor to chemistry." His eyes lit up as he spoke.

Max shifted uncomfortably, then got up to open and pour the Becherovka. *What was going on?*

I nodded. "I've always thought these old books are so much more beautiful than the laboratory items on the mantle."

Olivia scoffed from the couch, then resumed a conversation with Heather.

"Those are alchemical vessels on your mantle?" Ivan asked.

"I believe so," I said, trying not to show my confusion at Ivan's reply. Surely he knew what they were. But unless he was an extremely good actor, his surprise was genuine.

"I have only seen woodcuts and museum re-creations. Your pieces are much smaller than I imagined alchemical vessels would be."

"These are alchemy books?" Sam asked.

I nodded.

"Max!" Ivan called. "You would be interested in this."

Max returned to the table with the open bottle of Becherovka.

"You're interested in alchemy, Max?" I asked. I knew this party had been a bad idea. Nothing was turning out like I wanted.

"There's a similarity in the tools of alchemists and apothecaries," Max said, loosening his collar.

"Such a fascinating subject," Ivan said, resting the book on the table and flipping through the pages. "I never realized it until I began research for a chemistry book. Ah! This book, now I remember why it is familiar. I have seen a copy only once before, in the Klementinum in Prague. If I recall, it provided historical context for the work of John Dee. It is not widely available. Wherever did you find it?"

"I spend a lot of time at estate sales and flea markets," I said, mulling over Ivan's answer. He wasn't expressing interest in the aspects of alchemy that I would have expected for my theory. He seemed genuinely interested in the historical figures of alchemy, not the practical aspects of the alchemy. And why was Max so nervous? I had to do *something* to find out what was going on.

"Shortly after I began my research for my book on the history of chemistry," Ivan said, "the focus changed. I discovered connections to alchemy I hadn't realized existed."

I grabbed my cell phone and pulled up one of the photographs I'd taken of *Not Untrue Alchemy.* "Have you ever seen this?"

He studied the screen for a few moments. His face contorted, moving from interest to confusion to awe. His voice changed too. "Where did you find this?" The soft-spoken man was gone, a fiery zealot in his place. I wasn't the only one who noticed the change.

"I knew it!" Brixton shouted.

Everyone stared at the fourteen-year-old butler.

"It was you," Brixton said, pointing at Ivan. Tomato sauce covered the cuff of the sleeve. Everyone turned to stare at him.

"Brixton," I said, glaring at him and attempting to stop myself from throttling him, "this isn't what we—"

I caught a glimpse of Max out of the corner of my eye. He looked every bit as angry as I felt.

"You're the one," Brixton said, "who hurt Blue and took Do—I mean, took Zoe's books!"

"What?" Ivan sputtered, looking from Brixton to Max. "I don't understand. You think *I* had something to do with Blue's accident and what happened here?"

"Brixton," Max said sharply. "You need to stop."

"Nobody else had reason to steal Zoe's books," Brixton said.

Ivan turned to me. "You have more alchemy books, and they were stolen?"

"Including a very rare book that I'm betting isn't in the Klementinum or any other library—it's the book that includes this page you're so interested in."

Max ran his hands through his hair and took a large swig of his drink.

"If the page on your phone is like the rest of the book," Ivan said, "this is a phenomenal book. Max, have you any leads to get it back?"

"I'm not on the case, remember?" Max's jaw was set so tightly that it affected his speech.

"Max," I said. "What's going on? What aren't you telling us?"

"You really think I had something to do with these tragedies?" Ivan asked. He gripped the edge of the table. Sweat coated on his forehead.

"Well this *is* interesting," Olivia said. "Pray, do tell, Max. What *are* you keeping from us?"

"Are you all right, Ivan?" I asked.

"The excitement…" He wheezed as he spoke.

"Maybe you'd better—" I began, but it was too late. Ivan slumped over, dead to the world. I only hoped he wasn't truly dead.

CHAPTER 31

The tincture I'd given to Blue was in the pocket of my raincoat, hanging on the back of the door. Was it possible there might be a few drops left?

"Call 9-1-1!" Max shouted as he loosened Ivan's collar.

Before anyone had time do so, I pressed the liquid to Ivan's lips. At that moment I didn't care about what my guests might think. I had to try and save Ivan. I knelt down next to him, feeling relief as I felt him breathing. Confusion quickly followed. I hadn't detected any poison. How could I have missed something?

Ivan awoke with a gasp, causing Max to stumble backward.

"What the hell?" Max said. "Ivan, are you all right?"

Ivan groaned. "Did I faint? Please, everyone, put your phones away. This is nothing to worry about."

My attention had been focused on Ivan, but now I noticed that everyone except for Max, who'd been attending to Ivan, had their phones out to call the paramedics. They stood staring for a few moments; then everyone began to speak at once.

"We should still call—" Max said.

"It had to be that liquor—" Olivia whispered to Sam.

"Brix, honey, go see if he needs help," Heather said.

"You want help standing up?" Sam asked.

"Enough!" I said. "Party's over. Ivan says he's all right. It's his decision if he goes to a hospital. Ivan?"

"Thank you, Zoe. I'll be fine. This happens to me sometimes."

"Rest here for a bit, Ivan," I said as I picked up my guests' jackets. "Thank you all for coming."

"You can't kick us out," Brixton said. "I haven't even served tea and coffee yet!"

"Come on, folks," Max said. "Zoe's right. Let's give Ivan some space."

Olivia pursed her lips. While throwing her shawl over her shoulder, the tassels hit Max in the face. I didn't think it was an accident.

I felt safe with Max, no matter how suspicious he was acting. My instincts had served me well over the years, but I hadn't encountered many murders either. I put my hand on Max's elbow, holding him back before I showed Sam, Olivia, Heather, and Brixton to the door. Brixton didn't want to leave. His mom seemed disinclined to force him, so I insisted. I didn't want him there for what was going to follow either.

"What the hell did you give him?" Max asked as soon as I closed the door. "I can't just pretend I didn't see that."

"You think I gave him an illegal drug?" That was too much.

"Ivan," Max said, "how do you feel?"

"It's a simple herbal remedy," I snapped.

"Then why did it work so quickly? That's not how things work."

"If you hadn't noticed, I'm good at working with herbs."

"Then you won't mind if I see what you gave him."

"This is ridiculous!" I said.

"Leave it be," Ivan said. "My recovering quickly has nothing to do with anything Zoe gave me. This happens to me sometimes. I'm fine. I want to know what you were all talking about before I fainted."

Max shook his head and looked up at the cracked ceiling. "You, my friend, have been a person of interest in this investigation. Personal feelings aside, I had no choice but to look into your movements while I was the investigating officer."

"Me?" Ivan said. "Even if you think this of me, how could I? These past weeks, my health has been worse, as you can see evidence of tonight. That's why I haven't been at Blue Sky Teas as much as usual. I can barely hold a cup of tea these days. My doctor will confirm this."

"Why didn't you say anything when I saw you?" Max asked.

"I didn't know it was an interrogation! It's embarrassing, Max. I'm only in my fifties, but my body has other ideas. It thinks I'm an old man."

"I put a call in to your doctor," Max said. "He was out of town and we couldn't reach him to—" He broke off with a start.

"What are you staring at?" I asked. "Find something else you think is illegal and you want to report?"

He rubbed his eyes. "I could have sworn I saw the gargoyle statue move. That Becherovka must be some strong stuff."

"Why don't you two come into the kitchen." I gave a sharp glance at Dorian as I held open the swinging door for Max and Ivan. "I'll put the kettle on and make us all some tea."

"Zoe," Max said softly as he stepped through the doorway, "I'm sorry I reacted automatically when I saw you give something to Ivan. I'm trained to notice these things."

He was so close to me that I smelled the subtle scents surrounding him. He must have gardened in his yard earlier that day. His large brown eyes were downcast. I believed he was truly sorry, but that didn't mean I trusted him. Or that I trusted myself around him.

"How about I make the tea you brought, Max." I busied myself filling the kettle.

"Ah," Ivan said, "that'll make me good as new. In the meantime, Max can continue explaining why he thought I was involved in this madness."

"I was afraid," Max said, "when Zoe told me that one of the valuable books of hers that was stolen was an alchemy book, that you might have been involved."

"That's why you've been acting so odd this whole time?" I asked.

"I hated that I had to investigate a friend, but it goes with the job." He paused, looking at the espresso maker Dorian had purchased. "I thought you said you didn't drink coffee."

"It's for entertaining."

He nodded, but his eyes lingered on the open bag of coffee beans and the folded copy of *Le Monde* underneath it. He was a detective. It was natural he'd be observant. He could tell someone had made coffee recently and that someone who wanted to read a French newspaper was comfortable around my house. My lie about a French "friend" to cover up for Brixton was building on itself. Max now suspected my "friend" stayed over. My attempt at a simple life was nowhere in sight.

Max remained curt for the rest of our short conversation, clearing up that neither Ivan nor Max had any reason to want Dorian's stolen alchemy book. By the time I saw the two of them to the door, I wondered why I thought I could ever have a normal life.

It took longer than I would have liked to awaken Dorian from his stone pose. I had to shake his shoulders so vigorously that I was afraid I might break off a chunk of stone. Finally, he stirred.

"Mon dieu. I cannot believe we were wrong about the Czech professor! It was a perfect theory. Perfect!" He tried to flap his wings. It took a few seconds for his wings to respond to the flexing of his shoulders.

"Not exactly perfect," I said. "We were desperate, which blinded our better sense. We convinced ourselves about a far-fetched theory because we desperately wanted to find your book."

Dorian wriggled his toes and fingers. He continued to have difficulty moving his left foot, but the reversal of his life force hadn't yet progressed further. He looked from his claws to me. "Where does that leave us?"

"I don't know, Dorian. I wish I knew."

"I will clean up," he said, not meeting my eyes.

"You don't have to—"

"I am stiff from standing still. Washing dishes will be good for me. You will work on the book pages?"

Though I had come to the conclusion that I would need the full book to unlock *Not Untrue Alchemy's* secrets, what the gargoyle needed was hope. Even if there wasn't anything else I could do, at least I could give him hope.

"I'll study the pages," I said. "Maybe if I read them right before bed, my subconscious can work something out that has eluded me so far."

I brought the printed pages with me to bed, along with a glass of water with lemon. I couldn't concentrate, but it wasn't because of my fatigue. Knowing Ivan was most likely not a killer or thief, I now wondered if I could ask him for his help. Though I'd studied alchemy for a longer period of time than Ivan, my focus was less academic and more specialized. His interest in alchemy was the exact opposite. I had no doubt I was better at turning plants into tinctures, salves, and balms than Ivan, but there was a good chance he was better at understanding alchemical texts.

Once I'd made the decision to contact Ivan the next day, I fell into a restless sleep. I dreamt of alchemists in Prague.

A man with a long, pointed white beard appeared before me in the dream. I recognized him as the great scholar John Dee. The man had lived before me but was a legend to alchemists. We stood on the Charles Bridge in Prague, which in my dream was crowded with merchants from an earlier century in place of the hoards of tourists of today.

Dee beckoned to me. I followed him across the stone bridge. The fog became thick, swarming around us. I called out, but no sound came from my throat. I tried to run, but although my feet moved, I made no progress crossing the bridge. The fog overtook me. I could no longer see Dee or anything else. Fog had never frightened me, but in my dream, I had the strongest sense that I should be very afraid. Something dangerous lurked in the fog.

Almost as suddenly as the fog had swallowed me, the cloud lifted. But instead of scholar John Dee, charlatan Edward Kelley stood before me, balancing on the edge of the bridge. Kelley held a vial of mercury in one hand and wore a smirk on his face. As he steadied himself, the liquid metal bounced from side to side in its glass prison. Kelley caught my eye and winked. The man had fooled many people, including John Dee.

In his hubris at taking his eyes off the ledge, Kelley lost his balance. His shout pierced my ears, as if echoing against invisible walls that held me in place. He splashed into the water below.

My feet were my own again. I ran to the edge of the bridge and looked into the black water below. Instead of Kelley below me, the figure drowning in the water was Isaac Newton. He held the figurine of a dragon in his hand. His head sank beneath the water, yet he held the dragon tightly in his hand, keeping it above the dark waters.

As I reached out to him, I lost my footing. I would have fallen in myself had it not been for a hand steadying my shoulder. Without turning, I knew his touch. It was Ambrose.

As I turned to face him, Ambrose swallowed the substance of a glass vial. It was the vial of mercury Kelley had held in his hands. I tried to stop him, but he was now far away from me. His face contorted, as if feeling the effects of the mercury, then suddenly relaxed. He hadn't been poisoned after all. He smiled. It was the loving smile I remembered. I reached out to him, but a thick fog swooped in between us. There was nothing I could do to reach him. I reached for my locket, but it wasn't around my neck as it always was. Panic rose within me. The fog that carried Ambrose away was coming for me.

My arms fought to escape the confinement—until I realized they were fighting against tangled sheets, not ropes of fog.

I was awake.

I felt for my locket, damp with the sweat that covered my body. My heart was racing, but I breathed a sigh of relief. I didn't usually dream so vividly, yet I had done so multiple times that week. Perhaps I hadn't been ready to return to alchemy after all.

I took a sip of water from the glass on my bedside table, thinking over the dream.

Prague achieved a pinnacle of alchemical enlightenment a century before I was born. I had visited the city many times, but not while its most famous residents had lived there. My hazy dream world had melded memories of my own with legends I had heard of in its alchemical heyday.

The city of Prague holds an important alchemical legacy because it straddled the old ways of "magic" and new scientific methods. At the cusp of the Scientific Revolution, Rudolph II—a.k.a the Holy Roman Emperor, the King of Bohemia, and more—became a controversial leader because of his fascination with alchemy. Rudolph II's Court in the late 1500s to early 1600s hosted hundreds of alchemists, including John Dee—but not Edward Kelley. In an ironic twist of fate, Rudolph imprisoned Kelley not for being the charlatan that he was, but for failing to share his secrets for creating gold. The king never doubted Kelley's gold transformations were real.

Rulers like Rudolph wanted to control alchemists because they believed the alchemists could truly turn lead into gold, which would wreak havoc on currency values—unless the rulers controlled the gold themselves. It came to be commonplace for rulers to grant licenses to alchemists to practice. They couldn't have "just anyone" turning lead into gold.

Alchemists also needed patrons to have the resources they needed to pursue their intellectual curiosity. It wasn't gold or immortality that most alchemists were interested in—it was science. They were trying to understand the world around them, and they did make many breakthroughs that led to modern chemistry. Only long after his death was Isaac Newton publicly revealed to be an alchemist. He practiced alchemy in secret, and for years after his death the scientific community hushed up the secret that he had practiced alchemy, fearing of the impact of his scientific discoveries would be lessened. Newton's favorite substance was antimony: the Black Dragon. That's what he'd been holding in his hand in my dream.

I pushed the damp sheets aside and found the photographed pages of Dorian's book. I picked up a page that had an image of the Black Dragon, which symbolizes death and decay. Death and decay were a natural part of alchemy and of life in general, so I wasn't disturbed by the existence of such an image. What I had found fascinating and disturbing about the image was the rendering of the flames coming out of the dragon's mouth, which is why I had photographed it. I hadn't, however, photographed the opposite page, which would have held an explanation of the woodcut.

I shoved the troubling image into the drawer of the bedside table and finished the glass of water. Shedding so much sweat during my dream had left me parched.

The dream had pulled me in opposing directions: past and present, scholar and charlatan, mercury and antimony, poison and healing.

I don't believe dreams are magic any more than I believe alchemy is magic. But I do believe my subconscious was trying to tell me two things.

First, the mercury and other elements used by alchemists was for a purpose, unlike the poisonous mixture that had been used on Charles and Blue. *It wasn't gold or immortality that most alchemists were interested in—it was science.* The experiments of alchemists were dangerous *but pure.* The poison I was dealing with here in Portland was impure.

Second, this dream was fundamentally different from the "dream" I'd had after being poisoned. It was a hallucinogenic effect I'd experienced that day.

I had it wrong. We weren't looking for an alchemist who had stolen Dorian's book. We were looking for a poisoner who had killed Charles Macraith.

CHAPTER 32

In the morning, I found five text messages from Brixton on my phone. I felt bad that I hadn't thought to check the previous night. I texted him back that everything was fine, but we didn't know who had framed Blue. I asked him for Ivan's email address. It was a school day, so hopefully he'd be awake and heading to school. His last text message had come in at two o'clock in the morning, so I wasn't sure.

Two minutes later, Brixton texted me Ivan's email address— along with a passive-aggressive text thanking me for keeping him in the loop the previous night.

After a quick oatmeal breakfast to warm up, I met Ivan in Washington Park. He received my email on his phone and told me where he was, inviting me to join him. He said I could find him at the park's International Rose Test Garden. I wasn't sure why he would be at a rose garden in the dead of winter. Unlike the lush cemetery grounds I'd walked through earlier that week, the barren landscape of a winter rose garden gave me a cold, foreboding feeling. Dark clouds hung low in the sky, but the rain held off for the moment.

Ivan stood next to the brittle branches of a row of roses, their thorns more prominent for the absence of leaves and flowers. Though he wore a fedora, thick scarf, and a coat with the collar turned up, he was easy to spot. He was the only person there.

"You wonder why I come here in winter?" he asked.

"You appreciate the solitude?"

"It reminds me," he said, "that death is natural. My body is failing me, but I do not wish to feel sorry for myself. Sometimes," he paused and ran his fingers over the gnarled remnants of a rose bush, "I need a reminder."

"Would you like to talk somewhere inside, where it's warmer?" The chill in the air penetrated my coat. I could take it, but it didn't seem to be a good place for someone with failing health.

"The air is good for me." Ivan rubbed his hands together and shook out his shoulders. "Shall we walk?"

We walked side by side through the desolate rows of branches that had once been beautiful roses. I hadn't yet figured out what I should say to Ivan. I had to strike the right balance between getting the help I needed from Ivan and not revealing why I needed it, or why there was such urgency.

"I've been thinking about the woodcut illustrations you showed me," Ivan said as we entered the Shakespeare Garden. "They are unlike anything I have come across in my research."

"It's an interesting puzzle, isn't it? I was hoping you could help me figure out what the book is about."

"I miss an academic challenge, but would it not make the most sense to wait until the police have recovered the book itself?"

"I'm anxious to get started," I said. "It's the one mystery around me that I feel like I have some control over."

"This," Ivan said, "I can understand. Helplessness can lead to despair. Did you bring the images?"

I removed the printouts from my inner jacket pocket. Ivan took them from me. He stopped walking and examined them in silence. I couldn't tell if the frustration evident on his face was because of the tremor in his hands or what he saw in the images.

"What do you know of the history of the book?" he asked.

"I only found it recently, so when it was stolen I hadn't yet discovered its origins."

"And you found it—"

"In Saint-Gervais," I said, sticking to the truth as much as possible. That was the French town where Jean Eugène Robert-Houdin had been living when he brought Dorian to life. "I wouldn't be able to find the seller again. I didn't realize at the time what a find it was."

"That is unfortunate. Also unfortunate that someone stole it by accident, not realizing what they had."

I nodded but didn't speak for a few moments. Had it really been an accident? A crime of opportunity, that happened to result in the most precious item in my new house being stolen? That was too big a coincidence, wasn't it? Whoever took it had to know of its worth. The question was whether the thief took it for its monetary value— or if they wanted it to bring creatures like Dorian to life.

"*Non Degenera Alchemia.*" I pointed at the photograph of the title page. "Strangely convoluted, don't you think? Even for an alchemist."

Ivan laughed. "*Not Ignoble Alchemy.* Yes, very unnecessary. But alchemists have never been known for their simplicity. There are *hundreds* of words used to describe prima materia. Hundreds! The sun, the moon, water of gold, shadow of the sun, the garden, lord of the stones—the list goes on and on. No, it's not the obfuscation that I find fascinating about this book. What's most interesting here is that the book does not list an author."

The absence of an author wasn't common, but wasn't itself enough to signal that something was especially strange about the book. But along with the bizarre illustrations, I wondered why the author hadn't at least used a pseudonym.

However, that wasn't the most interesting thing Ivan had said. He translated the book's title as *Not Ignoble Alchemy,* whereas I'd translated *degenera* into *untrue.* That was an approximation, as any translation is. And my ecclesiastical Latin wasn't the best. *Degenera* could also mean something closer to degenerate or ignoble. But even if I'd done a sloppy translation of the title, that didn't help.

"I wish it was real," Ivan said. He spoke so softly that the wind nearly carried away his words before I heard them.

"I examined the book. I've been working with antiques for long enough that I know it's real. Hundreds of years old." Based on the style of Latin, and my observations of the book itself, it wasn't created before the Middle Ages, but dating the book could help me uncover its secrets—if I got it back.

"You misunderstand me." He pulled his scarf more tightly around him as the wind picked up, careful not to lose hold of the photographs in his hand. "I meant that I wished the theories expressed by the alchemists of history were true accounts of what could be accomplished with alchemy. That they could stop death."

Unlike the rose bushes that surrounded us, Ivan wouldn't return to life with the spring. "Even if it were true," I said, feeling my locket through the fabric of my sweater, "would you really want to live forever? It sounds lonely. So very lonely."

"That's not a sentiment I'd expect from someone your age. But you're right. Forever? No, I don't wish that. Right now, I would settle for living to my sixtieth birthday. Blue's teas have been part of the changes I've made to spend my last years as happily as possible. A few more years of good health is all I ask. That would be enough time for me to complete the book I've been working on."

"Related to alchemy?"

"About the intersecting history of alchemy and chemistry that scholars have missed. Isaac Newton is the focus of many books on the subject, and so are other famous alchemists, but many others have been forgotten. I suppose you could say I'm writing about the unsung heroes of science. Max and I have talked about it at length at Blue Sky Teas."

"That's why he was worried you might have done something drastic to get your hands on my alchemy books."

"He's seen me on some of my bad days, desperate to complete the book but thinking I would not have time… Come, let's continue our walk and mull over the meaning of these strange illustrations. You didn't come here to hear the problems of an old man."

"Maybe," I said, "but I don't see any old men around here."

"Ha! I knew I liked you from the moment I saw how you held your own with Olivia. She's not as bad as she seems at first—" He broke off. "Aha! I know what it is that was bothering me about these illustrations. I wonder if the person who carved these woodcuts did not realize the final image would be flipped once printed."

"You think they're accidentally backwards?" What had that made me think of? I took the stack of photographs from his hand and flipped through them. "That's not the only reason these illustrations are creepy."

"No," Ivan agreed, "but that is the thing that stands out. One cannot tackle all research problems simultaneously. You start with the ones that are easiest to identify, and then peel back the layers—"

"Ivan! I don't think this was an accident."

"They are clearly backward—"

"Because it's *backward* alchemy." The fear I had been keeping at bay returned head-on. I looked up at the dark sky that was threatening to burst. "The title, as you translated it, is *Not Ignoble Alchemy.* I had translated it as *Not Untrue Alchemy.* Those two things aren't different on their face, but there's a subtle difference. Something ignoble exists, but dishonorably. I think we're looking at alchemy's 'death rotation'—that's why it's not only the counter-clockwise motions that make the images look off. The distorted animals in these illustrations are *dead*."

"To symbolize the death rotation of backward alchemy. Very clever."

"But working backwards isn't possible," I said.

"I've read about some alchemists who tried it because it was quicker, but none of them claimed to have been successful, unlike the many alchemists who claimed to have succeeded at proper alchemy. Perhaps that explains the absence of an author identifying himself."

I couldn't tell Ivan what I had meant by my words. It was, of course, physically possible to follow the steps of alchemy backwards. But it wasn't right. It wouldn't lead to transformation and creation. Only death.

Earth, air, fire, and water. Calcination, dissolution, separation, conjunction, fermentation, distillation, coagulation. They all have a phase in alchemy, but the death rotation turns the process on its head. No good could come of it. Everything it created would eventually be undone.

"Sacrificing one element for another to complete a transformation," I said, feeling numb from the realization more than the cold. "Rather than striving for perfection, those alchemists were circumventing it. That would explain why any such transformations would deteriorate over time..." The full impact of what this would mean for Dorian was sinking in. If I was right, I could work with the book—but to do so, I needed that book.

"This *is* an interesting puzzle you've brought me," Ivan said. "It is delightful to speak with someone who feels so passionately about a theoretical exercise. I hope the book is returned to you soon so we can uncover more of its secrets. Do you realize the implications this book could have, if we're right?"

I realized, then, that this was much bigger than Dorian and myself. Not in the way Ivan thought. This wasn't about a theoretical history. There were real alchemists out there who had performed alchemy's death rotation. I had proof. It wasn't only Dorian this was affecting. Gold itself was crumbling.

I hadn't connected Dorian's deterioration with the thefts of gold statues from European museums, but now that I knew what I was dealing with, it was obvious. The journalists were wrong. There were no brazen thieves who broke into high security museums and left gold dust in their wake to taunt the authorities. *There weren't any thieves at all.* The gold statues were crumbling on their own. Turning to dust. The life force of the gold statues was fading—just as Dorian's was.

CHAPTER 33

After meeting with Ivan, I was so distracted that I nearly forgot I was going to stop at the library. I was now making daily trips there to get enough books for Dorian to read to stay awake. He spent several hours each day cooking, but I couldn't keep him cooking twenty-four hours a day. As it was, the fridge didn't have any more room for anything else.

Picking up the heavy bag of books from the truck, I lugged the mystery novels Dorian had finished reading into the library. Before picking out a new batch of books, there was something else I needed to do. I knew very little about backward alchemy. Nicolas Flamel had mentioned it to me only once, to say it was a force not to be used. The reason I remembered it was because of the ferocious look on his face when he'd spoken the words. He had spoken not with the calm voice I had come to know from my teacher. It had been a warning he didn't want me to forget. Because of that, I hadn't ever pursued the subject, not even when I was trying to save Thomas's life.

At a computer terminal, I looked up the library's alchemy books yet again. They were scattered across different sections of the library. It took me some time to track down the relevant tomes and surround myself with them on a long table. I was parched and hungry, but I had to figure out what was going on.

I searched through the books for hours, but only found the vaguest of references to backward alchemy and the death rotation. Whatever I was going to find out about Dorian's book, it wasn't going to be through library books.

~

I hadn't realized how much time had passed. By the time I reached home, it was after dark. Dorian was busy cooking dinner. I wasn't sure why; the fridge was already overflowing.

I wasn't yet ready to talk to Dorian about what I'd learned. Without the book, what I'd learned wasn't going to do us any good.

Brixton was having a hard time dealing with Blue's arrest, so I thought I'd kill two birds with one stone, getting rid of some of the food while checking on him. Max had said Brixton didn't want me to see where he lived, but I thought it was worth the risk to see him. Brixton hadn't been returning my text messages, but I found his address easily enough online. I was glad for that immediate result, but scared for what this level of online information meant for my future.

Heather opened the door of the apartment. Wet green, brown, and white paint covered large swaths of her arms.

"I thought you two might like some pie," I said, holding up two sweet potato pies of the six Dorian had baked.

"That's so sweet of you! Abel is out of town, though. I couldn't possibly eat so much pie. Do you mind if I give one to the neighbors?" She welcomed me inside and took the pies from me, setting them on a rickety card table that served as the kitchen table and grabbing a paint-stained towel to wipe paint from her hands and arms.

The apartment wasn't what you'd call spacious, but they had made good use of the space. In a corner of the living room next to a large window, an easel held the canvas Heather had been working on. I was surprised by how masterful it was. A sea of trees filled the canvas, the perspective so close that neither the sky nor the ground was shown. As I looked more closely at the trees, I saw eyes looking out.

"Feel free to share the pie with anyone you'd like," I said, "but I meant you and Brixton."

Her eyes narrowed in confusion.

"He's not home?" I asked.

"He told me he was staying over at your house tonight."

I froze. It was one thing for Brixton to be late coming home from school. That was bad enough with a murderer on the loose. But lying to his mom about where he'd be *all night* was something different altogether. Brixton was desperate to save Blue from a murder conviction. We hadn't been right about

Ivan being guilty. What would Brixton do to save Blue? Where was he and what was he up to?

"Heather," I said slowly, feeling the full extent of my worry creep through me, "Brixton isn't at my house."

Heather frowned. "He told me he was working on a gardening project for school, with Veronica and Ethan. He said you were helping them so they'd all be staying over at your place."

"You didn't think to call me to confirm?" I asked.

"I trust Brix." But as she said the words, her body tensed.

"Maybe you misheard him," I said, "and he's at Veronica's or Ethan's house?"

Heather's shoulders relaxed. "That must be it. He knows I don't approve of Ethan." She rooted through an oversize handbag, not bothering to wipe the remaining paint from her hands. She pulled out an old-model cell phone and scrolled through the contacts. Putting the phone to her ear, she tapped her foot while she waited. The seconds dragged out.

"Voicemail!" she said. "Ethan's phone went to voicemail. I guess I'll have to call his parents. I've got their number here somewhere..."

While Heather rooted through a stack of papers in a secretary desk next to the door, I stayed out of the way on the other side of the room, again looking at her painting. It was as if the eerie eyes in the middle of the impressionistic trees were watching me.

I pulled my eyes away from Heather's alluring painting and watched her speak on the phone to Ethan's father. She flipped the phone shut and stared at me.

"He said the boys were at your house."

"Same lie," I murmured. "They coordinated. Why didn't you tell Ethan's father they weren't at my house?"

She bit her lip and shrugged. "Let me try Veronica. There has to be a logical explanation for this. Maybe they're over there."

Veronica's cell phone went straight to voicemail. Heather called her parents, who were under the impression that Veronica was staying at Brixton's apartment, as she frequently did when she was younger. They hadn't thought anything of it when she said she was going to do so to work on a school project.

I could hear the voices of both of her parents on the line, their voices growing louder as they realized their daughter wasn't where she said she'd be. I couldn't make out their words, but Heather cringed. "Yes, but—no, I don't think—I really don't think—" She was barely getting a word in between the two irate parents. Her eyes grew wide in horror before she snapped shut the phone.

"They said they're calling the police," Heather said, biting her lip.

"Because some teenagers aren't where their parents think they are?"

"They're like that."

"I doubt the police will take them seriously," I said, pulling out my phone.

"Then who are you calling?"

"Max," I said into the phone. "It's Zoe Faust. Yeah, I'm sorry to bother you, but is Brixton hiding out at your place? He told his mom he'd be at my house, but he's not. He's been avoiding me. I know he's upset about Blue." I listened to Max for a moment. "I'm sure he'll turn up. I'll keep you posted."

I hung up and looked to Heather.

"It's only eight o'clock," Heather said. "Maybe they'll be home soon?"

"What worries me," I said, "is why would they make up the story about staying over at someone else's house, if they were planning on coming back at all tonight?"

Normally I wouldn't have been too worried about three teenage friends lying to their parents. There were any number of things they could have been doing that they didn't want their parents to know about. But with how worried Brixton was about Blue, I had a bad feeling about what they might have been up to. Dorian had been giving Brixton ideas about investigating. What if he had enlisted the help of Veronica and Ethan to help him clear Blue?

I suggested to Heather that she check Brixton's usual haunts and headed out to do my own investigating. It was after nightfall, so it couldn't hurt to pick up a creature who could see in the dark to help me search.

Dorian agreed with my assessment. So much so that he wanted to search without me, thinking I would slow him down.

"I'm going with you," I said. "I think I know where they might be. Remember that spelunking hat Brixton had?"

"You think they are in the tunnels."

"I do."

"I know a back way to get there, going underground close to here. Why are you looking at me like that? I have been exploring this new city. The tunnels here do not have the same morbidity as the catacombs under Paris, but there is a certain *je ne sais quoi*."

Since I wasn't capable of sleeping in, these late nights were getting to me. I made myself a simple yet energizing smoothie elixir in the blender with lettuce, ginger, chia seeds, and chocolate.

Knowing I'd be climbing up and down ladders and through who-knows-what, I left my long coat at home. To combat the effects of the chilly night, I opted instead for bundling in a wool turtleneck sweater, thick wool socks, and matching green hand-knitted gloves and hat a woman in Houston had made me after I helped her start a vegetable garden.

I knew that small sections of the tunnels were accessible to the general public on guided group tours. Tourists and history buffs met at a Chinatown restaurant, outside which an innocuous metal door in the sidewalk opened up to reveal a ladder leading to the tunnels below. But that was far from the only entrance to the tunnels. We entered through a metal grate I would never have noticed if Dorian hadn't pointed it out. It turned out the bundling wasn't necessary. As soon as we were underground, the temperature was in the sixties.

The tunnel we entered reminded me of caves I had once hidden in: nearly complete darkness with only a tease of light, a low ceiling to bump your head on if you weren't careful, and the smell of dust and desperation.

I was about to flip on my flashlight when the tunnel was illuminated from above, casting eerie shadows across the jagged stone walls, thick wooden beams, and dusty floor.

"I found the light switch," Dorian said. "This section of the tunnel is used by some tour companies."

We followed the lights a few dozen yards until the tunnel ended in two rooms.

"I think this is a dead end," I said.

"*Mais non.* I have been this way before."

He pushed gently on what looked like a section of rock just like the rest of the wall. It was, in fact, a wooden door covered in a false coating of rock.

There were no lights strung up in this section of the tunnels. We clicked on our flashlights. In the harsh glare of the flashlight beams in the darkness, every rock transformed into a malevolent creature.

A light up ahead flickered. It wasn't from our flashlight beams.

"Dorian," I whispered, grabbing his arm and shutting off my light. "Do you see that?"

"*Oui.*" He switched off his flashlight.

In the darkness that surrounded us, the light up ahead shone brighter than ever. The light came from around a corner, and it wasn't a solid light. It flickered, as if from a fire. Had homeless people snuck in here for a warm place to stay and lit a fire? I didn't smell smoke, though.

We crept closer, staying out of sight. People were speaking, but I didn't recognize the muffled voices.

I let go of Dorian's arm so I could feel my way along the wall without tripping. In the darkness, I couldn't see him. I knew he was smart enough to stay out of sight, so I wasn't worried about that. But it would have been nice to know he was close for whatever we might find.

The stone walls were strangely warm under my fingertips. I stepped closer.

Something was off about the voices.

Music began to play. It didn't drown out the voices. This wasn't the random sounds of people talking and playing music. I groaned to myself. It was a *movie*.

I peeked around the corner.

An old-fashioned movie projector beamed a James Dean movie onto a relatively flat wall. Sitting on blankets on the ground were Brixton and Ethan, with Veronica in between the boys with an additional blanket resting on her shoulders. In front of them were three open bags of popcorn and several old-style glass bottles of soda I didn't know still existed. Three spelunker hats lay askew next to the blankets.

"Good movie," I said, stepping into the room. "But everyone is looking for you."

Veronica screamed and jumped into Ethan's arms. Popcorn scattered across the floor. Ethan scowled at me—and Brixton scowled at Veronica, who wasn't moving from Ethan's arms.

"OMG!" Veronica said. "You gave me a heart attack, Ms. Faust!"

Once the kids were safely at home, I had time to think about what I'd seen. The kids hadn't merely found an old, boarded-up entrance to a section of tunnels once used for transporting goods. The door had been purposefully *disguised*. Whoever had done that wanted not only to keep people out, but to make it look like that section of tunnel didn't exist. I began to wonder why someone would want the tunnel to remain hidden.

CHAPTER 34

The next morning I was so groggy I was sure that even a strong green tea and a fruit smoothie wouldn't fully rouse me. I was wrong. Shuffling down the stairs, I was given a fright that raised my senses to a state of high alert.

Dorian's body contorted at an unnatural angle, his head hanging upside down with his hands and feet stretched out. I rushed to his side.

"Are you all right? Can I help?"

"You can position my hips," he said.

"What?"

"The lady on the video says my hips should be the highest part of my body. But since people do not have wings, do you think wings count?"

My laptop computer sat open on the coffee table, the screen displaying a video of a yoga class.

"Yoga?" I said, relaxing. The gargoyle wasn't dying. He was contorting.

"I thought it might help keep my body moving." He moved from downward dog to cobra pose. "*Zut.* This is quite unnatural."

I burst out laughing.

"Yes," Dorian said, righting himself. He stretched his shoulders as he stood up straight. "I can see you agree."

"I'm sorry," I said. "I'm sleep deprived. Is the yoga helping?"

He shrugged. "I can still shrug, so it is not hurting. At what time does the library open? Can you get me more books before you meet with Ivan today?"

As we fixed breakfast, the phone rang.

"Zoe, it's Heather. Brixton has run off again. He, Veronica, and Ethan didn't show up at school today."

"What is it?" Dorian whispered, watching my reaction to the phone call. I shook my head.

"Since they ran off last night," Heather continued, "and were just goofing off, the police think they're just ditching school. But... I don't know. I don't like what's been going on. I have a bad feeling."

I did too.

I thought back to that false door we'd gone through. The one that was clearly there to disguise the fact that anything was beyond it. While the kids were having their movie night, had they seen something they weren't supposed to see?

After I got off the phone with Heather, I tried Max. He didn't answer his cell phone. I didn't see him at Blue Sky Teas, either, which Cora was keeping open. As I headed to his house, wind whipped around me, blowing dark clouds overhead. I turned up the collar of my silver coat.

My repeated knocks on the door went unanswered. I was almost back to the sidewalk when I heard a noise behind me. Turning, I saw a bleary-eyed man standing in the doorway.

"*Max?*"

He wore a bathrobe and looked like he hadn't shaved in days. And what was he doing asleep at nearly nine o'clock? The wind was picking up. A gust blew open his bathrobe. I found myself surprisingly disappointed that he was wearing pajamas.

"This better be important," he said, synching the belt of the robe.

"It is. Put the kettle on. I'm coming in."

Twenty minutes later, Max was showered and shaved and we stood together in the warm kitchen, a storm raging outside. Heavy rain beat against the kitchen window box that contained his indoor herb garden.

"I should call this in," he said.

"Call in *what* exactly? That we have *a bad feeling*? The kids went missing last night and they were fine."

Max looked out the window, his jaw firmly set. "Tell me again what you know."

"I suspected Brixton and his friends might have been exploring off-the-grid sections of the tunnels when I saw Brixton's spelunker hat."

"Why couldn't they be a little older so their dares involved sneaking into each other's bedrooms," Max said mostly to himself.

"When I found them last night, they weren't in a normal section of the tunnels."

"You mean they'd gone past the tourist section, through one of the boarded-up doors."

"That's what I thought at first."

"What do you mean that's what you *thought at first?*"

"The door I went through wasn't a boarded-up door. It was a *hidden* door. It had been made to look like it was stone, to blend into the rest of the wall."

"How did you find it?"

I hesitated. It was Dorian who had found the door. "I heard the movie playing. I followed the sound."

Max nodded. "Could you find it again?"

"I think so."

"Then let's go."

~

After several wrong turns, we found the hidden section of tunnel.

Max swore. "I've searched here so many times... I never found this."

"You've searched here?" I pushed open the door in the same way Dorian had done.

Max shook his head at the fake stone.

"What were you—" I continued, but Max held up his hand for me to be quiet.

We walked in silence for several minutes, falling into step beside each other. Max set the pace, alternating between walking slowly and hurrying. Whenever he saw an object like an old wooden chest or a break in the walls that might have been a door, he stopped to examine it, then quickly moved on. I understood the unspoken motivation. If the kids had been taken against their will, we needed to find them quickly. Only when we reached the dead end room where the kids had been watching the movie did Max speak.

"Damn," he said. "There's nothing here."

"What did you think you'd find?"

"You asked me earlier why I was searching the tunnels. Remember I told you I fell through a trap door chasing people I thought were involved in a girl's death?"

"When you saw the monster." I shivered at the memory.

"Don't remind me about my vivid imagination."

I hoped that was all it was...

"I was following a smuggling investigation that led me here," Max continued. "That's why I think it's possible that the kids may have seen something they weren't supposed to when they were down here."

"What were people smuggling?" I asked.

"It's an ongoing investigation, Zoe. I can't just tell you whatever I want to."

"No," I said. "You just lie around your house drinking twelve-year-old scotch."

"I wasn't—"

"I smelled it on your breath when I got to your house. That's something I'm sure anyone would have smelled, regardless of their herbal skills."

He sighed. "I had a bad night last night. I'm no good at sitting on the sidelines."

My flashlight flickered. "I could have sworn I put new batteries in this."

"I don't want to get caught here in the dark. Not after what I've seen. Let's get out of here."

We made our way back the way we came. Max walked especially quickly. I wondered if he was thinking of monsters.

When we reached the entrance through which we'd climbed down, the sound of the rain echoed as it pounded on the metal door above. We were now in a section of the tunnels with electric light and earthquake-reinforced walls. Two empty soda cans littered the dusty floor. Max clicked off his flashlight.

The string of electric lights was dim compared to the harsh flashlight beam, but it was reassuring to be in a section of tunnel that felt like civilization.

"This is private, dry, and well-lit," I said. "Tell me what you know about this smuggling operation. If Brixton and his friends saw something—"

"There's been a resurgence of interest in herbal remedies in recent years," said Max, "especially in places like Portland."

It was one of the reasons I felt comfortable here. People wouldn't look twice at a young woman growing strange herbs in her yard.

"But herbs aren't illegal," I said. "They're not regulated by the FDA."

He hesitated. "We think it's tainted herbal remedies."

"You didn't think to mention this before?" I felt my body shake with anger. "That's why you were so suspicious when I detected poisons!"

"Herbal poisons aren't a common type of poison to use to kill someone," Max said. "You were new to town and knew a lot about herbs and poisons..."

If only we had been able to tell each other what we knew. "I understand why I might look suspicious, but why would someone sell herbs that were poisonous? That hardly seems like a good business model."

"The most educated guess we've pieced together is that these are tainted herbs coming in from China. The smugglers wanted to capitalize on this new herbalism craze, but they didn't know much about herbs themselves. They bought a large, cheap shipment from criminals, hoping to turn a quick profit without paying any taxes. And the tunnels were the perfect place to store the supplies. They didn't realize the herbs were tainted with poison until Anna became ill and killed herself. After that, they pulled back. We haven't seen anything lately."

"You think Charles Macraith was involved in it?"

"He had a work injury last year that made it impossible to work."

"I know," I said. "He told me my house was his first real job in a while. He'd been hired by the agent who put the house on the market just to do a walk-through to make sure prospective buyers wouldn't fall through any holes in the floors and sue her. He wasn't up for more than that while he recovered. The real estate agent is the one who gave me his name."

"Charles had to have been hurting for money because of his loss of work," Max said. "Sure enough, when we looked into him, we found a large sum of cash at his house."

"That's why you think Blue blackmailed him. Because she was hiding from her past, and she only accepted cash at the teashop so she would have access to large amounts of untraceable money."

"It fits."

"How does it fit?"

"He was known for being the kind of guy who inspires confidences," Max said. "You haven't been here long enough to know it, but even though Portland is a big city, its neighborhoods like ours have small-town characteristics—including the gossip. The community Blue created at her teashop fostered a lot of friendships, but Charles never gossiped about anyone. That's the kind of person people open up to, sometimes unwisely."

I had to bite my tongue. That was exactly why I had hired Charles Macraith in the first place.

"But it still doesn't make sense," I insisted. "Blue knows all about herbs. She would never buy tainted herbs. Even if I could believe she'd do something like that, she knows too much to buy and sell tainted herbs."

"I agree. I've known Blue for years. But that's the way the facts point."

"Except that she's under arrest, meaning it's someone else on the loose who's taken the kids."

"We don't know they've been taken," Max said. "They lied to their parents last night. All the facts point to the conclusion that they're playing hooky today."

"That's not what your gut says."

"No," he said. "It's not. The thing that's bothering me most is that I can't put my finger on *why* I think that."

"I know why," I said, the reason dawning on me. "Their parents were irate last night. There's no way the kids would do something stupid so soon after their last escapade. Something else is going on."

"I'm half-tempted to pull Sam out of school to get him to help us search the tunnels for the kids," Max said, "since that's where you found them last time. He teaches a section of his class on local history, including information about the Shanghai Tunnels. The students get really into it."

I frowned. "Brixton said he took them on an underground tour that involved sections of the tunnels not included on the tourist tours."

"That can't be right," Max said. "He wouldn't have taken them anywhere off-limits."

"He's the 'cool young teacher' who loves his students. Of course he would. But what I'm wondering is what *else* he knows."

"You're suggesting Sam is somehow involved in this?"

"I don't know what I'm suggesting," I said. "Something isn't right, though."

"I know. I feel the same way. I hate that I can't trust my own gut anymore. Ever since I saw that monster." He winced. It could have been from his injury, but my guess was that it was his chagrin for believing he'd seen a monster.

"I don't think you saw a monster," I said. The pieces clicked into place. Tainted herbs. My dream that had been hallucinogen-induced. The timing of the arrival of Dorian and his book. "When you saw 'the monster' the first time, it was on the smuggled herbs case, right?"

"What does that have to do with it? It was the fall that disoriented me—"

"I think," I said, "you were given something tainted with a hallucinogen."

There *wasn't* another creature like Dorian. Max had only equated the two after he caught a glimpse of Dorian. I let out a huge sigh of relief.

"You're *relieved* that I was drugged?" Max began to pace.

"The police never determined if there were drugs in the dead girl's system, right?"

"It was determined to be suicide. The family had the body cremated before

I was on the smuggling case, before I could see the two might be connected. So you're right. We never learned if there was a hallucinogen in her system."

"Did the lab test for hallucinogens in the poison you found at Blue's—"

"God, Zoe, I'm not even on this or *any* case anymore!"

We stared at each other for a few moments. The close air of the tunnels felt stifling.

"Fine," I said. "I'll find Brixton and his friends on my own. Have a nice life drinking good scotch alone in your house."

Max groaned. "Wait. Fine. Tell me more about what you were thinking about Sam. I didn't know he was such an expert on the tunnels."

"I was thinking he could have found tunnels nobody else knew about," I said. "But I'm grasping at straws now. Forget I said anything. There's nothing to connect him to this. Lots of locals are interested in the tunnels."

But Max wore a strange expression on his face, caught between concern and anger. "Not everyone has a pile of medical bills for a sick aunt who raised him. That's why Blue took him on at the teashop, to help him supplement the money he made as a teacher."

"I knew about that. But lots of people need money. They don't go around poisoning people."

"Not only that. Olivia was in the hospital at the same time last year as Charles Macraith."

"And both with bills they couldn't pay?" I asked, remembering what Olivia had told me about Sam taking on the second job at Blue Sky Teas to help with the bills.

Max nodded, his face looking hollow in the dim light of the tunnel.

"Wait, where are you going?" Max asked as I started up the ladder.

"Sam is teaching and Olivia should already be over at Blue Sky Teas since she's helping keep it open. I'm going to look around their house." I'd dropped Olivia off at her house earlier that week. I didn't remember the house number, but I'd remember the barren rose bushes and pink shutters.

Max swore. "Zoe, you can't go breaking into people's houses. I need to get a search warrant."

I paused on the stair ladder to look over my shoulder. "You think you have enough to get one?" He didn't answer immediately.

"I thought so." I continued climbing the stairs back to civilization.

"Zoe!"

Without pausing, I called over my shoulder, "If he's using the tunnels, he's got to have maps somewhere. I'm going to find them."

CHAPTER 35

Dorian narrowed his eyes. "You want me to climb into this suitcase?"

"It's a duffel bag. And yes. I promise it won't be for long. You want to help Brixton and me find your book, don't you? I don't know how to pick a lock. You have to come with me."

The gargoyle grumbled several words of French that weren't fit to repeat as he climbed into the duffel bag. Sam and his aunt Olivia's house wasn't too far from mine, but I wouldn't make it carrying the heavy bag of gargoyle. I'd need to take the car. I didn't like the idea of driving my distinctive car to a house I was breaking into, but I didn't see any other choice.

It was a good thing I'd added extra chia seeds and cocoa powder to my smoothie that day. I needed the extra energy to lift the heavy bag and place it in my truck. I tried to lift it gingerly, but it hit the door frame as I raised the bag onto the passenger seat.

"Oomph."

"Sorry, Dorian."

Things would have been much easier if we could have waited until night-fall, but there wasn't time. If the kids weren't playing hooky, we needed to find them, and the tunnels were our best lead.

"Wait here," I said as I parked down the street from Sam and Olivia's house.

"Where would I go?" was the muffled response from inside the duffel bag.

I did a quick circle of the house and found a side door. I let out a small sigh

211

of relief. Even though the neighbors appeared to be at work, it was all I needed to be caught with a gargoyle picking a front door lock.

I carried the bag to the side of the house and unzipped the bag.

Dorian made quick work of the lock with his claws. I'd seen some thieves at work before, and those claws were better than lock picks.

A vase filled with the white flowers I'd bought for Blue was displayed prominently on Olivia's mantle.

My cell phone buzzed in my pocket. Max's name flashed on the screen. It was best if he didn't know what I was doing. The phone went back into my pocket.

"I do not see my book," Dorian said.

"No, but take a look at this." I picked up a poster tube labelled "world map." I popped off the top and looked inside.

Rolled inside a laminated map of the world, tightly rolled thinner sheets of paper were visible. I pulled them out.

"The tunnels," Dorian said.

My cell phone buzzed again. This was getting ridiculous. I pulled the phone out to turn it off, but along with Max's name across the screen, I noticed something else. He had called *five times*.

I must have missed some of the calls while I was lugging the heavy bag with Dorian inside.

I picked up the phone, but I'd just missed him. I had a voicemail waiting for me. Dorian's eyes grew wide as he watched me listen to the message.

"Zoe," Max's voice said. "If you're where I think you are, get out of there. I tried to get hold of Sam to see if he would voluntarily help us with his knowledge of the tunnels. But he wasn't at school. He called in sick today, Zoe. He could be anywhere."

I hung up the phone, feeling my pulse race.

"We need to go, Dorian. *Now*."

"Uh, Zoe. A young man is approaching the front door."

"I have to put this poster tube back where I found it." I moved quickly as I did so, scanning the room to see if there was anything else we'd moved. I spotted papers strewn on the entryway table.

"Zoe—"

"One second."

"You do not have one second."

My ears pricked with the sound of a key turning in the door.

Dorian pounced. Not on Sam, but on the door. He reached it right as the deadbolt began to open. With his strong hand, Dorian held the handle of the deadbolt, keeping it from opening.

Sam twisted his key from the outside. "Come on..." he said. He must have thought the door was stuck.

I moved as quietly as I could toward the desk we'd disturbed. I put all the contents back, then nodded at Dorian. He held up his free hand, asking me to wait.

"Come on," Sam said again from behind the door. He gave the doorknob a shake, then pulled out his key. We heard the sound of his keys rattling. While he searched for the right key, Dorian and I took our chance.

We ran out the back and hurried around the side of the house. There was no time to get Dorian back into the bag. I peeled off my jacket and tossed it on top of him, then peeked around the corner of the house. Sam was shaking his head as he opened the front door.

We didn't stop running until we were inside the truck. I was glad I had the foresight to park my truck down the street instead of in front of the house.

When we reached the hidden entrance to the tunnels, I dropped the bag at my feet, unable to hold it any longer. I had made Dorian crawl back inside the duffel bag for our walk from the truck to the entrance.

Making sure there was no one around, I pulled open the iron grate.

"Hurry," I said to the duffel bag.

"*Grâce à Dieu*," Dorian stepped out of the bag. He glared at it with a look of disdain before coming to his senses about his exposed location and darting into the tunnel.

I climbed down after him, closing the grate behind me. Dust from the tunnel floor wafted up to my nose, causing me to sneeze. My shoulder ached as if I'd been carrying a boulder. Which, essentially, I had been.

I handed him a flashlight, but he shook his head. I spread out the map of the tunnels on the surface of a dusty wooden trunk, shining the light onto the sketch.

"I think we're here," I said.

"*Oui*," Dorian agreed.

"You don't happen to have a photographic memory, do you?"

"Unfortunately, no. But I have explored the tunnels on my own and I see much better in the dark. I will lead."

Dorian scampered ahead. Though he moved quickly, one of his legs dragged behind, giving him an awkward gait. My flashlight bounced off the gargoyle, showing me that his whole leg up to his knee joint was now a solid mass of stone.

I tucked the map under my arm and hurried to keep up with the limping gargoyle. The temperature in this section of tunnels must have been close to seventy degrees, but I felt myself shaking. It couldn't have been the temperature making me shiver. It couldn't have been poison, either. I had fully recovered from the effects of the small amount that had affected me.

I knew what it was: *fear*.

CHAPTER 36

At a juncture in the tunnels, Dorian turned and looked back at me.

"This way," he said.

A few minutes later, we reached the door that had been purposefully disguised. What we hadn't known until we found the map was that beyond that door there was a *second* disguised door. What looked like a load-bearing beam of wood was in fact a cleverly disguised entry to a hidden set of tunnels.

It was the perfect setup for Shanghaiers. If someone happened to discover their first false door, the interloper would carry on straight ahead, never thinking to look for *another* hidden passageway.

The two-foot section of thick wood stood directly next to the stone wall. It looked innocent enough, but we knew from the map that there had to be a way to make it move. It wasn't a structural part of the tunnels at all. It was a narrow opening.

I pressed against the wood from one side, and then the next. It didn't budge. I pushed it forward. Nothing. I grabbed the sides and pulled. That didn't work either.

"Perhaps there is a trigger mechanism," Dorian suggested.

"It could be in one of the stones." Dorian tapped on them with his fingers. "You are taller. Try the ones above."

I handed the map to Dorian so I could work the stones with both hands. I tried each of the stones surrounding the beam, quickly at first, and then more methodically after quick pushes didn't do the trick. I was now sweating from apprehension. I peeled off the bulky sweater I was wearing over a cotton blouse.

"*Mon dieu*," Dorian whispered. "Why does it not open? And why must you touch your necklace after you press each stone?"

I hadn't realized I was doing it, but he was right.

I pushed on the highest stone I could reach, then turned and rested my back against the wall.

"You know what the locket means to me," I said. "I can't lose someone else I care about."

"Your brother. Brixton reminds you of him, *n'est-ce pas?*"

"I suppose he does." I clenched my fists in frustration. "Why won't this open!?" I whirled around and banged my fists against the stone wall. Pain shot through my forearms, but I didn't care.

Dorian pulled me away.

"It will not help anyone for your arms to be bloodied," he said.

I sighed and slumped down against the beam.

"Turn off the flashlight," Dorian said.

"We're not giving up—"

"No, but the shadows from the light confuses things. I can see better in the dark. I will look to see if there is a mechanism we have missed."

The darkness that enveloped us was complete. I saw nothing, and heard only my own breath and the light sound of claws tapping on stone.

"The other man in the locket," Dorian said softly, "you are thinking of him as well?"

I didn't answer immediately. As I listened to Dorian tapping on stone, the darkness gave me the courage to speak. "His memory was what I was running from," I said, "when you first saw me in Paris, helping the *Commandant*."

"He died because he had not found the Elixir of Life you had found?" Dorian continued to examine the wall as he spoke.

"The opposite, actually." I laughed ruefully in the darkness. "It was *because* he found the Elixir of Life that he died in the manner he did."

"*C'est vrai?*"

"It would have been better had he died of old age. A natural death, I could have handled. I would have grieved, but it would have been a natural death. Not like what happened."

"Did he die of the plague, as your brother did?"

"It's worse than that."

"*Merde*," Dorian said. "My claw is caught in the stone." He paused, and a rustling sound filled the darkness. "Ah! It is free."

"Is it the lever?"

"No. Nothing has moved. Yet the map shows clearly that this is the second door!"

"Maybe we're looking at this in the wrong way." I clicked on the flashlight, this time shining the light toward the ceiling. "If it's a mechanism that triggers the door, it doesn't have to be part of the door itself. It could be anywhere around here."

I stood up to take a closer look at the wooden beams running across the low ceiling. I methodically traced each of the beams. Four metal objects shone as the light passed over them. The simple hooks looked like they had been placed there to hold oil lamps to illuminate the passage.

But one of them was different from the rest.

I stepped closer to get a better look. I know metals. This particular hook wasn't solid zinc iron alloy like the rest. It had been painted black to look like the other hooks.

I reached up and tugged on the hook. I was rewarded by the sound of a latch clicking.

"You have found it!" Dorian said. He scurried to the thick beam and shoved. This time, the beam gave way, revealing a narrow passage of darkness. He hurried inside, carrying the map and my sweater with him.

"Wait a second," I whispered. "We don't know if it will close behind us and trap us. We need to find the mechanism on the other side, so we can get back."

Dorian pointed to a visible lever. "On this side," he said, "they have no use for disguise."

"Let me see the map," I said, taking it from Dorian's outstretched hand. "Damn. There are two branches of this tunnel."

"We shall split up?"

"I don't think that's a good idea."

Dorian snatched the map back, grumbling to himself as he studied it. We followed the narrow passageway for several dozen yards before the tunnel forked. I shone the flashlight in both directions.

"To the right," Dorian said softly, consulting the map, "is the shorter distance."

"Both directions go on for quite some distance," I whispered, "so the right is as good a choice as any."

I clicked off the light and took a deep breath. "We should be careful from here."

"Agreed. Give me your hand. I will lead you through the darkness."

In spite of myself and the situation, I laughed. I was being led by a living gargoyle through a secret section of tunnels underneath Portland. I remembered Brixton saying "My life is too weird." I could relate.

"This is amusing?" Dorian asked.

"You've heard the expression that someone laughs so they don't cry?"

"*Oui.*"

"This is one of those situations."

We walked in silence, in the cavernous darkness, for at least twenty minutes. Dorian periodically whispered for me to duck or to be careful as I stepped forward. As we walked further into the tunnels, the air grew close and stifling. Dorian maintained a firm grip on one of my hands to lead me. With my other hand, I felt along the wall. The only sounds were our light footsteps and the sound of my heartbeat.

Dorian's hand was neither rough nor smooth, neither warm nor cold. It felt like I was holding an ocean-worn rock, warmed to the temperature of its surrounding environment.

As we rounded a corner, the air quality shifted. I saw no light, but I felt a gentle breeze.

"Where are we?" I whispered.

"*Zut!* We have reached the end!"

"The end?"

Dorian pulled me further. I hadn't switched on the light, but a dim light spread out before us. We stepped forward into a room with a metal grate above. Light poured into the room from above. As my eyes adjusted, I became aware of a rhythmic sound.

I groaned. "The river. We're somewhere along the Willamette."

"It appears this is another disguised entry point."

"I can't reach the grate," I said. "If I lift you up, you should be able to reach it."

He nodded, and I cupped my hands to boost him up with his good leg. By holding him on my shoulders, he was able to reach the grate.

"Rusted shut," he said. "This has not been used in many years."

"We went the wrong way."

"Come," Dorian said. "There is no longer the need to be quiet as we retrace our steps."

Using the flashlight this time, we were able to move more quickly. Still, it wasn't fast enough. I held the flashlight in one hand and my locket in the other.

"We will find them," Dorian said. "Have faith."

"Faith doesn't save people."

"You are a good person, Zoe Faust. Whatever happened, it could not have been your fault."

"You're wrong. Because of me, both Thomas and Ambrose died. That's why I first gave up alchemy and ran from everything— including myself."

"What you told me of your brother was not your fault. Failing to save someone from the plague is not your fault."

"But that's not what happened to Ambrose." I clutched my locket more tightly. "I should never have let him talk me into practicing alchemy again."

"What happened that is so terrible?"

"I already told you that after Thomas died, I left the Flamel's house, unaware I had discovered the Elixir of Life." I walked more quickly than Dorian, so he wouldn't see my face as I spoke. "After I knew what I had become and returned to the Flamel's house to find it burned to the ground, I felt as if I was cursed. I didn't think I deserved to live, but I at least wanted to help others. I used my herbal skills of plant alchemy to do so. I was never good at making gold, so I sold healing tonics to survive. I gave away more than I sold, so I barely survived. I could never turn my back on a needy person. There were so many of them..."

I tried to shake off the memory of so much suffering. Though I had helped many people, there were so many more I couldn't save. "The man in the locket was someone you could not help?"

"Ambrose," I said. "When I met him, I was an emaciated wreck, curing others while I lived on boiled meat and potatoes, barely surviving myself. I had learned that I was nearly as human as everyone else—feeling sick when I ate poorly, bleeding when cut, blistering when burned—but I hadn't felt worthy of healing myself. Not until I met Ambrose. He was a fellow alchemist, so he recognized me for what I was."

"Ah!" Dorian said. "So the tragedy is that he found the Elixir of Life, yet still died?"

"Worse. It won't make sense unless you know what he did for me. When we met, though Ambrose was a practicing alchemist, he hadn't yet found the Elixir of Life. I fell in love with him, and he with me. He helped me realize my life was worth living. That's when I began to eat a plant-based diet, which helped me heal my body and feel alive again. I believed my life was worth living again, so I wanted to feel alive in every way. We worked together for many years, happy in our shared alchemy lab. But he had a son. Percival."

"The son did not approve of you?"

"I didn't approve of Percival. Ambrose was devoted to his son, but I saw him for the mean-spirited man he really was. Ambrose tried to get Percival interested in alchemy, but Percival is a perfect example of why the world isn't ready for alchemy's secrets. Percival was only ever interested in quick fixes. He took opium to excess, and ate and drank with a similar indulgence. He never held a job for long, because he always knew his father could make him gold. Whenever I tried to broach the subject with Ambrose, he wouldn't hear of it. He would believe nothing bad about his son. Ambrose was the most brilliant alchemist I've ever met, but Percival was his weakness."

"This is what I understand it is to be a parent."

"Maybe so. I should have seen it coming. Maybe then I could have prevented it."

"What happened?"

"Working together in our laboratory—me working with plants to create healing elixirs and Ambrose working with metals to create the philosopher's stone—we complemented each other and increased each other's learning. Ambrose created his own philosopher's stone that led him to the Elixir of Life. In spite of my protestations that it wouldn't work to transfer it to another, Ambrose tried to transfer it to Percival. When it didn't work, Percival became irate. Cutting corners, he tried to create it for himself, envious that his father and I would live while he would die. Percival continued to age, becoming a bitter old man who wasted away and died. Ambrose couldn't take it. Knowing he'd caused his son so much pain and that he would go on living—Ambrose went insane."

"*Mon dieu.*"

"I tried to get him help, but he was taken away and placed in a mental institution. He couldn't live like that. He killed himself."

"I am so sorry, Zoe. But you should also realize you are lucky to have found Ambrose at all. To have found that even briefly, for this I am envious."

"Believe me," I said, wiping away a tear with my sleeve, "you don't need to be envious of my life."

"I have never met another like myself. My father was the only one who knew my true self. The blind men I worked for believed me to be a man, like them. They believed me to be disfigured, and this is why I wished to stay out of sight from others."

Guilt washed over me. I hadn't considered that Dorian's life had, in some ways, been lived in even more isolation than my own. "We've both lived lonely lives."

"Yet," Dorian said, "I still wish to live."

We walked in silence for a few minutes, the weight of Dorian's words hanging in the air.

"How much further do we have to go?" I asked.

"*Merde*," Dorian whispered.

"What is it?"

"Quiet," he whispered sharply. "Turn off your light."

I clicked off the light. "What do you see?"

"Wait here."

"We're not splitting up."

"I shall be back momentarily."

"Wait—"

"There are two more passageways I see," Dorian said, "*neither* of which are marked on the map, yet there is light ahead. Remain here."

I crossed my arms and waited impatiently as Dorian's footsteps faded.

A few minutes later, he still hadn't returned. I began to tap my foot anxiously. Where was he?

A faint tapping noise sounded. I stood still. The noise continued. It wasn't caused by my fidgeting.

In the darkness, I wasn't sure which direction Dorian had gone, so I couldn't tell if the sound was coming from the same direction. Keeping the light off, I edged forward, following the sound.

As I crept forward, the noise grew louder. It sounded like someone hitting metal. Or maybe someone's bones being hit with a piece of metal.

I gave up stealth in favor of speed. I turned on my flashlight and ran toward the sound. I ran for minutes, down the narrow passageway of heavy, dusty air. I nearly tripped on a pile of boxes stacked on the side of the narrow tunnel. My lungs heaved, but I kept going.

The tunnel jogged left at a sharp angle. As I rounded the corner, two lamps illuminated a larger section of tunnel. Jail cells lined one wall. Brixton, Ethan, and Veronica were trapped in one of the cells.

On the outside stood a woman in a distinctive red shawl. It was Olivia.

CHAPTER 37

Veronica stopped banging on the iron bars of the jail cell as soon as she saw me. After a few seconds of the harsh sound echoing through the tunnels, the sound ceased. All was silent.

Olivia raised an eyebrow at me, while the kids stared openmouthed from behind the bars of the Shanghaier's cell.

I mentally kicked myself. Everything that applied to Sam Strum also applied to his aunt Olivia. Olivia needed money for her medical treatments. Olivia was at the hospital at the same time as Charles Macraith. And sharing a house with her nephew, she would know about his local history research findings about the Shanghai Tunnels.

"Well," Olivia said, "are you going to just stand there, or are you going to help me rescue the children?"

"*Rescue* them?" I repeated.

Olivia pursed her lips. "Did I give you too much credit by thinking you were an intelligent young woman?"

"Mr. Strum locked us up," Brixton said.

"It was so creepy!" Veronica added.

"Wait," I said. "*Sam* locked you up?"

"Give the lady a prize," Ethan said. He stood with his back against a brick wall on the far side of the cell, mimicking a casual stance that was betrayed by the nervous twitches of his hands.

Veronica elbowed him. "Ms. Faust is here to help—um, aren't you?"

"I am," I said, eyeing Olivia.

"She's not working with her nephew," Brixton said.

"I didn't know what Sam had done," Olivia said sharply. "Are you going to just stand there, or help me unlock these cell doors?"

"Where's Sam?" I asked.

"He wouldn't hurt them," Olivia said. "He just needed them out of the way. You don't have to worry about him. He won't be back."

I wasn't so sure. Regardless of what I thought, we had to get ourselves out of the tunnels. We were so far from fresh air that I didn't know what would happen if we stayed there too long.

I joined Olivia at the metal door. "What have you tried so far?"

"Brute force. It didn't work."

I looked at my cell phone. No reception.

"Mr. Strum took the key with him," Veronica said.

I tugged on the door. "What happened?"

"The last time we were here exploring—" Brixton began.

"Spelunking," Ethan cut in.

"Yeah, spelunking," Brixton said, rolling his eyes. "Well, we found some evidence that looked like there was modern Shanghaiing going on. Well, not Shanghaiing, exactly. Smuggling, though. That's almost as cool, right? There was like a truckload of boxes from China. We thought Mr. Strum would think it was cool, 'cause of his interest in this stuff. So this morning when we got to school, we went to find him before classes started."

"To tell him about what we found," Veronica added.

Brixton gripped the bars. "He was totally into it. Said we should all ditch school today so we could show him what we found."

"We thought he was cool!" Veronica said, stamping her ballet flats on the dusty cell floor. "A teacher ditching with us. That was going to be, like, the best story ever. Instead, he locked us up in here! Right after we showed him the hidden boxes! I couldn't believe it. We totally thought it was a joke at first."

As she spoke, I knelt down to examine the lock.

"When we saw that it wasn't," Brixton said, "I tried to hypnotize him."

I glanced sharply at Brixton.

"I, uh, read about hypnosis online," Brixton said. "But anyway, it didn't work. He left us here."

"Does anyone have a pocketknife?" I asked.

"Tried it already," Ethan said, and Olivia held up a broken pocketknife.

Where had Dorian gone off to? He would be able to pick the lock, but he couldn't reveal himself openly. If only I had the map he'd run off with, I could have made my way out of the tunnels to get help. The tunnels stretched on for miles in so many directions that I wasn't confident I could find my way out without the map.

"Olivia," I said, "how did you end up here?"

"After Sam left for the high school this morning, he came back to the house to grab a key. I didn't think much of it until I looked out the window and saw the children in the car. I knew something was wrong. He'd been acting strange lately. I thought it was because he was tired from working two jobs. But when I saw what he was doing this morning, I began to put the pieces together..."

"So you followed them."

"I don't drive, you know. But I suspected where they were going. I took the bus to a tunnel entrance I knew about from Sam, and used the stories he'd told me to find my way here."

"Could you find your way back to get help?"

She hesitated. "I followed the sound of Veronica banging on the bars with a brick. But without a sound to follow on the way back..." "How did *you* find us here?" Ethan asked.

"Brixton's mom called me, worried after she got a call that you were ditching school."

"Why didn't you guys call Max?" Brixton asked.

"I did. I told him my suspicions about Sam using the tunnels for smuggling tainted herbal supplements. He said he needed a search warrant to search Olivia and Sam's house..."

"You broke into their house?" Brixton said. "Wicked."

Olivia clicked her tongue.

Another, louder click sounded a moment later. Everyone froze.

"Sam?" Olivia called out, her body tensing. She wasn't nearly as confident in her assessment of Sam as she wanted us to believe.

There was no reply.

"You see?" she said hesitantly. "He's not here. He's not going to hurt anyone."

I could have pointed out that Sam had killed not once but twice— the first time accidentally killing Anna West, the second time deliberately murdering Charles Macraith, and a third death was only foiled because I'd found Blue in time—but I held my tongue.

"I don't like it down here," Veronica whispered. She tugged at the sleeves of her sweater, then wrapped her arms around herself.

"You found Sam's map of the tunnels?" Olivia said to me. "Why didn't you bring it with you?"

"I had to leave it behind."

Olivia threw her arms into the air, her shawl stirring up dust. She coughed before speaking. "We should split up. That way one of us should be able to find our way out of here and get help."

"We shouldn't split up," I said. "We can't be sure Sam isn't coming back."

"I told you," Olivia said, "he wouldn't hurt them."

"Only imprison them."

"He only did this to help me!" she said. "I knew he had gotten extra money to help pay for my experimental treatments abroad, but I thought it was Blue who was paying him generously because she knew about our money troubles. He never meant to hurt anyone! He would never have hurt anyone on purpose. He couldn't have known he'd been lied to and given tainted herbs."

Ethan put two fingers in his mouth and whistled. "Can we focus here?" The normally unfazed boy was visibly rattled.

"I have an idea," I said. "Give me one second."

I retraced my steps into the darkened portion of the tunnel. I was hoping it was Dorian who'd made the sound in an attempt to draw me out into a private meeting. I walked forward a few yards until I was out of earshot.

"Dorian?" I whispered. "Dorian?"

Nothing.

I waited for a few moments, but didn't dare go forward for fear of getting lost.

"Dorian?" I tried one last time.

I sighed and walked back to the group.

"Well?" Olivia said. "What was your brilliant idea?"

"I thought I remembered which way to go," I said. "But I was wrong."

"Looks like we could use these," Brixton said, pulling a bag out of his backpack. It was filled with a dozen chocolate date balls. He took one and passed the bag around.

Dorian had made the dessert treats. He'd made an awful mess of the kitchen at the time, searching for flour that I didn't have. Instead of abandoning the ingredients he'd already mixed, he'd experimented without expectations and was able to create something even better than he'd initially envisioned. I breathed in the dusty air as an idea tickled the back of my mind. Giving up on expectations was exactly what I needed to do here.

"I've got it," I said, looking from the lock to the opposite side of the old jail cell door. The hinges were covered in rust. "Can I see that broken knife?"

Using the broken blade of the Swiss Army knife, I eased the pin out of the upper hinge. It made a horrid squeaking noise as it pulled out of its socket.

"No way!" Veronica said.

Ethan swore under his breath, mumbling something about how he should have thought of it himself.

"Mwmsm," Brixton said through a mouthful of dessert.

Olivia held the door as I removed the second hinge pin. Together, we swung open the door in the opposite direction than was intended.

Veronica leaped out of the cell and gave me a hug. "Thank you, Ms. Faust!"

"Now we can all get lost together," Ethan said.

The bright light of a flashlight came around a corner.

Veronica shrieked like a banshee, causing the boys to cover their ears.

Olivia and I stepped instinctively in front of the kids.

"He wouldn't…" Olivia whispered.

It wasn't Sam who came into view. It was Max. I let out a sigh of relief. Max's shirt was askew and his chest heaved. He must have been running.

"You're all okay?" he asked.

His eyes locked on mine while everyone spoke at the same time to say they were all right. I barely heard them. At that moment, I was no longer in a claustrophobic tunnel, surrounded by three teenagers and the aunt of a murderer, with a gargoyle somewhere in the shadows.

"Thank God," Max said, his eyes never leaving mine. He took a step forward and pulled me into a kiss. His lips tasted of licorice and spearmint. I found myself lost in the intensity of the kiss, something I hadn't felt in nearly a century. The feeling scared me. I wasn't afraid of Max himself, but the *idea* of Max. It was too much. We were too different. He was a skeptic who would never accept me if he knew the real me. I pulled back. As I broke away, the look on his face surprised me. The confident, stoic cop was *hurt*.

"Mr. Liu!" Veronica said.

Max cleared his throat. "It looks like everyone is all right."

"How did you find us?" I asked, clearing my own throat.

"An anonymous person left me a map of the tunnels with this section circled. It was accompanied by a note saying I'd find Brixton, Veronica, and Ethan here. Was that you, Olivia?"

"It wasn't me," she said.

"You don't have to protect Sam any longer," Max said. "We've got officers at the house arresting him."

"I only figured out what my nephew was up to this morning," she said, "and I have no idea who left you that map."

I knew the answer. I wondered how many Portlanders had noticed a stooped, child-size figure using a bulky sweater to cover himself as he ran through the streets, taking a great risk to rescue us from the cavernous tunnels deep beneath the city.

CHAPTER 38

Thanks to Max, the police had arrived at Sam and Olivia's house in time to find Sam packing hastily for a getaway. And thanks to Dorian, Max had the map to find us and lead us all out of the tunnels.

The kids were now safely at home with their parents, who'd left work when they heard what was going on. I was waiting at the police station to find out what was happening. I was torn. Part of me had wanted to return home to see Dorian, but the best way I could help Dorian was to learn what had happened to his book. If the police could break Sam, they might discover where he'd hidden it.

As I waited to hear what was going on, I thought about how it was his own guilty conscience that had done him in. If he hadn't acted, he would have been safe. The kids wouldn't have gone to anyone else with what they saw, and Sam could have gone home "sick" and disposed of the merchandise to cover his tracks, now that he knew the boxes had been discovered.

I knew about guilty consciences. But whatever blame I shouldered for the deaths of Thomas and Ambrose, it didn't include murder.

Max poked his head around the door of the waiting room. Was it my imagination, or was he blushing?

"Your idea to remove the rusty hinge pins to get everyone out of those old hidden jail cells garnered a round of applause," he said, "and Detective Dylan has agreed to let you watch the interrogation from another room."

I followed Max into a small room with a video screen.

Instead of sitting down, Max left the room, leaving me to contemplate the man on the video screen. Sam Strum looked at peace. Not *happy*, but as if a great weight had been lifted. It made sense, now, why he continued to go to the teashop that was a reminder of the innocent girl who'd died because of him. The sadness I'd seen in him that day had been his penance.

Max returned a minute later with two cups of tea.

"Are we waiting for his lawyer to arrive?" I asked.

"He's declined a lawyer," Max said. "Says he wants to get everything off his chest. All he asked for was his favorite tea from his house before he'd talk. One of the guys is getting it. That's what we're waiting on. Zoe, I—"

Another officer entered the room, causing Max to break off whatever he was going to say.

"Looks like they're about to get started," the officer said. "Took long enough to find that damn tea."

We watched Sam breathe in the steam from the tea. He smiled oddly before he spoke.

"I wasn't going to hurt Veronica, Brixton, or Ethan," Sam said. "It's important to me you know that. I was only going to keep them locked up until I could disappear. Then I was going to call in a tip so they'd be found."

"Why don't you start at the beginning," a voice from off camera said.

Sam nodded. "When my aunt got sick a couple of years ago, she couldn't live by herself. I moved in with her."

"That was a generous offer."

Sam shot a confrontational look toward the interrogator, but continued. "She'd essentially raised me, so it was the least I could do. Aunt Olivia doesn't have any children of her own, and she needed me. It was difficult for her, as she went through her cancer treatments. She'd had cancer before, and beat it. But this time was different. They didn't think she'd survive." Sam paused and ran his hands over his face.

"That's where you met Charles Macraith—at the hospital?"

"I knew him before, but that's where we got to know each other better. Aunt Olivia and I had been going to Blue Sky Teas ever since the first time she got sick. I'd seen Charles around there. We were friendly but not friends. But at the hospital... We got to talking about how he'd been out of work for so long that he was hurting for money. And me and Olivia? She couldn't work, so I took a second job at Blue's. It was enough for us to get by, but not enough to try an experimental treatment for her. I had to find a way to pay for that treatment. She was dying, you know? How could I not do absolutely everything I could?"

I knew that feeling. Sam's heart had been in the right place, at least at first. But he'd gone way too far. I shuddered. Max glanced at me. His hand moved toward me, but he immediately pulled it back. I pretended I hadn't noticed.

"So you and Charles came up with a plan," the detective prompted.

Sam shrugged. "Charles was the kind of guy people would open up to. He knew a lot of people from all the home renovation work he did. And people knew they could trust him. He was never one to gossip."

"Uh huh."

"We'd both seen how herbal remedies had been getting so popular. Olivia took some, to try to manage some of her side effects. I knew how expensive they were. There must have been a *tremendous* markup. So one day Charles and I were talking about our money problems and how expensive herbal remedies were, and he got all quiet. I mean, quieter than he usually was. Which was already pretty quiet. Then he said he knew a guy who could get us some Chinese herbal remedies in bulk. The guy had problems himself, so he was getting out of the business. He had all these unused, packaged herbal supplements that could help people. He was willing to sell them to us cheaply, and we could even take over a company he'd already set up, but we'd have to sneak the shipment into the country. It didn't seem too risky. I mean, herbs aren't regulated the same way pharmaceuticals are, since they're safe. That's what we thought. It was supposed to be easy." He paused to take a deep breath and have a sip of tea. "Nobody," he said through clenched teeth, "was supposed to get hurt."

"But then Anna—"

"You don't have to remind me. I'm getting to that. Because you need to know that was never supposed to happen. Charles and I scraped together the little bit of money we had to do this deal with the guy. I put in a higher percentage. Charles had the contacts on both ends, but what he didn't have was money. He worked on selling the various supplements. You have to realize neither of us understood much about these supplements. We trusted the guy who sold them to us. That was our mistake. Being too trusting." Sam took another deep breath.

Sam was justifying his actions, still believing he was in the right. That had to have been obvious to Detective Dylan, but he didn't aggravate Sam by saying so.

What Sam was saying also helped me understand what had gone on with the different experiences that I and others had with the tainted herbs. There were *different* herbal remedies that had all been tainted. A large shipment from China, and they didn't even know what they were getting. It was an idiotic plan, but I still felt a sliver of empathy for Sam. He'd acted irrationally because he wanted to help someone he loved.

"We didn't know the shipment he sold us was tainted," Sam said. "We didn't realize it until Charles's distributor told him they wouldn't take any more. Said there was something wrong with it. Nobody was dying, though. Not until Anna. She was a health nut. I had her in my class a couple of years ago, and I'd see her at Blue Sky Teas after school. When she killed herself—"

He closed his eyes and breathed in the scent of the tea he held in his hands. He brushed a tear from his cheek before speaking again.

"When I heard she killed herself, I didn't believe it. She'd been acting erratically in the weeks leading up to it, but I assumed it was boyfriend problems making her paranoid. Teenagers have a lot of drama. But when I talked to her mom, I realized she was taking a 'brain booster' herbal formula that was supposed to help her focus on her schoolwork. She was responsible like that." He laughed, and more tears rolled down his face. "She didn't want to take any of the 'real drugs' some of the other kids were taking. Ironic, right?"

Ironic, indeed. I knew what had driven Anna to kill herself. Mercury poisoning, also known as "mad hatter disease." Hatmakers in the 1800s came in habitual contact with mercury, which was used to treat the felt in hat manufacturing. Many an alchemist had been poisoned by mercury as well.

"It wasn't your intent," Detective Dylan said.

"I told Charles, then, that we couldn't sell the rest of the tainted supplements. He'd been trying to find someone else to distribute them, but I said it had to stop. I thought he agreed with me, but when Zoe Faust moved into that house, I knew he had no intention of giving up."

Max glanced sharply at me.

"Zoe Faust was involved?" Dylan asked, sounding surprised himself.

"She has an online shop called Elixir, with all sorts of apothecary items. The guy we bought the herbs from called himself an apothecary. I knew there had to be a connection. Charles told me he was going to work on her house because he was ready to go back to work and make an honest living. But when I looked her up, I knew that he was lying to me. I mean, who on earth would buy that house to live in? It gives 'fixer-upper' a whole new level of meaning. I suspected Charles found a sympathetic partner to buy the house."

"Why would you suspect that?"

"Oh, didn't I say? Because that house was the first place where we kept the shipment. It was abandoned and had a huge basement. I helped Charles make a false wall in the basement to hide the boxes. He knew the house wasn't going to be occupied, because he was paid to do an inspection when they were ready to put it on the market. He said there was no way, with everything wrong with it, that anyone would buy it. That house was the perfect location to store the shipment, which was another reason we thought our plan would be easy."

The lights! That explained the "haunted house" lights people had seen in the house when it sat empty.

Sam's suspicion of me also explained how it wasn't a coincidence that Charles Macraith had been killed at my house the morning after my arrival, but at the same time the murder and theft had nothing to do with me or Dorian. It was both related to me *and* not related to me.

"After Anna died," he continued, "we got spooked. We didn't want anything to tie us to that place. I'm a local history buff and had done a lot of exploring in the Shanghai Tunnels under the city, including finding some that nobody else knew about. Those tunnels were originally built to transport merchandise to downtown shops from ships docked on the river, but they hadn't been used for that in ages, and only a tiny fraction of the tunnels are open for guided tours. I thought the unused tunnels would be an ideal place to move the boxes. Charles and I thought that there, nobody would find them. I'd taken some of my students on a field trip to the tunnels, but never to the section where we hid the boxes. And just to be safe, I stopped taking the students on field trips to far-flung sections of the tunnels altogether."

"An officer was injured in the tunnels recently."

"Max Liu," Sam said quietly. "I really was sorry about that. It was a lot more work than we thought to move so many boxes to their new hiding place. Someone got suspicious and called it in, I guess. I couldn't let Max see me. I had to pull the deadfall lever. It was nowhere near the section of tunnel we were using, so I wasn't worried about him or anyone else finding our shipment."

"And Zoe Faust?"

"I told you," Sam said, "she bought that rundown house. Charles must have lied to me about giving up the business. I thought she was going to be his new partner."

"That's why you killed him?"

"He had to be stopped, or more people would die. I did what I had to do to take care of Olivia, but I didn't want any more innocent people to die."

"The day of Mr. Macraith's death, what happened?"

"I took some of the tainted herbs—the same ones Anna had taken. I went to his house, making up an excuse that I thought I'd left something. I put the herbal mixture in his coffee. He drank coffee so thick I didn't think he'd notice."

"But he did?"

"No. He didn't. But it wasn't as poisonous as I thought it would be. I had to follow him to Zoe Faust's house to finish… To do what had to be done."

"Why'd you steal from the house? To make it look like a robbery?"

"I know about history. When I saw those antiques and books, I knew they would be worth a lot of money. I was still hurting for money, so I took them. I didn't think anyone would notice, but then I heard someone coming, and I dropped a couple of things on my way out the back door. I never meant it to look like a robbery, though. I thought Zoe would be arrested and you'd find evidence linking her to Charles. But you didn't. That made me wonder if I was wrong that they were working together."

"Tell me about Brenda Skyler. Who you know as Blue Sky. Why did you make an attempt on her life?"

Sam sighed. "That wasn't my first choice. When it was clear you weren't going to arrest Zoe, I tried to take care of Zoe like I did Charles."

My breath caught. Max reached for my hand and gave it a quick squeeze. I needed it more than he knew. I now understood why I had detected a strange odor in my trailer after Brixton found "poison" that was actually the spice asafoetida. I had dismissed the feeling at the time, thinking it was merely an unpleasant mix of scent bottles Brixton had broken. I was wrong. Sam had tried to poison me.

"But she didn't drink it," Sam continued. "I didn't want to hurt Blue, but something had to be done. If I went to jail, who would look after Olivia? She was doing better after the treatment, but the cancer had come back once already." He laughed and shook his head. "I know Aunt Olivia can be brusque, but she's a good person. She believes the best of people. She actually believed Blue was paying me enough for me to cover the cost of the airline tickets and experimental treatment for her cancer. And the reason Olivia wears that red shawl all the time is because of its sentimental value. It was given to her by a group of women who knit clothing for cancer patients."

"So you framed Blue—er, Brenda—to protect your aunt."

"I knew Blue was hiding something from her past, the way she wouldn't even use a credit card, so I figured she was the best person to blame."

"Where are the rest of the books that are still missing?"

"I sold them."

I groaned. I closed my eyes, images of Dorian trapped in stone filling my thoughts.

"I told you I needed money," Sam was saying. "I drove a few towns over and sold them to a pawnshop. The guy gave me a decent price for some of the items. I planted the rest at Blue's house. Like I said, I wished I didn't have to do it. I'm glad she's okay."

Detective Dylan grunted.

"Is that all?" Sam asked. The same strange expression I'd noticed earlier was back on his face.

"That'll do for now."

"Good," Sam said. He swallowed the last of his tea. "Very good."

"You can get up now."

"No," Sam said, "I don't think I can."

"Oh no," I whispered.

Next to me, Max tensed. "What is it?"

"The tea," I said. "The special tea he asked for. It's—"

On the screen in front of us, Sam Strum vomited across the table and fell forward, his head hitting the table with an excruciatingly loud smack.

"Poison," I finished.

CHAPTER 39

I stayed up with Dorian, waiting for news about whether Sam would regain consciousness and be able to tell us more about where he'd sold the books he'd stolen. The police said they would investigate out-of-town pawnshops, but I didn't know if that would be soon enough. Dorian was running out of time.

While we waited, we learned that Sam had kept a container of poison disguised as tea, which he'd hidden in his fridge, explaining why I hadn't detected it when I was at his house. It was what he'd used on Blue and had tried to use on me.

Sam didn't make it through the night.

It was after midnight when I received a call from Max that Sam had passed away. Dorian limped to the kitchen to make hot chocolate. He was using blended cashews to create a creamy, comforting texture without dairy. While the mixture heated on the stove, he rooted through the fridge, settling on a plate of vegan éclairs he'd cooked earlier that week using whipped coconut milk to create the custard filling. French comfort food.

Sitting in front of the fireplace with Dorian, a cup of steaming hot chocolate in my hand, I watched the light of the fire flicker over the gargoyle's gray profile. The hardened stone progression was accelerating. Most of his left leg had now turned to stone. The same progression was beginning in his left arm. The fingers of his left hand hung stiffly, as if attached to invisible splints. The plate of éclairs sat untouched in front of him, slowly melting from the warmth of the fire.

"It is over for me," Dorian said, holding up his stiff hand in front of the fire. "I thank you, Zoe Faust, for trying to save me."

"It's not over," I said. "I don't accept that. I'll be back in a minute." I found my laptop and brought it back to the living room.

"What are you looking for?" Dorian asked.

"Pawnshops."

"They will not be open in the middle of the night."

"No," I said, "but we can create a list of them. Since we can't tell the police about the urgency of finding out what happened to *Not Untrue Alchemy*, I don't know how soon they'll look into it. But there's nothing to stop us from calling shops ourselves in the morning. How many pawnshops could there possibly be?"

As it turned out, there were a lot of pawnshops. I'd done the impossible before, so I wasn't going to let that stop me. I moved to the couch to get comfortable for a long night.

The next thing I knew, I was lying down, listening to a tapping sound. Not rain. The noise was different. It was the sound of fingers tapping on a keyboard. I opened my eyes, sat up, and stretched. I'd fallen asleep on the couch.

The fire had gone out, but Dorian had pulled a blanket over me. Though the room was dark, I felt that the sun was rising. It was nearly dawn.

"*Bonjour*," Dorian said, looking up from his perch at the dining table. "I have created a spreadsheet. There are some *magnifique* computer programs these days. They have helped me narrow the search to eighty-four pawnshops you should try."

~

By the time I'd had a tepid bath, drank a fruit smoothie, and taken a walk to clear my head, some of the pawnshops were open.

Since the title of the book was written in Latin on the cover as *Non Degenera Alchemia* in a script nearly unreadable to most people today, I wasn't optimistic about finding a storeowner who remembered the book by its title. But I had to try. I figured if anyone remembered buying a set of rare, old books the previous week, I could follow up and show them a photograph of Dorian's book.

While I sat at the dining table and made phone calls, Dorian plied me with food and drink to keep me going. Plenty of tea to wet my parched throat, dried blueberries plumped in creamy millet cooked in almond milk as a mid-morning snack, homemade chocolate truffles as a pre-lunch pick-me-up.

It was mid-afternoon before my ears perked up at what I'd heard on the other end of the line.

"You remember the book?" I repeated, standing and motioning Dorian over to me. I put the phone on the speaker setting.

"I know books," the man said. "Used to be a rare book dealer, back in the day. Now *that* was a fulfilling job. Strange clients, sure, but in an eccentric way. Not like the creepy characters I see nowadays. One guy even tried to sell me a knife that had blood on it! Can you believe that?"

"Um—"

"I told him, you've gotta wash off that blood before I'll take it. Can't expect me to be cleaning up other people's messes."

"You *took it?*" I asked. I knew I should have been steering the conversation back to the book, but after a statement like that, the words were out of my mouth before I could think.

"Sure. It was a great knife. Strange that the guy never came back for it. I made me a couple hundred dollars off it."

"About the books—"

"Oh, right, I got off on a tangent there. Yep, I used to be a rare book dealer, back when you could make a living doing such a thing. I know there are some folks who still do it, but the money isn't there anymore."

"Uh—"

"What book was it you were asking about?"

"*Non Degenera Alchemia.* It looks like a seventeenth-century book. It would have been sold to you with a few other historical alchemy books."

"Right, that's why I remembered it. Alchemy. Strange subject. Most books I see on occult subjects are modern books pretending to be old, but these ones were truly antique. Yep, I bought three alchemy books from a young fellow who'd recently inherited them. He didn't want to get them back; wanted to sell them free and clear."

"Can you save them for me behind the counter?" I asked, beaming at a wide-eyed Dorian. "I can be there in two hours."

"Oh, I don't have them."

"Wait, you don't?"

"Nah. Like I said, they were a good find. A couple days ago, someone bought them all. If I'd known there would be other interested parties, I would have held out for more money."

"I'll give you a finder's fee if you help me locate the buyer so I can buy the books."

"Wish I could help you, but he paid cash and didn't leave a name."

Dorian's wings flew out from the side of his body, knocking over a chair.

"Everything all right there?" the pawnshop owner asked.

"Fine," I said, staring at Dorian's shocked face. "Thanks for your help." I clicked off the phone.

Dorian's body shook. *"Mon livre,"* he whispered. "It is truly gone forever."

"There has to be another way," I said. "There has to be."

"I—" Dorian began, but was interrupted by a knock on the door.

"You'd better hide," I said. "I don't want you turning to stone. It's too risky. Go to the basement."

Dorian's face registered alarm. "I cannot seem to lower my wings."

The knock sounded again.

"Zoe?" It was Brixton's voice. "I'm here with Veronica and Ethan."

"One second!" I called. "Dorian, I'll help you down the basement stairs."

He nodded. I could see the fear in his watery black eyes.

After getting him into the basement, I opened the door for the kids. "Sorry, I was in the middle of cooking. Come on in."

Brixton raised an eyebrow as they walked inside.

"You went to school today?" I asked them, noticing their backpacks.

"Our parents said it was best if we went back to life as normal," Veronica said. "Did you hear about what happened to Mr. Strum at the police station?"

I nodded.

"I can't believe it," Brixton said. "I mean, if you can't trust someone like him, who can you trust?"

"It's like all anyone's talking about," Veronica said.

The entitled Ethan hadn't spoken, walking straight past his friends to the dining table, where he opened his laptop.

"I don't mean to be rude," I said, "but I've had a long day. Was there a particular reason you stopped by?"

"We thought you'd want to see this, Zoe," Ethan said.

"We could have texted you earlier," Brixton said, "but Veronica thought you'd give us some food."

Veronica elbowed him.

"Coming right up," I said, laughing at the resilience of youth. I returned from the kitchen with a platter of mini chocolate éclairs to find the three of them sitting around Ethan's laptop.

Veronica took an éclair and beamed at me. "Show her, guys."

Ethan turned the laptop around, showing me the screen. The browser was open to the website of an antiquarian bookshop based in Seattle. It showed a photograph of Dorian's book.

"How did you—" I began.

"Ethan is good at finding stuff online," Brixton said, not trying to hide a wide grin.

"I get bored during class," Ethan said with a shrug. "Brixton said this book meant a lot to you, and we heard today that Mr. Strum had stolen your stuff and wouldn't be able to tell anyone what he'd done with it. I thought I'd make it my project for the day. I found it during fifth period."

"I don't know what to say, Ethan," I said. "*Thank you.*"

"I hope you've got a credit card with a high limit," Brixton said. "You do, right? For your business?"

"Why?"

"Look at the asking price," Brixton said, pointing at the screen. It was a figure far greater than I had access to. My elation from moments before disappeared.

"Won't the police get it back for her?" Veronica asked. She took another éclair as Ethan turned the computer back around to face him.

"They probably can," I said, looking at Brixton, "but it might take a long time to go through those channels."

Going through the legal system to retrieve stolen property from an innocent business person was going to be a nightmare. And one that would take far longer than Dorian had. It was going to be hard enough to use what Ivan and I had realized about the book to stop Dorian's deterioration. I had even less faith that I'd be able to reverse the effects once he'd turned completely to stone.

Brixton's smile faded. "More bureaucracy? Blue is still in jail, and you don't get your stuff back? This is totally screwed up. Maybe if we call Max—"

"I doubt there's anything he can do." I sat down at the end of the table and put my head in my hands. "But thank you, Ethan. Thank you all for trying."

"It's done," Ethan said, leaning back and smiling. He popped an éclair into his mouth.

"What's done?" Veronica asked.

"See for yourself, V," Ethan said, pointing at the screen.

"No way," she said. "You *bought it?*"

"Of course I bought it. What else is my dad's money good for if not to thank the person who saved us from that cell?" Ethan shivered as he spoke of it. "Do you want to drive to Seattle by seven o'clock tonight to pick it up, or should I ask them to send it by express mail?"

CHAPTER 40

It was nearly ten o'clock by the time I got home.

I made good time on the three-hour drive to Seattle, including having the good fortune to avoid the speeding ticket I deserved. Finding the book dealer's shop was another story, but he generously agreed to stay open later so I could retrieve the book. Ethan paid enough for the book that he really had no choice.

I was thankful for Ethan's generosity, but I knew I couldn't accept it. As soon as I got my alchemy lab into proper shape, I'd transmute some lead into gold. Either that or become a much better businesswoman.

Brixton had wanted to accompany me on the drive, but I thought it best not to subject him to my anxious mood and the high speeds I planned on testing out in my old truck. The speedometer went to one hundred, and although I'd occasionally driven fast on the open road, most of the time I'd had the truck it had been attached to my trailer. It was time to test my truck, and it came through.

I slammed the door of the truck and rushed to the house, cradling the book in my arms. I left Dorian doing yoga stretches while reading the newspaper—two forms of distracting movement were better than one. As I came through the door, he was nowhere in sight.

"Dorian?"

"*Aidez moi!*" The panicked voice came from the kitchen.

I found him standing on his stool, facing the counter. His wings were askew, one of them partially unfurled as stone.

"Can you move?" I asked.

"I am so glad you have returned. My fingers are too stiff to properly stir the batter for these crepes! There are lumps. Lumps!"

I smiled to myself. I'd gotten home in time.

"We have more important things to do than make crepes," I said. "Get down from there and come with me to the basement."

With what Ivan and I had pieced together about backward alchemy, I had a much better idea about what I should look for in the book. I didn't have as many ingredients in my laboratory as I would have liked, nor did I have a full understanding of backward alchemy, but tonight I was going to perform a quick fix. I never thought I'd hear myself say that again, but that was the very nature of backward alchemy's death rotation: sacrificing one element for another to skip the laborious process of true alchemy.

My vibrant herbs were the sacrifice. They had been lovingly cared for, which gave them power. Turning the pages of *Not Untrue Alchemy* with shaking hands, I found a section that suggested, in coded illustrations, how to use mercury to dissolve plants without going through the usual steps that required weeks or months.

For the next two hours, I crushed and extracted the essences of the fresh herbs, working backward by beginning with fire. The resulting ashes weren't the true salt that alchemists strive to achieve, but was none-the-less salt. Of the three essential ingredients of alchemy, mercury is the spirit, sulfur the soul, and salt the body. Salt was what I needed to save Dorian's deteriorating body.

I didn't know if this strangely transformed salt should be ingested or topically applied, so I tried both. While I dissolved the salt in a tea-like decoction, I also made a paste to cover Dorian's skin. The gargoyle eyed the gooey paste skeptically, so we tried the tea first.

At nearly the stroke of midnight, the stone pieces of Dorian's body began to shimmer. His stone leg returned to gray flesh, granule by granule. He was able to move, but the skin on his leg was a lighter shade of gray than it had been. He wasn't the gargoyle he once was.

He smiled and hopped up into my arms to give me a hug. Terribly undignified for a Frenchmen, and my back nearly gave out under the heavy weight of his stone body, but I wasn't complaining.

"I knew, Zoe Faust, that I could count on you."

I hugged Dorian back, happy he couldn't see the mixed emotions flashing across my face. Though relief was at the forefront, worry was close behind. The unnatural alchemy I'd performed to stop Dorian's deterioration was a quick fix that hadn't fully healed Dorian. It wasn't a real cure. There was much more I would need to do to discover the book's secrets and stop Dorian's body from once again becoming a stone prison.

"This isn't a cure, you know," I said, setting Dorian down. "There's more work to be done."

"You said this book is backward, and takes from other life forces?"

"There's still a lot I don't understand, but that appears to be the case."

His snout quivered. "Does this mean," he said slowly, speaking barely above a whisper, "that I am evil?"

"No," I said, shaking my head and feeling tears well up in my eyes. "It doesn't mean that. I don't yet understand what brought you to life, but the gargoyle you are—the gargoyle I know—isn't evil."

"Someone else did not have to die to bring me to life? Only the plants?"

I hesitated. "Nobody died for this temporary fix. That much I know. As for a permanent solution… I wish I knew, Dorian. I'll figure it out, though. I promise."

I knew I should be happy in the present moment. Dorian was safe. But for how long?

~

The following week was a blur.

Blue was out on bail. Charges had been filed against her for the illegal things she did to change her identity, but Max thought there was a good chance she'd only get probation.

When I stopped by Blue Sky Teas, Blue greeted me with a proposition. She'd heard about what a great cook I was, and also that I was underemployed. She made me an offer to bake vegan treats for the teashop. I happily accepted on the spot, without consulting Dorian. I knew he'd love the idea of yet another excuse to experiment with recipes, plus it could be his contribution to the huge food bills I was incurring.

Nobody could believe what Sam had done. Once people heard he'd done it for his aunt, they realized it made a certain kind of sense. But when they remembered his aunt was curmudgeonly Olivia, it again made less sense. Olivia hadn't made an appearance at the teashop, so nobody was sure how she was doing.

Brixton was more dedicated to keeping Dorian's secret than ever, and he was enjoying the cooking lessons the gargoyle was giving him. I think he even appreciated the weeding he was doing for me. As we prepared the yard for spring planting, he peppered me with questions about plants and alchemy.

He, Veronica, and Ethan said they had given up their tunnel explorations, as well as every other type of dare they used to come up with for each other. I wasn't sure how long that would last, but I was pleased it sounded like the kids wouldn't get into too much trouble for a while.

Dorian was in denial that his health would again begin to deteriorate, so I was left to my own devices to decipher the book. Well, I wasn't completely on my own. Ivan was eager to help. Although he didn't know I was a true alchemist or that Dorian existed, he was happy to have found a fellow enthusiast of the history of alchemy. He'd been depressed after being forced into his early retirement, so he was overjoyed to have an ongoing alchemy project that would drive his passion to finish his book.

~

I was getting ready to return a two-foot-high stack of library books when Max Liu appeared on my doorstep.

Looking at him through the peephole, I paused with my hand on the doorknob. I pressed my forehead to the door and closed my eyes. *Should I open the door?* My heart beat a little quicker as I remembered his kiss. The electrifying kiss that I'd pulled away from.

He and I could never work. Rationally, I knew that. But that was my problem. I wasn't as rational as I wanted to believe. I tried to take a sensible course of action, living on the road, staying away from attachments, and giving up alchemy after it caused me so much pain. I'd once transformed myself accidentally, becoming an accidental alchemist. Maybe, just maybe, I was finally ready to transform myself on purpose. Here in Portland, I'd found a place that made me want to stop running from myself. I didn't know what would become of me, but I was open to the possibilities.

I took a deep breath, opened my eyes, and turned the doorknob.

"Peace offering," Max said, holding out a bundle of fragrant jasmine green tea. In his other hand he held a canvas bag with greens poking over the top.

"Peace offering for what?"

"I was way out of line the other day," he said. "First at your dinner party, and then in the tunnels. I was just so happy to see that you were okay—"

"I accept your apology for how you acted about my herbal remedy at the dinner party." I took the tea and ushered him inside, giving me a second to think. "As for what happened in the tunnels, there's no need to apologize."

"But your boyfriend..."

I let the question hang in the air for a moment. His assumption gave me the perfect excuse, but I no longer wanted it. "I was being serious when I said he's just a friend. Veronica has an overactive imagination. I have a friend who's French. That's it."

Max was smart. I thought it best to stick to the truth. By keeping things simple, I could do that.

"I was hoping that was true. In that case, could I cook you dinner?" He held up the bag with greens poking over the side and gave me an endearing smile that hovered between confident and shy. "I'm not nearly as good a chef as you are, but I feel bad about how your dinner party ended the other night. It's the least I can do."

I felt warmth rise in my cheeks. "I'd like that very much."

Max paused on our way to the kitchen. Something in the living room had caught his eye.

"What is it?" I asked. "Don't tell me there's something else falling apart in this house."

"You throw me off balance, Zoe," he said, breaking off with an embarrassed look on his face. "I mean that in a good way. It's your gargoyle statue. I could have sworn it scowled at me as soon as I made a move for the kitchen."

THE END

Get a free novelette and more recipes when you sign up for Gigi's newsletter. Scan the code below, or go to www.gigipandian.com.

Scan to subscribe to Gigi's newsletter!

Read on for Recipes and an Author's Note, followed by Book 2, The Masquerading Magician.

RECIPES

CHERRY WALNUT OATMEAL COOKIES (VEGAN)

Total cooking time: Under 30 minutes
Makes 12 cookies

Dry ingredients:

- 1 cup old-fashioned oats
- ¾ cup unbleached all-purpose flour
- ¼ cup coconut sugar or brown sugar
- 2 tsp baking powder
- 1 tsp baking soda
- ¼ tsp sea salt

Wet ingredients:

- ¼ cup maple syrup
- ⅓ cup olive oil
- 1 ½ tsp vanilla

Mix-in ingredients:

- ⅓ cup chopped walnuts (or substitute a favorite nut)
- ⅓ cup unsweetened dried tart cherries (or substitute chocolate chips or a favorite dried fruit, such as cranberries) *Tip: Even if you're not a fan of plain dried cherries, try them here at least once because this flavor combination brings out the best in them.*

Directions:

Preheat oven to 350. In a large bowl, combine the dry ingredients. In a smaller bowl, mix the wet ingredients. Stir the combined wet ingredients into the dry ingredients. Fold in the mix-in ingredients.

Place a sheet of parchment paper on a baking sheet. Form approximately 12 cookie dough balls with your hands, and place them on the baking sheet 2 inches apart. Bake for approximately 12 minutes.

KID-FRIENDLY GREEN SMOOTHIE (VEGAN)

Total cooking time: Under 15 minutes
Makes 2 servings

Ingredients:

- 1 green apple or 1 ripe green pear (use an apple for a tart smoothie, or a pear for a sweeter one)
- 1 medium cucumber, peeled
- ½ ripe avocado, skin and pit removed
- 1 ½ cups frozen broccoli *Tip: For creamy sweetness, frozen broccoli works much better than fresh.*
- 1 tsp fresh ginger, peeled (or more to taste)
- 1 heaping tbsp cacao nibs or unsweetened cocoa powder *Tip: If you use cocoa powder instead of cacao nibs, it will turn your green smoothie brown—similar to a chocolate milkshake.*
- 1 heaping tbsp peanut butter or almond butter
- Approx. 1 ½ cups of coconut water *Tip: You can find canned coconut water at health food stores, often in 11 fl. oz. cans that provide the perfect amount of liquid for this smoothie. If you can't find coconut water, substitute water plus a little bit of added sweetener of your choice.*
- Optional: a few fresh mint leaves

Directions:

Chop the above ingredients roughly, then blend together in a blender. Add more or less liquid depending on how thick you'd like it.

Variations for a less sweet smoothie:

- Greens substitution: a few leaves of fresh kale instead of frozen broccoli
- Protein substitution: a heaping tbsp of hulled hemp seeds or 2 tbsp soaked chia seeds instead of peanut butter *Tip: Unlike hemp seeds, chia seeds expand in water and benefit from soaking. Soak 3 tbsp dry chia seeds in ¾ cup water. Let sit for 10 minutes or longer, shake or stir the*

mixture to avoid clumping, then store in a sealed container in the fridge for up to a week.

- Liquid substitution: plain water instead of coconut water
- Additions: Lots of green vegetables work well in this smoothie, such as celery, spinach, and parsley—try out your favorites.

ROASTED BUTTERNUT SQUASH WITH LEMON TAHINI SAUCE (VEGAN)

Total cooking time: A little over an hour
Makes a side dish for 4, or a light main course for 2

Note: This is a great dish to serve meat-eaters who are skeptical that hearty vegan foods exist. The creamy, flavorful tahini sauce is a crowd-pleaser.

Ingredients for squash:

- 1 large butternut squash
- 1 large white onion (or substitute a smaller yellow onion; white onions are milder)
- 1 tbsp olive oil
- ½ tsp dried rosemary
- ½ tsp dried sage
- Salt and pepper to taste
- Optional: ¼ cup raw pepitas, a.k.a shelled pumpkin seeds
- Optional: paprika, for garnish

Ingredients for tahini sauce:

- ½ cup tahini *Tip: Tahini is a sesame seed paste. You can often find it in a jar in the peanut butter aisle or with Middle Eastern foods, but if you find it to be expensive or hard to find, you can always make your own from scratch. See www.gigipandian. com/recipes for a recipe to make tahini from scratch.*
- 3 tbsp fresh-squeezed lemon juice
- ½ cup water
- ¼ tsp granulated garlic (for a chunkier sauce, substitute 2 minced garlic cloves)
- ¼ tsp sea salt (or more to taste)
- Optional: cayenne to taste

Directions:

Preheat oven to 425. Peel butternut squash and cut into ½-inch cubes, discarding the seeds. (*Tip: If the squash is difficult to cut, pierce with a knife and microwave it for a minute or two to soften it.*) Peel the onion and chop roughly. Toss squash and onion with olive oil, then spread out on a parchment-paper lined baking sheet. Sprinkle spices on top. Bake for approximately 40 to 50 minutes, stirring once after 20 minutes.

While the squash mixture is baking, prepare the sauce. Whisk all the sauce ingredients together, then taste to adjust for salt and spice levels.

Tip: You'll most likely have extra sauce. It's a versatile sauce, which also works well as a salad dressing. Pour into a lidded glass jar and it will keep in the fridge for a couple of weeks.

Tip: You can use more or less water, depending on preferred consistency, keeping in mind that the sauce will thicken in the fridge.

Optional touch for a tasty garnish: Toast ¼ cup raw pepitas in a dry skillet on medium heat for a few minutes, until they begin to pop.

Tip: Always watch toasting nuts, as they burn quickly.

To serve: Transfer squash mixture to a serving bowl, drizzle with tahini sauce, toss pepitas on top, and sprinkle with a dash of paprika.

For more recipes and tips, visit www.gigipandian.com/recipes.

AUTHOR'S NOTE

Though this book is a work of fiction, *The Accidental Alchemist* is based on fascinating historical facts that were too good not to run with in fiction.

Dorian's "father," Jean Eugène Robert-Houdin, was a French stage magician who lived from 1805 to 1871. He's considered the father of modern magic, for donning formal attire and moving magic from the streets into theaters. The biographical information in the book is true—including the facts that Robert-Houdin was a clockmaker who stumbled across magic by accident, and that he was asked by the French government to avert a crisis in Algeria. He helped convince Algerian rebels that his "magic" was more powerful than that of local shamans, therefore impressing the Algerian mullah leaders and helping the French cause. Fiction takes over where Dorian enters his life; his autobiography does not include anything about bringing a stone gargoyle to life.

French architect Eugène Viollet-le-Duc (1814–1879) was a contemporary of Robert-Houdin. Viollet-le-Duc is famous for restoring Notre Dame Cathedral in Paris, not only repairing it but also bringing new life to the cathedral. It was he who added the gallery of gargoyles—technically "grotesques" or "chimeras" because they don't serve as functional water spouts.

I took the liberty of making the two men friends and having Viollet-le-Duc give a prototype stone gargoyle to Robert-Houdin as a gift. As far as history has recorded, no such exchange took place.

Nicolas Flamel was a fourteenth-century bookseller and scrivener in Paris.

He and his wife Perenelle donated large sums of money to charity, which Nicolas claimed was gold he had acquired through alchemy. The two lived exceptionally long lives for their time, and when their graves were exhumed years later, no bodies were found.

Many early scientists were alchemists who practiced their craft in secret. Isaac Newton was one such scientist who carried out alchemical experiments secretly, and it's speculated that a nervous breakdown Newton suffered may have been caused by mercury poisoning.

~

The Accidental Alchemist is very much my "cancer book." The month after my thirty-sixth birthday, I was diagnosed with aggressive breast cancer. The Elixir of Life was a powerful idea during that time, as was life transformation in general. For National Novel Writing Month during the year of my cancer treatments, I wrote a draft that became *The Accidental Alchemist*.

I've always loved all things mysterious, and have been fascinated by gargoyles from an early age. I run the Gargoyle Girl blog of mysterious photography (www.gargoylegirl.com) and had toyed with the idea of writing a gargoyle as a minor character in a book or a short story. When I began jotting down notes about Dorian, he refused to stay in the shadows.

The cooking thread of the book emerged because my husband and I had recently moved from a tiny apartment to a house with a large kitchen and a little bit of land in the backyard. A passionate gardener, my husband planted an organic vegetable garden. I took cooking classes, wanting to take advantage of the biggest kitchen I'd ever had, as well as the herbs and vegetables we were growing. I didn't expect it, but I fell in love with cooking.

After my cancer diagnosis made me take charge of my health, I taught myself to cook vegan meals from scratch that were just as good as—and often better than—anything I'd eaten before. Through a combination of more classes and experimentation, I discovered tricks that transformed foods into decadent savories *without using bacon*. Once I'd done that, I knew I was ready to write a book involving cooking.

I hope you enjoy the transformations in *The Accidental Alchemist*. Recipes, like life, aren't set in stone, so definitely try out your own variations on the recipes I've included here.

THE MASQUERADING MAGICIAN

BOOK 2

CHAPTER 1

Persephone & Prometheus's Phantasmagoria: A Classic Magic Show in the Modern World.

The giant poster was illustrated in the style of Victorian Era stage magic posters. Two figures faced each other from opposite sides of a stage, the larger one in a tuxedo and top hat, the smaller impish figure in a devilish red suit. The taller tuxedoed figure held a wand pointed upward toward an ethereal floating figure. The devilish man held a ball of fire in his hand.

I smiled to myself as Max and I made our way through the lobby, my fingers looped through his. Some things had changed since the Victorian era. The tuxedo-clad magician in the poster was a woman. Prometheus and Persephone were a husband-and-wife magic act with equal billing.

Their style reminded me very much of posters of King of Cards Thurston and Carter the Great, both of whom used ghost and devil imagery in their posters and shows to illustrate the motif that they were magicians able to control the spirit world. The ambiance felt more like Paris in 1845, on the day Jean Eugène Robert-Houdin took to the stage at the newly built Palais-Royal theater with his ingenious mechanical inventions and masterful sleight of hand. But this was a small theater near Portland's Mt. Tabor, over 150 years later. Seeing that poster made me feel like I'd been transported back in time.

I should know. I attended Robert-Houdin's show over a century ago.

Though I look outwardly like a woman in her late twenties with trendy dyed-white hair who's named after her grandmother Zoe Faust, the truth is far different. Long before I bought a run-down house in Portland, Oregon, three months ago, I was born in Salem, Massachusetts. In 1676.

A shiver swept over me as a memory of a different time and place overtook me. Casually dressed Oregonians with cell phones in their pockets became formally attired members of society who would remember this performance for a lifetime.

Breathe, Zoe.

I willed myself to remember it wasn't a taut corset constricting my breathing, but my own nerves. I had thought tonight's opening performance would be the perfect way to spend time with Max after he'd been away, but could I trust myself with him? I couldn't tell him the truth about my past, no matter how much I wanted to. Maybe this had been a terrible idea.

Max pulled me toward the ticket-taker. I was holding up the line. I took one last look at the floor-to-ceiling poster in the lobby. Though the artist had done a wonderful job projecting the ghostly feel of the first phantasmagoria acts, down to faux-faded edges, there was a twenty-first-century addition: across the bottom, a garish yellow stripe contained a warning to theater patrons that any attempt to photograph the show with cell phones or other recording devices would result in expulsion from the theater.

I didn't have time to think more about whether I'd made a mistake coming here tonight. Almost as soon as we found our seats, the lights went down. The dramatic opening of Carl Orff's *Carmina Burana* sounded from speakers overhead. The music was in the spirit of the era they were invoking, even though it hadn't been composed until the 1930s. A spark appeared in the far corner of the darkened stage. It was barely noticeable at first, but a moment later, flames erupted from the back of the stage.

A wave of murmurs and stifled exclamations rippled across the rows of the theater. Max swung his head around, presumably looking for the fire alarm.

"Relax," I whispered.

"There's no way this little theater is safe for this kind of fire," he whispered back. "We need to—"

"It's only an illusion." I put my hand on his arm. "I promise."

Max's reaction didn't surprise me. No matter if he was on duty as a detective or not, he was always looking out for others. He settled back into his seat and gave me a sheepish grin before turning his attention back to the stage.

The flames followed a course, like dominoes. The tiny spark that had ignited in one corner of the stage as a slow simmer was now a full-blown fire that followed the path of a rope that appeared on the stage floor. The flames then snaked upward in a renewed fit of energy, as if being chased, jumping to a hanging spiderweb made of rope. The flames followed the woven web, tracing the intricate pattern like rabid mice in a maze.

I inhaled deeply, making sure I was right that this was only an illusion. I didn't smell fire. Smoke and mirrors. Or, more accurately, glass and lighting.

As the false flames approached the middle of the web suspended over the back of the stage, the music swelled, culminating in a crash of cymbals at the moment the fire reached the center.

"Ladies and gentlemen," a disembodied woman's voice boomed from offstage. "This display of fire is the handiwork of Prometheus. Never fear. I know how to handle him."

The illusory flames extinguished as abruptly as if a tidal wave had blanketed the stage. A small man dressed in a bright-red tuxedo, with spiky red hair that resembled bursts of flame, walked out onto the naked stage.

"Persephone," he said in a more powerful voice than his slight frame suggested, "you're no fun." He turned toward the audience, raising his hand to the side of his mouth as if about to impart a secret. "Don't mind her. But don't be too hard on her either. I'd be in a grumpy mood too, if I had to spend time in the Underworld."

He turned his head toward the darkness offstage, the direction from which the disembodied woman's voice had come. I knew that's where he wanted us to look, so I looked elsewhere, wondering what would come at us next. I tilted my head upward, toward the lights above the stage.

And froze.

It had definitely been a mistake to come here tonight.

Prometheus turned back to the audience, but my own eyes darted back to the catwalk of lighting equipment above the stage as my hands gripped the armrests. I couldn't believe what I was seeing. No, that's not true. I completely believed it. I didn't *want* to believe it.

Max leaned over and whispered into my ear, "What's the matter? Were you wrong about this being an illusion?"

I shook my head. "Just my imagination," I whispered. I forced myself to pull my gaze from the catwalk. To look away from Dorian. Things could get very ugly if I called attention to the interloper.

My friend stood in the shadows high above the stage, watching the show from above like Quasimodo or the Phantom of the Opera. It wasn't that he didn't have the money to buy a ticket and sit in a proper seat. Dorian Robert-Houdin couldn't show himself in public. He was a gargoyle, once made of stone before he was unintentionally brought to life 150 years ago by Jean

Eugène Robert-Houdin, the "Father of Modern Magic" in more ways than anyone realized.

What was Dorian thinking? What if someone saw him?

I felt an overwhelming urge to protect him. Should I act? What could I do? He and I were two misfits, surprised to find ourselves partly immortal through alchemy. I'd accidentally unlocked alchemy's greatest secret, the Elixir of Life, at the turn of the eighteenth-century. The years that followed were filled with crushing pain from the loss of those I'd loved, but also unsurpassable joy from the time I'd been able to spend with them. In the last three months, Max and Dorian had quickly become important to me. How could I deal with Dorian without alerting Max to the existence of a living gargoyle?

I glanced around the theater. The thudding of my heart filled my ears as loudly as the cymbals that had sounded moments before. It faded ever so slightly as I realized that nobody else had noticed the three-and-a-half-foot gargoyle watching from above. All eyes were focused on the stage. Thank God the entertaining performance was holding the audience's attention. So far. Prometheus was still speaking, carrying on the silly patter that's essential for a successful stage magician to master. *Carmina Burana* continued to play in the background, its intense vocals adding effective background suspense, but the volume had lowered as the magician spoke.

I pulled my eyes from Dorian as a woman in a black tuxedo stepped into view. She crossed her arms and raised a theatrically painted eyebrow at Prometheus.

In lacquered black high-heeled shoes that shone brightly under the spotlight, she stood more than six feet tall. Instead of the typical leotard or evening gown you'd expect to see on most women on the stage of a magic show, she wore a tailored tuxedo with tails down to her knees. Sleek brown curls adorned her head in the heavily styled waves popular in the 1920s, and bright red lipstick made full lips stand out on a pale face. If it had been a century ago, I would have described her face as handsome. Broad-shouldered and bold, she held herself confidently. With a top hat in her hands, she was elegance itself.

"I am Persephone," her voice boomed. "Perhaps you've heard of me. I'm Queen of the Underworld. But don't worry. I'm also the Goddess of Spring Growth. We Greek gods are difficult to pin down, I know. Since this week marks the first week of spring, you get to see a benevolent Persephone tonight. It's Prometheus you need to worry about. But I'll protect you from his fire-starter tendencies."

"She's quite dramatic, isn't she?" Prometheus said, stepping forward out of the shadows. If ever there was a contrasting duo, it was the two figures on the stage. Where Persephone was large and powerful, Prometheus was a puny wisp of a man. Not frail, though. Even from where I sat several rows back, I could tell he had the lithe body of an acrobat. That was good. The audience would want to keep an eye on him instead of looking around—and up.

"I'm warning you, Prometheus," Persephone said. "No fire games for these good people tonight. They've come to see a classic magic show. I will impress them with my prestidigitation."

Prometheus snapped his fingers. A crackle far greater than the sound of snapping fingers echoed as a burst of flame shot from his fingertips. Simultaneously, a roar of flames surged through the stalk of a potted fennel plant in the back of the stage. The flames stretched upward.

It was only a matter of time before people in the audience looked up and saw Dorian.

If he was spotted, would he have the sense to stand perfectly still and pretend to be a stone gargoyle placed there as a joke? Or would he try to run? I hoped it wasn't the latter. Dorian was no longer the swift creature he'd once been. His body was slowly returning to stone. This night was a rare break for me from my research and experimentation with the secrets of *Non Degenera Alchemia*—*Not Untrue Alchemy*—the book Dorian hoped could save his life. He'd stowed away in a crate from France just to find me, but three months of alchemy work had yielded few results. After so many decades of denying my gifts, my gifts were now denying me.

I'd discovered a quick fix, a Tea of Ashes that temporarily reversed his deterioration. But if I failed to find a permanent solution, a fate much worse than death awaited my friend. Soon, Dorian would be fully awake but trapped in an unmoving stone body—and I didn't know if the condition could be reversed.

I stole another glance at Dorian. He was no longer stock still. I let out a breath of relief as I saw him inching slowly along the catwalk toward the wings. At least, that's what he was trying to do. One of his claws caught in the metal latticework. It was the foot that had been giving him trouble. He tugged at his leg with his hands. My chest tightened when I saw what was happening.

Dorian's clawed hands flailed as he lost his balance. I clutched the armrest, expecting to see him fall onto the stage in front of over a hundred onlookers.

CHAPTER 2

On the stage, Prometheus's illusory flames flickered and grew. High above, Dorian's hands flailed wildly at his sides.

I held my breath and considered what sort of distraction I could create to prevent people from noticing a three-and-a-half-foot gargoyle crashing into the audience.

Before I could act, Dorian caught hold of a metal railing and steadied himself. He stood perfectly still. If anyone looked up, they would assume he was simply a stone gargoyle. A carving that resembled the "thinker" gargoyle of Notre Dame de Paris, with wings folded behind broad shoulders and small horns poking out on top of his head, was certainly an odd choice for a catwalk decoration, but everyone knew theater folk were an eccentric bunch, right?

I swallowed hard. How could he be here? Dorian knew how important it was that he not be seen. It was difficult enough to keep his existence a secret without him appearing above the crowd of a sold-out show.

I also understood the impulse. The gargoyle was homesick. He couldn't resist the lure of a magic show with posters showing a classic performance more reminiscent of Belle Époque era Paris than dot-com era Vegas.

Persephone pointed a red-tipped finger at Prometheus. The fennel flames extinguished. Like a phoenix rising from the flames as it renewed itself, a metal tree sprouted from the top of Prometheus's head, pushing through his spiky crimson-tipped hair. The trunk inched upward, and green leaves emerged from the trunk.

"What are you doing?" Prometheus sputtered, holding onto his head as if the roots of the tree pained him as the metal branches continued to grow. "Fire is supposed to bring death and destruction, not *renewal*."

"Is it not all connected?" Persephone replied. "Your fire fed the soil for this tree to grow. This is your own doing."

Prometheus moaned as the mechanical tree grew slowly but methodically until it was over a foot high. Prometheus shook his head, causing a few of the false leaves to fall to the stage floor. In place of the leaves was an orange. Persephone walked across the stage, the tail of her black tuxedo flapping behind her, and plucked the orange from the two-foot tree now sitting atop her partner's head. This illusion was one that Jean Eugène Robert-Houdin had created—as Dorian must have realized too. That's why we were here on opening night. I wanted to see a classic stage show like the ones I remembered from a distant past, from a happy time that had been far too brief. I couldn't fault Dorian for wanting the same thing, especially since the gargoyle had a stronger connection to the great magician than anyone.

The posters hadn't been misleading. The suspense here was much more subtle than most modern shows I'd seen, building slowly and holding our attention with wonder rather than demanding it with glitz.

Of course, I couldn't tell my date that I'd actually seen the illusion performed by its original inventor well over a century ago.

Perhaps coming here tonight had been a bad idea. Perhaps it had *all* been an awful idea.

I couldn't worry about that now. I was too terrified that someone would see Dorian. I felt the warm pressure of the heavy gold locket I wore on a chain around my neck. I couldn't let this happen. *Not again.*

It was times like these I felt foolish for thinking I could have a normal life here in Portland. But I was so tired of running. Finding a community where I fit in seemed too good to be true. As did meeting a man whose herbal gardening skills rivaled mine and was handsome and intriguing to boot. Max Liu was dangerous for the same reason that he wasn't dangerous. He was simultaneously alluring and safe. A rational detective who'd learned the teachings of his grandmother, an herbalist and apothecary in China. He was in his early forties, single after his wife died years ago. Losing her caused him to live his life in the present rather than the past, and part of this mantra made him avoid all talk of the past. It was one of the reasons it was easy to spend time with him. He didn't push me to open up about a past I could never make him understand.

But I knew Max and I would never work in the long run, because even if he accepted me for who I was, he would continue to age naturally while I never would. Yet, I could imagine myself comfortably settling into life with him and the many friends I'd made here in a short time.

Persephone bantered with the crowd while she peeled the orange she'd plucked from the miraculous orange tree. This wasn't as elaborate an illusion as Robert-Houdin's original, but the audience was captivated. Persephone threw the peeled orange into the audience. A young man I knew caught the fruit.

"It's real!" he shouted, holding up the orange.

My young neighbor Brixton was attending the show with his friends, sitting several rows in front of me and Max. Dorian had gotten both of us excited about the classic magic act, and Brixton had convinced his friends Ethan and Veronica to attend the show.

Fourteen-year-old Brixton was the one person in Portland who'd learned my secret and Dorian's. It hadn't been on purpose, and I'd been terribly worried about it at first, until events that winter had cemented his loyalty. At first he'd tried to convince Ethan and Veronica that he'd really seen a living gargoyle, but that was long behind us. I hoped.

"May I ask," Persephone said, "if there is someone here tonight who would like to escape from Prometheus's trickery? I can send you away to the Underworld, where you will be safe." She paced the length of the stage, the spotlight following her deliberate steps. "In this early part of the evening, the spirits are only strong enough to carry one of you. I'll do my best to protect the rest of you. A volunteer?"

"Brixton volunteers!" Ethan shouted, raising Brixton's arm for him. Brixton snatched it back and scowled at Ethan.

"Thank you, my young friends," Prometheus cut in, "but in this modern age, unfortunately I must insist on a volunteer who is at least eighteen." The mechanical orange tree was now gone from his head. I didn't see it anywhere. We'd all been paying attention to Persephone.

"How about closer to eighty?" The spotlight followed the voice and came to rest on two elderly men. A bulky man with gray hair and huge black eyebrows was grinning and pointing at his friend, a skinny throwback to the 1960s in a white kurta shirt and with long white hair pulled into a ponytail.

Persephone ushered the smaller man to the stage and asked him his name.

"Wallace," he said with a calm voice that struck me as out of place on the dramatic stage. "Wallace Mason." He wore the Indian-style cotton shirt over faded jeans and sandals. While most of the audience had dressed up, he looked like a man who thought the embroidered neckline on his shirt *was* dressing up.

Persephone continued an easygoing patter with the crowd, the spotlight remaining on her while Prometheus prepped the man. A minute later, the stage lights flickered. As they did so, an astringent scent assaulted my nostrils.

"The spirits are ready," Persephone said. "They have sent ether to carry my friend here to safety." She raised her arms, and Wallace Mason began to float. His white hair fell free of its ponytail and flowed past his shoulders. As his feet left the stage, the image of a flowing evening gown appeared over his clothing. The audience laughed.

"Forgive the spirits," Persephone said. "They think women are most worthy of saving."

I knew what was happening. I'd seen various versions of the Floating Lady illusion over the years. All of them involved someone—or their image—hovering high above the stage. Unfortunately, it was the worst possible illusion for keeping Dorian hidden from view. One of the audience members was sure to spot him.

The theater plunged into darkness. All that was visible was the ghostly, floating form of a confused man—and, for anyone who looked up, the shocked gargoyle above him.

A ripple of murmurs from the crowd followed. I looked around to see what people were looking at. When I looked back up, Dorian was gone.

I jerked my head around, searching for the gargoyle. Since a hefty stone gargoyle hadn't crashed onto the stage or into the audience, that meant Dorian must have freed his foot and scampered to safety. I hadn't imagined his presence, had I?

Max put his hand on my arm. "Don't worry," he whispered. "He's not going to fall."

I tensed, then realized Max was talking not about the missing gargoyle but the volunteer floating above the stage.

"I'm just tired," I whispered back. Max knew how hard I'd been working lately. He was under the illusion I was busy with my job and fixing up my crumbling house, not my true actions of working to save Dorian's life. Lying to those you care about is one price to pay for immortality.

I forced my shoulders to relax. Once Max's attention was back to the illusion, I looked up, toward the spot where I'd seen Dorian earlier. There was still no gargoyle. Only the ghostly image of the volunteer in a superimposed evening gown. Wallace Mason's floating image reached the catwalk—and disappeared into the ether.

The lights went out again. A moment later, Prometheus and Persephone stood in the center of the stage, the volunteer in between them. The magicians took his hands in theirs, raised their arms above their heads, and gave deep bows. I applauded enthusiastically, clapping as much for Dorian's escape as for the illusion.

During the brief intermission, I excused myself to use the restroom, when in truth I wanted to make sure there was no sign of Dorian. I knew Dorian, so I knew the types of places he liked to hide. There was no balcony in this theater, so I went to the adjacent alley but saw no sign of him. Hitching up my dress, I climbed the fire escape to the roof. No sign of him there either. I hadn't found him when the sound of accordion music wafted up through the vents, signaling that it was time to return to our seats. *Where was Dorian?* I reached my seat as the lights were falling.

"I really wish you'd leave your cell phone on," Max said, looking slightly annoyed.

"Didn't you see the signs in the lobby? Using a cell phone here is punishable by death." At least that got a smile out of him.

For the rest of the act, the magicians told the story of Persephone's powers as the Goddess of Spring Growth, who possessed the ability to bring the dead back to the living. A good story is one of the secrets of a successful magic show. Illusions are simply tricks if they don't tell a story. *Persephone & Prometheus's Phantasmagoria* was a dark fairy tale. The magicians knew how to lead their audience where they wanted them to go. I wished I could relax and enjoy the show.

When the lights went up at the end of the performance, I turned to Max, trying to think of how to excuse myself to look for my living gargoyle.

Max and I had met that winter, the very day I moved to Portland. It was now the start of spring, and Max had missed the first blooming flowers while he'd been out of the country in China to celebrate his grandfather's 100th birthday. When he'd returned a few weeks ago, there had been a change in him. He said he'd been busy with a case at work, but was that all it was? Going to the magic show together was our first date in over a month. But if Dorian was stuck somewhere because of his unmoving stone leg, unable to make it home...

"How about I make us a pot of tea back at my place," Max said. "I brought back some oolong tea from China with a flavor that's the most perfect blend of peaches and honey I've ever encountered."

The warmth in his dark brown eyes as he talked about one of his passions made me temporarily forget about Dorian. Max's straight black hair flopped at an angle over his forehead, reaching past his eyebrows. The unkempt look was sexy, but also unlike him. What had happened in China?

"I'm really tired," I said. "I know we haven't had a chance to catch up much—"

"Yeah, you've been distracted for half the night."

"I'm sorry, Max. I—"

"It's okay, Zoe," he said with a smile that didn't reach his eyes. "Besides, I'm sleep-deprived from a case I'm working."

I looked down at the green silk dress I hadn't worn in years. I'd pulled it out especially for this evening that I'd wanted to be special. The dress was one of the few items of clothing that hadn't been ruined when part of my roof collapsed during a brutal winter storm, only saved because it had been in storage in my Airstream trailer. The material was only slightly disheveled from my rooftop jaunt. I'm used to being careful with clothes, a habit from a time when they weren't so easily replaced. Max had dressed up too, in a slim-fitting black suit and the black-and-white wingtips I loved.

"It's supposed to be a gorgeous weekend," I said. "Why don't you come over for a barbeque in my garden tomorrow afternoon?"

At that suggestion, Max's withdrawn expression transformed into a genuine smile.

And so it was that instead of staying out with a man with whom I could never be completely honest, no matter how much I wanted to, I went home to a crumbling house where I hoped a gargoyle with a failing stone body would be waiting for me.

CHAPTER 3

I drove through the Hawthorne district of southeast Portland and eased my old truck into the driveway. I sighed as I looked at the gaping hole in the roof, covered with a tarp that flapped in the wind. One day I'd have time to fix the old Craftsman house.

A skinny figure dressed in jeans and a hideous velvet smoking jacket was waiting for me in front of the house.

"Zoe!" Brixton said. "It took you long enough. You *have* to listen to this."

Since Brixton wasn't my kid, I hadn't been expecting to see him in my house at ten o'clock at night.

"One minute, Brixton. Let's get inside. What are you wearing? You look like Hugh Hefner."

"Who?"

"Never mind."

I stepped across the creaking porch and opened the front door of my house. The diffuse light from a gold-colored Chinese lantern illuminated the corner of the living room, casting a mix of light and shadows across my green velvet couch and Dorian's stack of library books, which was nearly as tall as he was.

"Dorian?" I called out after Brixton closed the door.

A light peeked through the kitchen door, and I heard a rhythmic scraping sound.

I pushed through the swinging door and found Dorian stirring a steaming pot. As usual, the gargoyle stood on a stepping stool to reach the stove. He'd become a chef after serving as a companion to a blind former chef in Paris, who believed Dorian to be a disfigured man. Now the gargoyle was my room-mate. A secret one who didn't need a bedroom, but a roommate nonetheless.

I was glad to see him safe, but his calm countenance made me question what I thought I'd seen that night. A flash of irritation rose within me. I'd been abrupt with Max because I was worried about Dorian, and here he was acting as if nothing had happened.

"You're all right, Dorian?"

"*Ce n'est rien,*" Dorian said, continuing to stir the pot. "It is nothing. My leg merely stiffened from standing still above the stage for so long."

"You shouldn't have been there in the first place! What were you thinking?"

"Hey," Brixton said. "Didn't you hear me outside? Don't you want to hear this?"

"I have lived safely in the shadows for over one hundred and fifty years," Dorian said in his thick French accent, ignoring Brixton as well as he turned to face me. "I know what I am doing."

"But you've never had your body start reverting to stone before." I studied Dorian's legs. His left leg was a darker gray than the rest of his body and hung at an awkward angle with his clawed foot turned outward. Something was happening that we didn't yet understand. "You almost fell. And anyone could have seen you."

"Yet I did not fall, nor did anyone see me." He turned back to the stove and switched off the gas flame.

"You were at the show?" Brixton asked.

"It was not remarkable, yet it had some high points. Now will you fetch three mugs?"

The sulking teenager obliged, shoving his cell phone into his pocket and selecting three handmade pieces of pottery, painted with vibrant reds and oranges. I'd bought the mugs in 1960s New Mexico from the craftswoman who made them. I smiled to myself in spite of the situation. I had a small collection of mugs, but those were the ones most people were drawn to. They were my favorites as well. The craftswoman had instilled a loving energy into the clay, transforming a lump of raw materials into something both beautiful and functional. I thought of craftspeople like her as artisan alchemists.

Dorian poured the thick steaming liquid from his pot into the three mugs. He gave a start when he looked up at Brixton. "What is this vulgar jacket you are wearing?"

"Like it?" Brixton asked, his earlier agitation suddenly forgotten. "Veronica thought we should dress up for the show. I found this in the back of my mom's closet."

"Hmm…" Dorian handed Brixton his mug.

Brixton took a sip. "I don't know how he makes hot chocolate taste so good without milk or sugar."

"Cocoa elixir?" Dorian looked at me with innocent black eyes that wouldn't have been out of place on a puppy dog. "I know you have been feeling sick. *Alors,* I made your favorite."

"It's a good thing you're such a good cook," I said, accepting the mug. "You know how to bribe me." I took a sip of the rich, chocolatey drink. It had hints of coconut and cinnamon. "See, I've already nearly forgotten you almost got yourself found out tonight."

Dorian grinned and jumped down from the stool. He stumbled, but caught himself before he fell flat on the linoleum floor. "*Merde,*" he mumbled.

"You're due for another infusion of alchemy," I said, knowing better than to ask if he was all right. "The garden is doing well enough that I've got plenty of plants to create salts for your Tea of Ashes."

"I much prefer the flavor of my cocoa elixir," Dorian said.

Using a combination of mercury and sulfur, I was able to turn my hand-grown plants into a salt-like ash through an alchemical transformation described in Dorian's peculiar alchemy book, *Non Degenera Alchemia.* Salt was one of the three essential elements for alchemists. Mercury is the spirit, sulfur the soul, and salt the body. Dorian's soul and spirit were intact. It was his body that was failing him. My Tea of Ashes worked by temporarily fooling Dorian's body into thinking it had been rejuvenated with a true alchemical salt.

Alchemy is usually a long, drawn-out process. It can't be rushed. The discipline of alchemy strives to turn the impure into something pure, be it transmuting lead into gold or turning a failing body into an immortal one. It's as much about the alchemist as it is the ingredients. It's a personal transformation, done in isolation in one's own laboratory while following a series of natural steps that transform the elements. Using earth, air, water, and fire, you calcinate, dissolve, separate, conjoin, ferment, distill, and coagulate. You get out what you put into it. And alchemical transformations of the body can't be transferred to others—a lesson I learned the hard way a long time ago.

That's the way alchemy is *supposed* to work.

But the book that brought Dorian to life wasn't like that. *Non Degenera Alchemia* was backward alchemy, a dangerous alchemical idea that involved quick fixes. I speculated that's why the title wasn't simply *True Alchemy,* but instead the convoluted double-negative *Not Untrue Alchemy.* Drawing upon external life forces to shortcut nature, backward alchemy was the antithesis of true alchemy. The "death rotation" described in the book's coded illustrations and Latin text told of backward actions that took minutes instead of months, and began, rather than ended, with fire.

The quick fixes in the book showed me that I could use my energy, along with that of the plants I'd lovingly tended in my garden, to hastily produce the end product of ashes. But it wasn't a permanent fix. I had only scratched the surface in my understanding of the book.

"Is there enough for seconds?" Brixton asked.

Dorian smiled and topped off Brixton's cocoa. "It is too bad the magicians selected the orange tree automaton," he said.

"I thought that was pretty cool," Brixton said. "That was a real orange that grew from the metal tree."

"It was nicely done," I agreed. "You take offense that they stole the idea from the great Jean Eugène Robert-Houdin?"

"*Non.* I would have much preferred them to have re-created Father's pastry chef automaton."

"Of course you would," I said, barely able to suppress a smile.

"*Bon soir, mes amis,*" Dorian said, leaving his empty mug on the counter. He limped out of the kitchen. I presumed he was heading out on his nightly excursion. Since it wasn't a good idea for him to go out during the day, when it would be too easy for people to see him, he explored the city and surrounding forests at night. Lately his nocturnal jaunts had been limited because a portion of the city's forests had been overrun by treasure hunters. The brutal winter storm that wrecked my roof had also caused a mudslide that unearthed a portion of hidden jewels from a decades-old train heist. Poor Dorian now had to share the woods with clandestine treasure hunters.

"That was weird," Brixton said.

So much of my life was weird that I couldn't be sure which part he was referring to.

"Doesn't he always insist on cleaning up 'his' kitchen?" Brixton continued.

"I think he's embarrassed that we saw him lose control of his body."

"That's exactly why I thought you'd want to hear this." Brixton attempted to raise an eyebrow enigmatically, but ended up lifting both of them.

"Right! You wanted to tell me something. Sorry, Brix. What is it?"

"The magician Prometheus"—he paused for dramatic effect— "*is an alchemist.*"

I let out my breath and smiled. Brixton had an active imagination. Ever since he'd broken into my house and learned I was an alchemist, he'd seen alchemists everywhere. Well, perhaps not *everywhere*. But it had happened on more than one occasion.

"Don't you see?" Brixton said. "He could help you!"

Brixton knew I'd accidentally discovered the Elixir of Life in my twenties. Aside from my hair, which had turned white centuries ago, the Elixir prevented me from aging. He also knew alchemists weren't exactly immortal. Even though some of us have unlocked the secrets that transform energy into eternal life, we're flesh and blood and can be sickened or injured. With my herbal skills, sickness is less of an issue, but I have several scars that remind me how precarious life is.

It was typical of the young that Brixton had never asked me when and where I was born. He knew I used to run a shop in Paris in the early 1900s before returning home to the US and traveling around the country in my 1942 Chevy truck and my 1950 Airstream trailer. He'd never asked, as Dorian had, for the details of my birth and upbringing, so he didn't know I'd been born in Salem Village in 1676, or that because of my way with herbs and plants, I'd been accused of witchcraft at sixteen. Both I and the world had come far since then.

"Oh, Brix—"

"Why are you looking at me like that?" Brixton asked. "I'm telling you—"

"The same way you told me about Mrs. Andrews?"

"That was different." He scowled and busied himself with the mug of cocoa.

Brixton had sworn that one of our neighbors hadn't aged in ten years, from Brixton's first memories at age four to his current age of fourteen. I'd taken him seriously—only to find out the woman had gotten plastic surgery.

"And Jonas Latham?" I said.

Brixton scowled again. "Even though I wasn't right about him being an alchemist, I was right that he was up to something."

While riding his bike to my house, Brixton had noticed a man carrying laboratory supplies that looked similar to my alchemy vessels. As the man slipped into his garage, Brixton caught a glimpse of his "alchemy" lab.

Again, I'd given Brixton the benefit of the doubt. When I went to investigate, the police were at the man's house, arresting him. Brixton claimed it was a witch hunt and that the police had arrested him for being an alchemist. I asked Max about it, inquiring as a curious neighbor. It turned out the man had been running a meth lab in his garage.

A woman who had plastic surgery. Then a man dealing drugs.

"All right, Brixton. What is it this time?"

CHAPTER 4

"Um..." Brixton appeared suddenly fascinated with the crisscrossed scratches in the linoleum floor.

"Brix."

"Well, the thing is... He looks really familiar."

"He looks really familiar? That's all you've got this time?"

"This isn't like the meth dealer or Mrs. Andrews."

"You probably saw posters of the magic show online before it came to Portland," I pointed out.

"Would you let me finish? The magician is familiar from *history*. I swear I've seen him in a history book." He paused to lift the last coconut cookie from the magic-lamp-shaped cookie jar on the counter and pop it into his mouth.

"A former president, perhaps?"

"Not funny, Zoe. Not funny. I'm being serious!" With a mouthful of gooey cookie in his mouth, Brixton wasn't making his case very effectively. "You didn't recognize him? There's not, like, a registry of alchemists?"

"It doesn't work like that."

"Well, it should. How am I supposed to remember everyone I've seen in a history book?"

"If this man is an alchemist who's discovered the Elixir of Life, do you really think he'd choose a profession where he could be famous? Wouldn't that make it much more difficult for him to keep his secret?"

"I know you've been good at making sure you never get publicity or anything, but there are a lot of people with bigger egos than yours. People who want the attention. And don't you remember how he said he needed a volunteer of legal age 'in these modern times,' like he'd known *previous* times?"

I frowned. The magic show that night was straight out of the 1800s, it had sparked an uncomfortable sense of familiarity, and Prometheus clearly enjoyed the spotlight. Was it possible Brixton was right this time? I shook my head. "Living out of the spotlight isn't a matter of personal preference," I said. "It's about survival."

"Immortals are always famous in the movies—"

"Exactly. In the movies. Not in real life. There are only a handful of alchemists out there who've succeeded in extending their lives. They stay so well-hidden that I haven't managed to find a single one since I started looking earlier this year."

"Which is totally why it's awesome that an alchemist is here in town. You should invite him over to the teashop."

Brixton was right that I needed help, but if he was also right about this man being a figure from history, that meant this alchemist was a dangerous wild card. Before approaching him, I needed to know more. Not only whether Prometheus could be an alchemist, but if he could be trusted.

I tried to think about how best to explain my concerns, but Brixton was no longer paying attention to me. "That's weird," he said, staring at the screen of his phone.

"What?"

"Nothing. Just a website that got hacked." He tucked the phone into the pocket of his jeans.

"Don't go anywhere," I said. "I'll be right back."

I climbed two flights of stairs to reach my attic office. A three-foot section of the roof was missing, but had been patched with a quick fix—like everything else in my life these days. The attic flooring below the rooftop hole had collapsed too. The gaping hole, located directly above my bedroom closet, was now covered with a sturdy wooden plank and a Qalicheh Persian rug.

A combination of plastic, plywood, and decorative coverings kept the rain out until I could reverse Dorian's deterioration and resume work on the fixer-upper house. Saving Dorian's life was a bigger priority than saving the house from dry rot. Besides, this hole in the roof provided an easier way for Dorian to come and go from the house without being seen. Unlike the rooftop opening he used to squeeze through, this one was large enough that he could maneuver through it and replace the tarp even with a stiff leg.

With the storm damage, my attic office rivaled the basement alchemy lab as a work-in-progress. The top of the Craftsman house contained my public persona; the lower regions hid my private one: Zoe Faust, the twenty-eight-year-old proprietor of the online secondhand shop Elixir, a descendant of the woman who'd started an apothecary shop named Elixir in Paris in 1872; and Zoe Faust, the 340-year-old alchemist who'd accidentally discovered the Elixir of Life 312 years ago, and who ran an online business because she was no good at transmuting lead into gold.

Stepping past a collection of antique books on herbal remedies, a row of Japanese puzzle boxes, and the articulated skeleton of a pelican, I grabbed my laptop computer. When I entered the kitchen a minute later, the fridge door stood open but Brixton was nowhere to be seen.

Then the crown of his head popped into view from where he stood behind the fridge door, and he kicked the door shut with his foot. In each hand he was balancing a stainless-steel storage container with a platter of treats on top.

"The desserts wouldn't have run away in the few moments you took to come back for them," I commented.

"Yeah, that coconut cookie made me wicked hungry and I couldn't decide what I wanted. It's cool, right? Dorian said there was more than you two could eat."

I lifted the more precariously-perched platter with my free hand and led the way to the dining table.

"I already looked them up while we were at the theater," Brixton said. "I knew that magician looked familiar as soon as I saw him, but it wasn't until the intermission that I could use my phone without Veronica punching me. But then I couldn't find you to tell you. Anyway, the magicians Prometheus and Persephone are a married couple, Peter and Penelope Silverman. They didn't announce their secret identities or anything."

"Now you think they're *both* alchemists?"

He shrugged. "I only recognized Prometheus, but who knows? That's why you should look into it. With two alchemists helping you, that could totally save Dorian."

I opened the laptop while Brixton inhaled a piece of chocolate zucchini bread. Peter Silverman's website bio was short, but as a magician he was well-known enough that an online encyclopedia had listings for both himself and Penelope, who was both his wife and magic show partner. They were both in their early fifties, and Peter was the child of Marge and Herb Silverman of Silver Springs, Ohio. Penelope Silverman, *née* Fitzgerald, began her career as a circus performer and she'd been an expert lion tamer and knife thrower before she ran away from the circus to become a magician.

Peter and Penelope met in Las Vegas, where they each had their own stage show. Penelope's page had a photograph from her solo show, and Peter's showed an illustrated poster of their joint *Phantasmagoria* act, similar to the one I'd seen that night. Before the two met, both of them were struggling, performing only as opening acts or at hotels nobody sober would stay at. About five years ago, they'd become the marginally successful team of Persephone & Prometheus. There was nothing controversial except for one thing: Peter had once punched a theater patron for taking a photo of the show.

I looked again at the poster illustrations. Their likenesses were approximate, but not photographic quality. There were no photographs on either their own website *or* the external listings. That was odd. I typed in an image search. Hundreds of images of Penelope popped up, most of them showing her as a young woman in a skimpy costume with a whip. Though Penelope was stunning in her fifties, she'd aged normally.

But I couldn't find a single photograph of Peter Silverman.

"What is it?" Brixton asked.

"Nothing." I tried one more quick search, finding more of the same. Penelope had several social media accounts, but Peter had none.

"What are you looking at?"

I closed the laptop. "I'm sure your mom is worried that you're not home yet. Let me put your bike in the back of the truck and give you a ride home."

It was a fifteen-minute drive to the cottage where Brixton and his mother were staying while Blue was gone. Brixton slipped on headphones as soon as he sat down in the passenger seat, which was fine with me. I needed time to think.

Peter Silverman was hiding something. That didn't necessarily mean he was an alchemist. In fact, it was more likely to mean any one of a dozen other things that had nothing to do with alchemy. Maybe he'd changed his name to get away from a life of crime. Or perhaps he was running away from alimony payments. I briefly considered that he could be a hero in the Witness Protection Program, but they'd never let him appear on stage.

Whatever it was, it couldn't be good.

After I dropped Brixton off at the cottage, I selected one of my favorite songs to listen to on the drive home. I had installed a compact cassette player in the early 1970s, about thirty years after buying the truck. I had a sentimental attachment to the countless mixed tapes I'd made myself for my long drives across the country, so I'd never upgraded. I found the cassette that included "Accidental Life," a 1950s song by an artist who called himself The Philosopher. It combined a spiritual sound with the danceable rock rhythms gaining popularity in the fifties. What I loved most about it was how The Philosopher used his deep, soulful voice to tell the story of a man who wandered the earth for a thousand years. It wasn't only the lyrics that spoke to me; there are some voices that simply feel like home.

The song ended long before I pulled into the driveway. I drove the rest of the way home through side streets, enjoying the late-night silence. In the driveway, I took a moment to breathe in the crisp night air. The spring scents of cherry blossoms, daffodils, and hyacinths came on a gust of wind.

Inside, I walked through the house to check that all the doors and windows were locked. After being burglarized shortly after I bought the house, it had become my nightly ritual. Despite the break-in, this dilapidated house felt like a real home. Aside from my Airstream trailer that I'd lived out of for decades, this was the first place that had felt like home in the last century.

Just as I was about to turn off the kitchen light, I spotted a wooden spoon that had fallen in the crack between the Wedgewood oven and counter. I reached it easily enough, but paused before washing it. The scent of vanilla, cloves, and cardamom wafted up from the spoon, along with a scent I couldn't place. Though I'd been cooking for many more years than Dorian, he was the one who knew how to bring different flavors together in unexpected, complementary ways. Once I came to think of myself as worthy of a good life, I began using vegetables, herbs, and spices to make healthful meals. But my own purpose of cooking was to be healthy, not necessarily to enjoy the taste. Though I know how to dry high-quality herbs and spices for my alchemical transformations, and can create healing tinctures, teas, and salves, before Dorian entered my life I'd never thought about using the same ingredients to transform simple foods into heavenly masterpieces. My little gargoyle gourmet was a culinary alchemist.

These days, I'm considered a vegan. When I began eating a plant-based diet around the turn of the twentieth century, it was known as a Pythagorean diet, named for the mathematician Pythagoras, who advocated eliminating animal products from one's diet. Dorian was horrified when he learned I didn't stock bacon, butter, and heavy cream as kitchen staples. He'd been taught to cook with the traditional French methods, so learning to cook with the ingredients in my kitchen had been an adjustment. He rose to the challenge, though, and now declared that his vegan creations were the most impressive gastronomic feats in this hemisphere. Not only the best *vegan* creations, but the most delectable foods, *period*. I never said he was modest.

Dorian was still off on a nocturnal walk. He didn't need sleep, so after his nightly walks he spent the hours before sunrise baking pastries at Blue Sky Teas, slipping out before anyone saw him. Baking vegan treats for the local teashop was Dorian's contribution to our household expenses. Because nobody could know he existed, I was his front. Everyone besides Dorian and Brixton thought I was the chef who rose before dawn to bake fresh breads and delicacies. I hated all the lies I had to tell to fit into normal society, but this untruth provided a reasonable explanation for why I'd been so tired lately. With that thought, I yawned.

My last stop of the night was the basement. When I opened the door I kept locked at all times, my senses perked up. The second yawn that had been about to surface disappeared, replaced with a surge of adrenaline.

"Dorian?" I called out.

Silence.

I descended the stairs.

Standing on the bottom step, I had a full view of the room. The scent of home-brewed beer that had been so strong when I moved in had been gone for months, as were the putrid scents of my earlier failed experiments. After accidentally poisoning myself, I was now rigorous in my cleaning and storage of alchemical ingredients, and I kept the room locked at all times. Yet the harsh scent of sulfur dominated the basement. How could that be?

I stepped farther into the room, thinking I must have been so tired I couldn't smell straight. This wasn't sulfur. It was the pungent scent of cloves. No, that couldn't be right either. It must have been mold from an old book. Figuring out which one wasn't important right now. I had enough mysteries to deal with without worrying about the natural decomposition of an antique book. Besides, I couldn't be sure what I smelled. The only thing I felt sure of that night was that the perplexing odor came from a bookshelf in the far corner. I paused before turning off the light, with one last thought flitting through my mind: how strange it was that the scent seemed to be getting sweeter, rather than more foul, with age.

CHAPTER 5

When I walked into my kitchen sanctuary shortly after sunrise, Dorian was already there, wearing an apron and standing tall on his stepping stool as he fixed himself an espresso. I took a deep breath and savored the energizing scents surrounding me. A bowl of freshly made wild blackberry compote mingled with the fragrances of yeast from a loaf of sourdough bread in the oven and freshly ground French roast coffee beans. Next to the espresso machine sat two grinders, one for coffee beans and one for aromatic spices.

I tugged at the sleeve of my blouse, which was poking out from an ill-fitted sweater. I hated nearly all of the new clothing that I'd picked up at a local secondhand shop after my clothes were ruined. I supposed it was better the splintered wood had fallen into my closet rather than my bed, but I was unhappy nonetheless. I've never gotten used to wearing off-the-rack clothes. Even when ready-to-wear clothing supposedly fits properly, no two bodies are alike; it's impossible to get a perfect fit without tailoring.

I hitched up my high-waisted, oversize jeans to avoid tripping, but my superficial concerns were forgotten as soon as my gaze fell to Dorian's left foot. Not only was it fully stone, but another claw had broken off. Would it grow back after I healed him?

"Morning, Dorian," I said, hesitating to mention his foot. I also thought better of mentioning the fact that there was a chance there might be another alchemist in town. It was much more likely that Peter Silverman was a criminal hiding from his past; that would explain why he hated photographs and shunned social media. Dorian had a habit of overreacting.

"If you visit Blue Sky Teas today," he said, tamping down the coffee grounds, "you will see a new cake named after Brixton. I found a large patch of 'wild treasure' blackberries, which the boy loves. Brixton's Blackberry Bread will be on the menu." He turned from the espresso machine and his black eyes grew wide. "*Mon dieu.* I thought you were a morning person."

"That bad, huh?" I hadn't lived with another person in nearly a century. I wasn't used to making myself presentable before breakfast. I ran my fingers through my tangled hair. I gave a start as a clump of hair pulled out into my hand. *It was happening again.* I quickly tossed the hair ball into the trash. Thankfully, Dorian didn't appear to have noticed.

"I would be happy to make you an espresso. Perhaps one that is *très petite?*"

Dorian had ordered the espresso maker on my credit card—without asking me. Since I don't drink coffee, the existence of the contraption caused people to think I had a "friend" who stayed overnight. Brixton's efforts had cemented the gossip that I had a secret French boyfriend. Before he realized he needed to protect Dorian from the world, he'd tried to expose the gargoyle. Though I'd foiled Brixton's attempts to share a video of Dorian, he'd gotten a voice recording of Dorian's deep French-accented voice that he shared with his friends. I couldn't completely deny the existence of a Frenchman, so I made up a story about a platonic friend who was disfigured and therefore shy of meeting anyone new. It was a messy lie, and one I hadn't wanted to tell, but I'd had to act on the spur of the moment to protect Dorian. I especially hated that Max thought I was keeping a male friend from him, though technically that was the case.

"Thanks, but I'll stick with tea." Since the plants and drugs I put into my body affect me so strongly, I've never been able to drink coffee. Decaf would work, but then what's the point? The amount of caffeine in black tea, green tea, or chocolate gives me a boost without turning me into a Berserker. I got myself a glass of water and turned back to the sickly gargoyle. Even though the transformation was hurting me in ways that scared me, I knew what I had to do. "I'll do another plant transformation today, to make your Tea of Ashes."

"*Non.*"

"What do you mean, *no?* Your foot—"

"It is killing you, Zoe." He stepped, rather than hopped, down from the stepping stool. "You think I cannot see what is happening to you? I can no longer ask you to do this for me."

"You're not asking. I'm offering."

The gargoyle's gray lips quivered. "I do not wish us both to die."

"*Neither* of us is going to die," I said firmly. I didn't think it would help anything to mention the fact that if I died it would be a natural death—nothing compared to Dorian's tragic fate of being alive yet trapped in unmoving stone.

"You are a good woman, Zoe. I thank you for trying."

"Dorian—"

"*Un moment.*" He opened the oven door and placed the loaf of bread onto a wooden cutting board. "Do you not wish to tend to your *potager?*"

Though he suggested it to avoid a painful subject, he was right that I wanted to check on my backyard vegetable garden.

"I will be in the dining room with breakfast and the newspaper," Dorian said. "If you wish to join me and speak of other things, I would be happy to save some bread for you."

Denial wasn't healthy, but who was I to judge? I'd done it myself for decades. I desperately wanted to be able to heal Dorian, but after I'd run from alchemy for so long, I didn't know if I alone was capable of that. Was it worth it to speak with the stage magician, just in case Brixton was right?

I left Dorian to his espresso and zucchini bread and went to check on my two gardens: the indoor window-box herb garden and the edible plants in the backyard. Though I'd started my new garden in the midst of a cold and rainy Portland winter, I knew how to coax the best out of plants. Because I wanted to get a good volume in a short amount of time to create Dorian's Tea of Ashes, I'd planted several quick-growing herbs and vegetables, including lemon balm, parsley, leaf lettuces, spinach, sorrel, nettles, and fennel. Most of them could easily take over the garden if not harvested, but that wasn't a problem. The thriving plants gave me a few minutes of peace, but they didn't tell me what I should do about approaching Peter Silverman.

After making sure the plants were tended, I made myself a green smoothie in my vintage Vitamix with greens from the garden plus a green apple for sweetness and a knob of ginger for kick. I wholeheartedly believe that both cars and blenders were perfected in the 1940s. In the modern world of disposable everything, I missed the time when things were built to last.

I found Dorian sitting at the dining table, an empty espresso mug at his side and flaky crumbs from the freshly baked bread scattered across the entire table. Ever the gentleman, he'd saved a quarter of the small loaf on a plate for me.

Directly in front of him were *Le Monde* and two local newspapers. He'd been obsessively reading every word of *Le Monde* for months, ever since the French paper reported gold thefts from European museums. It was an important story to follow because Dorian and I believed the "thefts" not to be thefts at all, but rather the handiwork of unscrupulous alchemists who'd died centuries ago but left false gold behind. Unlike real gold that could be created by true alchemists, the shortcuts of backward alchemy could be used to create false gold. Because intent is important in alchemical transformations, and the intentions of these backward alchemists weren't pure, their false gold was now turning to dust. There hadn't been any recent developments, but after so many years living itinerantly, I enjoyed having newspapers delivered to my doorstep.

"Good riddance!" Dorian declared.

"Did I miss something?"

"This local newspaper reports the last of the treasure hunters have left. My woods can now go back to normal."

The woods near River View Cemetery were one of Dorian's favorite places for nocturnal exploration, and it caused him grief that so many interlopers were sneaking around "his" domain.

"Did someone find the hoard?" I asked.

"That does not appear to be the case." He chortled.

"What's so funny?" I looked over his shoulder. "*THREE INJURED IN FALL NEAR RIVER VIEW CEMETERY.* That headline doesn't sound very amusing to me."

"Not that dreary article." Dorian pointed a claw at another column. "The gossip columnist is much more dramatic, writing of monsoons and masterminds. *Écoute.*"

LAKE LOOT TREASURE HUNTERS GIVE UP HOPE.

> *Amateur treasure hunters from throughout the Pacific Northwest flooded to Portland in February, after monsoon-like rains led to the discovery of jewels from a 1969 train robbery. Two months later, those treasure hunters have abandoned their quest. Graphic images of injuries sustained by three men caught in a second landslide were leaked to the press. Since then, no treasure hunters have been seen on the hillside.*
>
> *A source close to the police department told this reporter that the photographs were purposefully released to scare other amateur treasure hunters away from exploring the cordoned-off area still considered a high risk for landslides.*

"What else does the columnist say of interest? Mmm... *Oui... Bon.*"

I took the newspaper from his hands.

"I was reading!" he protested.

"You stopped reading aloud. Let me do it."

In 1969, mastermind Franklin Thorne robbed the wealthy Lake family's private train car and killed guard Arnold Burke. Thorne was subsequently killed in a shoot-out with the police. Since the brazen train heist, the stolen jewels, dubbed the Lake Loot, remained elusive... until February of this year, when torrential rains caused a landslide in the hills near River View Cemetery. Days later, a sapphire necklace from the robbery was discovered near the Willamette River by two boys playing at the river's edge. Since the boys found this small portion of the Lake Loot, treasure hunters flocked to the area."

"Zoe," Dorian cut in.

I looked up.

He held out a clawed hand. "May I?"

"What's the matter with how I'm reading it?"

"Your voice lacks a certain *je ne sais quoi.*"

"I'm not reading melodramatically enough for you?"

Dorian blinked at me. "It is a dramatic story. It calls for a dramatic reading."

"Here." I handed over the newspaper.

Worried about another landslide, authorities blocked off the area and declared they would arrest anyone caught trespassing. But the lure of missing train-heist loot was too great. This announcement was clearly a misstep, one that simply caused the treasure hunters to return under cover of darkness, under more dangerous conditions that led to three men sustaining critical injuries. Was it the thrill of the chase that lured Oregonians to danger? If found, the distinctive jewels must be returned to their rightful owners, the Lake family, who have offered a small reward. Julian Lake, the 80-year-old survivor of the 1969 robbery, had no comment on recent developments...

"That's not the end. Why did you stop reading?"

"Forty-six years," Dorian murmured. "People speak of this as if it is a long time!" He tossed aside the newspaper and cleared the table.

It was time for me to descend the stairs to my basement alchemy lab. Dorian may object to my continued production of his tea, but I wasn't about to let him simply return to stone. Instead of turning on the overhead light, I lit an oil lamp. It put me in a better frame of mind to practice alchemy.

But instead of peace, I felt confusion. The scent from the night before had vanished. It must have been my overly active imagination. Since I'm not a night person, I must have been too tired to think straight. I wished that my own body's reaction to creating Dorian's Tea of Ashes was nothing but my imagination. I was much sicker than I wanted to admit to either Dorian or to myself. If I didn't find a true solution, soon I would waste away as completely as the plants I was about to turn to ash.

CHAPTER 6

Inside my makeshift alchemy lab, I tried to focus. In the past three months, I'd made fourteen glass vessels explode, sent seven streams of green liquid shooting up to the ceiling—with a stiff neck from cleaning the ceiling to prove it—and had created four tinctures with scents so noxious I couldn't use the basement for days.

This wasn't how things were supposed to go.

In the eighty years since I'd pulled away from practicing alchemy, I'd lost my touch. Big time. Processes that were once second nature to me were now faded memories. When I recalled those years working side by side with my beloved Ambrose, my partner in both life and in alchemy for four decades, I felt as if I was watching an out-of-focus film about someone else's life. I'd continued working with herbs for food and herbal remedies, so my gardens always thrived, my dried herbs transformed boring soups into vibrant ones, and my tinctures and teas were effective remedies.

As for the more complex transformations I'd rejected for causing more grief than joy, such as unleashing the philosopher's stone— that's where I was blocked. I was unable to reach the white phase of a transformation where new energy rises from the ashes.

I reached for the locket I kept close but rarely opened. It was enough to feel the carved gold. I already knew every detail of the two faces inside, one a miniature portrait from 1701, the other a black-and-white photograph from 1904.

It didn't matter whether I worked in my alchemy lab with the plant transformations that used to come so easily to me, or whether I sat at my dining table surrounded by books that could shed light on the coded instructions in *Not Untrue Alchemy*. Nothing was coming back to me.

In the past three months, since meeting my unique friend, I hadn't made nearly as much progress on his strange alchemy book as I'd hoped. Perhaps my biggest failing was that I no longer knew how to find any true alchemists. I had wasted quite a bit of time that winter trying to find someone who could help, only to come up empty. I'd never finished my alchemical training, so there were missing gaps in my knowledge of the history of alchemy.

The thing about alchemists is that they love codes. After reading every word of the book myself and having the Latin translated by an expert, I felt I knew less than I did when I started. The Latin clearly stated that to reinforce the words, the practitioner must look to the pictures.

Retired chemistry professor Ivan Danko was helping me translate the coded messages hidden in the woodcut illustrations of the book. But despite his passion for alchemy as a precursor to modern chemistry, his assistance wasn't the same as having a true alchemist at my side. Ivan thought of our work as a scholarly exercise to understand history. He didn't know the true reason for my interest, nor did he know that alchemy was real. It was understandable that he devoted more time to his own historical research than to helping me with *Not Untrue Alchemy*.

And because I had to use so much strength to create the "quick fix" Tea of Ashes that kept Dorian alive in the short term, I didn't have the time and energy to fully devote myself to the larger issue of a solution that could cure the gargoyle for good. I knew there was a better solution within reach, though. I pulled Dorian's book from the shelf. It fell open to the same page it always did. The page with the Latin that had brought Dorian to life. *The book had to hold the key.*

This image of a basilisk had always disturbed me. The creature with the head of a bird and the body of a serpent was nothing unusual in coded alchemical illustrations, but this basilisk was different. His serpent's tail was wound counterclockwise and hung down at an unnatural angle. Yet instead of writhing in pain, the creature was void of expression. *Too* void; he was dead. His stiff body clung to the sole turret that remained in a wasteland of castle ruins. Through the union of a bird and a dragon, the basilisk symbolized the blending of mercury and sulfur.

I was distracted by a sweet scent. I glanced around my lab, wondering where it could be coming from. I looked up to the ceiling, where some of my exploding experiments were still embedded, looking rather like constellations. It was a fitting image, since alchemists look to the planets in the heavens for guidance about when to begin different transformations. I wondered if any flowers had germinated on the ceiling and made a mental note to take care of that. But for now, I turned back to the book.

Birds are highly symbolic to alchemists, because an egg is the perfect vessel, hermetically sealed and representing the whole universe. Different birds symbolized different alchemical processes. For example, a self-sacrificing pelican signified distillation, and a phoenix represented the final phase that produced the philosopher's stone. In this way, alchemists could instill their teachings in codes that could be passed down through illustrated books that only the initiated would understand. During the height of alchemy in the Middle Ages, coded messages carved into public buildings were the norm.

Other animals were used in alchemical codes as well. Toads symbolized the First Matter (itself a riddle), and bees signaled purification and rebirth. However, the bees in this book didn't seem to have gotten the message. In the woodcut illustrations in *Non Degenera Alchemia*, the skies were full of bees swarming in a counterclockwise direction, with rogue bees stinging the eyes of the people and animals on the ground. I shivered.

I turned the page to get away from the disturbing basilisk illustration, only to come to an even more disturbing one. This page showed the Black Dragon, which symbolized death and decay, and was a code for antimony. Antimony was Isaac Newton's favorite substance, because of its starlike crystal shape, which he thought could explain light and the universe. This Black Dragon was picking his way through another set of ruins. Death surrounded him, yet he appeared to be alive. Fierce flames escaped the dragon's mouth. I slammed the book shut, wondering if I was subconsciously avoiding working with it because of its psychological effect on me.

Something had to change. I couldn't keep this up much longer.

The book had shaken my ability to focus, so it would be pointless to either work in the lab or try to translate the obscure symbols in the book's woodcut illustrations. A knot formed in my stomach as the images from Dorian's book swirled through my mind. I had to get out of the house. *Away from the book.*

I nearly ran from the house as I left to take a walk to clear my head. I walked through Lone Fir Cemetery, a peaceful park not far from my house. I couldn't stop thinking about the strange scent from my bookshelf. I knew I must have imagined it. Books might become moldy and begin to smell stale, but not sweet. And even if my plant transformations had resulted in plant seedlings sprouting in the basement, they wouldn't give off the aroma I'd smelled. Clove-scented honey. *That's* what the sweet scent had been! The scents of spring that surrounded me in the cemetery made it impossible to ignore the memory.

I hurried home and went straight to the bookshelf in the locked basement. I again pulled *Not Untrue Alchemy* from the shelf. I brought the pages to my nose and breathed deeply. I inhaled the musty, woody aroma that I found in most centuries-old books. Underneath the obvious was the distinct scent of honey. This was where the scent was coming from. *Dorian's book.*

I've worked with a lot of old books, but I'd never encountered anything like this morphing sweet scent. I wondered if Ivan had.

I hadn't seen Ivan in several weeks. He'd come down with pneumonia at the tail end of winter, which hit him hard because he suffered from a degenerative illness. He didn't like to talk about the specifics, so I didn't know what was wrong with him. After getting back on his feet, he'd been intent on making up for lost time in his own research. I'd brought him a healing garlic tincture when he was sick, but I had respected his wishes and left him in peace to catch up on his own research now that he was well. But this wasn't the time to be polite. If Dorian's book was truly *changing,* this was a breakthrough I couldn't ignore.

I reached for my phone.

"*Dobrý den,*" Ivan's voice said on the other end of the line, and when I identified myself he switched to English. "I'm so glad you called, Zoe," he said in his Czech accent. "I wanted to thank you for the tincture you brought me when I was sick."

"I hope it helped."

"Do you want to know something about being Czech?" he asked. "People often think my accent sounds Transylvanian. They encourage me to dress up as Dracula for Halloween. Especially a young girl who lives next door to me. Her name is Sara. She wears a scarf around her neck each day. I thought it was a fashion statement for a seven-year-old finding herself, but I learned from her mother it was because she was protecting herself from Dracula. One night, when her parents did not realize what she was doing, she watched an old black-and-white Dracula movie, and it made her think she lived next door to a vampire."

With Ivan's graying hair and scruffy beard, I couldn't imagine him as the romantic Hollywood version of Dracula. But there was a stoic strength to Ivan. He didn't dwell on his health problems, instead undertaking an ambitious research project he wanted to finish before he died. His light blue eyes always shone with intelligence and determination. No, I couldn't see him as Dracula. But I could see him as Vlad the Impaler.

"Thanks to your garlic tincture," he continued, "Sara says there's no way I could be Dracula."

I laughed. "I hope it helped your infection too."

"That it did. *Děkuju*. I'm back to work on my book. Sara has christened herself my research assistant, fetching me the books in my home library I can no longer climb to retrieve."

"About your library," I said, "I have a question for you." I paused and chose my words carefully. "Have you ever encountered an old alchemy book that smelled sweet, compared to the more typical moldy smell?"

He chuckled. "Once, at the Klementinum, a patron was banned for sprinkling a rosewater perfume on a foul-smelling book."

"What about the scent of honey?"

"Honey?" Ivan hesitated, and when he resumed, there was a change in his voice that caused my skin to prickle. "It's curious that you mention honey. I think I may have something that would interest you."

I gripped the phone. "You have a book like that?"

"I remember it because of the unnerving nature of the woodcut illustration." He paused, and I could picture him shuddering. "I hadn't thought of it until you mentioned honey, but now I see it clearly in my mind." As he spoke, the tone of his voice changed from casual to agitated. "Perhaps it's best to leave it alone."

"Why?" I asked, the tenor of my own voice reacting to his worry.

"It's an image I don't know that I will ever forget, Zoe," Ivan said hesitantly. "I don't know if you want to see this."

CHAPTER 7

I assured Ivan that I could handle looking at a disturbing image. He told me he was at Blue Sky Teas and had his research with him on his laptop, so I told him I'd be right there.

The teashop was on Hawthorne, walking distance from my house. My mind always calmed down several notches as I walked through the door beneath the sign that read *"There is no trouble so great or grave that cannot be diminished by a nice cup of tea*—Bernard-Paul Heroux." Inside, a weeping fig tree stretched up to the high ceiling, casting peaceful shadows across the redwood tree-ring tabletops.

A woman in her late twenties rushed out from behind the counter so quickly her blond braids whipped around her head.

"Zoe!" Brixton's mom stood on the balls of her bare feet and threw her arms around me. "You really outdid yourself with today's treats. Can I double my order for weekend mornings? I'm nearly out of these oatmeal cakes. Who knew so many people would think vegan food was so tasty?"

"Definitely," I said, looking around at the long line of patrons. Dorian would be thrilled.

Blue Sky Teas was started by our mutual friend Blue, who'd been cleared of a murder charge but was currently serving a short jail sentence for a previous crime. During Blue's absence, Brixton's young mom, Heather, was keeping Blue Sky Teas open for limited hours, which helped both women. Heather was trying to become a professional painter. She had the talent to pull it off, but she hadn't made much money at it yet. I was surprised Brixton wasn't helping her today. It was midmorning on a Saturday, so maybe he was still asleep. When I was young, there was no way a fourteen-year-old kid would be allowed to sleep in. Then again, when I was young, fourteen-year-old's weren't thought of as kids.

Brixton and Heather used to live only a few blocks away, but they were now living temporarily at Blue's cottage in a field on the outskirts of Portland. At the cottage, Heather had more space for her painting. The recent floods that had swept through Portland inspired her to create a new series of paintings featuring water, and the cottage was strewn with painted canvasses in various stages of completion. Brixton had a stepdad, too, who he adored, but I hadn't met the man. Abel was out of town for work most of the time. The nature of his work hadn't been volunteered, so I hadn't enquired.

Heather retreated behind the counter, and I joined Ivan at a table near the window. A quart-size mason jar filled with yellow daffodils and white trillium declared that spring had begun. The vase of wildflowers dominated the table, dwarfing the emaciated man sitting there.

Ivan Danko hadn't been this small a man when I'd met him earlier that winter. Although his ongoing illness seemed stable, his recent bout of pneumonia had taken its toll. His blue eyes had a cast of gray, and his short beard was ragged. He'd barely touched his breakfast.

"I thought I had an image of the book on my laptop," Ivan said after we exchanged pleasantries, "but I was mistaken. I'm sorry to have sent you on a fool's errand."

My heart sank. Each time I thought I was coming close to a breakthrough with Dorian's book, something got in my way. It was as if the universe was teasing me. "Do you remember anything about it?"

"I don't know exactly how to explain it," Ivan said. "It would be easiest to show you."

I stared at him. "Wait, I thought you didn't have it."

"Not here. In my home library. I'm nearly done with my tea. Do you want to accompany me back to my house?"

"I'll get my tea to go."

Ivan lived in a small house on the north side of Hawthorne Boulevard. We walked to his home, breathing in the sweet scents of plum and cherry trees, newly blossoming as spring took hold after an especially brutal winter. I made an effort not to speed up our leisurely pace to the brisk walking I preferred, since I knew Ivan hadn't been well.

One look at his house made it clear that the retired professor of chemistry was a scholar. Ivan had transformed the largest room of his house into an alchemy library. He was writing a book about the unsung heroes of science—scientists who experimented with alchemy as part of their work. Isaac Newton was one of the more famous scientists who conducted alchemical experiments. Knowing how men of science viewed alchemy, Newton had hidden his work, yet he felt it was important enough to continue in secret.

Finishing his academic book on unsung scientists who worked on alchemy was Ivan's goal before he died. I was again struck by the collection he'd amassed.

"It's here somewhere," he said, rooting around in a stack of papers on a side table. "Now if only I could remember where I put it..."

While he searched, I looked around the room. The oak bookshelves had been custom-made to fit into the dimensions of the room, including a low bookshelf that ran underneath the window that dominated one wall. The window looked out onto evergreen trees that towered over the house, making this the perfect room for contemplative research. On the window sill were several photos, including a recent one of him and Max smiling as they held giant beer steins. The two men were friends who'd met as regulars at Blue Sky Teas.

A photo album lay open on Ivan's desk. An enlarged photograph showed Ivan as a young man. I stepped closer to his desk to take a better look at the photograph. Ivan was pictured with two other men in Staromestske Namesti, the historic Old Town Square in Prague, in front of the famous astrological clock. He wore a beard even then, and his hair was just as unkempt. The buttons of his white dress shirt were mismatched. I smiled, amused to see he'd always been an absentminded professor.

Ivan reached across me and closed the album.

"I've never asked you why you left Prague," I said. "Wouldn't it have been easier to write this book there, in the heart of alchemical history?"

He looked to the photo album, a mixture of joy and sadness on his face. "Too many painful memories. Someone so young will not fully understand—"

"I thought you said I was an old soul."

Ivan gave me a sad smile. "Before I came to be at peace with my illness, I behaved quite foolishly. I tell people my condition made it necessary for me to take early retirement. This is true—up to a point. Had I acted better, the university would have kept me on as a professor emeritus, with my office and research privileges." He closed his eyes and was lost in thought for a few moments. "But that choice was taken away from me, by my own actions. I couldn't accept that I was losing control of my body. I'd like to blame it on the illness affecting my mind, but that would be a lie; my mind is as sharp as it ever was."

"Which is its own curse," I murmured. "You're fully aware that your body is failing and everything that means."

Ivan's eyes lit up. "You do understand."

I thought of Dorian but didn't speak. I took Ivan's hand, which was far too frail for someone in his mid-fifties, and squeezed it gently.

"I was angry," Ivan said. "I lashed out at everyone around me and went down a self-destructive path. I went back-and-forth between looking for false cures and drowning myself with alcohol. The university asked me to take an early retirement, to avoid a scandal. It was too painful to stay in Prague, where I spent so many happy years in my youth. And I did not wish the people who knew me before to see this is what I became. In this modern age, research is possible anywhere."

"It's not the same."

"I had the choice of staying in Prague but being too angry to do my research, or going somewhere else where I could focus completely on my book before I die." He cleared his throat and looked away. I gave him space, but he didn't need long. "Ah! Here it is."

I took a piece of paper from his hands. Not only was it a printout of a scanned copy, but it was the image of a secondary source, not an original alchemy book. The top half of the page contained explanatory text in German, and the lower half showed a poor- quality photograph of an illustration in an alchemy book. The yellowed page looked like a woodcut, as was common for alchemical reproductions. Though the image was blurred, I made out the central image of a cherubic angel trapped in a prison of flames, with bees circling above in a counterclockwise circle.

Backward alchemy.

I felt myself shaking with fear and excitement as I took in all the details. On the edge of the image, outside the flames, two men were dressed as jesters. Though the book had been damaged, the image was clear enough to reveal that the bees were stinging the men's eyes.

The bees in Dorian's alchemy book were used in a similarly unsettling way. But here in this image, there was something more. I realized why Ivan had said the image was so disturbing. The hair on my arms stood up as my gaze fell to the eyes of the angel. The absolute horror in her eyes cut through my core, bridging the gap between the printed page and the ground beneath my feet.

"I told you it was alarming," Ivan said. "It is much worse than any horror movie, no?"

It had always amazed me how much life artists could breathe into an image, even when all they had was a knife and a piece of wood. "Why did my question make you think of this illustration?"

"Honey," Ivan said. "The scent of honey. This is a book *about* alchemy, not an original alchemy book itself. The author of this scholarly book made a notation that when working with this alchemy book, he detected the scent of honey. Apparently, honey was used as a preservative. Counterintuitive, but alchemists have always been known for being ahead of their time."

"Where did this book come from?" I asked. Ivan and the author's theory of honey as a preservative didn't ring true, but something was going on.

"The academic text is in a German university archive," Ivan said, "but unfortunately the original source is unknown. The woodcut illustration was found as three single sheets of paper in a French bookshop."

I nodded. "From the blackened edges, it's clear the book was badly damaged."

"Ah!" Ivan said. "That's what I thought myself at first. But take a closer look. This photograph is of the three pages *together*."

I squinted. "They're overlaid," I whispered.

"Alchemists and their codes," Ivan said. "Here, the author notes that the flames were from a subsequent page, yet when the pages are placed together, the flames trace the edges of the angel."

The way the images were overlaid created a *new* meaning. Was it on purpose? Or by accident? Looking more closely at the photographic image on the page, it looked as if the paper had been scorched at the edges. And were those granules of soot? Without the original, there was no way to tell.

"Can you read me the rest of the text?" I asked. I'm good at picking up languages, but I never learned German. To blend in completely—to hide in plain sight—I've found it best to become fluent in a handful of languages, rather than gaining a superficial understanding of many more. Along with a deep understanding of a few languages, I'm good at picking up the local vernacular of a certain time and place. Unlike some alchemists I've known who would cling to outdated speech patterns, I've adapted.

Ivan explained that the rest of the text on the page theorized that the image was a warning about the dangers of alchemy. I knew better. This image told of backward alchemy's death rotation. Ivan knew of my "scholarly" interest in it, but he hadn't connected this illustration with backward alchemy. I shouldn't have been surprised; it was an obscure subject, even for alchemists and alchemy scholars. His oversight drove home the fact that Ivan's help wasn't enough. I needed to find someone familiar with backward alchemy. I needed to find a true alchemist. The magician Prometheus?

"The passage ends," Ivan said, "by noting that half of the angel's body is stone."

I gave a start, and my eyes grew wide as I looked to the lower half of the angel's body. This was one thing the scholar was right about. With the blurry quality of the photograph I hadn't noticed before, but now that I looked for it, it was obvious. The angel's legs fused into a stone boulder, the two becoming one. She was trapped by her own body.

It was exactly what was happening to Dorian.

My phone buzzed, startling me out of the disturbing implications of this new information. A text message from Brixton popped up on my phone, saying there was an emergency and I had to get back right away.

WHAT EMERGENCY? I texted back.

He didn't reply. I called him. He hated talking on the phone, so I didn't expect him to answer. But he did.

"Zoe! He's here!"

"Who's *where?*"

"Get over to your house."

"Who—"

"It's the magician! I knew I was right. He's an alchemist—and he's right here—"

"He came to see me?" How would he know where I lived? And more importantly, *why* would he seek me out?

"No. He's a *criminal*, Zoe. He's—"

My blood went cold. "Brix, if he's breaking into the house"—the line went dead—"call the police," I said to dead air.

I tried to calm my breathing. One day that boy was going to cry wolf one too many times... But I'd never forgive myself if this was something real. I'd given Brixton a key to my house when he'd stayed with me for a few days. He rarely used it after that, but what if he was at the house and the magician-alchemist was trying to get inside? All I knew was that Peter Silverman was a criminal of some kind. And a kid wasn't going to stop him.

CHAPTER 8

Someone must have broken into the room and switched documents. Surely that was the only explanation for the content of the papers strewn across the architect's desk.

Eugène Viollet-le-Duc frowned. He looked from old architectural drawings of Notre Dame de Paris to sketches of the cathedral over the centuries. These records couldn't be right, could they? Yet Viollet-le-Duc could not fathom the purpose of such a deception.

The world-renowned architect and artist had been hired along with Jean-Baptiste-Antoine Lassus to restore the grand cathedral. To Viollet-le-Duc, "restore" was a broad term. He had plans to bring the outdated building into the nineteenth century. He dreamed of simultaneously restoring the previous glory of the cathedral and adding modern flourishes to show the new generation how glorious the Paris institution truly was.

To ensure his own additions would be perfectly integrated, the architect gathered official historical records and sought out artists' renditions of the cathedral over the centuries.

Now that he had both sets of records before him, something wasn't right.

The cathedral's construction had begun in 1163, and modifications had continued for centuries. The prolonged construction was due to both expanding the site's glory to God and taking advantage of new advances in architecture. Viollet-le-Duc planned to use modern architectural styles and techniques, as his predecessors had done with their own generations' discoveries. There was also more to be done than restoration and expansion. There was also rebuilding sections that had been destroyed. During the French Revolution of the previous century, which had ended shortly before his birth, the revolutionaries had destroyed anything they felt symbolized nobility. Religious symbols of the Kings of Judah on the façade of Notre Dame had been mistaken for Kings of France, and therefore defaced.

Yet if he could believe the drawings made by multiple artists, the old carvings on the façade hadn't simply been vandalized. At different points in the cathedral's history, the carvings on the façade had been altered to give them new meaning.

That meant not all of the destruction had been done to deface the monument, as he'd been led to believe.

Viollet-le-Duc hastily unfurled the official plans and sketches in his possession. None of them showed the strange writing carved into the facade. He turned his attention back to the drawings that showed the real carvings. With a magnifying lens, he looked more closely. *Riddles.* These words made no sense. What a strange thing!

And what was this? He looked more closely, focusing the magnifying lens. A drawing of the cathedral before the French Revolution showed a man holding a book. The stone book bore the Latin words *Non Degenera Alchemia.*

Viollet-le-Duc chuckled to himself. Stonemasons often bemoaned that they were uncredited for their efforts. To be remembered, they would sometimes carve representations of themselves into their work. The stone carvers who worked on this section of Notre Dame must have had a good sense of humor. They had put their own secret joke in a place that would be seen by scores of people. He appreciated the effort, and regretted that he was obliged to restore that section to its original meaning.

Suddenly seized with inspiration, he cleared the desk and sat down with his notebook open in front of him. With an expert hand, he began to sketch. A winged creature took form beneath his pen. This was no angel; it was a gargoyle.

He paused, picturing the current cathedral in his mind. Weathered stone gargoyles already surrounded much of the old church. Though far enough from the ground that one had to squint to see their details, those gargoyles had always inspired his imagination. It was a shame that their function as waterspouts also meant they naturally crumbled within decades rather than centuries. He wished to carve larger chimeras that could be appreciated both from the street below and up close. Grotesques that would not be hindered by being functional waterspouts. Viollet-le-Duc imagined a gallery high atop the cathedral, where commoners could climb to view the splendid city and also get a closer look at the architectural details of the cathedral itself. High above the stonemasons' alchemy joke, this would be his Gallery of Chimeras.

CHAPTER 9

When I reached the sidewalk in front of my house, the first thing that came into view was the rooftop tarp that covered the hole Dorian used to climb out from the attic. Since his stone form had been carved as a prototype for a statue on the gallery of gargoyles that adorned Notre Dame, he felt most natural coming and going through the opening high above the ground.

Rushing up to the house, I found Brixton sitting on the bench on my porch, calmly strumming his guitar. There was no emergency in sight.

"It's *him*, Zoe." Brixton set his guitar aside and picked up a hardbound book with library markings on the spine. "Prometheus. The alchemist."

I groaned. "Brixton! I don't have time for more theories. I was in the middle of something import—" I broke off when I saw the page he'd turned to. Brixton was holding the old library book open to a page with a photograph of the man we knew to be Peter Silverman. I lifted the book from his hands.

"The website where I first saw his picture is still down," Brixton said, "so I went to the library and got a library card to check this out to show you."

On the page was a photograph of the stage magician I'd seen last night. He looked roughly the same age he was now, around fifty, but with a different hairstyle and mustache. There was something eerily disturbing about this photograph. Something I couldn't quite put my finger on, but it wiped the smile off my face. I've never been a fan of mustaches, but that wasn't it. In this closeup photograph, the man I knew as the magician Prometheus stared past the camera with vacant eyes that sent a shiver down my spine.

"He's *dead*," I whispered, realizing what was wrong with the photograph. "This photograph was taken after he was dead."

"He was supposedly killed in a shootout with the police, after he killed some guy during a robbery."

I flipped to the cover of the frayed hardback book. It was a book about infamous Portland murderers throughout history. Brixton wasn't simply claiming Peter Silverman was an alchemist. The man in this photograph was a *murderer*.

The caption read: *Franklin Thorne, killed by Oregon state troopers in 1969.*

1969. *Nearly 50 years ago.* The murderous magician hadn't aged a day.

"I told you he's an alchemist," Brixton said. "He must have found the Elixir of Life like you did, so he wasn't really dead. Just pretending. Now you know he really could help you with Dorian's book! I told you my idea for a database of alchemists was a good one. It would have saved me from getting a library card."

I shook my head. "The magician from last night's show must be related to this man. I'm sorry I doubted that you recognized him, but you can trust me on this point. The simplest explanation is usually the right one."

I've been around long enough to know the most straightforward answer is almost always the right one. *Almost* being the key word. But I didn't want to admit my doubts to Brixton. It was still much more likely that the magician was simply related to this infamous murderer. Striking resemblances occur within families. That reality is why people readily accepted that I'm the granddaughter of a woman who looked remarkably like me. That's much more believable to people than the truth that I'm the same woman. But what if my secret situation was true for this man, too?

Brixton took the book back. "I looked up more about Franklin Thorne while waiting for you to get here. Truly, they're not related. This guy Thorne didn't have any family."

Franklin Thorne. Why did that name sound familiar?

"The Lake Loot!" I cried.

"Yeah. Duh."

The missing train heist loot had recently been discovered. That's what must have brought Peter Silverman to town.

I made Brixton wait while I looked it up myself. As far as I could tell, Brixton was right that the two men weren't related. And neither had any connection to alchemy.

"A publicity hoax!" I said. "Maybe he cultivated the look. It would be great publicity for a guy who goes by the stage name Prometheus to pretend to be immortal."

"He couldn't have altered this library book," Brixton said. "The pages are all faded."

"No, and he probably wouldn't have gone to all the trouble," I whispered. I knew it was technically possible to create an illusion with so many layers of complexity, but a hidden library book didn't make any sense. Why go to the effort? "Wait, you said at first you remembered this man from a history book, and then realized you originally saw this photo on a website?"

"Yeah, that Murderous Portland site I follow."

After being trapped by a real murderer earlier in the year, Brixton had given up on daring activities, such as the B&E that had caused him to meet me and Dorian. In place of this risky hobby, he'd taken to the more macabre, but safer, activity of learning about Portland's murderous history. He was enamored with a website set up by a graduate student at Portland State that was devoted to Portland's seedy past, from its founding in the 1840s through the end of the twentieth century. Brixton had seemed most interested in the earlier Wild West era, but apparently he'd read about more recent crimes as well.

"But the site was hacked and it's still down," Brixton continued. "What's the matter?"

"That's an awfully big coincidence for the site to be down as soon as Peter Silverman arrived in town. I don't like it. If this was a publicity stunt, Prometheus would want to get the photograph out all over the Internet. But instead, the biggest site that makes his photo available is down. It's as if he *doesn't* want to be found."

"That's what I said," Brixton grumbled. "It's like you're not even listening to me."

Brixton had cried wolf twice in as many months, but that's not what made me skeptical. It was the fact that alchemists were so few in number. Even when I'd been studying alchemy, before I ran from it, I knew very few people who'd discovered its secrets. Granted, I knew fewer alchemists than my male counterparts did. Aside from Nicolas and Perenelle Flamel, most were skeptical of female alchemists. I'd apprenticed to Nicolas at the start of the eighteenth century, two hundred years after he and his wife had faked their own deaths in Paris. Because he was a cautious man who valued his privacy, even Nicolas didn't know many true alchemists. And I'd lost track of the Flamels in 1704. I didn't even know if they were still alive.

There had once been a larger number of practicing alchemists. However, even in periods of time where there had been a flurry of alchemical interest and activity, few people unlocked the secrets of alchemy. Most alchemists died either accidentally poisoning themselves in their laboratories or naturally of old age. Very few of us had found the Elixir of Life. There were more plausible explanations as to why Peter Silverman resembled Franklin Thorne.

Still, there was no way the complexity of a publicity stunt included altering obscure library books. There was more going on here than I understood.

"Shouldn't you be getting over to the teashop to help your mom?"

Brixton rolled his eyes, but he stood up and slung the guitar over his back. He paused before hopping onto his bike. "You know you're wearing Mom Jeans, right?" he said.

"That bad?"

"Worse. So much worse."

That was the last straw. My bank account was too low to commission the tailored clothing I was used to, I didn't want to put in the hours required to sew myself clothing from scratch, and I doubted I could afford anything decent from a department store— not to mention the fact that I didn't understand the social mores of shopping in a multi-floor department store inside a mall. That was one modern invention I'd only watched from afar. One of the few times I'd ventured inside a mall, my senses had been assaulted by a barrage of perfumes and powders that the "helpful" sales clerks wanted to show me. I fled before making it through the cosmetics section. But I was only putting off the inevitable. I was too old to get better at transmuting lead into gold, but learning how to shop in a mall had to be marginally easier. Didn't it? As soon as I figured out how to save Dorian, I would reinvent myself.

"I'll look after the library book," I said. As soon as Brixton disappeared down the driveway, I hopped into my truck. I had my own destination to reach. I didn't know what to make of the alchemical woodcut that showed an angel turning to stone, but there was something much more immediate I could do.

The library's newspaper archives were extensive. I had no trouble finding scans of the original newspaper editions from the spring of 1969, when the infamous train robbery had taken place.

In the days following the crime that had killed guard Arnold Burke—and resulted in the thief's death as well—the local newspapers reported on different aspects of the train heist. Several reporters quoted conflicting accounts of the heist from eyewitnesses, one reporter wrote a profile of the heroic guard, and an enterprising investigative journalist dug into the past of Franklin Thorne so quickly that his story appeared the day after the heist.

There was also speculation about what would have driven Thorne, a toy maker, to become a thief. The most widely accepted explanation was that the Thorne family had once been quite wealthy, but had fallen on hard times a generation before. As wide-ranging as the stories were, all of the reporters agreed on one thing: aside from a childless older sister, Franklin Thorne had no family.

I read through newspaper stories from the first few days after the theft and shootings, then I rested my head on the library table and closed my eyes. The fake wood surface smelled of plastic and bleach. Peter Silverman, aka stage magician Prometheus, aka murderous thief Franklin Thorne, had nothing to do with me. He wasn't here to find a fellow alchemist. He was here to retrieve riches he stole decades ago, now that renewed interest meant that someone else could get their hands on it.

I lifted my head, and my hand moved instinctively back to the archives. I stopped myself. *Peter Silverman isn't your problem, Zoe.*

But if Brixton was right, could he be my solution?

CHAPTER 10

"Why are you sitting on the sofa in your *imperméable?*" asked my gargoyle, his dark gray brows drawn together.

"I was all set to go out and confront a problem, until I thought better of it." I sat stiffly on the green velvet couch, my silver raincoat buttoned over my awkward clothing and the keys to my truck in my hands.

If Peter Silverman was a murderer who was back in town to find the loot he thought was lost, why would he admit to being an alchemist? Even if I could get him to open up to me, was an alliance with a dangerous alchemist worth the risk? I've survived for centuries because I listen to my intuition. And my intuition was screaming at me that I should steer clear of Peter Silverman. But at the same time, if his help could save Dorian's life…

Dorian hopped up on the couch next to me. His feet didn't touch the ground. "I suppose it is too much to ask an alchemist to avoid speaking in riddles."

"I don't mean to be enigmatic. Take a look at this book." I lifted the library book from the coffee table and opened it to the bookmarked page.

"The Fire God magician," Dorian remarked. "Prometheus. I would not have thought him good enough to merit being featured in a book. It is an unflattering photograph, no?"

"Take a look at the title of the book. It's a book about Portland's infamous murderers."

Dorian's snout twitched as he looked from the front cover to the information about the photograph. "But this is... How is this possible? It says this man was killed by *les flics* in 1969."

"I think he's an alchemist. A real one who's discovered the Elixir of Life." Something was wrong with that picture, though. Alchemists aren't immortal. If he was truly dead, as this picture indicated, there were only two ways he could have come back to life. One, he could have faked his death in the first place. Two, it was possible he could have used backward alchemy, the same unnatural alchemy that had brought Dorian to life and was now killing him.

"*C'est vrai?* Is it true? But this is wonderful! You have had such difficulty locating another true alchemist all these months. Monsieur Danko means to help you, yet he is not a true alchemist, and cannot know your true mission. Why is your face grave, Zoe? Working with a learned alchemist who may have been alive longer than you, this could help you decipher my book, no?"

"He's a *murderer*, Dorian."

Dorian waved his hand through the air. "You fail to see the big picture. Ah! I am settling into American life so well that I am using American idioms! Did you hear?"

I sighed. "I'm glad you're feeling more at home in Portland, but the big picture generally includes staying *far away* from murderers who the police felt necessary to shoot several times."

"Yes, but—" He broke off. "*Attendez.* Why did he come back?"

"Look at his name."

"Franklin Thorne? Ah! He is the man who stole the Lake Loot that has enticed these meddlesome treasure hunters."

"He would have been forced to leave town quickly at the time, unable to get the loot without being found out. But now that enough time has passed, he most likely wants to retrieve the rest of it before someone else finds it, since part of the stash has already been discovered."

"*Mais,* why would he care for jewels?" Dorian asked. "He could simply make gold."

"As you've seen, not all alchemists are good at transmuting lead into gold."

Dorian frowned. "I thought you were a special case."

"It's a huge depletion of energy for anyone. It's the level of difficulty to complete the transformation, and how quickly we recover, that's personal. But we're getting off track. Dorian—if he truly died in that shoot-out, and it's the same man we saw on stage last night, he had to use unnatural means to bring himself back from the dead. He would have to be using backward alchemy."

"That is even better! He might understand my book." Dorian grinned, his wings wriggling in his excitement.

"If he doesn't steal it first." My hand flew to my mouth. I hadn't realized the implication of my words until I'd spoken them out loud. There was *another* reason besides the valuable jewelry that could have lured an alchemist who practiced backward alchemy to Portland in the first place. "An immoral alchemist," I said slowly, "might want *Not Untrue Alchemy* to use himself."

Dorian gaped at me, his dark gray tongue hanging over his light-gray little teeth. "You think," he said, "he is here to steal my book?"

I shook my head, shaking free of my confused thoughts. "I can't see how it's possible. Even if he knew of the book's existence, there's no way for him to know it's here." Alchemists can't sense each other from afar. Up close, there are subtle cues, mostly inadvertent slip-ups that show we were alive during periods of time we couldn't possibly have otherwise experienced. It's not like we're surrounded by an aura that other alchemists can see.

"The scent of the book is most strong," Dorian said. "Could he have sensed it that way? I have never smelled anything like the strange scents in this book. And as a chef, I have smelled many things."

"The sweet scents in the book aren't unique. It's only odd that they're coming from an antique book."

"I believe you are correct," Dorian said. "I cannot imagine my book is what drew him here. "

"The much more plausible explanation," I said, "is that he's simply here to find the rest of the jewels that washed up in that mudslide along the Willamette."

"*Alors*," Dorian said, purposefully widening his liquidy black eyes so he looked like a teddy bear gargoyle, "he is merely trying to find what is rightfully his. That does not sound like such a bad man."

"Dorian!"

"Yes, yes, the murders he committed—"

"Sounds like it was only one accidental murder." I cringed. Was I trying to excuse him?

Dorian's wings slumped. "I am sorry to pressure you into speaking with the alchemist, my friend. I wish for no harm to come to you. Yet if there is a way this man can help me without hurting yourself, do you not wish to explore it?"

"Of course."

"*Bon.* We can at least hear his side of the story."

"*We?*"

Dorian looked up at me with innocent eyes. "Alchemists who have discovered the Elixir of Life would not be afraid of me. I am going with you."

CHAPTER 11

An hour later, I dropped a hefty duffle bag at my feet and glanced around.

We would have been there sooner, but Dorian insisted on cooking us an early lunch to "keep our energy up." I didn't object as soon as I tasted his newest version of macaroni and "cheese" made from cashew cream.

"We're alone," I said as I unzipped the duffle bag. Sweat trickled down the side of my temple. That gargoyle was heavy. "But you should hurry."

"*Mais oui.*" Dorian stepped out of the bag, asking for my assistance with his left foot, then got straight to work on the lock in front of us. He had it open in less than a minute.

"*Merde,*" he whispered. "I do not think I will be able to relock this door from the inside."

"As long as we can get back out, that's fine with me."

I grimaced at the sound of the door's screaming hinges, even though rationally I knew that we didn't need to be quiet. Not yet.

The front of the theater was locked up. The staff and performers hadn't yet arrived to prepare for that evening's performance. I'd had Dorian pick the lock of the side door, located on a deserted alley that led to a backstage area.

With the dexterity of Dorian's clawed fingertips, it was like having my own personal locksmith. I thought of him as a "locksmith" rather than "burglar" because my intentions were pure—I wasn't planning on stealing anything. I wanted to take a look around to see if anything suggested these magicians were more than they seemed. Before confronting a potential murderer and showing that I knew his secret, I insisted we do reconnaissance. This was a long shot, since alchemists know how to be careful. But at the same time, since nobody expects alchemy to be real, it's tempting to let your guard down. That's what I was hoping Prometheus, aka Peter Silverman, had done.

Dorian could see in the dark, so he didn't need to turn on any lights. I, however, did. At least, if I was going to be of any use. But I found there was already a light burning.

"Zoe!" Dorian whispered in the deep, gravelly voice he erroneously believed was quiet enough not to be overheard. "We are not alone!"

"It's okay, Dorian. It's a Ghost Light." I pointed at the solitary bulb on a standing lamp in the center of the stage. It didn't mean someone was inside the theater. The theater tradition was an old one. The solitary burning bulb was meant to ward off ghosts. Or to protect the safety of anyone working late. The rationale depended on who you asked. The point was that it was an old tradition no longer needed with modern lighting. A few theaters still used it, but it would be second nature to someone who had worked in the theater a hundred years ago.

Dorian didn't notice my worry. He got to work exploring the theater by the light of the unadorned, ghostly bulb.

"Everything is locked!" he declared indignantly.

"Isn't that what I brought you along for? It was difficult lugging you inside that bag. I think you've been eating too many of the pastries you're cooking for Blue Sky Teas."

Dorian wrinkled his snout at me. "An important role of the chef is to taste his own creations! How else would culinary progress be made? Especially with these complicated vegan rules you impose."

"How can you say the rules are complicated? The only rule is no animal products."

"Semantics," Dorian mumbled. "*Alors*, these are locks beyond what my claws can unlock. I cannot imagine what foul magic lurks beyond these chains."

I knelt down to inspect the chain wrapped around a traveling trunk, then eyed the dramatic little gargoyle. "They're performers, Dorian. You know very well from your father that stage magicians are careful to protect their illusions. All this tells us is that they're magicians who create their own illusions. Which we already knew from seeing their show." I wished I was as confident as my words indicated.

I walked around the trunks, crates, and cabinets that had been locked with complex sets of metal chains. They were perhaps a bit on the paranoid side, but nothing out of the ordinary for stage magicians.

In the 1800s, several famous magicians stole cutting-edge acts from each other. Many magicians filed patents for their inventions, such as the Ghost, but spies infiltrated crews to gain enough knowledge to pretend they'd invented similar illusions on their own. I must have been lost in my memories, because I didn't hear anything until a voice rang out.

"Who left the lights on?" A deep female voice echoed through the theater.

"Perhaps it was the ghost," a male voice answered.

Dorian and I slunk into the shadows at the back of the stage as Prometheus and Persephone, sans costumes, strode down the center aisle toward us. If they turned on any spotlights, we'd be seen. I pulled Dorian behind a section of curtain and opened a fold just enough to peer out.

"Very funny, darling," Penelope said.

Peter shrugged. "I don't remember doing it, but you're right. It was probably me. Old habits..."

I felt my heart racing. *Old habits.*

"I thought you were over the need to leave a light on for the ghosts of the theater."

The two magicians hopped up onto the stage, just a few yards away from us. Though they were both dressed casually in paint-stained jeans, their hairstyles were already in place for their characters that night. Penelope's highly stylized curls pressed along the sides of her face, and Peter's flame-inspired spikes were stiff enough to impale someone.

Peter ran his hand across the edge of a beaten-up trunk wrapped in chains. "Being back in Portland has brought back a lot of memories, Pen."

Dorian tugged at my hand. The magicians were close enough to us that I dared not whisper a reply, or even shift to look at him.

"Nobody has messed with these locks," Penelope said. "I don't know why you insist on locking up *everything* like this. It takes so long to open."

"You know why."

"I swear," Penelope said, "I'd like to clock the person who started that damn rumor about 'The Scottish Play' being cursed and Gaston Leroux for writing *The Phantom of the Opera.*"

"Right. Let's focus. We don't have much time. The crew will be here soon. Let's get this trunk open and get out of here."

So Peter didn't trust the crew. I thought about the illusions the magicians had performed. Though the tricks were detailed and involved precision, they didn't require many players to implement them. I'd learned from Dorian (who'd learned from his father) that there were many ways to perform the same trick. Instead of using complicated rigging as some performers did, the illusions I'd seen the previous night involved ingenious tricks of light. The magicians hadn't used real fire, so they could have made do with one or two local stagehands.

Penelope opened two combination locks that held the chains in place around the storage trunk.

"Just one more—" Peter broke off. "Did you hear something?"

"The ghost, perhaps?"

"I'm serious, Pen. I think I heard something."

"I wish you didn't have to be so secretive."

Peter stood still for a moment, listening, then sighed. "You're right. It must be getting to me. I must have imagined the sound."

Only he hadn't imagined it. Dorian pointed up toward the catwalk above the stage. Two figures, barely visible in the shadows, were making their way across the walkway that held the stage lights.

CHAPTER 12

The area above the stage was cast in shadows, and I couldn't make out the faces of the two figures who crept along the catwalk. Yet from the glimpses I caught of the long-haired man, he looked vaguely familiar.

As he stepped past a set of metal lights and into the dim glow cast by the Ghost Light, I got a better look at his face. I stifled my gasp. It was the elderly volunteer from the show the previous night. Wallace Mason, who'd played the Floating Lady!

Between Peter and Penelope's strange actions and the lurking figures above us, I was more confused than ever. What was going on here? Stage show "volunteers" were often planted in the audience, themselves performers who were part of a show. It was an easy way to be sure the volunteer would behave exactly as they were supposed to in a complex illusion. But Wallace and his accomplice weren't revealing themselves to Peter and Penelope. They weren't part of the act.

As soon as Peter lifted the lid of the trunk, I temporarily forgot about the men spying on the magicians. Stuck to the inside of the trunk's lid was a poster for the Queen of Magic, Adelaide Herrmann. That's who Persephone had reminded me of the previous night. Adelaide Herrmann was the first famous female magician who had equal billing. Along with her husband, Alexander Herrmann, she had captivated audiences across Europe and America in the late 1800s.

The two magicians removed a child-size backpack from the trunk, secured the lock, then left. A heavy door clanked shut. It echoed through the empty theater.

Dorian and I didn't dare move. Any sound we made would alert the other intruders to our presence.

"They're gone," a somber voice said from above.

"Shhh."

"You're too careful."

"And you're not careful enough. I bet they've got it with them. There's no use staying here."

"We might as well look around. Since we're here."

The men climbed down from the rafters. They made enough noise on the rungs of the narrow metal stairs that Dorian and I nodded at each other and crept from our hiding spot behind the curtains. Dorian scampered toward the back door, but I hung back when I saw what he'd left in his wake. Another small piece from his left foot had fallen off and was rolling along the floorboards. Another claw? I had no idea if stone claws could grow back on their own, so I ran after it. If I was able to save Dorian's life, I wanted him to be as whole as possible.

Where had it gone? Footsteps sounded behind me. I didn't have time to find it.

I caught up with Dorian just inside the back door. He climbed back into the duffel bag just as the lights clicked on above us.

"I *told you* I heard something," Peter's voice said. I turned and saw him and Penelope staring at me and Dorian.

"What have you got there?" Penelope asked, indicating the lumpy sack that contained Dorian.

"She's stolen something. Only I can't tell *what* would be that shape."

"Stolen?" I said. "I wouldn't dream of it. I knocked and nobody answered, so when I found the door open—"

"The door is locked," Penelope said.

"Maybe one of your crew forgot to lock up," I said. "It was wide open. Try it yourself."

"Why would we do that?" Peter said. "If it's unlocked, all it means is that you're a good burglar. Pen, why don't you search her for lock picks."

Penelope crossed her arms and leaned against the black wall. She smiled as if she was watching an amusing television show she wasn't participating in. "If she's that good, Peter, I'll never find the lock pics. They could be under a fake scar, hidden in her mouth. She might even have swallowed them if she's a regurgitator."

Dorian made a gagging noise as she spoke the word "regurgitate."

I quickly coughed to cover up the sound, but Penelope looked to the duffel bag.

"I'm terribly curious," she said, "about what you've got in the bag. We like our possessions to remain inside the theater. I'm sure you understand."

"I'm sorry. I think we got off on the wrong foot. I live locally and run an online business called Elixir. We've got lots of really cool antiques that I thought could serve as props in your stage show. I brought over one of my statues to show you. Just to give you a sense of the kind of things I've got."

I hoped Dorian was up for playing dead as a stone gargoyle. I unzipped the bag. Inside I found a stone gargoyle, his snout flared more than usual and his face set in an angry scowl.

"Remarkable," Penelope said. "Peter, are you looking at this?"

He wasn't. He was tapping the screen of his phone. "Elixir, huh. This is your website?" He held up the screen.

"That's right."

"You expect us to believe you make a living off this site? It's not even mobile friendly."

"I set it up before smartphones," I said.

"How is that possible? You can't be older than twenty-five."

"I'm twenty-eight, actually." That was the age I was when I accidentally discovered the Elixir of Life.

"We'll take him," Penelope said.

"What?"

"The gargoyle. The reason you're here. We'll take him."

"Oh! Oh. This is an example. A prototype. He's not for sale. You can order a custom carving through me, to your specifications."

"We like this one."

"Great. I can have one made that looks identical." I named a price, hoping it would be too high.

"Perfect."

"Perfect?"

"Is there a problem?" Penelope asked.

"Of course not," I stammered, thinking I would have been better off letting them think I was a thief. Where was I going to find someone who could make a cast of Dorian? "I'll come by on Monday with some paperwork and to discuss materials options."

"We look forward to it," Peter said.

I cringed when the exit door squealed as I departed, even though there was no longer any need for secrecy. In the alley, I hesitated. Why hadn't they called the police? Isn't that what people would do if they found a burglar in their place of business? Unless they really did have something to hide.

But there was something more important than worrying about the magicians' motives. To hide, Dorian had turned himself completely to stone. Would he be able to bring himself back to life?

As I lugged the duffel bag to my car, I got my answer. The bag kicked me.

"That hurt," I said.

"Not as much as it's going to hurt me to have a plaster cast made of my body," the bag mumbled.

"You're lucky they didn't see you moving."

An older woman passing by on the sidewalk gave me a strange look. Better wait until we were inside the car to say anything else. I squeezed the bag into the space in front of the passenger seat on the floor of the pickup truck. Once we were both safely inside, I leaned over and unzipped a few inches. A pouting gargoyle looked up at me.

"You okay?"

"Why," he said thoughtfully, "did they not call the police when they saw you inside their theater?"

"That's what I was wondering."

"And why did you not tell Monsieur Silverman you know him to be an alchemist? This was the point of our expedition!"

"Hey, what are you doing? You need to stay inside the bag until we get home."

"I am attempting not to get out of the bag, but to stretch. I cannot move my legs."

My own legs felt weak at that news. "Let me get you home."

"*Non!*"

"What do you mean, *no?*"

"Do not worry about my present state. It is not what happens to me *today* that matters. The feeling is already beginning to return to my legs." He wriggled inside the bag. "It becomes more difficult each time, Zoe. You must confront the magician."

"You're forgetting something."

"I forget nothing. I simply do not say everything at once. I am a civilized Frenchman," added the face peeking out from the old duffel bag.

"The two intruders," I said.

"Yes. I recognized them as the volunteers from the performance last night."

"There was only one volunteer. The man with the long gray hair was The Floating Lady."

"The other man," Dorian said, "was the friend with whom he sat in the audience."

Where had the other trespassers gone? What were they after? And what was the item Peter and Penelope had removed from the trunk that Wallace and the other man had noted? *I bet they've got it with them,* he had said.

"I'm not going to rush off and confront anyone without knowing what's going on," I said. "I've got a better idea."

Dorian didn't experience heat and coldness the same way people do, so I left him inside my locked truck, hoping he didn't stretch so forcefully that he'd rock the truck and draw attention to himself.

I was in luck. The box office was opening. Opening night had been sold out, but I hoped the early box office hours meant there were still tickets left. I approached the ticket office and bought myself a ticket for that night's performance.

CHAPTER 13

It had been a long day already, but it was only mid-afternoon when I heaved the heavy duffle bag containing Dorian up my driveway. I set it down abruptly when I saw who was waiting for me at my front door with a bag of groceries in his hand.

"Max!"

"I thought you forgot about me and our barbeque plans."

"Of course I didn't forget about you," I lied. I had missed Max while he was gone in China more than I'd imagined I would, but now that he was back, I didn't have time for him. Dorian's dilemma was taking up all of my energy—both mental and physical. I felt a wave of anger, immediately followed by guilt for being so selfish. It wasn't Dorian's fault. I wished the world was a different place, one where I could tell Max where I'd been. One where I could have brought him with me. I knew he'd be able to help, and more importantly, he would understand me on the deeper level I wanted. Maybe I could—

"Did you want to say something else?" he asked. "Your expression—"

I shook my head. "I feel bad that I lost track of the time. That's all. You know how I get caught up in nature when I go on a walk."

"You drove up, Zoe."

"Of course." *Damn.* "That's because I drove to River View Cemetery to go for a walk *there.* I like some variety."

Max's relaxed stance stiffened. "I thought most of that place was roped off after the mudslides. It's dangerous up there."

God, I was awful at lying. I kept digging myself deeper and deeper. "It's so beautiful there. And only part of it is cordoned off."

"You didn't go to the unstable steep parts, did you?" Max asked as he came down the porch steps, a grave look on his face. I knew he was conditioned to be a stickler for law and order, but the concern on his face was far greater than the situation called for.

"Why the third degree?" I eased the heavy bag containing Dorian onto the front lawn.

"It's nothing. Can I help you with that... sack?"

"I'm fine. It's just one of my antiques. I was having it cleaned. I, um, picked it up on my way home." I needed to change the subject. "Let's see what you brought with you."

"Fresh from the farmer's market." Beet greens poked out over the edge of the brown paper bag he held. Several bunches of asparagus rested on top, and I spotted purple garlic and Brussels sprouts underneath. It was a bountiful spring harvest.

"I'm glad you brought food. Since I lost track of time, I didn't have a chance to go to the market."

"And this," he said as he handed me a bag of fragrant tea, "is the tea I mentioned last night. Hey, are you okay?"

I self-consciously tucked my hair behind an ear, careful not to tug too hard and pull out any more clumps. "What do you mean?"

"Last night, I thought it was the light of the theater, but you've got dark circles under your eyes. And your skin is pale."

I inspected the bag of tea, ignoring Max's skeptical gaze. "It's spring. I've got allergies. Nothing to worry about."

"This is the tea I brought back from China, but I'm getting my own spring garden started now, even though it's a little late. You'll find that one of the nice things about living in Portland is that we get enough rain that plants often thrive even during extended vacations."

I smiled at Max. "My secret is elderberry. You know it looks out for the other plants, to help them out." I turned to look fondly at the plant that used to be thought of as a garden's "protector," then looked at Max with equal fondness. "I'm glad you're back. And I'm glad you're here." I'd told him far too many lies in the last five minutes, but that statement was true. Even though I couldn't tell him as much as I wanted to, his very presence was comforting. I held out hope that one day I'd be able to tell him more.

"I missed sitting with you in my garden," he said softly.

"While the sun set."

"Then watching the night-blooming jasmine come to life."

"You know," I said, "you never revealed your secret for getting it to bloom off-season."

"You want to know all my secrets?"

"A little mystery is a good thing, but you could at least tell me how your grandfather's birthday party was."

"Didn't I? I told you he appreciated having his far-flung family gather around him one last time."

"But what about *you*? How was the visit for you?"

"Visiting China. It was... Let's just say it's relaxing to be home, Zoe." He took a step toward me, then abruptly jerked back. "What the—? Is that a battery-operated antique?"

"What are you talking about?"

"Your sack. It made a noise."

"There might be something else in the bag. Something with, er, batteries, like you said. I'd better get this bag inside. You can take the food into the kitchen." I sighed. "I'll meet you there in a minute." I let Max into the house before stepping back outside to retrieve Dorian.

"Set me in front of the hearth," the sack whispered as I heaved it up the porch steps.

"I'm taking you to the basement," I whispered back.

"I wish to stay upstairs," he whined.

I closed the rickety front door behind us. "That's not a good idea, Dorian."

"I do not trust that man in my kitchen."

"Did you say something?" Max called from the kitchen, poking his head into the living room through the swinging door.

"Just the creaking floors." I waited until Max disappeared back into the kitchen, then lifted Dorian's stone form from the bag and set him in front of the fireplace. It was a spot he liked, because even in his stone form he could see everything. I didn't feel good about leaving him in stone form for too long, but I couldn't have an argument with Max there.

When I stepped into the kitchen, the farmer's market vegetables were stacked on the kitchen countertop and Max was holding a mason jar containing one of my latest transformations—a sun-infused healing lemon balm tea I was drinking daily to stave off the effects of helping to cure Dorian.

"It's a solar infusion," I said.

He raised an eyebrow.

"Steeping dried herbs in the sun, rather than the kitchen, to unleash their healing powers," I explained. Alchemy draws upon all the forces of nature, the planets being some of the strongest forces. Alchemists generally consult planetary alignments before they begin any transformative processes. The more complex the operation, or the greater the desired impact, the more important that alignment becomes. Each planet also has an associated metal, such as lead for Saturn, quicksilver for Mercury, silver for the moon, and gold for the Sun.

"I know what a solar infusion is. My grandmother did something similar when I was a kid. You'd get along great with my extended family. It's never made sense to me why it's worth all the effort. Especially moon infusions she'd steep under a full moon, thinking it was possible to harness the moon's power."

"Max. You make your own tea. You have one of the most unique gardens I've ever seen. And not two minutes ago we talked about night-blooming plants!" If my hair wasn't so weak from the backward alchemy quick fix I'd been performing, I would have tugged at my hair in frustration.

"That's different."

"Is it?"

In Max, I saw someone who'd once believed in all the possibilities of the world, but who couldn't break free from what he'd become. I hadn't realized it so clearly until that very moment. Max was walking on a tightrope, caught between two worlds: his childhood, with his herbalist grandmother who was an apothecary, and his adult life, working as a detective with a set of procedural and scientific rules that dictated his understanding of rationality. I knew it was nearly impossible to change a person if they weren't ready to change, but I believed Max could recapture the openness he'd once known. It didn't have to be a choice between two extremes. Once he realized that, I could open up to him, and we might have a chance for a future together.

I took the mason jar from his hands and set it back on the counter.

"Can we change the subject?" Max asked.

"What did you have in mind?"

"As lovely and complicated as this solar infusion of herbs is, it's not anywhere near as lovely and complicated as the woman in front of me." Max stepped closer and ran his finger along my jaw. His breath smelled of fresh lavender and peppermint.

Max's dark eyes were different than those of anyone I'd ever known, because of what they showed me about his soul. I've known a lot of people in my lifetime. Faces blur together in my memories, but I've never forgotten people's eyes. Before the advent of photography, it was usually only wealthier people who had their likenesses captured through portraits, so I didn't retain physical reminders of many of the people I'd known. I remembered their eyes not because of a unique color or shape, but because eyes are tied to an outward expression that people themselves are unaware of.

"Last night," Max continued, "I was hoping that we could pick up where we left off."

"I'd like that."

For a fraction of a second, I was self-conscious about my cracked lips and frumpy clothing. But with his eyes locked on mine as he stroked my cheek, I quickly forgot all about my own failings.

A faint knocking sounded. The front door? I couldn't be entirely certain it wasn't my imagination. Max either didn't hear it or chose to ignore it as well.

"Yo, Zoe!" Brixton's voice called from the backyard. "You in there?"

I pulled away from Max.

"I thought we were barbequing for just the two of us," he said.

"I thought so too." I opened the back door of the house, on the far end of the kitchen.

Brixton and his friends Ethan and Veronica stood in my backyard garden. Veronica's gangly frame towered over the boys. Her sleek black hair flowed past her shoulders, and I was pleased that she looked much more comfortable in her skin than she had even months before when I'd first met her.

"Hi, Ms. Faust, Mr. Liu," she said.

"What's up?" I asked.

"Your face is flushed," Brixton said. "Are you feeling sicker?"

"Sicker?" Max asked.

"He must mean my allergies." I turned back to the kids. "Max and I were just getting a barbeque started."

"I love barbeque," Ethan said.

Veronica elbowed him.

Max laughed. "There's plenty."

～

The miniature charcoal grill I kept in my trailer was only big enough to cook for two at a time, but there was enough food in my kitchen to feed an army, along with their counterparts. I asked Max to get the grill started while I collected ready-to-eat goodies. I pulled a carafe of iced tea from the fridge, selected an assortment of nut milk cheeses and breads, and washed an assortment of vegetables.

Because of Dorian, I kept my curtains drawn most of the time. Now that he was hiding in his stone form, I pulled open the kitchen curtains. I looked out the kitchen window and watched as Max began grilling two dozen asparagus spears along with full garlic heads wrapped in aluminum foil.

I was about to leave the kitchen to carry statue-Dorian into the basement so he could change out of his stone form, when Veronica opened the back door. She joined me inside while the boys stayed outside with Max.

"Now that Blue Sky Teas is serving my cooking," I said to her, "I can't figure out your real motive for coming over."

Veronica blushed. "We didn't come over *just* for food."

"No?"

"Brix knows you've been working too hard lately," Veronica explained. "What with getting up in the middle of the night to cook for Blue Sky Teas and managing your online business, Brix said you were bummed you didn't have time to fix up your spring garden like you wanted to."

"That's why he invited you two over?"

She gave a shy smile. "Yeah, but he also promised Ethan you'd cook for us. Your pastries are so popular at Blue Sky Teas that they're usually gone by the time we wake up on the weekend."

"Ah." I looked on through the window as Brixton pulled back a giant stalk of fennel and let it go, snapping it directly into Ethan's face. I'd taught Brixton enough about gardening and plants for him to know the weed-like plant was hearty enough for roughhousing. He wouldn't dare mess with the dwarf lemon trees that were still finding their footing.

"Really?" Ethan said to Brixton, then sneezed. "That's the best you got?" He broke off a thick fennel stem and held it like a sword. The impact was diminished by the fact that the tip was a bunch of yellow flowers. Brixton snapped off a stem of cabbage left behind after I'd harvested the edible portion. As faux weapons went, Brixton's was a much better selection.

"So, um, Ms. Faust?" Veronica sat on a countertop with her cell phone in her hand. "Can I talk to you about something else?"

"Of course." With the grim look on her face, I wondered what could be on her mind. Was she worried about how Brixton would react if she started spending more solo time with Ethan? I'd seen how things were headed with the trio of friends.

"It's your website," she said somberly. "It isn't mobile friendly. Like, at all."

"My *website*?" Was it really that bad? "There was no such thing as a smartphone when I built the site," I said for the second time that day.

She gaped at me. "But how do you expect to sell anything?"

"I don't think my buyers are shopping on their cell phones."

Her confused expression deepened. "Um, I could help you with it. You know, if you wanted. I'm kind of good at stuff like this."

"I couldn't ask you to—"

"It's fun, so I'd be happy to. You don't have to use it if you don't like it, but I could play around and see if you like what I come up with. You at least need to fix your SEO."

"My what?"

"I think you'd like something like this." Veronica moved so we could both see the screen, and showed me an assortment of mobile-friendly websites for merchandise like mine. "Since you've got a bunch of items from China, I could draw Chinese characters that could go next to the English descriptions. And I'll ask my mom to check my work, to make sure I got them right. I think that would look really cool."

I smiled. I'd probably spent more time in China than Veronica's Chinese-American mother, and I could have checked the Chinese myself, but I didn't like to advertise the fact that I knew as many languages as I did; it invited too many questions. And I was pleased it would give Veronica something to do with her mom. Brixton had told me she was closer with her Italian dad, because of their shared love of soccer. "That sounds great, Veronica. You should pick out something from Elixir to let me thank you."

I wrote down the login information to get into my website. When I looked up and glanced out the window, instead of seeing Max at the grill and the boys fencing with plants, I saw the three of them gathered around something else: *Dorian's alchemy book.* The dangerous, secret book I could have sworn I'd locked up in the basement that morning before leaving the house. I'd been ambushed.

That was the real motivation for Brixton coming over. He wanted Dorian's book.

CHAPTER 14

The young doctor did not think of himself as anything special. He knew himself to be a competent doctor, a fair man, and a mediocre alchemist.

He had not discovered The Philosopher's Stone, yet his modest laboratory contained herbs he used to heal his wife and son when they were sick. He was not above feeling jealous of the men who had lived in previous centuries, when alchemy was in its heyday. He fantasized that, had he lived then, he might have been honored with a spot in Rudolph II's court in Prague, where men from across the world were said to have been given a stipend to practice alchemy. But the doctor had been born centuries too late for that. Here in the nineteenth century, he had to live out his fantasies through books.

It was this hobby that led to the most improbable day of his life.

Though the doctor and his family lived in Paris, the doctor's wife was originally from the town of Blois. He and his family frequently traveled there to visit her infirm mother. His love for books was well-known to his family, so they thought nothing of it when he spent the afternoon at a local bookshop. In truth, it was his desire to avoid the company of his mother-in-law at least as much as the pull of books that led him to the bookshop that afternoon.

He had learned not to openly express his obsession with alchemy. Even in the modern times in which he lived, alchemy was greeted with suspicion. Therefore he feigned an interest in a wide range of scientific subjects. Once he told the bookseller the range of topics that interested him, the stooped man without a hair on his head nodded and retreated to the back of his shop.

The doctor looked over the books selected for him, then politely asked if the man had anything that was perhaps... older.

The bookseller nodded with understanding. The doctor watched the small, elderly man climb to the top of a ladder, wondering if he should assist the bookseller, lest he fall from the high rungs as he clutched a large book in one hand. Before the doctor could make up his mind, the bookseller was back on the ground, pressing the book into the medical man's hands.

"This is more to your liking, sir?"

It was. The doctor paid more than a fair price for *Non Degenera Alchemia,* an amount that had the bookseller drinking fine wine for months to come. The bookseller was quite pleased, for he had not even purchased the book to begin with. It had been left on the stoop of his shop some years before. At first he thought the anonymous donor must not have realized its value, but when he turned the pages of the book, he guessed the donor's true motivation. A foul odor emanated from the book. When certain pages were opened, the stench grew stronger. But the bookseller was also a book-lover. He could not abandon such a carefully made book. Even after cleaning the book failed to remove the smell, he was unable to part with it. Instead, he climbed to the top rung of his ladder and set the book on top of his highest bookshelf, where the scent would not reach his nose. The scent would fade over time, he imagined. With the book far from his gaze, he promptly forgot all about it—until the day the young man with an interest in alchemy walked into his shop.

The doctor didn't notice anything odd about the scent of the book until he and his family returned to Paris. Was it his imagination, or did the book smell of more than dusty leather and mold? Perhaps one of the items in his medical bag had spilled onto it. He wasn't usually so careless, but with a young son, he was neither as methodical nor as well rested as he once had been.

He had a small collection of alchemy books, which he kept in the midst of a much larger collection of literature and scientific volumes. *Non Degenera Alchemia* was unlike any other alchemy book he'd seen. The transformations pictured were all wrong. Indeed, once he was back home in Paris, the doctor was no longer sure it *was* a real alchemy book. The tiny bookshop had appealed to his romantic tendencies. Perhaps he'd spent his money more on an idea than the book itself.

Now, it looked as if he wouldn't have a chance to find out. His wife insisted he remove the book that smelled like it had been stored in a stable of animals. He couldn't argue with her, and not only because she won every argument. In this case, he believed she was right.

He no longer knew any alchemists who might want to buy the book. He had once tried to join a secret society of alchemists in Paris, but he found them to be a very silly group of men. None of them had discovered alchemy's secrets, but all of them delighted in deciphering riddles.

Thus, with a heavy heart, he tucked the book under his arm and set out to find a bookseller who might pay him a few francs for it. Before leaving, he sprinkled a few drops of his wife's perfume onto the spine, hoping to mask the other odors. He hated to damage the book, but who would buy it in its current state?

His actions were for naught. A few steps out the door, the odor of the book returned. The perfume must have dispersed quickly in the dry air. Perhaps he could find a bookseller with a stuffed-up nose.

The doctor followed the path of the Seine River, the pleasant day balancing out his feeling of foolishness for his hasty purchase. As the spires of Notre Dame Cathedral came into view, the smell of farm animals dissipated, replaced with scents of the forest. So shocked was the doctor that he tripped. The book flew out of his hands, landing a few feet in front of him. He dusted off his trousers, which thankfully had not ripped, then lifted the book. Memories of childhood Christmases flooded through his mind as fragrances filled his nostrils.

Was he going crazy? Or could this be true alchemy?

CHAPTER 15

"What's the big deal?" Brixton said. "I was just showing the alchemy book to Ethan because he took Latin in private school before he moved here. I thought he could help translate some of the crazy stuff in there."

"It's a valuable antique," I snapped. "It shouldn't be outside. The spores from the garden will ruin it." It was true, though that's not what I cared about.

"Is that why it smells so weird?" Ethan asked.

"Mold?" Max chimed in. "I met a book restorer a couple of years ago, on a case. He might be able to help."

"Thanks," I said, taking the book from Ethan's hands. "I'll keep that in mind."

"I'm the reason you got the book back, you know," Ethan said.

My shoulders tensed, but I kept the book firmly in my hands. I'd never asked Ethan to buy the book from the innocent rare books dealer, but I was thankful *Non Degenera Alchemia* hadn't gotten caught in police red tape as I fought to have it returned to me after it was stolen in a break-in a few months ago. Ethan's family was wealthy enough that the charge on his father's credit card hadn't been a problem. I wondered if he'd even noticed.

"You know I'm grateful, Ethan. And I'm working on paying you back—"

"Whatever. I just thought it would be cool to see what all the fuss was about. After all, this is the book Brix made up all those stories about. Like how it's what brought your shy French friend to life. Nice one, Brix."

Brixton became suddenly interested in a wild maze of mint leaves that were snaking their way up the fence. He knew why he couldn't tell them the real reason I needed to decipher the book, but I hadn't realized just how much he'd told his friends shortly after meeting me.

"Are we going to eat or what?" Ethan said.

I took the book inside, not trusting myself to speak to Brixton while the others were around. I knew what he was doing, and he meant well. He saw that Dorian was dying and knew that my own efforts weren't working to save him. Since Ethan read Latin, it was a natural leap for Brixton to think Ethan might be able to help.

I trusted Brixton's intentions, but he was fourteen. In my youth, that age was considered nearly an adult. But a teenager today wasn't an adult. I couldn't assume that Brixton was. I'd become too careless in what I shared with him.

He would never *purposefully* reveal my secret and Dorian's, but his actions could still lead to dangerous situations. I wasn't worried about Brixton slipping up, or even purposefully telling anyone about me and Dorian. When he did so shortly after we first met, nobody believed him. People see only what their worldview enables them to see. It's like we're all walking around with x-ray glasses set to different frequencies. When most people are told about a living "French gargoyle," their imagination conjures the image of a disfigured Frenchman who was self-conscious about being seen, not a stone gargoyle who'd accidentally been imbued with a life force when an unsuspecting stage magician had read from the pages of a book he never suspected contained actual magic. The few people who'd seen Dorian move when he was hiding in plain sight assumed it was a trick of the light or that they'd had one too many pints of Portland's exquisite beer.

True, my life would have been easier if I didn't have to pretend I had a shy friend from France, but I didn't fault Brixton for trying to be understood. The problem was when he acted recklessly by taking matters into his own hands. When he did so, I couldn't anticipate all the unintended consequences.

After taking the book to the basement bookshelf, I carried statueDorian to the basement. Between gardening and taking long walks, I've never been a gym person. Honestly, the whole concept of a gym that doesn't involve competitive sparring baffles me. Doing unproductive physical work within the confines of a dark building, as opposed to working up a sweat in nature? But as I hefted Dorian into my arms, I realized that perhaps lifting weights wasn't such a bad idea.

I set him down at the bottom of the basement stairs, feeling a twinge in my lower back. After locking us into the basement, I told him it was safe to wake up.

"I can see that." He stretched his neck, flapped his wings, and flexed his fingers. Moving his hips as if he was playing with an invisible hula hoop, he frowned at his legs. They were taking longer to regain movement than the rest of him.

"You heard what happened?" I asked. He hated it when I fussed over his condition.

"Of course." He shook his head sadly. "I can see and hear very well when I am trapped in stone. I saw the food preparations being made. Such poor cooking technique! You did not wait nearly long enough for the coals to heat properly to grill the vegetables."

"Dorian—"

"And I have the perfect recipe for a tarragon sauce to accompany asparagus, but I cannot show myself to prepare it—"

"Dorian!"

"Yes?"

"I was talking about whether or not you heard that Brixton showed Ethan your book."

Dorian narrowed his eyes. "You are trying to change the subject because you have never liked tarragon."

"I like tarragon just fine, as you know full well. I don't grow it myself because it doesn't have as many healing properties as other herbs."

"It is the King of Herbs, Zoe. The King of Herbs."

"Would you please focus? I need to go back upstairs in a minute."

"Yes, yes. I heard you confront the boys. I was confused as to why you stopped Ethan from looking at my book."

"He's a *kid*, Dorian."

"Yet he is the one who enabled us to get it back."

"I remember, Dorian. I remember." When all this was over, I needed to work on creating enough gold to pay Ethan back. "But knowing how to type your wealthy father's credit card number is completely different from knowing how to comprehend an ancient and dangerous text."

"Fresh eyes. Is that not the expression?"

"Yes. He's a fresh set of eyes. But he's fourteen. And he doesn't know about alchemy. And did I mention he's fourteen! Look, I really need to get back. Lock yourself in here. Don't let anyone in. Don't let anyone besides the two of us look at the book."

"You show Ivan—"

"That's different. He's a scholar—"

The gargoyle threw his arms into the air in exasperation. "No *ham*," he muttered. "No *butter*. No showing my *own personal possession* to whomever I wish."

I sighed. "Do you really miss ham?"

He scowled at me. "No, I do not. But that is not the point."

"I give up. Stay here, Dorian. I'll make sure everyone leaves before too long."

Getting rid of my guests proved more difficult than expected. It was such a gorgeous afternoon for a barbeque that my outburst hadn't dampened the fun. When I stepped into the backyard five minutes after I'd left to deposit Dorian and his book in the basement, Max, Brixton, and Ethan were sitting in folding wood chairs in a semicircle around the grill while Veronica flipped pieces of asparagus.

None of them seemed to notice my foul mood. Dorian was right that I was failing in my own attempts to decipher his book, so it was no wonder he agreed with Brixton that any help was welcome. A kid who'd studied a little bit of Latin wasn't going to help. But an old alchemist was another story. Now that I knew Prometheus's true identity, I was eager to attend the *Phantasmagoria* magic show that night.

Since none of my guests were picking up on my impatient mood and suggesting they depart, it was time for another approach. I picked a stalk of ragweed to force myself to sneeze repeatedly. With a red nose and eyes, it was much easier to wrap up the barbeque. With my overzealous inhalation of ragweed, I was certain I didn't look like someone Max would want to spend the evening with, leaving me free to get ready for the magic show. I hated the continued deception. It never got easier.

I counteracted the effects of the pollen by taking a bath with chamomile bath salts, then dressed in an oversize black blouse far too long for my arms, and black leggings that left nothing to the imagination. In simple black, I hoped I'd blend into the background.

I arrived early and got myself a glass of red wine at the lobby bar. At least two dozen attendees were there ahead of me, holding drinks and chatting with friends. I smiled but didn't strike up any conversations. I was there to see what else I could discover.

While I looked around the wood-paneled lobby, I sipped the wine. The spicy and sweet flavors of cloves, pepper, and black currants danced on my tongue. I've never been a big drinker, since my alchemically-trained body experiences heightened effects of everything I put into it. But I enjoy the complex characteristics in wine. And unlike coffee, which can keep me up for days, too much wine puts me to sleep. After one more sip, I abandoned the half-full wine glass on the edge of the bar.

The lobby was filling up, providing the cover I needed. Mirroring the authority of the magicians in the illustrated *Persephone & Prometheus's Phantasmagoria* poster next to me, I walked purposefully to the closed doors that led to the seating area. Unfortunately, they were locked. That wasn't uncommon, and I should have expected it. Stage magicians wouldn't want anyone seeing their setup. I wished I knew how to pick locks as deftly as Dorian did with his claws. I had to wait until the audience was let in, which happened a few minutes later. I lingered next to the doors, so I was one of the first members of the audience ushered inside. I spotted two staff members dressed in black. One was in the sound booth, and one stood at the side of the stage, guarding the curtains from curious patrons who might be tempted to peek. To me, neither of them looked much older than Brixton.

Instead of finding my seat, I walked to the front row and caught the eye of the staffer hovering in the wings.

"This is a wonderful old theater," I said. "Have you worked here for long?"

He grinned. "Two years this May, when I graduated with a degree in theater."

"What about the guy in the sound booth?"

His grin faltered. "He's been here a little longer, but I know a lot about this place. Listen, I've got to finish setting up, but do you want to grab a beer after the show? I can tell you all about it."

The revealing leggings had definitely been a bad idea. I politely declined his offer. He'd told me what I needed to know. Peter and Penelope hadn't brought their own crew with them. They were working with locals.

At this Saturday evening performance, there were a few empty seats in the theater, but not many. I was heartened to see that people were still interested in attending a classic magic show. I wished I could enjoy it.

The lights flickered, signaling that the performance would begin shortly. I was seated in the back row, and I watched the stage carefully.

The curtains opened slowly, revealing a dark stage. A glimmer of light bounced off a piece of glass. I was surprised at the sloppy setup. The night before, it hadn't been immediately obvious that the fire was an illusion.

The magicians must have realized something was wrong too. Instead of the swell of music that had kicked off the previous night's show, the curtains began to close again.

But at the same time, something was happening on the stage. As my eyes adjusted, I made out the form of a tall cabinet at the side of the stage. It had been there the previous night, I remembered, but it hadn't been used. At least not in a way the audience could see. This time, though, the door of the cabinet was slowly opening. There was someone inside. He held himself stiffly, almost as if he was playing the part of a dead body.

This was definitely in keeping with the *Phantasmagoria*'s theme of death and resurrection, but I was surprised that the magicians would change their act so drastically between performances.

The curtains continued to close, but the heavy fabric moved slowly. I could still see the middle of the stage. And I recognized the man inside the coffin-like cabinet.

It was the Floating Lady volunteer I'd seen at the theater earlier that day. What was he doing there? Had he stayed at the theater to spy on the magicians and hidden in this cabinet, not knowing it would be used on stage? He was a little late to be sneaking out unnoticed.

Right before the curtains closed, my breath caught. Wallace Mason *wasn't* trying to hide. A dark patch of red stretched across his chest.

He tumbled out of the box just as the two sides of the curtains came together with a crash. Of course it wasn't the curtains making the noise. It was the sound of his dead body hitting the stage floor.

A murmur of voices echoed through the theater, as audience members turned to one another, presumably wondering about the strange opening of the show. Though magicians love morbid imagery, the scene on the stage had none of the previous night's dramatic flare. This was no act.

The magician had killed again.

And without revealing who I was, there was nothing I could do about it.

CHAPTER 16

Looking at my face in the mirror the following morning, I barely recognized myself. My skin was drawn like it had been before I began taking care of myself, and the dark circles under my eyes were even darker than the day before. A large chunk of hair fell off in my hairbrush. Even my teeth had a faint gray cast to them.

Dorian was right. Helping him was killing me.

Each time I made the Tea of Ashes, the effects lasted longer and were more severe. Still, I was in better shape than Wallace Mason. I couldn't get the image of his body out of my mind. I hadn't realized he was dead until he hit the stage floor.

Though I've seen my share of death over the years, seeing two murder victims within three months was unsettling, to say the least.

Had Wallace Mason seen too much when he was at the theater earlier that day? If it was the magician-alchemist who had killed him to protect his secret, how could I ignore the murder? I was entangled, whether I liked it or not.

I doubted the two young crew members had anything to do with the murder. The elderly usher who took our tickets didn't seem especially likely, either. I expected the police would dismiss them from suspicion, making the magicians the most likely suspects. Would the police figure out Peter Silverman's true identity? It would be like the Salem Witch Trials all over again—only this time, the accusations against me would be true.

As an innocent sixteen-year-old I'd been accused of witchcraft, because of my affinity to plants. I could work with plants in ways that most people couldn't, both in coaxing them to grow and in extracting their mysterious properties. People are frightened of what they don't understand. It was their fear that had driven me away from them and into the arms of alchemists. Now I had become something that people might truly have reason to fear, not because I would harm anyone—I had spent my life trying to do the opposite— but because I had unlocked powerful secrets that could be used for both good and evil.

Breathe, Zoe.

Now that I'd gotten a few hours of sleep, I began to wonder about my hasty assumptions. Had I jumped to the right conclusion? Was the magician involved? I was looking at only half of the picture—the magician-alchemist, not the man who'd been killed. The dead man's life would be examined by the police. The police would look into Wallace Mason's life and follow the trail wherever it led.

Pushing thoughts of murder from my mind, I fixed myself a cup of turmeric tea and a green smoothie for breakfast, then I tended to my window box and backyard gardens. Three mint varieties—lemon balm, chocolate, and peppermint—were getting a little carried away, stretching their roots and tendrils too close to the parsley. That wouldn't make any of the plants happy. My garden choices had been made in part so I could harvest fast-growing plants for Dorian's Tea of Ashes. If it hadn't been for that, I would have planted the mint in containers.

The familiar routine of touching the plants and giving them the amount of water they needed served to calm me, but my mind was still restless. I dressed in my ill-fitting jeans and a sweatshirt and set out on a walk to clear my head. But the scents of springtime Portland only served to remind me of the strange scents I'd imagined coming from Dorian's book, and the scent of ether the magicians had used in their performance.

Back at the house, I went straight to the kitchen with the intention of having another cup of tea. Before the mug reached my lips, a knock sounded on the front door.

I'd already given a brief statement to a police officer the previous night, when I was questioned along with the rest of the audience. I'd said I didn't know anything, so I couldn't imagine they were following up already. I knew I should have told them about seeing the two men sneaking around the theater earlier in the day, but I couldn't do so without incriminating myself. Doing the right thing was always a delicate balance for an alchemist. Telling the complete truth could easily lead to greater confusion and injustices. If I knew anything that could help, I would have spoken up. But in spite of my initial reaction, I didn't know what had transpired.

I took a deep breath and opened the door.

"You were *there* last night?"

"Nice to see you, too, Max."

He pushed past me into the house. "You didn't say anything about going back to the magic show."

"It was a last-minute decision. I wanted to see if I could figure out how some of the tricks were done. I told you I love old-fashioned magic shows."

Max stared at me. I suddenly felt very self-conscious about my hair and skin. "What are you keeping from me, Zoe?"

"Are you here officially?"

"No. I'm here as your... whatever the hell I am to you. But I suppose your answer shows me where I stand."

"Max—"

"A man is *dead*, Zoe."

"Why do you think it has something to do with me?"

"I didn't say that! I'm worried about you. That's why I came by. You were in the same place as a killer."

"Oh."

"You find it so surprising that I'd be worried about you?"

"No, it's just—"

"What?"

"Nobody has been worried about me in a long—"

A crash from the house interrupted us. I gave a start, and saw Max's shoulders tense.

"You attract burglars like anise hyssop attracts bees," Max whispered, then raised a finger to his lips.

Only Max would have thought up a simile that included anise hyssop instead of something simple like sunflowers. I put my hand on his and stopped him from heading to the house. "It's not a burglar. I was cataloguing my inventory and left a stack of books that wasn't very stable. I didn't anticipate being pulled away for so long."

"You sure?"

Another crash sounded.

"I'd better check it out."

"Max, really—"

I feared what he'd find inside. With solid stone covering a larger portion of Dorian's body each day, he might not be able to transform himself into the proper shape people had seen. I was already thought to be "quirky" for carrying my large gargoyle sculpture to different rooms of my house on a regular basis. That was fine. But how would I explain a strangely contorted gargoyle sculpture?

Ignoring Max's pleas for me to wait outside, I followed him up the stairs. Max cringed as each successive step groaned under our feet. Stealth was impossible in this old house.

The attic was crammed full of artifacts for my business, but empty of life. There wasn't even a stone gargoyle anywhere in sight. However, there *was* a pile of books scattered across the floor, even though I'd lied about a precarious stack. Was my *house* alive now? That was all I needed.

My attic was the exact opposite of Max's house. Instead of his sparse decor, in which an iron tea kettle, a white couch, two scenic paintings, and two personal photographs gave the house its personality, my attic was an involved mess of relics I'd accumulated over the centuries. For the decades in which I traveled across the United States in my truck and trailer, these books, artwork, and alchemical artifacts had resided in a storage facility in Paris.

The hardwood floor was pockmarked with water damage from the winter rains. You'd think that after all these years I'd be good enough at home repair that I could fix the damage quickly and resume my alchemical work on saving Dorian's life. But in my defense, I'd rarely lived in my own home. Most of the time I hadn't even lived in a proper house. This Craftsman house in Portland was a luxury.

"Wow," Max said, taking in the room.

I couldn't tell if he meant that in a good way or a bad way.

"These are all real antiques?"

"They're not exactly antiques. At least I don't think of them like that. They're all related to the science of healing. That's why the store is called Elixir."

"I didn't realize you were still working at your business." He shook his head. "I guess we don't know each other as well as I thought."

"Max—"

"I thought you were working as the chef at Blue Sky Teas."

"Part-time. Why did you think I wasn't running Elixir? You knew I shipped the storage crates to the house when I moved here. I wasn't hiding anything." Well, I wasn't hiding *that*. "Is it because I haven't invited you up to the attic before? As you can see, it's not the kind of room where I'd invite a guest. I haven't gotten properly settled in yet."

"That's not it."

"No?"

"I checked out your website."

I groaned.

"It looked like you hadn't updated it in the last decade," Max said sheepishly.

Three comments on my website in as many days? I was definitely going to take Veronica up on her offer to update the site. But I couldn't seem to care much at the moment. Dorian was dying an unnatural death. I was getting sicker by the day as I tried to save him. A murderous alchemist was in town, seeking his stash of loot, a stash which had led to the death of a guard and which had now washed up on the banks of the nearby Willamette River. And a man spying on the alchemist had been murdered, the body found in front of my eyes.

So yes, updating my website so I could make enough money to fix my house and pay Ethan back wasn't my top priority. I gave an involuntary shiver as I thought back to that damned theater, with Dorian's foot caught on the catwalk and the volunteer's dead body tumbling out onto the stage.

"You're thinking about the dead man, aren't you?" Max said. "I can see it on your face. I'm sorry you had to see that."

I nodded, but didn't trust myself to speak. I'd seen more death than I wanted to in my lifetime. It doesn't get easier. But that's a good thing.

"Is there something you want to tell me, Zoe?"

My throat tightened and anger flushed my face. Why was Max simultaneously the easiest and most difficult person to communicate with? "You really think I had something to do with his—"

"I didn't mean it like that! Of course I didn't mean that. Sometimes I feel like you understand me better than anyone, but sometimes… I can tell you're keeping something from me." He frowned as something in the corner caught his eye. He set down the cookbook of herbal remedies he'd picked up, and walked up to a whitewashed hutch that held glass jars with original vintage labels. "Imported herbal supplements? Really? After everything that happened last winter, how can you—"

"God, Max!" I snapped. "I don't know the man who was murdered, and these are vintage *jars*. With nothing inside. Nothing. These glass vessels were once used by famous scientists. That's why they're worth a lot of money."

"Really? People will believe Louis Pasteur used one of these *vessels*? Are his fingerprints on them?"

"Isaac Newton, actually, but yes. I don't have fingerprints, but I have documents that show—"

"You actually believe papers have survived that long and aren't faked? Jesus, Zoe. You do." He pinched the bridge of his nose. "I'm sorry. Look, can we change the subject?"

"Back to the dead man you think I have something to do with? I told you, I don't know the man. He has nothing to do with me."

"Are we fighting? How did that happen? I came over here because I wanted to make sure you were okay, that you hadn't gotten mixed up in—"

A cough sounded from the closet behind me. I knew that cough. I quickly coughed, hoping Max would think the first one was mine.

"I could use some tea for my allergies," I said. "They're affecting my throat. Why don't we go downstairs?"

"I can see myself out."

"That's not what I meant."

"We don't seem to be communicating very well today. I'll leave you to clean up this mess." He paused, a veiled look I couldn't place passing over his face. "Where's that gargoyle statue of yours? I didn't see it when I came through the house."

"Why?" My intuition kicked into high gear. Max knew I "moved" my statue around, but he'd never seen Dorian move on his own.

"Never mind. It's nothing." He paused. "I hope it's nothing."

"What's that supposed to mean?"

"I have to go, Zoe."

And with that, he left. *Why did he want to know about Dorian?*

CHAPTER 17

I rested my back against the closet door for a moment, allowing time for Max to drive away and for me to compose my thoughts.

When I was certain he was gone, I yanked open the attic closet door. "It's safe."

"I hope the boy did not ruin any of your books," Dorian said. His gray arm was wrapped around Brixton's shoulder. The two stood, and Brixton helped Dorian step out of the closet.

"He lost his balance," Brixton said. "That's why there was a crashing noise. We didn't know you were back until we heard you and Max raise your voices. So when Dorian fell down, I thought I'd better make this place look like you said it did."

"Max knows that *you* exist. Why didn't you just say you came over to raid the fridge or something?"

Brixton and Dorian stared at each other, both frowning.

"She is a smart one, this alchemist," Dorian said.

I pressed my fingers to my temples. I didn't remember signing up to take care of two adolescents.

"Don't be bummed, Zoe," Brixton said. "I'm sure Max'll come around." He made sure Dorian could stand without toppling over, then put his hand on my shoulder. Okay, sometimes he could be a thoughtful kid.

I looked at the two of them. "Why are you here, anyway? I didn't know you were coming over. I thought you'd be at Blue Sky to help your mom with the Sunday brunch crowds."

"Yeah, that was the plan, but then I heard about the guy who was killed by the alchemist—"

"We don't know for sure that's what happened."

"Alchemists," Dorian said, "are known to have gone to drastic measures to protect their secrets."

"You were the one who said we should give him the benefit of the doubt!" Brixton said, gaping at the gargoyle.

"My young friend," Dorian said to Brixton, "bring me the local newspaper, s'il vous plaît."

Dorian didn't usually ask for help like that. His left foot hung at an unnatural angle. He saw me looking and tossed a small throw blanket over it.

He cleared his throat and opened the paper. "Wallace Mason was an important enough man to have a short obituary in the newspaper. He founded a wellness center in Portland in the 1960s, where he extolled the virtues of vegetarianism and herbalism, and he took in many troubled people. He's survived by a daughter who lives abroad."

"That's it?" I asked.

"Hey guys," Brixton said, "there's a lot more online." He scrolled on the screen of his phone. "He was quoted in the media after that sapphire necklace from the Lake Loot was found."

"Aha!" Dorian said.

"He was one of the treasure hunters?" I asked. His presence at the theater took on a new meaning. "What did he say?"

"That they should allow people to search," Brixton said, still reading his phone's screen, "because that's the best chance at recovering the loot for the family. Why didn't he want it for himself?"

"Use your *little grey cells*," Dorian said, tapping his forehead and making me wish I hadn't checked out every single Poirot book from the library for him during the winter. "A 1960s wellness center. This means he is a *do-gooder*. Of course he would wish to find the *trésor* for the family."

"Unless he's lying," I pointed out.

Dorian scowled at me as he stretched his shoulders, his wings flapping gently as he did so. "We would know more if someone would confront the alchemist. Then we could learn if he might help us."

"We've already discussed all the reasons why that's a terrible idea."

"Yes, but this is a democracy," Dorian said. "The boy and I have outvoted you."

"This isn't a democracy."

"Of course it is," Brixton said. "I slept through a bunch of government classes, but even I know that."

"This *house* isn't a democracy," I said.

"But we will not confront him inside the house," Dorian said, his black eyes opened wide in a deceptively innocent expression.

I groaned. *A simple life, Zoe. You really believed you could have a simple life?* I wished I could say that if the magician was a murderer, the police would figure it out. But if he was an alchemist?

"Maybe Zoe has a point," Brixton said.

"Thank you," I said.

"I mean, Franklin Thorne is a really good magician, with his Prometheus character. If you confront him directly, he might capture you before you knew what was happening."

I tried to stop Brixton to tell him that wasn't what I meant, but he kept going.

"You were there at the show," he said. "You saw him. Prometheus is, like, *Houdini* good."

Dorian made a squawking noise I'd never before heard escape his dignified gray lips. "Houdini! *Non!* Ehrich Weiss stole my father's name and dishonored him! Houdini is but a poor imitator of the great Robert-Houdin! Those illusions you witnessed at the stage show? These were not inspired by the crass, escapist acts of Houdini. *Non.* Many were created by the prodigious Robert-Houdin."

Brixton stumbled backward as Dorian's heavy wings flapped back and forth.

"He's a bit overly sensitive on this topic," I said to Brixton.

"Overly sensitive?" Dorian parroted back at me. "I am not the egotistical man who could not understand a family's wish to grieve for their relation in solitude. That was Houdini. Since the day he was turned away from visiting his idol's grave, Houdini set out to destroy Father's name."

"Wow," Brixton said, reading his phone screen. "Son of a—" "Language," I said automatically.

"Sorry, D," Brixton said, ignoring me and speaking to Dorian. "I didn't mean anything by it. I just meant that Prometheus is a wicked good magician who probably has lots of handcuffs and stuff, so Zoe should come up with another good cover story before she goes and talks to him."

"I'm right here," I said.

"Yeah," Brixton said, "but you look like you're resisting coming up with a plan. So Dorian and I should come up with one for you."

I sighed and tried to think of anything I could say that wouldn't result in them skewing the intent of my words and investigating for themselves.

"As long as you two stay out of it completely," I said, "and I do mean *completely*, I'll look into it."

"*Bon,*" Dorian said. "In one hour I shall have lunch ready for you. That way you can keep up your energy for your investigation."

~

The scene outside the theater was much as I expected it would be. The building at the base of Mt. Tabor was roped off with crime scene tape, and officers milled around.

Peter and Penelope sat together on the bumper of a powerful, late-model SUV that loomed over the tiny Portland cars surrounding it. With a hitch on the back, I presumed they used the SUV for hauling a trailer of the items for their magic act. They were no longer wearing their stage makeup or formal wear from the day before, though the sleek curls of Penelope's hair were ready for any stage. She puffed on a cigar and looked at the sky.

"If it isn't our friendly neighbor," Peter said in a voice even a toddler could tell was sarcastic. "Come to tell us our new gargoyle is ready? I'm so sorry, but as you can see, it's the world's worst time for a visit."

The man struck me as far too immature to have been alive for 100 years. He was immature even for 50. I've known alchemists who've lost sight of their humanity, but it tends to express itself in a different tenor. Aloofness and a lack of empathy, yes. But sarcasm? Not that I'd encountered. But then again, I'd never known any alchemists who practiced backward alchemy. And that's what he had to be, coming back from the dead.

"I'm so sorry for your loss," I said, though what I was really thinking was how murders followed Peter Silverman wherever he went.

"We didn't know him," Penelope said, blowing smoke rings into the sky. She gave what appeared to be a heartfelt sigh, then extinguished the cigar. "But yes, it's a tragedy nonetheless."

"I assumed you knew him, since he was a volunteer."

"Everyone thinks they know how a show works," Peter said with a resigned smirk. "That's *cheating*, my dear."

Penelope turned her sharp gaze to meet mine. "Don't mind him. He's upset that the police are wrecking all of our earthly possessions as we speak."

"Looking for the murder weapon?"

"I don't know what they're doing," Peter said, "but that's certainly not what it looks like."

My phone buzzed in my pocket. "Excuse me," I said, scowling at the phone.

"Zoe, thank God you picked up," said the voice on the other end of the line. "There's an emergency. Listen—"

"You can't keep crying wolf, Brixton," I snapped.

"You don't understand! It's Ethan. I found out he took a photograph of a page in the alchemy book—"

"That's okay. It's not like the existence of the book is a secret—"

"You're not *listening* to me, Zoe! He read it *out loud.* The Latin. He brought a stone garden gnome to life."

CHAPTER 18

FRANCE, 1855

With trembling legs, the young doctor clutched *Non Degenera Alchemia* and walked to a nearby café, where he drank copious amounts of wine.

He had once read about a sect of alchemists from the sixteenth century who met in the crypt below Notre Dame de Paris. He had dismissed the notion as rumor, for even when he asked fellow alchemists about it, they had dismissed this "backward alchemy" as myth. But what if it was true? It was only when he returned to Paris that the book gave off a strong scent. And it was only when he came upon the cathedral that the odor changed.

Stumbling now, he made his way to the cathedral, unsure whether it was the wine or alchemy that made the book feel as light as a feather in his hands. He climbed the steps to the new Gallery of Chimeras and looked out over the city. So many great men had shaped Paris. He knew he would never be one of them. *Unless this book could turn him into a true alchemist.*

From high atop Notre Dame de Paris, the drunk doctor read from the pages of the strange alchemy book, hoping against reason that here in this sacred historical site, the knowledge would seep into his veins and make him more than the simple man he knew himself to be.

Directing his attention to the stone chimera in his path, he recited the Latin words. The stone began to shift. He must have been more intoxicated than he thought. He had only hallucinated once before, when given an incorrect dose of laudanum. The horned gargoyle stepped off of its pedestal and stood in front of him. What sorcery was this? He wasn't able to answer his own question, because he promptly fainted.

When he awoke, he was in a jail cell for drunkenness. He could no longer remember whether the events of the night before had been real or a dream. A sprained wrist was the only indication that something had taken place that night.

Had the book truly made it possible for him to bring a stone creature to life? It wasn't possible! Alchemical transformations could not be transferred in such a way. Yet he had seen it with his own eyes. He held his hands before him, half expecting his fingers to turn to stone.

When he was released from his jail cell, the book was returned to him. Ignoring the pain in his hand and wrist, he ran to Notre Dame, earnestly hoping that the events that had transpired there had only been a nightmare. When he reached the gallery, he found an empty pedestal where the gargoyle had once stood. Was he mistaken? Had there been a figure there at all?

For days, the doctor searched for the creature he was half convinced he'd imagined, but never found it. He read the newspapers each morning and evening, wondering if its presence would be reported. Nothing.

If this was what alchemy had driven him to, he had no right to try to be more than the unassuming man he was. That day, when his wife was in the park with their son, he tossed the book into the hearth.

It didn't burn.

He tossed more wood into the fire. Still, the book did not catch fire. He threw one of his most boring books into the flames. It popped and sizzled in the heat and was soon reduced to ash. *Non Degenera Alchemia* glowed in the fire, yet did not burn. Of this he was certain. Today he was completely sober. This was no hallucination.

The young doctor screamed with confusion as he pulled the book from the fire with a poker. He wrapped the book in a blanket, fearful to touch it once more. He wrote a note for his wife, then took his leave.

When he returned a week later, the young doctor no longer looked so young. But the book was safely hidden where he hoped nobody would find it ever again.

CHAPTER 19

"What's the matter with your hand?" I asked.

"I took Ethan's phone from him," Brixton said, hiding his bloody knuckles. "He wasn't happy."

"You *hit him?*"

"What was I supposed to do? Anyway, he hasn't posted it online."Brixton swallowed hard. "Yet."

Dorian swore in French.

"We'll talk about your methods later," I said. "Play the video."

Brixton, Dorian, and I were huddled in my attic after I'd rushed home at Brixton's news.

The video image was bumpy and unstable. Ethan wasn't using a tripod. Someone was there with him, making the recording. It must have been Veronica.

On the screen, Ethan stood in a large garden of immaculate stone walkways and expensive potted plants, all ornamental rather than edible. Stone cherubs and garden gnomes poked out from behind three of the waist-high pots. In the distance, a high wooden fence enclosed the yard. This must have been Ethan's home.

"A book of ancient magic," the boy said to the cell phone camera, "has recently come into my possession. I'm going to conduct my first experiment for the world to see. I'm told that these Latin words are known to have brought monsters to life—"

Dorian huffed. I put my hand on his shoulder.

"Today," Ethan continued on the video, "I'm going to prove or disprove the 'magic' of this old book. I'm going to see if I can bring Harry here to life. He will be 'Harry, the garden gnome who lived.'"

He took a few steps down one of the well-tended stone paths. The screen went blurry for a moment as the person holding the cell phone camera zoomed in closer. It came to focus on both Ethan and a two-foot garden gnome wearing a pointed red hat and an evil grin. This was not good.

Ethan picked up a weathered antique book. It wasn't *Non Degenera Alchemia*.

"What's he doing?" I asked. "That's not Dorian's book."

"Look more closely," Brixton pointed. "I watched it five times while I was waiting for you. You can see a piece of paper sticking out of that old book. He's being dramatic, like he loves to do. He must've found that old book in his parents' library and put a printout of the picture he took of Dorian's book inside."

"To pretend he's reading from a real magic book..." I murmured as Ethan read the Latin words. He wasn't half bad. I hadn't expected his Latin to be good, but he was a smart kid. Brixton was friends with him, so it figured.

"What the—" Ethan abruptly broke off. His expression changed from a confident, smug smile to wide-eyed horror. The camera zoomed in on his face. "No!" he shouted. "Don't film *me*, Veronica. Get Harry!"

The camera swirled around from the sky to the ground, its focus landing in the spot where the garden gnome, apparently named Harry, had stood. The figure was gone.

The video went black.

"Ethan called me," Brixton said, his voice shaking. "He's totally freaked out. What do we do?"

"You didn't have anything to do with this?" I asked.

"Of course not! Ethan was making a joke about what I told him right after I met you guys, when I wanted him and V to believe me about Dorian. Only it didn't turn out to be a joke. So, what do we do?"

"We find Harry," I said. My heart thumped in my throat, but I had to remain calm for Brixton's sake. I turned to Dorian. I hadn't known him to ever be at a loss for words, but the gargoyle stood dumbstruck. "Dorian, think. When you had been brought to life, what did you do? Where did you go?"

He ruffled his wings and blinked at me, as if coming out of a trance. "Where did I go? It was a confusing time, at first. Since the words that brought me to life were Latin, I was born speaking and understanding Latin. But no other languages. Not until Father taught me French."

"The library?" Brixton suggested. "That's where Latin books would be."

"Or a Latin professor at a university," I said.

Dorian waved his hand to dismiss both ideas. "This garden gnome will not know any of these things. He is a child right now. He needs guidance and tutelage. He will not have gone far."

"Maybe you could lure it here to Zoe's house with your cooking," Brixton said.

"I wish I shared your enthusiasm for this idea, my young friend. It would provide an excuse to ask Zoe to buy the expensive ingredients she does not think are important for my gourmet cook—"

"Hey!" I cut in. "We need to focus."

Brixton paced back and forth, his thumb rhythmically flicking his phone screen like it was a security blanket. "Yeah, there's a little baby monster—"

"I am not a monster!"

The phone dropped from Brixton's hand and clattered to the attic floor. None of us made a sound. The only one moving at all was Dorian, whose chest was heaving. His snout flared and his black eyes narrowed. If I had any doubts about Dorian, I would have feared for Brixton's safety. As it was, I wasn't entirely comfortable with how quickly his moods changed these days.

After a few seconds, Brixton scooped his phone from the floor. "I didn't mean anything by it," he mumbled.

"There's power in words," I said softly. "Always remember that. Brix, why don't you take your bike and see if you see anything weird out there. Start at Ethan's house, and circle the streets."

"What are you two going to do?"

"I'll do the same thing, but in my truck. Since we can't ask anyone else for help, we need to split up—"

"What about the alchemist?" Brixton asked.

"You're staying away from that man, Brix. I mean it."

"Whatever."

"What are Ethan and Veronica doing?"

Brixton rolled his eyes. "I think Ethan is 'comforting' Veronica. He said she was totally freaked out."

"You didn't see her?"

"Only for a second. She wouldn't look at me. I thought this was urgent. That's why I took his phone…"

"Good work, my young friend," Dorian said.

Now was not the time to explain that punching a friend was anything but good work, especially for a kid who had a juvenile record. "Call me if you see Harry," I said. "Don't approach the gnome on your own."

Brixton blinked at me. "He's a little tiny garden gnome."

"Still."

"When we find him," Dorian said, his earlier anger apparently forgotten, "I could tutor him. He could become my apprentice."

"A garden gnome junior chef," Brixton mumbled. "My life is so weird."

"Once the sun sets," Dorian said, "I will begin the search. For now, I will remain here. I shall compose a list of ideas of where he might go."

"Good," I said. "We'll meet back at the house at sunset."

Brixton and I left Dorian in the attic. I took a last look at his gray face. It now bore a wistful, almost happy, expression.

～

I drove to rose gardens, cemeteries, and parks looking for any evidence of a rogue gnome. I stopped frequently to check the news on my phone, hoping I wouldn't see news reports of a living garden gnome.

My heart sank along with the sun. This was hopeless. I checked my phone for the hundredth time for sightings in the news or a message from Brixton. Nothing.

Brixton was already in the attic with Dorian when I returned. His knuckles were still bloody and his hand had swelled up in the intervening hours. I admonished myself for not tending to it right away. I retrieved a healing salve, applied it, and wrapped his hand in a clean bandage.

"Ethan called me," Brixton said. "He's pissed off. He wants me to come over and give his phone back. Should we do it? I already downloaded the video and then deleted it from his phone."

"We're going to have to tell him something…"

Not knowing what else to do, I drove us to Ethan's house in silence. Even though people believe only what they're ready to believe, seeing an inanimate object come to life would be difficult to explain away.

Ethan opened the door with a stoic expression. His cheek was red, as was half his nose.

"Look," Brixton said, "I'm really sorry—"

"For what? I fell off my bike while doing a trick. No way did I let anyone sucker punch me."

"About why I had to—"

"My parents are out at some fundraiser tonight, so we can talk inside." Ethan invited us into an opulent living room with high ceilings, a grand piano, and ultramodern black-and-white furniture that looked like it belonged in a cosmetic surgeon's waiting room, not a home.

Brixton handed the phone back to him.

"Took you long enough. What have you been doing all afternoon?"

"Looking for Harry, of course!"

Ethan gaped at us. "You guys took me seriously?"

Brixton gaped right back at him. "The video—"

"It was a joke! God, you really believed it?" Ethan laughed so hard his injured nose started bleeding again. He dabbed it with a tissue from a porcelain container next to the couch I didn't dare sit on.

"You got Veronica to go along with it?" Brixton said, his face red with fury and embarrassment.

"Yeah, that was tough," Ethan said in between fits of laughter. "I'm not sure if she's more pissed off at you for hitting me, or at me for making her play a joke on you."

"It wasn't funny," Brixton said. His face flushed bright purple with either anger or embarrassment. Probably both.

"Yeah, you're right," Ethan said with a straight face before again bursting into laughter. "It's not *funny*. It's *hilarious!* Can't you take a joke, Brix?"

"You're quite a moviemaker, Ethan," I said. I didn't dare speak too much. My own emotions were far from under control. A combination of relief, anger, and confusion swept through me.

"I didn't think it would work," Ethan said. "No offense, Zoe, but I thought you'd set Brix straight."

Brixton flung open the front door and stormed out.

"Hang on!" Ethan ran to the open doorway. "You guys should stay for dinner! I'm going to order takeout from that Vietnamese place you like but say is too fancy. My parents are at a stupid charity event all night. I've got my dad's credit card. Anything on the menu you want. Come on, Brix. Brix?"

Ethan's shoulders slumped. I walked over to stand with him in the entryway. From where we stood, I could see Brixton standing at my truck with his arms crossed, looking into the distance.

"We'd better go," I said. "But thanks for the invitation."

When Ethan turned toward me, nodding half heartedly, there was no mistaking the loneliness on his face. "Tell him it was just a joke, okay?"

"He'll get over it, Ethan," I said. I hoped I was right. In spite of his shortcomings, Ethan was a good kid. He thought of himself as a rebel, but in his world that meant buying designer clothes to mimic the style of James Dean and refusing to participate in the numerous extracurricular school activities his parents pressured him to join. Brixton and Veronica had been best friends since childhood, and Ethan found his first true friends in the two of them.

I walked through the excessively pruned front yard that could have been featured in a modern landscape magazine, and glanced back at the house as I unlocked my truck. The oversized front door was closed, but I thought I saw someone peeking out from behind the heavy white curtains.

"I'm going to kill him," Brixton said, slamming the door of my old truck.

"You know," I said, sitting still for a moment before starting the engine, "his joke tells us something important."

"That Ethan is the biggest jerk—and Veronica too. She's why I never doubted it was true!" He sank down into the seat.

"Brixton, he read the words. He read the real Latin that Dorian knows brought him to life."

"Yeah, I know."

"*It didn't work.*"

"You mean that's not how Dorian came to life?"

"There must be something *else* that has to trigger the Latin words," I said. "There's more going on." The book, I now realized, was far more dangerous and enigmatic than I'd suspected.

CHAPTER 20

"The answer," Dorian said, pacing across the creaking attic floor, "must be that the boy was not reading directly from my book."

"Maybe," I said. "Or maybe it's because the gnome was made of plaster, not stone." I thought back on the backward alchemy illustration Ivan had shown me, with the angel turning to stone. But even as I spoke the words, I wasn't convinced.

"There is one way," Dorian said, "to find out."

"We talked about this already. It's too dangerous." I didn't want to mess with implementing the dark forces of backward alchemy, only combatting them. That's why in all of my research into rejuvenating Dorian, I had never tried to bring an inanimate object to life. But desperate times call for desperate measures.

"Your face betrays you, Alchemist. You are as curious as I."

"It's not about curiosity," I snapped. "I never wanted to be an alchemist in the first place. I was happy as an herbalist. Spagyric alchemy was a way to understand more about the properties of plants. But this?" I flipped my white hair, my daily reminder that alchemy had saved the rest of my body from the ravages of time, while my hair and the rest of the world aged around me. "Sometimes I wish Nicolas and Perenelle had never seen my potential and taken me in. Then I might have been able to cure my brother the way I'd always done before I met the alchemists, because I wouldn't have wasted time chasing the false hope that I could find the Elixir of Life for him."

Dorian blinked at me. "But then you would not be here with me. And where would I be without you?"

"You would have found a more competent alchemist to help you." I picked up the object closest to me, a puzzle box missing the key that told how to open it. I threw it across the room as forcefully as I could. It bounced off the wall and landed on the Persian rug that covered the hole in the floor. It didn't break. I was even a failure at expressing angst. The thick wood pieces were linked in such a manner that I doubted anything besides a sledgehammer, or fire, could break it open.

Dorian limped over to me and rested his head on my elbow, then wrapped a wing around my shoulder. "If smashing objects helps you feel better, I can scavenge many things that would make the world a better place if they were broken."

I laughed, and a tear escaped to roll down my cheek. I extricated myself from Dorian's wing to pick up the puzzle box on the other side of the room. I didn't want him to see how upset I was. Was I so desperate for answers that I was seriously considering purposefully bringing a stone object to life? Would it tell me something that I couldn't hope to otherwise understand?

True alchemy is a focused, heightened state of natural processes, but backward alchemy turns nature on its head. I didn't understand nearly enough about the "death rotation" illustrated in *Non Degenera Alchemia*. In spite of my lack of understanding, I was certain with all my heart that although Dorian had been brought to life by the book, he wasn't evil like the backward alchemists who had created *Non Degenera Alchemia*.

"Intent," I said aloud, feeling hope rise within me.

"*Pardon?*"

"I was thinking through what we do know." I placed the carved box back on the shelf and looked at the articulated pelican skeleton. Pelicans are an important symbol in alchemy because of the sacrifice they make for their young. "*Intent* is important for an alchemist's work. Since alchemy is about transforming the impure into the pure, the alchemist's intent is as important to a transformation as are the ingredients."

"Intent," Dorian murmured.

"You weren't corrupted by this book, even though the backward alchemy inside shows so much death along with power and resurrection. I wonder if Ethan's incantation didn't work because of his intent. He *knew* he was playing a joke."

"*Non,*" Dorian said, shaking his head. "My father was not an alchemist. He did not know the words he read would bring me to life."

"But he read the words with purpose. He was planning on building a gargoyle automaton that would 'come to life.'"

Dorian gasped. "*C'est vrai!* This was his intention. And this will be your intention when you read the words."

"I still don't know if we should mess with the dark forces of backward alchemy."

"If you are not willing, I can enlist the boy's help."

"No. That's not going to happen." I'd taken Brixton home after our enlightening visit with Ethan, so it was just me and the gargoyle in the house. I'd already involved Brixton more than I should have.

"He would be happy to help."

I rubbed my temples. Sometimes there was no arguing with a desperate gargoyle. If I didn't help him, I had no doubt he would try it on his own or with Brixton. My unwillingness to take risks was causing us to spin our wheels. There were too many unanswered questions. Compared to approaching a murderous backward alchemist, bringing a baby Dorian to life seemed like the safer choice.

"If we do this," I said, "you follow my lead. Whatever happens, you do as I say."

Dorian mumbled something under his breath in French about narcissistic alchemists who think they know best. I ignored him and closed the attic door, locking us in, then set a foot-high stone carving of Buddha on the floor.

I opened *Non Degenera Alchemia* to the page Jean Eugène Robert-Houdin had read from all those years ago. The disturbing woodcut illustration showed a dead basilisk perched atop the ruins of a crumbling building, and bees circling overhead in a counterclockwise rotation. In stark contrast to the desolate image, the sweet scent of flowers wafted up from the faded page. Underneath the stronger aroma of cloves and honey I detected the scent of roses.

Dorian frowned. "Buddha is a bad choice."

"He's got a full body, just like you. He's made of a similar stone. This statue is a perfect choice."

"But it is *Buddha*."

I considered. "You think it's blasphemous?" I asked.

"*Non,*" Dorian said. "Boring. If I am to have a companion, he should be someone who enjoys great food. The Buddha would insist on eating simple meals. The words 'simple' and 'meal' should never be used in the same sentence. *Non*. That will not do."

"I'm not bringing to life the spirit of the Buddha, you know. We don't yet

353

know where the power comes from, but surely you see you're not the devil you look like."

Dorian touched his horns with his stone hands, his eyes opening wide. "You think I am a devil?"

I sighed. "Of course not. I don't know what Viollet-le-Duc had in mind when he carved you, but I'm certain it wasn't the soul of a gourmet chef. You've become your own person, Dorian. Just as this little Buddha will be. If this works."

"*D'accord.* You may try it." He scowled at Buddha, then retreated into the corner.

I held the book in trembling hands and read the Latin. I'd studied this page to such an extent over the past months that I knew the words by heart. But I was careful to read the words from the page, with my energy and intent directed at the stone Buddha statue.

I finished the incantation and looked to the stone Buddha.

CHAPTER 21

"He does not move," Dorian said, poking the Buddha statue with a clawed fingertip.

"No," I agreed. "I read the words perfectly. You're sure that's all Robert-Houdin did?"

"That is what he said. And yes, he was a man of details. This is how he was such a successful stage magician. He would not have left out any details when he told me what happened. Perhaps it is my presence?"

Over the next hour, we tried everything I could think of. Different figurines of different materials and sizes, different locations in the house, and with Dorian both present and absent from the room.

Nothing worked.

"Perhaps it is your clothing," Dorian suggested. "The forces of nature must not believe you are an alchemist. Before the flooding, your clothes were much nicer."

I looked down at my frumpy jeans, remembering the torn dress that had been the only thing I owned for the first year after my brother and I fled Salem Village. "It's not my clothes."

"*Alors*, I am truly a freak of nature."

"Dorian—"

"You are exhausted. It is nearly ten o'clock, and we have not yet eaten dinner. I will cook."

"I'm going to bed."

"Zoe, you have not eaten for half the day. Your skin is drawn. Your eyes are bloodshot. Your hair scatters the floor. You *must* eat."

He was right. There was a time when I didn't take care of myself at all, and it was surprisingly easily to let those bad habits take hold again while under pressure. We descended the steep stairs from the attic. Dorian moved slowly, no longer the agile creature I'd met three months ago.

"Ah!" he cried out.

I saw what was happening but couldn't reach his flailing arms in time.

He tumbled down the steep attic stairs, living stone crashing into each thick wood step. I cringed as I watched his gray body contort and land with a crash on the hardwood floor in front of my bedroom.

"My left wing!"

I hurried down the steps and knelt next to his prostrate body. "It didn't break off."

"I cannot move it." His lower lip trembled.

"You need to let me give you another infusion of alchemy."

The gargoyle struggled to sit up, yet he brushed off my attempts to help him. His left leg was now fully stone, and he was unable to bend it to balance. After pushing himself up with his working wing, he grudgingly accepted my help to limp down the flight of stairs that led to the living room.

"If you let me cook you a hearty dinner tonight," he said without meeting my gaze, "I will consent to your assistance with another batch of the Teas of Ashes."

I awoke the next morning with the sun, unsure if I felt optimistic or defeated. I knew both more *and* less about Dorian's book.

Ethan's prank had forced my hand into making the discovery that invoking the power of the words in the book wasn't enough to bring a piece of stone to life. I now had more information. Yet at the same time, I felt as though I was further from unlocking the secrets of the book. And even if I could, unlocking the coded messages of the book still might not be enough to save my friend.

I needed help. I again came back to the question of whether it was worth the risk to ask Peter Silverman, the murderous magician alchemist, for help. Should I make a deal with the Devil to save an innocent?

That was a question I first grappled with 300 years ago. That time, I waited too long to make my own decision. It wasn't literally a deal with the Devil, but it felt like it all the same. My brother had suffered and died because of it. I'd gone on a fool's errand that took me from my brother during his last days on earth and cursed me to live on.

My little brother, Thomas, died of the plague in 1704, when he was just twenty-six years old. At the time, I didn't believe my shattered heart would ever heal. I already knew heartbreak, of course. Between disease, distrust, and death, life in the "Age of Enlightenment" was brutal. I watched three of my siblings die in infancy, watched my mother and father stand mutely by as I was accused of witchcraft for my connection to plants, and heard the whispers as my former friends abandoned me one by one.

It wasn't Thomas's death *itself* that broke my heart; it was the cause of it. It was Thomas who helped me escape being burned as a witch. At age sixteen, I fled from Salem Village, Massachusetts, to London, England, with the help of fourteen-year-old Thomas. He was the only person to stand with me through the next twelve years. And I let him down. I might have been able to save him if I'd been there for him instead of abandoning him to study alchemy.

I spent his last weeks on earth trying to find the Elixir of Life. I ignored the advice of Nicolas Flamel, refusing to believe I wouldn't be able to transfer an alchemical protection to another person. Nicolas had advised me to enjoy Thomas's company for his last days on earth, making him as comfortable as possible. Instead, I discovered the Elixir of Life for myself without realizing it, and Thomas died alone.

It was my deal with the Devil. Asking for immortality so I could save my brother, but being granted it only for myself, cursed to live out my endless days alone. I've never forgiven myself for that youthful mistake. I spent the next hundred years trying to atone for my sins, helping everyone except myself. I didn't feel worthy of receiving my gift of immortality. An accidental alchemist, I atoned for my sins by healing others. Sometimes it was enough; and sometimes it wasn't.

I didn't want to repeat the same mistake again.

I pulled on the thick wool socks I kept at the side of my bed and put on a robe. Even though it was spring, the house was cold from the drafts that had crept in during the night, a result of not having properly fixed up the place. One day.

In the kitchen, I got myself a glass of water with fresh lemon slices. I was still full from the late dinner Dorian had cooked of roasted asparagus with a tarragon and avocado sauce, a French lentil salad, and cashew cheesecake, but I knew I needed to eat breakfast if I was going to have the energy to make Dorian's backward alchemy tea.

I took a mug of steaming green tea to the back porch along with a pen and notebook, and one of Dorian's oat cakes. I watched the sun begin to cast light over my incongruous garden: half of the backyard filled with thriving greenery, the other half barren dirt where I'd pulled plants from their roots to mix into the backward alchemy that began rather than ended with fire.

With the Venetian fountain pen, I started a list of what I knew: One, I needed help with Dorian's book. Two, Peter Silverman was an alchemist who was most likely in town to retrieve his lost hoard before someone else took it.

As for what I didn't know, that list was much longer:

Was it safe to approach Peter openly? Would Peter admit what he was, or get defensive and attempt to silence me, as he might have done to Wallace Mason? Was Wallace's friend in danger, too? I paused in my scribbles. If that was the case, didn't I have a moral obligation to warn him? If it was indeed the magician-alchemist who had killed Wallace, the police would never be able to unlock the motive. I could only hope they had enough physical evidence to lock him up. But, as evidenced by his presence here, the police hadn't stopped him before.

Speaking of the police, why had Max expressed an interest in my gargoyle statue right before he left? I hadn't had time to think about it while worrying about Ethan's garden gnome, but anything that drew attention to Dorian filled me with unease.

I wished I had someone else I could confide in besides a teenager and a gargoyle. But alchemists were so few and far between. A bad feeling tickled my cold fingertips and spread through me. Since finding the Elixir of Life is personal, it was rare for both members of a couple to find it. True, both Nicolas and Perenelle Flamel had managed this, as had Ambrose and I. But we were the exceptions. Could Penelope be an alchemist as well? If so, knowing now what I knew about backward alchemy and how I suspected Peter's involvement with it to fake his death, he could have used it to help Penelope achieve the same degree of unnatural immortality. At the very least, she must know Peter's secret.

I couldn't trust the magician-alchemists. Nor could I get the help I needed from my teenage ally or the dying gargoyle. Ivan's theoretical knowledge of alchemy was helping, and though I couldn't trust him with my secret, I knew he was on my side. But his help was coming too slowly.

I finished my tea and oat cake, got dressed, then gathered enough plants from the garden to fill a copper bucket. The plants that looked most energetic this morning were stinging nettles and sunflowers. I avoided my thriving lemon balm. Paracelsus, the sixteenth-century doctor and alchemist, called lemon balm the Elixir of Life. Lemon balm tea worked wonders for me, but when I'd tried to work it into Dorian's Tea of Ashes, it resisted the unnatural process. Now I stuck to weedier plants.

I descended the stairs to the basement. For half the morning, I transformed the healthy plants into ashes that I dissolved with sulfurous fire and mercury. Like Paracelsus and other alchemists before me, I focused on the *tria prima* of mercury, sulfur, and salt.

I knew firsthand how dangerous mercury was. Many an alchemist had been poisoned by it. It was a dual-faced rebus, capable of both healing and hurting. I kept mercury on hand for true alchemy, but it was also an ingredient of backward alchemy.

As I stirred the mixture counterclockwise and performed the steps of alchemy in the hastened, backward way explained in the book, the energy from the plants and my own body transferred to the ashes. The plant leaves wilted. My lips and the tips of my fingertips shriveled in a way I now recognized—a cross between soaking in a bathtub for too long and being stuck under the desert sun. I blinked to combat my aching eyes that felt as dry as the ashes I'd created.

Success. I held up the unnatural ashes in my weakened hand.

A normal alchemical operation of this importance would have taken months, even years, to perfect. But because this was backward alchemy, the Tea of Ashes took only a small fraction of that time. The problem was its effects. They were severe and long-lasting. The first time I made the unnatural tea for Dorian, I hadn't realized the sacrifice it involved—or how much it could hurt me.

My "success" was a disingenuous one. Each time I went through the process, I felt it pull more of my own life force out of me.

After steeping the ashes in hot water, I found Dorian in the attic. He sat on the floor reading another science fiction novel that he'd requested I pick up at the library for him. His left leg was askew.

He shifted under my gaze. "I was extra careful on my way to and from Blue Sky Teas during the night. The baking is done, and nobody saw me." He set the book aside and looked up at me with concern.

"You've been reading a lot of science fiction lately." I handed him the Tea of Ashes. Before I'd discovered this quick fix of the Tea of Ashes, Dorian had to keep moving to avoid turning to stone. The movements could be small, so he'd had me check out dozens of classic mystery novels from the library to stay awake through reading. Before he met me he'd been a literary snob, but

I'd expanded his horizons. Most recently he'd been giving me lists of science fiction novels, like the one he had in his hand.

"There are more beings like me in science fiction than in detective novels." He accepted the sour-smelling concoction. "Though I'm not sure I enjoy the ambiguous endings. Next time, I will ask you to bring me more cookbooks as well."

"The last time I did that, you scribbled notes in the margins throughout the books. You can't do that to library books."

"They should thank me!" he replied indignantly.

Dorian's snout scrunched as he drank the thick, grainy tea. As soon as he handed the mug back to me, with only sediment remaining, the near-black color of his left leg and wing lightened. A moment later, his wing flapped, and he was able to bend his knee.

"*Merci, mon amie.*"

He bounded down the stairs. I was glad his newfound energy had given him the speed to depart quickly. That way he didn't see me falter. My legs no longer had the strength to hold me upright. I tried to push myself up from the floor, but my shriveled fingertips felt as if they were still clutching the leather binding of Dorian's book. I tried to breathe, but I imagined I was still smelling the confusing scents from *Not Untrue Alchemy*. My vision clouded and I collapsed onto the dusty floor.

CHAPTER 22

The retired magician lifted the book from the dusty shelf. A jolt of electricity caused his fingertips to tingle as the leather spine touched his skin.

The scent of the volume pushed its way through the still air of the old magician's study, seeming stronger than anything that could possibly emanate from the leather binding and onion skin pages. He identified cloves, honey, and dung, accompanied by an imprecise hint of decay. It was as if the book was greater than the sum of its parts.

The magician shook his head. He knew that wasn't possible. He was becoming fanciful in his old age. Yet there was something mysterious about the antique book. He hoped others would sense its power.

Though officially retired, Jean Eugène Robert-Houdin wanted to keep his mind sharp. The Father of Modern Magic had moved to Saint-Gervais to write his memoirs.

When the French government had taken him away from his writing, calling upon him to serve his country by intervening in Algeria to help divert a military crisis, he had been skeptical. True, he was arguably the most famous stage magician in the world, but his sleight of hand wasn't magic. Nobody was more surprised than Robert-Houdin when his new way to perform the bullet-catch illusion convinced Algerian tribal leaders of France's power. They believed he was performing real magic.

Perhaps most unexpected was his own reaction to his assignment. Instead of discomfort at the dangers he encountered, Robert-Houdin found himself craving further adventure. No longer content to sit in his study and write his memoirs, he wished for a continued audience. Not necessarily on the stage in Paris where he once performed, but creating new illusions he could show to his family and friends.

It was for this end that he selected the curious book with a Latin title. It would be the perfect prop for an automaton he was building.

Robert-Houdin carried the hefty volume to the draw ing room, where a meter-high stone carving rested in the corner, underneath a sheet. He chuckled to himself. His wife hated the gargoyle given to him by his friend Eugène Viollet-le-Duc, and tossed a covering over it whenever her husband wasn't looking.

The carving was unlike other gargoyles Robert-Houdin had seen in his travels across Europe. First, it was not technically a gargoyle, in the original meaning of the word, for it did not function as a waterspout. This stone carving was purely ornamental. Viollet-le-Duc had been commissioned to renovate the great cathedral of Notre Dame de Paris, and he had the fanciful idea of creating a gallery of monsters looking over the saints below. The stone creature sitting in Robert-Houdin's drawing room was an early prototype of Viollet-le-Duc's that the architect realized was too small to sit aloft the cathedral's high walkway.

Robert-Houdin pulled the sheet away from the stone carving. Folded wings curled around the stone beast. The little gargoyle looked remarkably like *Le Styrge*, the carving of Viollet-le-Duc's that held a prominent spot next to the stairway entrance to the cathedral's gallery of monsters. An impish grin adorned the creature's face. Yes, this gargoyle would be perfect for what the great Robert-Houdin had in mind.

The magician was known for his ingenious engineering as much as for sleight of hand. His most well regarded invention was an automaton that could both write and draw, a creation which he had shown to King Philippe before it was sold to P.T. Barnum. His favorite, though, was his orange tree. Symbolizing spring renewal and rebirth, the mechanical tree "grew" from a withered stump into a lush patchwork of leafy branches that sprouted real oranges. Mechanical birds appeared in the tree, which was impressive enough, but these birds would then perform yet another feat for the audience. They flew above the tree and revealed a ring "borrowed" from an audience member. The mechanical tree was his crowning achievement—until now.

Robert-Houdin had given a metal plant life. Now, he would bring a stone chimera to life. His own personal golem. He allowed himself a sly smile nobody was there to see. The feat wasn't real, of course. Merely an illusion. He would craft a metal automaton and cover the moving parts with a dummy made in the mold of Viollet-le-Duc's stone creation. Then, on stage, he would recite a few words of "magic" from an ancient book, bringing the creature to life.

He stroked his chin. He would have to time it perfectly, by adding a winding mechanism to the automaton so it could be wound up several minutes before springing to life. But for a former clockmaker, this was a trifling task—far easier than lifting an assistant above the stage with ether.

First, however, it was time to practice. The most important part of any illusion was the drama surrounding it. Without expectation, an illusion was a simple trick, easily forgotten. And Jean Eugène Robert-Houdin did not wish his work to be forgotten.

Sitting in an armchair in front of the creature, he leafed through the book. The intermingling scents were stronger now, as if the book had been dropped in a farmer's field. But no damage showed upon the pages. Odd, that.

No matter. The book was almost twenty centimeters by fifteen, large enough to be easily seen from a stage, especially in a small theater with only a dozen people in the audience.

The book was written mostly in Latin, but many pages were filled with woodcut illustrations rather than text. Robert-Houdin had seen many things in his life, both horrible and wondrous, but the illustrations in this book sent a shiver from his head of gray hair down to the bunions of his feet in his patent leather shoes.

An admirer had given Robert-Houdin the book as a gift, and now Robert-Houdin would put it to good use. Yes, this antique book plus his new gargoyle automaton would create the performance of a lifetime.

Non Degenera Alchemia, the title read.

CHAPTER 23

I wasn't unconscious for long, but it was longer than I would have liked. The taxing act of creating the Tea of Ashes caused me to have disturbingly vivid dreams. In my unnatural sleep, the pages of *Non Degenera Alchemia—Not Untrue Alchemy*—came to life before my eyes and transformed into Jean Eugène Robert-Houdin's stage magic performance I'd seen in 1845. The bees rose from the dead and circled sluggishly around me, as if by the magical ether that raised sleeping people above the stage in the theater. When I woke up, I was shivering. I half expected to see a dead bee next to me.

My legs and arms shook as I climbed down the attic stairs. I drew a bath, the most comfortable option in a house with pipes that insisted on alternating between scalding hot and freezing cold water. I applied a poultice of plantain and salt to my skin to suck out any toxins from my alchemy. The wild plantain weed was from the equally wild yard in front of Blue's cottage.

My skills were only one of the reasons I made my own remedies. I'd lived through times when supposed medicines were filled with poison. The "blue pills" dubbed as cure-alls during Victorian times were full of mercury, and many medicines for babies had contained opium. Though I was born in New England during Colonial times, I think of myself as a Victorian more than anything else. I left home at sixteen, and it was during the Victorian era that I settled down for a time after a long period of travel. Therefore the fears and mores from that era were etched into my mind more firmly than the culture of other places where I lived for shorter periods of time.

Right now, I wished there was a cure-all that would be as easy as swallowing a pill. I knew I should fix myself a healing tea or tincture, but I couldn't fathom doing anything besides sleeping after my bath, so I dressed in flannel pajamas and crawled into bed. I was planning on taking a nap, but as soon as I lay down I detected the fragrant scents of berries and cream.

I opened my eyes. Dorian stood at the foot of the bed, carrying a tray of food.

"Is it lunchtime already?"

"Brunch. You had a taxing morning, so I have made crepes for you. One is filled with chocolate, the other coconut cream and wild strawberries. The English cannot compete with the French when it comes to any food invention —besides Vindaloo, of course—yet their idea for this extra meal of brunch is quite a good one."

I smiled with my cracked lips, happy to see Dorian back to his old self. "I don't think it's supposed to be an *extra* meal, but I'll take the crepes. I'm famished."

He set the tray on the side table and hopped up on the edge of the bed. "This is my fault," he said, his gray legs dangling without touching the floor.

"You're apologizing for the food? That's a first." My throat was so dry that I barely recognized my voice.

He clicked his tongue. "You are sick. I was unsure which herbal remedy you would like, so I brought food. I will return with tea, once you tell me which one you would like."

"There's a glass jar in the backyard labeled Lemon Balm Infusion. Would you bring it to me?"

When he returned a few minutes later with the sun-infused tea, I had nearly finished the first crepe. That morning's transformation had expended a lot of my energy.

"Are you are strong enough to hold the mug yourself?" Dorian asked.

I nodded, unable to conceal a smile, and accepted the giant porcelain serving carafe in which he'd warmed several servings of tea.

"*Bon.* Then I will read you the news we have missed." He jumped up onto the bed and spread *Le Monde* in front of him.

"What's the matter?" I asked as his wings drooped.

"For the past month, I have not found any more news of gold statues crumbling in Europe."

"I noticed that too."

"Does this mean the false gold is already... dead?"

I knew what he meant. Just as Dorian's life force was reversing for a reason

I had yet to identify, false gold in Europe had begun to crumble into dust at the same time. The newspapers had reported the missing gold as thefts, but we knew better. Whatever was happening to both Dorian and the crumbling gold, the gold had already wasted away. Or as Dorian had put it, the gold was dead. I shivered. My Tea of Ashes alchemy might be the only thing keeping Dorian alive.

At that moment, with the scared look on Dorian's face, I abhorred the backward alchemists with the strongest conviction I'd felt this century.

There have always been rogue alchemists. I'd learned from Nicolas Flamel, who was my mentor for a brief time, that the core group of men who'd practiced backward alchemy in Europe were long-since dead. It was an inevitable outcome, since backward alchemy is dangerous and unsustainable. But a break-off sect of alchemists from the heyday of Western alchemy had set forces into motion that were coming to a head half a millennium later.

What I didn't know was why this was happening *now*. The backward alchemists were dead. *What was it they had done?*

I'd failed miserably when I tried to find true alchemists, some of whom should still be alive. But I was out of my depth. I had to try again.

I wasn't well enough to leave my bed, so I asked Dorian to bring me my laptop. From the bed, I searched for any leads I might have overlooked before. I'd searched before, but the Internet rabbit hole had many winding paths. I decided to join a chat group of alchemy enthusiasts. What can I say? I was desperate.

After joining the online group, I was allowed to look through the discussion archives. An hour later, I was certain these alchemists were an assortment of well-meaning amateurs across the spectrum of alchemical interests.

All alchemy is about transformation, but it's approached in different ways. The three core elements of alchemy are sulfur, mercury, and salt. Sulfur is the soul, mercury is the spirit, and salt is the body. Over the centuries, alchemy has involved transformations of base metals into gold, of the mortal body into an immortal one, and of the corrupted spirit into something pure.

In the past, the first two were primarily what alchemists studied, thus acting as a precursor to modern chemistry and medicine. More recently, spiritual alchemy had become more prominent. That's what the members of this listserv were mostly concerned with. The few new members who asked about making gold were met with derision, and they quickly left. Interesting how times had changed.

Though I didn't learn anything on that website, it showed me that perhaps expanding my search would lead me somewhere. I wondered if any of the few real alchemists I'd once known had gotten involved with spiritual alchemy to ease their discontent with outliving everyone they cared about.

With renewed hope, I felt a surge of energy. I scoured the Internet for spiritual alchemy gatherings. I felt my stomach rumbling and was about to give up, when my hands froze above the keyboard.

I knew the light hazel eyes of the spiritual alchemy speaker in the photograph on the screen. I knew the man not from my many travels throughout the United States since 1942, but from long before.

Or at least, that was my first impression. It couldn't be true, though. Toby was a man I'd known in the late 1850s, during the time I spent with the Underground Railroad. He'd been a sickly man when I first encountered him and nursed him back to health. Nothing like the vibrant man in the photograph named Tobias Freeman. Toby had known nothing of alchemy, and I hadn't taught him. I was heartened, though. This strong resemblance must have meant that Toby had survived and had children.

Because I was good with herbal remedies, my role in the Underground Railroad was to help slaves who were too weak to make the journey north, nursing them back to health to give them a fighting chance to make it. Tobias was one of the weakest men I'd cared for. He was close to six feet tall, and I doubt he'd weighed much more than 100 pounds when he was brought to my doorstep.

But there was no mistaking those light hazel eyes, so light they shone like gold.

The online conference program listed an email address for Tobias Freeman. Nothing ventured...

My friend Levi Coffin recommended I get in touch, I wrote in an email from my Elixir email account, signing my name simply as *Zoe*. Levi had been involved in the Underground Railroad, so if this was the same man I'd known, I hoped he'd pick up on the reference. If not, I'd simply get a polite message telling me I was mistaken.

Not five minutes later, an email reply pinged on my phone.

Zoe Faust. I never thought I'd see you again, my friend.

CHAPTER 24

I hadn't yet decided how much would be prudent to tell my old friend—that a living gargoyle was living with me, that a murderous alchemist had recently come to town, or perhaps that a book of dangerous backward alchemy was in my possession—when he sent me a second email.

Too much to say over email, he wrote. *Checked my schedule and I've got a couple of days off work this week. As long as you're in the U.S., I can catch a flight to see you.*

I agreed there was too much to say over email. In person, I would also be able to confirm that he was still the same good man I'd known over a century before. Some things about people change over time, but some don't. I hoped Tobias was still the pure-souled Toby I'd once known.

We made plans for him to fly to Portland in two days. I also had an email from Veronica, apologizing for the joke she and Ethan had played and saying she'd started work on my website. I sent quick email replies, then practically flew down the stairs in search of Dorian, my sickness nearly forgotten.

"*Salut!*" the gargoyle said as I came through the kitchen's swinging door. He hopped down from his stepping stool and wiped his hands on his flour-covered apron. His balance was a little off, with two missing stone toes, but he quickly recovered. "You are well enough to venture to the market! I have made a shopping list."

"Dorian, I found someone who can help us." I didn't even care that flour and some sort of red paste covered a swath of the kitchen walls, including the curtains that prevented curious onlookers from spotting Dorian. I took the list and set it on the countertop.

"You are feeling braver about the magician?"

"No, I found a man I *trust*." I accepted a miniature red velvet cupcake from Dorian's outstretched hand, and told him about Tobias.

"And he will be here in two days?" Dorian asked once I concluded.

"He's flying in on Wednesday. Can I have another cupcake?"

"*Non.*"

"No?" That was a first.

"You have not yet eaten lunch." He gave a sniff. "Have I taught you nothing about being a civilized person in these months we have known each other?"

I threw my arms around the gargoyle.

"Nor have I taught you enough about being dignified," he mumbled, though he hugged me back. "Your fidgeting is making me nervous, Zoe. I can see you do not wish to be cooped up in the house with me today. I will pack your lunch as a picnic basket to take with you."

"Take with me?"

He gave a Gallic shrug. "Your friend is not arriving for two days. Plenty of time for exploring more leads that might help us, *n'est pas?*"

With a heavy picnic basket loaded into the passenger seat of the truck, I drove to the theater. I didn't know what I hoped to find, but Dorian was right. There was so much going on that if I was well enough to leave the house, I should be doing something productive.

As I approached the theater, I caught a glimpse of Penelope's distinctive hair. She was driving the SUV I remembered, with Peter in the passenger seat. They were pulling away from the theater.

Should I?

I followed them for several minutes, careful not to get too close in my distinctive 1940s truck. It turned out I was *too* careful. In a city of narrow bridges with hidden entrances, it was impossible to hang back and still see where they turned. I lost them.

I pulled off the road and realized I was next to River View Cemetery. Could that be where they'd gone? The cemetery land was on a hillside overlooking the Willamette River, near where the sapphire necklace from the Lake Loot had been discovered by the young boys. I put the truck into gear and eased up the winding hillside drive that lead through the cemetery.

I could see why Dorian liked this graveyard, one of the forested areas he frequented under the cover of night. River View Cemetery cultivated a peaceful beauty, from its welcoming walkways and weeping cherry trees to its personalized headstones and mausoleums, each in its own style rather than dictated by the cemetery board. It didn't have as many ornately carved statues as some, such as Highgate Cemetery in London, but it was calm and hospitable.

I felt myself fading, so I was glad Dorian had insisted on packing me a picnic lunch. My body was too exhausted to carry the picnic basket far, so I found a sunny spot on a patch of cut grass with views of the river, a small grouping of ornate mausoleums, and headstones with loving memorials from families. I spread out a blanket and opened the basket from Dorian. The heaping picnic basket contained enough food for at least four people. I found two homemade baguettes with vegetables flavored with olive and walnut tapenades, an assortment of fruit, a thermos of chai tea, and a large mason jar of homemade green juice made with apple, celery, parsley, spinach, and ginger. I knew what was in the juice because of a handmade label with Dorian's distinctive French handwriting that adorned the outside of the jar. While he'd taught me many things about transforming food through cooking, I'd taught him the importance of labeling all of one's transformations.

Though picnicking in cemeteries has fallen out of fashion, the Victorians loved it. Society wasn't always death-phobic in the way it is today. Death used to be much more integrated into life. It was difficult to dismiss it so easily when it was more common, but it also wasn't hidden from sight when it did happen. Though sorrow was involved, it was a natural part of life, and therefore it was celebrated as such, in part through beautifully constructed cemeteries.

I wondered how I would one day die. Through violence while helping someone? An incurable sickness? Or simply a car accident I never saw coming? I thought of it often. Though I had achieved a degree of immortality in a more natural way than alchemists who practiced the "death rotation" of backward alchemy, I hadn't purposefully sought out this aspect of alchemy. Yet I would never end my own life as my old love Ambrose had, when he took his own life after he outlived his son. My life wasn't easy, but it brought many joys, including many new ones I'd found here in Portland.

The reason most true alchemists seek out the Elixir of Life is so they may live long enough to achieve a greater understanding of life. Especially in past times when life spans were so much shorter, there was so much unfinished business. Therefore a longer life goes hand in hand with alchemy's quest to turn the impure into the pure. The Flamels used their longer lives and alchemical skills to transmute gold that they gave to charities. I and others I had once known used our herbal healing skills to help others, such as what I'd done for Toby. We couldn't purify all of the world's evils, but maybe one day the world would be ready.

I sipped Dorian's chai tea and wondered what it would be like to see Tobias (as I should now call him, apparently) again, until I was startled out of my thoughts.

I was under the impression that the treasure hunters had packed up and left the area, but that didn't appear to be the case. Not completely. A fence was in place in an attempt to keep people out of the unstable areas where a minor landslide had occurred due to the winter flooding, but I spotted two men with metal detectors. They were cutting through the cemetery on their way to the steep public lands beyond that had suffered the brunt of the landslide. That was the area where experts speculated the sapphire necklace had come from before it washed down the hillside.

I froze when I spotted a third man with a metal detector. This man stood out. *I knew him.* A thick head of gray hair that fell to his shoulders and hearty black eyebrows gave him a distinctive look. This wasn't someone who could be easily forgotten. He was one of the two men I'd seen sneaking around the theater. The friend of the dead man, Wallace Mason.

CHAPTER 25

"Hello there!" the dead man's friend called to me.

Dammit. I'd been staring.

"I couldn't help notice you looking at my metal detector." He walked over to my picnic blanket, eyeing it suspiciously. "You here for the same thing? Got one concealed in that gargantuan picnic basket of yours?"

"I read about the treasure hunting in the paper." I stood and extended my hand. "I'm Zoe. And I'm not here searching for the missing loot. Only enjoying the view."

"Earl Rasputin." He took my hand. His hand was rough, calloused. It matched his gritty, deep voice.

I also noticed his eyes were rimmed with red. Of course. His friend had been murdered.

He scratched his stubbly cheek. "You look familiar. Have we met?"

Had he seen me inside the theater with Dorian? Had he and Wallace still been there when I spoke with Peter and Penelope? I would have seen him if he'd been in my line of sight, but perhaps he'd heard my voice. That could have been why he thought I was familiar.

"You look familiar to me too," I said. "I've got it. You were with the man who volunteered for the *Phantasmagoria* magic show."

"You were there?"

"I love a good magic show." I cringed inwardly at my inept response. Clearly it wasn't just my body that was lacking at the moment; my mental faculties weren't at 100 percent either. Plus, his bushy black eyebrows were distracting.

He sighed. "You haven't seen the news."

"Oh, how stupid of me. Yes, of course." I fiddled with my hands, trying to appear flustered as if I'd only just now remembered that Wallace was dead. It wasn't difficult, since I was flustered for another reason. I tried to think of a good segue to warn him about the magician without sounding crazy. I also needed to find out what he knew about the loot that had led him to spy on the magicians, when nobody else seemed to have made the connection. But all I came up with was, "I'm so sorry. I did hear about the man who was killed. He was your friend?"

"You get to be my age, and you lose a lotta friends," he said. "It's not an enjoyable experience, but you learn to live with it. But this one's different. I'm not used to losing friends through violent death—if you don't count war." He paused and his dark eyes bore into me. "In the face of death, what you learn most is that you've gotta keep on living. That's why I'm out here today."

I looked around. A lot of trees and birds, but not a lot of people. "His funeral?"

"Nah, the police still have him."

"That's awful." I shivered, and I wasn't acting for Earl's benefit. When I thought of Wallace Mason's dead body falling onto the stage floor, the image replayed itself in slow motion in my mind, as if I could have done something to prevent it. "Do you know what happened?"

"He went and got himself stabbed to death." Earl shook his head. "He always had a temper, so who the hell knows who he pissed off this time. Stupid bastard. Gets himself killed just when we're so close!"

"So close?" *What did he know about Franklin Thorne, aka Peter Silverman, and his loot?*

"Wallace and I are treasure hunters. Been doing it for close to a decade now. Instead of sitting at home alone drinking the bottle of rye he bought me for my last birthday, I thought I'd honor his memory by coming out here today. See if I can find the treasure."

"You're talking about the Lake Loot? I thought everyone had given up on it."

He looked from me to the picnic basket, his eyes narrowing as he did so. "You know a lot about it for someone who says they're not here for the treasure. You having a party here? Where are the rest of your friends hiding?"

"It's just me. Would you like to sit down and have something to eat? I was hungry, so I overdid it."

"You got that right." He set down the metal detector and a fanny pack, then hitched up his jeans and sat down on the plaid picnic blanket. Apparently he'd decided I was harmless. I wasn't so sure about him, though, when I caught a glimpse of what was in the fanny pack. Flyers about Bigfoot sightings. *Bigfoot.*

Yes, I'd just invited a conspiracy theorist to join me for a late lunch in a cemetery.

Well, since he was already sitting down, I might as well sit back down, too, and give him a sandwich. After all, I needed to warn him to stay away from the magician-alchemist.

"What's a pretty little lady doing all alone in a cemetery?" Earl asked, taking a bite of the olive tapenade and vegetable sandwich.

"It's peaceful here." I pressed my locket to my chest, my daily cemetery reminder. "I'm surprised they allow metal detectors in here. Seems like that's an open invitation for grave robbing."

"Some poor sap was arrested for that very reason. Nah, they run a tight ship here. You stick a shovel in the ground and they'll stop you before you toss the first pile of dirt over your shoulder. But I know what I'm doing. I was just passing through to the landslide area." He waved his hand over to where I'd seen the other treasure hunters headed.

"The landslide area that's blocked off—"

"You work for the police, missy?"

"No, but—"

"Then maybe you should mind your own business."

I contemplated skipping the warning to stay away from the alchemist's hoard, but my conscience got the better of me. "I was only trying to help. It seems awfully dangerous. It seems like you'd be doing a disservice to your friend to get arrested or die trying to find the loot."

"Neither is gonna happen."

"Do you know something more than the others about the Lake Loot?"

Earl narrowed his eyes at me.

"Don't you think it's suspicious," I said, "that your friend was killed right when you two were so close to finding it? I don't mean to be nosey, but I'd hate to see the same thing happen to someone else."

"Like I said, Wallace had a temper. He was a good man, and helped me out years ago when I was going through a rough time, but lots of people would say he had it coming. I already told the police. Don't you worry about it. *Damn.*"

My skin prickled. Had he remembered something? "What is it?" "This is the best sandwich I've eaten in years. You a chef?"

I sighed. "I cook pastries for a café part-time. But you've got me curious. What do you know about the loot?"

"I used to work as a chef."

"You did?"

He nodded. "I was born at the wrong time. I owned a food truck twenty years before they became popular."

"What did you cook?"

"Chocolate fondue. Now, I can tell what you're thinking. That's pretty dang messy for a food truck. But that was the genius of it. I've got a knack at tempering chocolate, bringing it to the right temperature so it doesn't melt when you don't want it to. Each morning dip an assortment of sweet and savory foods in chocolate, then pop 'em into the truck's fridge. Voilà. I'd have fresh chocolate-covered fruit, scones, bacon, you name it. I'd take custom orders. Those were the most popular. I never understood grilled cheese sandwiches dipped in chocolate, but to each his own." Earl shook his head. "I'm a man ahead of my time. When I was ready to retire I sold my truck to a young punk for a song, and now the kid's got lines down the street for some sort of curried chick pea burrito. Baffles the mind."

"And now you look for lost Oregon treasures?"

"You've got talent, young lady." He tucked the last piece of a sandwich into his mouth and closed his eyes as he chewed, giving me a chance to study his face. As he ate in blissful silence, his weathered skin accentuated the lines around his mouth and eyes. He gave a contented sigh, then his dark eyes popped open and startled me with the intensity of his gaze. "I don't give out praise willy-nilly. You mind?" He indicated the basket.

"Help yourself. And thanks. But you never answered my question. What's your secret information about the Lake Loot? You've got me intrigued."

He squinted his eyes at me. "If I told you, how do I know you wouldn't take it for yourself?"

"Why would I do that? I don't understand why *anyone* is after it. Whoever finds it can't keep it. It belongs to the Lake family."

"You're forgetting about the reward."

"You're in it for the small reward?"

He picked up a second sandwich and stood up. "You wouldn't understand. It's the thrill of the hunt, honey. The thrill of the hunt. And now that Wallace is gone, I'm going to find it to honor his memory."

~

After Earl left, I again felt like I knew less rather than more. Earl was a strange fellow. Bigfoot sightings? An inside track on the treasure? He knew a lot more than he was telling me, but what? It couldn't be a coincidence that he'd been sneaking around the theater. What had he discovered about Peter Silverman's connection to the Lake Loot? If he believed in Bigfoot, did he believe in alchemy? Or could it all be an act? Could he have killed his friend once they were close to finding the treasure?

I was tired of thinking. At least Earl had saved me from lugging a heavy picnic basket back to the car. He'd eaten almost everything.

I was still tired from the effort I'd expended that morning, but a walk would do me good. I was cold despite the warm spring air and my thick sweater, another indication that my energy was depleted in ways that food couldn't heal. Either that or this polyester sweater wasn't nearly as warm as my favorite wool sweater that had been impaled by a sharp piece of ceiling.

I followed a winding path past a set of mausoleums. Either by accident or design, the plants circling several of the raised crypts mirrored the family names. I imagined that in late summer, giant sunflowers shadowed the Sun family mausoleum. The Thorne mausoleum was surrounded by thorny rose bushes, destined to bloom vibrant and fragrant. And a skilled gardener had somewhat successfully coaxed blackberry bushes into growing up the outer stone walls of the Blackstone crypt.

There weren't any funerals taking place that Monday afternoon, so I had the place mostly to myself. Until a figure caught my eye. Though he was on a path below me on the hillside, it was impossible to miss him. He was juggling three pine cones in his left hand. In his other hand, he held the hand of a woman who stood a head taller than him.

Peter and Penelope Silverman. The magician-alchemists.

CHAPTER 26

It wasn't a fortuitous coincidence, after all, that had led me to the cemetery that afternoon. When I'd lost Peter and Penelope two hours before, I wasn't far from the entrance to the cemetery. They must have seen me following them and waited to come to the cemetery.

"Good afternoon," I called down to the path below me on the hill.

"Hello!" Penelope said. If I hadn't known she was so successful at acting the part of her role of Persephone on the stage, I would have believed she was genuinely happy to see me. Peter, on the other hand, dropped the pine cones he was juggling.

They cut across the grass, walking briskly up the steep incline to meet me. Peter's hair was no longer red and spiky, but medium brown and combed back. And in place of his bright-red suit he wore a sedate combination of khakis, polo shirt, and loafers. The difference was so striking that if I'd seen him in the street I would have assumed he was a banker or an accountant on his day off, but never a magician or an alchemist.

"We're here visiting family," Penelope said. Unlike Peter, she looked much the same as her stage persona with her perfectly rolled sleek curls. She was dressed in a flowing black dress that wrapped elegantly around her tall frame.

"I didn't realize you were from Portland," I said. "The show is a homecoming of sorts."

"Something like that," Peter murmured, studying my face. "Are you feeling all right?"

"I'm fine. It's just spring allergies. I've been wandering the grounds. I didn't see any Silverman headstones."

"Distant relatives with a different name," Penelope said without missing a beat.

The family connection clicked. One of the mausoleums I'd passed was for the Thorne family. *Franklin Thorne.* They'd postponed their visit when they thought I was following them. Why didn't they want me to see them visiting the cemetery? Did they think I'd connect Peter to Franklin Thorne and the loot?

"It was *you,*" Penelope said, staring at me with a horrific recognition on her face. The Goddess of Spring Growth had turned on me, becoming Queen of the Underworld.

My throat constricted. Penelope had to have known Peter was an alchemist. Could they tell that my sickness was brought on by practicing backward alchemy? By letting them see me in my weakened state, had they figured out I was a fellow alchemist, despite my lie about having bad allergies?

"Zoe Faust," she continued, ignoring the confused look on Peter's face, "who is the reason the police searched through every inch of our possessions."

"I don't know what you're—"

"Your cheap knock-off statue, Zoe. The gargoyle you brought to the theater was such a shoddy piece of work that a piece of him must have broken off."

I froze.

"That," Penelope said, "was what the police were looking for."

"My statue?" I croaked.

"Wallace Mason," she said. "That poor man someone murdered and planted in our set piece—the police found a fragment of a stone statue clutched in his dead hand."

Dorian's toe. That's where it had gone.

The dead man had it.

I drove like a madwoman on my way back to the house. I couldn't reach him any other way. Dorian didn't have a cell phone. Not because it would be ridiculous for a gargoyle to have a cell phone— even though we both agreed that would be true as well—but because he had trouble using small keyboards, and touchscreen phones didn't respond well to his touch. I had a land line so he could make outgoing calls. But because he wasn't supposed to exist and live with me, he didn't answer the phone.

Max was waiting for me on the rickety front porch.

"I'm so sorry, Zoe," he said.

"For what? What's going on?"

"I really hoped the piece of evidence would match something found at the theater, but it didn't. They'll be here any minute. I had to tell them."

"Tell *who, what?*"

"About your gargoyle statue. The crime scene guys were looking for a piece of evidence relating to something the investigating officer found. They didn't find a match in the magicians' props. But that gargoyle of yours… The magicians said you brought him to the theater. Zoe, it may have been used in the commission of the crime."

The world around me spun in and out of focus. Stars flashed in my eyes. I couldn't let myself faint. I focused on Max's deep brown eyes, trying to steady my breathing.

"You don't understand," I said, raising my voice. I hoped Dorian would hear me inside the house and hide, rather than turning to stone as soon as a guest appeared, as he usually did.

"Then why don't you tell me?"

I opened my mouth but couldn't speak.

"What's going on with you, Zoe?"

"I need to go inside."

Max stepped in front of me. "I can't let you do that."

"What are you talking about? This is my house."

"There's a search warrant on its way."

I clutched his arm. "You have to let me inside, Max. My statue isn't simply a statue."

Max frowned, but at the same time he took my hand in his and squeezed it gently. "Our guys know how to be careful. They won't break it. But really, Zoe, I didn't know you were so attached to physical objects."

I'd respected Dorian's wishes that we not share his existence with anyone else, and I agreed with him about the need for secrecy. But this was an emergency. I had to trust Max.

"You're not listening to me. He's not a statue." I took a deep breath. And another. "He's my French friend."

"Oh, you mean you borrowed him from that shy friend of yours? Don't worry, he'll be able to get his statue back after the investigation."

"Listen to me, Max. The things you saw your grandmother do when you were a child, when she helped people as an apothecary— there were parts of what she did that you thought were magic, before you decided you didn't believe in it. *You were wrong.* It's not a supernatural magic that apothecaries and alchemists perform, but their work is real.

Alchemy brought the statue to life." I held my breath and waited for him to respond.

"Zoe," Max whispered. "I know you've been under a lot of stress lately, moving to a new place, buying a house that was a bigger fixerupper project than you thought, and getting up in the middle of the night to bake for the teashop. I've seen how tired and ill you've been. And between my trip and work I haven't been around this month—"

"I'm not going crazy, Max! I'm trying to open up to you and tell you what I've been holding back. Come inside with me. I'll show you."

I took a frantic step toward the door, but Max's gentle hold on my hand turned into a firm grip. He held me in place and shook his head as a police car drove up and parked in the driveway.

I stared mutely at the duo who walked up to us.

"It'll be easier," Max said softly, "if you let them in and let them have the statue. I'll get you some help, Zoe. Fighting us right now will only make things worse."

I closed my eyes and breathed. This couldn't be happening. It was daytime, so Dorian would be somewhere in the house. I couldn't warn him. As soon as he heard voices in the house, he'd turn to stone. A defenseless stone statue that the police could take in as evidence. And the longer he stayed in stone, the harder it would be to awaken him.

I nodded numbly and unlocked the door.

The police found a three-and-a-half-foot gargoyle statue standing in the kitchen, next to the fridge. It was missing a pinky toe that matched the piece of stone clutched in Wallace Mason's hand. But he was very much a stone statue, not the living creature I'd tried to tell Max about moments earlier. I watched helplessly as they carried Dorian from the house.

CHAPTER 27

"Non Degenera Alchemia," the retired magician read aloud.

Something to do with alchemy. Robert-Houdin knew basic Latin, and he knew of alchemists. He, in fact, had many books on the subject. Not one but two rooms of his home had been designated as libraries, filled with over a thousand volumes both accumulated by himself and given to him by friends. He devoured books the way some men devoured bottles of wine. It had been an obsession of his ever since he was a young man. While studying to be a clockmaker, he ordered a set of books on the subject. After the books arrived, he unwrapped the paper packaging and found there had been a mistake. Not truly a mistake, though. It was *fate.* Instead of books on the craft of clockmaking, he had been sent books on the mechanics of magic.

Instead of returning the books, he read them. To the curious boy, the idea of true magic opened up a world of possibilities. But where the books explained the technical structure of magic tricks, it seemed to Robert-Houdin that they failed to elevate the conjuring tricks into a true art form. Why was magic lower-class entertainment of the streets? Would French society not appreciate skillfully enacted illusions in the comfort of the theater?

From that moment on, the clockmaker was no more. The formally dressed stage magician who became the Father of Modern Magic was born.

He performed on stages across Europe, honing his craft. He spoke often of the fated books that showed him the path to his true destiny. He wasn't sure he actually believed in fate, yet it made for a good story. Because of it, friends and well-wishers often gave him strange books on a wide range of subjects. Alchemy was as strange a subject as one could find, and therefore several dozen acquaintances had brought him alchemy books over the years.

But *Non Degenera Alchemia* enticed him more than the others.

He ran his weathered fingers over a woodcut of a globe encircled by flames. He hadn't noticed before that the globe was also a face. It screamed in agony.

A knock on the drawing room door startled him. He'd been so caught up in the wonderful and horrible illustrations that he'd lost all track of time.

"Well, *mon ami*," he whispered to the stone beast, "our illusion will have to wait." He closed the book. Was it his imagination, or did the scent of decay permeating the room disappear as soon as the book snapped shut?

When Robert-Houdin returned to the drawing room the following day, the strange alchemy book lay open on the side table. He narrowed his eyes. His wife knew he hated it when she fussed with his books. At least she hadn't covered up the carving again.

He glanced at the clocks in the room, all of which kept perfect time, from the grandfather clock next to the window to the glass clock on the mantel. Three hours until dinner. He would not let himself get distracted by the illustrations again. He wished to find a passage to read that would sound mysterious to his audience, providing the drama to elevate his illusion to the perfection he demanded.

Ah! There it was! He took back what he was thinking about his wife. She'd selected—accidentally, almost certainly—a page with a perfect section of text. It was almost as if it was calling to him…

He shook his head, feeling the aches of old age as he did so. As he lifted the book into his hands, the pain in his joints lightened, as if the book itself were affecting his body. "*Bof!*" He was definitely growing fanciful in his old age. It wasn't the book itself. It was the anticipation of creating a new illusion that made him feel young again.

He mouthed the Latin words on the page. Three lines of text. A strange combination of words, he could tell, even though he didn't speak Latin well. He'd studied Latin in school, of course, but the method of study was so rote that he'd memorized written passages without understanding their meaning.

He formed the words of the first sentence. In spite of his incomprehension, the first line rolled off his tongue. He practiced it again. Yes, he liked the sound of it. Very theatrical. The first two were easy, the last more difficult. He decided he would try again later.

That night after dinner, he moved the statue onto the small stage he'd erected at the house. The automaton would take much more work to complete, but in the meantime he could practice timing with the stone beast.

Alone in the miniature theater, Jean Eugène Robert-Houdin licked his dry lips, looked out over the empty chairs, and read the incantation. His shoulders drooped. The words fell flat, and not because of the lack of an audience. The words were incomplete. The first two lines screamed to be read with the next. He licked his dry lips and read the last line of text. His tongue stumbled over the foreign words.

Squaring his shoulders, he tried again. The words again came haltingly, as if he were trying to speak backward. He knew an English magician who read backward to pretend he was conjuring the Devil. This Latin evoked a feeling at least as dangerous.

He read the words again. Better. They became easier each time he tried. Having practiced, he turned at a right angle to the empty seats, facing the stone carving, and read the three lines together.

The heavy book became light in his hands, as if an illusion using ether were in play. He glanced upward, annoyed. Someone was surely playing a joke on him, using fishing wire hanging from the ceiling to lift the book without him seeing the mechanism. Yet he saw no wires. His eyesight was not as good as it once was. To be sure he wasn't missing anything, Robert-Houdin held the newly light book in one hand and swiped his other hand above the book. His fingers did not find any wires. What type of illusion was this?

He looked back to the stone gargoyle—but the creature was gone.

CHAPTER 28

Dorian was gone, taken into police custody as evidence.

I didn't know how my life could get any worse. My closest friend had been forcibly removed. The longer he stayed in police custody, the more likely it was that he'd remain trapped in unmoving stone forever. The first man I'd been interested in in years thought I was insane. I was a failed alchemist, unable to create enough gold to make any of my other problems go away. My hair was falling out. And now, after decades of not drawing attention to myself, I was being questioned by the police for the second time since moving to Portland.

Max hovered nearby while the investigating officer asked me a few questions. The pitying look on his face made it easy for me to ignore him. I kept my focus on the other officer as I explained how I brought the statue to the theater to tell the magicians about my business, because I thought they might like some of my wares as props. The magicians would back up my story. I had no connection to Wallace Mason, and I had no idea why he would be interested in a stone toe that rolled away. He was a treasure hunter, so had he thought it was a treasure?

I again neglected to mention that I'd seen Wallace Mason and Earl Rasputin sneaking around the theater. That admission would bring further scrutiny. Scrutiny I couldn't afford. All it would do was lead the police down a path they would never believe.

"You have a roommate?" the detective asked.

I looked at him closely for the first time. As tall and thin as Ichabod Crane, his drawn face and dark craters under his eyes completed the look.

"No," I said. "I started cooking earlier and haven't yet cleaned up." Luckily Dorian hadn't started the oven, or I would have had more explaining to do. The detective raised an eyebrow at my messy housekeeping, but seemed to accept my explanation.

I didn't have to go to the police station to answer further questions, but I had the distinct impression they'd be looking into any possible connections I had to the victim.

Max stayed behind after the other officers left. The look of concern on his face was too much.

"Maybe you could take a few days off," he said softly. "The teashop can survive a few days without your cooking."

"Sorry for my emotional outburst." I couldn't look him in the eye. "I just need to get some sleep."

"Maybe you could talk to someone. I hated when the department made me talk to a psychologist, but—"

My gaze snapped to his. "I'm *not* crazy."

Memories flooded my mind of what different societies have done to "crazy" people over the years. Doctors had explained and treated mental illness in many different ways. What was called "hysteria" in the 1800s became known as "nervous complaints" in the early 1900s, then a "mental breakdown" in the 1940s, followed by what we currently categorize as depression. Many of the poisonous drugs and physical traumas inflicted upon patients did more harm than good.

But many of us who institutionalized our loved ones did it because we truly wanted to help them. When Ambrose snapped after his son died, psychiatrists were still called "alienists," and I believed they could help him get better, or at least prevent him from harming himself while he took the time he needed to recover on his own. One of the ailments Ambrose was diagnosed with was "dementia praecox," a condition later recharacterized as schizophrenia. I was able to find him one of the most humane asylums that existed in early-twentieth-century France. Charenton was located only a few miles outside of Paris, so I was able to visit Ambrose regularly—until he took his own life.

I steadied my breathing enough that I could continue speaking. "I was simply trying to explain my emotional attachment to my statue. I got a little carried away."

"But you said—"

"I want to be alone, Max."

What I *really* wanted was to try telling Max the truth again. But with how he'd reacted by not even giving me a chance to explain, how could I? It pained me that no matter how much we had in common and how much we were drawn to each other, his worldview was so different from mine in so many important ways.

Even if Max would listen to me, I didn't know the whole truth of what was going on. Why was Wallace Mason clutching Dorian's stone toe?

~

Without Dorian, the house felt strangely empty. After all these years, I was surprised by how quickly I'd become accustomed to living with someone. Though Dorian left the house during the darkest and quietest part of the night, he was always here for breakfast, lunch, and dinner. Not to mention tea, appetizers, desserts, and snacks.

A tear slid down my cheek when I noticed what Dorian had been cooking in the kitchen. The thoughtful gargoyle had been fixing me an extravagant dinner with my new favorite dish—a smoked paprika macaroni and "cheese" made of creamed nuts. Soaking raw nuts ahead of time, then blending them with water and a little salt and lemon juice created a thick cream more decadent than the heavy cream Dorian used to cook with before he came to live with me. My old blender was far more versatile in the gargoyle's hands.

I called Heather and told her I was sick and that I'd be unable to bake pastries for Blue Sky Teas the next morning, or for the foreseeable future until I was better.

Brixton would wonder what was wrong with Dorian, since the gargoyle was the real chef, but I didn't have the heart to tell him. Maybe I could figure out what was going on and get Dorian back before Brixton knew he was gone.

But how could I get Dorian back? After cleaning the kitchen and fixing some of the healing lemon balm tea I'd been drinking regularly to combat the effects of backward alchemy, I tried to sleep. I failed miserably.

There was no point in lying in bed not sleeping while Dorian was trapped in a police evidence locker, slowly dying. His capture was only obscuring the real motivation and clues surrounding Wallace Mason's death.

I dragged my tired body out of bed, unlocked the door to the basement, and lit every candle. I didn't know what I could do to get Dorian back, but once he was returned to me, I needed to have a real cure figured out. It was my best hope for being able to awaken him from stone after having to hold still for so long.

I pushed all thoughts of Max out of my mind. Intent is essential in alchemy, and focus is key. I couldn't let myself be distracted with regrets about Max. Maybe it was for the best that he hadn't believed me. If Max had seen Dorian in living form, how would he have processed the information? With his attachment to the rule of law, would he have let Dorian escape, or would he have captured Dorian as a suspect? I didn't want to know the answer.

I brought *Non Degenera Alchemia* to the best viewing table in the lab, a slanted wooden desk once used by monks painting illuminated manuscripts. The desk was one of the high-end items for sale on my website, but until it sold, it was a great book stand. Standing in front of the old pages that had weathered the years so well, I willed my mind to understand the morbid woodcut illustrations. My vision blurred as I stared at the counterclockwise circle of bees. Through my unfocused eyes, the black ink of the dead animals underneath blended into a smoky haze.

My focus snapped to attention.

Why did the image trigger a disturbing memory as soon as my vision blurred? I stared at the bees, as if the intensity of my gaze could capture the animals through sheer will. The memory slipped from my grasp.

I needed to get away from the book for just a moment. I stepped back and sat down in front of the table containing the glass vessels and the mortar and pestle I'd used to make Dorian's Tea of Ashes. Though I'd cleaned it well, I could still smell the ashes. Backward alchemy called for using fire too early in the transformation, burning too hot.

Fire and ash.

My eyelids felt heavy.

The next thing I knew, a faint glow of light was coming through the narrow frosted glass window high on one of the basement walls. It must have been shortly after sunrise. While I'd accidentally slept, the candles had extinguished themselves and the dim sunlight was the only light in the room.

A lurch in my stomach reminded me that Dorian was gone, and a kink in my neck told me I'd slept all night with my head resting on a table. Damn. I'd tried so hard to stay awake! But it's not my nature to be awake in darkness. Ever since I was a small child, the perceptiveness that made me understand plants affected my body the same way. When plants slept, my eyelids drooped. I was called a "simpler" at the time. The people in Salem Village thought of it as magic. But being observant of the natural world isn't magic. If I'd been born in the late twentieth century and was the age I looked, I would probably have been a botanist. As it was, I became a plant alchemist.

The planetary cycles and light and darkness don't affect all alchemists equally. Living with Ambrose in early-twentieth-century Paris, I begged him to go out to the *bal-musettes* without me, since I needed to sleep and renew my energy. There was no need for my weakness to prevent him from enjoying himself. He wouldn't hear of it. He argued I was the best herbalist around and could make myself an energizing tonic so I could go out dancing with him all night. It usually got me through to midnight.

I unlatched my locket chain and looked at the images inside—a black-and-white photograph of Ambrose and a miniature portrait of my brother. I had a larger photograph of Ambrose somewhere. I'd kept it hidden from sight for so long because it was too painful to have a daily reminder of my loss. But the more I thought about it, that was backward. Suddenly, I desperately wanted to find that larger photograph.

Aside from my journal of alchemical notes, I've never kept a proper diary. But my notebooks serve much the same purpose, holding pressings of flowers, ticket stubs, sketches, and photographs. The photograph wasn't in my notebook that encompassed 1935, the year of Ambrose's death. I ransacked the attic in search of the photograph. It wouldn't be in an articulated bird skeleton, an apothecary jar, or any glass vessel. It must have been inside one of my notebooks. Half an hour later, I found it tucked inside a palm-sized sketchbook from the 1950s, the book I'd carried with me for the first few years I traveled around the country in my brand-new Airstream trailer that was now six decades old.

Ambrose's kind eyes smiled up at me. For many years after his death, his image had caused me pain. But looking at him now, I felt hope. Ambrose would have told me he had faith in me.

I thought back on what I'd been working on before falling asleep. My eyes had glazed over while staring at the pages of Dorian's book. No, that wasn't quite right. They hadn't glazed over. My tired eyes had made the illustrations blur together. Much like the blurry image of the German book Ivan had showed me. I'd gotten sidetracked by too many other things to research that academic book. I hadn't prioritized it because the scholar who wrote it clearly didn't have an understanding of the backward alchemy illustration he'd included.

But what about the backward alchemy image *itself*… an angel turning to stone? Or was it a stone angel that had been brought to life? Death and resurrection. Mercury and sulfur. *Fire and ash.*

I needed to talk to Ivan. It was too early to talk to him now, but after watering my garden and fixing myself two cups of tea, I called him.

I brought Dorian's book to his house, along with the printout from the art of alchemy book he'd given me with the disturbing image of the stone angel, dead jesters, and bees.

"This substance," I said, pointing to the sooty markings on the edge of the page. "Do you have any thoughts on what it might be?"

"No," Ivan said with a shake of his head, "but I take good notes about where I find all of my reference materials." With unsteady hands, he searched through an electronic document on his computer.

A few minutes later, he found the location of the German book that had been written by a nineteenth-century scholar of alchemy. Ivan had found it digitally archived by a Czech university. Not much was known about it, but the cataloguing librarian's notes indicated that the book had been damaged by a fire, and some soot remained on the pages.

Fire and ash.

"You have a working fireplace, don't you?" I said to Ivan.

"Is it cold today? I hadn't noticed, since I'm always cold these days. I rarely use the fireplace. Would you like me to turn up the central heat?"

"That's not what I meant. Can I see your fireplace?"

Ivan gave me a strange look, but motioned me through to the living room.

I scooped up a handful of ashes from Ivan's fireplace and brought them back to his study. There, I smeared the ashes onto the page of *Non Degenera Alchemia* that the book always opened to, the one with the Latin that had brought Dorian to life.

"What are you doing?" Ivan cried. "You will ruin the book!"

"I don't think so." I spread the cold gray ashes across the paper. "If I'm right, I'm revealing its true meaning."

I had assumed that the ruined stone buildings illustrated in *Not Untrue Alchemy* were what they appeared to be: fragmentary ruins that symbolized death. But that was only half of the story. Death *and* resurrection. That's what we were missing.

Before our eyes, the ashes turned the opaque pages translucent. Remaining on the transparent paper was the black ink of the illustrated plates. The individual woodcuts that showed desolate landscapes with crumbling ruins weren't what they had seemed. They weren't barren landscapes at all. Five illustrations were lined up, and their individual pieces made up a coherent whole.

The backgrounds of crumbling remains weren't ruins at all. Together, they revealed one intact building.

A cathedral.

CHAPTER 29

There was even more to *Not Untrue Alchemy* than I had imagined. Alchemists love codes, using them out of necessity from a time when they were persecuted, but also, I suspected, because they like to feel clever. This was a deeper level of hidden meaning than I'd ever encountered. The woodcut illustrations weren't only coded images themselves, but worked with a trigger.

But even with my breakthrough in the book, I didn't know enough to save Dorian. The cathedral had no identifying features. It could have been one of a hundred cathedrals. Even if I could identify which one, what did that tell me?

It was mid-afternoon when I returned home, but I'd been too sick with worry to eat anything. I was falling into old patterns. I forced myself to drink the last of my healing lemon balm–infused tea, and I found lentil and cucumber salad leftovers. I brought the late lunch to the back porch over-looking my half-thriving, half-depleted garden, and forced myself to eat. Before I'd finished, I heard the sound of someone approaching. A moment later, Brixton dropped his bike next to the porch.

"Aren't you supposed to be helping your mom at the teashop after school?"

"Since there aren't any pastries today, there's hardly anyone there. My mom's teas aren't nearly as good as Blue's."

"Come inside, Brix. There's something I need to tell you."

"Mom said you were too sick to cook today, so I already know it's Dorian who's sick. What's wrong with him? I thought you were going to heal him. I brought over some Stumptown coffee for him."

"That was thoughtful. But he's not here."

Brixton gave me a look that suggested I'd sprouted a second head. "It's daytime. He has to be here."

"That's the problem," I said.

"His mind is going, too, and he wandered off? That sucks. Why aren't you out looking for him?"

"He's not outside. The police took him into custody. My stone gargoyle statue is a piece of evidence."

"How can they do that?" Brixton sputtered. "Did he get caught somewhere he wasn't supposed to be and turned to stone to save himself?"

I forced myself to keep my voice calm in front of Brixton. "You've seen how his left leg has been turning back to stone more quickly than the rest of him. His toe broke off at the theater. The man who was killed was found clutching it in his hand."

"That doesn't make any sense! Why would he care about a piece of stone?"

"I don't know. But Dorian is now evidence in the investigation."

"Prison break," Brixton said. "That's your plan, right? We can't leave him in there."

"I don't have magical powers that allow me to walk into a secured evidence facility."

Brixton balled his fingers into fists. "Then what are we supposed to do?"

I hesitated. Though Brixton was the one person I could talk to about Dorian, he was still a kid. He was on the verge of becoming a man, but his actions continued to remind me that the transformation wasn't yet complete. I couldn't tell him that I'd had a breakthrough with Dorian's book but that it wasn't enough. That I needed the help of a backward alchemist—both to unlock the secrets of *Not Untrue Alchemy* and to wrap up the murder investigation so I could get Dorian back.

"I'm thinking about what to do," I said. "Right now, I need to do a few things around the house. You can raid the last of Dorian's cooking from the fridge before you go."

"You have a plan you're not telling me, don't you? That's why you want me to leave."

"I have a friend coming to visit. I need to get ready—"

"A *friend* is coming to visit? Don't you care about Dorian at all?"

"Of course I care!" I snapped. I was surprised by how much his words hurt. "That's why Tobias is coming for a visit. He's an alchemist. I thought he could help."

"I thought you didn't know any alchemists anymore. Or are you lying to me about everything? After what happened earlier this year, and after Ethan and Veronica's *joke*, I thought you were the one person I could trust."

I'd hurt Brixton too. He'd been let down by so many people. Not only had a trusted authority figure betrayed his trust earlier that year, but his stepdad's absence must have weighed heavily on him. He refused to talk about his mom's absentee husband, Abel, so I didn't know the whole story. But because of Brixton's refusal to speak of him, I suspected it wasn't good.

"I only just found Tobias. I knew him a long time ago, but we lost touch and until yesterday I didn't even know he was alive."

Brixton squinted his eyes with confusion. To someone raised in the modern world, it's pretty unbelievable to not have instant access to anyone you wanted to find.

"He's flying to Portland tomorrow," I continued. "Only..."

"What?"

What I wanted to say was that since Dorian was gone, I didn't know what good Tobias's visit would do. Instead, I said, "I wish I didn't have to wait until tomorrow for Tobias to arrive."

As soon as Brixton left, I climbed to the attic and rooted through a box until I found the object I was after. I held it up. The copper hadn't even rusted. *Perfect.*

I waited five minutes, then slipped out of the house. I put "Accidental Life" on the cassette player to give me courage, and drove to the theater.

～

The police tape had been removed, and the magicians' SUV was parked in front of the theater. I banged on the back door until Peter opened it.

"I told you not to open the doors," Penelope's muted voice could be heard behind him.

"I know what you are," I said, pushing my way past Peter into the dark backstage area, and onward to the stage where I could see them clearly. "And I know what you're doing here. I'm not interested in exposing you. I don't care that you're after the Lake Loot—"

"Call the police, Pen," Peter said. "Zoe Faust is unwell. Delusional, I'd say."

"Hear me out," I said. "If you help me, I won't tell the police that I know the real reason you're in town—"

A cell phone materialized in Peter's fingers. His sleight of hand was good.

Penelope put her hand on top of Peter's. Her red lacquered nails caught the light and for a moment it looked as if her fingertips had been dipped in blood. "We're not calling the police."

"But—" Peter protested.

"Didn't you hear what she said? She *knows*, Peter. I could tell she knew. That ruse with the gargoyle..."

"How?" The muscles on Peter's neck looked like they were ready to pop out. I only hoped he didn't have an aneurism before he could help me. "How did you know? I took steps so no one would piece it together."

"Never allowing your photo to be taken was a good try," I said, "but there's a photo in a book from the 1970s on Portland murders."

"Damn. I went to all the trouble of taking down that website, but a real book..." He shook his head and pursed his lips.

"How did you do it?" I asked. "It was backward alchemy, wasn't it? I'm not judging you. It's why I think you can help me—"

"Help you?" His eyes widened and then narrowed. His mouth followed suit, as if he was struggling for words.

"Don't lie to me!" I said. "I have nothing more to lose."

For the next few moments, the three of us stood staring at each other, sizing each other up.

Penelope cleared her throat. The sound echoed through the empty theater. "Are you wearing *chain mail* under your blouse?"

Chain mail was the object from my boxes that I'd taken as a precautionary measure. I may have been acting somewhat recklessly by venturing to the theater alone, but when confronting a man who had killed before and his knife-throwing wife, I wasn't going to be *completely* defenseless.

"Are we on *Candid Camera*?" Peter asked. "As you know, I *hate* cameras. I'll never consent to being featured on television."

"I don't care what you've done," I said. "I'm not going to turn you in. Going to the police is against my interests as well."

"We didn't kill that man," Penelope said. "That hasn't got anything to do with the loot. We're not doing anything illegal."

"Even better," I said, playing along. "Then you won't mind helping me with this." I pulled two photographs of Dorian's book from my bag. "Please. It's important. It's a matter of life and death, or I wouldn't be asking."

Peter's expression was even more perplexed than before. "What does this have to do with the riches my father was accused of stealing?"

"Your *father*?"

"Franklin Thorne. You said you'd figured out my secret and that we're back in Portland to find his hidden treasures. But you've only got half the story. I don't care about the money. I'm back because he was innocent. I'm here to clear his name."

CHAPTER 30

"You're not Franklin Thorne?" I said.

"What are you talking about?" Peter said. "He was killed in 1969. I know theater makeup can do wonders, but you really think I'm ninety-five?"

Peter Silverman *wasn't* an alchemist who'd used backward alchemy to recover from a shootout with the police after he killed a man. I had the same biases as everyone else. I saw what I expected to see. What I *wanted* to see.

Before I could think of how to respond, someone else spoke up.

"No way!" a young voice said from the shadows.

Brixton? It couldn't be. He stepped onto the stage, the squeaking of his sneakers' rubber soles the only sound in the nearly deserted theater.

"I don't know how you're here," I said, "but we're leaving." I put my hands on his shoulders to steer him back outside. "Sorry to have intruded," I called over my shoulder.

Brixton shrugged free. "You should be better at checking the back of your truck before you drive off," he said. "I could have been an axe murderer! Anyway, I knew you were up to something. Hi guys, I'm—"

"*Not* telling them your name," I said sharply.

"How very maternal of you," Penelope said. "He's too old to be your son. Younger brother?"

"Neighbor," Brixton said.

"I can read your mind," Peter said casually, slowly circling the two of us, "so there's no need for you to voluntarily tell me your name."

"Very funny," Brixton said.

"I thought so, Brixton Taylor," Peter said.

Brixton's voice caught.

"Stop joking around," Penelope said. "Zoe thinks we're coldblooded killers. That's why she doesn't want us to know her young friend's name."

"How did you—" Brixton began.

"Check your pocket, Brix," I said. "I bet he lifted your school ID card."

"If I were to have done such a thing," Peter said, "it would already be back in his pocket." His graceful steps carried him across the stage in a flash, and he sat down at the very front of the stage, dangling his feet over the edge. "I can see how curious you both are. I can assure you, we're not murderers."

"We're supposed to just, like, take your word for that?" Brixton asked.

Peter exchanged a look with Penelope. "Since you know the truth about why I'm here, you might as well know everything." He pointed at the front row of seats a few feet in front of him. "Why don't you get comfortable?"

Brixton jumped down from the stage and sat in front of Peter. Short of tossing him over my shoulder, I wouldn't be able to get him out of the theater. But now that I knew Peter Silverman wasn't a reckless backward alchemist, the immediate danger went up in smoke along with the motive I'd theorized. I sat down next to Brixton.

"What are you wearing?" Brixton whispered. "This outfit is even worse than those jeans."

"Never mind." I tugged at the heavy chain mail.

"I changed my name because of my father's infamy," Peter explained. He twirled three tennis balls in one hand, his fingers deftly looping the balls around one another. "I spent my childhood under the dark shadow cast by being the son of a murderer." In the space of a heartbeat, the three tennis balls became two. In another beat, one ball became half the size of the other— father and son.

"That wasn't the worst part," Penelope added from the other side of the stage. "It was knowing that Peter's father was framed. Franklin Thorne is innocent."

"How'd you do it?" Brixton asked, his wide-eyed gaze fixated on Peter. "How'd you erase your identity so completely? I mean, I really thought you were like a Doppelgänger or something." Brixton glanced briefly at me, making sure I realized he was keeping my alchemy secret. "A *library book* says he didn't have kids. My friend Ethan changes stuff on Wikipedia all the time, just for fun. But a *library book*?"

Of course Ethan, the bored and entitled rich kid, would alter history for fun. But even more reliable books weren't the absolute truth. I should have known better than to take the book at face value. Recorded history isn't objective. Everyone has an agenda. Most of the time historians get much of the story right, but I've lived through plenty of events with history book descriptions that diverged from reality.

"You two both really thought *I* was the man in this photograph?" Peter's eyes darted from me to Brixton. It must have been a trick of the light, but his eyes glowed red for a fraction of a second. "You thought I could help you with cheating death? You mentioned… What was the phrase? *Backward alchemy?*"

"I was trying to act crazy," I said with a nervous laugh, "to get you off-guard so you'd open up. The police confiscated my gargoyle statue, so they think I'm involved somehow. I was hoping I could get you to confess. Dumb idea, I know."

"Dumb, indeed," Penelope murmured. She strode across the stage, watching me closely, and stopped next to where Peter was sitting at the front of the stage.

"It's really disturbing to be under suspicion," I said. "I'm sure you can imagine."

"I can imagine a lot more than a nosy girl who dyes her hair white for attention," Penelope said. She sighed and sat down next to Peter, letting her long legs dangle next to his. "Peter has spent his whole life running from a past that he had no choice in creating."

"How'd you run?" Brixton asked.

"I had a skip-tracer help me write myself out of Franklin Thorne's story," Peter said. "That's how I learned about deception and illusion, and that led me to become a magician. Being ridiculed as a boy caused me to retreat into magic. It made me simultaneously invisible and powerful. I guess you could say I'm an accidental magician."

I groaned. Along every step of the way, I'd seen only what I wanted to believe. People dismiss anything that suggests I'm older than twenty-eight because it doesn't fit their worldview, and I was just as guilty. Because *my* worldview involves alchemy, that's how I'd interpreted the clues. But Peter Silverman wasn't a centuries-old alchemist who hung onto old-fashioned ideas; he was a lonely boy who'd latched onto ideas from the past because they were more comforting than his present-day reality.

Even the theme of death and resurrection in the *Phantasmagoria* stage show didn't necessarily suggest Peter was a backward alchemist. The macabre theme is common across cultures and eras, and just because it wasn't popular in this form at the moment, I'd jumped to my own erroneous conclusion. The little things he did that I took as clues were simply the actions of a skilled performer playing the role of Prometheus.

"It's not about big changes," Peter said, "it's the *small* changes that count. Feeding tiny errors to different sources—a different error each time. That obscures everything."

I'd known other children who had to grow up too fast, my brother and myself included. Years after growing up, it's easy to forget how much young people are capable of when they're thrown into adverse circumstances. Especially when they're shunned by their peers.

"So you just erased yourself from history?" Brixton asked.

"Not exactly. Pieces of me are there. First, one agency was informed that there was a mistake in their records. Franklin Thorne didn't have a son; he had a daughter. Another agency was given a different birth date. And another a note about a foreign adoption, with no biological children at all. When my mother had a breakdown, she moved us across the country to live with her sister, my aunt, providing another opportunity. She started using her maiden name, Oakley, to distance herself from the Thorne scandal. I registered for school with a different surname. For the first time, I was my own man. "

"Wicked," Brixton whispered.

"As for my first name, I wasn't born Peter. But I played Peter Pan in high school. I was smaller and had more muscle strength than all the women, so they cast me. The nickname 'Peter' stuck. And when I turned eighteen, I took my aunt's married name, Silverman. Of course if anyone *really* looked into my past, they'd be able to figure it out. But I was more concerned with getting through my life each day. In time, people forgot about me. But they never forgot about him. *A murderer.*"

"But even the press reported Franklin Thorne had no family aside from an older, childless sister," I said.

Peter nodded. "Those first few days, sure. I remember it well. My aunt on my father's side was fiercely protective. She took over and answered all the calls from the press." He laughed sardonically. "As a kid, I thought she was protecting us—my mom and me. But she was only protecting herself. She talked about him being a loner and having no family. She wanted to distance herself from him, and not make him seem sympathetic by having a family. She needn't have worried. As soon as reporters did a little digging, they found us. It took ages to undo what they put me through."

If only I'd read more newspaper accounts, I would have discovered Franklin Thorne had a son! It was the same problem I was having with Dorian's book. I was pulled in far too many directions. The necessity of studying the "quick fix" to prevent Dorian's immediate death had kept me from delving deeply enough into my alchemy practice to find real answers.

"My aunt had it all wrong, though," Peter continued. "He was *innocent*. You thought we killed that man to keep the secret that we're here to find the Lake Loot and keep it for ourselves?"

"He and his friend were treasure hunters," I said, "so I figured they were on to you."

"If they were," Peter said with a shrug, "I had no idea."

"Why do you think your dad is innocent?" Brixton asked.

"And how do you think you can clear him?" I added.

"As *lovely* as this evening interlude has been," Penelope said, "now that your big mystery is resolved and you know why we're here and that we had no reason to kill anyone, why do you two care?"

"The police confiscated my statue," I said through clenched teeth, "and they think it might have been involved in the murder. I'm involved whether I like it or not."

"The murder," Penelope said, "has nothing to do with us." She paused, then shook her head and swore. "You think that poor man found out that Peter was Franklin's son, and thought Peter could tell him more information that would lead him to the loot?"

Peter began to juggle three oranges. I wasn't sure where they came from, and I wasn't entirely certain Peter did either. The look on his face made me wonder if juggling was such an unconscious action that he didn't realize he was doing it.

"If that's true," Peter said, "I suppose you think that gives me a motive. But I didn't kill him. I didn't even know he was here before the show that night."

"Zoe," Brixton whispered to me as Peter ranted. "Look at your phone."

Brixton had texted me, presumably as a more secretive way of passing along a message: WALLACE WAS IN THE NEWSPAPER AS TREASURE HUNTER, REMEMBER? P & P MUST HAVE KNOWN. THEY'RE LYING.

CHAPTER 31

I finished reading the text message and looked up at Brixton. His eyes were wide and he was trying to raise a pointed eyebrow, but both were raised. In the half-lit theater, the effect made him look like a demented clown.

I gave my head a subtle shake. Brixton was jumping to unfounded conclusions in thinking the magicians were lying to us. People who weren't conducting their own investigation wouldn't necessarily read up on the history of a murder victim. An equally rational—or, it could be argued, *more* rational—approach would be to let the police handle things.

"You asked how I know my father is innocent," Peter said. He continued to juggle, but his eyes were locked on Brixton's. "You read that book, so you know the thief is supposed to have pulled off countless heists throughout the 1960s. But they never identified the culprit until this last heist. There's *no evidence* it was my father. Only the fact that he was killed by the police that day."

"But the media—" Brixton began.

"I lived with him," Peter snapped. The juggled oranges swooped higher into the air, nearly reaching to the catwalk. "Don't you think I would have noticed? He was a woodworker who made children's toys. We didn't have much money. My father's family once had money, generations before I was born, but that's not how we lived. He was a simple man who made an honest living. He didn't deserve this."

"Franklin Thorne was accused of killing the guard, Arnold Burke, in cold blood," Penelope said. "But really, Franklin was a hero. It was Burke who was the thief."

"How did everyone get it wrong?" Brixton asked.

"Franklin Thorne and Arnold Burke looked similar," she said. "Nothing like how much Peter resembles his father. But both men had mustaches, brown hair, and were close to fifty years old. *Witnesses mixed them up.*"

"Eyewitness accounts are *always* unreliable," Peter said. "It's the same principle that makes magic shows successful. People see what they want to see—and what they're led to seeing. Nobody wanted to believe a trusted guard who'd once been a policeman was actually a master thief, so they didn't see it. But the truth is that my father was the guard's hostage, not the other way around."

It was an all-too-common story. I'd seen it play out across the world through the centuries. In many ways the world progressed toward more just societies, but this wasn't one of those areas. But it's a noble failing. Nobody wants to believe that a dependable member of society would betray their trust. That's why our minds fill in the blanks with unreliable, yet well-meaning, eyewitness accounts.

"The story the police tell," Penelope added, "is that Franklin held up the train car, and when confronted by the guard, Franklin took him hostage. But really, the guard was the thief. That's how he'd gotten away with so many robberies. When Franklin stepped up to stop the corrupt Burke, he was himself taken hostage."

"They escaped," Peter said, "but the police caught up with them later that day. That's when the shoot-out took place. Both men were killed, and my father was blamed for the whole thing, instead of being hailed as the hero he was for trying to stop the jewel heist."

"But you *are* here because of the sapphire necklace that was found," I said.

"In a sense," Peter said. "But not for the money. I'm hoping there will be evidence that shows it was found in Arnold Burke's hiding spot. That will prove Burke was the thief all along."

"We were performing in Reno when we heard about the discovery of the sapphire necklace," Penelope said. "We were booked through the end of last month, but we made plans to perform a run of shows here as soon as we could."

"You look skeptical," Peter said. For a change, the sarcastic edge from his voice was gone, replaced with a flat, resigned tone. "It's a look I know well. But let me ask you this: The jewels are identifiable. Utterly unique. How could I profit from selling them? I'd only get the reward money, which isn't much.

Those treasure hunters were in for the fun of it. Maybe some of them came for the trivial reward. But nobody besides the Lake family cares as much as I do. Nobody."

"What've you found out so far?" Brixton asked. "You going to be able to clear your dad's name?"

Penelope took Peter's hand in hers. The three oranges he'd been juggling fell to the floor at my feet. She sighed. "Our first lead was a bust. We thought the guard's old house must have been in the area affected by the winter flooding. On a map it looked like it was. But the flooding didn't affect that area much. I was wrong. We've also tried to talk to Julian Lake, but he's quite elderly and a notorious recluse, so he wouldn't see us."

"We got so busy with the stage show that we haven't had time to think of next steps," Peter said. "But nobody is more motivated to find the truth. I'll get there."

I was filled with a combination of relief and disappointment. There wasn't a dangerous alchemist in town, so no one was going to expose my secret. But at the same time, I could no longer hope there was a backward alchemist I could turn to for help with Dorian's book.

If it hadn't been for Dorian becoming entangled, at that moment I could have walked away from Peter and Penelope Silverman. I didn't know how serious a suspect I was, but I did know that Dorian was now central to the investigation. The magicians' motive had gone up in smoke, and Dorian's stone toe in Wallace Mason's hand was confusing the line of inquiry. With the focus on Dorian obscuring the facts, I had little faith the investigation would be resolved quickly. I feared for my friend, trapped in both stone and police custody.

CHAPTER 32

The following morning, I drove to the airport to pick up Tobias Freeman.

A practicing alchemist was my best hope for saving Dorian. However, the more I'd seen of backward alchemy, the less sure I was that a true alchemist could help. Also dampening my optimism was the fact that Dorian was still in police custody. Now, even if Tobias had insights about *Not Untrue Alchemy*, it might be too late for him to help.

Yet I still found myself looking forward to seeing an old friend who would understand. Especially after Max's rejection of the very idea that alchemy could be real.

I spotted Tobias as he walked slowly through the secured section of the airport. He was no longer the sickly man I'd known as an escaped slave, but a muscular man standing tall as he helped an elderly couple with their bags. He winked at me from afar, his brown skin crinkling around his golden-flecked hazel eyes in a manner that told me he often smiled. He waited to greet me until he'd left the couple with their grown grandson.

"Zoe Faust," he said, shaking his head, "as I live and breathe." He swallowed me in a bear hug.

"I never thought I'd see you again, Toby," I said into his shoulder, feeling my eyes well with tears.

"Hey," Tobias said as he let me go. "No need to cry. But why do I think those tears have more to do with the reason you reached out to me than me being here?"

I wiped the tears from my cheeks. "Let's get out of here first."

He grinned. "All those years ago, I *knew* I was right about you being an alchemist."

I took his elbow and led us toward the parking garage. "I can't say the same about you. I thought of you often for many years. I hoped you'd made it to Chicago and were growing old in peace, sitting on a rocking chair on your own front porch, as you said you dreamed of doing." Was this man who looked like he could star in an action movie really the same man I'd nursed back to health so many years ago? If it wasn't for his unusual eyes and his familiar voice, I wouldn't have believed it.

"You didn't notice that I was paying attention to what you were doing all those weeks you looked after me."

"You were barely conscious."

"You were single-mindedly focused on what you were doing, I doubt you would have noticed if the livestock from the farm next door had run through the house."

"Nice try. I remember when that happened. I seem to remember the pig— Charlene?—took a liking to you."

"Charlene was a nice pig! They're smart, you know. I think she sensed I was sick and was trying to keep me warm."

I stopped at the edge of the parking garage and turned to face Tobias. "If it wasn't for that voice, I'd swear I was only imagining you were the same man."

"This voice of mine nearly got me into a whole world of trouble."

I raised a questioning eyebrow.

"You're right that we should get away from here before we talk," Tobias said, glancing around the gray and confining cinderblock-like structure.

"This way."

Tobias took my elbow and held me back. "Let me pick."

"Pick what?"

"I bet I can guess which car."

"Cars didn't exist when we knew each other."

"But cars have personalities. Take me to the right floor, and I'll guess yours."

"You're on. And this is the right floor."

"I get three tries, right?"

"Something tells me you won't need it."

Tobias walked directly up to my green Chevy truck. It was certainly one of the oldest cars in the parking garage. I saw a couple of others from the 1960s, but nothing besides my pickup was from the forties.

"That obvious?"

"I may have cheated. You've got myrrh in here. Who has myrrh these days? I can smell it. I still could have guessed right in three tries, even without the scent of myrrh." He pointed at a black Mustang. "That would have been my first guess. You hated bicycles. I figured you'd be a car person. But myrrh?"

"It's a good air freshener. And you really were a lot more observant than I gave you credit for."

"When you're in servitude," he said, leaning against the truck with a confidence I would have expected in a man who grew up with servants of his own, "you learn how to speak little but see everything."

I unlocked the truck. Tobias gave a low whistle as he climbed inside.

"You fix this up yourself?" he asked.

"I did. Like you said, I'm a car person. Fixing the interior and the engine has a similar energy and rhythm to working in an alchemy lab."

He picked up the cassette sticking out of the tape player. A flash of anger—or was it confusion?—crossed his face. "If you *knew* what I was, why didn't you ever try to find me?"

I frowned. "I was about to ask you the same thing. But I didn't know what you were until I saw your photograph online yesterday—"

"This *tape*, Zoe. This is my song. 'Accidental Life.'"

I stared at him. The reason for my love of the song clicked into place. "*You're* the Philosopher?"

He returned my shocked stare with a grin. "You really didn't know?"

That's why his voice had felt so familiar. Like home. A man I'd once cared for who'd become an alchemist. I shook my head and laughed, feeling tears escape my eyes again. "I was always drawn to this song, but I never knew why."

"Truly?"

"By the time that song came out, you should have been about a hundred years old."

"It was my hundredth birthday. That's why I wrote the song. I realized I couldn't give this 'gift,' if that's what it is, to anyone else, and I needed an outlet to deal with that. I never dreamed it would take off. When you're on the way to being famous, everyone wants a piece of you. You can't have any privacy."

"And you can't have any secrets—not ones you want to remain secret, anyway. Which is no way to be invisible, like we have to be."

He nodded.

"I always wondered why The Philosopher never recorded another song."

"Now you know why. It was reported that he moved to Mexico to find himself. He was a philosopher, after all."

I shook my head as I started the car. We drove in silence for a few minutes as I exited the parking garage.

"Even though I didn't know you'd become an alchemist," I said slowly, "you knew about me. Why didn't you contact me? You didn't think I'd help you again? I understand you'd want to put those times behind you—"

"Shoot, Zoe. That wasn't it. You know those were different times. I did try to find you once. I heard that you'd moved to Europe. I never got involved with the society of alchemists—mostly a bunch of traditional white men, especially at the time. Are they hassling you? Is that why you're so upset and why you tried to find a friendly face from your past?"

"Not exactly. It's complicated—"

"You're preaching to the choir."

"My story will make more sense if I can show you something I've got at my house. An alchemy book that's unlike any other. We've got a few minutes until we get home. Why don't you tell me how you became an alchemist? And are you in touch with other true alchemists?"

Tobias ran his long fingers from the dashboard to the eight-track and shook his head. "I don't know any true alchemists, in the way that you mean it. The spiritual alchemists are kindred spirits in many ways, but they're interested in perfecting their own souls, not seeking out the Elixir of Life. I've watched them age."

"But you saw through me in such a short time."

"I saw much of what you did with herbs to heal me, so the next time I fell ill, I sought out herbalists. It was then that I realized nobody else was doing what you did."

"Lots of herbalists use family Bibles and put their own energy into the tinctures they create to heal people," I said. "What made you think what I did was anything more? I was careful—"

"That you were. But not everyone's favorite book is in a strange code, and not everyone works only when they think nobody else is looking. I doubt anyone else noticed."

"But you did."

"I didn't think much of it for years. Then once I learned to read, I read everything. It was about ten years after you knew me that I found a word for what I saw you doing: alchemy. I was intrigued, because you were unlike anyone else I'd ever known. I was lucky to know many kind people in my life —conductors, other abolitionists, and just plain old folks who didn't like to see another human being suffer. Alchemy had been pretty much discredited by then, so books were cheap to come by. I liked so much of the philosophy—transforming one's life. Taking the impure and making it pure. Plus"—he paused and laughed his deep laugh—"I enjoyed the puzzles of the coded pictures."

"And you always liked puzzles."

"You remember that?"

"I'd forgotten until this very moment."

"About fifteen years after I started toying with alchemy, I had my break-through."

"The Philosopher's Stone and the Elixir of Life."

He nodded. "I transformed myself from that scrawny, scared pile of bones into a spiritually and physically healthy man."

"You look great, Tobias."

"You look pretty damn good, too, Zoe. You used to be skin and bones yourself. I hardly ever saw you eat, and you always had dark circles under your eyes. But even though you look healthier than when I knew you, there's something..."

"When you knew me, I didn't feel I deserved to be taken care of." I felt for my locket. "I healed others, but never myself. I didn't take care of myself until decades later. A fellow alchemist helped me realize that if I wanted to heal others, I first needed to heal myself." I smiled at the memory. "That's when I transformed myself by eating to take care of my body. Cooking with the plants I used in my laboratory."

"But..."

"But what?"

"I can see there's something wrong with you, Zoe. *You're sick.*"

I stole a glance at Tobias as I shifted gears and turned off of Hawthorne. Was it still that obvious? I thought I was doing better that day. "You can tell?"

He shrugged. "I help acutely sick people every day. You're not at that stage yet, but it looks like you're on your way. It's not only your sallow skin, but your jeans are at least two sizes too big. That can't be good."

I sighed. If I survived the week, I was going shopping. "I'm getting over the effects of a taxing transformation."

"Whatever type of transformation it is that you're messing with," Tobias said, "you're in dangerous waters. You need to stop before it kills you."

CHAPTER 33

"I shouldn't judge," Tobias said. It was clear he regretted his directive from a moment before. "I haven't seen you in two lifetimes. I don't know what's going on with you."

"You're right that I'm sick," I said. "But don't worry. It won't last much longer." I spoke the truth. Either I'd figure out how to get Dorian back and cure him, or I'd die trying.

"I always wondered something," Tobias said. "I feel bad even asking, since you gave so much of yourself to the cause..."

"You can ask me anything. You're probably the oldest friend I've got." I reached for my locket. I'd lost so many people I cared about. It was nice, for once, to find someone.

When he spoke, his voice was almost a whisper, so soft I could barely hear him over the hum of traffic around us. "We were all so poor."

"You're wondering," I said, "why I didn't simply make gold?"

"Knowing what I know now, it's a fair question."

"I'm great at spagyrics—"

"Plant alchemy, sure."

"The thing is..." I paused as I pulled into the driveway. "I never got the hang of making gold."

"Truly?"

I sighed as I turned off the engine. "Why does everyone think making gold is easy?"

"Damn, woman, *nothing* worthwhile is easy to come by."

"Did you forget you're talking to the woman who saved your life?"

He laughed heartily. "I wish I had some gold left to say thanks. It looks like this house could use a top-notch repairman." He stepped out of the truck and eyed the tarp that covered a sizable chunk of the roof. As he reached back inside to lift his overnight bag, I was again struck by his physique. Tobias was at once the same good man I'd known 150 years before, and also a completely different person.

I pointed at the roof. "That's why I'm wearing ill-fitted clothing. A winter storm did in a section of the house and ruined most of my clothes. I haven't had time to shop for anything that fits properly."

I led him into the house. Tobias dropped his bag next to the green velvet couch and followed me to the kitchen. Out of habit, I looked around for Dorian, even though I knew he was across town in police custody. The gargoyle was either in an evidence locker or in a lab being examined for trace evidence. If I ever saw him again, I'd never hear the end of it.

"You looking for someone?" Tobias asked. "You live here with someone?"

"That," I said, "is a more complicated question than you realize. Let me get us some sustenance first. Coffee or tea?"

"I've never met an alchemist who could stomach coffee."

"Come to think of it, I believe you're right." I opened the curtains, lit a burner, and set a kettle on the stove. "But that espresso maker isn't mine."

"Oh, the mysterious roommate." Tobias stood in front of the espresso machine and breathed deeply.

"You said you didn't like coffee."

"I didn't say I don't *like* coffee. I said I can't drink it. The scent of coffee is one of my favorite things on earth. Sometimes I'll brew a pot to act as potpourri. But the last time I fell off the wagon and drank a double espresso, I was awake for days."

"The trace amounts of caffeine in chocolate is all I can take," I agreed. "I didn't realize that metallurgic alchemists were sensitive to plant compounds."

"I'm primarily a spiritual alchemist. Couldn't you tell from the lyrics of 'Accidental Life'?"

"But you mentioned you've been making gold."

"I've become somewhat of a generalist—by necessity. You been to Detroit lately? They need all the help they can get."

"Your email didn't mention what you're doing there. You said you help acutely sick people, and I noticed you wear a bloodstone on a necklace chain. Let me guess. ER doctor?"

"EMT. An emergency medical tech. The paperwork is easier than if I were a doctor, but I still get to heal people. Some of the guys who ride with me in the ambulance were wary that I keep a bag of herbal remedies with me, but ever since I saved a man from bleeding to death using cayenne pepper, they don't give me grief."

"Ouch. You didn't learn that one from me. I prefer less painful ways to slow bleeding."

Tobias moved away from the espresso maker and looked past the glass window box above the sink into the backyard garden. "Your backyard is both a medicine cabinet and a chef's dream garden."

"Speaking of which, have you eaten breakfast?" I lifted a domed copper lid from a platter of misshapen blueberry scones, oatmeal nut cakes, and whole grain three-seed muffins. Dorian always brought home the less aesthetically pleasing baked goods from Blue Sky Teas. He was convinced that only the most perfectly shaped creations were worthy of being sold to customers at the teashop. Personally I preferred the misfit pastries. "They're all vegan. And none of them have coffee in them." At my insistence, Dorian had ceased making espresso ginger cookies that looked identical to chocolate cookies. The ginger masked the smell of coffee, and I'd accidentally nibbled on them more than once.

But Tobias wasn't paying attention to the platter. He was still staring out the window. "What happened to that corner of the garden?" He tilted his head toward the section I'd pulled to make Dorian's life-saving tea.

"That's what I wanted to talk to you about. It's—" The kettle gave a high-pitched scream. "Why don't you pick a tea, then I'll get the book I wanted to show you and explain everything." I opened the cabinet that held an assortment of loose-leaf teas. They were hand-dried herbs stored in glass jars.

Tobias selected a flower blend of goldenseal, calendula, and chamomile. The kitchen was bursting with fresh and preserved foods and had no room left for a kitchen table, so Tobias carried the platter of breakfast pastries to the dining table in the large living/dining room. I brought a steeping teapot along with two mugs looped around my fingers to the solid oak dining table, then went to retrieve Dorian's book.

Tobias was already biting into a second deformed pastry when I sat down at the table.

"Ignoring their odd shape, these oat cakes are heaven on earth, Zoe. Heaven on earth." He gave a contented sigh as he ran his calloused fingertips along the edge of the table. "And this table is older than I am."

"Not quite. I bought it from the man who carved it in France shortly after the Railroad wrapped up and I was no longer needed."

"You were still needed, Zoe. I wished I'd had you around so many times... Now—" He clapped his hands together. "Is this old book what's making you look so sick and sad today?"

With a dangerous backward alchemy book, a dead man, a dying gargoyle, and missing loot... "I don't know where to start," I said.

"I do," a deep French voice cut in. "She needs help because of me."

CHAPTER 34

Under the moonlit sky, the shadow creeping slowly across the roof might have been mistaken for a man. But this man was smaller than most—and had wings.

Jean Eugène Robert-Houdin wondered if his years of creating illusions had played with his mind. Was the belief that he had brought a stone gargoyle to life some form of insanity? The creature seemed so real! But perhaps it was an illusion. He, of all people, knew the power of illusions. They convinced the mind that the impossible was true. This could be an elaborate hoax constructed to fool him. Yes! That must have been what was going on, for what other explanation could there be?

It took him several days to revise his opinion. There was no illusion on earth that could explain the living, breathing creature who looked to him for answers he didn't have. Nothing except for the possibility that the alchemy book he'd read from contained *real* magic.

His wife had a strong constitution, so Robert-Houdin considered sharing the secret with her. But he knew what she would do. She would say it was the work of the Devil and send the gargoyle away. But Robert-Houdin knew the creature was no devil. He was as innocent as his own children upon their birth.

The creature did not cry like a baby, but in other ways he was much like a child. He craved food and attention, as all newborns did.

However, unlike a newborn, the gargoyle spoke some Latin and possessed an acute intelligence; though Robert-Houdin's Latin was poor, that much was clear. It was impossible to deny the creature's existence, nor would he relegate him to a freak show. He would raise the creature as his own flesh and blood. Was it not his own work that had brought the gargoyle to life?

But calling him "creature" wouldn't do.

"Dorian," Robert-Houdin said. "I will call you Dorian."

To his family, it appeared that Jean Eugène Robert-Houdin isolated himself as he worked in secrecy on the greatest illusion of his career. Nobody was allowed to enter his studio. No one. Under any circumstances. If anyone dared defy him, they would be written out of his will.

Needless to say, they all obeyed.

In the solitude of his studio, the old magician taught Dorian, whom he came to think of as Dorian Robert-Houdin. Dorian quickly picked up several additional languages, and also excelled at stage magic.

Unlike most men who worked in seclusion, Jean Eugène Robert-Houdin didn't forget to eat. If anything, his family observed that his appetite doubled, perhaps even tripled, in size. On top of that, he became a picky eater, insisting on the highest-quality foods.

In truth, Robert-Houdin's appetite lessened as he came to grips with the import of what he'd done, and he cared not what he ate. It was Dorian who had a voracious appetite and who craved superior meals. When not given the finest foods, he would sneak out at night to obtain them himself. It wouldn't do to have Dorian seen, so Robert-Houdin made sure to bring the gargoyle his favorite foods.

In this way, the gargoyle's unique personality became apparent, convincing Robert-Houdin that Dorian was as much a man as any other. Robert-Houdin was happy that some of Dorian's preferences mimicked his own. Like his father— which is how Dorian came to think of the man who had given him life—Dorian devoured great books. Authors like Flaubert, Baudelaire, Molière, and Dumas opened up a whole new world to him. He grew into a proper French gentleman.

CHAPTER 35

I jumped up. "Dorian!"

The gargoyle descended the stairs with a limp so pronounced it was painful to watch. He thought of himself as a self-reliant gentleman, so I knew how much it pained him emotionally to show such physical weakness. Staying still in stone must have sped up his progression back into stone.

As he reached the bottom of the stairs I threw my arms around him. "You escaped!"

Tobias handled the appearance of a living gargoyle better than I could have hoped. He broke only one mug as he pushed back from the table to stand defensively. The solid oak dining chair remained in one piece as it hit the floor with force.

"Don't be frightened," I said. "He's a friend."

"Ah." Tobias chuckled nervously. "Channeling Georges Méliès, are you?"

"Not exactly," I said. "He's not an automaton."

Tobias's face clouded. "Damn, Zoe. What are you messing with? You can't control a homunculus. Surely you know that. You need me to help you kill it? Why didn't you say so in the first place?"

Dorian's eyes opened wide with distress. "Zoe?"

"Nobody is killing anyone," I said.

"You sure?" Tobias said.

Dorian pinched the ridge of his snout and shook his head. "I am not a homunculus, nor am I a golem, a robot, or an automaton. I am a gargoyle."

Tobias stood in a fighting stance as he stared at Dorian.

"Tobias Freeman," I said, "meet Dorian Robert-Houdin."

"A man trapped in stone?" Tobias asked, his shoulders relaxing slightly.

"He's a good soul," I said. "The two of you are among the best men I've known in my life."

Tobias stepped forward hesitantly, then stuck out his hand for Dorian to shake.

"We are not sure *what* I am," Dorian said, "yet I appreciate and will accept your gesture of friendship."

The formerly stone gargoyle and the former slave shook hands.

"Amazing," Tobias said, gripping Dorian's rough gray skin. "You didn't think this little man was worth mentioning until now, Zoe? I thought he'd be the first thing you told me about when we walked through your door."

"Speaking of which—" I ran through the house to make sure the curtains were drawn and returned a minute later, breathless. "It's no longer safe to stay here."

"What have you pulled me into, Zoe?"

"We should tell him," Dorian said to me, then looked up at Tobias. "I believe you are trustworthy, Monsieur Alchemist."

"You heard him praise your cooking, huh?" I said. If the gargoyle continued to use an endorsement of his cooking as a signal to trust people, we were in big trouble.

"*Mais oui.* From the bannister above, I spied his reaction."

Tobias looked from the half-empty platter to the gargoyle. "*This* little fellow cooked all this? You've gotta give me the recipe for the oat cakes. The muffins too."

Dorian puffed up his gray chest.

"Don't encourage him," I said.

"You're right. I don't know what came over me asking about food when there's a living gargoyle in front of me."

Dorian blinked at Tobias. "That makes more sense than anything that has befallen me, Monsieur Freeman. Food is the key to understanding the soul—"

"Dorian," I cut in.

"*Oui?*"

"Why don't you skip the philosophy and tell Tobias what's going on. You also need to tell me how you escaped. Did anyone see you? Do they know you're gone?"

The gargoyle sighed. "Americans. Always so impatient." He flexed his shoulders, causing his wings to partially unfurl.

Tobias's jaw dropped.

"Let's get upstairs into the attic," I said. "If the police raid the house in search of their missing statue, you can crawl out the hole in the roof to hide where they won't find you."

"But I wish to go to the kitchen," Dorian protested. "I am hungry. They did not feed me—"

"I'll bring food," I said. "Tobias, can you take Dorian and this book up to the attic?"

I joined the two of them five minutes later, carrying a platter of day-old bread along with curried hummus, sliced cucumbers, and olives. They had their heads together over the alchemy book, and Dorian was pointing at the disturbing woodcut illustration of bees swarming around dead animals.

"No fruit?" Dorian asked, looking up.

"He's a particular little fellow," Tobias said.

"One who's about to tell us how he escaped from police custody."

"The *police* in this town know about him?" Tobias asked.

"Not exactly." I briefly told Tobias how Dorian was brought to life with the backward alchemy book, then explained how he could shift back into stone at will, and that it was his stone statue form that was thought to have been used in a crime. "But what I don't know," I finished, "is how he found his way back here from police custody."

Tobias and I looked expectantly at the gargoyle as he finished eating a mouthful of bread slathered in hummus.

A small burp escaped Dorian's lips. "*Pardon.*"

"Amazing," Tobias whispered.

"I do not wish to relive the humiliating ordeal," Dorian said, "but for the sake of our investigation, I will. The first indignity was a fine powder they dusted over my whole body."

"Looking for fingerprints?" I asked.

His eyes narrowed. "*Oui.* They did not find any. This frustrated them. They were not very nice when they carted me to a storage facility. It was from this room that I escaped."

"You were careful?"

"Am I not always careful? I took care of myself long before I met you, Zoe. It took me quite some time to make all of my limbs move again after being still for so long. Once I was confident I would be able to walk, I took a blanket and covered myself, in case there were video cameras. This was shortly before sunrise—"

"That was hours ago!"

"Yes, I made it to my attic entrance before the sun rose."

"You've been here this whole time? Why didn't you come downstairs?"

"I could not get my legs to move," Dorian said slowly, his wings wilting at his sides. "You see, Monsieur Freeman, I am dying."

"I'm going to find a way to save you, Dorian," I said. "I'm getting closer."

"That's why you wanted my help," Tobias said.

I nodded. "But now a murder has gotten in the way—"

"A murder?" Tobias repeated. "What on earth is going on here, Zoe?"

"It's a long story," I said.

"Ah!" Dorian said. "I nearly forgot." He scampered, lopsided, to a corner of the attic. He retrieved a gallon-size plastic bag with a shiny object inside, which he then handed to me.

"A *knife?*" I said, a horrible realization dawning on me. "You took this knife from the evidence room?"

"*Oui.* This is the knife used to kill Monsieur Mason. You did not wish the police to learn the secret of the alchemist, and this is his knife—"

"He's not an alchemist, Dorian!"

"*Pardon?*"

"I was so worried about you that I went to confront him last night." I explained how Peter Silverman was the son of Franklin Thorne, and that although we were right that Peter and Penelope had returned to Portland because of the discovery of the sapphire necklace, the real reason they wanted to come back was to clear Peter's father's name.

"He's just a regular guy who can't help us with your book," I concluded.

Dorian's wings crumpled. His whole body seemed to deflate, from his horns down to the stone foot that was missing its toe.

"Why did you think this man in particular would be able to help you?" Tobias asked. "I get that you thought he was an alchemist, but it sounds like you thought he was a special kind."

"You did not tell him what is peculiar about my book?" Dorian asked.

"Tell me what?" Tobias asked.

"Perhaps," Dorian said, "I should leave the two alchemists to discuss matters further."

"You're staying right here in the attic, Dorian. And keep the knife with you. If the police come and you have to flee, take it with you. You can't let the police find it—or you—here."

"So," Tobias said, "our only chance to save this little fellow is to keep him out of sight while the two of us figure out what's going on with his book. Shouldn't we get started?"

CHAPTER 36

I led Tobias to my basement alchemy lab. The light switch at the top of the stairs turned on a solitary twenty-watt light bulb. It was one of my many fail-safe's to make sure nobody looked too carefully at what I was working on in the basement. I'd removed bulbs from the other light fixtures in the basement and used a combination of kerosene lanterns and candles to light the laboratory for my work. They served the dual purpose of keeping prying eyes from easily seeing what was there, and providing the natural energy of fire that fueled my alchemy.

I found a match and began lighting lanterns and candles.

"How is it possible that Dorian is dying?" Tobias asked. "Isn't he made of stone?"

"Dorian was once a piece of stone. He was a gargoyle carved by the architect Eugène Viollet-le-Duc, as a prototype for a gargoyle on the cathedral of Notre Dame in Paris."

"Wait. Robert-Houdin. You said that was his surname. Like the French magician?"

"One and the same."

"You're telling me that magician was an alchemist who somehow transformed himself into a gargoyle during one of his experiments? It certainly gives a whole new meaning to his being the Father of Modern Magic."

"I didn't mean it like that. Jean Eugène Robert-Houdin was Dorian's father —in a way. He was reading from a book of 'magic' as a prop for an illusion he was creating. He didn't realize it was alchemy, or that it could bring a piece of stone to life."

"It can't."

"That's what I thought too. But you saw Dorian with your own eyes."

"There's got to be something else going on with him."

"I think there is." I finished lighting candles and swept my arm across the room. "That's why I've resumed practicing alchemy after decades. I was planning on setting it up properly and easing into it, but Dorian sped up my plans."

"None of this is very stable for laboratory experiments," Tobias commented, eying the folding tables serving as countertops. "It isn't very *secret* either."

"The best laid plans..." I murmured to myself in the flickering light.

"What was that?"

"When I bought this place at the beginning of the year, I did it with the intention of fixing up the whole house. It's so rundown that it was the perfect cover for doing extensive renovations. I hired a jack-of-all-trades contractor to fix the roof, patch up the house, and create a true alchemy lab in the basement."

"So what happened?"

"It didn't work out." I didn't need to distract Tobias by telling him about how the handyman ended up dead on my front porch.

"What you've got here is what you did yourself?" he asked.

I nodded.

"In that case, you've done a pretty decent job."

"Not the world's most ringing endorsement. I put a lot of effort into this."

"You know there's still a garage sale tag on that card table. And it smells like beer."

"Touché."

"And what's that on the ceiling?"

I sighed. "I couldn't get all the nettle spurs off the ceiling, so I'm pretty sure it germinated."

Once Tobias stopped laughing hysterically, his mood shifted. His hazel eyes flecked with gold could show great warmth, but now their brightness turned fierce. The transformation was jarring. Tobias grew more serious than I'd seen him since picking him up at the airport that morning.

"This isn't like you, Zoe. The haphazard nature of this lab. It's not true to alchemy. It's not true to *you*. Why don't you tell me what's going on with that little gargoyle gourmet? What are you holding back? What's really going on?"

I hesitated. I couldn't bring myself to say the words *backward alchemy* out loud to another alchemist.

"*This* is why you're sick, isn't it?" His angry eyes flitted across the laboratory. "You're practicing alchemy, but you're not doing it right. Is he forcing you—"

"No, it's nothing like that."

"What's going on, Zoe?"

"This isn't what I wanted. I haven't practiced true alchemy in ages. You saw my trailer parked in the driveway. I was living out of it, for most of the time, since the fifties."

"Since we can never stay in one place for too long..."

"When I came through Portland, I felt such a longing to put down some roots, at least for as long as I could. For a few years at least. I thought I could at least have that."

"As much as I'd love to get caught up properly and discuss all the things I can't talk about with anyone else, that's not why you asked me here. I've gotta tell you, you're even better at avoiding the subject than your stone friend. Why don't you tell me what's really going on with him?"

I looked up at the nettle hooks on the basement ceiling. "Whatever is killing him, it's only affecting his body. Not his mind. You saw his limp. He used to be able to turn from stone into flesh and back again with ease. Now it's getting harder and harder for him to do so. But when he's trapped in unmoving stone, he's perfectly conscious. If I don't figure out a way to save him, he'll be awake but trapped in a stone prison."

"Damn. Not dead, but trapped in a stone coffin. That's worse than death."

"I know, Tobias. I know."

"You two go way back?"

I gave a weak laugh. "I only met him three months ago. He hid out in my shipping crates when I had them sent from a storage facility in Paris. The only thing he had with him was an old book."

"The alchemy book the magician read from?"

"At first, I didn't think it was alchemy." I paused and lifted it from the bookshelf. "*Non Degenera Alchemia*. Which roughly translates to *Not Untrue Alchemy*."

But Tobias wasn't paying attention. Instead, he picked up the framed photograph of Ambrose.

"I wondered about him," Tobias said.

I froze. What was going on? Tobias couldn't have known Ambrose. I hadn't yet met Ambrose when I knew Tobias. A tickling sensation ran from my spine to my nose. "What do you mean? I know different alchemists are sensitive to different things, but I didn't realize any of us were capable of being psychic."

"What's my knowing him have to do with being psychic? We're scientists, Zoe. There ain't no such thing as a psychic."

"When I was helping the Underground Railroad, I hadn't yet *met* Ambrose. You couldn't have seen this photograph."

Tobias gave me a strange look, a cross between bewilderment and enlightenment. A look common to the faces of alchemists.

"I mean," he said, "I knew him in person."

"How wonderful! So you knew him in the late 1800s, before I did? We didn't meet until 1895. I knew he'd spent some time in America, but I didn't realized he worked with other alchemists."

Tobias shook his head. "It had to have been the 1950s." He closed his eyes for a few seconds, then nodded slowly. He opened his eyes and snapped his fingers. "1955."

I felt myself shiver. "That can't be right. Ambrose killed himself in 1935."

Tobias gave a start, then looked intently at the photograph. "I didn't mean to shake you, Zoe. You know that over time, faces begin to blur together. I must be mistaken." But his words were too quick, stumbling over one another. Whatever Tobias really thought, he didn't think he was wrong.

Was it me who was mistaken? Was there any way that Ambrose could have survived? The asylum had shown me his body. *Unless it had been an illusion.* My stomach lurched. Why would they have lied? There was no reason for them to have done so.

There had to be another explanation. Ambrose had had a son, Percival, who hadn't taken to alchemy. But maybe Percy had fathered a child, unbeknownst to us. He had never married, but it was the kind of thing the cad would do. It must have been a family resemblance that Tobias had seen in the man he met in the 1950s. After all, that had been the case with Peter Silverman. It was the easiest explanation. Was it the right one?

CHAPTER 37

"Zoe, you with me?" Tobias's voice pierced through my confused thoughts.

"What? Sorry. I was distracted."

"I feel wretched that I rattled you so badly because I thought I recognized the man in the photo. I've seen so many faces over the years. I was wrong in this case."

"I know. It's just been a long time. I miss him." I set the frame down and turned it away. "Let's get back to work. With your interest in alchemical codes, you might be able to shed some light on this. I had the text translated by an expert, to make sure I had a good handle on it."

"I've gotta warn you," Tobias said, "I always hated Latin, so I'm not sure how much I'll be able to help you with this book. I learned alchemy from deciphering the riddles in the pictures, not from solving coded Latin."

"Even better. The text states that the answers are *in the pictures*. And the illustrations inside aren't like any alchemy I've ever seen. I recently figured out that the woodcut illustrations showing cathedral ruins make up one coherent cathedral when ashes are spread onto the pages to make them blend together. But it's a generic cathedral, so I can't figure out what it means."

"I think you misspoke, Zoe. You mean acid, not ashes, right?"

I shook my head, then I spread the book open on the angled scriptorium desk and stood back and watched as Tobias slowly turned the faded pages. Only, the pages weren't quite as faded as I remembered them.

"I see what you mean," he said, startling me. "These illustrations. Are you sure this is truly old? It doesn't have the scent of an old book."

"It's the strangest thing," I said. "At first, I thought I was imagining it. But now I'm sure it's not my imagination. The scent of the book keeps getting *sweeter.*"

Tobias's breath caught.

"What is it?" I asked. "You've encountered something like that before?"

"I've read about codes that involve all of the senses, but I've never come across one."

"I think I know why you've never seen one before." I hesitated, still feeling hesitant to speak the words aloud. "This book is backward alchemy."

Tobias gave a low whistle and quickly closed the book. "*That's* why you've been so evasive since I got here. That's what you didn't want to tell me."

"You know about it?"

"Only that you should steer clear of it." He stepped away from the book and crossed his arms. "The death rotation. You sure about Dorian?" He paused and ran an anxious hand across his face. "I mean, if this book is what gave him life—"

"I've never been more certain of anything. Whatever he is, he's a good soul. Unlike the intent of the backward alchemists who made this book, Robert-Houdin's intent was pure. Dorian is an innocent victim."

"His *intent,*" Tobias repeated. "You think that's what kept Dorian from being corrupted?"

"It's not working for his body, though, since it's reverting to stone."

"You know," Tobias said slowly, "you might not be able to save him."

I reached for my locket and steadied my breathing. "I have to try."

Tobias relaxed his arms and stepped slowly back toward the desk. "I'll do what I can to help you two, but…" He hesitated briefly, then opened the book again and shook his head. "I'm sorry, Zoe. Even though I enjoy codes, I'm primarily a spiritual alchemist. I only practice my own form of alchemy, and I don't know anyone who works with this type of whacked alchemy."

"Normally I'd say that was a good thing."

"Back up a sec." He looked at the book as if seeing it for the first time. "Why is this happening *now?* What changed?"

"That's what we can't figure out. We think it's happening to other things too. Several works of art made of gold have been crumbling in European museums."

"You mean the gold thefts in the papers earlier this year?"

"They *weren't* thefts. The culprits were reported to be cheeky thieves who left gold dust in place of the items they stole, but it happened at the same time Dorian began to return to stone. I think it's related."

"Damn. But you don't know why?"

I shook my head.

"Then we'd better get to work."

For the next several hours, Tobias and I went through the book's woodcut illustrations.

His interest in puzzle codes led us to a coded reference I hadn't picked up on—the placement of the flying bees relative to the planets in the different illustrations.

"The bees," Tobias said. "If you take all the images together, looking at which planets are represented in each image, it's as if they're telling you to follow a path."

"The ladder of planets," I said. "I thought of that already, but it doesn't lead anywhere. The Tea of Ashes I'm creating for Dorian isn't like any other transformation I've done. Beginning the process under a certain planet doesn't increase its strength."

"You're looking at this too literally, Zoe."

"That's always been one of my problems with alchemy," I grumbled. "What did you have in mind?"

"The planets have forces that pull different metals to them. Codes convey ideas without being literal about the example."

"Right. Like how the Language of Birds only symbolically involves birds, and hundreds of different dragon symbols have nothing to do with finding a real dragon."

"Exactly. A planetary pull is a strong one, controlling massive oceans through the tides, even keeping us glued to the ground instead of flying off into the universe."

"But you just said this didn't have to do with planets." I forced myself not to tug at my hair in frustration.

Tobias heard the defeat in my voice. "Let go of literal thinking, Zoe," he said softly.

I closed my eyes and breathed deeply, visualizing the melded illustrations of death and resurrection, the ruined cathedral now whole. "The cathedral," I said, my eyes popping open.

Tobias grinned. "*That's* the planet."

"It's trying to pull the book toward it."

"You've gotta find this cathedral."

"I don't see any identifying markings," I said, "but the book dates back at least to the sixteenth century, so it's not a modern cathedral."

Tobias sighed. "Most of them aren't, so that doesn't narrow it down much."

"Thanks for your optimism."

Tobias held up his hands. "Don't shoot the messenger."

"Dorian was originally a carving meant for Notre Dame in Paris," I said, then shook my head. "But the book came into his possession in Blois."

"Is there a Blois cathedral?"

"I'm pretty sure there is. But there have got to be hundreds of cathedrals in France alone. There's got to be something else…"

My cell phone rang.

"You're not answering the door," Brixton said on the other end of the line. "Dorian says you've got him held hostage in the attic and you're starving him to death. How come you didn't tell me he got out?"

I winced. "I'm so sorry, Brixton. So much is going on that I didn't stop and think. He's only been back for a few hours. How did you find out? Don't tell me it's on the news."

"Nah, Dorian emailed me. He's on your laptop in the attic."

Of course he was.

"I think your 'B' key is broken. He kept spelling Rixton."

"You can let yourself in. I'm in the basement and I'll meet you in the kitchen in a second." I hung up the phone.

"Who was that?" Tobias asked.

"The only other person who knows who I really am."

Dorian refused to stay in the attic. He claimed it was safe enough to be inside with the curtains drawn. With Tobias and Brixton at the house, he insisted on cooking all of us a celebratory welcome-home dinner.

"The police must show you a warrant if they wish to come inside, no?" he asked, his arms crossed and his snout flaring.

"Yes, but—"

"My legs are functioning well enough for me to make it upstairs before you let them in. If they come for me, I will be gone before they find me."

I gave up arguing with the gargoyle and let him cook a gourmet dinner for the four of us. I didn't have much food in the kitchen, having been preoccupied by other things, but Dorian created a feast out of the staples in the cabinet and the greens he sent Brixton to harvest from the backyard *potager*.

While Brixton was outside, I considered telling Dorian about the revelation Tobias and I had about the cathedral. But without a solution, I decided against it. I'd at least let him enjoy this evening.

Dorian had been giving Brixton cooking lessons, and he thought it would be a great lesson for Brixton to see how to create a feast when a pantry was nearly bare, so he invited us all to join him in "his" kitchen as he cooked.

"Now that Dorian is back," Brixton said when he returned to the kitchen with a basket full of assorted greens from the garden, "and you've got T helping you with the book, we can help Peter clear his father's name, right?"

There were so many things wrong with that sentence that I didn't know where to start.

"Dorian is on the lam," Tobias said first. "That's not a fun place to be."

"You escaped from jail, too?" Brixton asked with wide eyes. "Wicked." Only after staring at Tobias with wide-eyed awe for a few seconds did it occur to him that this might not be cool. He cleared his throat and let his eyelids droop into a pose of indifference.

"A jail of sorts," was all Tobias said on the matter. "But he'll never be free until the police are no longer searching for him."

"We must point the police in a different direction," Dorian said. He drummed his clawed fingertips together.

"Here's a crazy idea," I said. "Now that you're safe at home, we should stay out of the investigation. It doesn't have to do with us."

"But Peter's whole life was ruined," Brixton protested. "And all because of what people thought of his dad."

"Helping the magician clear his father's name is a worthy goal," Dorian agreed, "but Zoe is correct. This is not our concern."

"How can you say that?" Brixton asked. "People think his dad is a murderer. It sucks when people don't understand what's really going on with your dad."

"I thought you did not know your father," Dorian said.

"I mean my stepdad."

"People do not understand him?" The gargoyle blinked at the boy. Dorian knew a lot about the local community, but he missed out on a lot too.

"He works out of town," I said gently.

"Doing what?" Dorian asked.

"It doesn't matter," Brixton mumbled. He looked away.

"Yet you said—"

"Drop it, okay?"

"How about I put on some music," Tobias suggested. "I think we've all had an exhausting day."

"I've got a better idea." I put on a recording of the *Adventures of Ellery Queen* radio show. We listened to the 1940s classic detective radio broadcast as Dorian and Brixton cooked.

"Why do their voices sound so pretentious?" Brixton asked.

"It's not pretentious," Tobias and I said simultaneously.

"It was the style at the time," I added.

"Why don't you talk like that, then?" Brixton said. He stopped stirring.

"Before the days of reality television," I said, "there was more of a distinction between how actors spoke and how people spoke in real life. I was never an actor."

"I must insist," Dorian said, his snout flaring, "that if you remain in the kitchen, you do not distract my young assistant."

"Amazing," Tobias murmured as Dorian showed Brixton how to deglaze a pan containing a fragrantly charred mix of shallots and spices using a small amount of broth before adding the lentils and homemade vegetable broth to stew a red lentil curry. I wasn't entirely certain whether Tobias was amazed that a gargoyle was cooking, that Dorian was creating a gourmet feast from nearly barren shelves, or that a fourteen-year-old boy was enthusiastically helping.

To go with the curry, Dorian made a cashew cream sauce with the last of our raw cashews, speeding up the process of soaking the cashews by plumping them in boiling water. Dorian sautéed minced garlic in olive oil infused with chili peppers, added a splash of water to steam the heaping bunch of nettles Brixton had picked in the garden, and right before turning off the heat he added the arugula greens also from the garden. I normally ate the arugula raw in a salad or added to a smoothie as a zesty kick, but the brief sautéing brought out its peppery flavor.

Dorian gave Brixton the assignment of dipping freshly picked wild treasure blackberries in melted dark chocolate, giving him a coarse sea salt to sprinkle on top. Brixton was once skeptical of how Dorian added salt to just about everything, including desserts, but he'd come around once he tasted the results. A small amount of high quality salt could transform a dish into a heightened version of itself. The salt worked all too well with the chocolate-covered blackberries; Brixton ate more of them than were added to the parchment paper–covered plate that was supposed to go into the fridge to harden while we ate dinner.

I didn't grow up eating chocolate (I couldn't imagine what Brixton would think of that), but once I was first offered it in France, there was no going back. Many high-quality chocolates don't contain any dairy, such as the barely sweetened dark chocolate I preferred.

The sun was beginning to set when Dorian turned off the stove and declared dinner was served. We were eating an early dinner because Brixton had to help his mom clean up at Blue Sky Teas after it closed for the day. Before we sat down at the dining table, I triple-checked that the house was securely locked up and all the curtains drawn.

I was the last one to sit down at the table. I noticed Brixton had taken large helpings of everything except for the nettle mélange.

"You missed this one of the serving dishes," I said.

"They stung me when I picked them. You guys are crazy to eat those weeds."

I was reminded of a story about Frederick the Great, the King of Prussia in the mid-1700s. Many of the poor were starving, but they wouldn't eat a plentiful new food: the potato. Using reverse psychology, the king placed armed guards around the royal potato field. Sure enough, the peasants snuck into the field to steal the potatoes. The French had been similarly tricked into realizing the goodness of the potato by Antoine Parmentier earlier in the century, which is why potato dishes in France often contain the world "Parmentier" in the title.

"I'll fight you for the rest of the Parmentier nettles, Dorian," I said.

"There is no potat—ah! *Oui*. I mean *non*. This is my celebratory dinner, so I wish to eat all of the nettles. You understand, of course, *mon amie*."

"Just a little bit. The curry won't be the same without them."

"Hmm," Dorian grumbled. He wasn't a bad actor. "I am feeling magnanimous this evening. Please, take the nettles."

I served a scoop to both myself and Brixton. He didn't say a word, but he ate every bite.

When Brixton reached across the table to collect our empty plates at the end of the meal, Tobias noticed the callouses on his fingertips.

"You must play that guitar a lot." Tobias nodded toward the guitar case backpack Brixton had left in the corner.

Brixton shrugged.

"It looks like you've got some time before you've gotta get back to help your mom. How about we make some music?"

As Tobias sang "Accidental Life" and taught Brixton how to play it on the guitar I almost started to feel optimistic. Dorian clapped along until the claw of his left pinky finger broke off.

"*Merde*," he whispered. He scampered after the claw.

Brixton ceased his strumming and Tobias stopped singing. The sound of Dorian's claws on the hardwood floors echoed through the house.

"You said you were doing better," Brixton said.

"I am," Dorian said, holding the broken claw in his hand.

"I'm old enough you don't all have to lie to me," Brixton said.

"We're not—" I began.

A brisk knock sounded at the front door.

"Dorian," I whispered, "go up to the attic. If you hear *anyone* coming up besides me, crawl onto the roof. And don't forget to take the knife with you."

CHAPTER 38

As Dorian limped up the stairs, I caught snatches of the words he mumbled under his breath, but chose to ignore them.

After I heard the attic door squeak shut, I opened the front door to a familiar face.

"Yo, Max," Brixton said. He gave the detective a fist bump.

"Sorry to interrupt your… dinner party?" Max said, his gaze floating to the dining table in the open living/dining area.

"This is my old friend, Tobias," I said. The two men silently appraised each other and shook hands.

"Can I talk to you in private?" Max asked. He was speaking to me, but he kept glancing at Tobias. Was he *jealous*?

I already had a good idea that Max was here to tell me that my gargoyle statue had been stolen from the evidence lock-up. But I hated how we'd left things, so I invited him in rather than stepping outside for a brief chat. I left Brixton and Tobias playing music in the living room, and took Max through to the kitchen.

"What's up?" I asked. I crossed my arms and leaned against the counter.

"I wanted to give you the bad news in person." Max stood awkwardly, unsure of what to do with his hands and equally unsure how close to stand to me. He shook his head. "It'll keep. I shouldn't have come in person. I didn't think you'd be entertaining. Stupid of me. I'm intruding—"

"You're not intruding, Max."

"It's not a date?"

"With Tobias?" I laughed. He *was* jealous. "Brixton is here, too, in case you've already forgotten."

"Right. So you and Tobias—"

"He's a dear old friend. Just like I said. And he's only in town for a couple of days."

Max stepped closer and lowered his voice. "I'm here about what you told me the other day."

Panic seized me. He couldn't be here to have me committed, could he? Had my own past deeds come back to haunt me, because I'd once helped institutionalize the man I loved?

"I wasn't myself that day," I said. "I mean, I don't mean I have psychotic breaks and become another person." I was making this worse. "Let me start over—"

"We all get tired sometimes, Zoe. It's okay. I know you're into this New Age stuff."

I swallowed a nervous laugh threatening to surface. The term "New Age" was entirely backward. Being in touch with nature and our own bodies was as old as the world. It was only in recent times that we'd forgotten about it. But Max's words knocked me back to my senses. "I get carried away sometimes."

"I know you're attached to that statue. That's what I meant about why I'm here. It was stolen, Zoe. The statue was taken from evidence. That's what I wanted to tell you. You must've been right that it's more valuable than we thought."

I kept my mouth shut, the easiest way to avoid lying about what I already knew. I should have known it wouldn't take long for the police to realize their evidence was missing.

"You're in shock," Max said, his voice full of concern. "Can I make you some tea? Or should I get your friend? I'd understand if you wanted me to leave. I told you that you could trust me with your valuable possession, but I was wrong. I hope you can forgive me. But really, I'd understand if you simply want me to go."

When I heard the tenderness in his voice, I knew what I wanted. And it wasn't for him to leave. "Please stay."

"You sure?"

"Very. But you don't look so sure yourself. What is it, Max?"

"I can't let it go. I just—I don't understand what happened."

My heart beat in my throat. "You didn't see the thief, did you?"

Max rubbed his brow. "No. We didn't see them. It was a professional operation."

My body was now completely tense. "Why do you say that?"

"Someone hacked into the security system."

That wasn't what I'd expected him to say. "Really? How do you know?"

"The video only shows a figure *removing* the statue from the evidence locker. They had a blanket draped over themselves so as not to be seen by the cameras. At the door, they picked the lock, again under the blanket. But none of the cameras caught him *entering*."

People only see what they want to see. It never occurred to the police that a piece of evidence could have walked out on his own, so they assumed it was a much more complicated operation than it was.

"Am I under suspicion?" I asked.

"No. I showed the detective your website. He knows you couldn't have pulled this off."

"Thanks. I think."

"I can't figure out why it was taken." Max paced the length of the small kitchen, from the window box herb garden to the off-kilter back door. "There were no fingerprints or trace evidence on the statue."

"I could have told you that. I keep him—it—well cleaned."

Max stopped pacing and took my hands in his. They were warm and comforting. "I don't like this, Zoe. I don't like it at all. We don't know what we're up against."

"I'll be careful, Max. I promise."

The sound of Tobias's sonorous voice and Brixton's guitar sounded through the door.

"Brixton has gotten really good at the guitar," Max said with a smile that reminded me why I loved having him in my life. "Your friend has a great voice too. He a musician?"

"Not professionally. He's singing to cheer me up. That's why he came to visit. It's been a rough couple of days. I feel like I've aged two years in the last two days."

"I know you've been through a lot, Zoe. Losing your little brother when you were young, and now encountering two violent deaths this year."

I felt my locket against my skin, keeping my brother close to me. "This might sound silly," I began hesitantly, "but one of the things that helps me deal with death is to embrace it. The Victorians, and other cultures, had a custom of having picnics in cemeteries. Would you like to join me for a picnic at River View Cemetery? It helps me clear my head—"

"Have you been going back there again, Zoe?" Max snapped, anger flashing in his eyes.

His outburst was so unexpected that I jerked backward and bumped into the swinging kitchen door. "What's the matter with you, Max? Ever since you got back from China—"

"I'm sorry, Zoe. I shouldn't have snapped at you. I've been thinking about a lot of things differently since that trip to my grandfather's 100th birthday party. I don't want to lose you."

"Why would you lose me? We're just getting to know each other. Why are you being so cryptic?"

Max gave a long sigh. "You know I lost my wife, Chadna, not long after we were married. You asked me before what happened to her, but I didn't want to talk about it."

I thought back to the times I'd been to Max's sparse house. There were only two photographs. A black-and-white one of his grandmother, and one of his wife in vibrant color. His grandmother was photographed inside her apothecary shop in China, her lips unsmiling but her eyes alive. The photograph of Chadna was taken in a field of tulips. Her long black hair flowed almost to her waist, and the loving smile on her face told me Max had taken the photo.

"You weren't ready to tell me," I said. "That's okay, Max."

"That wasn't it. It's not about you. It's that I've always wanted to think about the future, not the past."

That was one of the great things about Max. He didn't press me to tell him about my own past.

I waited for him to go on, but instead he said, "I should go. I'm interrupting your party."

"They seem perfectly happy without me. Is that the Spinners they're singing now? I'd say you've got quite a while before they even realize I'm not in the room. You were talking about not living in the past."

"And I was completely wrong. Grandfather had the traditional big sixtieth birthday party when I was a toddler, here in Portland, but this one was different. He's going to die soon, but he was the happiest I've ever seen him. Family and friends from across the world and from every stage of his life visited over the course of a week. They spoke of being helped by him and my grandmother in ways that couldn't possibly be true. The transformations Grandmother made out of herbs weren't magic. She was an apothecary—just a precursor to a pharmacist. But two of Grandfather's guests in particular made it sound as if my grandparents had transformed their lives with magic. And people Grandfather hadn't seen in seventy years made the trip, so he'd truly touched their lives." He paused. "Looking back *was* looking forward."

"That sounds beautiful."

"It also sounds crazy. What's crazier is that I was starting to believe it."

I squeezed his hand, feeling hope rise within me. Was he closer to understanding than I thought? "It doesn't sound crazy, Max."

"If you really mean that, then I know you're ready to hear the reason why I became so overprotective when you've mentioned going up to the mudslide area. It's about Chadna." A sad smile consumed his face. "I should start at the beginning. Her older sister died of cancer when she was young. It's why she wanted to become a doctor in the first place. She thought she could channel her grief into something concrete. She was so driven. I met her during her fourth year of med school. In the ER."

"She was your doctor?"

"That would have made a nice story, right? But that's not what happened. A friend of mine called me in the middle of the night, needing to go to the emergency room. I drove him, but I'm no good in the middle of the night, and you know I hate coffee, so I promptly fell asleep. She woke me up." He cringed.

"What's so bad about that?"

"She woke me up with smelling salts. She thought I must have come into the ER for myself and been in such bad shape that I'd passed out. She was brand-new to the ER so she didn't know about proper procedures or anything. She broke the smelling salts right under my nose, and I head-butted her nose. There was blood everywhere."

My hand flew to my mouth and I tried to stop laughing, but my efforts were in vain.

"It's okay," he said. "It's impossible not to laugh at that story."

"It's a wonderful story, Max. That's the kind of thing that keeps a memory alive."

"It's definitely unforgettable."

"Was your friend you took to the ER injured on the job?"

"No, he wasn't a cop. I hadn't yet joined the police force. I was aimless until I met Chadna. She was the exact opposite of my woo-woo family." He laughed sadly. "I told you my grandmother taught me a lot about herbs when I was kid. She and my grandfather lived here with my family until she died, and then my grandfather returned to China. It was my grandmother who was passionate about herbal medicines, talking about the energy of plants and the intent that goes into creating herbal remedies. I always regretted that, shortly before she died, I told her how stupid it all was." He ran a hand through his thick black hair. "Chadna was nearly finished with her residency when she received her own cancer diagnosis."

"How long did you have left with her?" I asked, wondering if he was acting so strangely because of how sick I looked. Did he think he'd lose me to cancer too?

"She had a year of cancer treatments. She never lost her smile through the whole thing, but it was even brighter when she beat it."

"Wait, she was *cured?*"

He nodded. Tears welled in his eyes. "Two weeks after she received the news that she was cancer-free, we were on a weekend getaway to celebrate. We were hiking. We came across a boulder that looked like it would give us a gorgeous view. We climbed up it, and the stone shifted."

My breath caught.

"She fell," Max said. "We were supposed to have our whole lives together, but in that moment, it was all taken away."

"I'm so sorry, Max. That's why you don't want me trekking around that unstable ground above the river."

"I don't want the same thing to happen to you." He stepped closer and ran his fingers through my white hair that he, like everyone else, thought was dyed. "There was nothing I could do, but I still blame myself, you know?"

"I know. I—" I broke off. Should I try telling Max the truth again? What would he do if he saw Dorian?

"I should go," Max said. "You should get back to your friends."

"Don't go." I put my hand on his arm and took a deep breath.

CHAPTER 39

As the end of his life grew near, Jean Eugène Robert-Houdin feared for what would become of his not-quite-human son. Inspiration struck one day, out of a tragedy.

A famous personage in France, Robert-Houdin knew others in high society as well as men at the tops of their professions. One such man was a well-regarded chef who cooked *choucroute garnie* with such exquisite results that people traveled for miles to partake of his delicacies. The chef developed an ego, as most men do when told repeatedly how great they are. One day, a grease fire began in the kitchen. It quickly engulfed his establishment. The chef made sure all of his workers made it to safety. He was the last one out. It never once occurred to him that the building would dare injure him. Yet a wooden beam struck him, trapping him inside the burning building. Before he was rescued, the fire scorched his head and hands. He escaped with his life, but without his sight and former dexterity.

As he'd never married, the former chef sat alone in his large house. There was no life in the house, save for the domestic servant who came twice a day to clean the house and bring him barely tolerable food. The chef might have withered and died from desolation had it not been for the occasional interesting visitor, such as his old friend Jean Eugène Robert-Houdin and an odd fellow Robert-Houdin brought with him.

437

Dorian was introduced as a distant relative of Robert-Houdin's who had been disfigured in an accident and was therefore wary of being seen by people, who could be cuttingly cruel. Oh, how the chef understood the cruelty of men! The people who once adored him would no longer look upon his burned face and hands. The saving grace of his blindness was that he himself did not have to see what his once-handsome face had become.

The chef was the first person aside from Robert-Houdin with whom Dorian had conversed. On one visit, the topic turned to food, as it often did. Robert-Houdin went to the window to look upon the barren trees that swayed in the wind. Winter would be upon them soon. He sensed it would be his last winter in this world.

Robert-Houdin's human son had recently died in the Franco-Prussian War, and the Hessians were threatening Paris. What more did an old man have to live for?

When he pulled himself out of his own thoughts and returned to the sofa, he realized that he had not been missed. Looking between the two outcasts, a flash of inspiration overwhelmed him.

"Martin," Robert-Houdin said. He rose out of habit, even though the chef could not see him. "I have had the most inspired idea. You and my relation Dorian are both men shunned by society through no fault of your own, and you both appreciate eating gourmet food."

"Why must you bring up my failings?" Martin asked, holding up his burned hands. "I can neither see nor hold a knife. I must rely on the vile porridge and stews that wretched woman brings me."

"Yet Dorian," Robert-Houdin said, "has the best eye sight of any man I have met, and is nearly as accomplished at sleight of hand as I. Would it not be possible for you to teach him to cook? He is looking for somewhere to live where he will not need to hide from people who look upon him unfavorably because of his disfigurement. In exchange for food and lodgings, he could cook and clean for you. I cannot imagine a more perfect plan."

And so it was that one of the greatest cooks in France would teach Dorian Robert-Houdin the skills that enabled him to become a gourmet chef.

～

The war brought challenges that year, but the Robert-Houdin household survived by hiding from the Hessians in a cave. Having gotten his affairs in order, Robert-Houdin passed away that summer, at peace.

Upon the old magician's death, the family unlocked his studio. Everyone was disappointed to find no great creation waiting for them. What had the man been working on all those years? His mind must have left him.

The family was less surprised by a trifling fact of far greater significance. Upon Robert-Houdin's death, his friend Viollet-le-Duc came to pay his respects. He asked if he could see the magician's stage props. Since the architect was not a magician competitor, Robert-Houdin's family saw no harm in allowing an old friend to visit his studio. They didn't expect the elderly architect to erupt in a rage when he could not find the gift he'd given his friend years before. No matter, they thought to themselves. They were sorry for his grief, but could he really have expected that his friend would keep his atrocious gift? When the architect began raving and asking questions, claiming that Robert-Houdin had been an alchemist, they set him straight and politely asked the man to leave.

CHAPTER 40

"I want to tell you something, too," I said. "So please, don't go."

Max stepped back to give me space, but took my hand in his. I smelled jasmine as he ran his index finger along the life line of my palm, even though I knew his Poet's Jasmine wouldn't be blooming again until summer. "I'm glad you're feeling better after your meltdown the last time I saw you."

Meltdown? I steadied my breathing. As much as I wanted to tell Max the whole messy, unbelievable truth, I'd been overly optimistic that I could tell him everything. He wasn't ready to believe me. Not yet. "Hey, *meltdown* is a bit harsh, don't you think?" I forced a laugh. "There was a search warrant for my house, so I was entitled to a freak-out."

"Fair enough." Max laughed along with me. "What were you going to tell me? After I told you that embarrassing story of how I met Chadna, you know you can tell me anything."

I couldn't, though. If he thought my talking about a living gargoyle was a meltdown, he'd certainly have his own meltdown if I convinced him it was true. But he was still straddling that line of what he'd let himself believe. One day soon, I hoped he'd be ready. And in the present, it was still true that I didn't want Max to leave. He understood what it was like to lose a loved one under tragic circumstances, and I needed to open up to someone about Ambrose. The memories that had bubbled to the surface were too distracting, and talking with Tobias was no longer an option, since Tobias mistakenly thought he knew Ambrose long after he'd died. Max was who I wanted to talk to, and there was a lot I could tell him that was true. All I had to do was leave out irrelevant details that wouldn't have fit with his understanding of the world.

The sound of melodious guitar chords and a booming baritone continued in the background, lulling me into a sense of safety I hadn't felt in years. Even though the people around me didn't understand all of me, I was surrounded by people who cared for me, and who I cared for.

"It's not only my brother I lost," I said. "There was someone I once planned on spending my life with. I never talk about him either. Until this week, I kept his photograph hidden inside an old notebook. But you're right. When we try to forget them, we're not fully living in the present. I want to tell you about him."

I pulled free from Max's hand. I didn't want him to be able to sense the difference in my pulse when I changed irrelevant facts that would make him question my recollection. As an excuse, I opened a glass mason jar filled with chocolate ginger cookies. I offered one to Max, but he declined. I ate the chewy cookie quickly, barely tasting it. Dorian would have been appalled. He also would have been appalled that I detected a hint of bitterness in the cookie.

"Ambrose was a fellow gardener and herbalist," I said, choosing my words carefully. "Until I met him, I had never really gotten over my brother's death. Not the fact that Thomas died, but the fact that I couldn't save him from the virus that killed him." It was the Plague that had killed my brother in 1704. Dumb luck that a small outbreak swept through France while we were there, and a dumber sister who thought seeking a cure in her alchemy lab could be more useful than simple loving care. "I got him the best care I could, but I should have been there with him."

"You thought you could be a miracle worker with your herbal remedies. I understand the impulse to save everyone, especially those we care about. But I wonder if I could have done something differently that day with Chadna, so I understand how you can still blame yourself."

"I traveled around for several years after that." For over 150 years, if I wanted to be precise. Which I didn't. I ran from my apprenticeship with the Flamels, ran from my alchemy research, and ran from myself. I traveled through the Far East and the fledgling United States of America.

I carried only one satchel, though in my unhealthy state even the single bag was often burdensome. I'd abandoned alchemy when Thomas died, so I was no longer encumbered by the tools of an alchemy laboratory. My bag contained the bare essentials for creating tinctures, tonics, balms, and salves, along with a few items of dirty clothing, a dusty blanket, and stale bread. I walked in the one pair of shoes I owned, with my gold locket around my neck, and kept several gold coins tucked into a hidden pocket. Only in winter did I travel with dried herbs. Throughout the rest of the year, I found plants to work with wherever I went. They were there, if you knew where to look. After many years, I found myself back in France.

"After I got tired of traveling," I continued, "I went to work at my grandmother's shop in Paris—the shop I now run as my online business Elixir. Ambrose was English, but I met him there in France. What are you chuckling about?"

"Ambrose, such an old-fashioned name. I was smiling because it suits you so well. You've always struck me as wiser than your years. *Immortal.*"

I froze.

"Doesn't the name Ambrose mean 'immortal'?" Max continued.

"It does." I relaxed, but I felt my hands shaking. To cover up my nervousness, I absentmindedly bit into another cookie. The meaning of his name was one of the reasons Ambrose had been intrigued by alchemy in the first place. "Ambrose was an aspiring gardener when I met him. You would have been horrified by his sad garden. But he wanted to learn."

One day in the 1890s, when I was bringing an herbal remedy to an ailing household outside of Paris, I came across a striking figure. He wasn't the most handsome man I'd ever seen, but there was something that drew me to him. Something beyond his thick black hair, dark blue eyes, and gently crooked nose.

Next to a cottage along the dirt path, a man was kneeling in the dirt next to a row of unhealthy salsify. The spectacles that adorned his face shone in the sunlight. I watched as he ran a hand through his unruly black hair. Despite the failure of his *potager*, his face showed contentment instead of the frustration I expected. I couldn't resist setting him straight about caring for his struggling garden.

Just as I had never excelled at alchemy involving metals, Ambrose had never been good with plants. Yet he never gave up. In spite of years of failure, he continued to keep a range of plants in his garden and struggled to keep them alive. That was Ambrose. Never giving up. Until the end. We were at once opposites and the perfect complements to each other. *I can't believe I'd have forgotten you, but do we know each other?* Those were the first words Ambrose had spoken to me, on that first day of our acquaintance, when he caught me pausing to look at him. *No,* I replied, *but I know that poor salsify plant you're strangling the life out of. May I show you how to care for it?* After that, we had never left each other's sides.

"Even though I was always good with herbal remedies and healing others," I continued, "I didn't start taking care of myself until I met Ambrose. That's when I began eating the healthy plant-based foods I eat today, to heal both my body and soul. It was a whole new way of life for me, and it was wonderful for a while. Until—" I needed a moment to compose myself. "Until Ambrose killed himself."

"I'm so sorry, Zoe," Max said gently. "The look on your face. It's guilt. You look like you blame yourself for his death too."

"Part of me does." I stopped myself from saying more. That Ambrose had gone insane after hearing that his son Percival had died of old age. He couldn't deal with the weight—the curse—of living indefinitely, so he ended his life.

"When someone takes their own life," Max said softly, "it's about them. Not you."

"That doesn't make it any easier."

"No, it doesn't," Max said, a look of understanding dawning on his face. "That's why you spent most of your twenties on the road."

My twenties. "That's part of it."

"Are your parents still alive?"

I shook my head. "I lost them a long time ago." I'd lost them long before they died. When I didn't adopt the norms of our time and was accused of witchcraft, they didn't support me. If it hadn't been for my brother, I would have been killed before my seventeenth birthday.

"I'm sorry, Zoe. You're so young to have lost so many people."

"I'm not so young, you know." Why had I said that out loud?

"I know. You've been through so much more than most people your age. But…"

"But what, Max?" I tapped my foot nervously on the linoleum floor. Why was I so jumpy?

"We're at such different places in our lives. You're just starting out in life. Portland is a fresh start for you. I don't want to hold you back."

"If you're trying to say you're too old for me, I don't care that the age listed on your driver's license is greater than mine." Nor did I care that I'd been born before his great-great-great grandparents.

The older I get, the more I've seen how after adolescence, it's our physical bodies that age us and constrain us. Shared experiences give people within a generation an affinity for each other that makes it easier to connect. While that's a real connection, it's also a superficial one. Aside from my relationship with my brother, all of the other meaningful relationships I've had in my life have been with people—and a gargoyle—who've had vastly different life experiences from mine. Different ages, classes, languages, races, religions, nationalities, occupations, passions. The more I saw people's superficial differences, the more I learned those things weren't important.

In alchemical terms, our bodies are the salt that ages, our spirits are dual-faced mercury that changes with the times, and sulfurous fire is the key to our souls across the ages. Our soul is our true self, regardless of age or history.

One of the reasons I didn't mind falling out of touch with true alchemists was that they often lost sight of their souls. The older some alchemists got, the easier it was for them to abandon their humanity. I sometimes wondered whether I didn't look hard enough for Nicolas and Perenelle Flamel because I feared it had happened to them.

Thinking of them made me fidget even more. That was unlike me. Though I'd been more scattered than usual as I desperately sought out Dorian's cure, my alchemical training has taught me how to focus.

"I wonder if I've been selfish," Max said. "You're only twenty-eight—"

"I'm *not* twenty-eight." I clamped my hand over my mouth, horrified by what I'd admitted.

I looked at the cookie jar. The label on the jar had been typed up on the antique typewriter Dorian used to make the labels I insisted on. These weren't ginger chocolate cookies. They were *coffee* and ginger chocolate cookies. I'd just ingested several cups worth of caffeine.

Max frowned at me. "Are you okay, Zoe?"

"This has been great! Hasn't this been great? Opening up to each other." The caffeine was making me manic. Would it act like a truth serum? I had to get Max to leave before it made me say something I couldn't undo. I took Max's hand and pulled him toward the back door.

"You're trying to get rid of me? What did you mean you're not twenty-eight?"

"Just like you were saying earlier, that I'm an old soul, from everything I've gone through."

"Okay..." His furrowed brow said otherwise.

"Old Soul! That's a great name for a band, don't you think? I should suggest that to Tobias and Brixton. They're so talented, don't you think?"

"Your hands are sweating. Are you sure you're okay?"

"It's later than I thought. I should get back to my guests." I pulled open the back door. "You should go."

CHAPTER 41

After Max left, clearly displeased by his abruptly requested departure, I gulped two glasses of lemon water. I mentally kicked myself for being so abrupt with Max, but I couldn't trust myself not to say too much. Beads of sweat covered my face. The corner of my lip twitched.

I slammed down the empty glass and stormed into the living room. "Dorian made *coffee* cookies!"

The music broke off with a discordant guitar chord coming to a metallic screeching halt.

"Dorian!" I shouted. "Dorian!"

"I'll go get him," Brixton said, stumbling away from me as quickly as he'd fled from me the first day I met him.

"It was impossible not to hear the piercing banshee wail," Dorian said from the top of the stairs. "I am sorry, *mon amie*, but did you not read the label I created as you asked?"

"I asked you not to bake caffeine into anything, because I knew this might happen." My legs twitched nervously. "Before he left, I let it slip to Max about my not really being twenty-eight. Who knows what I would have told him next if I hadn't gotten him away from me."

"Max isn't still in the kitchen?" Brixton asked.

"I shoved him out the door before I accidentally told him about you lot."

"You're sweating an awful lot," Brixton said. "Are you poisoned? Do you need to go see a doctor?"

"She's got someone better right here," Tobias said, feeling my forehead. He shook his head.

"I'm not poisoned," I insisted. "But I doubt I'll sleep for days."

Tobias checked my vital signs and agreed this was nothing more than a case of an alchemist's reaction to coffee.

"Not cool," Brixton said. "It must suck to be an alchemist. Except for the super-human part. That's pretty wicked." At fourteen, Brixton was already a coffee convert. I expected that wasn't abnormal in Portland, although the amount of sugar he added to his coffee also explained it.

After he was convinced Tobias was medically qualified and I was all right, Brixton pulled the chocolate-covered blackberries out of the fridge. The kid, the gargoyle, and the former slave ate a simple yet delectable dessert. As for me, I walked up and down the stairs a few dozen times, then lay down on the couch and put a compress over my eyes. Neither worked. Nor did the herbal remedy Tobias insisted I try. I sprang up the stairs to try one more thing.

Brixton was packing up his guitar when I returned with a hula hoop in hand. It was time for him to meet his mom at Blue Sky Teas to help her clean up the teashop.

"You can let your mom know I'm feeling better and can bake pastries for the morning," I said.

"But you're not feeling better," Brixton said. "You said—"

"Since your mom thinks I'm the one who bakes the teashop pastries, we need to keep up the pretense. Now that Dorian has escaped police custody, he can resume his baking." I put the hula hoop around my waist and began moving my hips. The hoop spun around me, with the sound of the tumbler inside following my movements. "I bet he'll make some great items tomorrow, happy to be a free man again. Or, I suppose he's a free *gargoyle*, and it's technically tonight, since Dorian will be baking before any of us are awake in the morning. Except for me. Since I won't be sleeping. For days. Dorian, do you need any ingredients? You must need ingredients. I could go to an all-night market if you—"

"Uh, Zoe," Brixton said, "you're babbling. And you look ridiculous. I'm leaving." With a departing eye roll at the sight of the 1950s hula hoop, he slipped out of the house. Tobias locked the door behind him.

"Well, *mon amie*," Dorian said. "Now I realize why caffeine is not a method you wish to use to stay awake in the night. You are quite useless at present. Monsieur Freeman, may I interest you in a nightcap before it is dark enough for me to leave the premises?"

"Zoe, do you want to join us?" Tobias asked.

"Can't talk. Hula hooping."

~

An hour later, I was still twitchy, but I'd calmed down enough to have a sensible conversation. Which was a good thing, because Tobias had to catch a flight the next day. This was our only evening together.

I found him in the attic with Dorian, drinking sherry with the gargoyle out of ornately etched cordial glasses. A nearly empty crystal decanter sat on a silver platter between them.

"You didn't tell me this little fellow could drink me under the table," Tobias said.

"Moi?" The gargoyle chuckled.

"I'm glad you two are getting along so well. Especially since tonight I alienated one of the few friends I've got here."

"Monsieur Liu is not good for you," Dorian declared.

"He seemed like a good man," Tobias said. "We've all been around long enough to be good judges of character. And I judged him to be a kind man who cares for Zoe."

Dorian raised his clawed index finger to make a point. "A good man? Yes. A trustworthy one? No."

"You're just saying that because he's cooked in your kitchen."

"Mais non! This is a problem, yes, but I am not being frivolous. Max Liu is the arm of the law. His men locked me up! How can you trust this man?"

"It doesn't sound like that was his fault," Tobias said.

"Yet it would not have happened if Zoe could tell him the truth about she and I!" The dramatic statement was rendered less powerful because it was followed by a hiccup.

"If you two are done determining my love life," I said, "maybe Tobias and I can get back to work on *Non Degenera Alchemia.* Toby, you said you wanted to see more about the Tea of Ashes."

"Catch you later, little man," Tobias said, shaking Dorian's hand.

"It has been a pleasure." Dorian bowed his head.

The stairs creaked under my enthusiastic steps as we made our way down to the basement. We'd left Dorian in the attic with a stack of science fiction books from the library. I wondered what a drunk gargoyle would make of them.

"I wish I could stay," Tobias said as I unlocked the basement's secure lock, "but I've got a shift tomorrow and I'm needed back home. There isn't anyone to cover for me."

"Is your station short-staffed with medical techs?"

"Something like that."

I wasn't up for creating the Tea of Ashes in my present agitated state, or so soon after having done so that week, but I walked Tobias through the process I'd pieced together from the counterclockwise motions in *Non Degenera Alchemia's* illustrations.

"Slow down," Tobias said as I flipped through the pages. "You're going to destroy the book."

He was right. I took a step back. "I should let you handle the book until the coffee is out of my system."

"I don't know what it is about that stuff that messes up alchemists so badly. I'd wager it rivals mercury with its dangerous dual-faced properties. But only for us."

"It's our own faults for being overly connected to nature's transformations."

"Let's get back to these unnatural transformations here." He pointed at the page I'd nearly ripped out of the book. "Jumping right to fire and ash. That can't be good."

"It's not. Each time I light the fire with the intent of practicing backward alchemy, the effects begin. My skin begins to shrivel along with the plants I'm turning to ash."

"The salt of the body. That makes sense."

I nodded. "That's why it temporarily stops Dorian's body from reverting to stone."

"I keep coming back to the gold thefts in Europe," Tobias said. "The ones that you don't believe are thefts at all."

"I'm almost positive," I said. "We looked up the dates of the 'thefts' where the thieves left behind gold dust, and they correspond precisely to when Dorian began to return to stone. The impure becoming the pure—and now transforming back again into dust."

"And they're both connected to this cathedral." Tobias tapped on the page of the book.

"Tobias!"

He jumped back.

"I didn't mean to startle you. I haven't thought much about the crumbling gold since I realized the book illustrations form a cathedral. This means there could be a *pattern* to the gold that's crumbling. It's not that *all* alchemical gold is in danger of disintegrating."

"Are the gold pieces religious relics?"

"Not all of them. They aren't similar pieces. There's no pattern. At least that's what I thought—until now."

"There's a pattern there, Zoe. You just need to find it." Tobias yawned and his eyelids drooped.

I shook his shoulders, even more adrenaline surging through my engorged veins. "Are you all right? Is the book having an effect on you?"

He shook his head. "I worked the night shift right before flying in to see you this morning."

"Why didn't you say so?"

"We don't have much time together. I didn't want to waste it sleeping. But after that sherry…"

"Come on, Toby. You know there's no sense working on alchemy when you're so tired. I'll fix up a bedroom for you."

Between the coffee's physical effects and the mental strain of thinking about Ambrose, the cathedral, Dorian's deterioration, and Peter's quest, I knew I'd never sleep. After I saw Tobias to his room, I heard him speaking softly to someone on his cell phone, followed by snoring that was anything but soft. I scribbled a note and grabbed my silver raincoat.

A light misty rain fell from the night sky. I breathed in the scents of fresh rain and blossoming fruit trees as I set off on a brisk pace. I had no destination, but I needed to keep moving. It was early enough in the evening that other people were out, but as soon as the rain began to fall harder, I found myself mostly alone on the sidewalk.

I walked past the restaurants and bars on Hawthorne, past the signs for hand-crafted beer, hand-poured coffee, and hand-made clothing and hats. Turning off the main drag, I passed households watching television for the evening, and parks vacant from the rain. The rainwater streamed down my face, nourishing my unnaturally dry skin. Once my hair was soaked, I began to get a chill, so I came home. The front door creaked loudly enough to awaken the dead bees in Dorian's book in the basement.

"Zoe!" Tobias's voice in the living room startled me. He leaped up from the green velvet couch. "Thank God you're back. You didn't take your cell phone with you."

"I've never gotten used to taking it with me everywhere. What's the matter?" I stood there dripping onto the floor.

"I woke up thirsty after drinking all that sherry, so I went to get myself a glass of water. The house was really quiet. Too quiet, like houses get when everyone is sleeping."

"Dorian doesn't sleep."

"I know. You told me. That's the problem. You said he shouldn't go out this early in the evening—especially now that the police will be on the lookout for a stone gargoyle."

"He's hiding in the attic," I said. "He's probably reading quietly."

"I climbed up to the attic, Zoe. I wanted to be sure, so I checked the whole house. The gargoyle is gone."

CHAPTER 42

PARIS, 1871

Sleep was not a necessity for the gargoyle. Without knowing any other state of existence, Dorian thought this neither a blessing nor a curse—until his father died. Jean Eugène Robert-Houdin passed away from pneumonia, not long after the tragic news of his son's death due to injuries suffered in the Franco-Prussian War. Dorian found himself more alone than he imagined.

His new employer, the blind chef, understood Dorian's grief at his relative's death. But Dorian could not tell him this was the first person in his life he had lost to death. He had been brought to life only eleven years before, yet with his deep voice and keen intellect, it was important for him to maintain the illusion that he was a much older man. And a man, not a gargoyle, of course.

Luckily, Dorian found himself without much time to be maudlin. Between the distractions of Paris and the cooking lessons from his employer, Dorian could have filled more than a twenty-four-hour day.

At first Dorian objected to the part of the agreement that involved cleaning, but after some grumbling, he found washing dishes and dusting could be contemplative exercises. It was but a small price to pay for the lessons in French gastronomy he received.

The chef could not have been more pleased with how well Dorian took to the demands of French cooking. Dorian did so well that the chef pleaded with him to allow some former friends to come over for dinner parties, as he wanted very much to showcase the gourmet cooking of his successor. Yet Dorian was resolute. He had been traumatized by his disfigurement, he said. Nobody could be allowed to see him.

To keep up the pretense, Dorian pretended to wear the clothes his father had given him for the charade that was to be his life. To add verisimilitude, on his nocturnal explorations Dorian would bring a handful of clothes with him, which he would toss in the dust. Therefore he was able to have his clothing laundered with the chef's clothing without raising suspicions.

Dorian learned not only how to cook everything from creamy *aligot* to succulent *magret de canard*, but also how to find his way through the world without being seen. He learned through trial by fire, as he was in Paris during the short-lived War of 1870.

While the chef slept, Dorian pretended to use the very nice bed chamber created for him, when in truth he was exploring the City of Lights under the cover of darkness.

PARIS, 1881

Ten years later, when the chef approached the end of his life, he wrote Dorian Robert-Houdin a reference so he could be a home companion to other blind people who did not have families to care for them.

Upon Martin's death, a small inheritance was bequeathed to Dorian. The gargoyle was unaware of the money until a letter reached him at the home of his next employer, an *avocate* who had long ago retired from practicing law and had recently been widowed. Not realizing the true form of his disfigured friend, the chef did not have the foresight to give Dorian his gift in person. Now, it seemed Dorian would not be able to claim his inheritance without being seen. But all was not lost. By that time, Dorian, even more than his father, was a master of illusion. His greatest skill was *not being seen*.

Dorian's penmanship was superb. This was not an easy feat, considering his clawed hands, which Viollet-le-Duc had never intended to hold a pen. Holding a whisk and beating eggs was one thing. But it was important for Dorian to rigorously practice writing, for written correspondence was his connection to most of the world.

Upon receiving news of his modest inheritance, Dorian asked his new employer, the barrister, for counsel. Explaining that he was far too embarrassed to show his disfigured face to anyone, Dorian gave the barrister permission to act on his behalf, and the lawyer declared under oath that the tragically disfigured Dorian Robert-Houdin lived at his home and was who he claimed.

It was with methods like these that Dorian made his way in the world.

He moved from place to place with only a small travel case in which he kept a few remembrances of his father, including *Non Degenera Alchemia*. Dorian appreciated art, but he didn't especially care for the illustrations inside the alchemy book. He kept the book because it reminded him of his father, but whenever he opened the book, he felt a strange sleepiness overcome him. He suspected it was his imagination, that it was sadness he was feeling as he thought of the man who gave him life and raised him. The man who was no longer on this earth. His father had explained to him that something in this book had brought him to life, but Dorian was not a philosophical creature. He was a gourmand who appreciated the finer pleasures in life, not a philosopher. If it had been a cookbook, he might have spent time unlocking the book's coded messages. But why dwell on things that had no bearing on his life?

CHAPTER 43

It wasn't yet ten o'clock. Far too early for Dorian to be out of the house. He never left the house until the dead of night, when fewer people would be around. Did he think that because of the rain it would be safer?

"Maybe he went to hide the knife." I cringed at the thought. One of these days, I was going to have to sit the gargoyle down to talk about police evidence.

"The knife is in the attic."

Great. Just great. All I needed was for the police to raid the house and find a murder weapon inside.

I texted Brixton to ask if he knew where Dorian was. Less than a minute later he texted me back.

He went to see Julian Lake.

I groaned.

"What is it?" Tobias asked.

"He went to see Julian Lake of the Lake Loot. How can he do this? What does he hope to learn by spying on the man whose family heirlooms were stolen decades ago?"

"That's nice of him, though. The little guy is helping Brixton with the magician's quest to clear his dad."

"It's *not* nice. It's not safe for him to leave. His leg is effectively broken, and the police are looking for a missing gargoyle statue."

Another text popped up from Brixton. HE LEFT A WHILE AGO. HE'S NOT BACK YET?

I made a mental note that I should never leave the two of them alone together.

DON'T WORRY, HE'S PROBABLY WAITING UNTIL IT'S LATE ENOUGH TO SNEAK HOME MORE EASILY, I typed. I half believed it. No need for both of us to suffer a sleepless night.

TEXT ME WHEN HE'S BACK, Brixton wrote. We both cared about the gargoyle.

I felt marginally better after I looked up Julian Lake. He was eighty-five years old *and blind*. If Dorian was able to catch him alone, the sightless Mr. Lake would assume he was a man.

Up in the attic, Tobias and I sat on the floor playing gin rummy and drinking cocoa that wasn't nearly as good as Dorian's, while we waited anxiously for his return. With my favorite wool sweaters ruined from the destructive winter storm, I wrapped a blanket around myself to stay warm. As Tobias dealt the cards and light rain tapped at the tarp securing the roof, a comforting familiarity washed over me. I was still worried about Dorian, but the edge was gone from my worry. I had friends who wanted to help.

"You can go back to sleep, you know," I said.

"Not a chance." He paused before picking up the hand he'd dealt. "It's good to be here, Zoe. Even under these screwed-up circumstances, I'm so glad it led you back to me."

"I am too."

For the next hour, we caught up about life and where our travels had taken us. We learned we'd almost been in Albuquerque at the same time, and because we were both on the road so much we'd learned to fix up cars ourselves. Tobias owned fewer possessions than I did, so all his belongings fit into a 1956 Cadillac Eldorado.

"What's so funny?" Tobias asked when I laughed so uncontrollably that I dropped my cards.

"The two of us. Could we have picked more conspicuous cars?"

"In this life we lead, we've gotta take our enjoyment where we can get it. Though my wife hates that car."

I froze before I could pick up my scattered playing cards. "You're *married*? Why didn't you say so earlier?"

"It's complicated."

"Isn't everything in our lives? Does she—"

"She knows. It would be impossible for her not to."

I no longer felt like playing gin. I looked from Tobias's resigned face to the strewn cards. The King and Queen of Hearts stared up at me. "She's grown older than you."

"So much so that when we moved to Detroit we couldn't tell anyone we were married. I don't talk about it out of habit. Since I'm an EMT, we tell people I'm her live-in companion to help with her health."

"Why didn't you tell me? Is it okay for you to be away from her?"

He chuckled. "I knew you'd be concerned about her if you knew. That's why I didn't tell you when we emailed. I wanted to come see you. And you would have stopped me."

"Of course I would have stopped you!"

"She's okay. One of my friends is looking in on her while I'm gone. And it's just two days. But Rosa is the most important reason why I need to get home."

"What's the matter with her? Is there anything I can do to help?"

"Nah. I've got it covered. And there's no disease or condition to treat." A wistful look passed over his face. "Simply old age."

"When did you tell her?" I asked, thinking of Max.

Tobias stood up and walked the length of the attic, coming to a stop in front of a shelf of antique books on gardening and herbal remedies. "Too late," he said. "I told her too late."

"Once she'd already fallen in love with you."

He gave a single curt nod. "Even though I pretended I gave her a choice, I didn't give her a fair one. If she'd always known, she could have steered clear of me, and had someone to grow old with."

"You seem like you love her very much. Haven't you had a good life together?"

"We have. I would have made the same choice to be with her. I just wish I'd given her an honest choice."

We stopped talking as a faint scratching sounded on the roof. The noise was followed by the appearance of a gargoyle squeezing through the rafters and carefully reattaching the tarp. A cape of black silk was fastened around his neck. It looked suspiciously like the cape I thought was hanging inside my old trailer parked in the driveway.

"Ah!" Dorian cried out when he spotted us. "You wish to kill me by a heart attack, so I will not become trapped in stone?"

"We know where you went," I said.

Dorian stepped to the empty corner of the attic. He unfurled his wings and shook off the rainwater. *"Magnifique,* is it not?"

"No, it is not."

"He is blind, Zoe! It was the perfect mission for me."

"You were able to talk with him?" Tobias asked.

"I thought he didn't take visitors," I added.

"He does not like most people, yet I believe he is lonely. His caregiver is a spiteful woman. And she is a terrible cook." The gargoyle sighed wistfully. "His kitchen is four times the size of this one."

"Hey," I said to the little ingrate.

"He has two refrigerators, each of which is twice the size of this—"

"Dorian."

"You distracted me with your talk of food."

"I didn't mention food. You did."

"Semantics. Where was I? Ah, yes. Not only was I able to talk to him, but after I presented him with a slice of chocolate cake—my new recipe, which is my best yet, if I do say so—"

"Dorian. I'll grant that the cake is good. Back to Julian Lake."

"Oui. I could not carry much with me and remain nimble, but I knew chocolate would be a good choice, because most people favor it. In this, I was not disappointed."

Tobias put his head in his hands. "Is he always like this?"

"Pretty much."

"Impatient Americans," Dorian grumbled, then cleared his throat. "Very well. I learned a very important fact. Monsieur Lake was present on the train Peter's father, Franklin Thorne, was accused of robbing. He has a great memory. He remembers the guard, Burke, very well. It is not possible that the guard was the guilty man. It is as the police reported. Peter Silverman's father was the thief and murderer. The magician is lying about his motive for returning to Portland."

CHAPTER 44

I texted Brixton that Dorian was home safe and sound, in hopes the kid would get some sleep. I needed more time to figure out the best next steps, and I didn't want Brixton running off doing anything foolish.

If Peter was lying about his motivation, could he also have a motive for murder we didn't know about? Or was he simply an innocent victim who incorrectly believed his father to be innocent? He was only a child at the time of his father's death.

"Something strange is afoot at *Persephone & Prometheus's Phantasmagoria*," Dorian said. "Do you think he is framing you for the murder of the treasure hunter, so he may find the loot for himself?"

I briefly considered his suggestion that I might have been framed in such an obscure way, but dismissed it as the lingering effects of the coffee. "I don't know, Dorian. That seems pretty far-fetched that he'd find a stone toe in the theater, associate it with me, and leave it in the fingers of the dead body in hopes that it would lead the police to me."

"*Oui*, without facts it is only a theory. But magicians are masters of misdirection. We must investigate!"

"Hold on, you two," Tobias cut in. "I understand that you've been pulled into this inquiry because of Dorian's missing toe, but investigating *yourselves*?"

Dorian blinked his black eyes at Tobias. "Have you not read the works of Agatha Christie? She was an Englishwoman, yes, but her investigative skills are unparalleled. She has taught us that it is the amateur sleuth who is most capable of using his *little grey cells* to solve the most complex of crimes."

"That's fiction," Tobias said. "Anyway, Poirot wasn't an amateur."

"Semantics," Dorian mumbled. "He was not *un flic*. He was not a policeman. Those who work outside of the law are privy to more—"

"The backpack!" I cried.

Dorian grinned. "*Merci*, Zoe, for proving my point."

"What backpack?" Tobias asked.

"Dorian and I saw Peter and Penelope taking a small backpack out of a trunk in the theater. They were acting in secret, and at the time I believed he was an alchemist, so it made perfect sense that he'd be acting secretively. I didn't give it another thought. But since his secret is that he's Franklin Thorne's son who's looking into clearing his father's name, *what was in the backpack?*"

"I remember thinking," Dorian said, "that it looked like the possession of a child."

"It did. It wasn't a briefcase of research papers. It looked like a child's backpack. I wish I could remember what the two of them said to each other."

"Let us return to the theater," Dorian said.

"No," Tobias and I said simultaneously.

Dorian scrunched his snout. "Dual-faced alchemists! I thought you were on my side."

"I'm so much on your side that it would kill me if you were taken into police custody again. We take no unnecessary risks, which means we don't return to a crime scene."

Dorian's wings slouched. "Your heart is in the right place, Zoe Faust. No matter. It is nearly time for me to return to Blue Sky Teas to bake for the upcoming day. You need not remind me to be careful."

After spending the night in the basement fruitlessly rereading *Not Untrue Alchemy* from cover to cover, Tobias, Dorian, and I breakfasted on the misshapen leftovers Dorian brought back from the teashop kitchen before sunrise. Today it was a feast of chickpeaflour pancakes. Though his recipe was tasty, he decided pancakes didn't work well for the teashop's glass pastry display cabinet. Presentation was an important last step of Dorian's culinary alchemy. A strong flame under a cast-iron skillet could transform flour, water, ground seeds, and a few herbs into a stack of blissful breakfast. But transformation wasn't always pretty. Dorian didn't think his pancakes were attractive enough to entice people from a display case.

Tobias and I prepared breakfast plates in the kitchen. Tobias inhaled deeply as he fixed an espresso for Dorian, who was waiting impatiently in the attic, then made a pot of tea for himself. I was still drinking my restorative tea blend to combat the effects of creating Dorian's Tea of Ashes and accidentally eating coffee-saturated cookies. This morning I had an extra cup, since I hadn't slept a wink. My large solar infusion batch was nearly used up.

"I wish I didn't have to leave," Tobias said as he lifted a tray of tea and coffee in one hand. "Rosa and the job need me. I'll think about your problem, though. Maybe I'll come up with something that'll help you from afar. I keep thinking that the crumbling gold has to play into this puzzle."

"I'm glad we found each other again, Tobias."

"Even if it took a pickle of a mess to drive you to seek out other alchemists, I'm happy you did, too, Zoe. I'm happy you did too."

I scooped up the second tray, and we joined Dorian in the attic's safe haven with his escape route in the slanted roof above.

"You carry that tray with such alacrity, Monsieur Freeman," Dorian said, "that I believe you must have been employed as a waiter in your past." He took a sip of the espresso Tobias had fixed. "*Oui*. This espresso is *très bon*. I am correct, no?"

"Guilty."

"You do not look pleased! *Le garçon* is a worthy profession. You help the chef present his creations."

"You're an optimistic fellow for a Frenchman, Dorian."

"But of course."

"And a great chef. If only you weren't a gargoyle, you could head any restaurant."

"You are a sly one, Monsieur Freeman. You are leaving momentarily for a flight, which will not provide edible food. I will prepare a basket of sandwiches and snacks to see you safely home."

Encumbered with enough food for Tobias and his wife to eat all week, I drove Tobias to the airport to see him off. As I drove, he looked through the assortment and chuckled.

"What's so funny?" I asked. "The amount of food?"

"Dragon's tongue, dragon carrots, and even dragon's mugwort. There's a pattern here."

"I doubt it. You're the one who likes patterns, so that's what you see."

"I'm not kidding, Zoe. He's got them all in here."

"I'm sure he does. He loves using Tuscan kale, purple carrots, and tarragon. Texture, color, and flavor."

Tobias rewrapped a fragrant baguette sandwich in its parchment paper. "You've got a point. Gardeners might have even more vivid imaginations than alchemists."

~

The drive to the airport was far too short. After I saw Tobias off, I couldn't help thinking more about him and his elderly wife. It was the right choice for them. Would I be able to have that for myself? Did I even deserve it? I wasn't even sure I could save my closest friend from an unnatural fate trapped between life and death.

I listened to "Accidental Life" on the drive home, keeping my old friend near me.

When I got back to my house, two unexpected guests were waiting for me: the magicians. They'd made themselves comfortable on the porch in front of my Craftsman. Peter juggled d'Anjou pears that looked suspiciously like ones from a neighbor's tree, and Penelope sat on the top step while twirling a cigar deftly between her long fingers.

I slammed the truck's door. "How did you find me?" Like Peter Silverman, I knew how to stay under the radar. I walked cautiously toward them.

"Your young friend had a card for Blue Sky Teas in his pocket the other night," Peter said. As he spoke, the pears vanished. They didn't drop to the ground, but I didn't see where they could have gone.

"The young woman with bare feet was incredibly helpful," Peter continued.

I groaned to myself. He had to be referring to Brixton's mom, Heather, the free spirit who would never entertain the notion that she was being conned.

"She was so sorry to hear you'd left your locket at the theater," Peter continued.

My hand flew to my locket. It was there. He certainly had the skills to remove it without my noticing, so I was relieved he hadn't actually lifted it as part of his ruse.

"I didn't mean to worry you," he said. "Especially since I came here for help. May we come inside?"

"Now's not a good time." I willed myself not to look toward the attic.

The front and back doors to the house could be opened by a skilled lock-picker, but the attic and basement doors had extra locks on them, so I wasn't too worried about whether they'd already let themselves into the house. Disturbed at the thought, yes; worried by it, no.

"I'm sorry I butted in before," I added. "I wish you luck on your quest, but I can't help you."

"We were looking at your new website," Penelope added.

"My new website?" I said. I'd forgotten Veronica was working on that.

"You've got some antique puzzle boxes for sale," Peter said. From the small backpack I recognized from the theater, he pulled out a carved puzzle box made of sandalwood. It was smaller than the palm of my hand and the irregularly shaped flower carvings told me it had been hand carved. He handed it to me. The words "ashes to ashes" were carved on the bottom.

Don't engage, Zoe. The box is intriguing, but it's not your problem.

"What's this?" I asked, running my fingertips over the soft wood. A raised rose was carved onto the box, with thorns circling the edges.

I'd seen that image before.

"I'm hoping you can help me open it," Peter said. "It has nothing to do with the matter you came to see us about, but being back in Portland to clear my father's name has made me sentimental. This box belonged to him. He made it in his toy studio, and he left it to me."

His father, Franklin Thorne, the supposed thief and murderer, had made the box.

"I know what this is," I said, a disturbing realization dawning on me.

"That's great," Peter said. "I knew you'd know how to open it. Didn't I tell you, Pen?"

"Quite," Penelope said, her eyes never leaving mine.

"Could you show me?" Peter asked.

"I didn't mean that I know how to open it," I said. "I doubt anyone besides the person who put it together could open it without breaking it."

Peter frowned.

"I know that's not the answer you were hoping for," I said, "because I know you don't want to break what's inside."

"This is ridiculous." The muscles of his lithe body tensed. "How do you possibly know what's inside?"

"I saw the Thorne family crypt at the cemetery," I said. "The carvings on the mausoleum walls are etched into the stone. They're carvings of roses and thorns that match this box. You think this puzzle box contains a key to the

Thorne family crypt. But there's only one reason you'd be secretive about your motives—"

"There's nothing secret about my motives," Peter said with false calmness.

"That's where your father's plunder is hidden, isn't it, Peter?" I said. "You know he's the thief—you've *always* known—but you haven't been able to get inside the stone mausoleum to get at his hidden loot."

CHAPTER 45

Peter stared mutely at me.

"Well," Penelope said, "she's certainly much more clever than we gave her credit for." She stood up and walked down the porch steps, stopping uncomfortably close to me. She was taller than me, so I saw it for the power play that it was. "How did you know?"

"At the time I didn't realize what I'd seen at the cemetery." I stepped away from Penelope and walked a few paces toward the barren elderberry bushes that lined the side fence. Simply being near the garden protector made me feel more in control. "But the Thorne mausoleum isn't too far from the mudslide area."

"The police already searched it after he was killed," Peter said. "The cemetery keeps a key."

"To the main entrance, sure," I said. "Not the hidden one."

Peter had a fit of coughing.

"Little things you both said didn't add up," I continued. "You didn't approach the police to access the records, but you spent time at the cemetery. The item you were protecting in a locked trunk wasn't part of your research, but a child's backpack containing a puzzle box given to you by your toymaker father. No, your actions weren't those of people researching historical facts to clear a man's name. They were the actions of the treasure hunters. I didn't put it together until a friend of mine talked to Julian Lake. He said there's no way the guard was involved."

"Nice try," Penelope said. "But Julian Lake is a recluse. He doesn't talk to anyone."

"My friend is good at getting people to open up to him."

Penelope narrowed her eyes at me.

"It's not illegal to search for the Lake Loot," Peter said, recovering his voice.

"No, it's not. You're admitting that you knew your father was the thief all along?"

"It's not Peter's fault his father was a criminal," Penelope said.

"Pen—"

"Oh, do be quiet, Peter. Do you want to resolve this once and for all or not?"

Peter gripped the railing of the porch but remained silent.

"We already told you how Peter spent his whole life running from people's assumptions about him," Penelope continued. "Is it any wonder he wants to at least get something out of it? Returning the jewels to the Lake family and getting a reward will bring him closure."

"Why didn't you just say so in the first place?" I asked.

"After hiding his past for so long, I'm sure you can understand the desire to wrap things up out of the spotlight, so to speak." She gave me an inscrutable smile. "In case he wasn't able to find the hidden loot and return it to the Lake family to redeem *himself*, he didn't want to reveal his identity and open himself up to mockery."

It did make sense. It was an impulse I often felt in my own life. I needed to conceal so many parts of my life that hiding became second nature. But after they'd lied repeatedly, how could I be sure Peter and Penelope's intentions were pure?

"I'm sure you won't mind if the police accompany you to the crypt to open it." I returned Penelope's enigmatic smile.

"Of course not," she said. "But unfortunately, you yourself said there's no way to open it. Without destroying whatever is inside."

"I didn't exactly say that."

Peter dug his fingernails into the wooden railing, and the muscles on his neck looked as if they were going to pop out. "Anyone ever tell you that you like to speak in riddles?"

"I'm not the one who wrote a clue on the box itself."

"It's not a clue," Peter seethed. "I tried every possible letter substitution. It doesn't tell me how to open the box."

"To open a box like this," I said, turning the box over in my hands, "the best way is to know the correct spots to push, in the right order, as you know. The person who built it would know how to do that. But without having a key, the box needs to be destroyed to get at what's inside. Breaking or burning are your options, but if you don't know what's inside, it's difficult to know which would ruin the protected item. If, however, you believe it to be a key, that key won't burn. The box itself tells you that much."

"Ashes to ashes," Peter whispered.

"It was a simpler clue than you imagined. If you want to open the box without breaking the key inside, you have to burn it."

Peter groaned. Before I realized what was happening, the box disappeared from my hand.

On the other side of the porch, Peter applied a putty-like substance to the rose carving on the box. With swiftly moving hands, he peeled it off and handed the putty to Penelope. He jumped over the porch railing, landing gracefully on the stone path, and with a snap of his fingers, a lighter appeared in his hand. He lit the box on fire.

"Wait!" I cried. "It's only a theory."

Peter gave me a devilish grin. "That's why I made an impression of the box carving. Just in case you're wrong."

The box smoldered and caught fire. When the flames extinguished, an iron key was left, its dark metal glowing in the ashes.

～

"I need your help," I told Max.

I'd pushed aside all thoughts of how I'd shoved Max out the door, and called him. It was the best thing I could think to do.

He sighed audibly at the other end of the line. "You mean you want a recommendation for a psychologist?"

"I'll explain everything later, Max, but I need you to meet me at River View Cemetery. At the Thorne family mausoleum. It's near where the mudslides took place."

Now it sounded like he was choking.

From my front lawn, I explained that I wasn't going hiking in a dangerous area as he feared, but that the magicians had come to me with help on their puzzle box because I had several of them for sale through Elixir. And I told him about Peter's connection to Franklin Thorne and the Lake Loot. I managed to convince Max that since the information wasn't directly related to the murder investigation that another detective was handling, he had every right to accompany me to River View Cemetery to check out my crazy idea.

"He's coming?" Penelope asked.

"He'll be there as soon as he can."

"Good," Peter said. "We'll meet you there."

"We go together." There was no way I was letting the magicians out of my sight. "Your SUV is big enough for all of us."

They exchanged a quick look that confirmed my suspicions that they were up to something. But I'd called someone who knew I was with them, so surely they wouldn't do anything to harm me. At least not here. Not today.

That was the logical conclusion, but people don't always behave in a rational manner. My heart skipped a beat when Peter reached into the backseat before stepping into the driver's seat. It turned out he was grabbing a coat.

Though it was a warm spring day after the rains of the previous night, Peter bundled in the puffy snow coat. That was odd. Perhaps he was getting sick. In spite of the situation, I found myself thinking through the simple herbal remedies from my backyard garden that might help at the onset of a cold, such as one of my mints.

I was more worried about a different danger. A glimpse in the side mirror confirmed that my health was getting worse. I feared that might be the case, but I'd pushed the thought from my mind because I didn't want it to be true. The effects of making Dorian's Tea of Ashes were catching up with me. I had to find a real solution soon.

We parked in the main lot next to the chapel and walked from there.

I was unsurprised to see Earl Rasputin on the steep hillside adjacent to the cemetery, walking methodically with his metal detector in hand. Peter, Penelope, and I continued to the Thorne mausoleum.

Earl must have seen us, too, because as soon as we reached the mausoleum, he wandered over.

"Afternoon," he said, tipping the rim of the baseball cap shielding his eyes from the sun. Peter and Penelope gave no indication of recognizing him. Was their reaction genuine? Earl had remained in the audience on opening night, while his friend volunteered on stage. So if the magicians were telling the truth that they had nothing to do with Wallace Mason's murder, it made sense they wouldn't recognize Earl.

"Let me give you each a flyer." Earl pressed a flyer into my hands: *Baby Bigfoot. Have you seen this creature?*

It was a more detailed flyer than the one he had the day I met him. In addition to the text, this one included a sketch of a hairless gray creature with horns and wings.

Oh, God. Baby Bigfoot was Dorian. He'd been outed by the conspiracy theorists. I groaned to myself, but forced myself to smile as I took the flyer. It was a rudimentary sketch, lacking incriminating details, but it was clearly Dorian, as if seen from a distance.

A normal life, Zoe. You really thought you could have a normal life?

"Do you want me to help pass out your flyers?" I offered. Perhaps if I was enthusiastic enough about the cause he'd give me all of his flyers, and then I could destroy them.

"That's a great idea," Penelope said. "I'd love to help too."

That threw me. Had she seen Dorian moving, too? Was that why she'd been fascinated when I showed her his stone statue?

Earl grabbed a stack of flyers and started to hand them to Penelope. But as he did so, a gust of wind picked up, and the Baby Bigfoot flyers scattered. Penelope and I knelt down to pick them up. The wind didn't make it easy. Moisture from the grass damaged a few of them, but most were no worse off.

The treasure hunter gave his thanks, but lingered even after we retrieved all of them.

"Do I know you?" Peter asked.

"Earl Rasputin. I attended your performance on Friday night. I could tell how you did the ghost trick, you know."

Peter narrowed his eyes. "And I can tell that you're a—"

"Max!" I called out. "We're over here."

We didn't get to hear the end of Peter's comeback, because as soon as he saw Max, Earl said his farewells.

Max apologized for running late, but said that Ivan was back in the hospital for pneumonia and he'd promised to visit him during visiting hours that day. I hadn't realized Ivan was in the hospital. I knew I should visit him as soon as I could too.

I traced my fingers along the intricate carvings on the white granite that belonged to Peter's family. These rose carvings were far older than Peter's father. But if I was right, the toy maker who knew how to carve clever puzzle boxes would have also been able to add nearly-undetectable segments to an existing structure. It's a trick alchemists have employed for millennia. For our work to remain hidden, we learn how to hide things in plain sight.

I focused my intent on the pattern, ignoring the people around me. Besides the main door, nothing on the front of the raised crypt looked like it might fit a key. I stepped back and circled the structure. That gave me the answer. The back wall had aged differently than the other walls. Most people wouldn't have noticed the difference, but I saw it because different plant spores had settled on this surface.

On that wall, I found a tiny hole disguised in a thorn of the rose carving.

"Do you want to do the honors and make this official?" I asked Max.

The slightly charred key fit perfectly.

The key opened a hidden compartment that wasn't connected to the main family crypt. As Peter had previously said, in 1969 the mausoleum was opened by order of the police, but nothing unexpected had been found inside. This hidden compartment was never found because Franklin Thorne had added a *new wall* along the back of the mausoleum, making it two feet larger than its original construction. It was a large enough space to hide stolen items, but was small enough to avoid detection.

The interior of the narrow space was filled with moist dirt. There was no proper floor. Franklin might have been a clever thief and craftsman, but he wasn't a good architect. Rainwater had drastically damaged the hidden compartment. That was how the sapphire necklace became dislodged.

"The Lake Loot," Peter whispered.

Lying in the uneven, damp dirt, half a dozen jeweled necklaces sparkled through their bed of mud.

Peter took a step forward.

"Don't touch it," Max said.

"I was just looking."

But I wasn't paying attention to either of the men. Next to the half-buried jewels, I noticed something else. The dirt in the far corner had been disturbed. An indentation in the earth told me we weren't the first people who'd been there recently. It wasn't a footprint, but rather an imprint, as if an object had been removed.

I looked from the hiding spot to the Baby Bigfoot flyers clutched in my hand. What was going on?

CHAPTER 46

I dangled the Baby Bigfoot flyer in front of Dorian. "You were seen."

"Mais non! How can this be?"

The magicians had dropped me off at my house, where thankfully I'd found Dorian in the attic. He hadn't gone off on any new ill-conceived adventures.

"We're not being careful enough," I said. "Once your foot and leg became a problem, we should have kept you in the house. I'll tell Heather I can't bake pastries for a while—"

"It is not possible," Dorian insisted. "I have been wearing your silk cape over me whenever I leave the house. Even if someone saw me, they would not see me as myself, *n'est pas?*"

"You're wrong," I snapped. "You must not have been careful enough. We have enough to worry about without Bigfoot hunters flocking to Portland."

He stamped his working foot on the creaky attic floor. "You have not told me what has happened! You have been gone for many hours, yet I cannot see or hear anything in this attic. You said you were taking Monsieur Freeman to the airport, yet you did not return. I thought I heard your loud engine earlier, but you did not come inside, so I believed I was mistaken. You expect me to read your mind? Where did this Baby Bigfoot flyer come from?"

My shoulders sagged. "You're right, Dorian. It's been a morning full of surprises. I'm sorry."

"*Merci.*"

"I'm sorry for not having a chance to tell you what was going on this morning," I said. "But I'm not sorry for telling you to be more careful."

Dorian mumbled something under his breath that I chose to ignore, though it sounded suspiciously like the insult *casse couille*, a vulgar way to express irritation.

"What we need," he said, "is a code ring."

"A code ring? To decipher the coded illustrations in the book, you mean?"

"*Non.* I speak of the telephone. You do not wish me to answer it, since nobody besides you and Brixton believe me to live here. I am a clandestine companion. A lonely lodger. A secret chimera—"

"Dorian."

"Yes, yes. As I was saying, you do not check email on your phone, so we have no way to communicate about urgent matters."

"Normally the house is perfectly safe. We couldn't have foreseen that search warrant from the police."

"No, but who knows what the future holds? We must institute a coded system of telephone rings."

I considered the idea that must have come from one of the Penny Dreadful detective novels he'd read that winter. "That's not a bad idea," I admitted.

"I thought so. We will work out the sequence of rings later. For now, you must tell me what has transpired."

"Remember those treasure hunters you were worried about because they might sully your woods next to River View Cemetery? They're the ones who saw you."

"*C'est vrai?* I do not see how—"

"It's true. Earl, the treasure-hunting friend of the dead volunteer, was passing out these flyers at the cemetery."

"But why did you return to the graveyard in the first place?"

"When I got back from the airport, Peter and Penelope Silverman were waiting for me here at the house."

Dorian gasped and protectively curled his hands around his ears. "I did not hear you and the magicians downstairs. I am losing my hearing as well!" His wings flew out at his sides in agitation. "*Quelle horreur!*"

I put my hand on his shaking shoulder, careful to avoid his flapping wing. "There's nothing wrong with your hearing. I didn't invite them inside. And they wanted my help, so they didn't aggravate me by picking the lock, even though I'm certain Peter has the skills to do so."

"Excuse my outburst." He folded his wings and sniffed. "I am oversensitive at present."

"We're all on edge. Those magicians aren't helping. They lied to us about being in town to clear Peter's father's name. They've known all along that Franklin Thorne was the murderous thief. Peter wanted to find the loot for the reward and to save face himself."

"The missing Lake Loot."

"It's not missing any longer, Dorian. We found it."

Dorian sputtered and rolled his eyes as theatrically as a stage performer. "You found the *tresor*! Yet this was not the first thing you said when you came home!"

"The treasure doesn't matter. Your safety—"

"*Bof.*" He sat down and patted the floor next to him. "Tell me."

I sat down next to the gargoyle and explained how Peter had a complex puzzle box from his father, like the ones I sold at Elixir, and that I'd figured out it contained a key that opened a secret hiding spot at the Thorne family mausoleum at the cemetery. Franklin Thorne had hidden his stolen loot in his hiding place before the police caught up with him later that day, but not thinking he'd be killed that day, he hadn't had a chance to convey the information about his hiding spot to his wife and son. "But when we went to the cemetery together," I concluded, "I could tell someone had already gotten into the mausoleum, because the dirt inside the secret room had already been disturbed."

"Yet you said there was only the single key," Dorian said. "And you were the one who found it, *non?*"

"Yes. I also took the precaution of going with Peter and Penelope to the cemetery and asking Max to meet us there. That way the magicians couldn't get into the crypt ahead of me. I wonder if I underestimated Earl Rasputin, though. If he saw what we were doing... Could he have found another way in?"

The gargoyle drummed his fingers together.

"What are you thinking?" I asked.

"Tell me everything. Every detail, no matter how small." He raised a clawed index finger into the air to make his point.

"To what end?"

"As I said, something strange is afoot with these magicians."

I was wary of my little detective taking things into his own hands. Again. But I could use his insights. I described our trip to the cemetery, from the carving of roses and thorns on the mausoleum to the rose bushes that surrounded the raised crypt, from the tiny hidden room to the indentation in the dirt. I told Dorian how Peter had bundled up like he was cold or feeling under the weather, how we'd met Earl Rasputin handing out Baby Bigfoot flyers with an illustration that vaguely resembled Dorian, that the wind had blown some of the flyers away, and that Max had arrived late at the cemetery because he had to visit Ivan in the hospital.

"It is as I thought!" Dorian exclaimed, jumping up from his perch-like sitting position.

"You know what happened?"

"To test my theory, I have but one question for you." His claws made a crisp tapping noise as he drummed his fingertips together. "When the flyers blew away, whose hands were they in?"

"Earl was handing them to me and Penelope."

"Penelope, eh?"

"We both offered to take some flyers. I wanted to destroy them rather than hand them out, and I was afraid Penelope was intrigued because she recognized you."

"It is obvious what has happened," Dorian said. "Obvious!" He drew his hands behind his back and paced the floor. He was enjoying this. "The magician, Peter Silverman, has stolen something from the crypt."

"That's not possible. I was the one who figured out they had to burn the box. They didn't have the key until then. I was with them the whole time."

Dorian dismissed me with a wave of his hand. "Have I taught you nothing in these last months, Zoe Faust?"

"What does cooking have to do with this?"

He pinched the bridge of his snout. "The magicians! Peter Silverman got into the crypt while you were distracted by his wife and Earl Rasputin."

"You think they're working together?"

"Perhaps, but I think not. Any good magician knows how to read their audience. I believe that because there were two of them and only one of you, they seized on the distraction of Monsieur Rasputin to carry out their deception."

"If Franklin Thorne used the mausoleum as a hiding place for one treasure…"

Dorian nodded. "He would have used it for *all* his treasures he wished to keep hidden. This is why the magician was bundled in a heavy coat, though it is a warm day. If he was an even better performer, like my father, he would have feigned illness to complete the deception. But he did not see this illusion through, and you noticed it as odd. Therefore you remembered he was wearing a coat—a coat he used to hide the additional valuables he pilfered."

I groaned. "Peter Silverman didn't want to restore his own good name by returning the Lake Loot to Julian Lake and receiving a reward. He wanted to get his hands on the bigger stash he knew his thieving father had hidden."

CHAPTER 47

I called Max to tell him what I thought was going on with Peter, that the magician had retrieved other items his father had stolen. Max said he'd pass along the information to the investigating detective.

Next I texted Brixton to tell him the news, then drove to his high school, where classes would soon be ending for the day. I had no confidence he'd heed my words and refrain from confronting the magicians.

Brixton rolled his eyes when he saw me, but his demeanor changed when he climbed into the truck.

"I'm supposed to help Mom at the teashop, but I don't feel like it. Can you drive me home?"

"How about we still go to Blue Sky Teas but I join you for a cup of tea first? It might help."

Another eye roll. "I know you guys think tea solves all the world's problems. But it really doesn't."

I had a good idea why he was upset. "You're disappointed about Peter Silverman, aren't you?"

"He lied to me, Zoe. He never wanted to help his father's reputation. It was all a lie." He stared out the window as we drove past rows of blooming spring flowers. "How am I supposed to trust anyone?"

We drove in silence to Blue Sky Teas. When we arrived, Brixton took his mom's place behind the counter without a word, and Heather joined me at a small tree-ring table. Today, the mason jars were filled with a rainbow of tulips, and the whole teashop smelled like a flower garden.

"I'm worried about Brixton," I said, keeping my voice low. I hesitated. "Can I ask you about his stepfather?"

Heather's eyes lit up. "Abel. He's the best thing that's happened to me since Brix."

"Brixton seems to idolize him, and I know he gave Brixton that guitar he loves. Why won't he talk about what Abel does?"

"What does that even mean, *what we do?*" Heather studied her paint-stained hands for a moment before she looked back up at me. "Such a loaded expression, don't you think? I mean, am I a painter because I paint, even though I don't make much money at it? Or do I work in a café, since that's what I'm doing for money?"

"I wasn't trying to be philosophical. I'm trying to help Brixton. He's really upset, and I think it has to do with Abel."

Heather looked to the counter. "He looks okay to me."

I sighed and tried a different track. "Brixton doesn't have anything to be ashamed of, so why won't he tell me what keeps Abel out of town?"

Heather plucked a yellow daffodil from a braid of her blonde hair and picked the petals off one by one. "It's embarrassing," she whispered.

"Is he in jail or something?"

She crushed the flower stem between her fingers. "In a way, it's worse. If he was in jail, it wouldn't be by his own choice."

I wasn't sure I followed that logic, but I went with it.

"He works for Big Oil," she said, her voice so soft I could barely hear her.

"Oil?"

"Shh. Yes, it's awful, isn't it? I protest them all the time! He doesn't want to do it, but he's great on the oil rig."

I looked up to the faux blue sky above the weeping fig tree and laughed.

"What's funny?" Heather's face flushed. "See, I'm so embarrassed just talking about it to you. I told Brix it would be better if everyone thinks he's a painter like me."

"I'm so glad that's all it is. And you've just reminded me how easy it is to be wrong about people."

I was too tired to stay awake for dinner that night. I didn't fight Dorian when he brought me a tray in bed and put me to sleep.

At midnight I was awakened, I wasn't sure by what. I'm used to the patter of Dorian's feet on the roof.

I got up to walk through the house. I found the source of the noise almost immediately. Dorian had dropped a hefty notepad in front of my door. There was a note on the top sheet.

You are sicker than you will admit. Ivan is in the hospital, so I have taken the liberty of taking my book to his home library. Do not fear, it is not missing. I am a fresh set of eyes (how American I am becoming!) and will return home with new ideas.

I sighed. *A simple life, Zoe. A simple life.*

I drove my truck toward Ivan's house. It was walking distance, but the truck would be the easiest way to get Dorian home without him being seen.

A plume of smoke rose in the distance, coming from Mt. Tabor. A bad feeling clenched my stomach. It looked like it was coming from the theater. But unlike the fake fire in the Prometheus and Persephone stage show, this fire was very real. My tires screeched as I turned and headed toward it.

I found Dorian outside the back of the theater, hiding next to a dumpster. His wings flapped in earnest. He was horribly upset.

"I went inside because I thought I heard a voice calling out for help, but it was too hot. I dropped my book! It is inside, burning."

The sound of sirens sounded in the distance.

"Hide, Dorian."

"I know!" he snapped. "I hid from the men in the theater last week, as I will hide now."

He'd "hidden" from Wallace Mason and Earl Rasputin, yet Earl had posters that resembled Dorian. Could it really be that simple?

"Dorian," I said. "I know what happened."

Dorian heard the urgency in my voice and stopped.

"They didn't see you in the woods by the cemetery," I said. "Wallace Mason and Earl Rasputin saw you *in the theater*. Both of them, when they were spying on the magicians just like we were, when they hoped to get inside information about the location of the Lake Loot. That's why Wallace was clutching your stone toe, and why Earl had a knife. They were defending themselves from Baby Bigfoot, and in the confusion and darkness, *Earl stabbed the wrong man.*"

A faint cry of distress interrupted me.

"*Merde,*" Dorian whispered. He gave me one last look, then followed the sound of the anguished cry into the burning theater.

CHAPTER 48

The flames crackled and burned brightly.

The cloudy mixture bubbled in its glass vessel. The gray bubbles turned to white. The alchemist smiled to himself. He loved watching his transformations take form. He gained a deep satisfaction that his patience and pure intent could transform impure natural substances into something greater than the sum of their parts.

Ambrose looked up from his experiment as footsteps sounded on the stairs leading down to his alchemy lab. The thick wood sagged under the weight of the hefty man entering the secret laboratory.

"Father?" the petulant voice called out. It would have been excusable in a boy, but the boy was now fifty.

"Percival!" Ambrose stood to greet his son. "Good to see you, my boy. I wasn't expecting you until Saturday."

"It *is* Saturday, Father."

"Is it true?" Ambrose extinguished the flame underneath his alchemical creation. All the time and energy he had poured into that vessel, now abandoned at the appearance of his son.

"You forgot about me," Percival said without humor. "I suppose that means you haven't prepared any food for dinner."

"Zoe is gone for a few weeks, and I'm afraid the vegetables miss her touch.

I've been eating bread and beer. But we can walk down to the pub for something more substantial."

Percival nodded with approval, his ample chin jiggling as he did so. Even in the dim light from the glowing athanor furnace, the streaks of gray in Percival's hair were apparent. The two men no longer passed as father and son. Percival was now five years older than the age Ambrose appeared to be. In a few years' time, it would look as if Percival were Ambrose's father.

As Nicolas Flamel had warned Zoe Faust many years before, it wasn't possible for one alchemist to transfer their personal Philosopher's Stone to another. Knowledge could be transferred, but transformations themselves were personal. Yet like Zoe before him, Ambrose refused to believe it. He was convinced he could help his son achieve the immortality he craved.

The father and son who now looked like brothers climbed the stairs, then replaced the trap door and rug that hid the laboratory. On the cool autumn day, the cabin was warm with the heat of the burning stove that masked the smoke from the secret athanor furnace of their lab. It was only a short walk from the warm cabin to the local pub. Ambrose had spent many years in France—and he was thankful he had, for it was there that he had met the love of his life—yet he was happy to be back in England. The friendly people in his native land supported each other, and ubiquitous public houses were their gathering spot. He mused that there must have been one pub for every thirty men. He was happy that he and Zoe could live in this welcoming community for at least a few more years before people began to notice they weren't aging like the rest of them.

In a far corner of the dim pub, Percival shoveled mutton into his mouth while Ambrose drank beer and told his son of his latest alchemical discoveries, which he hoped Percival would try. Ambrose did not believe the longer lifespan granted by the Elixir of Life was essential to have a fulfilling life. Yet he considered the quest for the Philosopher's Stone, the penultimate step to the Elixir, to be rewarding for what it could tell a man about the world, and about himself.

"It's useless, Father. I can't do it without your help—"

"We already tried that," Ambrose said, the sharpness in his voice surprising himself as much as Percival. "You know how it turned out."

"You're giving up on me?"

"Of course not, my boy. This very month I found you a new book. An obscure treatise by Roger Bacon. It may help—"

"A book?" the no-longer-young man scoffed. "You think *a book* can help

479

me, Father? Only the apocryphal book you once mentioned could help me. Yet in the same breath you told me it was an unnatural abomination."

"But Percy, surely it's worth a try—"

"If you really wanted to help me," Percival hissed, "you'd find that book created by the sect of alchemists who worked at Notre Dame."

Neither man spoke for a few moments. In their darkened corner, they listened to the boisterous laughter surrounding them, but escaped the attention of the other men.

Ambrose lowered his voice. "I never meant for you to cling to those ideas of backward alchemy. I only mentioned it as part of your education—"

"Then why mention it at all?" Percival straightened his shirt, the buttons straining under his corpulence.

"I found the Elixir by immersing myself in every aspect of alchemy."

"I don't believe you. When you told me of backward alchemy, it was only when that woman was away. *You didn't want her to know.*"

"Zoe is a pure soul." Ambrose's voice was barely above a whisper now. "She wouldn't have understood."

"You don't trust her?"

"It's not about trust. Zoe didn't need to be burdened with this dark knowledge I learned of. She had already discovered alchemy's secrets when I met her."

"Which she didn't share with us."

"You know she couldn't."

"Do I? If you choose to believe that…"

"You'd fare better if you believed it too. Then you would be free to gain your own understanding. You could write your own translation of the Emerald Tablet, as every alchemist must—"

"I disappoint you because I'm not a scholar."

Ambrose knew his son had never possessed the temperament to be a scholar, yet he refused to give up on him. If Percival gave up on his futile quest for the Elixir of Life, Ambrose believed his son could enjoy his remaining years on earth by gaining a greater understanding of this miraculous, interconnected world. But if Percival insisted on seeking out immortality, his father wouldn't deny him. He would simply guide him in the right direction. Wasn't that what a parent was for?

"Knowledge is never a bad thing," Ambrose said. "It gives you the tools to choose what's right."

"More knowledge doesn't always work out for the best. It led to you choosing that foul woman. She ruined our lives the day she forced her way in."

"That's enough," Ambrose snapped.

Percival hefted himself up from his seat. "I need another pint of ale."

Ambrose wondered where he had gone wrong with Percival. The boy's mother had died in childbirth, so he lacked a mother's love. Ambrose had tried to make up for that, but had he gone too far and spoiled him? When Percival was a child, Ambrose hadn't denied his son any comfort he could supply. And as an adult, Percival's indulgent lifestyle was only made possible with alchemical gold from his father.

That was all in the past. Ambrose had to decide what to do about Percival in the present. He knew more of the dangerous backward alchemy book than he'd spoken of. A book created in France, many centuries before, that told of death and resurrection not through the true alchemical process of natural rebirth, but through an unnatural fire that ignored the world around it and quickly created artificial ashes.

Unnatural fire and ash went against everything true alchemy stood for. But it was knowledge nonetheless.

Percival returned to the table.

"My son," Ambrose said. "I have something to tell you."

CHAPTER 49

"Can you tell me anything?" I asked the firefighter.

"Everyone got out safely." His face was coated in soot, and his kind eyes showed relief. "Whoever you're worried about, they got out and were taken to the hospital."

I knew the fireman believed he was speaking the truth, but there was no way paramedics had taken a gargoyle to the hospital. I'd been waiting on the outskirts of the blaze, and I hadn't seen Dorian through the thick smoke. Had he made it out? If I sifted through the rubble, would I find the charred remains of a stone statue? I might be all alone in this world once again.

"Zoe!"

I turned and saw Max running toward me. He swept me up in his arms and held me in a comforting embrace. I didn't want to let go, but after a few moments he stepped back and looked up at the smoky night sky.

"Why doesn't it surprise me to find you here?" He took my hand and pulled me farther from the smoldering wreckage. "Are you all right? You look like someone died. It's okay. I heard on the scanner that everyone got out."

"Death and destruction follow me," I whispered.

"Don't talk like that. We've both had our share of—"

I stopped his voice with my lips. He didn't object. Across the street from the glowing ashes, I let myself exist purely in the moment. For a few minutes, I lost myself in the kiss, enveloped in a combination of warmth, caring, and the scent of vanilla.

It was the scent that shattered the dream and brought me back to reality.

"Whatever happens in the future," I said, pulling back, "I want you to know that's how I feel about you."

"What do you mean, *whatever hap*—hey, where are you going?"

I slipped out of his arms and backed away. "I need to check on something."

I didn't trust myself to drive, so I ran home on foot. I heard Max calling after me, but I didn't turn back. With my silver raincoat billowing behind me, the rows of shops and houses passed by in a blur.

I'd traveled around the United States for decades, all alone in my truck and trailer with my window box plants as my only living company. I'd been foolish to think I could stick around Portland for a while, no matter how much the city and its people spoke to me. If Dorian was dead, being back on the road would make it easier to hang onto my fond memories of him, and of Brixton, Max, and the other friends I'd made here.

When I reached my front lawn, I wasn't sure if my heart was pounding so hard from physical exertion or from the fear of returning home to an empty house.

"Mon amie!" Dorian called out as I closed the front door. He flung his arms around my waist, and curled his wings around me. "When you did not return home immediately, I was afraid you had followed me into the theater when I went in because I heard Earl Rasputin's voice. With so many onlookers, I could not return."

I hugged Dorian back, glad he couldn't see the tears of joy in my eyes. "That was brave of you, Dorian. I think you saved his life."

"Oui. It is true."

My immodest friend led me to the dining room table, where he was eating a large dinner after exerting himself, and told me what he knew. Earl had indeed been trapped in the theater. But either from the effects of the smoke or from seeing a heroic gargoyle, Earl passed out before he could tell Dorian anything.

"I left him in the back alley," Dorian said. "I could not find you, but I watched until I saw the ambulance. I knew, then, that he would be safe. As for my book—you will see if there is anything that can be recovered?"

"There are too many people there tonight, but as soon as I can, I'll search every inch of the ashes for what we can save. Whatever happens, I'll do whatever I can to save you."

Dorian blinked his liquid black eyes at me. "I know this, Zoe."

I didn't dare tell Dorian I was convinced we wouldn't find anything. As I'd experienced that very evening with Max, living in the moment, however temporarily, could be a wonderful thing.

Now that I knew Dorian was safe, I wanted to return to the theater to get my truck and drive to the hospital. I've always been uncomfortable inside hospitals, because of what they used to be like many years ago with treatments that often did more harm than good, but I wanted to visit Ivan and find out what had happened to Earl. I checked the clock—I had less than an hour before visiting hours ended.

The optimistic gargoyle insisted that I eat something before leaving the house. I wasn't sure I could stomach anything, so Dorian fixed a delectable consume with freshly toasted croutons.

I hugged Dorian and kissed the tip of his head between his horns, causing his cheeks to turn dark gray with embarrassment, then grabbed my silver coat and slipped out the door.

My own cheeks flushed red when I found Max at the hospital. He didn't bring up my confusing actions from earlier that night, but simply led me to the hospital café. As we drank tepid peppermint tea, he filled me in about what he'd learned.

Earl was awake and recovering. Thankful to be alive, he confessed everything that night. As I'd suspected, he admitted to accidentally killing his friend. The two of them had broken into the theater to spy on Peter Silverman, and Earl spotted a Baby Bigfoot hiding in the shadows. Wallace didn't believe him, so Earl snuck away from his friend in an attempt to find the creature. When Earl felt a hand on his shoulder, he was frightened it was Baby Bigfoot attacking him. He lashed out, only to realize too late that it was his friend.

Earl had spent time in a psychiatric ward in his youth, so he was afraid of what would happen if he came forward with the truth. I thought back on Wallace Mason's obituary, which had mentioned how he took in troubled souls, and how Earl had told me about his rough times Wallace had helped him through.

Earl and Wallace had figured out that Peter Silverman was really the son of thief Franklin Thorne, and they thought he'd have the inside track to recovering his father's lost hoard. Seeing us all at the cemetery, especially with a detective, had spooked Earl. He thought there was additional evidence he'd left behind that the police would put together with him. He set fire to a portion of the theater to cover up his crime, but the blaze got out of control. Earl hadn't realized the flames in the show were fake and that the theater wasn't specially equipped to handle a contained fire.

Earl maintained it was Baby Bigfoot who saved him from the fire. The doctors chalked up his overly active imagination to a near-death experience.

I would have laughed, but I wanted to cry. Dorian's book, and the secret to save him, must have burned down with the theater. It didn't matter that I'd photocopied and photographed the pages. As I'd learned since then, the pages had a life of their own through backward alchemy. It was the book itself that mattered.

"You look exhausted, Zoe," Max said. "Can I drop you at home?"

"I've got my truck here, but thanks."

We walked to the parking garage together, and Max kissed my cheek before he got out on his floor. I hesitated for a moment, then pushed the button to return to the hospital.

It was now the middle of the night, certainly not visiting hours, but I wanted to at least try to look in on Ivan. Max had mentioned where his room was located, so it was worth a shot. I expected I'd find his door closed, but it was ajar. I poked my head inside.

"Zoe, is that you?"

I stepped inside the narrow private room. "I'm sorry to have woken you. I wanted to see how you're doing."

"It's real," he wheezed. "Isn't it?"

"Yes, I'm really here. You're not dreaming. But you should go back to sleep." I moved back toward the door.

"Why didn't you tell me?"

"Tell you about what?"

"About alchemy." His voice rattled. "That it's *real*."

I froze in the doorway, half of my body in the gloomy darkness of the room, half in the fluorescent light of the sterile hallway. Shivers ran down my spine to my toes. "You're dreaming, Ivan," I said. My voice shook.

"The more I thought about what you did to that book, the more I saw—"

"You *are* dreaming," I whispered. "Go back to sleep."

Ivan sat up in the hospital bed. "Turn on the light." What his voice lacked in strength it made up for in severity. This was a command I couldn't ignore.

I turned on the light and walked to his side. "Whatever you think you saw—"

"You know how I got involved in the study of forgotten alchemists?" Ivan asked sharply.

"You were a professor of chemistry. Alchemists were early chemists."

"I understand chemistry. Science. What you did to that book, at my home, defied the natural order."

"The ashes," I whispered, closing my eyes. After Dorian's disappearance, I'd been so desperate that I'd slipped up and let Ivan see what I was doing. I'd been too upset to think about acting secretly.

"Why didn't you tell me?" The edge was gone from his voice. In its place was disappointment.

"Would you have believed me?"

"If you had showed me—"

"You would have thought it was a magic trick," I said. "People have never been ready—"

Ivan snorted. "You think of me not as a friend but a mindless member of the public?"

"It's because you're a friend that I didn't want to burden you with the truth."

"A burden? You think the Elixir of Life would be a burden to a dying man?"

Now I understood. "I don't know how to find the Elixir of Life, Ivan. I wish I did—"

"But you did find it once, didn't you? You're not simply an old soul, as you always joke with me. Your body is old too."

As much as I wished it were Max who was ready for my secret, it was Ivan who was more than ready to believe me. I nodded slowly. "I don't know how I found the Elixir, though. It was an accident."

"Surely your notes—"

"They're gone."

The look of desperation in his eyes pained me. I didn't know what I could say that would comfort him.

"*Non Degenera Alchemia*," Ivan said. "You're deciphering it to find the knowledge you once lost?"

"Not exactly." I couldn't tell Ivan about Dorian. That wasn't my secret to reveal. "Backward alchemy is dangerous, and I want to understand what's going on with this book—but *not* use it."

Ivan's eyelids drooped. He nodded. "I must sleep, but when I'm released from the hospital, you will come see me, to tell me what you know?"

"I will," I promised. "But Ivan—"

He chuckled sleepily. "I know what you are going to say. The world has never been ready for alchemy. This is what the alchemists have said for years. Don't worry. I will not speak of this to a soul."

I slipped from the room and flattened my back against the hallway wall. How could I have been so stupid? I had behaved recklessly after Dorian was confiscated, and now Ivan knew my secret. If I thought it could have helped him, I would have told him before. I worried that I'd given him false hope. But maybe, just maybe, false hope was better than no hope at all.

~

Fire crews were still at the site of the theater fire, so I couldn't yet search for the charred remains of *Non Degenera Alchemia*. Dorian wasn't at home, and after finishing off the last of my solar infusion in the kitchen, the large house felt eerily empty. I tried sleeping, but the stressful events of the day prevented me from nodding off. I popped my "Accidental Life" cassette into the car stereo, and drove around the city that was beginning to feel like home.

Shortly before dawn, I saw that there was no one left at the theater. I parked on a side street and snuck into the wreckage, clinging to my own false hope. A fragment or two of the book might have survived. I didn't care if the roof fell on my head. My best friend was dying.

As I stepped through the smoldering wreckage, the scent of honey wafted through the soggy, charred remains. Was it only my imagination? I followed the scent to its origin in a lump of ashes. Reaching into the sodden mess, I pulled a book into my hands.

Non Degenera Alchemia was intact. It hadn't burned.

It had seemed too much to hope for. A gasp of joy escaped from my lips before I tucked the book under my coat and retreated to the safety of my truck.

I opened the book. It fell open to the page it always did. The scent of honey and cloves overwhelmed my senses so much that I nearly shut the book again. Only one thing stopped me. On the melded cathedral illustration were details that hadn't been there before.

The fire had done more to the pages than the ashes I'd used. Background details appeared on the page, giving life to the cathedral. The intricate stained glass rose window. The island. It was the Île de la Cité. This was Paris in the 1500s. This was Notre Dame de Paris.

And rising up from the cathedral was the outline of a fierce phoenix flying upward, away from the flames. Death and resurrection.

The difference between Dorian and the garden gnome and Buddha statues wasn't their different materials. It wasn't intent. The difference was that Dorian himself was connected to Notre Dame. That was the key.

CHAPTER 50

Dorian was so thrilled with the new discovery that he was moved to experiment with new vegan recipes inspired by Paris. He handed me a long shopping list and pushed me out the door.

When I returned from the market close to lunchtime, Dorian showed me what he'd discovered in the news. The police had found Peter and Penelope with a whole stash of riches that had been stolen from several Oregon heists in the 1960s. Also in the magicians' possession was a letter from Franklin Thorne to an associate asking about selling his full "collection." It looked as if Peter's father had been about to retire from the business. If only he'd done so one job sooner, multiple deaths could have been avoided.

Penelope claimed ignorance of the origins of the treasures. Having observed her intelligence, I wasn't inclined to believe her. But neither of them were killers, so I supposed it didn't really matter as much. Peter was arrested, and Penelope told a reporter that she was looking for a fresh start. She'd reinvented herself before, moving from a circus performer to a skilled magician, and I had no doubt she'd succeed in whatever she did next.

Reclusive Julian Lake consented to be interviewed by a television reporter, but the clip we watched online made it clear that he wasn't there to comment on the discovery of his family's lost riches. Instead, he was offering a *new* reward. This time, he sought the help of the public to find the mysterious French chef who'd visited him that week. It was the best meal he'd eaten in years, and he wished to hire the chef.

After Dorian saw to it that I ate every last bit of a roasted vegetable sandwich on fresh-baked sourdough bread with garlic hummus, I called Tobias to let him know what had happened, including my discovery that the illustrations in the book had pointed to Notre Dame Cathedral in Paris. He again apologized for upsetting me by misidentifying the photograph of Ambrose in my alchemy lab. I told him it was all right. I surprised myself by actually believing it.

"One last thing, Zoe," Tobias said. "I found an old tincture that never worked for me, but my notes say it helps with the symptoms you're experiencing from backward alchemy. I'll overnight it to you."

"And let's not wait another 150 years before we see each other this time, okay?"

"It's a deal."

~

Brixton made up with his friends. Veronica and Ethan came to the teashop while he was working behind the counter, and they brought him a peace offering: a wind-up gargoyle that Ethan had commissioned from a specialty shop.

Ethan confessed he'd been sneaking around the burned theater after the fire, for kicks, and thought he saw the Baby Bigfoot shown in the posters around town. It made him realize that there might be more going on in this world than he understood. Maybe there *was* a Bigfoot. Brixton went along with Ethan's version of the truth, and didn't give up Dorian's secret.

While the boys caught up at a table filled with Dorian's pastries, Veronica sat with me and showed me my new and improved website on her phone.

"This can't be right," I said. "It looks like I've already sold two of my most expensive items in the last twenty-four hours."

"You haven't checked your email or your bank account?" she asked.

"I've been a bit busy." I'd need to pack up these items right away. I looked more closely, to see which pieces had sold. If what Veronica had showed me was right, I now had enough money to pay Ethan back *and* perhaps enough left over to hire someone to fix my roof. But first, I was buying myself a new wardrobe.

I settled back in my seat and enjoyed the convivial atmosphere. The painted blue sky on the ceiling and the live weeping fig tree in the center of Blue Sky Teas mirrored the sunny spring day outside. Two of Heather's water-themed paintings were now hanging on the walls. Though they'd been inspired by the winter flooding, the dramatic blues and bright whites were in perfect harmony with the spring flowers that filled the café.

"May I join you?" The voice startled me from my thoughts.

"Hi, Mr. Danko," Veronica said. "How are you feeling? I heard you were in the hospital."

"Much better, thank you." Ivan sat down and set a Czech newspaper onto the tree-ring table. He *did* look much better. Perhaps hope was breathing new life into him.

I couldn't say the same thing for myself. As I caught a glimpse of Ivan's newspaper, I felt as though the life was draining out of me. The sensation was surreal, like being in a dream.

I pointed to a grainy photograph in the newspaper. The focus of the image was a statue on Charles Bridge, the famous stone bridge that stretches across the Vlatava River in Prague. The bridge was lined with statues of saints, but this particular statue didn't match the rest. It was a gargoyle.

"What's this?" I asked, tapping a shaking fingertip on the newsprint image.

"Ah," Ivan said. "That is an interesting story. It seems that a stone gargoyle was found this week on Charles Bridge."

"Why is that weird?" Veronica asked. "Aren't there gargoyles all over Europe?"

"They don't usually appear without warning," Ivan said, "especially not 150 years after they disappeared."

I looked more carefully at the image. Though it didn't look like Dorian, there was something familiar about the style.

"This gargoyle," Ivan continued, "was identified as having been stolen from Notre Dame around the time the Gallery of Chimeras was opened to the public."

Like Dorian, this must have been a carving by Viollet-le-Duc. Was it another piece of the puzzle?

"Wasn't your gargoyle statue stolen, too, Ms. Faust?" Veronica asked. "There's, like, a gargoyle thief on the loose."

"Mine reappeared under mysterious circumstances too," I said, forcing a laugh.

I told everyone that my missing gargoyle statue had been dropped off on my porch during the night. The same "anonymous donor" had returned the murder weapon to the steps of the police station. A security camera video showed only a hunched figure under a black silk cape.

Max was unsettled by the fact that they hadn't caught the thief, but when he found me in my garden the following day, his response surprised me.

"If I had to choose between catching the guy who broke into the evidence locker," he said, "and having your gargoyle returned to you, I'm glad it turned out this way."

"I do believe you're learning to unwind, Max Liu."

He started to speak, but was interrupted by his cell phone. "Damn. I'm sorry, Zoe."

"I know, you have to go."

I had more to worry about than a complicated love life. And also more to celebrate. Dorian was safe from police scrutiny and could go back to being his usual self.

My Tea of Ashes remedy was still taking a toll, so I had opened the package from Tobias with anticipation. I lifted the carefully wrapped dark blue glass jar. The label was faded with age. As Tobias had said, the notes indicated this preparation could help with shriveled skin and hair loss. An accompanying note from Tobias said he'd held onto it for sentimental reasons, because the small man who had given it to him shortly after he met me in 1855 had been another kind soul during that dark time. The tincture hadn't worked for him, which is why he'd never used it up, but because my symptoms were identical to those described, he hoped it might work for me.

I looked from Tobias's note to the label on the glass jar. They had been written by different people, but the writing on the label looked familiar. I found a magnifying glass to examine the label. Was it my imagination, or did a tiny scribble at the bottom of the label say *N. Flamel?*

I sniffed the tincture, then put a drop on my tongue. I'm not sure whether it had a placebo effect or whether it was real, but I felt more energetic than I had in months.

Maybe it was hope that filled me with a renewed energy. I had my first solid lead on Dorian's book. Ivan might be of even more assistance, now that he believed alchemy was real. Now that I knew the book was tied to Notre Dame, I realized something must have changed at the cathedral. What was it that had set in motion the gold statues crumbling into dust and Dorian turning to stone? It had been months since I'd been in Paris. It was time for a trip back. This time with purpose.

I doubted the French customs officers would allow me into the country in my current slovenly outfit, but I was about to remedy that problem. Heather and I had made a date to go to the mall together. The huge department store again overwhelmed my senses, but I allowed Heather to lead me inside. The perfumes, the bright lights, and the endless rows of clothing struck me as unnatural. But on this visit, with a little bit of help, I learned that if you went beneath the surface, you could find the pieces that fit your own unique shape *and* personality. Two hours later, I emerged a new woman. I walked out of the mall wearing the first pair of comfortable jeans I'd ever owned, a green cotton sweater over a tailored white blouse, and silver flats.

I dropped Heather off at her cottage that sat at the edge of a wild field. There in the untamed meadow, the first leaves on the rosebushes were beginning to unfurl.

Brixton came outside before Heather reached the door.

"Hey Zoe, you promised you'd cook me that new dish you're perfecting," he said, giving me what he assumed was a surreptitious look. "Is tonight good?"

"Right. That new dish." Brixton must have been in touch with Dorian.

Heather said she wanted to work on a new painting, but asked if I would send Brixton home with leftovers.

The scent of caramelized onions had thoroughly permeated the house by the time Brixton and I walked through my front door. Dorian cooked a bountiful spring feast for the three of us, and after dinner, he put on a living room magic show with illusions his "father," Jean Eugène Robert-Houdin, had taught him a century and a half ago. Illusions that relied on sleight of hand—or in his case, sleight of claw.

THE END

～

Get a free novelette and more recipes when you sign up for Gigi's newsletter. Scan the code below, or go to www.gigipandian.com.

Scan to subscribe to Gigi's newsletter!

Read on for Recipes and an Author's Note, followed by Book 3, The Elusive Elixir.

RECIPES

CHOCOLATE ELIXIR

Drink your chocolate in 2 ways:
Hot Chocolate or Chilled Chocolate Smoothie

Serves: 2
Cook time: 10 minutes

Ingredients:

- 2 tbsp cacao or unsweetened cocoa powder
- 1 tbsp coconut sugar
- 1½ cups of your favorite non-dairy milk (e.g., almond, rice, coconut)
- ½ tsp vanilla extract
- ½ tsp cinnamon, preferably Ceylon
- ¼ tsp ginger powder
- ⅛ tsp cayenne pepper
- ⅛ tsp sea salt

Directions:

Place all the ingredients in a blender and puree until smooth. For hot chocolate, warm the blended mixture on the stove. For a chilled smoothie, add 8–10 ice cubes to the blender and puree.

Variations:

- Substitute the ginger with cardamom.
- Substitute the coconut sugar with 2 or 3 dates. For easier blending, soak the dates in hot water for a few minutes before adding them to the blender.

CASHEW CREAM MAC & CHEESE

Serves: 4
Cook time: 40 minutes

Ingredients for pasta:

- ½ lb. small pasta, such as elbow macaroni, conchigliette shells, or fusilli

Ingredients for onion mixture:

- 1 medium yellow onion, diced
- 5 cloves garlic, diced
- 1 tsp olive oil
- ¼ tsp salt

Ingredients for sauce:

- 1 cup unroasted cashews, soaked in water overnight (or for at least 4 hours) and drained
- 2 tbsp tomato paste
- 1 tsp salt
- ¼ tsp black pepper
- 1 tsp smoked paprika
- 1 tsp turmeric
- 1 tbsp yellow mustard, powdered or liquid
- 1 tbsp nutritional yeast (optional; add extra ¼ tsp salt if not using)
- 1 tbsp corn starch
- 1½ cups water

Directions:

Preheat oven to 375. Start a large pot of boiling water and cook pasta according to package instructions.

While the pasta is cooking, sauté the garlic and onions with ¼ tsp salt for approximately 10 minutes. When the onion mixture is translucent and slightly browned, remove from heat and set aside.

Combine sauce ingredients in a blender. Add half of the cooled onion mixture to the blender mixture. Blend for a few minutes, until creamy.

In a large bowl, combine the cooked pasta and sauce. Add the pasta and sauce to an oven-safe baking dish (a 9-inch glass baking dish works well). Sprinkle the remainder of the onion mixture on top for a flavorful topping that will crisp in the oven. Bake for 15 minutes.

Variations:

- Want to add vegetables to the recipe in a way that makes the sauce even creamier? Cauliflower works great with the flavors in this recipe. While the onions are sautéing, break a small head of cauliflower into florets and steam for 10 minutes. Add the steamed cauliflower to the sauce ingredients in the blender. Follow the rest of the instructions above.
- Don't want a crispy onion topping? Use a smaller onion and blend the whole onion mixture into the sauce.

ROASTED ASPARAGUS & BRUSSELS SPROUTS WITH TARRAGON
AVOCADO SAUCE

Serves: 4
Cook time: 20 minutes

Ingredients for roasted spring vegetables:

- 1 lb. asparagus
- ½ lb. Brussels sprouts
- 2 tsp olive oil

Ingredients for sauce:

- 1 large avocado (or two small ones), peeled and pitted
- 2 tbsp olive oil
- 2 tbsp fresh lemon juice
- 2 tbsp water (more or less, depending on desired thickness)
- 1 tbsp fresh tarragon, chopped
- ¼ to ½ tsp salt, to taste
- 1 tsp granulated garlic or 1 large garlic clove
- ¼ tsp black pepper

Directions:

Preheat oven to 425 and prepare a baking sheet with parchment paper. Cut off the tough ends of the asparagus, and cut the remaining spears into 2-inch pieces. Quarter the Brussels sprouts. Toss the vegetables with 2 tsp. olive oil, then spread evenly on the prepared baking sheet. Roast for approximately 15 minutes.

While the asparagus is cooking, prepare the sauce. Put all the sauce ingredients into a blender and puree until creamy. Toss the roasted vegetables with sauce.

Variations:

- Asparagus and Brussels sprouts are a nice combination of seasonal late-winter and spring vegetables, but if you feel like making the dish during the winter, the sauce works well with potatoes. Cut 1 lb. of potatoes into $\frac{1}{2}$-inch pieces (red or Yukon gold potatoes work well, either peeled or scrubbed), toss with olive oil, and roast for about 30 minutes. Toss potatoes with sauce.

- For a more garlicky dish, toss several smashed garlic cloves with the roasted vegetable mix. Roast along with the other vegetables. The garlic will be softer if you leave the skin on while roasting, but remember to peel the skin off before serving.

AUTHOR'S NOTE

The Masquerading Magician is a work of fiction, but the historical backdrop is real.

Jean Eugène Robert-Houdin (1805–1871) is the French stage magician known as the "Father of Modern Magic." The astonishing history of his life in *The Masquerading Magician* is accurate except for the following: he was not known to be a book collector, he never possessed the fictional alchemy book *Non Degenera Alchemia*, and he was not given a gargoyle by his contemporary Eugène Viollet-le-Duc (1814–1879). Viollet-le-Duc was the architect who created the Gallery of Chimeras on Notre Dame, including the carving Dorian is based on. As far as history recorded, the two famous men did not know each other.

Records suggest that alchemists used to meet at Notre Dame many centuries ago, and there are theories of a backward "death rotation" in alchemical transformations. However, as far as I can tell, there never existed a break-off sect of backward alchemists.

It's true history that the façade of Notre Dame de Paris was defaced during the French Revolution, and there is indeed evidence that alchemical codes have been carved into Notre Dame in the past. My addition of *Non Degenera Alchemia* to the façade is fictional. As for the real carvings that once existed, some scholars have attributed them to fourteenth-century alchemist Nicolas Flamel.

Nicolas Flamel and his wife Perenelle claimed to have discovered the

Philosopher's Stone, granting them the power to transmute lead into gold and extend their lives. Is there any truth in this assertion? The Flamels did possess an ancient alchemy book, donated large sums of money to charity, lived exceptionally long lives for the time, and when their graves were unearthed the coffins were empty. The less fanciful interpretation of these facts is that Nicolas Flamel was a bookseller who owned many books, his wife was wealthy and had money to donate, and graves in the fourteenth century were not especially secure. But doesn't it make for great fiction?

Dorian the gargoyle was inspired by the many mysterious gargoyles I've visited over the years. My gargoyle photography can be seen on the Gargoyle Girl blog at www.gargoylegirl.com.

Though Dorian is fictional, his culinary alchemy is based on my own exploits in the kitchen. A cancer diagnosis challenged me to completely transform the way in which I ate, and instead of giving up meals I loved, I challenged myself to learn how to cook healing foods from scratch that would nourish both my body and soul.

In addition to the three vegan recipes in the back of this book, recipes are included in each book in the Accidental Alchemist mystery series, plus more recipes can be found online at www.gigipandian.com/recipes.

THE ELUSIVE ELIXIR

BOOK 3

CHAPTER 1

The woman was still behind me.

She was so close to me on the winding, irregular stone steps inside Notre Dame Cathedral that I could smell her breath. Sourdough bread and honey.

I could have sworn I'd seen her at the *boulangerie* near my apartment earlier that morning. Now her unwavering gaze bore into me. She must have been at least eighty and wasn't more than five feet tall. She didn't fit the profile of someone worth being afraid of. Most people would have dismissed it as a coincidence.

Unless you're someone like me, who always has to be careful.

We emerged from the cramped corridor onto the narrow Gallery of Gargoyles, high above Paris. I shielded my eyes from the sun. A warm wind swept my hair around my face as I looked out through the mesh fencing that covered the once-open balcony.

The gargoyle known as *Le Penseur*, "The Thinker," sat regally with his stone head turned toward the City of Lights, as he had for over 150 years. Unlike my friend Dorian, this gargoyle of Notre Dame wouldn't be stepping off his stone mount.

For a few brief seconds, the stunning details Eugène Viollet-le-Duc had added to his chimeras all those years ago made me forget about the woman. The grandeur even made me lose sight of the real reason I was at Notre Dame that day. My quest was never far from my thoughts, but for those fleeting moments, I allowed myself the space to appreciate the splendor of the crafts-manship of generations of artists and laborers.

A girl around eight years old squealed in delight as she noticed a set of smaller gargoyles perched overhead, grinning maniacally at us. Her younger brother began to cry. His father explained in a thick Welsh accent that gargoyles weren't to be feared. They weren't even real, for Heaven's sake! His father was right—in this particular case.

If I didn't get rid of my shadow and get what I needed here at Notre Dame, the Welshman's words would be true for all gargoyles, including my best friend. I followed the tight walkway for a few steps until I saw it. An unfin-ished slab of limestone where a gargoyle might have perched.

This was the spot.

I glanced behind me. The woman stood a few paces away. In stylish sunglasses with a perfectly knotted silk scarf around her spindly neck, she was simultaneously frail and glamorous. Unlike the crowd of tourists excitedly scurrying past each other on the balcony that was never meant for this volume of visitors, the woman stood stock still. She held no camera. Her gaze didn't linger on the dramatic cityscape or on the unique stone monsters that surrounded us.

She looked directly at me, not bothering to conceal her curiosity.

"May I help you?" I asked, speaking in French. Though the woman hadn't spoken, the style and care of her clothing, hair, and makeup suggested she was Parisian.

She pulled her sunglasses off and clenched them in boney hands. "*I knew it*," she replied in English. "I knew it was you." Her voice was strong, with the hint of a rattle in her throat. The forcefulness of her words seemed to surprise her nearly as much as it surprised me.

My throat constricted, and I instinctively reached for my purse. Empty except for my phone, notebook, wallet, and homemade granola bars packed in parchment paper. I was thankful I'd had the sense to leave Dorian's alchemy book safely hidden far from me. I willed myself to relax. Things were different now. This wasn't a witch hunt. Being recognized wasn't necessarily a bad thing.

I'd flown from Portland to Paris earlier that week. Because of the urgency of the situation, while I was recovering from an illness and too sick to climb the steps of Notre Dame, I'd stayed busy with people I thought might be able to help me, several of whom blurred together in my mind. Librarians, acade-mics, amateur historians, Notre Dame docents, rare book dealers. Still, I found it surprising that I'd completely forgotten this woman. No, that wasn't entirely true. Now that she'd removed her sunglasses, there was something vaguely familiar about her... And if she was one of the people who worked at the cathedral, that would explain how she was fit enough to keep pace with me on the hundreds of stairs.

"Please forgive me," I said, switching to English, as she had done. "I seem to have forgotten where we met."

She shook her head and laughed. "So polite! We have not met. You're Zoe Faust's granddaughter, aren't you?"

I let out the breath I'd been holding and smiled. "You knew *Grandmere?*"

The woman gave me a curious look, her eyes narrowing momentarily, but the action was so quickly replaced with a smile that I might have imagined it.

"During the Occupation in 1942," she said. "My name is Blanche Leblanc."

"Zoe Faust," I said automatically.

The quizzical look on her face returned.

"Named after my grandmother," I added hastily, stumbling over the words. I'm a terrible liar. Personally, I think it's one of my more endearing qualities— who wants to be friends with someone if you never know if they're being honest?—but in my life it's also a most inconvenient trait. "It's lovely to meet you, Madame Leblanc." That was a lie too. I'm sure she was a nice person, but I didn't need this complication.

Three out-of-breath tourists, the stragglers of our group, burst through the top of the winding stairway. While they caught their breath, I led Madame Leblanc away from the crowded section of walkway next to the gargoyles. There wasn't much space on the gallery, but by stepping back a few feet, at least we wouldn't be jostled.

"You look so much like her," Madame Leblanc said, speaking more softly now. "When I was a young girl, my mother once brought me to her shop. What was the name?"

"Elixir."

"Yes. Elixir. Many foreigners left Paris, but your grandmother stayed and helped people during the war. Her healing remedies saved many lives. But then she left. After the fire..."

I returned her sad smile. These days, people think of me as an herbalist. In the past, people thought of me as an apothecary. Not many people have ever known the truth, that I'm an alchemist.

I've never gotten the hang of turning lead into gold, but ever since I was a small child I've been able to extract the healing properties of plants. My ability to heal people was one of the things that made me think my accidental discovery of the Elixir of Life wasn't entirely a curse. But the dangers of living a secret life created a heavy burden. My "grandmother" Zoe Faust is me.

Since I've always been good with herbal remedies, I've been able to help both sick and injured people.

And war leads to far too many of both.

"Yes," I said, "*Grandmere* finally left Paris to help a family that was fleeing with a child too sick to travel."

Madame Leblanc's painted lips quivered. "My first thought was the right one, *n'est pas?*" Her silk scarf swirled in the wind.

"Are you all right?" I asked.

"Don't touch me," she hissed, twisting away from me. "My mother was right. *You are a witch.*"

The Gallery of Gargoyles was loud with the excited voices of tourists of all ages, but suddenly I couldn't hear anything except the beating of my heart. The multilingual voices of the tourists around us dissipated as if sucked into a vortex. It felt like the only two people left on the Gallery of Gargoyles were me and Madame Leblanc. My stomach clenched. I wished I hadn't eaten a hearty breakfast from that *boulangerie*. "You're confused, madame."

"You were in your late twenties then. *You have not aged a day.* There is no anti-aging cream that good. I know. I have tried them all. You stand before me through witchcraft or some other deal with the devil."

I choked. "I'm told my grandmother and I look very much alike," I said, trying to keep my breathing even. "These things happen—"

"I am eighty-two years old," Madame Leblanc cut in. "My eyesight is not what it once was, but my hearing is perfect. Even with the cacophony around us, I would know your voice anywhere."

"I'm told that I sound like her, too—"

"I remember the voice of the soldier who told me that my father was dead." Her words were slow. Crisp. "I remember the voice of the nurse who handed me my healthy baby girl. And I remember the voice of the apothecary named Zoe who saved many lives in Paris— but not that of my mother."

Momentarily stunned by the heartfelt speech, I was at a loss for words. I looked from the woman to the gargoyles surrounding us then out at the Eiffel Tower stretching into the blue sky, Sacre Cour's manmade grandeur, the flowing river Seine, and wisps of smoke from chimneys. Air, earth, water, fire. Elements I worked with and craved.

"I don't know what sort of bargain you made with evil forces to be here today," Madame Leblanc said, her voice nearly a whisper, "but that woman was not your grandmother. She was *you*. I know it is you, Zoe Faust. And I will find out what you are. You cannot hide any longer."

CHAPTER 2

My heart galloped loudly in my ears. I feared I might be overcome with vertigo high atop the cathedral. This was a complication I didn't need.

"My grandmother always said she felt bad about the people she wasn't able to help," I said, forcing myself to speak calmly. "What was your mother's name? Perhaps she mentioned her to me."

"Oh, you tried to help her," Madame Leblanc said, a snarl hovering on her wrinkled lips. "You gave her a tincture that day she brought me to the shop. But at home, she refused to take it. She said it was witchcraft. She said that nobody's herbal remedies could be as good as yours without the work of the devil."

"I'm sorry," I said. "My grandmother wasn't—"

"Stop lying!"

The breathless tourists glanced our way before edging their way past, giving us as wide a berth as possible on the narrow parapet. Maybe my hope of salvaging the situation was misguided. I looked longingly at the exit, wondering if Madame Leblanc would be as quick on the stairs down as she was on the way up.

"The strong family resemblance has confused you," I said.

"I'm not crazy," Madame Leblanc said.

The ferocity in her eyes shocked me. Had she harbored this grudge against me since she was a child? I felt bad for her, but I couldn't say more. The world wasn't ready to know about alchemy.

"I'm going to find out what you are," she said. "You made a grave mistake returning to Paris."

"Madame—"

I broke off as a security guard approached us. He asked if everything was all right, but his bored eyes told me he was more concerned about moving us through the narrow stone gallery than with finding out what our disagreement was about.

With the distraction from the guard, I wondered if I could make a run for it.

Six months ago, my life had turned upside down. Perhaps not quite as upside down as it had in 1704 when I accidentally discovered the Elixir of Life, but it was the second-biggest shakeup in the intervening 300 years. Half a year ago, I learned that dangerous backward alchemy was real.

Alchemy is a personal transformation. Its core principle is transforming the impure into the pure, be it lead into gold or a dying body into a thriving one. Backward alchemy's Death Rotation skips the natural order and sacrifices one element for another. Backward alchemy takes more than it transforms. Backward alchemy and the Death Rotation are based in death, not life.

I've been running from alchemy for a long time, so I didn't make this discovery on my own. I'd been sought out by Dorian Robert-Houdin to help understand a book of backward alchemy, *Non Degenera Alchemia*, which roughly translated to *Not Untrue Alchemy*. Dorian's fate was linked to that of the mysterious book filled with disturbing woodcut illustrations and strange Latin text. The book was changing, and so was Dorian. He was dying an unnatural death. He would soon be alive but trapped in stone—a fate that struck me as far worse than death. I couldn't let that happen to the quirky fellow who had quickly become my best friend.

Did I mention that Dorian is a gargoyle?

Dorian Robert-Houdin was originally carved in limestone for Notre Dame's Gallery of Gargoyles. He'd been a prototype carving by Notre Dame renovator Viollet-le-Duc, created for the brand-new Gallery of Gargoyles built in the 1850s and 1860s. The statue turned out to be too small for the balcony, so Viollet-le-Duc gifted the creation to his friend Jean Eugène Robert-Houdin, the French stage magician credited with being the father of modern magic. Neither man was an alchemist, but a stage show magic trick went very wrong one day when the retired magician picked up a beautiful alchemy book. The gargoyle statue came to life as the magician read from the alchemy book he believed to be merely a stage prop. On that day in 1860, Dorian the living gargoyle was born in Robert-Houdin's home workshop.

Madame Leblanc and I were now nearly alone with the gargoyles and the security guard. Tourists were divided into groups that the staff sent up the stairs of the cathedral in waves, to prevent an unsafe level of crowding on the gallery. While Madame Leblanc assured the guard we'd be moving on shortly, I tried to ground myself in reality.

In addition to the stragglers who'd only recently reached the gallery, the only other person nearby was a man in a priest's collar who was staring intently at one of the gargoyles. Now there was a respectable fellow. If a living gargoyle came to him for help, I bet it would be a calm, well-mannered creature—not like the opinionated Dorian, who thought of himself as a French Poirot and was constantly getting into trouble. Though my fellow misfit Dorian was dear to me, he didn't listen. Ever.

I clung to the small amount of relief that I hadn't followed Dorian's advice for me to take him with me to Paris. He could shift between life and stone within seconds, so he'd suggested I carry him around Paris in a backpack in stone form. I had no doubt that he would have peeked out of the bag regularly and ruined any hope I had of convincing Madam Leblanc she didn't need to tell the world I was an immortal witch.

The guard left us to scowl at two teenage backpackers who were attempting to reach through the mesh barrier to touch a gargoyle. When I turned back to Madame Leblanc, she was blushing.

"I'm sorry," she said. Her lips were pinched. It was a difficult phrase for her to utter. "I have been foolish, no? I don't know what came over me. I hope you will forgive an old woman. It is only that you look so much like her."

"De rien," I said. "Think nothing of it. Good day, madame." I turned away, giving my attention back to the perch I wanted to verify with my own eyes. There was no doubt in my mind that this section of molding had been constructed to support a gargoyle. *It was true.*

Another gargoyle *had* once perched here. Local history held that a group of drunken Parisians had stolen the stone creature 150 years ago. But I knew the truth. A gargoyle much like Dorian had once stood here. *A gargoyle that had come to life and vanished.*

A hand touched my elbow.

"I would very much like to hear your memories of your grandmother," Madame Leblanc said. She stood uncomfortably close to me in the confined space. "Your fond memories of her will help me push my mother's angry memories from my mind. I do not wish to die with such bitterness. It will also allow me to apologize for my foolishness that must have disturbed you. May I treat you to lunch?"

"It's truly not necessary to apologize," I said. "And I, uh, have a phone call I need to make."

"I insist. I will wait for you to complete your call. You only bought enough bread for breakfast at the *boulangerie* this morning, so I know you haven't already prepared lunch."

I'd been right about seeing her at the bakery next to the apartment I was renting. She must have known where I was staying. It wouldn't be easy to back out of the invitation. And in spite of my discomfort, I didn't want to leave this woman with so much anger over an old misunderstanding.

Taking advantage of my hesitation, Madame Leblanc wrapped her bony hand around the crook of my elbow and led me toward the exit. Her cold fingers tightened around my arm like the brittle fingers of a skeleton, making it impossible for me to break away discreetly.

I didn't trust that her change of heart was genuine. But if it wasn't, I could use this opening to convince her I *wasn't* over 300 years old. I just had to lie convincingly.

No question, I was in trouble.

CHAPTER 3

We exited the cathedral through a twisting metal gate, a modern affront to the majesty on the façade above. I stole a glance up at the limestone carvings that adorned the front of the iconic cathedral underneath the Rosetta stained glass window. Hidden in the Christian imagery were a few alchemical symbols that had been added over the centuries. As an accidental alchemist, I had taken months to brush up on the more obscure alchemical codes in Dorian's book, but the symbols on Notre Dame were straightforward—if you knew what you were looking for.

In a row of saints, a saint was shown defeating a dragon that looked suspiciously like an ouroboros, the serpent who swallows its own tail, thus representing the cyclical nature of alchemy. In a different panel, a salamander was engulfed in flames but not burning, symbolizing how the animal can protect itself from fire, just as Dorian's alchemy book had done when caught in a fire. As we hurried along to reach the quieter side of the cathedral my eyes flicked to an unassuming carving of a simple man holding a book. If you looked closely, you could make out the chiseled letters NON DEGENERA AL. *Non Degenera Alchemia.* The alchemy book that had brought me here.

In the walled park behind Notre Dame, filled with Parisians walking their dogs, Madame Leblanc deposited me on a wooden bench. She strolled along the path, giving me privacy to make my phone call.

I'd been bluffing that I had a call to make. Yet after being shaken, I had an impulse to call Dorian or Max. I wanted to hear a friendly voice. I scrolled through the photos on my phone of my life in Portland. A hurricane-strength wave of homesickness nearly knocked me from the bench. I hadn't felt the emotion in so long that it took me a few moments to identify it. Homesick? The bittersweet emotion meant that after all these years, I truly had a home.

From my small phone screen, the image of my sort-of-boyfriend Max Liu looked up at me from behind a jasmine bush in his backyard garden. Max didn't yet know everything about me, but we'd come to care deeply for each other since I moved to Portland.

The photo of my misfit best friend was far less personal, because I didn't want to risk anyone else seeing the image of a supposed statue cooking up a storm in the kitchen. Therefore my photo of Dorian was of him standing next to the fireplace in the posed form he took when he returned to stone. I liked this particular snapshot for the mischievous gleam in his eye.

The sun hadn't yet risen in Portland. Max would be sleeping, but I wouldn't be stirring Dorian from slumber. The gargoyle didn't need to sleep, and the predawn hours were his favorites because he could move around most freely. I slipped earbuds into my ears, made sure there was nobody behind me, then hit the button to call him for a video chat.

"I am so pleased you called," Dorian said in his thick French accent. The formal voice didn't match the excited grin on his face. "I have made the most amazing discovery."

"You have?" In spite of the shock I'd received from Madame Leblanc, Dorian's enthusiasm was contagious. "What have you discovered?"

"Avocado!"

"You discovered... avocados?"

"Yes. They are *magnifiques*! Once you are home, we must share this with the world."

I let out a breath and lamented the fact that my dying friend was far more skilled at culinary creations than alchemy. "I'm pretty sure people already know about avocados."

A blur of claws flashed across the screen as he waved away my concern. "*Oui.* But do they know they can use avocado *in place of cream* to make a perfect chocolate mousse, pudding, or even frosting?" He was sitting so close to the screen that his horns bumped into the monitor.

"Is something wrong with the video camera?" I asked. It was mildly disconcerting to have such a close-up view of stone pores.

"*Pardon?* No, I am simply busy baking. I was skeptical of the skinny women on the Internet at first, but the flavors of cocoa and salt are stronger than the flavor of the avocado. It works perfectly! But I am speaking over you. You have something to tell me as well? Have you seen my brother yet? Yes, this must be why you are calling!"

"No, I'm sorry, Dorian. I haven't been granted access to see the stone gargoyle yet."

"Oh. *C'est regrettable.*"

"But Dorian, I found his empty perch at Notre Dame."

"*Vraiment?* This supports our suspicions that he is a creature like me."

"It does. I'll find a way to see him."

He narrowed his liquidy black eyes. "The professors continue to hold him captive?"

I wouldn't have described the study of an unmoving statue quite so dramatically, but he wasn't wrong.

Shortly after the Gallery of Gargoyles opened in the 1850s, one of the stone gargoyles was stolen. It was thought to be a prank, perhaps perpetrated by drunken artists or writers inspired by Victor Hugo's *Notre Dame de Paris* who found a stone chimera not properly secured and therefore made off with it. The great cathedral had been defaced many times before in its long history, so Parisians gave a Gallic shrug and moved on. The gargoyle wasn't seen again for over 150 years—until last month.

A gargoyle that looked suspiciously like the missing stone gargoyle was found on the Charles Bridge in Prague and repatriated to France from the Czech Republic. My friend and I suspected he was another creature like Dorian, who'd been brought to life but was reverting to stone. The Charles Bridge gargoyle had turned completely back to stone more quickly than Dorian. Was he alone in the world without an alchemist like me to help him?

"He's still under lock and key at the university," I said. Since the statue's pose was anomalous, architecture scholars at a local university were studying the gargoyle.

"You will find a way. But... you have other news, no?"

"Why do you say that?"

"Your face. It reads like an open book."

Now that I had him on the line, what was I going to tell Dorian? There was nothing he could do to help, so did I really want to worry him by telling him that I'd been recognized by someone who could expose me?

Furthermore, he would probably *try* to help, which would only make things worse. I could imagine him suggesting I find an underworld contact in Paris who could "convince" Madame Leblanc to leave well enough alone. In addition to being a food snob and a talented chef, Dorian was an avid reader with a vivid imagination. Since he lived a relatively solitary life out of necessity, Dorian had more interactions with fictional characters than real people, and his ideas about real life needed reining in. Frequently.

"I was worried about you," I said. "I wanted to see how you were doing." It was the truth. His backward transformation had been speeding up. Every day his progression back to stone was happening more quickly.

"My arm is not troubling me."

"Your arm? There's something wrong with your *arm* now?"

"I think we have a bad connection," he shouted. *"Allo?* I cannot hear you, *mon amie.* I will sign off and return to my new recipe. I seem to have misplaced my cardamom. *À bientôt."*

His face disappeared from the screen and I was left alone.

I'd left my Portland home a week ago in order to save Dorian's life. When I moved to Oregon earlier this year I'd been hoping to have a semblance of a normal life for a few years. With its quirky people, respect for nature, and health food culture, the city of Portland spoke to me from the moment I'd rolled into town with my Airstream trailer, thinking I'd stay for a brief time. I'd gotten far more than I'd dreamed. Friends as dear to me as any I'd ever had, a guy I was falling for, and a house that truly felt like a home. I'd put all that on hold to come here. Madame Leblanc had thrown my carefully constructed plan into disarray.

I looked across the park toward the Seine. Parisians strolled with their heads held high, walking dogs, puffing on cigarettes, meeting lovers. An artist with a hat to collect donations was sketching on the pavement in colorful chalk. Next to the surrealist image of pigeons with musical notes in place of eyes, he'd lettered in bright yellow chalk, *Life without art is stupid.*

I wasn't feeling the pull of the romantic City of Lights. Alone in a city that wasn't home, across the world from everyone I cared about, the only person in Paris who cared at all about me was a tenacious woman who could very well expose my secret and prevent me from saving Dorian's life.

CHAPTER 4

Ten minutes later, I found myself seated at an impossibly tiny table squeezed into the darkest corner of a café in the Marais neighborhood, walking distance from Notre Dame. The scent of cigarette smoke lingered in the air, seemingly from ghosts but more likely from centuries of smoke-filled conversations the walls had absorbed.

"There was hunger, fear, and death during the war," Madame Leblanc said, "but it elevated our senses. That's why I remember your grandmother so clearly. She was a flame that burned brightly. Too brightly, some said. That's why they said she was a witch."

I shivered. "She never told me that." I'd been called a witch many times, but until now I hadn't realized people in Paris had thought the same of me. I'd been careful here. Though I owned my shop for decades, I'd only stayed for a few years at a time, leaving the shop in the capable hands of an alchemy student while my beloved Ambrose and I were living in England or traveling elsewhere.

Madame Leblanc kept her eyes locked on mine as she raised a glass of wine to her lips. Her makeup was perfect. I didn't even want to think about what I looked like. I'd been sick in the weeks leading up to my trip to Paris, due to an alchemy experiment gone wrong. I've always been good at taking care of myself with healing foods, tinctures, and teas that I make myself, but understanding backward alchemy was taking a huge toll on me. I never would have left my cozy midcentury kitchen and gotten on an airplane had time not been running out for Dorian.

"Being so young, you would not understand how different things were," Madame Leblanc said. "The war... It's not like in the movies. We weren't living in black and white, or even sepia. It was a more vibrant, heightened state of existence."

I knew what she meant. Being an alchemist is both a blessing and a curse. I've helped thousands of people, but I've also seen many of them die. I've seen more of this wondrous world than most, eating and drinking and laughing and crying with people from cultures simultaneously identical and poles apart. In those travels, I've seen the best and worst of humanity. This was especially so during traumatic times like plague, famine, and war.

But I couldn't say that out loud. I had to check myself before I spoke—it would have been all too easy to reminisce with her. Digging my fingernails into the palm of my hand, I reminded myself that I was twenty-eight-year-old Zoe Faust of Portland, Oregon, who'd been living out of her silver Airstream trailer for the last few years, bumming around the United States after a bad breakup, not my namesake who'd owned a shop in Paris.

I had closed my shop and returned home to America in 1942. Ambrose had died a few years before, followed a short time later by a fire at Elixir. My collection of herbs, tonics, and elixirs was destroyed, along with the *potager* back garden where I grew herbs and vegetables. The alchemy student who'd helped me at the store off-and-on, Jasper Dubois, had already left Paris, so there was nothing keeping me there. The side of the shop with alchemical equipment was spared, which allowed me to stay afloat selling paraphernalia at flea markets across the US. I had put the larger items that survived the fire into storage, wondering if they'd survive the war and whether I'd ever return to Paris.

Instead of answering Madame Leblanc, I took a bite of my arugula salad with roasted chickpeas and potatoes, which I dressed with olive oil and vinegar. Madame Leblanc ate a crème fraîche and steak tartar tartine. I'd declined sharing a carafe of wine and opted instead for tea. I needed to keep a clear head.

"You appear to be more lost in your memories than I am, mademoiselle," Madame Leblanc said.

"I was thinking of how little I knew of my grandmother's life here. What were your impressions of her and her shop?"

She sat back and inhaled deeply. The lines around her mouth grew deeper as she pressed her lips together. Her hands tugged at the starchy cloth napkin in her lap. I wondered if she was nervous that her recollections might upset me. No, she didn't seem like one to shy away from controversy. I thought it more likely she was craving a cigarette.

"At first," she said, "I didn't know it was your grandmother's shop, because an elderly man was there when my mother first took me. But a few months later, your grandmother appeared. She was much more pleasant, no?"

I smiled. Jasper had been a young man when he began minding the shop for me. He was a student of alchemy. Not *my* student, because that would never do for Jasper. He was a product of the times. Born into a title but no money, he was convinced of the superiority of the French, the bourgeoisie class, and the male sex. I doubt it had ever occurred to Jasper that I could have taught him anything. I discovered alchemy's secrets accidentally and therefore wasn't prepared to take on apprentices, but Jasper had never asked how I found alchemy so he didn't know my transformation had been accidental. He simply appreciated the availability of an alchemical laboratory behind the shop, making it a mutually beneficial relationship. Every decade we would switch places as the proprietor, and Jasper continued to age while he sought out a worthy alchemy teacher. The last time I'd arrived in Paris, I found the shop closed and Jasper gone. I was never sure if he'd found the alchemy teacher he was looking for, or if the war had scared him off.

Madame Leblanc returned my smile. "In spite of what my mother told me that soured my memories, I remember that your grandmother was beautiful, like you. She had gone prematurely gray too. No no, don't be self-conscious. I can tell you haven't dyed your hair white to be *avant-garde*, but the color suits you."

"Thank you," I said simply. It wouldn't do to elaborate. My hair turning white was what had alerted me to the fact that I had indeed discovered the Elixir of Life. It was the one part of me that aged.

"My mother told me your grandmother gave remedies even to those who could not pay, and her *potager* was the envy of the neighborhood. That garden flourished even in winter. It was unnatural. That is what convinced my mother it was witchcraft."

I was about to speak when a police officer appeared in the doorway, his eyes methodically scanning the cafe. His stiff stance and uniform suggested he was with the military branch of the police, the *National Gendarmerie*. Tall, dark-haired, young. Most people look young to me these days, but he was truly a boy, only a year or so out of university, I guessed. His gaze came to rest on my table.

Madam Leblanc waved him over. "My grand-nephew," she said to me, beaming. As she turned to the young man, her smile tightened, shifting from pride to a different emotion. *Scheming.*

"Gilbert," she said, "this is Zoe Faust. I trust you had time to look into what I told you?"

I gripped the table. I was being ambushed.

While Madam Leblanc had considerately given me "privacy" at the park outside Notre Dame, she'd made her own phone call. She called her *gendarme* grand-nephew. But surely he couldn't believe a fanciful tale that his grand-aunt was lunching with a 300-year-old woman, could he? Why was he here? Humoring his auntie?

"*Bonjour, mademoiselle,*" he said, bowing his head in friendly greeting as he sat down at the table.

"Is there a problem?" I replied in English. Better to play American tourist Zoe Faust.

"Could I see your identification *sil vous plait?*"

"What's this about?" *Breathe, Zoe.*

He shrugged as if he had not a care in the world. Turning away from his aunt, he gave me a conspiratorial smile. "I expect it is nothing. Your passport please?"

I handed him my US passport. I wasn't too worried. It was a real passport. Every decade I received a new birth certificate from a man who'd been a prop-maker in Hollywood in the 1950s before his career was destroyed by the McCarthy hearings. I'd helped him through an illness when he was destitute, and even though he didn't understand the reason why I needed those birth certificates in my name, he'd always happily supplied them until his recent death.

The smile evaporated from the police officer's face as he looked at my passport. "Zoe Faust? You? *C'est vrais?* This cannot be. *Tante* Blanche?" He looked to his aunt.

"I was named after my grandmother," I explained.

"Ah." A chagrined smile appeared on the *gendarme's* innocent face. "But of course. Is your grandmother still alive, mademoiselle?"

Madame Leblanc scowled at the young man as he accepted my statement.

"Why are you asking about my grandmother?" I asked.

"It is believed that she has information about a fire in 1942. It killed one…" He paused and consulted his notes. "Jasper Dubois."

I stared at him. "Jasper?" I whispered. "Jasper died in the fire?" My God. Poor Jasper. I always believed he'd been a coward and had run off when the war began. It wasn't as simple to find people in those days.

"Aha!" Madame Leblanc exclaimed. "You admit you were alive in 1942."

My shoulders shook. "My grandmother mentioned him often. He helped her with the store."

"Yes," Gilbert said. "The shop called..." He consulted his notes again. "Elixir."

"Yes, that was my grandmother's shop. But I didn't realize anyone was killed, or that the police would investigate such an old fire."

"There's no statute of limitation on murder, mademoiselle."

"Murder?"

"The fire was arson. The person who owned that shop is quite possibly a murderer."

CHAPTER 5

A murderer? A murderer. A. Murderer.

My brain was having trouble processing the information. Slipping up and being found out to be over 300 years old, I could understand. But a murderer?

"There must be some mistake," I said. "I—my grandmother, she wouldn't have killed anyone."

"We all think we know people," the policeman said in his heavily accented English, "but we do not truly know the depths of their souls."

What an utterly French thing to say. Under other circumstances, I would have been amused, and perhaps had a conversation with him about Sartre or Foucault.

"You say she is dead?" he continued.

"Yes. Many years ago."

"Where is she buried?"

"What? Buried? No, she was cremated."

"At what crematorium?"

"I have no idea. My mother was the one who handled it."

"Where can we find your mother?"

"She died many years ago too." My head throbbed. "Why do you need that information?"

"We need to confirm your grandmother is truly deceased. You must understand, she has been on the run since 1942. What is it you Americans say? On the lam?"

My mind raced as I willed hazy memories to come into focus. The fire had been an accident, started by someone trying to stay warm, and nobody had died. But what if that wasn't true? What if the fire that drove me from Paris had been deliberately set, and had killed Jasper?

Who would have done that? And why hadn't I known?

It was the fire that had prompted my immediate departure from France in 1942, but I'd been ready to move on. Ambrose, the man I loved, had killed himself several years before, after the death of his son Percy had driven him insane, so there was nothing keeping me in Paris.

I still felt this policeman must be mistaken, but I thought back on that place and time, so different than today. In Paris during the Occupation, the rules of life were different. People looked out for each other on an individual level more than in times of peace, but at the same time, authorities had more pressing problems than sorting out the aftermath of a fire that seemed to be accidental.

After Paris was taken, an underground network sprang up that made it possible to travel to neutral European countries and leave for the United States from there. I'd left with a family that was fleeing Paris with a sick child. One of their daughters, Cecily, was stricken with influenza and shouldn't have been traveling at all, but the family insisted it was more dangerous to stay in the city. Ambrose and Percy were dead and my shop was destroyed, so I took the opportunity to help Cecily and start anew. I'd been so focused on administering to the child and hurriedly packing the intact half of my shop that I hadn't sought out the authorities to make an official report. It wasn't the kind of thing that mattered at the time.

"I'm truly sorry to have distressed you, mademoiselle." Gendarme Gilbert's demeanor shifted. He appeared genuinely distressed to have upset me.

"I know you're only doing your duty." I looked at his young face, which might not have been as young as I originally suspected. As he leaned across the small table, I saw that his skin was drawn and sallow, especially around his eyes. He wasn't sleeping well. I found myself thinking of tinctures that might help him.

I shook off my natural inclinations and got back to the matter at hand. "I can look into the information you requested, but it will take time. I simply can't imagine... Can you tell me more about the fire?"

A shrug. "I do not have all of the details. It was only my aunt's call that alerted me and caused me to make inquiries. I'm not sure how much you know about the French police, but this is not my jurisdiction. I am not with the *Police Nationale*." Another shrug. "But my aunt is a persistent woman."

"I understand," I said, wondering what a Leblanc family Christmas was like.

"The crime did not come to light at the time but was noted after the war. Perhaps it was disguised as a casualty of war by the person who owned this shop." He paused and consulted a palm-sized notebook. "Yes, the murderer had intimate knowledge of the shop. A note was made in *l'ordinateur—comment dites-vous?*"

"She understands French," Madame Leblanc said. "She knows you said *computer*."

"*Bon*," he continued. "A note was made on the computer decades ago when the records were entered in, but no suspects had been found. *Alors*, it was forgotten. Until my aunt called me today."

"I see."

"In this modern age, forensics can find many things that were once not possible. Again, I am sorry to have distressed you! You look like an honest woman, mademoiselle. You are too young and innocent to have this burden." He shook his head. "If you give me your word that you will send me evidence of your grandmother's cremation, I see no reason to confiscate your passport. But if you do not—"

"Gilbert!" Madame Leblanc cut in abruptly. Her face flushed. "You're letting her *go*? I remembered the dead man found in the shop after she left and called you to exact justice, yet you betray me?"

"*Tante*, what can I do? This woman was not even alive in 1942. She is not responsible for anything that happened seventy-five years ago."

What *had* happened all those years ago? Killing is the antithesis of what true alchemy stands for. It chilled my 300-year-old blood to think I could have been so close to a murder and not prevented it.

Alchemy is about life, not death. Alchemical transformations strengthen and purify the basic nature of both inanimate objects and people. Corrupted metals being transmuted into pure gold and mortal people stopping the deterioration of their bodies. The Philosopher's Stone and the resulting Elixir of Life are found through rigorous scientific study and focused pure intent.

We alchemists aren't immortal. It's an oversimplification to say the Elixir of Life is a path to living forever. We *can* be killed; we simply don't age in the same way as normal people. It's a science that the world hasn't proven ready to embrace. Those of us who've gone public have rarely met with a good end. That's why there was no way I was speaking up now.

I felt the gold locket I wore around my neck, with a miniature painting of my brother and a photograph of Ambrose. I'd always felt responsible for the deaths of my little brother and the man I'd loved with all my heart. Was I responsible for Jasper's death, too?

"This is very serious, you understand. I realize she is your grandmother, but if we find you are shielding her because she is elderly—"

"I'm not."

"I'm trusting you, mademoiselle."

I nodded in what I hoped was a show of meek acquiescence. One of the advantages of looking young is that people underestimate you. Even when I truly was only twenty-eight, most people had no idea what I was capable of. I was an accomplished simpler—a person especially good with plants—by the time I was a teenager, and I unlocked alchemy's deepest secrets a decade later.

"I am truly sorry about your grandmother," Gendarme Gilbert said. "I hate to see it trouble you so. Remember her for the woman you knew. You are not the same woman as she, not responsible for her deeds."

I stole a glance at Blanche Leblanc. She wasn't convinced.

The world is a constantly changing place. Technological advances made it both easier and harder to hide. Yet I've always found that the best way to stay safe is to hide in plain sight. I was so certain I would no longer know anyone in Paris. It never occurred to me that a *child* would remember me.

I tossed a handful of Euros on the table and fled from the ambush. It took every ounce of my willpower not to break into a sprint as soon as I stepped out of the café. When I turned the corner, I ran.

My chest burned. I was still weak. Too weak to be running across Paris from a threat out of the past.

I was out of breath and wheezing when I unlocked the heavy blue door to my building, pushed on the thick brass knocker in the middle of the door, and used the worn wooden railing to pull myself up the three flights of stairs. My lungs were on fire by the time I reached my apartment. I caught my breath and bolted the door behind me.

In addition to my pounding heart and burning lungs, my ears buzzed. At first I thought it was the stress of the situation taking over my whole body, but then I saw the source of the sound—half a dozen bees circled outside the kitchen window. Though I'd wrapped *Non Degenera Alchemia* well, it wasn't good enough. Its scent was still attracting bees. Not the musty scent of a decaying antique book, but the smell of sweet honey and spicy cloves. It was as if the book was aging *backwards*.

I walked across the main room to the kitchenette. A wood-framed window of thick glass separated me from the bees. I wasn't normally frightened of the small insects. They lived in harmony with nature and were essential to the plant cycle of life. But these bees... I looked more closely. One of the swarm flew away. I hoped his comrades would follow suit. And then I saw my mistake. The bee that had flown away hadn't given up. He was giving himself space to achieve more speed. He flew straight at the window. I jumped back as he smashed the glass with a splat. His fuzzy body fell to the window sill below.

I looked away and shivered. I didn't want to end up like the kamikaze bee. I hadn't yet found what I needed to in Paris, but how could I risk what would happen if I stayed?

There was no way to prove Zoe Faust from 1942 was dead, because she wasn't. I'd have to fake a death certificate, which was possible but inadvisable. I keep my secret by being careful, and the one man I knew who could forge documents was dead. Plus it would take time I didn't have. If I remained in Paris, I risked bringing my secret into the open. My life would be under a dangerous level of scrutiny, especially with Madame Leblanc and forensic evidence to fuel the accusations.

I lit a burner and set a kettle of water on the stove. Tea would replenish my body, calm my nerves, and allow me to think. As I contemplated my options, a knock sounded on the door.

"I know you are inside, Zoe Faust," Madame Leblanc's voice echoed through the door. "I have the information about your past that you crave. I can tell you what my nephew cannot."

CHAPTER 6

I flung open the door and immediately regretted it. Though I was careful about leaving any evidence of alchemy in the open, I hadn't been expecting guests and hadn't taken stock of what was visible at the moment.

"What do you want?" I stood blocking the doorway.

"I want the truth," Madame Leblanc said. "In return, I will tell you what you wish to know."

I gripped the side of the door, hesitating with the door open barely wide enough to see all of Madame Leblanc's face.

"The reason I remember you so clearly," she continued, "enough to know the truth that you and your 'grandmother' are one in the same, is because the image of that man, Jasper Dubois, is seared into my mind. I will never forget it."

"What did you see?" My heart beat in my throat.

"When the ashes from the fire were cleared, my friend Suzette and I played in the ruins. We were five years old. We were the ones who found him."

"I'm so sorry," I said. I meant it. What an awful discovery for a child to make.

She tilted her head in acknowledgment of the sympathy.

"My grandmother didn't tell me that Jasper was still in Paris when the fire broke out," I said. Had he been hiding from me?

"You are either wrong or lying. This is why I called my nephew. Jasper Dubois did not perish in the fire. He was *stabbed to death*."

I didn't have time to react because a precocious bee had squeezed its way through a joint in the thick window frame. It flew straight toward Madame Leblanc. It landed on her wrist. She swore creatively and slapped her hand. The dead bee fell to the floor, but not before it left its stinger in her tender flesh. She pulled up her sleeve and I caught a brief glimpse of a black tattoo on her forearm. Had she been branded by a concentration camp? Was the discovery of a body one of her last memories of childhood freedom?

"Come inside," I said, my mood involuntarily softening. I could never resist helping people when I had the resources to do so. Refusing assistance wasn't in my nature. "I have a calendula salve that should help the sting."

Madame Leblanc gave me a curious look. She hesitated for only a moment, then followed me inside and accepted the salve.

"You should—" I began.

"I know how to apply a salve. I'm familiar with most forms of medicines. Getting old has as many frustrations as it does pleasures. I do envy you."

"My grandmother taught me—"

She snorted. "Grandmother."

"You truly believe in witchcraft, madame? I'm sorry it's disturbing that I look so much like my grandmother."

Madame Leblanc walked to the narrow kitchen window overlooking the courtyard.

"Those must be fragrant flowers in the window sill. I have never seen so many bees." She closed her eyes and swayed.

"Can I offer you a seat?"

"You are still as kind as you always were," she said, refusing the seat and standing as tall as her frail frame allowed. "But this is not over. You may be able to fool the rest of the world, but I know you are the same woman who disguised a murder as an accident. I will be sure Gilbert uncovers the truth about what you did to poor Jasper Dubois. My nephew will figure out what you did—and I will figure out what you *are*."

With that she tossed her silk scarf across her shoulder and turned on her designer heel. "*Au revoir*, Zoe Faust," she called out from down the hallway. "For now."

Standing stunned in my doorway, I wondered where I'd gone wrong. My plan had seemed so simple a week ago. The book that had brought Dorian to life had pointed the way to Notre Dame. It was here I would find the last piece of the puzzle to save Dorian's life.

Only it hadn't proven that simple.

I'd been naïve in thinking Paris would hold obvious answers. I'd been hopeful because I hadn't known about Notre Dame's history with backward alchemists until Dorian's book caught on fire that spring. Instead of reducing the book to ash, the fire had brought forth hidden ink and revealed its connection to the cathedral. The unexpected transformation was significant, I knew, yet I couldn't see what exactly it told me about Notre Dame. I was missing something.

I thought the second living gargoyle might shed light on the solution. Unfortunately because I wasn't an academic, an architect, or a stone carver, I'd been refused access to the gargoyle who was trapped in stone. The university's staff studying the bizarrely posed statue didn't realize a living being was trapped inside, and I couldn't very well tell them. I had to find another way to see the creature. And until now, I thought I'd have time to do so.

I also wondered if there might be other backward alchemists out there. If there were, they might be able to help me. I hadn't been able to decipher parts of Dorian's backward alchemy book, which wasn't surprising since alchemy is filled with secrets, obfuscation, and codes. Most alchemists learn through a combination of personal experimentation in a laboratory and an apprentice-ship with a mentor. I hadn't worked with a mentor since studying with Nicolas Flamel nearly three centuries ago, and I'd fled from my training before it was complete. I was only in touch with one alchemist—a former slave, Tobias Freeman, who hadn't studied alchemy formally either, and who didn't know any alchemists besides me. Even among properly educated alchemists, most don't know each other because secrecy and suspicion are so ingrained in our training that we hide the truth from everyone. There was no one to help me.

In other words, my trip had been a bust. And now, on top of everything, there was the murder of Jasper Dubois. What had I gotten myself into by returning to Paris after all these years?

I locked the apartment door and breathed deeply. I closed my eyes, but the buzzing of the bees prevented me from relaxing. Rooting through drawers, I found a roll of tape and sealed the joints of the war-time building's window frame to foil the bees.

I wished I could call Tobias to think through my dilemma. But there was nothing more my one true alchemist friend could tell me about backward alchemy or alchemy's connection to Notre Dame, since he'd had even less formal training than I'd had. It was his nonjudgmental friendship I craved.

But I couldn't bring myself to burden him. Not now. Though I knew he'd want to help me, he had his own life-and-death situation to deal with. He was caring for his wife of sixty years, Rosa, who was dying of old age in their home in Detroit. Rosa wasn't an alchemist and had continued to age. Still, Tobias and Rosa had loved each other for more joyous years than most of us get.

Instead I sat down, pulled out my phone, and searched for references to Jasper Dubois online. Millions of hits, but none of them my Jasper. Narrowing the search, I found reference to the 1942 fire in a French library's online newspaper archives. It was only a small article, providing no insights. Much more space was devoted to the war. I wouldn't find answers with the tools of the modern world.

My fingers hovered over the screen for a moment, then typed a search I hoped I wouldn't use until I had an answer about how to save Dorian's life. Flights home to Portland.

The more affordable flights connecting to Portland left in the morning, but Madame Leblanc's nephew would probably look for me the next day. I bought a ticket for the last flight that left that night. I would arrive home in the wee hours after a nineteen-hour journey, but I had little choice.

I opened the floorboard under which I was hiding *Non Degenera Alchemia*. I'd chosen this apartment rental because the building had been around for centuries. I knew it would have little nooks where I could hide things I didn't want anyone to find. Not that I was expecting trouble, but old habits die hard. Now I was glad I'd taken the precaution.

The book was safely ensconced in its hole. In spite of my overzealous wrapping, two now-dead bees had made their way underneath the top layer of plastic. They had squished themselves to death in their quest to reach the book. Bees are a minor symbol in alchemy and they are used even more in backward alchemy. Many of the disturbing woodcut illustrations in Dorian's book showed bees circling counterclockwise above a menagerie of dead animals. Beyond the scent of honey that permeated the pages as it aged, was there something more drawing the insects to it?

I didn't have to open the pages to see the woodcut illustrations. The twisted imagery was unforgettable. My mind saw bees filling the skies in a counterclockwise formation, stinging the eyes of the people and animals that writhed on the ground.

From those unsettling coded images in the book, I'd taught myself how to create an alchemical Tea of Ashes that temporarily stopped Dorian from returning to stone. Superficially, the process looked easy—mixing ingredients in fire that quickly transformed into salt. Much easier than true alchemy, which in addition to basic ingredients involves pure intent, time, and energy. Backward alchemy is a shortcut, a straight line through what should be a labyrinthine maze of discovery leading to true knowledge. Because the short-cuts here were backward alchemy, it was a delicate balance between adding life to Dorian and taking it from me.

Before leaving Portland I thought I'd found the right balance to make Dorian a large enough batch of Tea of Ashes for him to stay healthy while I was gone in Paris. I was wrong. The transformation had failed, and even worse, it left me sick for three full days—too sick to travel and too sick to do anything much beyond lie in bed. I'd lost so much time, and now I was being forced from Paris after less than a week.

But I wasn't giving up. I had five hours until I was due at the airport.

The question was, with five hours left in Paris, could I do what I hadn't been able to do in five days?

CHAPTER 7

Sitting at the edge of the sagging bed in the small apartment, I rubbed a bee sting on my arm that was still noticeable and looked through the small set of tinctures and salves I'd brought from home. Traveling with the preparations was a force of habit, but in this case it was also necessary after I'd been sickened by the Tea of Ashes and stung by bees interested in Dorian's book.

After arriving in Paris I'd taken *Non Degenera Alchemia* to Notre Dame to compare its illustrations to the carvings on the façade of the cathedral. For the record, bringing a book of unknown power to an ancient cathedral to which it's tied is a very bad idea. That experiment led to many stings as I shooed bees away from the book; I used my photocopies for reference after that. I'd also visited many libraries and bookshops in hopes of discovering obscure references to Notre Dame's connections to alchemy that I hadn't been able to find in my own alchemy books or in mainstream publications.

One of the places I'd visited was a narrow bookshop within view of Notre Dame. Appropriately, it was called *Bossu Livres*—Hunchback Books. It was presumably named for the famous character Victor Hugo's *The Hunchback of Notre Dame*. The bookshop's specialty was the history of Paris, with a large section on Notre Dame Cathedral. The bookseller thought I was a graduate student conducting research for my dissertation, so he didn't bat an eye when I asked about information on any secret societies that used to meet at Notre Dame. I bet it wasn't even the strangest research question he'd received. He was the only bookseller who'd taken my request seriously and spent more than a few minutes looking through his files. Though he hadn't been able to help at the time, he'd told me to check back in a few days.

Hoping to continue the research Madame Leblanc had interrupted that morning, I hurried across Pont Notre-Dame to the small Île de la Cité island where the cathedral stood. Normally I took time to appreciate my surroundings, especially when I was in a city as storied as Paris. But not today. If I let myself slow down, I knew I'd imagine Madame Leblanc and her nephew over my shoulder and the ghost of Jasper Dubois in front of me.

It was a warm day, close to the start of summer, and the scents of Paris swirled around me. Strong coffee, smooth wine, freshly baked bread, and… something smoky that stirred a memory I couldn't quite place. I glanced upward. The Gallery of Gargoyles was visible from the ground, though the personalities of the stone creatures were left to the imagination at this distance. "What are your secrets?" I whispered.

I pulled my eyes from the limestone façade, once painted brightly but now a natural golden tan, and continued to the narrow street that housed the bookshop. The shop was barely wider than I was tall, probably the same square footage as the interior of the Airstream trailer that was parked in my driveway in Portland. The small space was filled with treasures, stacked from floor to ceiling.

I pushed on the solid door, painted a bright blue. It resisted. The brass handle didn't budge either. I peeked into the window. A ray of sunlight shone over a display in the window of Paris-based poets from the nineteenth century. Aside from that illuminated corner, the interior of the shop was dark. A sign in the window read *Fermé*. The shop was closed.

I leaned against the stone wall and tried to keep my spirits from being completely crushed. At every turn, I faced another obstacle.

I gave a start as the bell jangled and the door of the bookshop swung open.

"I didn't mean to frighten you, mademoiselle," said the man who opened the door.

"It's quite all right. I'm pleased to find you're open after all."

He waved me inside. Only then did I realize it was the same bookseller I'd previously spoken with. A plain man in his forties, he had a forgettable face. The impression was rounded out by thinning brown hair, leathery skin, and the hint of a stoop. If he were to lean against a shelf of his leather-bound books, I had the feeling that he'd blend in and be invisible to customers. He'd told me his name just yesterday, but I struggled to recall it. "It's good to see you, Monsieur Augustin."

"Please, call me Lucien." He turned the sign from *Fermé* to *Ouvert*.

My eyes swept over the shelves as I breathed in the scent of books made over the centuries from various wood pulps and animal skins. These books were decaying as normal books did, with a faint hint of mildew detectable in the older ones and nary a bee in sight. Normally I loved spaces crammed full of books, but the haphazard nature of this room kept me off balance. If they had a filing system, it was unlike anything I'd ever encountered.

"I was wondering if you'd had a chance to look for the book on Notre Dame secret societies you mentioned," I said. "I know I told you I'd check back with you in a few days if I didn't receive a call from you, but I'm leaving Paris sooner than expected."

"Finished the research for your thesis already?" Though he spoke with a French accent, the inflection in the question suggested he'd lived elsewhere for a time. Under other circumstances I would have asked him about it, because linguistic nuances tell you so much about a person, but that conversation wasn't meant to happen today.

"Unfortunately a family emergency came up. I have to leave Paris immediately." I feigned interest in a photographic history of the cafés of Paris to avoid meeting his gaze as I lied.

He frowned. "I'm so sorry to hear that. Because I found something of interest."

My eyes snapped up. "What is it you've found?"

"A slim volume, probably produced in the fourteenth century." He hesitated. "Probably not what you're after. Never mind."

"No, please tell me what you found."

"It's called *The Backward Alchemists of Notre Dame.*"

My breath caught.

"Bizarre, no?" Lucien said. "I didn't think it was what you were looking for," he added with a shake of his head, misinterpreting my expression. "*Dommage.* I thought it was worth a try. It sounded like a secret society. The type of thing you mentioned as a possible interest for your thesis."

"I'd love to see it." Hope welled in me again. It was exactly what I needed. *This could lead me to a backward alchemist.*

"*Bon.* I am glad I requested it. The book is being sent here to the shop from a storage facility. Perhaps if you came back tomorrow morning—"

"I'm leaving Paris tonight." I didn't want to think about what awaited me with Madame Leblanc pressuring her nephew to flag my passport.

"Let me check on the status of the shipment. Maybe we'll get lucky." He disappeared through a door shaped like an embrasure of a castle and nearly as narrow as an arrow-slit. I let my eyes wander across the high shelves crammed full of books in a dozen languages, all related to the history of Paris, but none of them organized with any system I could discern. I picked up a book on unique Parisian architecture from the nineteenth century with a focus on abandoned buildings. I turned the pages, stopping at a photograph of *le Cabaret de L'Enfer*. As was typical of the French, the old nightclub was a complete embodiment of its theme: The Nightclub of Hell. It typified the quirky French ethos.

I knew the famous nightclub. *Le Cabaret de L'Enfer* had been one of Ambrose's favorite late-night clubs in the early 1900s. He was a country lad at heart and always felt most comfortable when we lived in the countryside. But because I could help more people when we lived in more populated areas, we always returned to Paris. After a time, he came to love it as I did. *Le Cabaret de L'Enfer* was one of the places that captured his imagination. He wasn't alone. His son Percy had once thought of opening a similar club in London, but he was a lazy, lazy man, so his talk never turned into action. But more ambitious entrepreneurs had opened a parallel nightclub next door to the Paris cafe: *Le Ciel*. Heaven.

I was stirred from the memory of a bygone Paris by a movement at the corner of my eye. Lucien had returned, shaking his head. *"Je suis desolé, mademoiselle.* No luck."

"Could you mail it to me in Oregon? I'll pay in advance for expedited shipping. Plus extra for your trouble."

"Extra is not necessary, mademoiselle. But you are kind." His eyes turned to the book in my hands. *"Le Cafe de L'Enfer.* You know of this landmark? It has quite a history."

"I've read about it. It's too bad it wasn't preserved."

"I have something you might like. I believe I have an old postcard of the Hell-mouth doorway."

He flipped through a stack of postcards on a stand near the cash register, then drew his hand back abruptly. *"Merde.* Damn these frail fingernails."

I winced as he held his finger, clearly in pain. "I might have something that can help, monsieur."

I wound a finger around my white hair as I reached into my purse with my other hand. I carried a tincture with me that would be good for frail fingernails. It was an herbal remedy that helped me with my hair, which would have been thin and brittle without extra care. Through healthy eating and topical treatments, I was able to keep it looking and feeling similar to how it did when I was young. Though I'd never again have thick, long hair, my hair was healthy enough to fool people into thinking I dyed it white as a trendy fashion statement and that I followed a vegan diet because it was the latest fad.

Lucien gratefully, if skeptically, accepted the tincture. I wrote out instructions for how to use it while he completed my order. I'd just have to hope that the book would provide useful insight whenever it did arrive to me in Portland.

The bell above the door sounded. Lucien's friendly eyes turned dark as the young woman with an overzealous application of eyeliner asked if he had any books containing maps of the catacombs of Paris, the tangled tunnels lined with human bones.

"*Je suis desolé, mademoiselle,*" he said, and the customer departed.

"I think I saw a book on the subject in a pile over there." I pointed to a jam-packed bookshelf. "I bet I can catch her."

Lucien shook his head firmly. "*Moutards.* Maps of the catacombs are not for them. They sneak into the catacombs with complete disregard for their history. They use it as a *bôit de nuit,* their own personal nightclub. As if it were *le Cafe de L'Enfer.* This desecration of the catacombs has become acceptable!"

"Urban explorers," I said.

He narrowed his eyes at me.

"I'm not one," I added hastily. "But I've heard about it. Adventurers, kids staging raves, artists." They seemed harmless enough to me. Kids enjoying their youth in Paris. I was too old to understand the appeal myself. Or perhaps the underground crypts disturbed my alchemical sensibilities. Relics like human bones were to be revered, not made into entertainment. I'd visited the ossuary once, shortly after the underground graves had been opened to the public in the late 1800s, when an appreciation for macabre curiosities turned the rows of skulls and bones into a tourist attraction. I'd never had a desire to return.

The bookseller looked from his dim sanctuary to the vibrant street outside. "I do not know what this old city is coming to."

The wind was picking up as I stepped out of the shop. I turned up the collar of my silver raincoat, touched a hand to my locket, and glanced at my watch. I had time for one more errand. It was time to see a possible member of the family: Dorian's brother.

CHAPTER 8

The previous month, a gargoyle resembling the chimeras of Notre Dame had been found on the Charles Bridge in Prague. There were no witnesses aside from a drunk who slept outside near the bridge. The man swore the five-foot statue had limped onto the bridge by itself as dawn was breaking. Needless to say, his testimony was dismissed as the ravings of a drunken fool.

Authorities thought there must have been at least one other witness, because a half-empty bottle of absinthe was cradled in the statue's stone arms. The liquor had been bottled this year. Yet no witnesses could be found. It must have been a prank, the police surmised. Someone who shared a similar sense of humor with the thieves who were leaving gold dust in place of gold figurines in museums across Europe, offering no trace of how they got in or out.

I knew the true explanation for both of these occurrences. There were no thieves, and there was no prankster. Gold created through backward alchemy was reverting to dust. And this was a gargoyle like Dorian, who was brought to life but was now reverting to stone.

Architectural scholars recognized the statue as being one of Viollet-le-Duc's creations for Notre Dame, and it was quickly asserted that this was the stolen carving that hadn't been seen in over a century.

Only sketches of the gargoyle existed, and without any photographs it was all scholarly speculation. It was determined that more study was needed, and that architects and stonemasons would be the most appropriate people to study the beast.

The Czech authorities readily handed it over to France. Now the gargoyle frozen in stone was under study at a Paris university's architecture department.

In spite of my deferential tone and fluent French, I'd been denied admittance to study the statue by the scholar in charge, Professor Chevalier. I'd been confident I'd win him over with enough time, but time was no longer an option. An idea began to take shape in my mind. One that my young friend Brixton would undoubtedly call "wicked."

As I walked back to my apartment to pick up *Not Untrue Alchemy*, I made a phone call to check with Professor Chevalier's secretary, making sure he wasn't allergic to bees. I claimed to be a nurse who wanted to check how an allergic patient was doing, and the secretary assured me I had the wrong number, because she was certain the professor wasn't allergic to bees. If I wished to hear it from his own ears, I could call back when she expected him to return to his office within half an hour.

Perfect.

I freed *Not Untrue Alchemy* from its hiding place, made sure the book was carefully bundled, and pressed the few possessions I'd brought to Paris into my rucksack. Hurrying down the stairs and into the courtyard, I cast what might be my last glance at the centuries-old building. Would this be the last time I was ever in Paris? Instead of walking toward the university, I made a two-block detour to a spot I'd been working my way up to visiting.

Two minutes later, I stood outside the Auberge Nicolas Flamel, the Michelin star restaurant and oldest house in Paris. It had also once been the home of my mentor.

The plaque that adorned the building began with the words *Maison de Nicolas Flamel et de Perenelle sa femme. Pour conserver le souvenir de leur fondation charitable.* The home of Nicolas Flamel his wife Perenelle, honoring their charitable work.

I ran my fingertips across the rough stone that had stood since they built their home in 1407, and that had served as a restaurant for over a hundred years. His building had stood the test of time much better than the building that had housed Elixir. Because of the fire... I pushed thoughts of poor Jasper Dubois from my mind.

Alchemical symbols were carved into many of the stones on the Auberge Nicolas Flamel, though I knew for a fact they hadn't been made by Nicolas or Perenelle. The carvings came later, long after they had faked their deaths and abandoned their city home for the French countryside. These symbols hadn't been made by true alchemists, but were instead laymen's ideas of what alchemical symbols would look like, added once Nicolas had become infamous. The decorative letters and animals of the faux alchemists had worn smooth over time, but were still visible. As was a loose stone.

That was odd. In a section of solid stone, nonexistent joints of a brick shouldn't have been able to crumble.

Had someone purposefully defaced the building? Though it hadn't been Nicolas's home for centuries, the violation of the home he'd crafted infuriated me. Ignoring the sharp glare of a waiter smoking a cigarette on his break, I stepped onto the windowsill to see what was going on. The light backpack weighed heavily on my shoulders, reminding me how weak I still was.

On the loose stone was an alchemical carving. A real one. *Could this have been carved by Nicolas himself?*

The waiter muttered about uncivilized tourists as I tugged on the stone that bore the ouroboros. It didn't give. Then I thought about the symbol itself. The ouroboros—the serpent eating its own tail, representing the cyclical nature of alchemy. Following the meaning of the symbol, I gave the stone not an outward tug but a clockwise twist. That set it free.

Behind the ouroboros stone was a faded note on vellum.

Addressed to me.

My heart pounded in my ears and the voice of the aggrieved waiter faded away. The familiar hand of Nicolas Flamel had scrawled a note in old French: *Dearest Zoe. If you find this one day...*

The rest of the note was illegible. *No, no, no.* This couldn't be all there was! With shaking hands, I felt around behind the false brick. Nothing. I grabbed at the edges of the rough stone hole, getting nothing for my effort except a scrape across my knuckles.

I pulled my hand away, ran my fingertips over the soft, faded paper, and willed my eyes to see text that wasn't there. Was there anything left of the ink?

The waiter had brought a compatriot from inside the restaurant, a regal woman with leathery skin. She was at least twice my size and carried a rolling pin in her hand.

I could deal with the note later. I shoved the ouroboros brick back into place, making sure I heard a click, then jumped down from the windowsill and sped away from the house, the note from Nicolas in my pocket.

CHAPTER 9

I walked to the university in a haze, passing elegant women expertly maneuvering cobblestones in perversely high heels, shopkeepers reminiscent of centuries past closing up shop for the day, and sidewalk cafés radiating the mingling scents of cigarettes, wine, and espresso.

What had Nicolas wanted to tell me? And when had he left the message? It wasn't before I left Paris during the war, was it? I'd visited his home then and hadn't noticed the carving. Yet the vellum looked old. I hadn't been in hiding while living in Paris before the war, so why hadn't he sought me out if he was alive and in Paris? And if he was angry with me for leaving my apprenticeship so abruptly centuries ago, before I completed my training, why reach out to me at all? It didn't make sense.

Reaching the Left Bank, I saw groups of college students dressed up for a night out on the town. Evening was quickly approaching. With my distracted thoughts, I bumped into a young couple with their arms draped around each other. They were stopped in the middle of the sidewalk, a map in their hands. They folded the map and nodded at each other, but instead of walking toward a metro station, café, or bar, they knelt down and pried open the manhole they were standing on. On any other occasion, I would have been curious about a young couple climbing into the sewers, but not today. With a note from my mentor in my pocket and a gargoyle to meet, I continued on my way.

I couldn't stop thinking about Nicolas. If he was still alive, would he be able to help me with Dorian's backward alchemy dilemma? No. Of that I was certain. He'd once warned me of backward alchemy. True alchemy is about personal transformation and requires a personal sacrifice to create the Philosopher's Stone and the Elixir of Life. Backward alchemy, in his eyes, was the antithesis of alchemy's purity. Nicolas wouldn't even speak of it, except to warn me away from it.

I stopped in front of a slanted Linden tree and steadied myself on its trunk. The bark was smooth and comforting under my raw fingers. Being with a small piece of nature in the loud and crowded city took the edge off of the troubling realization that even if I found Nicolas, he would fight me rather than help me if my quest involved backward alchemy. Being the purist that he was, I could imagine him insisting that Dorian was an unnatural creature who shouldn't be alive. He would also be furious that I'd been so careless as to be recognized by Madame Leblanc, who was threatening to expose alchemy.

I reached the university without walking into traffic or crashing into a light post, which was about as much as I could hope for at the moment. When I reached the professor's door, I took Dorian's book out of its three layers of taut plastic.

"*Bonjour, monsieur*," I said from the doorway. "I was hoping to show you the architectural woodcuts in this antique book. I think when you see them, you'll understand why I'm so interested in seeing the gargoyle." I nodded toward the gargoyle standing in the corner of the office. More than a foot taller than Dorian, and with rougher edges, the gargoyle wore a pained expression on his stone face. Dorian had taken to calling him his "brother" ever since we learned of his existence the previous month.

"Chimera," the professor corrected me with a stern frown. "The sculpture is a chimera, not a gargoyle. Let me see this book."

I forced a smile and handed *Not Untrue Alchemy* to the professor. Technically, the term *gargoyle* only refers to a carving that serves as a water spout, with the stone creature's mouth and throat serving as the drainpipe. But the word *gargoyle* has become a general term for a range of stone creatures that perch on buildings. Even Dorian refers to himself as a gargoyle.

"Of course," I said. "The chimera. Do you mind if I open this window?" I moved to open it before he had a chance to reply.

He looked up from the book. "I'd prefer you did not—"

His words were drowned out by another sound. The buzzing of bees. The noise began softly, as a hum, but quickly rose to the level of a biblical swarm of locusts.

At least a dozen bees flew into the room. They circled the professor's hands. He dropped the book onto his desk and cried out as the stinging began.

It took all of my willpower to stop myself from rushing to help him. *Deep breath, Zoe. He'll be fine.*

Professor Chevalier swore and rushed from the room. I donned gloves and whisked the book into a plastic bag with an airtight seal. Half a dozen bees were trapped inside with the book. The rest followed the professor.

I closed the office door and locked it. I knew I didn't have much time, so I'd make the most of it. First things first: I left a salve on the desk that would help with the bee stings.

Next I slid *Not Untrue Alchemy* from the bag, careful to keep the bees inside. The book fell open to the page it always fell open to. These were the words that had once accidentally brought Dorian to life, when Jean Eugène Robert-Houdin had read the words as a dramatic addition to his stage show.

I began to read the mysterious words aloud.

Here in Paris, I felt the power of the words so deeply that I was caught off guard. My body began to sway as strongly as when I'd been on a fishing boat during an unexpected typhoon. I braced myself against the wall with my free hand and looked at the gargoyle, hoping he wouldn't begin to shake as much as I was. Then he'd be sure to fall and shatter.

The gargoyle didn't move.

I sat down on a nearby chair and cradled the confounding book on my lap. Reading from an alchemy book alone shouldn't direct so much power toward myself. And certainly not this quickly. Alchemy involves practicing in solitude in one's own alchemy lab, going through the processes of calcination, dissolution, separation, fermentation, distillation, and coagulation.

But this book was *backward* alchemy, where shortcuts abound and one element is sacrificed for another. Alchemy can seem like magic, because we can't see the mechanism of the transfer of energy under a microscope. But it's not any different than theoretical physics. You don't have to see science to believe in it. Alchemists were early chemists, but because of "puffers"—the fools who only saw alchemy as a way to make money and sought favor with kings by transmuting lead into gold for political gains—alchemy was squashed, twisted, and discredited. Across time, whenever true alchemists have tried to come out from the shadows, it has ended badly.

Still feeling like I was seasick, I focused my breathing. *Think, Zoe.* I read the incantation again. The gargoyle again failed to come to life.

There was one more thing I wanted to try. I had a packet of tea with me, leftovers of the Tea of Ashes I'd made for Dorian before coming to Paris to stave off his backward transformation into stone. I'd saved the remnants of the ash-like substance that I'd created from the living plants in my garden.

The gargoyle's mouth was frozen half open, revealing a dark gray tongue and sharp teeth. I rubbed the ashes onto his stone tongue. The gray powder coated the rough surface, disappearing into the stone pores.

I stepped back. Nothing.

The sound of a buzzing bee interrupted the silence. One of the bees inside the book's wrapping was frantically trying to escape. I shut the book and pushed it back inside. Let the bees have it. It wasn't doing me any good.

The buzzing subsided, but the room wasn't silent. There was now another sound.

Wheezing.

My eyes flew to the gargoyle's dark face. His gray eyes began to water.

"*Peux-tu m'entendre?*" I asked. Can you hear me?

The gargoyle wasn't able to move his stone body, but his eyes were alive. I felt a jolt of pity as his sad eyes locked onto mine. Gray stone lips twitched. I wished I'd been wrong. I wished what the scholars believed was the truth, that this was simply a gargoyle carved by a stone carver with an offbeat sense of humor. Not this— a living soul trapped in stone.

I also wished I'd been wrong about Dorian's book. It had led me to the recipe for the Tea of Ashes and to Notre Dame, but it appeared to have served its purpose. It wasn't a miracle that could save the gargoyles from reverting to stone.

"*Aidez moi,*" the gargoyle croaked in a deep gravelly voice. "Help… Help me."

The last words were barely audible. The wheezing stopped. His lips froze, but for a moment longer his liquid gray eyes bore into mine. He blinked once more, then went still.

CHAPTER 10

Dorian's black eyes opened wide and he blinked at me.

"*Mais c'est formidable!* It is true I have *un frère—a brother!*—and he is being held captive—" He broke off with a curse that had been popular a century ago and began to pace across the creaking hardwood floor. "*Mais attendez...* your visit to Notre Dame did not yet yield the answers we need, yet you are home."

I hadn't had trouble leaving Paris and my connecting flight had touched down in Portland shortly after midnight. Dorian and I sat in my Craftsman house's attic, which I'd half converted into an office for my online business, Elixir. I hadn't slept at all on the flight. Flying affects my body's natural rhythms more intensely than it does most people, because the planetary alignments go by too quickly. It scrambles my head. I much prefer to travel by car or boat, or on foot. I'd felt so alone on the long flights, fleeing both the country and the prospect of finding my mentor Nicolas, who I hadn't seen since I'd run away from alchemy.

"Did you fear they would arrest you for sending bees after the bad man who is keeping my brother captive?" Dorian asked.

I sat down on a hefty crate I'd pushed into the corner next to the sloping ceiling. How to explain what had happened? "Not exactly."

"She comes home speaking in riddles," Dorian muttered.

Home. That was exactly how I felt. Like I was returning home. I *was* home. I was again reminded that this was the first time in decades that I felt I had someplace besides my trailer to call home. I was simultaneously comforted and terrified. I loved the friends I'd made since moving to Portland several months ago. But if I failed to unlock the secrets of backward alchemy, my newfound best friend Dorian would suffer a fate worse than death. If I failed to convince a man who once believed in magic that believing in alchemy wasn't to be feared, I would lose my relationship with Max, my first chance at love in nearly a century. And now, if I dared return to Paris to finish what I'd started, I'd risk exposing my own secrets and the secrets of alchemy that the world wasn't yet ready for.

With Dorian in front of me, I couldn't bring myself to tell him about the complicated accusation of murder from 1942. Telling Dorian of my own entanglement in a disturbing death from so many years ago wouldn't help anyone. Nor could I tell him that I realized true alchemists like Nicolas Flamel might not understand that Dorian wasn't inherently evil. I didn't want to crush his hopes.

"How bad is your arm?" I asked, watching Dorian's awkward stance as he limped back and forth across the room, his clawed feet tapping on the floorboards with each step he took.

"*Ce n'est rien.*"

"In that case, move your left arm for me."

"I told you," he snapped, "it is nothing." He flapped his wings impatiently. "A kidnapped fellow gargoyle and the riddle of my book are much more important."

"I'll figure it out. I'm closer than ever before, Dorian."

Dorian stopped pacing and studied my face. "What else is wrong? What are you not telling me?"

"Why do you say that?"

He narrowed his liquidy black eyes. "I have known you for long enough to have learned your expressions, Zoe. When you are sad, your shoulders fall. When you are angry yet pretend you are not, you purse your lips. And when you are frightened, you tug at your hair. *You are frightened.*"

Apparently I would be a bad poker player. I put my hands into my lap.

"What has you so scared, *mon amie?*" Dorian asked. "I have faith you will help me. Help *us.*" He hopped up onto the crate next to me—he was only three-and-a-half feet tall—and patted my shoulder with his wing. His wings were heavy stone but simultaneously soft and malleable.

"I'm tired. That's all. I've got killer jet lag."

"For someone so old and wise, have you yet to learn you are a terrible actress?"

"You may recall I did fine on my own before you showed up in my living room."

"Yes. But you do much better when you do not lie."

I couldn't argue with that. Since one of the core tenets of alchemy is purity of intent, that's how I live my life. I don't feel comfortable lying. Whenever I can avoid it, I do. When I bought the crumbling Craftsman house in Portland, Oregon, earlier in the year, I didn't make up a story that I was a renovator or a house-flipper. When you act naturally, it's easier for people to believe what they want to. Real estate agents filled in the blanks that made sense to their worldview. They believed I was a young woman who wanted a bargain and didn't know what she was getting herself into. And my new neighbors assumed I was a good fit for the artsy Hawthorne neighborhood because I dyed my hair white to be trendy. In truth, I'm 340 years old, my hair turned naturally white nearly 300 years ago, and I wanted the falling-apart house so I could build myself an alchemy lab without people wondering what the construction was all about.

"You're an insightful gargoyle."

"*Oui.* I know this."

How could one refuse to answer an insightful, arrogant gargoyle? "Something happened yesterday," I said.

I gave Dorian a brief overview of the unexpected turn of events that had driven me from Paris, telling him about Madame Leblanc, who'd known me when she was a child, and the murder of my old shop assistant. "Madame Leblanc said that her policeman grandnephew would figure out what *I'd done*," I concluded, "and she'd figure out what *I am*."

Dorian's eyes grew wide with horror as I spoke. "*C'est terrible.* Of course you made the right decision to leave Paris. You could not risk yourself." He jumped down from the crate and began to shake. A seizure? This was a new development.

"Are you all right? Are you feeling yourself turn to stone all at once?"

He shook his head. "I have had a thought most *horrible.* This woman—she might have attempted to put a stake through your heart!"

I smiled for perhaps the first time since Madame Leblanc had confronted me at Notre Dame.

"It is not humorous, Zoe. If other people fail to take her seriously, she might resort to violent action. You are a pale woman who has been alive for centuries. What was she supposed to think?"

"I'm not that pale."

Dorian crinkled his forehead, causing his horns to wriggle. "All the hair on your body is white. People do not come much paler than you."

"You think she might think I'm a vampire? That's crazy. Vampires don't exist."

"Neither do alchemists, according to most people."

"Fair point. But what was I supposed to do? I couldn't tell her the truth. Besides, she already told me her mother thought I was a witch."

Dorian sputtered. "This is worse! Being burned at the stake would be even more painful. Fire takes longer to kill. Your skin would blister—"

"Hey," I cut in, "nobody is getting staked through the heart *or* burned alive."

"You are the one who said she was after the truth."

"Which isn't much better, I agree, but she doesn't want to kill me—only expose me."

"You did the only reasonable thing by leaving. You cannot help me if you are in prison. Or on the run in France. Or dying with a wooden stake in your chest."

"I get the point." I cringed at my unintended pun.

The gargoyle was right. He was a lovable and infuriating combination of adolescent puppy dog and wise old sage. Madame Leblanc was not someone to dismiss. I'd known people like her in different countries and different times. Women who were too easily dismissed when they should not have been. Some of them suffered in silence. Some of them formed communities of like-minded souls. And some of them took revenge.

"What are we to do?" Dorian asked.

"I've been thinking about that. I need to tell you about the other gargoyle—"

"My brother."

I hesitated.

"Why did you purse your pale lips?" Dorian asked. He tilted his head. "Perhaps you should buy some lipstick. That might squelch the vampire rumor."

"There's no vampire rumor."

"Whatever you say, ashen alchemist. Why were you pursing your pallid lips?"

"It's not good to think of him as a brother. You don't know him, Dorian."

"What is there to know? He is my brother."

He blinked at me so innocently that I felt tears welling in my eyes. "You shouldn't get too attached to the idea of another living gargoyle. We might not be able to bring him back from stone. When I saw him—"

"You *saw* him?" Dorian flapped his wings and wriggled his snout. "You did not tell me this! You said he was being held captive by a mad professor—"

"I'm fairly certain I didn't say that. But it's true, I did see him after I sent a swarm of bees after the professor so I could sneak into his office."

"*Bon.*" Dorian slapped his good hand against his knee. "Is my brother arriving later in a crate? I cannot believe you neglected to tell me of this upon your arrival."

"I didn't mention it first thing because I couldn't get him out of Paris, Dorian. He's more than a foot taller than you—there was no way I could carry him out of the university."

"Why did you go to see him without an escape plan? You caused harm to the professor but not so you could free my brother? This makes no sense. What were you thinking?" He flapped his wings.

"I'm most concerned about you. I needed to test what we thought we knew about your book and the Tea of Ashes."

"A test? You think *mon frère* is a test?" He harrumphed.

"If it worked, it would have helped him."

"Yet it failed." His wings folded around him.

"The Tea of Ashes transformed him for a brief moment. Only long enough for me to know he's still alive in there." I trembled at the memory of the gargoyle's pleading gray eyes.

Dorian peered intently at me. "The great Dorian Robert-Houdin knows what you need. I will bring food. Wait here. I will return shortly. Then you will tell me all about my brother."

I gave Dorian a hug. "I missed you, my friend."

"*Moi aussi, mon amie.*" He cleared his throat. This level of emotion was terribly undignified for a Frenchman born in 1860.

CHAPTER 11

Maybe Dorian was right that I'd have a clearer head after eating something. Especially Dorian's cooking.

Dorian had taken over my kitchen pretty much the day I moved into my crumbling Craftsman. Shortly before his death, Dorian's father, Jean Eugène Robert-Houdin, had the idea to serve as a reference for his adopted gargoyle son. Robert-Houdin explained that his "distant relative" Dorian was badly disfigured and did not feel comfortable being seen in public, but was a good man who would be a great help as a companion to a blind person. Dorian's first job was for the chef who'd lost his sight in a kitchen fire. Dorian learned to cook from the famous French chef. He took to it so well that he'd been a culinary snob ever since.

When Dorian followed me to Portland to seek my help last winter, he was horrified to learn that I eat only plant-based foods. Since alchemists aren't immortal, I learned long ago to take care of my body. I've been following a vegan diet since before the word was invented. I was a "Pythagorean" at one time—the mathematician also preached the merits of a plant-based diet. It's been a challenge at times to live in the United States, England, and France, which is why I always appreciated my sojourns to India. I was hopeful when Sylvester Graham's Grahamite diet caught on in the United States in the 1930s, but was dismayed that while he endorsed vegetarianism, he shunned spices. What good is a long life without some spice?

In the months since Dorian and I began sharing the house and the kitchen, he experimented with how to cook the decadent French foods he loved with vegan ingredients. Cashew cream replaced heavy cream made of dairy. Smoked salts and spices replaced bacon. Mushrooms replaced meat. Though it took him a while to admit it, he loved his new recipes more than his old ones. Before I left on this trip to Paris, he'd already declared himself to be the greatest vegan chef in all of Portland.

I smiled at the thought. Then yawned. The adrenaline that had kept me going was wearing off.

Dorian returned to the attic a minute later with a stack of three containers balanced in his right hand. I again noticed his inability to move his left arm, but I knew that bringing it up again before he was ready wouldn't get me anywhere.

The snacks he carried included a spread of morel mushrooms cooked simply in olive oil and spices, including a black salt sprinkled on top. I scooped up a mouthful with a piece of bread. It was exquisite, as expected. When I took care of myself, I ate well but far more simply than this.

"Brixton found you these mushrooms at the market?" I asked. Our four-teen-year-old neighbor, the only person in Portland besides me who knew of Dorian's existence, had been bringing Dorian groceries while I was out of town. Brixton was also tending to my backyard garden, which was the excuse he gave for coming over to the house while I was gone.

"Not Brixton," Dorian said.

"You promised you'd tell me if you were going to use my credit card again."

"This is what you think of me?" His snout twitched. "*Non.* I have my ways."

"Your ways?"

"A gentleman must keep his secrets."

"Dorian."

He shrugged. "While you were sick and then out of town, I was unable to cook for Blue Sky Teas, since they believe it is you who cooks there. I was bored. I wished to experiment with new recipes— ones that would work with only one good arm. You slept even more than usual while you were sick. It was quite tedious."

"That doesn't answer my question."

"No? Did you not taste the nut bread? It is superb. The perfect texture and the ultimate balance of sweet and savory. What else do you need to know? I have told you everything important that transpired last week—unlike *some* people. You still have not told me of my brother. *Bof.* I am so distracted thinking of my brother that I did not even remember *serviettes* with our snack. You are dripping oil and we have no napkins."

"It's not a long story," I said, grabbing a tissue to serve as a napkin. "Once I got into the office on my own, I read the backward alchemy incantation from the book." I glanced nervously at the book, its sweet scent of cloves and salty scent of the ocean filling the attic. "The words didn't affect him as they did you all those years ago, when Jean Eugène read from his 'prop.' But when I placed the Tea of Ashes in his mouth, he awakened and spoke—"

Dorian gasped.

"Only a few words," I whispered. The pleading terror in his eyes was something I'd never forget. I hoped Dorian couldn't see the horror on my face. "He was only awake for long enough to ask for help."

"*Alors*," Dorian said. "So it is true. This is the fate that awaits me."

"Not while there's an ounce of breath left in me."

Dorian frowned. "I am humbled by the sentiment. Yet you have already lost too much weight in this last month. Soon you will have completely wasted away." He pointed a clawed hand at the decadent snack that would have looked more natural at a sunny wedding reception than the silent shadows of an attic at three a.m. "Eat."

I obliged.

"How's Brixton?" I asked.

"Happy that it is now summer vacation. He is a good boy. He has been tending your garden, as you asked, and also bringing food to both me and Ivan."

"Ivan needs people to bring him meals? He said he was feeling better." I wondered if Ivan had told me that so I would answer his practical alchemy questions instead of telling him to rest.

Retired chemistry professor Ivan Danko had an interest in the history of alchemy as a precursor to modern chemistry. Like most modern-day scientists, he hadn't believed alchemy was real. Ivan suffered from a degenerative illness that left him with a weak immune system and a crushed spirit. His last wish was to finish writing his book before he died. At least, that was his wish before I'd been reckless. I'd accidentally shown Ivan that alchemy was real. I couldn't be a proper mentor to him (unlike Jasper Dubois, Ivan had asked), but because Ivan understood the need to be discreet about alchemy, I agreed to answer his questions as best I could when he set up his own alchemy lab. He was a good man and I wanted to help.

I was far from confident that Ivan would find the Elixir of Life that had consumed and eluded so many intelligent men over the centuries. I would have discouraged him from trying, save for one thing: it gave him *hope*. That hope gave him renewed energy for life. He might yet finish his book before he died.

"I do not trust that man," Dorian said.

"You don't trust anyone who knows the secret that alchemy is real."

"That is not so. I trust you and the boy."

"You trust me because you purposefully sought me out, and you didn't trust Brixton for months."

"This is true. But it is dangerous to trust others—as your trip to Paris proves. Brixton is young and naïve. So yes, the thoughtful boy brought Ivan a meal when he was recently home from the hospital, but this gave me an idea. Visiting Ivan was a perfect way for Brixton to keep him under surveillance during the daytime, when I could not watch him."

"Watch him?" I felt my eyes narrowing. "Why do you need to watch Ivan?"

"To see if he is up to nefarious deeds. Did I fail to mention we have been visiting Ivan?"

I rubbed my temples. "Are you trying to tell me that you and Brixton have been spying on Ivan?"

"*Spying* is a strong word. I prefer to call it gathering intelligence."

I closed my eyes and breathed deeply. "This is a bad idea."

"The boy can move about freely during the day—"

"He's fourteen."

"He did nothing unsafe. What is the harm? You are the one who believes we should trust Ivan."

I rolled my eyes at Dorian. "People don't generally react well when they learn they're being surveilled."

"Have you ever known us not to be careful?" he asked.

I opened my mouth to speak, but he cut me off by saying, "I withdraw the question."

CHAPTER 12

In spite of the late night, I awoke with the sun, thinking of Jasper Dubois, who hadn't simply decided to move on from dangerous wartime Paris but had been killed.

My body is attuned to planetary alignments, so I always awaken with the first rays of sunlight. Alchemists have different strengths— some of us excel at transmuting corroded metals into pure gold, some of us feel the energy of gemstones, and some of us, like me, have a connection to plants—but all of us are affected by nature, from the scents that drift through the air to the rotations of the celestial planets above.

In the light of day, my immediate situation didn't seem as dire. I doubted the French authorities would spend limited resources to follow up on such an old crime, especially since I'd left France and the suspect was most likely dead. Ivan was a good man who would laugh if he learned Brixton was keeping an eye on him. An apprehensive feeling tickled at the edge of my consciousness, but with so many unanswered questions, that was to be expected. Jasper's death was an unsolved tragedy, but he was gone. Dorian was alive and needed me.

Since I'd arrived in the middle of the night, I hadn't yet seen my backyard garden. As a plant alchemist, the garden wasn't simply a hobby; it was an extension of my being and my salvation. Feeling the energy of the plants, from their roots in the earth to their soft, fuzzy, or prickly leaves, touched my soul. When my aptitude was discovered by an alchemist who assumed it was my brother's work, I learned that the alchemical term for creating healing medicines using the ashes of plants was spagyrics. I prefer to think of myself simply as a plant alchemist.

I was apprehensive as my bare feet touched the cool wood of the back porch. Breathing in the chilled air, I saw that Brixton had done a great job. Especially flourishing were the beets, parsley, and an assortment of salad greens. My young neighbor had more of an aptitude for gardening than I'd anticipated. I laughed as I noticed the plant that was doing the worst: nettles. Normally the tasty, healing plant that most people thought of as a pesky weed would grow under any circumstances, pushing out other plants. Brixton was afraid of the stinging leaves, so he must have ignored it. Now that I was home, I'd pour some extra energy into the nettles.

Simply stepping into the sanctuary helped calm my mind, which was still racing with all the confusing facts being thrown at me. The lavender made my head spin in a different way—it made me think of Max. I'd missed him more than I'd imagined I would. I shouldn't have been surprised. We shared so much in common, from our gardens to devoting our lives to helping people, and the chemistry between us was something I hadn't felt in decades. Was it enough to overcome the chasm in the foundation of our understanding of the world that made Max skeptical of anything he couldn't see?

After watering the garden and fixing myself a revitalizing green smoothie for breakfast, I came to a decision about what to do with the illegible vellum note from Nicolas Flamel. As much as I wished to learn what had become of the generous man who'd briefly been my mentor, I couldn't risk what he'd think of Dorian's connection to backward alchemy. I made sure the note was safely hidden away in an empty jar of Devil's Dung in my basement alchemy lab, where nobody would ever look, then climbed the stairs to the attic. The door was latched from the inside, so I knocked.

"I am at the denouement of a book that is giving me a *frisson*," Dorian called through the door. "Come back later, *s'il vous plaît*."

I wondered if it was true he was reading a thrilling novel, or if he didn't want me to see how poorly he was feeling. It distressed me to see my friend in so much pain, and it scared me to watch his body reverting to stone. Dorian used to shift between life and stone as easily as a person would move between standing up and sitting down. But now each time he transformed into stone, it was more and more difficult for him to regain movement. I needed answers. I hoped the bookseller would send me the book on backward alchemists as soon as promised.

Since the garden was thriving, I collected two buckets of parsley and beet greens, then went inside and unlocked the door to my basement alchemy lab. I hadn't had a chance to build a proper alchemy laboratory, just as I hadn't finished construction on my fixer-upper house, but both were holding their own. After things with my contractor didn't work out, my underemployed locksmith had made sure the house was in good enough shape that the neighbors wouldn't complain, and I'd cleaned the basement and made it my own. Both solutions were painfully close to the quick fixes I abhorred in backward alchemy. My imperfect alchemy lab served as my daily hypocrisy check. It was a good reminder that we do the best we can, but life isn't black and white.

I set the buckets of greens down on my work table, feeling an uneasiness creep over me as I did so. Something was amiss. There was nothing obvious, but I knew I wasn't wrong. The *energy* of the basement felt different. I glanced around.

I'd purposefully kept the room sparse, with two simple yet solid wooden tables, alchemy ingredients ranging from cinnabar to gold dust, and only candles and kerosene lanterns to light the space. Those sources of light served two purposes. First, they transported me to the right mental state to begin alchemical transformations. Second, they made sure that anyone snooping would have to take an extra step to cast light on their surroundings.

Had Dorian tidied the room in an attempt to be helpful? Though his body was failing him, he was a helpful little guy. I wanted to make another batch of Tea of Ashes for him. I knew if I told him what I was up to, he wouldn't let me go through with it. That's why I wasn't going to tell him in advance. Besides, this would be a small batch, not like the unwieldy batch that had backfired and made me so ill before going on my trip.

I followed the backward steps, beginning with fire. Extracting the essences of the fresh greens through this backward process left me with ash that wasn't alchemy's true salt, but mimicked it closely enough to work temporarily.

Two hours after beginning the Death Rotation, I had an ash-like substance to dissolve in hot water for Dorian to drink as medicine.

My joints ached as I climbed the steps leading out of the basement. At the top, it took a minute for me to catch my breath. It took all my energy to boil the water to make the tea for Dorian. Luckily, the scent was so pungent that he smelled it from the attic and came downstairs before I began dragging my tired legs up the stairs. He shook his head but accepted the tea.

"I'm going to rest for a little while now," I said. Dorian helped me to the couch. Between his limping gait and my wilting body, we were a sad sight. My eyes fluttered shut as soon as I hit the couch cushions. I felt Dorian place a blanket over me as I drifted off to sleep.

I woke up abruptly, with a gargoyle poking my arm with his claw and waving a bunch of fragrant roses under my nose.

"The roses worked!" he declared.

I rubbed my arm and sat up. My throat was so parched it took me a moment to speak. "I need sleep, Dorian."

"You have slept for many hours. You at least need to drink liquid." He set down the roses and handed me a glass of water. I sat up and drank it, then lay back down and pulled the blanket over me.

Dorian tapped me again.

"I'm serious, Dorian. I need more sleep."

"Zoe." The gargoyle gently tapped a claw on my forehead. "I do not wish to worry you, but you have been asleep for more than a day."

CHAPTER 13

Against the will of my aching body, I sat up. "I slept for a whole twenty-four hours?"

"*Oui*. This is why I needed a strong scent to wake you." Dorian waved the roses in front of my face again. "Your phone rang many times, yet you did not awaken. It was Max."

"Max? Did you—"

"Of course I did not answer. He phoned many times. He must have missed you very much." Dorian frowned. "But the ringing was most distracting. I asked Brixton to tell him you had horrific jet lag and needed sleep."

"A *whole day*?" At least it was one day closer to receiving the book from Paris in the mail. I stretched my cramped neck. My velvet couch wasn't the most comfortable bed. "I slept for an entire day?"

"Is your hearing affected?" Dorian shouted into my ear. "Yes! A whole day!" He raised his arms above his horns to pantomime the rising and setting of the sun.

"My hearing is fine. At least it was until a moment ago."

"Ah, I understand. You were being incredulous at the amount of time you slept."

"Where's my phone?"

Dorian scampered across the room and brought it back to me. Ivan had left me a voicemail asking me to call him because he had something to show me, and my sort-of-maybe-boyfriend Max Liu had sent me several welcome home text messages. In spite of everything else going on, I couldn't wait to see Max. In his last message he said he was working on a case today, so unfortunately I wouldn't get to see him quite yet.

I looked up from the phone and felt a pang of guilt that I'd been thinking of Max and ignoring a problem right in front of me. "Your left arm and leg," I said, abandoning my phone on the coffee table. "The Tea of Ashes didn't work?"

Dorian hopped up onto the couch next to me. "Yes and no. They are easier to bend than before you returned home, yet I still cannot control them very well."

"I'm so sorry, Dorian." I groaned. "I know what must have gone wrong. Brixton was the one who's been keeping up the garden. The plants I sacrificed didn't have much of my own energy in them."

"*C'est rien.* The book will come and you will capture a backward alchemist. Then he will tell you what we need to know to save me and my poor brother."

"I don't know if it will be that easy."

"*Oui.* You will need assistance to get them to reveal their secrets. I have read many thrillers with ingenious methods of torture."

I gaped at Dorian. "We're *not* torturing anyone."

"It is not difficult. And your basement is perfect. Brixton has returned the books to the library, but I can ask him to check them out again."

"Absolutely not. No torture."

"But the professor is probably torturing my brother as we speak! Chipping away at his stone flesh. By the time we rescue him, there may be nothing left of him!"

"The professor doesn't want to destroy the statue—"

"Statue?" Dorian sniffed and stood tall. The dignified stance was only slightly marred by his limp and awkwardly hanging arm. "This is what you think of me? That I am nothing more than a piece of stone?"

"Of course not. All I meant is that the other gargoyle is in stone form right now. And yes, the professor will probably take small samples of stone to test—"

Dorian's good hand flew to his mouth and his black eyes opened wide with horror.

"He'll be fine," I added. "You were fine after your toe chipped off."

Dorian squirmed uncomfortably. "If you would be so good as to ship me to Paris in an express delivery crate, I could stage a hostage rescue."

"The book that I hope will lead us to a backward alchemist should be here any day now—"

"No books arrived in the mail while you slept. Only advertisements. These Americans and their advertisements…" He shook his head. "You are confident about this book?"

"It sounds like a good lead. If there are any practicing backward alchemists left."

Dorian narrowed his eyes. "You suspect there are."

"I do. But until we find one—"

"You are the smartest, bravest person I have ever met, Zoe Faust. Even more so than my father."

"Flattery won't convince me torture is okay."

"No?"

"No."

Dorian muttered something under his breath and hopped down from the couch. "It is almost eight o'clock in the morning. The market will be open. I have taken the liberty of drawing up a shopping list. Brixton was helpful, but he could only do so much."

Dorian used to slip meat products into his lists, hoping I wouldn't notice. "No bacon?"

He pointed a claw. "Smoked salts are even better."

"No cream?"

"I have five pounds of raw cashews."

"Maybe my hearing was affected after all. I could have sworn you said *five pounds* of cashews."

He beamed at me. "Wait until you taste the new recipes I have created during your absence."

~

Three pints of lemon water, a mug of healing ginger and turmeric tea, and almond butter and sea salt drizzled on freshly picked fruit gave me the energy I needed to start a nettle infusion and pick up groceries.

Making a full alchemical preparation, with the steps that distill the core essence of a plant into ashes, takes time. To extract energy from my nettles more simply, I poured hot water over a tangle of nettles in a mason jar and left it to steep on the back porch.

I usually walked to the market, but the length of Dorian's list and the heaviness of my legs led me to the truck in my driveway. My 1942 Chevy took a couple of turns of the engine to get started, but I'd taken good care of it over the years and it repaid my love with reliability.

An hour later, I hauled in five bags of groceries. Dorian jumped up and down with glee. With his good arm, he pulled his stepping stool to the counter next to the bags.

"You're happier to see a kitchen full of food than you were to see me," I said.

He pulled his snout out of the bag containing grains and dried beans. "Would it offend you if I admitted to equal amounts of happiness?"

I left him to his food and went to the other room to make my phone calls in private. With the time difference I couldn't call the bookstore proprietor to check on the status of my book delivery, but I could call Max and Ivan. Max's cell went straight to voicemail, so I tried Ivan next.

Though Ivan knew alchemy was real, he didn't know that my interest in unlocking *Not Untrue Alchemy*'s secrets was to save Dorian's life. Everyone aside from Brixton and Tobias believed I owned a gargoyle statue that I liked to move around the house and had an interest in alchemy because of the business I used to run out of my Airstream trailer and now ran out of my attic. Ivan assumed I was passionate about understanding alchemy because I was an accidental alchemist who wanted to understand more. Ivan was a scholar, so that's what made sense to his own worldview. Alchemy was a quest for knowledge.

But I'd been *too* passionate in my attempts to understand the bizarre woodcut illustrations in Dorian's book. Approaching the problem from an academic angle, Ivan had insights that hadn't occurred to me. These insights had helped me understand some of the book's illustrations. I'd subsequently let my guard down and accidentally allowed Ivan to see that alchemy was real.

"*Dobrý den*," Ivan said when he picked up the phone.

"My friend, how are you?"

"Me? Never better." The enthusiasm in his voice came through over the phone. I knew what it was: hope. His realization that alchemy was real had given him hope.

"I'm glad to hear it."

"I have a newfound appreciation for alchemical riddles," Ivan said. "I'm so glad you called. I wish you were back from Paris so we could talk in person, but this will do."

"That's actually why I'm calling. I'm home."

Ivan paused for so long that I wondered if the connection had been dropped. "Where are you?" he rasped. "Can you come over?"

"Are you all right?" I waited for a reply that didn't come. "Do you need me to call a doctor?"

"No, no. I'm fine," he said. But the tone of his voice said otherwise. "Zoe, now that you are home, there's something you must see."

CHAPTER 14

Books on chemistry, history, and alchemy filled the giant study in Ivan Danko's house. Had he bought more research books in the month since I'd been here? I didn't remember his library being so labyrinthine.

I maneuvered around a pile of books on Chinese traditions in alchemy that partially blocked the study doorway. I couldn't stop myself from straightening the precarious stack. It wasn't the quantity of books that had changed, I realized; it was their organization. The bookshelves were only half full. Books that were once shelved in a methodical way were now stacked in haphazard piles. I tensed as I stepped over a toppled stack of leather-bound books to enter the room. Pages ripped from a disassembled book lay on the desk.

"Ivan, what have you done?" My heart ached at the sight of the damaged books. As someone who collected antiques before they were antique, I hated to see so much knowledge and craftsmanship treated so poorly. "Practicing alchemy requires you to respect your materials. You've completely ruined this book." I picked up the skeletal remains of what had once been a museum-quality book from the sixteenth century.

He waved off my concern. "The opposite. Quite the opposite, I assure you."

My eyes fell from his sunken eyes to his scruffy beard. Ivan hadn't looked healthy for as long as I'd known him, but his eyes held a desperate tint I hadn't previously seen. His dress shirt and slacks were pressed and pristine as usual. It was only his surroundings that had changed.

Still, this wasn't like Ivan. Forced into early retirement from his job as a chemistry professor in Prague because of his illness, he liked to be in control of other things in his life, such as his library. He stressed the importance of order to properly organize his thoughts for his book on the history of early chemists—in other words, alchemists.

"Is everything all right, Ivan?"

"I'm so pleased you've returned. A photograph didn't capture the necessary nuance, so I thought it best to wait to show this to you." He took a labored breath but grinned as he lifted a hefty book with pages so dark they were nearly black. "Now that you can see it in person—"

"You *burned* this?" The memory of the fire at Elixir filled my mind. The fire that disguised the murder of Jasper Dubois.

"Not burned. I put ashes on the pages, as you did with *Not Untrue Alchemy* to reveal hidden meaning in the pages."

"That book is unique. I haven't come across anything like it in the centuries I've been an alchemist."

"But," Ivan said with fire in his eyes, "you were never looking." He pointed at the charred pages of the sad-looking book.

"What am I looking at?"

"Don't you see?" He jabbed a shaking finger at the blackened page. "The ashes reveal the page beneath, making the flying bees on this top page circle the dragon on the page below. That symbolizes—"

"It's a coincidence, Ivan. Alchemy books are filled with woodcut illustrations. Of course they'll end up on top of each other like that."

"You don't know that." His Czech accent became more prominent as he became agitated. How could I balance helping him feel like all his efforts hadn't been in vain with getting us back on track?

"When I left for Paris to do my own research there," I said, "you talked of reading your books in a new light as a first step on the path to alchemy, not experimenting on them in an attempt to replicate the bizarre codes from my backward alchemy book—"

"You don't have all the answers, Zoe. You said so yourself. You don't fully understand alchemy. If you did, you could help me find the Elixir of Life more quickly. I've done good work to help you understand the strange book in your possession and also to help my quest for the Elixir. What do I care if I ruin books? Even if you're right that I've destroyed them, what good are they to a dead man?"

"But your book—"

"I would rather live on than leave a book behind."

I squeezed Ivan's gaunt shoulder. When it comes to ideas about what's most important at the end of life, comfort is better than words. I've seen people deal with looming death in many ways. Some find consolation in what they leave behind for their children or the world, some wish to surround themselves with loved ones, and some push it from their mind altogether.

"I'd at least like a few years longer," Ivan continued softly, taking my hand. "At this rate, I might not have time to finish writing my book, even if I tried."

"I'm sorry, Ivan," I whispered.

"I know, Zoe. And I know why you have this drive to solve the riddle of this book."

I pulled my hand away.

"Don't be embarrassed, Zoe. I know you feel sorry for me. You wish me to be healthy again, as I do."

I bit my lip. Dorian's existence wasn't my secret to tell, and I *did* want Ivan to be healthy again. He was a good man and a rigorous scholar who could likely unlock alchemy's secrets. But that would take time—more time than Ivan had. The Elixir of Life was something each person had to discover for him or herself. I couldn't do it for him. And while I could play a small part in mentoring Ivan, saving Dorian was my first priority.

"I do, Ivan. I really do. But applying backward alchemy to your own practice isn't going to help you. It's not true alchemy. Backward alchemy takes life in order to give it. That's not right—"

"I understand that," he barked. "My books aren't backward alchemy. I only wish to learn from that book of yours, not to use it. You're the one who brought it to me in the first place."

"Ivan, I—"

"Forgive me. I'm sorry I snapped at you. We can figure it out together."

"*Without* backward alchemy's Death Rotation."

He smiled. "Let me show you the laboratory I set up in my garage."

To the average Portlander, it probably looked as if he was setting up a space to make home-brewed beer. Prominent on one table was a distillation vessel with an alembic retort to distill vapors, a round cucurbit for boiling, and a receiver to collect distilled liquids.

"I never imagined I'd be putting what I read into practice," he said, "so I'm sure I've got it all wrong."

"Not bad at all, Ivan. Not bad at all."

The doorbell chimed. Ivan went to answer it while I studied some hand-written notes in a notebook.

"Thank you, Max," I heard him say from the other room.

"Max?" I hurried from the garage. Max Liu stood in the doorway holding a bag of food truck takeout in one hand and a stainless steel thermos in the other. He dropped them onto the floor and swept me up in a hug. Everything else faded away. I'd missed his scent, his touch, and everything about him. He pulled back from the hug and cradled my face in his hands for a moment. His brown eyes held an intensity that combined delight, regret, and longing.

I'd thought about Max so many times while I was in Paris, wishing he could have been there with me. Even though I knew he wasn't ready to hear the whole truth about my past, I could be myself with him in so many important ways. I hoped he'd be ready to know the whole truth someday soon. But for now, it was easiest if I kept the alchemical part of my life separate. Max knew I was interested in alchemy, but he thought it was because of the alchemical artifacts I sold in my online store.

It had taken me a long time to realize an essential truth: I *could* have connections with people who didn't know I was a true alchemist. Thinking otherwise was a misguided idea born out of self-pity. Most human interaction doesn't take place on the spoken level. Before I'd come to realize that, I kept myself shut off from anything beyond the most superficial of friendships.

I'll never forget the moment I embraced that truth. It was a day that had started out without hope. I'd been lost and was suffering from heat exhaustion in the south of India. A young family took pity on the strange, pale foreigner. They invited me into their modest clay home for a meal. That scorching, dusty day, I learned to cook dosas and poori as people on the Indian subcontinent had done for millennia, grinding the flour by hand, adding spices that killed germs and healed the body, and watching the bread bubble on an open fire. I taught their toddler English nursery rhymes that made him laugh and squeal with delight. I don't think any of us under the thatched roof understood a single word we said to each other that day, other than our names. But I will always remember them.

Max stroked my cheek and drew me into a kiss. As I lost myself in the embrace, I remembered the special evenings we'd spent together that spring, sitting together in Max's backyard garden drinking tea, sometimes talking and sometimes simply reading in the twilight. The important thing wasn't what we talked about, but the feeling of togetherness, easy comfort, and electricity.

Ivan cleared his throat. I opened my eyes and saw him leaning in the doorway, shaking his head and smiling.

Max pulled back from his kiss, but he didn't blush. He kept his eyes locked on mine and his fingers entwined in mine.

"Since Ivan hasn't been feeling well," Max said, "I thought I'd bring him some lunch and tea while I've got a break. I'm so glad I caught you here too. I have to run, and today is going to be a long one for me, but how about dinner tomorrow night?"

"I'd love that."

Max gave me a quick kiss goodbye before departing.

"He brought more than enough for me," Ivan said after he shut the front door. "You're welcome to stay for lunch. Let me clear off the kitchen table."

I followed Ivan to the kitchen but stopped before stepping inside. The kitchen table was covered with more than a dozen alchemy books—each one of them destroyed.

Ivan hadn't experimented on only one book with questionable results. He'd obsessively taken apart at least fifteen antique books. Some had been soaked in water, some smeared with ashes, and some charred by fire.

Ivan had unnecessarily destroyed priceless history on a fool's errand. He was no longer simply a dedicated scholar. He was obsessed.

CHAPTER 15

I gave Ivan an excuse and made a hasty departure. I needed to think, and I knew the perfect place to do so. I went on a long slow ramble to Lone Fir Cemetery, named for the single tree growing in the cemetery when it was founded in the 1840s. Since then, nature has become as much a part of the graveyard as anything else, with hundreds of trees creating a serene atmosphere for contemplation.

The Victorians held many beliefs I disagreed with—such as the prevalence of dresses that made it nearly impossible to walk through a room without knocking things over let alone breathe—but their view on cemeteries mirrored my own. A calming atmosphere with well-tended landscapes and remembrances of loved ones provided a perfect setting for a thoughtful walk or picnic. In a cemetery, there was no rush. You could think about people past and present without the burdens of the outside world.

Ivan had clearly crossed the line from passion into obsession. I'd done that myself once, so I couldn't blame him. It was how I'd found the Elixir of Life without realizing I'd done so. I was obsessed with finding a cure for the plague that had afflicted my younger brother, and I'd foolishly wasted his last days. I hadn't listened to Nicolas or Perenelle about what was possible, nor did I heed their warning that I would regret it if I didn't spend time with Thomas making him more comfortable before he died.

I remembered that raw emotion well, so I knew there was nothing I could say to Ivan to make him believe he was approaching alchemy incorrectly and that his time would be better spent with his friends or writing his book.

Jasper Dubois had never listened to me either, but for different reasons. What had happened to him all those years ago?

I'd walked for only ten minutes, but the serene cemetery no longer felt peaceful. Death is one thing, but not knowing what happened to someone was another. Without consciously realizing where I was going, I walked out of the cemetery and found myself heading to Hawthorne Boulevard.

Blue Sky Teas was half full—much less crowded than it had been two months ago. Still the same was the weeping fig tree that stretched to the high ceiling in the center of the teashop, and the thick tree-ring tables that filled the cozy space.

It was partly my fault the teashop wasn't doing the brisk business it had been. I was Dorian's front, so while I was sick and then gone in Paris, he wasn't able to supply home-cooked treats for the teashop. Dorian baked vegan pastries in the teashop kitchen before dawn, but everyone thought it was me who was the chef who got up early to bake while they slept. I can transform herbs into healing remedies, but it's Dorian who's the culinary alchemist, transforming basic ingredients into decadent feasts. When "I" was unable to bake because of illness or travel, there was no way to explain fresh-baked treats showing up when the teashop opened.

The other reason for the drop in business was the fact that the owner, Blue Sky, was in jail for a past crime that we all wished hadn't resulted in prison time. Blue created teas and decoctions that rivaled anything I'd tasted in Munar, delighting the senses and healing the body and soul. She was due out soon, but in the meantime our friend Heather Taylor was running the teashop.

Heather stood behind the counter this morning. Her teenage son Brixton sat at a corner table next to a man with dark brown skin, long black hair, and a tattoo of interwoven metal bars winding up his neck. At first I wondered why Brixton wasn't at school, but then I remembered summer vacation had begun. His wealthy friend Ethan was organizing a fifteenth-birthday trip to London that summer, paying for his friends to attend.

"Zoe!" Heather called out. "Welcome home." The words warmed my soul. It wasn't a one-sided feeling that this was my home. "One second, then I'll introduce you to Abel." She turned back to the customer at the counter, but at the sound of his name, the dark-haired man sitting with Brixton looked up, as did Brixton. So this was Brixton's stepfather. He worked out of town a lot of the time, so I hadn't met him yet.

Abel stood and extended his hand. It was calloused and his handshake firm. "The famous Zoe Faust. Thanks for looking after Brix. He's been telling me all about your garden. I know he started helping you in the garden so you wouldn't press charges after he broke in, but it's been really good for him. Thank you."

Brixton rolled his eyes.

"How could anyone resist the lure of the neighborhood haunted house that someone was finally moving into?" I said. "I don't blame Brixton. If the tables had been turned, I might have broken into your house to see what was going on."

"So can we change the subject or something?" Brixton said. "I didn't think you were coming back so soon from your trip to visit your grandmother's friend in Paris."

I hoped Brixton wasn't paying enough attention to notice the flush I felt on my cheeks. I'd forgotten how close the lie I'd invented for my last-minute trip to Paris was to the truth I'd discovered, though Madame Leblanc couldn't rightly be called a "friend."

"The visit wasn't what I imagined it would be," I said truthfully.

"Well, I'm glad you're back," Abel said. "This way I get to meet you." He moved a banjo from a chair to make room for me.

"Pretty cool, huh?" Brixton said. "Abel brought it back for me. Did you bring me back something cool from Paris?"

Abel elbowed Brixton. "Manners."

"What?" Brixton said. "Isn't that what people do?"

I smiled. I could already tell that Abel was a good influence on Brixton. He wasn't Brixton's biological father, but they held themselves in a similar way. Abel actually looked like he could have been Brixton's half brother. He was in his twenties, a few years younger than Heather, who wasn't quite thirty. Without her then-boyfriend's support or her family's blessing, Heather had dropped out of high school when she became pregnant with Brixton at fifteen. Whenever Heather's flaky behavior frustrated me, I reminded myself that her father had left the family when she got pregnant, never to be seen again. I hadn't seen my own family since I was sixteen, so I knew how difficult that could be.

"Not hungry?" I asked, looking at the half-eaten sandwiches on the table.

"Mom thought of getting fresh herbs for tea," Brixton said, "but she forgot about making sandwiches at lunchtime. So she's making mint and basil baguette sandwiches." He rolled his eyes. "It's your fault, Zoe. Not only were you gone so we didn't get fresh food, but now that I've eaten Dor—I mean, *your* cooking, I can't stand these pre-made sandwiches she picked up for behind the counter."

Able shifted his position so the weeping fig tree would block him from Heather's view. "We're going to get out of here in a little while to get some real lunch," he said quietly, a conspiratorial grin on his face.

Something was different about the setting. It wasn't just the people and food. Had the tree been trimmed? No. It was the paintings that now hung on the walls. I recognized the style.

"Heather's new art is remarkable," I said.

Brixton shrugged, and a look of pride spread across Abel's smiling face. "She sold two of them the day she hung the series on the wall," he said.

"I can see why," I murmured.

In contrast to Brixton's mom's bubbly personality, she used unusual colors of paint to create dark and deep images. In her latest series, she'd added metallic accents to black, brown, and green forest landscapes. The gold and silver peeked out of the trees like eyes watching the viewer.

These new paintings were close-up studies of women's faces, but there was more to them than portraiture. The reflections in the eyes and the wrinkles on the skin each told their own stories, as if transforming from one meaning to another as the viewer looked more closely. In the painting closest to me, the reflection showed a raven in flight, and a crease on the woman's cheek was two simple line figures dancing.

"I think Mom needs help with the lunch rush," Brixton said to Abel. "Would it be cool if you helped her so I can catch up with Zoe?"

It didn't look very crowded to me, but Heather was taking orders and grabbing pre-made sandwiches from the display cabinet. Abel tousled Brixton's hair and stood up. "Glad you're not too cool to think of your mom."

Once Abel made it to the counter, Brixton hunched his shoulders over the table and spoke softly. "I didn't really expect you to have brought me a gift from Paris, you know. That was just part of my cover, pretending like you were on vacation with your grandma's friend like you told everyone."

"That's what you wanted to tell me privately?" I whispered back.

"Nah. Did Dorian tell you what's up with Ivan?"

"Yes. About that, it's a terrible idea."

"Why? You don't care about what we learned?"

"I already know that Ivan is obsessed with alchemy. You need to distance yourself from him. Desperate people can change."

"Yeah. Whatever. Fine. But that's not what I'm talking about."

"It's not?"

"No. It's not just me and D keeping an eye on him. There's a creepy guy spying on Ivan."

CHAPTER 16

Someone was spying on the alchemy scholar? I felt my temple twitching furiously.

"A creepy guy?" I repeated.

"Well, maybe *creepy* isn't the right word. But he was totally spying on Ivan yesterday."

"Dorian neglected to tell me that." Why hadn't he told me? The vein in my temple was now fully pulsating. I knew why Dorian hadn't told me himself: he knew I'd disapprove.

"You need to stop," I said. "Now."

Brixton rolled his eyes. "I have the daytime shift, so it's not like it's dangerous. What? You're friends with Ivan. He, like, helps you with stuff. You said so."

"There's so much going on right now that we don't understand. It's safest for you to stay away from anything that involves spying."

"Whatever. So do you want to hear about the guy I saw or what?"

I glanced at the counter. Abel and Heather had a good rhythm together. They weren't paying any attention to us. "Who was he?"

Brixton shrugged. "Just some boring-looking guy. He was spying on Ivan, like in a movie."

"Define *spying*," I said.

"Did you forget English while you were in France?"

I sighed. "I know what the word means. I want to know why you think someone is spying on Ivan, not visiting him. What exactly was he doing?"

"Looking in the windows. That totally counts as spying, right? When he first walked up to the house, I thought he was some professor Ivan knew. But then instead of knocking on the door, he looked in all the windows, and then flattened himself against the wall to make sure Ivan didn't see him."

That certainly sounded like spying.

My senses tingled. I was experiencing the feeling of being followed myself. Was it real or an overactive imagination? I scanned the tables and the side-walk that was visible beyond the large front windows, half expecting to see Madame Leblanc hiding behind a potted plant, stealing a glance at me through her designer sunglasses. But that was crazy. The bushes on the side-walk weren't big enough to conceal a person, even a small one. Besides, she didn't know where to find me. Still, I was uneasy as I watched several people walk past. None of them resembled the persistent Madame Leblanc or anyone else I knew.

"Without making obvious movements," I said to Brixton, "look around and see if you spot the man you saw spying."

"Wicked."

My pulse raced. "You see him?"

"No. He's not here. But we're totally in a spy movie."

"I'm being serious, Brix."

The eye roll. "I'm being serious too. There's seriously a guy spying on Ivan. That's why you need my help. Something is going on."

"When did your stepdad get back?" I asked Brixton.

"Yesterday." He scowled. "You don't think he—"

"No, that's the opposite of what I meant. You want to spend some time with him, right?"

"Yeah. That's not lame. He's really cool."

"I can tell. Spend the time with your family, and with Ethan and Veronica. Forget all about Ivan. Forget all about me and Dorian for the time being too."

"What's going on, Zoe?"

"I'm not sure. That's what worries me."

"You're kind of freaking me out."

"Sorry. Nothing freak-out worthy. You know me. I'm old. I worry."

"You're worried about saving Dorian, aren't you? Why did you leave Paris so soon if you hadn't figured stuff out?"

"I've got a lead." Would the book be in today's mail? "I should go check it out, actually. No more surveillance, okay?"

"Cool."

As I stood up, I fought the urge to tousle Brixton's hair as Abel had done.

On the sidewalk, my skin again prickled. There was no sign of anyone I didn't wish to see, but for a fraction of a second the profile of a man turning the corner reminded me of Ambrose. I felt for my locket. My encounter with Madame Leblanc had brought up too many painful memories. My long-ago lover who'd died by his own hand, my brother who'd been claimed by the plague, and Jasper Dubois, my assistant who'd met a murderous end. Death followed me. Why did I think I could save Dorian?

I hurried home. *Backward Alchemists of Notre Dame* hadn't arrived in the mail. I'd looked up the title after the bookshop proprietor told me of its existence, and I understood why I hadn't found it before. The only reference to it was a footnote in an obscure text I didn't own, according to the comments of one of the many blogs devoted to "the Secrets of Paris." In the modern age, people often assume they can find anything online. They don't realize how far from the truth that is.

I needed to get that book as soon as humanly possible. I'd already paid Lucien Augustin for the book, but it wouldn't hurt to reach out to rare book dealers I knew in the States.

I found Dorian standing on his stepping stool in front of the stove. With his right arm he stirred a fragrant pot of tomato sauce, heavy on the garlic. His left arm hung awkwardly at his side. It was even worse than it had been before my latest attempt at creating another batch of Tea of Ashes. I wondered if I should fix him a little sling.

I crossed my arms and stood over him. "You didn't tell me about the spy."

"Ah. You spoke to the boy." He continued stirring. "I wished to wait until we knew more. There was no sense speaking of it before I knew what was going on."

"I told you everything I know about the other gargoyle, about Jasper Dubois, and about all of my Notre Dame leads, even though I have no idea what's going on with any of those things."

"Using my little grey cells," Dorian said, setting down the wooden spoon and tapping his head with his index claw, "I have taken the liberty of diagraming a chart of possibilities for all of these problems—both yours and mine."

Dorian thought the famous Poirot expression "little grey cells" was especially appropriate to him because his body was gray.

"A chart," I repeated.

"*Un moment.*" He stepped down from the stool and opened the drawer with scratch paper and pens. He rummaged until he found the notepad he was after, then cleared his throat.

I sighed. "All right. What have you figured out?"

"*Bon*. We will begin with Ivan. He is Czech. He has defected, and therefore we can assume he is a spy—"

"Let me stop you right there. What was the last novel you read from the library?"

Dorian frowned. "Do not use the fact that it was a John Le Carré book against me."

"This isn't a spy novel," I said. "I'll let you finish cooking dinner, and then you can tell me what you think might be a realistic theory."

I left him grumbling in the kitchen and stepped through the back door to get the nettle infusion that was waiting for me on the porch. It was ready, so I strained the liquid into a clay mug and took it with me to the basement.

I sipped the energizing liquid as I descended the steps. When I reached the bottom, I nearly dropped the mug. Something was very wrong.

Someone had been inside my alchemy lab.

CHAPTER 17

A sweep of the room assured me there was nobody besides me in the room, but my heart refused to stop pounding. Because this time, I wasn't imagining that someone had been there. My dragon's blood had been moved from the front of a row of glass jars to the back. I twisted the lid, tilting the jar away from me as I eased it open. The contents were right, so nobody had added anything. I didn't keep a record of measurements, so I couldn't be certain if they'd taken any or simply looked.

Was this the same person who'd been spying on Ivan? How did they get in? And why look through my alchemy lab? Was someone spying on *alchemists*? Was I right after all that Madame Leblanc had tracked me down to expose me?

I abandoned my nettle infusion and raced up the stairs. "Dorian!"

"What is the matter? Is there news of my brother?"

"Someone has been in the house."

His horns twitched in horror. "*Mais non. C'est impossible.* You installed security locks on the doors and windows, and no human can enter via my rooftop entrance."

"You weren't doing anything in the basement alchemy lab, were you?"

"How can you think this of me? I know you do not wish it to be disturbed. What did you detect had been taken?"

I sighed. "Nothing is missing." But I hadn't imagined that the bottle had been moved, had I?

"You have not yet recovered from making the Tea of Ashes. It was foolish of you to make it again. But I forgive you. I will cook a satisfying early summer meal. That will help you think straight." He took my hand and dragged me back to the kitchen.

"*Alors*," he said, "no word of my brother?"

"I'm sorry," I said, wondering what Professor Chevalier's reaction would be if the woman who'd brought a swarm of bees to his office called for an update on his gargoyle—excuse me, his *chimera*—statue. I also wondered how soon a locksmith could get here to rekey the house. With so many unexplained mysteries circling me, I at least wanted to feel secure in my home. I stared at an unfamiliar basket on the kitchen counter.

"Where did these wild mushrooms come from?" I asked.

"The forest."

"You know how to safely forage mushrooms?" Eating poisonous mushrooms was a complication not worth risking. I'd seen the effects on people who'd eaten foraged mushrooms that looked nearly identical to safe varieties. Sometimes I'd been able to help the unlucky people who'd simply been trying to feed their families, but more often it was already too late once the first symptoms appeared.

"Do not worry," Dorian said. "They are safe."

I couldn't imagine a forager taking a gargoyle along with him on a forest walk. "How do you know?"

Dorian looked everywhere in the kitchen except at me. He coughed. "Did I neglect to mention I have a job?"

"A job? You? Without me as your cover?"

He sniffed. "I had many jobs before I met you. I have impeccable references."

"You brought your references to Portland?"

"It was not necessary. You remember Monsieur Julian Lake? Yes, of course you would. You may recall that the elderly gentleman is blind. What you may not have known is that he appreciates gourmet cooking. Unsurprising for someone from such a distinguished family. However, his housekeeper is a terrible cook." Dorian shook his head and pursed his lips. "After Monsieur Lake tasted my cooking, when I was pumping him for information earlier this year, he desired more meals cooked by the great Dorian Robert-Houdin. Monsieur Lake wished to employ the services of the disfigured Michelin-star chef who does not wish to be seen."

"You have a Michelin star?"

Dorian sniffed. "Not officially, no. One needs to be associated with a restaurant to receive the honor. May I continue?"

"Please."

"His invitation was so insistent that I could not refuse without being rude. He would have gone to extreme lengths to find me, had I not accepted. He is a man used to getting what he wants."

"I see. How long have you been secretly working for Julian Lake?"

"It is not a secret."

"You didn't tell me about it, and I had no other way to find out. That makes it a secret." Something seemed fishy.

"I did not wish you to worry."

I thought about that. "I'm not really worried. He's blind and you know how to hide from others. Why would you assume I'd worry?"

"No reason." Dorian became overly interested in brushing dirt from the mushrooms.

"Dorian."

"Yes, all right." He turned from the counter and looked up at me. His liquidy black eyes were imploring. "I did not wish you to think you had been replaced."

"Replaced?"

"*Bon.* I should have known you have a big enough ego that you would not feel threatened. One would hope so, after living for so long."

"You were worried about me being *jealous?*"

"It is a natural emotion, no? And Zoe, if you saw his kitchen! It is a thing of beauty. No, I shall never show it to you. For then you might succumb to a tremendous fit of jealousy. Modern stainless steel appliances including a subzero freezer, a five-burner gas range, and an island larger than your whole kitchen. Of that you *should* be jealous. And of the covered pizza oven near the backyard pool."

"There's nothing wrong with this kitchen. Or my backyard. Modern amenities and square footage are overrated."

Dorian waved his good hand in a dismissive manner. "Yes, yes, I know of Julia Child learning the art of French cooking in her closet-size kitchen. *Peutêtre.* I will grant that you might be right about space not being a necessity. Yet modernity has brought such wonders."

I pointed at the vintage blender that had been my travel companion in my Airstream trailer since 1950, up to the simple copper pots hanging from the ceiling in the cozy kitchen, and down to the glass bottles I'd filled with infused olive oils, vinegars, and salts. "This is the height of kitchen technology right here. Haven't you noticed the resurgence of young people embracing traditional methods?"

Dorian rolled his eyes. He and Brixton were a bad influence on each other. "I do not understand your resistance to modern food preparation techniques," he said. "You embrace modernity when it comes to language. You pick up modern vernacular like a house on fire."

"That's not quite the right idiom—"

"You have proven my point. You understand slang in ways I never could, yet you do not try to adapt your methods of preparing healing foods."

"Adapting to language lets me fit in without raising suspicions." At least it did when my worlds didn't collide. I tensed as I thought about my carelessness in Paris. The city had transported me back to a century ago, and I'd spoken the French that I'd spoken at that time, not thinking how it would sound. "But preparing foods, teas, and tinctures isn't something I do publicly. The old methods are what speak to me."

"*D'accord*. We shall agree to disagree, as always, *mon amie*."

"How did Julian Lake find you in the first place?" I asked. "He didn't come over to the house, did he?" A worrisome thought.

"*Non*." Dorian jumped off his stepping stool and opened the recycling bin under the counter. He pulled out a wrinkled newspaper dated earlier in the month. He opened the pages to the Classifieds section and shook it in front of me. "Modern technology has not completely replaced civilized communication."

"Stop shaking your fist. I can't read what you're trying to show me. Let me guess. Missed connection, seeking a Frenchman who'd visited him with vegan pastries this spring?"

"Close," Dorian said. "Very close. The newspaper advertisement is what caught my eye. Only I never told him the pastries I brought him were vegan. This advertisement offered a modest reward for anyone who put him in touch with the disabled French chef. When I called him, he remembered my voice." Dorian's snout twitched as he gave an indignant sniff. "Can you believe that he gave me a test before hiring me? A test! He did not trust that I had baked the food I brought him."

"Sounds like a smart man."

Dorian chuckled. "He would not accept my suggestion of plant-based cooking. I knew right away he was not a man to lose an argument, so I stopped arguing. Instead, I simply did not tell him I was not using the meats he purchased to use as starters in my soups and casseroles. He declares he has never eaten so well. Between smoked salts, infused oils, and creamy nut sauces, he never had a chance."

"With Julian Lake's setup, I'm surprised you're still doing any cooking in my kitchen at all."

Dorian pointed a clawed fingertip at my midsection. "You are skin and bones, Zoe. What would you do without me cooking for you? When I met you, though you did not cook feasts on par with mine, you ate well. You took care of yourself by fixing yourself smoothies with vegetables from your garden, soups with oils and salts you infused yourself, and an assortment of healing teas you created with the power of the sun and moon."

I twirled my hair around my finger. "I still do those things." Did I, though? I'd let Dorian bring me food while I was sick before leaving for Paris. While in Paris, I'd bought fresh food daily, like other Parisians, but I didn't have my blender, which is what allowed me to make healthy meals easily. And since returning, I hadn't followed my usual morning practice of starting the day with a glass of lemon water, tending to my garden, and fixing either a smoothie of fruits, vegetables, and nut butter or a bowl of slow-cooked porridge with dried fruits, nuts, cinnamon, and sea salt.

"You have not noticed that we are out of half of the flavored salts in the cabinet," Dorian said, "nor that I used the last of your favorite cayenne-infused olive oil."

"We have enough left. My first priority is finding a cure for you."

"*Food is life*, Zoe. I appreciate the sentiment, but you must first slow down and take care of yourself."

A faint buzzing sounded. My shoulders tensed for a fraction of a second before I realized it was my phone. Not bees. I went in search of my phone and found that I'd missed a string of text messages from Brixton, as well as two voicemails.

A fist banged on the front door so loudly that I dropped the phone.

I opened it to find a trembling Brixton. When he spoke, his voice shook as well. "He's dead, Zoe. He's dead."

CHAPTER 18

The frazzled teenager pushed his way past me into the house. He ran his hands through disheveled hair and took several deep breaths. "I've never seen a dead body before."

"Who—"

"It's not like it is in the movies, or even photos of real corpses."

"Brix—"

"I tried calling you, Zoe." He shoved his hands deep into the pockets of his jeans and paced the length of the living room. "When you didn't answer, I called Max. I didn't know what else to do! I didn't want the killer to get away."

Killer? "You *saw* someone murdered? Oh, God, Brixton. Who—"

"I didn't see the actual killing, just the dead guy with a gash in his head." Brixton broke off and flung himself onto the green velvet couch. He put his head in his hands. He brushed off my attempt to put my hand on his shoulder, so I gave him space.

When he looked up at me, his face was calm. So was his voice. "I screwed up, Zoe. I was far enough away that the killer slipped out without me seeing where he went." He punched the coffee table.

I cringed. So much for forced calmness. I'd get him a poultice later to help with the inevitable bruise. For now, an injury was the least of my concerns for Brixton. If a killer had seen him, he'd have suffered a lot worse than a sore hand. "You did the right thing getting away and calling the police. You should have called them first. Why did you call me?"

I dreaded the answer I expected: that it was someone I knew.

"Didn't I say? It wasn't a random dead body I saw. The killer was the same man who Dorian and me saw spying on Ivan."

"Ivan." I sank onto the couch, my legs no longer steady enough to support me. "He killed Ivan?"

Brixton swore. "I didn't mean it's Ivan who's dead. Sorry to scare you. I don't know who the dead guy is. I mean, I kinda thought he looked familiar, but I probably just saw him around somewhere. But Ivan is probably in danger now, right? Since the spy who was spying on him killed someone?"

I desperately hoped Brixton truly had been far enough away that the killer hadn't seen him, otherwise he'd be the one in danger. "You told all this to the police?"

"Yeah, Max was on some other case and said he couldn't just assign himself to whatever case he wanted. But he made sure some cops showed up real fast. I told them everything. They made me call my mom too. Not cool. She totally freaked."

I could imagine. "Brixton. Back up a sec. *How* did you find the dead body?"

"You know we've been following Ivan, right? How Dorian had the idea to figure out what Ivan was doing now that he knows alchemy is real—in case he was going to expose you and D." Brixton's voice shook as he spoke. "So, this dude we saw at Ivan's, we didn't have a clue who he was." Brixton hit the coffee table with his fist again. At least it wasn't as hard a punch this time. "It doesn't matter, really, cuz we know the important thing now—that he's a killer."

"We should get Dorian," I said, surprised he hadn't heard us and come downstairs already. I ran up to the first flight of stairs and called to him. He had to have heard me, but he didn't reply. "Hang on one second, Brix." I continued up to the attic, slowing only on the narrow steps leading up from the second floor to the attic. The attic door was closed. I turned the handle, but it was locked. "Dorian, let me in." I shook the handle. "Dorian?"

"He's not there?" Brixton startled me from the landing below me. "Weird."

"He must have snuck out just now. Now that he has my cape, I think he's getting more brazen." I whirled around. "Don't follow his example."

He rolled his eyes. "Like I'd imitate a gargoyle."

A perfectly sensible response. "Let's go back downstairs. You were telling me how you found the man."

The detour to look for Dorian seemed to have given Brixton the time he needed to collect his thoughts. He was more relaxed when he continued.

"There's this cabin that looks like an old shack. It's in the woods past Ivan's house, in one of those greenbelts in between housing developments. The cabin is boarded up and there are signs saying to keep out. It's where Dorian saw this guy go a couple of nights ago. So I went to check it out during the day today."

"And you stayed, even after you saw there was a dead body? You stayed in the woods with a killer out there?"

"I went far enough away." Brixton rubbed his hand.

Brixton's temper worried me. He was a teenage boy, so some outbursts were to be expected, but I hoped he would grow out of the uncensored temper that had already given him a juvenile record. "All that matters is that you're safe. Next time you see something like that, you get the hell out of there. No, there's not going to be a *next time*, because you're not going to be involved in this. Or anything like this. Ever. Again. Is that clear?"

Brixton rolled his eyes. "I had to see what was going to happen."

"I know a crime scene can seem intriguing—"

"That's not what this is about! The shed, Zoe. God, aren't you listening to me? It wasn't a normal shed. The stuff inside—" He broke off and shook his head. "It's why the killer was following Ivan. What they have in common. It's what *you* have in common with them too."

I felt a cold shiver tickle its way down my spine. The look on his face terrified me.

"It was an alchemy lab, Zoe. The dead guy and the killer, they were practicing *alchemy* in the woods."

I stared at Brixton. This wasn't a joke. "You're sure?"

He nodded "What's going on? I mean, I thought there weren't hardly any of you guys around. There are more alchemists here in Portland?"

"I didn't think so," I said, but I wasn't so sure. My head swam. Had I been drawn to Portland on a subconscious level not because of its welcoming people, splendid food options, and lush greenery—but because alchemists were here? Could that have been the reason Portland felt immediately like home? As a female alchemist, I'd always been an outsider. Only Nicolas Flamel, who thought of his wife as an equal, had deemed me worthy of an apprenticeship. But I'd left abruptly, after a personal tragedy, and had lost touch with him.

"Tell me what you saw." My throat was so dry that my voice cracked.

"Do you need some water or something?" Brixton took me by the hand and led me to the kitchen. His hands were clammy but strong.

I was still in a daze as he poured me a glass of water. It was the people that drew me here to Portland—normal, everyday people like Brixton, Max, and

Blue. Alchemists aren't drawn to each other like that. We're not magical beings. We're simply people who've tapped into different energies, performing different experiments than mainstream science.

There was another explanation, but I didn't like it one bit: that alchemists were here in Portland because of me, Dorian, and his backward alchemy book.

I accepted the glass of water from Brixton and drank it in five gulps. The liquid revived me. "I'm the one who's supposed to be taking care of you, kiddo."

Brixton shrugged.

"I'm all right," I said. "I don't know what came over me. Go ahead and tell me what you saw."

"I don't know how to describe it exactly." The frustration was clear in every aspect of the boy in front of me. The expression on his face hovered between innocence and angst, between boyhood and adulthood. "Stuff like in your alchemy lab."

"You haven't taken chemistry yet, have you?"

"No, I just finished freshman year. Chemistry is later. Why?"

I grabbed my phone and looked up a photo of a chemistry lab. I handed the phone to Brixton. As he hesitated, I relaxed. "You've only seen my alchemy lab a couple of times. Come with me."

I unlocked the door to the basement and lit the candles that illuminated the room.

"I still think it looked more like this than the photo you showed me," Brixton said.

"Have you been inside a chem lab?"

"I saw that meth lab before it got shut down."

"And that's it?"

"I'm not making this up. I'm not."

Was he trying to convince me or himself? "I didn't say you were. It must have been really upsetting to see a dead body."

"I'm not a kid, Zoe. I'm not imagining things." His voice broke and he swallowed hard. "I know what I saw."

That's what worried me. If Brixton had seen a murderer, that meant the murderer might have seen him too.

CHAPTER 19

I made sure Brixton had told the police everything he'd seen and extracted a promise that he wouldn't investigate further. I wasn't sure how much good that promise would do, so I insisted on tossing his bike in the back of my pickup truck and driving him home.

From my seat I watched Abel open the door and give Brixton a bear hug in the doorway. Abel mouthed "thank you" to me and waved. I drove home in silence, save for the sound of the engine I'd tended for more than half a century.

I turned off the engine once I reached the driveway in front of my Craftsman house. I sat there for a few minutes, unsure of what to think, feel, or do. This couldn't be Madame Leblanc's revenge on me, could it? It wasn't impossible that she could have tracked me to Portland. But this was far too subtle a way for her to frame me through alchemy. This murder wasn't meant to be discovered so quickly. The discovery in the remote area had occurred because Brixton had been following the killer.

Gripping my keys, I walked over to the Airstream trailer that had sat in the other half of the driveway since I'd moved in. I unlocked the creaking door that needed oil, then lay down on the built-in couch.

Though I'd cleaned out most of the contents of the trailer when I moved into the house, subtle scents from years of love and life lingered. The musty postcards I'd sold at flea markets across the country for decades. The fresh, uplifting mint from the tendrils of lemon balm and peppermint plants that had lived in my traveling window box garden. And the salty scent of the sea—a combination of the flavored salts I used to flavor simple meals and the trailer's long stretches driving across snow-covered country roads and through sandy beach towns.

I wasn't maudlin enough to truly believe that death followed me wherever I went, but I was at a loss to explain the deaths surrounding me. Jasper's death in my Paris shop couldn't be connected to a dead body found in a shack in the woods in Portland—yet they were both connected to alchemy.

I closed my eyes and let the fragrance of salty, musty mint carry me back to a time when life had been simpler. Only that was a false memory. My life had never been simple. From the time I'd been driven from Massachusetts for having an "unnatural" aptitude with plants, to ignoring Nicolas Flamel's warnings about how to study alchemy, to finding love with a man who'd killed himself after his son failed to find the Elixir of Life along with him. Those hadn't been simple times.

The years I'd spent traveling across the United States in my truck and trailer were simple on the surface, but if I was honest with myself, I knew I'd been running away. There was always a cloud lingering over my head, even when I would park my trailer in a nice town and settle down for a year or two at a time.

The quirky friendliness of Portland's residents and the greenery the city insisted on maintaining was an inviting combination that made me think I might finally have a simple life, at least for a little while. Though that illusion had been shattered the day I moved in, I still held onto hope. If I could figure out the last piece of the puzzle to save Dorian, put these unsolved deaths behind me, and spend time with Max—

My eyes popped open.

I was having dinner with Max that evening. The thought filled me with a mix of emotions, ranging from desire to comfort to apprehension. Part of me wanted to cancel, because how could I possibly think of enjoying myself with everything that was going on? But life has always been complicated. I'd seen too many people regret spending their time worrying instead of living. With one last look around my empty trailer, I went inside the house and picked out a dress to wear that night.

I walked to the restaurant on Hawthorne with the sun high in the sky above me. It was the start of summer, but it was also an early dinner. Max knew I wasn't a night owl. Even though he didn't know how closely my body's reactions were tied to the cycle of the sun and the planets, he understood that I felt most comfortable in the earliest hours of the evening.

Max had suggested this restaurant because it served organic vegan food, and as I looked through the front windows, I realized the restaurant was even closer to my own way of eating than I'd imagined. Patrons were being served on wooden plates.

Even as the world moves towards progress, a pendulum is also in play, swinging between different ideas that societies embrace at different times. When I was growing up in Salem Village—not to be confused with wealthier Salem Town—in the late 1600s, we grew our own food and ate off of shared wooden plates called trenchers.

Today's young people had embraced much of what I remembered from my childhood, going back to the land and appreciating slow food, the idea that food should be locally sourced and respected for its traditions and transformative processes rather than thoughtless calories that immediately appear out of thin air at a takeout counter. As a bearded man in the window took a sip of dark beer from a mason jar, I smiled at another parallel. In my day, beer was often drunk for breakfast with porridge. I'm sure today's hipsters would have approved.

A heavily tattooed couple stepped past me. The one with an intricate black dragon wound around his elbow and a fedora on his head held the restaurant door open for me.

Max was already in the lobby. He was dressed in a slim-fitting charcoal suit and skinny silver tie that made me want to reach out and touch it. I resisted the temptation, but Max didn't. He greeted me with a brief kiss that tasted of lemon and rose hips. I pulled back but left our noses touching for a moment. That made him smile.

"I'm glad you're home from visiting your grandmother's friend," he whispered.

If you want a lie to be believable, stick as close to the truth as possible. When I left for Paris, I told Max and most of my Portland friends a believable lie: that my grandmother's dear friend was quite elderly and wanted to see me before she died.

"I'm glad to be home too. Thanks for making sure Brixton was taken care of today. He came to see me after he was done talking to the police."

"Poor kid. He seemed really shaken."

"Does he need protection?"

Max pursed his lips. "Why would he need protection? People used to deal drugs out of that place, but not since it's been boarded up."

The hostess interrupted Max's strange answer and led us to a corner table.

"Are we talking about the same thing?" I asked once we were seated. "He told me he found a dead body and saw the killer. I know he says he hung back far enough and the guy didn't see him, but what if he was wrong? I'm still worried he'll be in danger."

"Brix either let his imagination get the better of him or he was trying to get a rise out of you. I can see him doing that." Max's deep brown eyes softened. I wished I hadn't brought up the murder.

"He wasn't acting, Max."

"The body is at least a decade old, Zoe."

"But Brixton said—"

"I don't know what Brixton was playing at when he talked to you, but the victim has been dead for quite some time. For whatever reason, Brixton lied to you."

CHAPTER 20

"Maybe it wasn't a deliberate lie," Max continued. "Brixton loves dark things, like how he's into Portland's murderous history."

"Not so much anymore," I murmured, thinking of where that interest had led us earlier that year.

"His imagination probably got the best of him. But I'd have thought he'd find it exciting to find a mummified dead body."

"*Mummified?*"

"That's not exactly the right word, but I'd rather not talk about decomposition over dinner. Brix really didn't tell you that? Maybe he was trying to tell a macabre joke that backfired and he didn't know how to talk his way out of it."

I shook my head. Something wasn't right here.

"I'm surprised you kept our date if you thought Brixton was in danger," Max said. "I'm glad you came, and that I could put your mind at ease."

My mind was far from at ease, though. Brixton could be immature, but this wasn't right. "Brixton told me there were alchemical items like the things I sell." I took a moment to take a sip of the water placed on the table, deciding how much I should say to Max. "I suppose you're going to tell me that was Brixton's imagination, too, since he knows I collect healing and alchemical artifacts for Elixir?"

Max swore softly and shook his head. "I'd have thought the guys would tell him not to talk about the case. Don't you want to talk about something else?

How was your trip? How was the visit with your grandmother's old friend? Did the boxes she found in her attic belong to your grandmother like you thought?"

"Yes. No. I mean, I don't want to change the subject yet."

Max rested his elbows on the table. "What can I tell you so we can properly begin this meal? At first the guys thought it was a drug lab, but it turns out Brixton got the part about alchemy right."

"*He did?*" Brixton was right about alchemists being in Portland, but not about the state of the dead body?

"It wasn't exactly like the stuff in your shop, though," Max said. "Someone was using it as a lab to practice alchemy. Can you believe in the twenty-first century there are still people who believe in that nonsense?"

My shoulders tensed, and I instinctively reached for the gold locket hanging around my neck. A waitress came to take our orders, so I was saved from saying something I'd regret. If cayenne-spiced bean burgers with a seasonal early summer salad and white wine didn't make me feel better, I didn't know what would.

"I'm glad you ordered some wine," Max said, his eyes lingering on my locket. "You still look tense. Don't worry about Brixton. He'll be all right."

"Your grandmother wouldn't have called alchemy nonsense, Max."

"Being an apothecary is different." He crossed his arms defensively. "That's about healing people. It's like the herbal remedies we both use, but with a different name."

"That's not how you talked about it before." Sometimes it seemed like Max was so close to being open to the ideas I wanted to share with him, but other times he was closed off, as if two sides of himself were fighting with each other.

"I can get fanciful when I think about my childhood. False memories from photographs." He gave me a shy smile and relaxed his arms. "I hope you like the guy in front of you more than eight-year-old Maximilian."

"Not Maxwell?"

"Nope. Now you know everything about me."

I couldn't help but smile. "I doubt that."

The waitress dropped off our glasses of wine, and we raised them in a toast. "To eight-year-old Maximilian," I said, "who saw the world as full of wonder, and who believed anything was possible. May we find him once again."

Instead of laughing, Max frowned. What had gone wrong with my date?

~

On my walk home—alone—I replayed Max's words again and again. Someone had been practicing alchemy in the woods. That was the relevant fact. But what I couldn't stop thinking about was that Max thought my beliefs were idiotic. Of course, he didn't know they were my beliefs. Not exactly. How could I tell him, especially now? But I had more urgent things to worry about.

I still couldn't quite believe that Brixton had been right. I had to see that shed in the woods.

I climbed the stairs to my attic. The door was locked from the inside.

"Dorian?"

"*Un moment!*"

The door swung open a minute later. A gargoyle with one of his arms hanging limp at his side looked up at me. "I thought you were out on a date."

"I was. It ended. Why did you have the door locked?"

He flapped his wings defensively. "You are the one who says I must be careful."

"Tonight isn't a night to be careful," I said. "It's a night for action. I need you to show me the cabin in the woods."

While we waited for it to be late enough for Dorian to safely venture outside, I made myself a chocolate elixir in the blender, which I needed for energy to stay awake so late into the night.

Two hours later, I doubted the caffeine had been necessary. Adrenaline was more than enough to keep my eyes wide open as Dorian and I snuck across the grass in the no-man's land between two neighborhoods.

From the outside, the cabin in the overgrown section of woods looked abandoned. Though a public path cut across this narrow swath of forest, a sign nailed to the cabin's door marked it as private property. Holes and broken pieces of wood indicated the front door had once been nailed shut, but jagged pieces of wood now hung loosely around the door frame. The door itself, musty and half decayed from years of neglect, pushed open easily.

Stepping through the crime scene tape across the rickety threshold, it became obvious that the disrepair was only an outward disguise. Though the police had taken most of the objects from inside the cabin—presumably why they hadn't left an officer to guard the shack—enough remained to assure me that Max and Brixton were right. This was the workspace of practicing alchemists.

It was the scent that hit me hardest. Honey, charred salt, and ash. It smelled like Dorian's Tea of Ashes.

This wasn't simply an alchemical lab. *This was backward alchemy.*

A branch snapped in the distance.

Dorian's horns twitched. He'd heard it too.

I turned off the flashlight and felt my way to the window on the far side of the cabin. I tensed as a weak floorboard moaned under my foot, but I needed to get to that window. That was the direction from which the sound had come. Dorian shushed me, but I had no choice. I had to see what was out there. Like the door, the window had been boarded shut long ago. Unlike the door, the window hadn't recently been opened. My only view was through the uneven spaces between rotted boards.

Only a small sliver of moon hung in the sky, leaving our surroundings nearly pitch black. But it wasn't too dark for me to make out the shadow of a figure, perhaps fifty feet from the cabin. A man.

"We need to leave," I whispered. "*Now.*"

"What do you see?"

"There's someone out there."

"Let me see. You know I see better in the dark."

"Cover yourself in your cape."

Dorian didn't fight me. I heard the sound of cloth flapping as he flipped the cloak around his wings. He took my hand and remained mute. Thank heaven for small favors.

My eyes hadn't adjusted to the darkness, but Dorian could guide us. He led the way out the front door.

"*Un moment,*" he whispered.

"Don't—"

But it was too late. He'd already let go of my hand.

It couldn't have been more than a minute that I stood alone in the crisp darkness of the cabin porch in the sinister woods, willing my eyes to adjust and for Dorian to return. But it felt like an hour. Every sound made by nocturnal creatures and plants blowing under the pressure of the gentle wind set my senses on edge.

I jumped as a familiar hand took mine. My eyes had adjusted to the dim moonlight enough for me to make out Dorian's cape-shrouded form.

"A man," he whispered. "With my leg, I cannot risk getting a closer look. But you are right. A man is out there. Watching."

Dorian tugged at my hand, pulling me away from the cabin. "If we go this way, the cabin should block us from his view. As long as he cannot see in the darkness as I can, this path should be safe."

I followed Dorian's lead, creeping between the thick groupings of trees on our way out of the woods, hoping the man out there didn't have night vision goggles. At the edge of the greenbelt, we waited in silence for a few more minutes before walking to where my old truck was parked. We didn't need to speak. Both of us understood we had to be sure we hadn't been followed.

"This is bad, Dorian." I turned the ignition, cringing at the sharp sound of the engine revving. No sense in keeping quiet now. I opted for speed instead. The tires screeched as I peeled onto the street and pointed us homeward.

"It will be worse if you are given a speeding ticket."

I gripped the gear shift.

"I wish to hear 'Accidental Life,' " Dorian said.

The cassette was already in the player, so I hit the play button. Tobias Freeman's booming voice filled the car. He'd written the song for his 100th birthday, in the 1950s. After I'd nursed him back to health when I met him in my work on the Underground Railroad, Tobias had discovered the Elixir of Life. His loved ones had not. One by one, he had watched them age and die. It was a lot to grapple with, as I knew well. He'd recorded the track under the moniker The Philosopher. The soulful song by my friend immediately made me feel calmer.

"*Bon,*" Dorian said with a grin.

"You asked me to play the song so I'd feel better, didn't you?"

"*Oui.* I know you wish Tobias could be here. Now he is."

Careful to drive the speed limit, I watched the nighttime greenery bounce off my headlights, then give way to houses. "What's going on, Dorian? A long-dead man was found in a backward alchemy lab. Another man, 'creepy guy,' who must have known about the dead body, was following Ivan—possibly the same person followed us back there by the cabin."

Dorian peeked out from the folds of the cape. He was sitting on the floor of the passenger side of the truck. "Do not forget the woman in Paris who wishes to expose you."

The brakes screeched as I came to a stop at a red light. Dorian bumped into the glove compartment. "How," I said, looking down at the scowling gargoyle, "could I possibly forget her?"

"You are upset," Dorian said. "Perhaps we should continue our discussion in the morning."

Feeling the effects of being awake so late at night, I had to agree with Dorian. Talk could wait for tomorrow. But I had one more thing to do before I could sleep.

I dialed the Paris bookseller's shop to check again on the book he was sending. It was early afternoon in Paris, yet there was no answer at the bookshop. As the phone continued to ring, a disturbing thought tickled my brain. Someone was following alchemists. They'd spied on Ivan and they'd broken into my house. Had they also been following me in Paris when I'd visited the bookshop? Had they done something to the bookseller?

What had become of the bookshop proprietor?

CHAPTER 21

I dreamt of a fierce sea.

Dressed in a feed-sack dress with scratchy fibers that bore into my skin, I watched from a rocking boat as water serpents gracefully spun their lean bodies through the water, circling each other in an underwater dance. What at first looked like a benevolent action morphed into a scene of battle. The creatures curled their bodies around one another and bit into each other's flesh. Above them, bees circled and toads fell from a dark sky.

A pelican swooped from the air and caught a toad that was about to fall on my head. She nodded at me, then flew back to her nest, where she would give the toad to her offspring. I watched her flapping wings until the bird disappeared in the clouds. These dream clouds weren't the clouds of reality. They were faces of women.

These were the faces from Heather's new paintings, with reflections in the women's eyes. One of the reflections was of a man. Was it her father who'd fled? No, I recognized this man. It was the Frenchman who owned the bookshop, Lucien Augustin. His body was bound in thick ropes, and he'd been lashed to the mast of a ship. The ship that I was on. The raven I remembered from one of Heather's paintings appeared behind him, only the bird was no reflection. The black bird flew out of the clouds and dove straight for me. The ominous feathered being would have crashed into me had it not been for a toad I had assumed dead. The amphibian jumped from the boat at the last moment and caught the bird in its mouth.

I woke up.

The cotton sheets of my bed were tangled around me like tentacles. I was drenched in salty sweat. If I'd been fanciful, I would have sworn the salt came from the sea of my dream.

Sometimes I really hated that Freud was right about our subconscious speaking to us in our dreams. I'd found him to be a terribly arrogant man, but I grudgingly admitted he was a smart one. In alchemy, serpents represent the life force that's exchanged in each transformation, pelicans represent sacrifice, and toads represent the First Matter that both begins and ends the creation of the Philosopher's Stone. My subconscious was definitely trying to work out the confusing events around me.

A sweet aroma brought me back to reality. The scent of fresh apricot tarts told me that Dorian was back from his predawn baking at Blue Sky Teas and had brought back misshapen pastries, as usual. The treats tasted as good, but customers were less likely to buy a lopsided tart, so he brought these malformed treats back to the house... if he didn't eat them first.

I made myself a cup of jasmine green tea from tea leaves Max had given me and sat down with Dorian at the dining table. Built by a craftsman I met in the south of France shortly after the turn of the twentieth century, the table had been in storage during the years I'd lived out of a trailer. It was nice to have a home again, even if I always made sure to keep the curtains drawn tightly so that Dorian could have the run of the house.

Even at the familiar table that had brought me joy from the moment it was handcrafted, with a perfect breakfast and my best friend at my side, I couldn't relax. I was plagued by the troubling idea that the bookseller had been harmed by whoever was following me and Ivan. Could the book he found be more important than either of us thought? Could *Backward Alchemists of Notre Dame* hold a real clue to finding a backward alchemist? And if so, was someone trying to stop me from getting it?

"Breakfast is unsatisfactory?" Dorian asked, his horns twitching in alarm. "I will cook fresh food. I suspected I had gone too far trusting the malformed atrocities. This scone resembles your Richard Nixon, no? It is the chin." Dorian frowned at the scone. "What would you like? Buckwheat crepes? Chickpea pancakes? Almond milk porridge?" He jumped down from his chair, falling onto the creaky hardwood floor in the process. His left ankle was now unbending, solid stone.

"These pastries taste perfect, Dorian." I helped him back into his chair and held my tongue about his stone lower leg. "I simply didn't sleep well."

"If you are certain."

"I am." I took a huge bite of a heavenly apricot tart to prove my point.

"*Bon*. Then we can get to work. My little grey cells have been mulling over this most unusual problem: not one but *two* old alchemy murders. Both of which are distracting you from helping me and my brother." He tapped his claws on the wooden tabletop. "When we have eliminated the impossible, the only thing that remains, however improbable, is the truth to which I will apply my little grey cells."

"I'm pretty sure you're mixing your fictional detectives."

"I am being most serious, Zoe. Murders across time and location, yet they have one thing in common: *you*."

"The connection," I said emphatically, "is alchemy."

Dorian shook his head even more emphatically. "This week has stirred up two alchemical murders relating to you. You cannot think this is a coincidence."

"Jasper was killed in France seventy-five years ago. The unknown man in the cabin was killed in Oregon around a decade ago. I was careless in Paris and Brixton was snooping in Portland because we want to get alchemical answers to help you. In that sense, you're right: they're connected. But only because of dangers we both stepped into."

"You miss the logical next step, *mon amie*. You being recognized in Paris could have set forces in motion—"

"I can't think straight. Everything seems connected right now. Even Heather's paintings remind me of alchemy."

"*Oui*. She has a vivid imagination. I can see why the themes of transformation remind you of alchemy."

"You've seen the paintings?"

"When I arrive in the café's kitchen at three a.m., before removing my cape I look around to make sure there is nobody there."

"Now you think Heather is an alchemist? *Heather?* The woman who dropped out of high school at sixteen, who can't be bothered to wear shoes for half the year, who's more interested in weaving daisy chains in her hair and finding the perfect shade of green paint than making sure where her son is?"

"I agree, it does not make sense that all of Portland is overflowing with alchemists. I have explored enough to know that is not the case. There is something else at play, Zoe. *You*. You must investigate the unknown dead man to find out his connection to you—"

"The police are already doing that."

Dorian flapped his wings at his side. "But there is a connection to the man who has been spying on Ivan!"

"The only thing I have to investigate is the alchemy that will save you. I'm so close to understanding what's going on, Dorian. So close to saving you." I swallowed hard, willing my eyes not to fill with tears. "As soon as that book from Paris arrives, I'll be able to find a backward alchemist and have the last piece of the puzzle."

"And in the meantime?"

"The book will be arriving soon. Maybe even later today." If someone hadn't gotten to Lucien first.

"*Alors*, the meantime? We are well equipped to solve these past mysteries, you and I."

"I know you're careful, but you can't move your left arm. And your foot..." I let the words trail off as I looked at his poor foot. His stone ankle was frozen at an awkward angle. Was it painful?

Instead of protesting, as I suspected he would, Dorian's wings folded as he nodded sadly. "I nearly fell from the roof the other day. No, no. Do not worry. I have since compensated and know how to hold on with one hand and foot. But you are right that I cannot investigate as I once could. Yet I have other skills to assist you. In addition to reading the entire Christie canon, I read Tey's *Daughter of Time*. Twice."

I crossed my arms and stared down at the gargoyle. "Then you should stay in the attic instead of following phantoms. If memory serves, the hero in that novel about solving a centuries-old mystery didn't leave his hospital bed the entire time."

Dorian's snout twitched. "Well played, Alchemist. Well played."

"If you want to play armchair detective, why don't you help me look through online archives of newspaper accounts from 1942 Paris?" I didn't think learning more about Jasper Dubois's death would help, but it couldn't hurt, and it was a safe line of investigation for Dorian. I handed him my laptop.

"I have already done this."

"You have?"

"You thought I would not use my little grey cells to help you?" His shoulders and wings fell. "I searched for clues for many hours, while you slept. Alas, I have not discovered any new facts, only theories. This is why I have not spoken of my findings. As for my brother—"

"The other gargoyle," I corrected.

Dorian narrowed his eyes.

"I should run to the market," I continued. "There's a farmer's market today."

"You are a *très intelligent* woman, Zoe. You knew the one thing you could say that would not cause me to object to ending this conversation."

～

Though it was early summer, an unexpected rainstorm had blown in that morning, though I probably shouldn't have called it "unexpected" since this was Portland. I grabbed my silver rain coat and walked to a local farmer's market. I found myself looking over my shoulder the entire way. Could Dorian be right that the two murders were connected to me? It wasn't possible. Jasper's death might have been connected to me, but I wasn't in Portland a decade ago.

I was so distracted I barely noticed the early-summer fruits and vegetables. I was vaguely aware of a pyramid-shaped stack of apricots, but didn't stop wandering until I reached a stall that sent me back to another century.

The farmer had freekeh, a preparation of durum wheat in which the young green stalks are set afire to stop the process of the wheat aging and to give the grain a smoky flavor. It would be a perfect complement to the green onions from my garden. And I knew Dorian would love it. For a brief time he'd missed the smoky flavor of cured meats, but he'd been delighted to discover a whole other world of smoky spices and grains.

The more I got to know Portland, the more I loved my new home. A stab of frustration overcame me. I was *so close* to having a happy life here. If only I could solve the riddle of Dorian's alchemy book to save him and rid myself of the murderous mysteries that had followed me, I knew that life was within reach.

I was almost hopeful on my walk home. I let myself appreciate the moment, taking in the scents of the smoky freekeh and sweet summer peas in the bag over my shoulder, and the roses and pine from the nature that surrounded me.

I quickened my pace as I approached the house. A package was sticking out of the mailbox. I'd let my imagination run wild in thinking something bad had happened to the bookseller. I tore into the package.

It wasn't the book from Paris.

The book-shaped package contained a bound stack of magazines. I flipped through the pages. All back issues of a vegan magazine Dorian had recently discovered.

It was probably still true that I was jumping to conclusions about the bookseller. An unsettling thought about Lucien crossed my mind: The French police could have tracked me down to the bookshop. If they told the bookseller about Jasper's murder in 1942, Lucien might have decided that he didn't want to help a criminal.

Or worse. If the authorities had traced my movements in Paris, could they have traced me back to my house in Portland?

Dorian had an escape-hatch in the roof of the house; if anyone entered the house with a search warrant, he could make an easy escape. What did it say about my life that I'd already had to think about such matters multiple times this year?

Being traced here didn't seem especially likely, though. The supposed granddaughter of a possible criminal who was most likely long dead wouldn't merit the French authorities sending their American counterparts to follow up with me. But Madame Leblanc cared enough. I tensed as I remembered her high-end clothing. She could very well have the resources to hire a private investigator to look into anything related to alchemy in Portland.

I couldn't sit at home doing nothing, so I walked to Blue Sky Teas. It was early afternoon, but as I drew near I saw that the teashop was dark and the sign set to CLOSED. A little rain never stopped a Portlander. I peeked in the windows but saw nothing amiss.

IS EVERYTHING ALL RIGHT? I texted Brixton.

WHERE ARE YOU? he texted back.

TEASHOP.

MEET ME AT THE MORGUE.

The morgue? This couldn't be good.

CHAPTER 22

"Mom is supposed to identify the body," Brixton said. "They think it might be her dad."

"Oh God, Brix. I'm so sorry." In the sterile hallway outside the morgue, the astringent scent in the air was stifling. It didn't help that none of this made any sense. *Brixton's grandfather?* Brixton and his mom didn't have anything to do with alchemy.

"Why do they think this man—"

"Unsolved missing persons cases from that time. Mom's dad was one of them. Her mom filed a report after he disappeared."

"I didn't realize. I thought he…" What was a nice way to say his grandfather fled instead of sticking around to support his young daughter and grandson?

Brixton shrugged. "Yeah, Mom thought he ran out on the family. You don't have to look so uncomfortable, Zoe. I never knew him." He shrugged again, trying to look aloof but fooling nobody. "Looks like he might have been killed right here in Portland."

And Brixton was the one who found the body.

"All these years we hated him," Brixton whispered.

Abel tried to give him a hug, but the kid shrugged him off, opting instead to shove his hands into the pockets of his hoodie. Abel tapped his foot nervously. Brixton fidgeted and began to bite his fingernails.

Abel straightened and put his hands on Brixton's shoulders. I followed his gaze. Heather was walking down the hallway toward us. Her blonde braids were a mess, her face set in a stoic mask unlike any expression I'd seen on her before.

Heather could be an immature flake, but she was always full of vitality and hope. Until now. This was the first time I'd seen her with a cloud over her face. Even when Brixton had been in trouble in the past, she met the challenge with energy and love. The woman in front of me wasn't the same person. Her face was cold. Defeated. When she reached us, I could see her arms were shaking.

"Was it him?" Abel whispered.

For a fraction of a second, I could have sworn she stared at him as if he was a stranger who had no business talking to her. When she recovered, her reaction wasn't much better. "How could I tell? Tell me, Abel, how am I supposed to know what that *thing* was?"

I cringed. The body had been decomposing for more than a decade.

Abel's muscles tensed. "They showed him to you, even though he was beyond recognition?"

"They thought I might recognize identifying markings."

I would have expected her to shudder or break down. Instead she was emotionally distant.

"Let's get you home," Abel said.

"The teashop," she said. "I have to open Blue's teashop."

"It's okay for it to be closed for a day."

"But there's no need. I don't know who that poor man is." She paused, and I saw the first hint of emotion cross her face. "He didn't have any teeth— they'd all been removed." She shuddered. "Dental records won't work, so they might have to do a DNA test to identify him. They're sure to get an answer. A real answer. Oh, God, Abel. What am I going to do if it's him? All this time, I thought he hated me. But what if, what if he went off and did something dumb, trying to get money for me? What if that's why he never came home? He might have sacrificed himself for us, and I never knew it."

I left the morgue understanding far less than I'd known going in.

Had Brixton and the police been wrong about the old cabin in the woods being an alchemy lab? The person Brixton had seen leaving the shack had been spying on Ivan, and possibly on me, but that man wasn't necessarily here in Portland years ago when the murder took place.

Did we even know it was murder, and not just a recluse who'd died of natural causes? That would be a less gruesome answer for why he didn't have any teeth. Why hadn't anyone found the body before? Had it been hidden until now? Had the man spying on Ivan moved the body?

The more I thought about my unanswered questions, the more my theories fell apart. Was I being narrow-minded to think these deaths were connected to me? Or, at the very least, to alchemy? Guilt at being so self-absorbed replaced my confusion. Heather's dad, Brixton's grandfather, might have been cruelly taken away from his family. Was it him in the morgue? Did he die with regrets, or was he happy to have died trying to provide for his family?

I drove home past the combination of parks and forests, bridges stretching across the river and urban neighborhoods, wondering what secrets were hiding beyond what I could see. The brief summer storm had felled an old tree that had crumpled a small car, and a detour rerouted me onto a different street. If I were to be killed by a falling tree branch, would I die with regrets? I was doing everything I could to help those I cared about. But what about my own life? I was pushing Max away for stupid reasons.

When I got back to my house, a bouquet of amaryllis was waiting for me on the porch in a simple hourglass vase. The red flowers streaked with white were the perfect choice, for the scent was beautiful but subtle. It struck the right balance: heartfelt but not too pushy.

The card read *Peace Offering. I'm cooking a veg curry for an early dinner tonight. There's plenty.* The card wasn't signed, but it was Max's handwriting.

I brought the flowers inside and placed them in the center of my beloved dining table, then picked out a bottle of wine to bring to Max's house. I would have asked Dorian's opinion, because he was the one who created our wine list, but he wasn't home that I could see. Was he cooking at his new employer Julian Lake's house? I couldn't help worrying that he would struggle with his arm and foot while away from home.

I was used to living on my own, so the stillness of an empty house didn't usually bother me. But with the unexplained deaths surrounding us, being in the house alone filled me with apprehension. I walked through my basement alchemy lab and watered my plants, then methodically checked the locks on all of the windows and doors. My locksmith friend had come over as soon as I'd called him. The house was secure. I checked again. And maybe one last time. Third time's a charm, right?

I picked up the bottle of organic Zinfandel and walked to Max's house.

Max opened the door with his black hair spikier than usual, wearing a once-white apron over his black clothes. He grinned sheepishly as he wiped his hands on a clean corner of the apron and accepted the bottle of wine.

I knew a fair amount about wine from when I lived in France, but it was Dorian who forced me to get caught up to the twenty-first century. He didn't believe in using cooking wine or table wine. According to the little chef, the wine used in cooking had to be every bit as good as a wine you'd order to drink. Since Dorian couldn't come to the local markets with me, I photographed the wine shelves and he gave me lessons on which ones to buy for different dishes. I wasn't completely convinced it mattered as much as he thought it did, but there was something to the idea of pairing.

"This wine goes well with spicy food," I said. "From the smell of sizzling cumin seeds and cayenne, I think I chose wisely."

Max sniffed the air and bolted for the kitchen. His modern kitchen was sparsely decorated but simultaneously full of character. Teacups and a kettle from his grandmother gave the room an elegant simplicity that embodied Max. A philosophically decorated room.

"I didn't know I was getting in over my head when I started this curry," he said as he stirred the pot with a bamboo spoon. "It always looked so easy when I watched it being prepared."

"Thanks for the flowers, Max. And for inviting me over."

"When I heard about Heather's dad, it made me realize how stupid our fight was. I mean, it wasn't even a *fight* fight. But I didn't like it."

"I don't even know what we were fighting about anymore." I felt for my locket. My security blanket.

His eyes dropped from my eyes to my neck, where I held my gold locket between my fingertips. "You're holding me at arm's length, as usual. Your actions speak louder than words. I know you're not completely over your ex."

I stopped fiddling with the locket. *That's* what this was about? Jealousy?

"It's supposed to be a difficult thing to work through," Max continued. "We each have our baggage. Plus I'm too old for you."

"What are you saying?" Had I misinterpreted the flowers, and this whole invitation? "Is this a break-up dinner?"

"I said it's *supposed to be* difficult." He set the wooden spoon on the counter and took my hands in his. "But it's not. When I'm with you, the hours pass like minutes. I like being with you. So much. Can we forget about all that other stuff? And just be here in the present?"

Ever since I'd met Max, that's what I'd been hoping for. I was about to verbalize my answer, but as soon as I smiled, Max drew me into a kiss spicier than the curry cooking next to us.

The coconut milk curry and basmati rice pilaf ended up slightly burned, but neither of us cared. The hours passed without me realizing where the time had gone or feeling tired.

When I helped Max clean up the kitchen after dinner, I noticed the recipe. In a wrought iron cookbook holder sat a three-ring binder of recipes. Facing forward was a hand-written notecard behind a plastic sleeve. The handwriting wasn't Max's. Was it his grandmother's? I set down the dish rag in my hand and flipped through the binder. More than half of the recipes were for Indian foods. This binder had belonged to Max's dead wife, Chadna.

I felt my cheeks burn with a small pang of jealousy. I willed myself to push away the baseless feeling. Why was I being so silly? I'd been in love before, too, and it didn't change my feelings for Max.

I set the binder down as Max placed the last dishes into the cabinets.

"That was perfect," I said.

"When did you learn how to lie?"

"I mean it. You make it so easy to relax and enjoy life, even if I only get a few hours' break from it. Thank you for the perfect evening. But I should go. I've got an early day."

"I've gotta be up early too."

I hoped I didn't show my disappointment. Part of me had hoped Max would try to convince me to stay. A big part of me.

"But the thing is," Max continued, "I don't seem to care."

I didn't either.

❧

I crawled out of Max's bed at 4 a.m. I'd remembered to set my phone alarm for the time everyone thought I got up to bake for Blue Sky Teas. I glanced back at Max, who was sound asleep. I sent Dorian an email that he shouldn't worry if he didn't see me when he came home, then crawled back into bed.

My locket felt cool on my chest. I realized I hadn't thought of it all night. That hadn't happened in... I couldn't remember how long. I fell back asleep with a contented smile on my face.

I woke up next as the sun rose shortly after 5:30. I rolled over onto my stomach, enjoying the comfortable warmth of Max's bed. Thin rays of sunlight pushed their way through breaks in the curtains. The top of Max's head poked out from the duvet. He was always so put-together that I smiled at the sight of his sleek black hair askew on his forehead.

I was so contented that I must have dozed off again, because I awoke to the sensation of kisses on my bare shoulder.

"I'm glad you came back after baking," Max said.

"I wanted to be here with you when you woke up."

"I'm glad." He propped himself up on one elbow and ran his hand through my hair. "I always assumed you dyed your hair. I mean, the bright white suits you. It adds to your beauty. But..." He ran his finger down my arm. "*What happened*, Zoe? Every hair on your body is white."

"Life," I said. Honesty is the best policy.

"You told me about the stuff you went through losing your family so young, and I've heard of people getting streaks of white hair from stressful encounters. But *all* of your hair?"

"We all experience life differently, Max." I put a finger to his lips as he tried to speak. "I'm glad I'm experiencing mine here with you. What's up with the skeleton at the end of the hallway?"

"You're changing the subject."

"It's a fair question, considering I spent the night with a detective who might moonlight as a homicidal maniac."

Max laughed and covered his face with a pillow. "I'm not very good at disposing of bodies, though, am I?" he mumbled.

I pulled the pillow from his handsome head. "Maybe you're just a body snatcher."

He grinned and grabbed me. "You caught me. I'm a body snatcher." He ran his hands over my hips. "You're not too tired after getting up in the middle of the night?"

I shook my head. "I'm a morning person."

"Good."

An hour later, I stepped out of the bathroom, drying my hair with a towel, and found Max putting on his shoes.

"I really do have to get to the office to finish the paperwork on this case," Max said. "Want to grab a cup of tea at Blue's before I head on to work?"

Max and I both lived in the Hawthorne neighborhood within walking distance to Blue Sky Teas. The storm from the previous day had passed, and we walked to the teashop under a bright blue sky.

Heather stood behind the counter and waved at me as we walked through the welcoming door of the teashop.

"Here she is," Heather said to a man who stood at the counter.

He turned around. My balance gave way. It felt as if the world was spinning out of control. Max steadied me. My heart raced and my limbs went numb. I grasped the locket hanging around my neck, but I could barely feel it between my fingers.

Though I hadn't seen him in nearly a hundred years, I knew the man. Or at least, I had known my beloved a century ago. Before he died.

Ambrose.

CHAPTER 23

Noisy voices swirled around me. I blinked and saw blue sky and clouds above me. No, that wasn't right. It wasn't real sky. A dream? No, I was awake. I was looking up at the painted ceiling of Blue Sky Teas. I was lying on my back. A group of people stared at me from above. I struggled to focus on the blurry faces.

"She's coming to," Heather said. "You guys, give her some room."

Max and another man helped me up. A familiar man I'd known a century ago.

"Hello, Zoe," he said in an English accent. "So sorry to have startled you."

Could it really be Ambrose? I clutched my locket as my eyes focused on the handsome face in front of mine. No. This wasn't Ambrose.

"Percy?"

It was Ambrose's *son*.

The Old English accent was more refined than I remembered, as was the man. Gone was the plump insolent man suffering from gout, replaced by a younger, fitter man with a humbler tone of voice.

"It's been a long time," he said.

That was an understatement. Percy had died in 1935.

I closed my eyes. This wasn't real. I was hallucinating. I must have fainted and hit my head after seeing a man who reminded me of the great love of my life. Percy had the same black hair, distinctive nose, and striking eyes as his father. The similarity hadn't been as strong when I'd known them, because

Percy's fondness for beer and overindulgence in rich foods had given him a pudgy layer and a ruddy tinge.

Max put his arm around me and pressed a glass of water to my lips. "Do you want me to take you to a doctor? Work can wait."

"I'm all right. I usually eat first thing. Must be low blood sugar."

"Help her to a chair," Heather suggested.

Max and Percy lifted me to a chair. Much more forcefully than was necessary, I thought. I looked sharply at them both as they lifted me off my feet. Were they each trying to prove they were stronger than the other? Percy's flab had been replaced by lean muscle. He wore a leather jacket over a white dress shirt and trendy fitted jeans.

"Let me get you one of your carrot cake muffins," Heather said. "Lot of natural sugars."

I nodded. Even though I was pretty sure it was shock that had caused me to faint, one of Dorian's treats couldn't hurt.

"Max Liu," Max said to Percy, extending his hand.

"Percival Smythe."

I raised an eyebrow involuntarily and hoped Max didn't catch the gesture. I wondered how long Percy had been using that surname. Though the last name he gave was false, he was very real. Rage and regret swirled inside me, feeding each other. Ambrose and I had been told Percy was dead, and Ambrose had bitterly mourned the loss of his son. Our lives would have been more different than I could fathom had we believed otherwise. Ambrose might still be alive today.

Percy had never had the patience and demeanor to become an alchemist. It had been painful for him that both I and his father had found the Elixir of Life while he continued to age, so he'd moved far away from us. Ambrose and I hadn't seen Percy's body, but we had no reason to doubt the news of his death. If only we'd known it had been a lie, Ambrose would never have killed himself.

"So you're an old friend of Zoe's?" Max asked, pulling up a chair protectively close to me.

"Percy is Ambrose's son," I said.

"Ambrose?" Max said. He knew I'd traveled across the US in my Airstream trailer after the man I was involved with died. Max didn't know those travels had stretched over decades rather than just a few years. I could see the unspoken question on his lips. Percy looked like he was in his mid-twenties, the same age I claimed—far too old to be the son of a man I'd been involved with.

"I was hoping we could get caught up," Percy said.

Heather saved me from answering by setting a carrot cake muffin in front of me. "I've gotta get back to the counter, but give me a holler if you need anything else."

I didn't feel hungry, but I forced myself to take a bite. Pecans and cranberries, salt and dates, a sweet and savory blend to awaken my senses while feeding my lightheaded body. Dorian continued to outdo himself.

"You want me to leave so you can get caught up with him?" Max asked. His voice was sharp, and I recognized the emotion. Jealousy. It was a stronger version of the same feeling I'd experienced the previous night when I realized the recipe I'd just enjoyed had come from Max's dead wife. I couldn't worry about Max's jealousy now. My unfinished past trumped my love life.

Percy lowered his eyelids, giving me a hint of the petulant man I remembered.

I had never liked Percy, but I had to talk to him in private, without Max looking on.

"Go file your paperwork," I said to Max. "I'm all right. I'll stay here and catch up with Percy."

His lips set in a frown, Max nodded and left.

"I really am sorry about all this," Percy said. "I—"

"You *died*," I whispered sharply.

"Rumors of my death were greatly exaggerated."

"Very funny. While you were *not dead,* I see you've had more time to become well read. I can't remember you opening the pages of a single book when you stayed with me and Ambrose."

Percy was already a young adult when I met Ambrose. His mother had died in childbirth, and Ambrose had done the best he could. It was far better than most men had been able to do at the time, even the ones who'd been able to maintain custody of their children. But Ambrose had spoiled the boy.

Percy sighed. "I deserve that. But I'm a different man than when you knew me, Zoe. I've turned my life around."

"Where have you been all these years? You discovered the Elixir but didn't tell us? And now, all of a sudden, you decided it was time for a reunion? This isn't the best time—"

"That's not why I came. I'm here because I need to warn you. A dangerous alchemist followed you here to Portland. I believe you met him at a bookshop in Paris."

The plain man from the bookshop? "Lucien? He's an alchemist?"

Percy nodded. "Not just an alchemist. A backward alchemist."

CHAPTER 24

I'd found a backward alchemist and hadn't even known it.

Worse yet, the backward alchemist had turned the tables. While I'd been blindly seeking someone like Lucien, he knew exactly who I was. And he'd followed me to Portland. But why? He'd taken the time to lead me on with talk of the obscure book that could have helped me locate backward alchemists, but it now seemed he never meant to send the book at all.

"Why?" I croaked. "Why is he here?"

Percy seemed surprised by my expression of horror. Had he expected me to be surprised or disbelieving instead?

"I take it you know what that means, to be a backward alchemist," he said, his gaze unwavering. "I didn't figure you for the type to know about that kind of thing."

"What kind of thing?"

"Not untrue alchemy."

Not Untrue Alchemy. The translated name of Dorian's book.

"That's what they call it these days, you know," Percy continued. "'Backward alchemy' is so passé."

"What they practice isn't true alchemy," I murmured mostly to myself. "But it's not completely false either. So they practice not untrue alchemy." He was talking about a *phrase*, I realized, not the name of Dorian's book itself.

Percy nodded. "Lucien Augustin is a very dangerous man."

"Percy, what the devil is going on? A backward alchemist is following me—and you! You let us think you were dead."

"I didn't have a choice—" He started to raise his voice but glanced around the café and broke off. "I know you've got no reason to trust me," he continued in an earnest whisper, "but I want to help you."

"Why? You never made a secret of the fact you despised me."

"Half a century can do a lot for one's maturity. It took me awhile, Zoe, but I've grown up. I may look nearly as young as the day you last saw me, but I've had a lot of time to think. You and I may not have always gotten along—"

"An understatement."

"—but you're the only family I've got."

I, too, had lost my entire family long ago. Aside from my beloved brother Thomas, I hadn't been close with my immediate family. They didn't question the ways of Salem Village and were quick to judge when I was accused of witchcraft simply because I had an "unnaturally good" way with plants. My connection to plants and aptitude for plant alchemy weren't witchcraft. My only "crimes" were helping the vegetables and grains on my family's plot of land grow more robustly than our neighbors.

My brother and I fled the village instead of waiting for me to be condemned to death as a witch, but Thomas died only a few years later. It wasn't until I met Ambrose that I felt like I had a family again.

I looked straight into Percy's eyes. "Ambrose would want me to hear you out," I said. "His love of you was so great." My voice broke. Of all the unexpected things life had thrown my way, I never thought I'd see *Percy* again. And looking so much like his father.

"Once, that didn't mean as much to me as it should have," Percy said. "I know I took Father for granted. And you too. Like I said, I've grown up." He gave me an embarrassed smile before his eyes darted around the teashop again. "Look, is there somewhere we can talk in private? I'll tell you everything, but I'm worried about Lucien. I don't know where he is, and I don't want him to find me here in Portland."

"Stay here. I'll be right back."

"But—"

"Stay inside and I'll be right back."

I rushed outside to call Dorian. My hands shook as I dialed, but I relaxed slightly after getting a good look at the people on the sidewalk near Blue Sky Teas. They were all far too hip to be Lucien, even in disguise.

So Lucien had followed me to Portland. That explained why he hadn't answered the phone at the bookshop. It also meant there was probably no book that would give me the answers to save Dorian. Well, maybe there *was* a book that held answers about people who'd died at the hands of backward alchemists practicing at Notre Dame, but not one that he'd share with me. But why had Lucien followed me here?

I thought that if I could find a backward alchemist he could answer my questions, but I hadn't thought through the reality of the situation. Lucien must have known what I was to follow me to Portland, but he didn't reveal himself to me. He wasn't going to let go of his secrets easily. My grand plan was in shambles.

After completing our special sequence of coded rings, Dorian picked up the phone.

"I'm bringing someone over to the house who shouldn't see you," I said. "Get whatever you need to stay in the attic for a couple of hours."

"Max is moving in?" an indignant gargoyle replied.

"What? No. Why would you say that?"

"He is why you did not come home last night, was it not? Yet you do not sound happy, like people in the movies after they have—"

"Max has nothing to do with what's going on this morning. Ambrose's son Percy is here."

A pause on the other end of the line. "I thought he died many years ago."

"I thought so too. I need to talk to him in private, so I'm bringing him over to the house."

"You can trust him?"

I hesitated before answering. "Not completely. That's why I want you—and *Non Degenera Alchemia*—out of sight."

"Why is there such fear in your voice?"

"I'll explain everything as soon as I understand it myself."

"No matter. I will simply listen through the pipes."

"Fine. Wait, *what?*"

"From the attic, there is a way to access the audio qualities of the plumbing in the house."

"You're telling me you've been able to listen in on downstairs conversations all this time?"

"I only recently discovered it, during the party. And you have been away—"

"What party?"

Dorian cleared his throat. "I misspoke. My English, it is not so good."

"Your English is perfect, Dorian. What party?"

Dorian sighed. "Brixton and his friends wanted to have an end-of-the-school-year party. They were supposed to have it at Ethan's home, while the boy's parents were out of town, but his parents came home unexpectedly. Brixton asked me if they could have the party at your house. He already had a key…"

"Do you realize all the dangerous elements in my alchemy lab—" Was that the reason the items in my basement alchemy lab had been askew when I arrived home? Oh God, if *kids* had gotten in there…

Dorian clicked his tongue. "You think I did not consider this? The basement and the attic were securely locked. The children were only allowed on the first floor. I listened through the pipes to make sure they did not get into trouble."

"How could you—"

"If I had not allowed them use of the house, they would have gone somewhere else—perhaps somewhere more dangerous, like those Shanghai Tunnels they used to sneak into. But… *qu'est-ce que* a 'jello shot' I heard them speak of while giggling? When I cleaned up the last mess that Brixton made, I did not see a dessert mold."

I groaned, but I had more important things to worry about than unchaperoned fourteen- and fifteen-year-olds getting drunk off jello shots. Even though he could be infuriating, Dorian would take care of Brixton and his friends. A trustworthy gargoyle chaperone was better than no adult oversight in the dangerous tunnels under the city.

"Percy and I will be there in a few minutes," I said.

In front of Blue Sky Teas, I looked through the large windows to where Percy sat under the weeping fig tree, with his hands wrapped gently around a mug of tea. My throat tightened. He looked so much like his father.

Were my feelings for Ambrose getting in the way of a rational decision? Was I fooling myself that I could trust a word Percy spoke?

CHAPTER 25

"The twenty-first century suits you well," Percy said, resting his elbows on my dining table and tapping his manicured fingertips together. Like his diction, the way he carried himself was more refined than the slovenly man I'd known. "Vegan restaurants are everywhere in this strange new century, you can buy unusual herbs and minerals without being hunted as a witch, and your white hair looks good in this short, modern hairstyle."

"You look good too, Percy. For a dead man."

"I'm sure you've guessed that I found the Elixir."

"Mmm. What I can't guess is how you found *me*."

"This is where things get tricky." Percy pushed the chair back from the table and began to fidget. He tapped his breast pocket, and for a moment seemed surprised to find it empty.

"Recently gave up a smoking habit?"

"Something like that."

"Nobody followed us back to the house. You don't have to be so nervous."

"If you knew what I know, you'd be nervous too."

"You're stalling, Percy. Why don't you tell me what it is you know?"

"You have to hear me out—the whole story—before you pass judgment. Will you do that for me?"

I didn't answer for a moment. What was his game?

Percy jerked backward as my phone beeped, nearly toppling the chair. What was he so frightened of?

The phone was set to only make a noise if one of a few people contacted me. I reached for the phone while keeping one eye on Percy. The phone notification was an email from Dorian. I expected he was in the attic along with my laptop, listening to us through the pipes.

Hear Percy out, Dorian's message said.

"I owe it to Ambrose to give you the benefit of the doubt," I said.

Percy's lip quivered, giving his face the humanity of his father. "I never meant for any of this to happen. I didn't know what I was getting myself into. When I found Lucien, he told me so many wondrous things about not untrue alchemy. Things you and Father never told me."

"Oh, God, Percy." The skin on my cheeks prickled, my mouth went dry, and I felt like I was looking through a tunnel. "What have you done? You found the Elixir through backward alchemy?"

I should have realized it as soon as I saw him. Both because he didn't have the temperament for true alchemy and also because he was *younger* than he was the last time I'd seen him. He hadn't simply stopped aging; he'd reversed the clock. I hadn't seen it at once because of my feelings for Ambrose. I hadn't wanted to believe Percy capable of such evil; I was already subconsciously giving Percy the benefit of the doubt. Ambrose and I had tried to teach alchemy to Percy and failed. But because Ambrose always held out hope, I did too.

"You said you'd hear me out," Percy said, a flash of the petulance surfacing. There was the young man I remembered. "I told you it wasn't an easy story to tell. Please, Zoe. Please let me tell you. Maybe then you'll understand."

I bit my lip and nodded. This was what I'd wanted: a backward alchemist who could explain to me how it worked. What was he going to tell me? Would it be possible to save Dorian's life?

But now that I had a backward alchemist right in front of me, I was frightened of what he might say.

"Go ahead," I said through trembling lips. "I'm listening."

"I know now," Percy said, "that there was a reason you didn't speak of not untrue alchemy. But I couldn't see it then, could I? I never had the same sense of discipline as you and my father. Back then, I blamed Father for spoiling me. Lucien told me I could be more. And that I could achieve it without the years of effort that might not ever pay off. He was so charismatic in how he talked about it—"

"Lucien? Are we talking about the same man? The bookseller at *Bossu Livres*?"

"He might not be charismatic now, but that's only because he's been alive so long that he's begun to lose his humanity. He was different back then."

It was one of the dangers of any type of alchemy. The longer you lived, the easier it was to disassociate from normal people, to begin thinking you were something more. I wondered if that was one of the reasons I hadn't searched as hard as I could have for Nicholas Flamel. He'd been alive since the fourteenth century. If I found him and Perenelle again, I wasn't sure I'd like what I found.

But something wasn't quite right about Percy's analysis of Lucien's change. If an alchemist lost a firm grip on human emotions, it wouldn't have made him less charismatic. Could it be that Lucien wasn't the man I'd met?

"I was young and foolish," Percy continued. "He told me my sacrifice would be cutting ties with the people I knew. Lucien was the one who arranged for the plot in the cemetery and a telegram with news of my death. I didn't want to do it, but he insisted. That's how we've lived without being found out."

"How many of you are there?"

"Not many. Around a dozen at the time of my transformation, but only three of us left that I know of. It seems like a lonely existence, I know. But I believed the stories Lucien told me." He broke off and shook his head.

"How does it work?" I asked. "How do you get a life force back?" This was the moment I'd been waiting for. The last pieces of the puzzle.

"There was a book, and we followed the formulas in the illustrations."

My heart raced. "What's the code?"

Percy blinked at me. "There's no code."

"There's always a code, Percy. We're alchemists."

He shook his head and smiled. "The whole point of backward alchemy is *shortcuts*, Zoe. The founders were lazy, lazy men. Lucien and Olav."

"Who's Olav?"

"A Viking. Exceptionally strong, but very stupid. Like the Vikings were."

I reminded myself this wasn't the time to combat Percy's stereotypes.

"The two of them were complementary," Percy continued. "With Lucien's brains and Olav's brawn, they bullied alchemists into sharing the codes of true alchemy, then used the Death Rotation to cut through the clutter and skip straight to the Elixir."

"But if there's no code in backward alchemy, then what's the secret?"

Percy swallowed hard. He sat back down at the table and reached for his water. After drinking it in one gulp, he slammed the glass down and met my gaze. "Are you going to make me say it? You're a smart woman. You already know, don't you?"

"Sacrifices," I said without realizing I was speaking out loud. "You're talking about the necessary sacrifices. It was *people* you sacrificed, wasn't it?"

Percy nodded gravely.

I'd suspected as much, but I hadn't let myself believe it because I was terrified about what that would mean for Dorian. I'd been able to keep him relatively healthy through *plant* sacrifices that also drained my own energy, but that wasn't enough. Even with the knowledge a backward alchemist could give me, I would still have to go through with a sacrifice.

It was an impossible situation. I could never purposefully take a life. There was no way I could convince myself it was right to sacrifice a life, even if it was to save another.

My phone buzzed. I scooped it into my hand so Percy wouldn't see Dorian's message.

No sacrifice, Dorian's email read. *If it is my fate to live trapped in unmoving stone, so be it.*

I swallowed a sob as I set the phone facedown on the table. Even if Dorian was ready to accept his fate, I wasn't.

CHAPTER 26

"Lucien didn't tell me about the sacrifices." Percy's chest rose and fell. He wiped sweat from his forehead with a handkerchief. "Not at first. It wasn't my fault. I was already in too deep when I found out. He started me off performing processes that weren't so different from the alchemy you and Father practiced—except that these processes involve counterclockwise Death Rotations shown in a book, skipping the long, boring steps. So it's not necessary to use a long-burning athanor furnace to cook the vessel that becomes the Philosopher's Stone. Only fire is needed, just like the book illustrations showed. The result is an ash-like substance."

"The Tea of Ashes," I whispered.

"What did you say?"

"Nothing. I'm thinking aloud. Go on."

"The result is Alchemical Ashes." Percy cleared his throat. "Could I get some more water?"

I filled Percy's glass with more water from the kitchen. It gave me a moment to think. Now I knew the real term the backward alchemists used: Alchemical Ashes. But it was the same substance as in the tea I'd been making Dorian: ashes. I'd followed the coded instructions successfully. I *wasn't* missing anything. Only the sacrifice.

"And the sacrifice?" I said as I handed the glass to Percy. I remained standing over him as he accepted the water with shaking hands.

"It's the sacrifice who stirs the transformation that results in Alchemical

Ashes." Percy lowered his voice and his gaze. When he continued, he whispered his words to the table. "That's how the energy gets transferred: through an apprentice who gives his life."

"An apprentice 'gives his life.' As in gives *up* his life?"

"Or *her* life, I guess I'm supposed to say, now that it's the twenty-first century." Percy forced a laugh as he again wiped sweat from his forehead. "But as far as I know, it's only been men."

And I thought *my* alchemy apprenticeship with Nicolas Flamel had been difficult. Staying awake through the night to watch the fire burning steadily in the athanor furnace was nothing compared to an apprenticeship that ends with losing your life. "Apprentices *willingly* sign up for this?"

"Well, the thing is…"

"They don't know what they're signing up for, do they?"

"I didn't either," was Percy's indignant reply.

"You killed someone to be here today."

Percy wouldn't look up at me. "*Not* directly."

"That's splitting hairs, Percy."

"It's not, you know." His gaze snapped to mine. "I *couldn't have* killed anyone directly. The boy signed up for it himself."

"Have you ever taken responsibility for anything in your life, Percy?"

"I didn't mean to, Zoe! Please forgive me. I've never forgiven myself, but if you could forgive a child's mistake—"

"You were far from a child."

"When nobody ever treated me like an adult, how was I supposed to grow up?"

I tried to steady my breathing. "I don't want to fight with you, Percy. I want to know why you came to me. I want to know what Lucien is doing here."

"I'm getting there. I told you, you need the whole story if you're going to understand." He nervously tapped his fingers on the table. "I broke off contact with Lucien years ago, once I knew what he was. I was able to stay young through my plant sacrifices—never hurting another person, I swear. You were so good with gardening. I paid attention to that. I learned from you. I've got a garden now, so I make my own Alchemical Ashes every year or so, whenever my life force begins to fade. It's only that first transformation that requires an external sacrifice."

"It doesn't hurt you to do that?"

"To do what?"

"Make the Alchemical Ashes."

"Why would it hurt me?"

I didn't want him to know I had the backward alchemy book and had made the Alchemical Ashes for Dorian, so I had to choose my words carefully. "Based on how alchemy works, I would assume it would be extremely draining."

"It's not so bad."

"No?"

"Well," Percy continued, "it's not so bad as long as you only need to do it once a year. More frequently and you're looking for trouble."

"How do you know?"

"That's what I'm getting to." The petulant boy was back. "It's why I'm here. Even though I broke off contact with Lucien, he kept tabs on me. Several months ago, there was a change that caused our backward alchemy to become unstable. Lucien got in touch with me to see what I knew."

"Wait, you mean he *didn't know* what the change was?"

"I don't know either. That's the problem. None of us know. Several of us have already died."

This wasn't how I imagined things would go when I found a backward alchemist. They were supposed to know what was going on. "Nobody knows?" I echoed.

He shook his head. "I don't have the answers. That's what we're looking for. The book I mentioned, it's called *Non Degenera Alchemia*."

I held my tongue, even though part of me wanted to confide everything I knew. I was so close to answers. But I was also close to an unknown danger. Could I trust Percy?

"The book spelled out the secrets of not untrue alchemy," Percy continued. "It was lost or stolen ages ago, but it didn't really matter, because we had other practicing not untrue alchemists to pass down the knowledge. Lucien and Olav created the book at Notre Dame, and after that, a small secret society followed their work, meeting at Notre Dame."

That explained the book's connection to Notre Dame. And how Dorian had been brought to life by accident. He'd been created specifically for Notre Dame. Life forces were linked.

"Why did Lucien need the information in the book if he's the one who created it?" I asked.

Percy shrugged. "Maybe he forgot. That's the reason he wrote the information down, right? So he wouldn't have to remember it."

"But you just said he, Olav, and others passed down the knowledge."

Another shrug. "Maybe there's something special about the book itself."

"You don't know what's special about it, though?"

"I already said that, didn't I?"

I called upon every ounce of my will power to avoid strangling, or at least slapping, the lazy man in front of me. "If you had this book, would it save you? Is there something in there that would stop the shift? Something that doesn't involve another sacrifice?"

"It doesn't matter, because how would we find it? It's been gone forever."

"Nobody looked for it?"

Percy shrugged yet again. "Why would we? We'd already gotten what we needed from it."

I shook with frustration. Backward alchemists and their shortcuts! They didn't see the power of true knowledge. I circled the table. Clockwise. Was I subconsciously trying to counteract the backward Death Rotation?

"But now," Percy said, "our energy is fading. It's fading at different speeds, but fading all the same. Even mine."

"You could have saved yourself a lot of my skepticism if you'd come right out and said you wanted help. That's your real motivation for coming here, isn't it?"

"Lucien really did follow you here from Paris. I'm not making this up."

"I didn't say you made it up. I believe you want to help me too. But it's not your main focus. You want to save yourself."

"Is that so bad? For all of time, man has been interested in self-preservation."

"I'm all for self-preservation. Just not when it involves murdering others."

"I didn't kill anyone on purpose, I swear. And I stepped back from it once I knew. I'm not a bad guy. I didn't have it in me to do it again. It was only Lucien. After the inexplicable shift, he made another sacrifice—"

I gasped. "He killed someone else? Now? This year?"

"The sacrifice didn't work, though. He's still aging rapidly. All of us who are left have been aging quickly for the past few months."

"That doesn't make sense, Percy. That would mean you were, what, twelve years old last month? Or ten?"

Percy smiled. I couldn't believe he actually smiled moments after telling me a man he knew had recently murdered someone. "It's thanks to you that I'm spared, Zoe. I was a few years younger a few months ago, and because of my thriving *potager* garden, I've been able to keep myself relatively young." His smile faltered. "But I've run out of plants. We're all desperate to discover what changed. Lucien thinks the answer is in *Non Degenera Alchemia*."

"What does that have to do with me?"

Percy stood up and crossed his arms confidently. Several inches taller than me, he positioned himself to look down his nose at me. "Why were you in Paris, Zoe?"

"I used to live there, you know."

Percy stood so close to me I could feel his stale breath on my face. Yet I refused to back away.

"You went to Lucien's bookshop in Paris," Percy said, "asking questions about alchemy. You made him suspicious. Lucien now believes you have this book. That's why he's here. He wants that book, and he won't stop until he gets it."

CHAPTER 27

"It's ridiculous of Lucien to think you've got the book," Percy continued. *"Zoe Faust* in possession of a backward alchemy book?"

"Absurd," I murmured. It was my turn to avoid his gaze.

I thought back on all of my interactions with Lucien. I couldn't imagine him as the charismatic leader Percy had described. What had I said to Lucien to arouse his suspicions that I was a true alchemist, let alone that I had his backward alchemy book? It couldn't simply be the interest I expressed in alchemy. There were many people out there like Ivan, who weren't true alchemists but who had an interest in alchemy. That's why there were so many modern books on the subject.

"Why would Lucien even think I have this book?" I asked as casually as I could.

Percy shrugged. "Something you said made him suspect it. He mentioned that you two talked about the Cabaret de L'Enfer, but I don't know why that would mean you had *Non Degenera Alchemia.*"

I groaned. "I do. Or rather, I bet I know why he suspected me of being an alchemist. He saw me looking at a photo of a Hell-mouth door that led into the nightclub I once knew well—a hundred years ago. He asked if I knew it. I said I'd read about it, but I'm sure my face revealed the truth." Caught up in those memories, I also might have slipped into colloquial French. Not a problem in and of itself, since many Americans speak fluent French, but my conversational French is from a century ago.

"Lucien didn't realize you were someone I cared about," Percy said, "or he wouldn't have told me he was going to get the book *by any means necessary*. I didn't like the tone in his voice when he said it. I didn't like it one bit."

"He admitted that to you?"

Percy's eyes darted nervously around the house. "He, uh, might have thought I was on his side. Because I, uh, told him who you were. Don't get angry! I didn't mean to do it. He caught me off guard. I hadn't seen him in ages, and he showed up on my doorstep with a photograph of you. He took it on his mobile phone while you were browsing at his crummy little bookshop. I asked him why he had a photo of Zoe Faust... He'd heard of you because you're one of the few women alchemists taken on as apprentices with a master. You can't blame me for that, can you?"

"It's not your fault, Percy," I said, half believing my words.

"I'm glad you can see that. Lucien said you left Paris abruptly. Otherwise I bet he would have stolen the book from you in Paris."

"The book I don't have, you mean."

"I meant he would have *attempted* to steal it from you in Paris. I don't know how he found you in Portland, though."

I put my head in my hands. "I gave him my address."

"I know he can be a charmer, Zoe, but giving a strange man your address—"

"For him to send me a *book*, Percy. He's a bookseller."

"Oh."

"How did *you* find me?" I asked.

"I knew the name of your apothecary shop." He pulled out a cell phone and scrolled for a minute. He held up the web page to my online business, now an "antiques" store as opposed to an apothecary. Brixton's friend Veronica Chen-Mendoza had overhauled the website. The bottom listed my home address. Veronica didn't know I was hiding.

"I came to your house this morning but nobody was home," Percy said. "I peeked into the recycling bin outside and saw a takeaway cup with a stamp that said Blue Sky Teas." He said it like riffling through someone's trash was the most natural thing in the world. "I knew I had the right house, because you've got the oldest car on the block. Is it from the forties? I don't know how you keep it running."

"It's called hard work."

The dig was lost on Percy. "Aren't you worried you might give yourself away with the alchemical artifacts you sell through Elixir and that old truck?"

"Apothecary wares are cool again, hadn't you heard? Hiding in plain sight has been working well for me." *Until last week.* "Let's get back on track, Percy, since there's a madman out there."

"God, I could use a beer."

"It's ten o'clock in the morning."

"It's six o'clock in the evening in England. Seven in France."

"No beer." My phone buzzed. I ignored it. I'd forgotten Dorian was listening to our conversation through the pipes, but I knew perfectly well there was beer in the kitchen for a beer-battered vegetable tempura recipe. "I think it would be helpful for me to understand more about this book."

"You've never come across it over the years, have you? You sell so many antique books. If you and I find it before Lucien, we could use it to help us. Not sacrificing anyone again, of course. But I'm already immortal; I only need to figure out how to stop whatever change happened."

"We're not immortal, Percy."

"Speak for yourself." He flexed his muscles, clearly pleased he had the toned body of a twenty-five-year-old.

"Your cells have stopped aging, but we can both die. You realize that, don't you?"

Percy frowned. In denial, as always.

I weighed my options and made a decision on instinct. I trusted that Percy didn't wish to harm me, but I didn't trust him to keep my secrets under pressure.

"I came across photographs of the book you spoke of," I said. "That's what sent me to Paris to research alchemy's connection to the cathedral of Notre Dame. When overlaid, the woodcut illustrations pointed to the cathedral." Everything I said was true except that I possessed the original book, not only photographs. And that it was fire that had shown me how the illustrations fit together.

Percy nodded vigorously. "That's where the not untrue alchemists used to meet. Where did you find the photos? Do you have them?"

"Not here. They're at a friend's house. He's an alchemy scholar—" I swore.

"What is it?"

"Someone was seen spying on my friend Ivan—the alchemy scholar I mentioned. I'm sure it was Lucien. And you don't know about the murder victim who may have been an alchemist, do you?"

"*Murder?*" Percy flipped his head around. Was he making sure Lucien wasn't hiding behind the couch?

"It's an old murder. A decade old, something like that. But the odd thing is that the body was found in a cabin in the woods with alchemy supplies, and I think Lucien was seen there too. What was he doing there?"

"He's after the bloody book, Zoe. Your friend is in danger, as are we. Even though Lucien can't kill you directly—"

"Of course he could kill me. Especially if he's as bad a guy as you're making him out to be."

"You don't know?" Percy blinked at me. "Of course you wouldn't, since you've never killed anyone." Percy shook his head and spoke as if addressing a toddler. "The Elixir of Life is a transformation of the life force. If an alchemist kills a living being directly, their own life force is taken away. That's what I was talking about earlier, how the sacrifice has to be volunteered. You understand?"

Was he attempting to lecture me on alchemy? Not only was he condescending, but he was completely wrong.

"Percy, that's an old wives' tale. There's nothing stopping anyone on earth from killing another person. Aside from their moral compass. Or fear of being caught."

"No, it's true. That's why Lucien hasn't killed the rest of us. He's a very bad man, Zoe, but he's afraid he'll die if he goes too far. The sacrifices are different, because they're *willing* participants. Unwitting, but it's still their choice to sacrifice themselves."

"Then why do you think Lucien is so dangerous?"

Percy bit his lip. "There are many things that can be done to a person without killing them."

I shivered. It was an absurd theory, but if Lucien and Percy believed it...

"Give me a minute," I said.

I stepped into the living room, keeping my eyes on Percy while I called Ivan. Thankfully he picked up the phone immediately. "This is going to sound strange," I said, "but I need you to take what I'm going to say seriously."

"With you, Zoe, I've ceased thinking of anything as strange."

"There's a man called Lucien who's stalking people and places related to alchemy."

"This man is harassing you? How can I help?"

"Yes, and he might harass you too. And he could be dangerous."

"I'll be careful. What does he look like?"

"He looks like..." I closed my eyes and tried to think about how to describe such a nondescript man. "Average-looking guy, but don't underestimate him."

When I opened my eyes, Percy was gone.

"I can take care of myself," Ivan was saying, "but I thank you for your concern. I'll be careful."

Percy was a bigger concern, so I ended the call with Ivan. The kitchen door swung open a moment later. Percy emerged with a platter of misshapen vegan pastries.

"God these are good," he said. "Why didn't you cook like this when I knew you? I'm starving after that long flight."

"Where are you staying?"

"Nowhere yet." He indicated the small satchel he'd dropped inside the door.

"That's the entirety of your luggage?"

"I've never understood why people in this century feel the need to travel with so many possessions."

"In some ways you're very much your father's son."

"I'm so sorry about what happened to him, you know." His face was filled with such sincerity that my eyes welled with tears. "I wish—I wish I could take it all back."

I didn't completely trust Percy, but I wondered... Could we help each other?

CHAPTER 28

Dorian stomped across the tiled kitchen floor. "How could you do it? How could you let him stay here?"

Percy had gone to a restaurant for lunch, so Dorian and I were alone in the house. As tasty as Dorian's pastries were, Percy had insisted there was no way he would eat a vegan lunch. Dorian and I were in the kitchen with the curtains drawn, as always. I was making a summer salad with a bounty from the backyard garden that Brixton had been keeping up, and Dorian was slicing freshly baked French bread for sandwiches.

"You keep talking about the perfection of Julian Lake's kitchen," I said, "and the delicacies he'll order for you. Why don't you stay there for a few days—and take your book with you. I want to keep Percy close and the book far away."

"*Je ne comprend pas.* Do you or do you not trust him?"

"I haven't yet made up my mind. But he's a backward alchemist. We need the information he can give us."

"You do not need to pretend with me, Zoe. I heard every word. I know there is no hope. I will not stand for the sacrifice of an innocent to save me."

"We don't know that's the only way."

Dorian didn't answer. Instead, he selected a paprika-infused sea salt and handed it to me. "This one will be good with the salad."

Though I'm not the cook Dorian is, I've always been intrigued by how salt can bring out the flavors of the simplest foods. Unlike some unnecessary culinary flourishes, salt fulfills a body's basic needs. Throughout history, salt has played an important role in society and culture because of how essential it is for the body. It's why salt, along with sulfur and mercury, is one of the three essentials in alchemy. In that *tria prima*, salt represents the body, and is the child of sulfur and mercury.

As Dorian skillfully tossed a salad using only one hand, my phone buzzed. It was a text message from Brixton, asking if Dorian could prepare a feast for two dozen people—tonight. I called Brixton back to tell him it was bad timing. To my surprise, he picked up his phone.

"I got your message, Brix, but that's awfully short notice. We can't just—"

"Blue's home," he said. "She's out of jail."

I could hear the joy in his voice. It was so innocent and blissful that I nearly forgot the tragedies swirling around me. "That's wonderful. I didn't know she was being released so soon."

"She didn't want to tell any of us in advance. I guess she didn't really believe it was going to happen, until she was actually out. Isn't it wicked awesome news? Especially with Mom so upset about her dad maybe being dead. Blue's sure to cheer her up. Have you noticed she has a way of doing that?"

I smiled even though neither the teenager on the other end of the line nor the gargoyle absorbed in his cooking could see me.

"She definitely does have a way about her," I agreed.

"She showed up at her cottage today. Mom and Abel thought having a welcome home party for all of her friends would be even better than keeping her to ourselves. Is Dorian there? Can I talk to him?"

"He's busy. But I'm sure he'd be happy to cook."

"I am not busy," Dorian called out behind me. He hopped down from his stepping stool and snatched the phone from me. "Allo? *Oui. Oui.*" He nodded thoughtfully. "This is a superb idea. If only Zoe had not banished me from my home—"

"I didn't banish you." I tried to grab the phone back. Dorian shushed me and scurried away. "I'll keep Percy out of the house this afternoon, so you can cook before you move into Julian Lake's house for a few days."

"*Merci.*" He handed the phone back to me.

"I'll make sure Dorian has everything he needs to cook," I told Brixton, "then bring the food to the teashop tonight."

"Cool. This is going to be wicked."

"You're going to be with Blue and your parents the whole afternoon, right?"

I swear I could hear the sound of his eyes rolling. "Sure, probably."

"I'm serious. There's a killer—"

"No, there's not. Those cops told me I was wrong and the guy had been there for years. That's why they think my grandfather—"

"I know. I'm sorry, Brix. But the man you saw spying on Ivan is a very dangerous man. I don't know what he has to do with the man who was found, but he's killed before."

A pause came from the other end of the line, then a swear word I chose to ignore. "Seriously?"

"Seriously. You need to stay far away from him. Don't go anywhere on your own."

After I hung up the phone, I had to figure out how to keep Percy out of the house all day. He was expecting me to pick him up in a little over an hour, so I had time to figure it out.

I drove to the market to get the ingredients on Dorian's shopping list. Usually I walked to local shops or farmer's markets every few days, to supplement the vegetables from the garden and the staples in the pantry, but today I was both in a hurry and needed to buy in bulk. After surviving the fluorescent lights at the supermarket, I dropped off four bags of groceries with Dorian. I was about to head back out to pick up Percy, but Dorian stopped me as he looked through the sacks of food.

"Where is the garlic?" he asked.

"We already have plenty of garlic." I pointed to four heads of garlic, Purple Stripe hardneck, and Western Rose softneck.

Dorian narrowed his black eyes. "I need more for this tomato sauce recipe."

"Are you sure garlic pasta is the way to go for a party?"

He chuckled. "If everyone eats the garlic, they will not mind."

"Remind me to pick some parsley from the backyard to mute the effects."

"Garlic will welcome your friend home with luck."

I paused at the swinging kitchen door. "I didn't realize you were superstitious."

He clicked his tongue. "Not superstitious. Food has cultural significance, as you of all people should understand. It feeds both the body and the soul. Everything I am creating for tonight will welcome Blue Sky home."

I leaned in the door frame and looked over the left half of Dorian's body that was rapidly turning to stone. He didn't dwell on his limitations. "Thank you. That's so thoughtful."

Dorian waved off the comment, and moved his stepping stool to unpack the last bag of groceries. The simple task took longer than usual, since he could only use his right arm to lift the stool.

"I can help when I get back," I said.

"It is unnecessary. I have selected recipes that only require the use of one good arm." Dorian said the words casually, but he didn't look at me. He peered into the grocery bag containing the first tomatoes of the season and shook his head. "I will make do," he muttered, dismissing me with a wave of his clawed hand.

I smiled and left Dorian to the feast preparations. I did a quick walk-through of the house, making sure it was tightly secured and thinking about how different my life had been six months ago. I used to eat for healing and nourishment, with pleasure coming in last on my list of priorities. Since Dorian had come into my life, he'd shown me that delectable foods didn't have to be unhealthy. Which was an accidental discovery.

When Dorian showed up on my doorstep—or, in a moving crate in my living room, to be more accurate—he learned I didn't keep bacon, butter, or cream in the house. Dorian respected my eating habits, but he refused to eat the same "boring" food I ate. I used my flavored oils, salts, and vinegars to season simple soups, stews, and salads, but in cooking with what I had on hand, he showed me how easy it was to turn simple meals into mouthwatering feasts.

I knew why I was thinking so much about food. I was starving. I'd been feeling so anxious I hadn't stopped to take care of myself. I knew better than to disregard my body. I stuck my head back into the kitchen to grab a snack to take with me. The thoughtful gargoyle was one step ahead of me. He handed me a toasted baguette sandwich wrapped in parchment paper.

My friend and I were so alike but also worlds apart.

And that gave me the perfect idea for what to do with Percy. I slipped up to the attic before leaving the house.

I picked up Percy from a local brewery where he was enjoying an extended lunch accompanied by beer and a pretty young woman. She wasn't happy to see me, but she perked up when Percy whispered something in her ear before paying the bill.

"Not too worried about Lucien after all?" I said once we were on the sidewalk.

"I was in a darkened back booth, so I knew I'd see him before he saw me."

I led Percy to the truck. My myrrh air freshener was no match for the scent of batch brewed beer that had ensconced itself in Percy's clothing.

"I thought you lived in the other direction," he said as I pulled onto the highway.

"I need the house to myself to cook for a good friend's welcome home party tonight, so I've got another idea—"

Percy gaped at me. "I'm dying and you're having a party?"

The words bristled. Percy was in much better shape than Dorian. And one of the lessons I'd learned after being alive for so long was that you need to slow down and enjoy the small moments in life. Not only did they make existence more meaningful, but they helped you see things more clearly. I was going to give myself this evening to celebrate life with Blue, Brixton, and Max. I didn't know what would happen the next day, but time with them tonight was a gift I could give all of us.

"I'm going to help you help yourself," I said. "I found the photocopied pages of that book we were talking about." I pointed to my purse that lay at Percy's feet. He lunged for it and greedily scooped up the pages.

"You have it," he said. "You have it! Where did you find these?"

"I used to do a lot of research. I found those pages years ago. You're the one who's the backward alchemist. I'm going to leave you at a library."

"A library? Zoe, are you serious? I can stay out of the way at your house."

"I need to concentrate, and so do you. You can read these pages and see what they tell you."

"But—"

"I'll pick you up in four hours. You can come to the party with me."

"Can we have dinner first?"

"Didn't you hear me? I'm going home to cook for the party."

"But you're cooking vegan food."

Family.

CHAPTER 29

Long before I saw her, I knew Blue was there. The fragrance of her homemade teas filled the cozy space. I'm sure it was my imagination, but even the weeping fig tree in the center of the cafe appeared to have perked up that night. The illusion was created because the tree-ring tables that normally circled the living tree had been moved aside to make room for the crowd that had gathered to welcome Blue home.

I'd dropped off Dorian's feast before picking up Percy from the library. Unsurprisingly, Percy hadn't gleaned anything useful from the hours surrounded by information.

As Percy and I walked into the party in full swing, everyone was facing the back of the café. The sound of two acoustic guitars strumming with two voices harmonizing echoed through the teashop. Abel and Brixton were performing "Imagine," a perfect choice for the occasion. Their voices blended to create perfectly imperfect harmony. Their arms moved in rhythm on their guitars.

The song concluded. Heather whistled and the crowd applauded. I caught a glimpse of wild gray hair moving stealthily through the crowd, toward Brixton. My heart skipped a beat as I thought about how easy it would be for someone to get to Brixton if they wanted to. Blue snuck up behind Brixton and gave him a hug. He turned nearly as red as the beets in my garden but hugged her back.

I saw another smiling face in the crowd. Max Liu. He must have felt my eyes on him, because his gaze met mine. I felt my stomach give a little flip-flop as his smile grew wider.

"These two are way too good," Blue said to the crowd. "I'm calling for a forced break so you'll all eat this wonderful spread of food Zoe prepared for the occasion. Eat!" She caught my eye and winked.

"First," Max said, "a toast to the heart of the neighborhood." He raised a clay mug of tea. "Blue, you were here for me during a rough time in my life, and you made me feel at home. I can confidently say that every person here feels the same way. Thank you, Blue."

"Hear, hear!" several voices chimed in.

Blue wiped a tear from her eye. "I'm only crying because the food is getting cold." She laughed and cleared her throat. "This is the first place that's ever truly felt like home."

I knew the feeling more acutely than she or anyone else in that room knew. I wished I could have told Blue how much I related.

We all knew Blue Sky as the owner of Blue Sky Teas, the woman who knew how to brew exquisite teas, who'd helped Brixton with his homework at the teashop since he was in elementary school, and who brightened any room with her infectiously relaxed demeanor.

But the woman who let her curly gray hair run wild and lived in baggy jeans also had a past that nobody knew about until earlier that year.

"Thanks for welcoming me back," Blue concluded. "Now eat!" I could barely imagine blissfully chubby and exuberant Blue Sky as Brenda Skyler, a stick-thin workaholic who wore power suits, dieted, and worked for her husband's legal practice, where she unknowingly helped him with illegal schemes. She wasn't culpable for the crimes she didn't know about, but she was guilty of forging documents and faking her own death to begin her new life.

The woman in the teashop that evening was a mix of the two. She'd lost weight in jail, and her radiant face, usually full of natural color from the time she spent wildcrafting outside, was pale.

The party guest list included me, Brixton, Heather, Abel, Brixton's best friends Veronica and Ethan, Max, and a dozen of Blue's friends who I hadn't previously met, as well as Percy, who I'd brought along with me. Ivan wasn't feeling well enough to attend.

The teashop usually closed at seven o'clock in the evening, but tonight it was open for this private party. Two of the tree-ring tables had been pushed together for the spread of food prepared by Dorian in my kitchen that afternoon. I needn't have worried about his infirmity. He'd outdone himself with a freekeh and parsley salad, freshly baked bread with garlic tomato sauce for dipping, bowls of nuts, each home-roasted with a different spice mix, plus a dessert tray of miniature tarts and mousses. Everyone congratulated me on the food.

"How did you get the tomato sauce so creamy?" Heather asked, popping a bite of sauce-dipped bread into her mouth.

"A chef never reveals her secrets," I said. I'd have to ask Dorian later. She was right. A delicate flavor I couldn't place added depth and balance to the flavorful garlic.

Heather had woven a banner out of wildflowers that was supposed to read WELCOME HOME BLUE. But some of the flowers refused to be tamed, so by the time the party started the string of letters read EL ME HOME BLUE. Blue loved it.

The teenagers took photographs of people standing under the sign to share on social media. Percy and I ducked out of the way as photos were snapped.

"It was so much easier before every bloody man, woman, and child had a damn mobile phone," Percy whispered.

During a short break for everyone to fill their plates, I introduced Percy to my friends. Brixton and Abel resumed the live music, with Brixton still on his acoustic guitar, and Abel switching to a banjo. I wished Tobias could have been there to sing, but I knew he was exactly where he needed to be, spending precious last moments with his beloved Rosa.

Max brought me a lemon tart. "Penny for your thoughts."

I took a bite of the tart, giving myself a few moments to think. "The tart is more tart than I expected," I said. *Smooth, Zoe.*

"You didn't taste them at home?"

Damn. "Too many things to sample. I trusted the recipe." *Please don't ask what's in it,* I thought to myself. Although from the flavors dancing on my tongue, I could guess most of the ingredients, the two dominant ones being coconut oil and lemon.

Max nodded and bit into a chocolate mousse tart.

The connection between us from the day before was missing, and I knew why. He kept glancing distractedly at Percy.

"You asked what I was thinking about," I said. "I was thinking about how beautiful it is that so many people came to celebrate with Blue at the very last minute."

"It's lovely," Max said. Unlike our generic conversation. Max stole another glance at Percy, who was on the outskirts of a small group with Blue.

"You never told me the story of the plastic skeleton in your house," I prompted.

"It was Chadna's during med school."

Great. He was jealous of Percy and I'd asked about his dead ex-wife. But instead of the reaction I was expecting, a grin spread across Max's face.

"She refused to tell me why she kept it so long. On each of my birthdays, she'd tell me a little bit more of the story. That way she said I'd be forced to live a long life with her, to hear the end of the story."

"That's beautiful."

The smile on Max's face faded as I felt a tap at my elbow. Percy.

"I'm going to get more food," Max said.

"What's up, Percy?" I asked.

"I'm tired. I thought I'd go back to the house for an early night. Could I have the key?"

"You don't have to lie to me," I said.

"Fair enough." Percy shrugged. "I was trying to be sly about giving you some time with your beau and letting you have fun at the fete."

Maybe Percy had grown up, after all. I gave Percy a key and made sure he remembered how to walk back to the house.

"GPS," he said, shaking his phone at me.

Brixton and Abel amped up the music. Blue began to dance with her friends. I was reminded of my love for Portland when I couldn't tell the difference between Blue's forager friends and the group of lawyers who'd come to her aid. Perhaps they were one and the same. Brixton was busy playing guitar and his friend Ethan was too cool for dancing, so Veronica joined the group of older women and let loose. At fourteen, she was already the tallest woman in the group. Her cascading black hair tossed from side to side in rhythm with the music. The awkward young woman I'd met six months before was slipping away, innocent adolescence sacrificed for a more fully formed young adulthood.

Max pulled me from the corner in which I was hiding to dance with him. Looking into his eyes, my stomach fluttered. Things were starting to feel like they had before Percy arrived in Portland—until Max abruptly stopped dancing.

His eyes narrowed and he walked to the door of the teashop without a word.

Two men in suits stood at the door. Even though they weren't dressed in policemen's uniforms, their stance and Max's interaction with them suggested they were detectives. With the volume of the music, from across the teashop I couldn't hear what they were saying, but Max was shaking his head. *No no no.* Had I dismissed the French police too soon?

The two men were insistent. Max shook his head one last time, then led them around the weeping fig tree in the center of the teashop. Not to me.

To Heather.

With an abrupt jerk of his arm, Abel broke off strumming his guitar. He smiled as he stood and whispered to Brixton to continue playing. I knew that look of bravado on Abel's face was a mask applied for the benefit of his stepson. Brixton tried to argue but ultimately listened to his stepfather.

As soon as the music resumed, people forgot about the interruption. They went back to dancing and eating. Nobody else seemed to notice that the newcomers weren't welcome guests. I followed Max and Abel to the corner where the detectives were talking with Heather.

"It'll be easier if we talk to you both down at the station," one of them was saying to her.

"What's this about?" Abel asked. "Did you confirm the identity of the man Brix found?"

"You are?"

"Her husband."

"It's okay, hon," Heather said, stroking Abel's arm.

"Please step aside, sir," the detective said. I hoped Brixton was too busy on the guitar to see the look the detective directed at Abel, or I feared the impetuous teenager might try to punch the detective.

"You have no right to interrupt this private party," Abel said, his voice rising. Brixton's guitar riff ended with a discordant crash. He flung the instrument aside and ran to his mom. All eyes followed him.

"It's okay, Brix," Heather said. "They only want to talk to us."

"Us?" Brixton asked.

Heather linked her arm through Brixton's, stood on her tiptoes to kiss him on the side of his head, then nodded to the detectives.

"Now?" Brixton said, pulling away from his mom. "They can't just—"

"It's okay, sweetie," Heather said softly.

Brixton looked to his stepfather. With a clenched jaw, Abel nodded at Brixton. Then Max, Abel, and Brixton followed the detectives out the door.

Blue tried to assure everyone that it was a private family matter and nothing to worry about, but the party broke up after that.

I walked home alone, wondering what the detectives had found out about Heather's father. Why wouldn't they answer Abel's question? It seemed simple enough.

Walking up my driveway, my senses tingled. I haven't survived as long as I have without listening to the subtle cues surrounding us that we pick up as intuition. Something was different, but what? I chastised myself. I had a house guest. I must have noticed the subtle movement of him moving behind a closed curtain. I continued walking, but stopped as soon as I passed my Chevy truck and Airstream trailer.

The front door was ajar.

I ran to the door and pushed it open. The living room had been ransacked.

"Percy?" I called out.

No answer.

I ran through the house. The lock to my basement alchemy lab had been broken open. I grabbed a heavy flashlight and crept down the stairs. With each step, my heart pounded more loudly in my ears.

At the base of the basement stairs, Percy lay unconscious on the concrete floor, his hair wet with blood.

CHAPTER 30

"I'm all right," Percy croaked. But he clearly wasn't. Blood covered the side of his head.

"I'll call an ambulance."

"No." He grabbed my wrist. "Too many questions. You know that."

He was right. But he was also in bad shape. In worse shape than my natural remedies could fix.

"All right," I said as Percy struggled to sit up. "Let go of my arm and I promise I'll get supplies, not call an ambulance."

He obliged then sank back to the floor. I rushed upstairs to get supplies.

After I'd cleaned his head wound, I saw he wasn't as badly off as I'd feared. Head wounds tend to bleed a lot, but the gash itself wouldn't need my sloppy stitches after all. I led him to the bedroom he was using, exchanged his bloody shirt for a fresh one, and applied a healing salve that would serve as a natural antibiotic.

"Was it Lucien?" I asked, holding an ice pack to the side of his head.

He nodded and winced in pain.

"I don't suppose you have any Paracetamol? No, I didn't think you would."

"He was after *Non Degenera Alchemia*?"

"It appears that way. I'm so sorry I couldn't stop him—"

"I'm sorry I left you alone. Neither of us should be on our own right now."

A knock on the door sounded from below.

"You'll be all right." I tucked him into bed before running downstairs.

At the front door I found Max. He looked infinitely more frazzled than he had an hour before. Brixton sat on the porch steps behind him, a banjo slung over his back.

"Abel is with Heather at the police station," Max said. "I thought I could look after Brix—"

"I'm almost fifteen," Brixton cut in. "Nobody needs to look after me."

"But I was called into the station," Max continued. "So I can't keep an eye on him. I hate to impose upon Blue the day she's out of jail. Can he hang out here until his mom can pick him up?"

I hesitated for long enough that Max picked up on the delay. At the sound of creaking floorboards overhead, he stepped in front of Brixton and shifted into a combative stance.

"It's fine," I said. "Everything is fine. I just have a visitor. Ambrose's son Percy is staying here."

"Oh," Max said, his voice curt. "I didn't realize he'd be staying with you. We can go. Sorry to have bothered you. I'll figure out something else."

"It's no bother," I said. "Brix, since the party got cut short and you were busy making music, I bet you're hungry. There's a lot of food in the fridge."

"I'm not hungry." Brixton glared at me. "But I'll pretend to eat something so you two can talk." He pushed past us and disappeared through the kitchen's swinging door.

"Smart kid," Max said.

"I don't think he likes being treated like a kid. Come inside. What did you want to talk about?" I took a step toward Max, but he turned away. He strode across the living room and gripped the back of a dining room chair.

"What's going on, Max? Is the man Brixton's grandfather? Why the secrecy?"

The sound of scales being played on a banjo came from the kitchen.

"This case keeps getting stranger," Max said. "The lab guys got things wrong. This isn't an old case after all. Some of those chemicals we found in the shack's laboratory messed with the speed of decomposition. The man Brixton found was killed *this past week.*"

Oh no… "That means Brixton *is* a witness to a murder." Had Lucien killed a new apprentice in a makeshift alchemy lab here in Portland? Was that what Percy was hinting at?

Max swallowed hard and nodded.

"Then why," I asked, "were the detectives interested in Heather and Brixton, if it's not Brix's grandfather after all?"

"I didn't say that."

"So it *is* Heather's father? That's why they're questioning her?"

"Not exactly."

"What does that mean, *not exactly?* It's both her dad and *not* her dad?"

"He hasn't been identified yet. There are no teeth to test for dental records, and DNA testing doesn't work that quickly. But now that we know it's a new death, it's unlikely to be Heather's father."

"Then why—"

"Those guys don't have the best social skills. Because of the new information about the probable timing of death, they wanted to get more details from Brixton about what he saw. As a minor, they needed his mom present."

"So it was Brixton they wanted?"

"At first." Max rubbed his eyes. "But Heather's manner made them suspicious."

"So now they're talking more with her alone."

Max nodded. "She wasn't doing herself any favors. The first time they talked with her, she wouldn't agree to a voluntary DNA swab when they thought it was her dad, which could prove or disprove a familial match, since there weren't teeth for a dental match."

"She had every right to refuse an invasive test."

"It's a swab across her cheek, Zoe."

"Which you said was *voluntary.* Of course she'd decline." I feared the day when modern technology would make it impossible for me to keep my privacy. I'd already avoided many educational and job opportunities because I didn't want to be in more databases than necessary.

"Even when it could have helped her learn if it was her dad?" Max said. "Look, never mind. I don't want to have a stupid fight. I get it that privacy rights are important. *I* don't think she behaved suspiciously. But it's not my case."

"Meaning you're going to let them—"

"They're good cops, Zoe. We all want the truth."

"How's Brixton doing with all this?"

"Not great. If he was okay, he'd be fine on his own at home." He glanced at his phone. "Look, I've gotta run. You sure it's okay for Brixton to be here with you while your houseguest is here?"

"Positive." With Lucien on the loose, I wanted Brixton close.

"You two aren't..." He cleared his throat. "You sure you don't need privacy?"

"He's Ambrose's son, Max."

"Yeah, but he's a lot closer to your age."

"Age is meaningless." I took his hands in mine. I believed the words I spoke, and he must have seen it in my eyes. He squeezed my hand and gave me a slow kiss on the cheek before departing. The fresh scent of citrus lingered even after he was gone. A small piece of his comforting presence remained with me.

～

In spite of his claims that he wasn't hungry, I found Brixton eating a sweet potato pie straight from the pan.

"I thought you and Max were a couple," Brixton said through a mouthful.

"We are." Maybe. I hoped.

"Then who's the guy singing in the shower?"

"Percy. You met him tonight." From the kitchen, if I listened carefully, I could hear the singing coming from the bathroom above us.

"Your ex's kid? No offense, but he's kind of a tool."

I tried not to laugh.

"See?" Brixton said. "I'm totally right, aren't I?"

"I wouldn't say you're wrong."

"So is alchemy, like, hereditary?"

"It's easier to find out about alchemy if you know an alchemist," I said, "but it's not inherited."

Brixton nodded thoughtfully. He set down the half-empty pan of pie and hopped up onto the counter. Dorian hated it when he did that, but I liked how it made the house feel more like a home.

"I don't want you to teach me, Zoe. I don't want to learn alchemy." He picked up a sprig of spearmint from the kitchen's window box and twirled it in his fingers, looking at the spinning green pinwheel in his fingertips as he spoke. "I know Ivan wants to learn, since he's dying. But I think it would suck to outlive Veronica and Ethan, and anyone else I'll ever care about. I'll probably already outlive Abel and Mom." He squished the mint in his hand, releasing the scent into the air.

"Max told me what the police discovered."

"About the skin under his fingernails?"

"I meant how long the man had been dead. They found skin under his fingernails?" Was that the real reason they wanted Heather to voluntarily give her DNA? I decided now wasn't the time to worry Brixton about his mom. It wouldn't be her DNA under his fingernails regardless.

"I told you I wasn't lying about the body being new."

644

"We need to talk about something else serious." I lowered my voice. "Quickly, in case Percy is feeling better and comes downstairs. I hate to do this right now, when I know you've got so much else on your mind."

"It's cool."

"Percy came to Portland because he knows the man you saw spying on Ivan. The man's name is Lucien, and he's a dangerous backward alchemist. Percy fell in with him a century ago, and got caught up in backward alchemy, but Lucien is after Dorian's book, so Percy wanted to warn me."

"Whoa. He doesn't seem like the kind of guy who'd look out for other people."

"With everything that's happening around here, I'm glad you've got good intuition." Even though I could hear Percy still singing Spice Girls songs in the shower, I kept my voice low. "You're right. I don't trust him completely, so I haven't told him about Dorian or that I have Dorian's book. He's not the most altruistic of men. He also wants my help. He's suffering the same alchemical fate as Dorian."

"His body is returning to its original form?" Brixton asked.

I groaned. Brixton's concise summation made me realize I'd made a significant oversight. I knew that with his life force deteriorating, Dorian would be alive but trapped in stone *because he was originally made of stone*. With a *human* backward alchemist's life force quickly deteriorating, they'd transform into their original flesh and bone—as their flesh and bones would have with age.

"Zoe, are you okay? You look like you've seen a ghost or something."

"Something much worse. I think I've seen the truth about a backward alchemist."

"Wicked. What is it?"

"I need you to tell me exactly what happened when you saw Lucien go into the shack in the woods."

"I told you, I saw that Lucien guy, who'd been spying on Ivan, go into the shack and then kill some guy."

"But you didn't see him do the actual killing."

"No."

"You saw Lucien sneak out?"

Brixton hesitated, and I knew I was right.

"I might not have actually seen him," Brixton said. "But it was all loud, like a fight, and then it was quiet."

"You didn't see anyone else coming near the shed?"

"No. I waited a while, and after it was quiet for a really long time, I looked inside. That's when I saw the dead guy."

"A dead man who didn't look like Lucien."

"No, this guy was way older. That's how I knew Lucien must have slipped out the back when I was too far away to see him."

"You didn't see the body until a few minutes after he died."

"So?"

"That means," I said, "that the dead man is Lucien."

"I saw the guy, Zoe. He's not—"

"Lucien was a backward alchemist. His life force was reversing, so once he died, his body would wither much more quickly than that of a normal person. That's what's confused this whole situation. You saw him shortly after he died and thought he was an old man. The police saw him a short time later and thought he'd been dead for a decade."

Brixton kicked a kitchen cabinet. "And the police don't know about alchemy, so once they figured out the body was changing they thought it was the chemicals from the alchemy lab. So, he did an experiment wrong or something?"

I gripped the edge of the counter. "I don't think so. Percy isn't here to warn me. He fooled me, making me think he was being thoughtful tonight when really he wanted time alone in my house. Percy followed Lucien here to kill him and to steal Dorian's book for himself."

· And by telling him I had a copy of the contents of the book, I'd pretty much admitted to him that I had it.

CHAPTER 31

"Whoa." Brixton looked from me to the kitchen ceiling. The singing from overhead had stopped.

"We're leaving," I said. "Now."

I scribbled a note to Percy about having to go to the police station for Heather, so he wouldn't think I'd discovered his secret, grabbed my silver coat, and shoved Brixton out the door.

"The scent in this truck is always so weird," Brixton mumbled as he climbed inside.

"It's not weird," I said as I put the key in the ignition of the truck. "Myrrh is a great air freshener. It works well in toothpaste too."

"I remember. Like frankincense, from the Bible. My life is too weird."

"Frankincense is too strong for an air freshener. Seatbelt." Brixton rolled his eyes but obliged.

"Is it possible that Lucien was already injured when he made his way to his alchemy supplies in the shed?" I asked, trying the engine again. That's what I got for having a 1942 Chevy. I hated to think that Percy was stealthy enough to get into and out of the cabin without Brixton seeing him.

"Yeah. He was kind of disoriented, but I figured it was because he'd forgotten exactly where the shack was. It's pretty overgrown out there. You think that could explain why I didn't see Percy or anyone else?"

"Because Percy had already dealt him a fatal blow."

The engine of my truck turned over three times before finally starting, just long enough that I wondered if Percy had disabled it. I gave silent thanks as we peeled out of the driveway.

How could I have been so stupid as to think Percy believed the old wives' tale about alchemists not being able to kill people? He'd been trying to misdirect me this whole time. Had I fallen for it because he looked so much like Ambrose? Or because I'd wanted so badly to believe him because of my love for his father? Or maybe it was simply because I wanted to believe in the goodness of humanity.

Percy must have knocked himself out to cover his tracks after he searched my house for Dorian's book. A superficial head wound was a good choice. Even a minor wound in that location would bleed profusely and could easily look more serious than it was. He hadn't left the party to give me and Max space; he left so he'd have time alone to search my house. And I'd sent Dorian away, so I had no way to prove it. At least I'd asked Dorian to take *Not Untrue Alchemy* with him.

"Where are we going?" Brixton asked, gripping the dashboard as I turned a corner faster than was prudent. He winced.

"Is your hand still hurting?" I glanced at Brixton, expecting to see a bruise forming. Instead, I saw a bleeding scrape. "You didn't tell me you cut yourself on the table."

"It's nothing." He wrapped his sleeve around his hand. "And you didn't say where we're going."

"Your mom didn't do anything, so I'm guessing they're going to let her go soon."

"We're going to hang out at the police station?" Brixton rolled his eyes. "I should have brought the rest of that pie with me."

"How can you be so relaxed?"

"That guy Percy doesn't seem like an evil mastermind. You and I could totally take him on. And with Dorian in the mix, he wouldn't stand a chance."

I pictured Dorian clawing at Percy's perfect hair and burst out laughing. It was nervous laughter, brought on by the stress, but it was a welcome release of tension.

"See?" Brixton said. "You sure he could really be the killer?"

"I'm not taking any chances."

～

I left Brixton with Abel, apologizing for not being able to hang out with Brixton because my houseguest was unwell.

When I got back to the house, Percy had his feet up on the couch with an icepack on his head and a tray of ginger cookies on his lap, watching a sitcom on his phone. He'd found the beer in the fridge. Two empty bottles sat on the coffee table, and a third was open on the floor next to the couch.

"How's your friend?" he asked.

I was done playing things safe. I had to find out what was going on. "Lucien is dead," I said.

The platter of cookies dropped to the floor, as did Percy's phone. The screen cracked as it struck the hardwood floor. He left it where it lay.

I could have sworn Percy's reaction was genuine. Unlike his sincere expressions of regret from earlier that day, this was true shock.

"You saw him? Where?"

"He's the dead body they found in the woods."

The color drained from Percy's face. "But you said—I mean, how—?"

"I know you lied about Lucien being the one to ransack my attic and basement in search of *Non Degenera Alchemia*. It was you." I yanked the icepack from his head and pulled back his hair.

He howled with pain.

"It's only a scratch," I said. "It stopped bleeding right away. You didn't even bother reapplying bandages after your shower. You also didn't back up your lie by breaking down the door to get inside. You unlocked the door with the key I lent you—which you're going to give back to me. Now. Did you think keeping track of your lies wasn't necessary because I trusted you?"

"How can you—"

"Your most convincing lie was that you believe that silly legend about alchemists not being able to kill anyone." I let go of his hair and let him sink back onto the couch.

"It's true!"

"How can it possibly be true when you're the one who killed Lucien?"

"I would never. I *could* never. It was awful with Father—" Percy stopped himself.

Ambrose? My heart beat furiously in my throat. "What did you say?"

"Nothing." He clutched his head in his hands. "I'm in shock over hearing that Lucien is dead. I don't know what I'm saying."

"What was awful with Ambrose?"

"Nothing. Truly. I didn't mean anything."

"Yes, you did. When you tell the truth, you lose the cocky tilt of your head. You did it a moment ago. That means you didn't know Lucien was dead—I stand corrected there. I believe you about that."

"Why are you looking at me like that, Zoe? You're scaring me."

"You believe that old wives' tale from *personal experience*." My pulse raced. "Did Ambrose find out you had turned to backward alchemy, and that's the real reason he killed himself? No… Oh God, Percy, was your father's suicide the death you needed?" With Percy providing no answers, my imagination began running wild with horrible thoughts. The room spun. I couldn't catch my breath.

"You're unbalanced, Zoe. You always were."

My focus snapped to Percy. The spoiled little man who only superficially resembled his father. The physical similarities were striking, but not their souls. "I've never been more clear-headed," I said. "I've always worked to protect the people I love."

"What does that have to do with—"

"You don't understand everything that's going on, Percy. I'm someone with nothing left to lose."

Percy tried to stand. I pushed him back onto the couch and stood over him. His beautiful eyes, so like his father's in appearance but not spirit, opened wide with fear.

"This is how it's going to go," I said. "You're going to tell me the truth about what happened to Ambrose."

Percy's eyes filled with tears. "I never meant to hurt either of you. I only wanted what you had. Can't you understand that? It was so easy for you. Not for me."

"What happened with your father? And what does it have to do with that stupid superstition?"

"You don't know that it's stupid, Zoe. You didn't believe backward alchemy was real at first either."

"That's different. The death rotation makes sense. It's sacrificing one element for another, or even one living being's energy for another's." I thought of how creating Dorian's Tea of Ashes depleted my own energy. "If anything, killing should make a backward alchemist *stronger*, not kill him." I regretted the words as soon as they left my mouth. But alchemy is science, and that's what made sense scientifically.

"How would you know?" Percy snapped. "Have you ever killed anyone?"

"Of course not."

"Then you don't know. It would kill you—or, if you're strong, only bring you to the brink of death." Percy's lower lip trembled. The shaking spread to his whole body. He truly believed what he was saying; he truly was afraid of something.

"Oh God, Percy. What did you do?"

"Nothing," he said too quickly. "I'm not talking about myself." His eyes didn't meet mine.

"What did you do?"

"I told you—nothing! I didn't mean to do it. It was Father's fault. And yours. The more I think about it, it *was* your fault. You put him in that awful place. That's why it happened."

"Why *what* happened?" I'd had no choice about sending Ambrose to Charenton Asylum. I was worried he would harm himself. The psychiatric hospital was known for its humanitarian treatment of patients, unlike so many other "lunatic asylums" of the time. It had been good for him, even though in the end they hadn't been able to stop him from taking his own life. But that couldn't have been what Percy was talking about.

"I don't want to talk to you anymore. You're a bully. You always were."

I stared at the stranger in front of me; funny how the resemblance to his father faded more with every passing moment. Ambrose had been generous to a fault, never petulant or petty. "I've always showed you kindness, Percy. Always."

"By rubbing my nose in your own perfection? By stealing my father from me?"

"Is that what you think I did?"

"He didn't tell you everything, Zoe. My father is the one who told me about Lucien and Olav. He's the one who told me how I could find the backward alchemists." In my stunned silence, Percy rose and pushed past me.

"No, he would never—"

"You don't know everything." Percy rolled onto his heels and thrust his chin out, the same spoiled mannerism he'd had when he was twenty. Yet, he hadn't regained control of his quivering body. He wasn't nearly as confident as he wanted to appear.

"Sit down, Percival," I said in my most commanding voice. "You're going to tell me exactly what you've been dancing around. What do you know about Ambrose being in the asylum?"

He snorted. "Why would I tell you anything?"

I drew a deep breath and took a huge gamble. I could have played more on his superstitions, but there was a seed of a good man in Percy that I hoped I wasn't mistaken about.

"Because you're not a bad man, Percy. You never were. You're weak, though. Whatever you're holding in is what's killing you even more quickly. The weight is crushing your soul."

"I'm dying anyway, Zoe." Percy closed his eyes. His lips moved, but no sound came out. Was he praying? When he opened his eyes, I caught a glimmer of humility in them.

"I might as well die with a clean conscience," Percy said. "My father didn't kill himself."

CHAPTER 32

"The story begins," Percy said, "when I came back to Paris to see someone. A woman."

Of course, I thought to myself.

"I didn't visit you and Father," he continued, "because you believed me dead. I had no choice but to let you believe that. They forced me—"

"Stop with the excuses. If you want to die with a clear conscience, you need to own up to your actions."

Percy nodded, but the motion was erratic, as if he was battling himself. "Lucien kept an eye on you and Father when you were in Paris," he said with a trembling voice. "He knew that Father was raving about alchemy after *you* put him in Charenton Asylum. He was going to ruin alchemy for all of us. He shouldn't have been in that asylum."

"I believed it to be for the best," I said through my tightly clenched jaw. "He was distraught when he thought you'd died. He thought he'd failed you as a father, that it was his fault you were so unhappy, even though he'd given you everything he possibly could. He was talking about hurting himself."

"Instead," Percy said, "his actions threatened to hurt all of us."

"They believed him a mad man, Percy. Nobody took his ravings about alchemy seriously. He also talked about how he'd opened the gates of Hell at the *Cabaret de L'Enfer*. Which obviously wasn't true."

Percy grunted. "You thought you were so much better than him because you hated nightclubs."

I clenched my teeth. Percy was the type of man who thought he understood everything, even if he only had a small sliver of the truth.

I had rarely accompanied Ambrose when he went to *le Cabaret de L'Enfer* nightclub. Not because I didn't appreciate the macabre beauty or the dancing, but because staying awake late into the night has always been a challenge for me. Ambrose understood that, and he went out of his way to bring me the joys of the nighttime I otherwise would have missed.

The memory washed over me. One winter morning, nearly a century ago, Ambrose had awakened me a few minutes before dawn with a wicked grin on his face. "I have something to show you," he'd said. "Put on your dancing shoes." He'd discovered how to sneak into the nightclub while it was closed. While most of Paris slept but my own energy was surging, he lifted me onto his shoulders and helped me squeeze through a narrow window with a faulty latch. Once inside, I let him in through a larger door. He lifted two glasses from behind the bar and poured us drinks from the bottle of claret he'd brought with him. Carvings of devils and imps hung from the walls. Like the debated purpose of gargoyles, it was unclear whether the inhuman creatures were there to warn revelers or to tempt them. As the sun rose above Paris, Ambrose spun me around and around on the dance floor we had to ourselves.

"They could have believed his rantings," Percy said, shattering the memory. "He could have revealed everything. That's why Lucien asked me to visit Father and talk sense into him."

I bit back tears. I didn't want to hear the rest of the story.

"We looked alike, he and I," Percy continued. "That's what made it possible. I approached the gates of Charenton, pretending that I was Father and that I'd escaped. I couldn't very well walk in as a visitor, as I was supposed to be dead." Percy ran a shaking hand through his dark hair that was so like his father's. "As I expected, a nurse opened the gates for me, letting me inside. She was such a tiny thing, with a fragile heart-shaped face, I don't know how she could work in such a place. It was easy to administer the chloroform. I didn't hurt her. She was asleep before she knew what was happening. With her keys, I let myself into Father's room. *He* was the one who became violent. Not me. I only meant to talk sense into him."

Percy was pacing furiously now and knocked over the coffee table, but he didn't seem to notice. I barely noticed either. This couldn't be happening. This couldn't have been how my beloved Ambrose spent his last moments on earth.

"He must have been forced to take drugs or something that made him crazed. It wasn't my fault. I did only what I had to do to save myself. He said I was a hallucination sent there by God, telling him to reveal alchemy to the world." Percy's voice shook. His eyes darted around the room, looking every-where but at me. "It was the exact opposite of what I meant to achieve. I didn't know what I was doing. It was an accident. I was only trying to stop him shouting, blurting out our secrets. My hands went around his neck—"

He broke off in a sob as I felt myself crumpling onto the velvet couch. Instead of feeling soft and comforting, the texture was like razor blades. The asylum had found Ambrose with a broken neck. They told me he'd hung himself.

"When I stopped," Percy whispered, "it was too late. He was dead, and I was nearly dead myself." He continued through hiccupping sobs. "It took all the strength I had to get myself out of there. Lucien had to take care of me while I recovered. I w-w-was lucky to survive."

Percy was bawling by now. My normal instincts to comfort and heal were absent. I couldn't find it in me to forgive the man who'd killed Ambrose. He'd felt such guilt that it sickened him to the point of feeling like he was going to die. He wasn't an evil man, but I couldn't look at him for one more second.

"Get out," I said. "I never want to see you again."

CHAPTER 33

I was shaking so much that I could barely shove Percy's bag into his arms and lock the door behind him. I somehow got the door bolted before sliding down onto the floor.

I didn't cry. I couldn't. I was too numb from shock. I'd grieved for Ambrose, but this was different. Yet strangely, along with my horror, I also felt a sliver of *peace*.

Ambrose had grieved for his son. He'd lost himself in his guilt over finding the Elixir of Life when his only son could not, and he found it difficult to move on in the months that followed Percy's supposed death. But he *hadn't* been so lost that he'd taken his own life.

I gripped the wallet in my hand. As I'd shoved Percy's bag into his arms, I'd also lifted his wallet. It was done sloppily with shaking hands, but he'd been too upset to notice. There were still many blanks about Percy's current situation, but I couldn't bear to keep asking him questions. I hoped the wallet would provide some answers.

I took several deep breaths and picked up the coffee table Percy had knocked over. The simple action gave me a measure of reality to focus on. By the time I'd collected the books and newspapers that had fallen to the floor, I had mostly stopped shaking. I sat down on the couch and opened the wallet. Percival Smythe had a driver's license from Britain with an address in London, a membership card for a gym in a town in a suburb of Paris, and a library card from Edinburgh. A black credit card and several hundred dollars in cash indicated he was living well.

Two photographs were tucked inside the wallet. The first photograph was of Percy and a glamorous young woman. They sat together at a Parisian café, a cigarette in her hand and a pipe in his. They weren't looking at the camera, but at each other. She looked like a movie star. She reminded me of an actress from a 1930s Charlie Chan movie.

The other photograph was a faded black-and-white picture of Ambrose. The print was nearly worn through in the center, as if fingers had run over its surface many times. Percy had saved the photograph of his father and looked at it countless times. Damn. I couldn't dismiss him as completely heartless.

A tentative knock sounded on the front door.

"Zoe?" The voice was hesitant. "You don't have to look at me again, but I think my wallet fell out. Could you check the couch cushions?"

If it hadn't been for that well-loved photo of Ambrose, I wouldn't have opened the door. But now…

I opened the door and pressed the wallet into Percy's hands. "I hope you find peace before you die, Percy. But never show your face here again."

"I'm sorry," he said softly. "For everything."

By the time I locked the door again, my anger hadn't subsided, but it was a calmer rage. Clarity washed over me, showing me an important fact.

Percy was either one of the world's greatest actors, or he truly felt remorse over killing his father. He wholeheartedly believed the myth that alchemists can't kill one another without suffering grave consequences, and thought it was this old wives' tale that had brought him to death's door, not his own guilt. I would have bet my gold locket that he sincerely believed he'd nearly died from the wrath of a magical legend.

Meaning he couldn't have killed Lucien.

Filled with a confusing mix of fury and anticipation, I couldn't stand to be indoors. I went out to the backyard and stepped into the garden. It was a clear, crisp night. Pinpricks of stars dotted the indigo sky above. Amidst the sorrel, garlic, and nasturtiums, I breathed in the early-summer scents.

A desperate sound escaped my lips, half laughter and half sob. Finding a backward alchemist had been a distraction, not Dorian's salvation. An experienced backward alchemist had died because he came to Portland in search of

Non Degenera Alchemia, and a less experienced one wasn't able to tell me anything truly helpful. All Percy had done was devastate me.

I lay down in the garden, not bothering to look at which plants were beneath me. I didn't mind that I happened to be in the midst of blackberry brambles. I took pleasure in the pain of the thorns pricking my skin. It was a distraction from the mess of a situation I had to climb out of. I stared up at the star-filled sky.

I'd wasted too much of my life wallowing. Five minutes was enough time to compose myself. I had a gargoyle to save.

I brushed the brambles from my hair and clothes and went back inside to climb the stairs to the attic. There, surrounded by my alchemical and healing artifacts, I emailed Dorian to tell him I'd kicked Percy out.

I can come home? he emailed back immediately. *Tres bién. Julian Lake's housekeeper does not like me. She is suspicious that I will not let her see my visage. I believe she will try to sneak into my bedchamber tonight—little does she know I do not sleep!*

It's not late enough for you to walk across town, I wrote back. *I'll pick you up at the end of his driveway in 20 minutes.*

On the drive across town, I second-guessed everything I'd done not only that day, but since deciding to leave Paris several days ago. If I had stayed in Paris, how would things have played out with Lucien?

I pulled up in front of Julian Lake's estate. *House* wasn't a big enough word to describe the castle-like mansion, complete with stone lions standing guard. I didn't plan on walking up to the house and ringing the doorbell, so I idled the engine and waited with my thoughts.

A hunched figure in a black cape carrying a small satchel sprinted across the lawn. His bad leg gave him a limp, but it didn't slow him much. He looked rather like a hunchbacked Little Red Riding Hood with a book-shaped picnic basket.

Dorian climbed into the truck with *Non Degenera Alchemia* tucked under his arm. On the drive home, I filled Dorian in on what had happened with Percy. He replied with a string of profanities.

"I am so sorry, my friend," he said once he'd exhausted all the profane words he knew in both French and English, some of which I'd never heard. "Never fear. Dorian Robert-Houdin is on the case. I will put my little grey cells to work."

That's what worried me.

CHAPTER 34

I couldn't fall asleep that night. My mind was racing and refused to calm down enough for my body to get the sleep it craved. I got out of bed and lit a candle. The natural light of the flame was better to get into the mindset of alchemy, and that's exactly what I needed to do. Through Percy, my life had been connected to backward alchemy for far longer than I'd realized. I rubbed my gold locket, smooth for the decades it had comforted me.

How was everything connected?

The sulfurous scent of the candle and a mug of cashew milk cocoa calmed my nerves and awakened my senses. I unlocked the basement door and followed the stairs to my alchemy lab. As I lit a kerosene lantern and sat down at the solid wooden table I'd used for countless alchemical transformations, I thought through the confusing backward alchemy events that had happened.

I reached for my cell phone. My fingers hesitated for a moment before I sent Tobias a text message. I couldn't help chuckling to myself. When I was nursing Tobias back to health over 150 years ago, hiding in plain sight on a farm that was part of the Underground Railroad network, neither of us ever imagined a future when people could communicate instantly from hundreds of miles away, let alone without wires on a tiny device that fit in the palm of my hand.

It was the middle of the night, so I wasn't expecting him to answer. The very act of sending a message to my oldest living friend was comforting. I gave a start when my phone rang.

"Sitting up with Rosa?" I asked. I thought of Max, allowing myself a brief moment of the hope that that might one day be me and Max. It was a false hope, I knew. But that didn't mean I didn't want it.

"Is mind reading an alchemical skill I should be trying to hone?" Tobias replied good-naturedly.

"No supernatural skills required to know how much you love her. How is she?"

"Why don't you let me take care of you for a change. Are things not going well in Paris?"

"I had to leave."

A pause. "You're back in Portland? But that means it's the middle of the night for you too. You don't do nighttime, Zoe."

"I know." I hadn't thought Tobias would reply, much less call me. Where did I begin?

"I've seen you after you stayed up all night." His voice transformed from concern to anger. "You were no good to anyone after that."

"That night we had to run," I whispered, staring into the flames of the kerosene lantern and remembering the wretched night that left me with scars from harsh thorns and brambles.

"Are you in physical danger right now?"

"Not exactly."

"Then hang up and get some sleep."

"Please, Toby."

A long sigh sounded over the phone line. "What is it that has you reaching out in this darkest hour of the night?"

"I'm drowning. I know less than I did two weeks ago, before I went to Notre Dame."

"If I'm a sounding board, why don't you call me back in the morning?"

"I'm afraid." I clutched my gold locket.

A faint rustling sounded on the phone line, followed by the creaking of a door. Softly in the distance came the hum of crickets. I wondered if the lights of Detroit allowed him to see the constellations.

"I was awake because Rosa was dreaming. She kicked me in her sleep, but when I looked over at her, I couldn't fall back asleep. When she dreams, I see the same young woman I fell in love with over sixty years ago. I can't tell her that, though."

"She'd think you love her less now, because she aged. Even though it's not true." I thought again of Max, wondering if I'd ever be able to tell him just how different I was.

"If anything, knowing it wouldn't last forever has made me cherish her all the more." He cleared his throat. "I'm not letting you stay awake just to get philosophical. Tell me, why are you so afraid?"

After a moment's hesitation, the story spilled out of me. Tobias already knew about the unknown shift that had taken place six months before, when anything and any*one* who'd been helped along their way by backward alchemy began to have their life force reverse, from gold figures in museums turning to gold dust to living gargoyles returning to stone. And he knew about how, five months ago, Dorian had sought me out so I could help him decode *Not Untrue Alchemy*.

I smiled at the memory of my dear friend looking up at me from the wreckage he'd created in one of my shipping crates. I hadn't smiled at the time; I'd been terrified to find a living gargoyle, not to mention quite unhappy that he'd disturbed my carefully packed glass jars filled with alchemical ingredients. Dorian had apologized profusely and explained that he'd been hungry and was looking in the jars for food. When Tobias had visited, he'd been nearly as frightened to meet Dorian, and I hadn't known how to broach the subject of a living gargoyle who wasn't a homunculus to be feared. Since then, the two had bonded.

Now I told Tobias about what'd I'd recently learned of the formal origins of backward alchemy, in which a group of lazy men living in the 1500s, one of whom was Lucien Augustin, had found out how to shortcut true alchemy by using sacrificial apprentices, and had recorded their findings in a book that was meant only for themselves. Since alchemy connects as it transforms, the book took on the properties of backward alchemists, getting younger with age and not responding to fire as science would normally dictate.

In the flickering light of my half-finished alchemy lab, I grabbed the notebook on the table I used for recording plant transformations and began to scribble the ideas I was telling Tobias about.

"Why'd they create a book at all?" Tobias asked. "Sounds like they were selfish men who didn't want to share their twisted miracle."

"They're the laziest of men, Toby." I thought of Percy and snapped the pencil in my hand. "They didn't want to memorize even their most simple alchemical transformations. But they were so lazy they lost track of the book a couple hundred years ago."

"You don't know how it works yet?"

"Sometimes I feel like I'm so close to understanding, and sometimes I think I'm so far away I wouldn't understand it if I lived another three hundred years."

"Notre Dame didn't hold the key? I was so sure there was something it could tell you."

I hated to admit to Tobias how careless I'd been, but why had I contacted him if I wasn't going to be honest?

"Zoe?" he prompted.

"I was recognized. I had to leave before I was done."

Tobias swore.

"That's what started the mess I'm in. I thought at first the elderly woman who recognized me had sent a private investigator after me, but it was worse than that."

"Worse?"

"Two backward alchemists followed me home." I was glad he couldn't see my face as I explained how I'd learned a man I once knew in Paris had been murdered, seen a second stone gargoyle come alive for the briefest moment, and been tricked by Lucien about a nonexistent book that I hoped could lead me to a knowledgeable backward alchemist. I explained how I'd learned that Ambrose's son, Percy, was a clueless backward alchemist who'd killed his own father and that Lucien had died and shriveled inside an alchemy lab he'd set up in an abandoned cabin in Portland. It was all the more personal because Brixton had been a witness and now the police were suspicious of him and his mom, but I was so exhausted I was seeing alchemy everywhere I looked, even in Heather's paintings.

As I rambled, I picked up the shard of pencil and continued writing. Pouring my soul out to both Tobias and my notebook, I kept waiting for something to click. It didn't.

"I can see why you can't sleep," Tobias said.

"None of it makes any sense."

"On the contrary, it makes perfect sense."

"I remember you being a philosopher, not a comedian."

"I'm serious. *You're the one* everyone believes can figure it out. That's why they've all come to you."

"Misguided faith in an accidental alchemist."

"You really believe that?"

"Which part?"

"It wasn't an accident, Zoe."

"I never meant to find it—"

"You never meant to find the Elixir of Life for *yourself.* But you worked all hours to find it to save your brother's life. That's purpose. *Intent.* Not an accident."

"This isn't a problem with my ego. I know I'm great at many things. I can grow a thriving garden under the harshest of conditions, I can use spagyrics to create healing elixirs for an assortment of ailments, and I can fix the engine of just about any car produced before 1985. But I'm a terrible liar, I'm awful at turning lead into gold, and I never finished my alchemical training so I don't know how to decode formal alchemy."

"Do you realize the confusion you've told me about tonight sounds much more similar to listening to plants and putting a broken engine together than to speaking the secret language of some old white men?"

I swore. Why are we so blind to seeing what's right in front of us?

"I believe they're right that you can solve this," Tobias said. "As long as you get some sleep, kiddo."

"Kiddo? I'm almost two hundred years older than you."

"Then start acting like it. Stop thinking of what you don't know and focus on what you do. You know more than you think, my friend."

CHAPTER 35

I woke up at dawn, after approximately four hours of sleep, with a furious headache and a dry mouth that felt like it was filled with stinging nettles. Tobias was right—I shouldn't have stayed up. Was he also right that I knew more than I thought I did? With my brain in a fog, I wasn't much good to anyone at the moment.

Dorian saved the day. A breakfast feast was waiting for me. The spread took up half the dining table. Dorian had spent the predawn hours baking for me. He'd created variations on several of my favorite foods from my youth, from creamy almond milk porridge to cranberry nut bread. On the other half of the table, Dorian had arranged a set of notecards, written in his impressive cursive script. I helped myself to a serving of porridge and a slice of bread while Dorian explained the notecards.

"Each card is a piece of the puzzle," he said. "It is similar to the notes you wrote last night. By writing each separate point on its own notecard, we can move these items around in ways that are not simply chronological. My method is much more fruitful than yours."

"You snuck into my room and took my list?" I'd carried the notebook upstairs with me after talking with Tobias, hoping I'd have further revelations during the night. I didn't.

Dorian blinked at me innocently. "You left your door open. This was a sign you wanted my assistance."

It was a sign it had been a warm night, but no matter. "So you've rearranged my notes in a different order so they make more sense?"

"*Oui.*"

I stared at him. "You have?"

Dorian tapped one of his horns and raised a stone eyebrow. "I have cracked the case!" He grinned triumphantly. "Lucien was not an alchemist! Percival has misled you, Zoe."

"We know Lucien is the dead body. Brixton saw him."

Dorian waved away my concerns. "Brixton is an impressionable boy. Yet buried in your notes are dismissive descriptions of Heather, the very woman the police believe to be behaving suspiciously. It is *she* who is our most viable suspect."

I popped a bite of cranberry nut bread into my mouth and thought about how to refute the ridiculous idea. Dorian hadn't had an opportunity to interact with Heather. He could see in stone statue form, so he'd once stood still next to the fire place during a dinner party I'd given, and had observed Heather then. But most of what he knew of people was what Brixton and I told him.

"Heather wouldn't kill anyone." I saw Dorian open his mouth, so I quickly continued. "No, you're right. Anyone could kill someone, given the right circumstances. But for Heather, this doesn't make any sense. That's the more important point. Since you read my notes, you know I don't think those detectives are a good judge of character."

"*Non.*"

"No?"

"It is your own thoughts that betray you."

"My own thoughts?"

"You forget that you and Brixton have both said how strangely she has been behaving of late."

"It's true," I admitted. "But people have all sorts of things going on in their lives. Heather has a teenage kid and a husband who works out of town. That's not easy. But she doesn't have any connection to Lucien."

"How do you know there is no connection?" Dorian asked. "Her paintings at Blue Sky Teas—"

"We're reading too much into those paintings, Dorian. Brixton told her about the things I sell at my shop, and she's really creative."

"You are missing the point, Zoe. The motive could be any number of things we do not have enough information to understand. It is impossible to see into the hearts of men. No, my point is that your notes contain many points in history that are linked to one another in theory, such as the unfortunate coincidence of being recognized by a woman who knew you when she was a child. But there is only one true fact: science does not lie."

While science doesn't exactly lie, it's subject to the same human limitations as anything else. Accepted science in one era is later looked upon as laughable. Bloodletting to restore the balance in a sick body, mercury to treat syphilis, aether to explain light and gravity. Concerning forensics, DNA evidence was evolving as other tools had before it. And science didn't tell the whole story.

"Alchemy is science," I said, "but that doesn't do us any good because they don't understand it—"

"Yes, alchemy may be *foreign* science to these investigators, but they are seeking DNA evidence. You said they have the DNA of the killer, and yet Heather *refused* to submit to the test!"

"Do you remember the Phantom of Heilbronn?" I asked.

"The Phantom of the Opera? Have I told you about the time I snuck into a theater performing the musical and newspapers wrote that the phantom himself had appeared at the show?" He chuckled.

"No. Heilbronn. An example of when DNA science lied. A supposed female serial killer in Europe who killed dozens of people."

"Oh, yes. One of her crimes was committed in France."

"She didn't exist, Dorian. Laboratory results were contaminated with 'sterile' cotton swabs. It was the DNA of a factory worker."

"This is not bad science. It is human error."

"That's my point. It's perfectly reasonable to fear what will become of your DNA."

"Ah, so." He scratched his gray chin.

I looked at the set of carefully placed notecards and thought about how to turn the police onto Percy without revealing alchemy. Percy, whose wounds I'd washed. Aside from his head wound, he didn't have any scratches on his body.

But there was someone else who did. I felt as if the room was spinning around me.

"You are ill?" Dorian asked, his gray forehead creasing with concern. "Your face has gone as pale as a ghost from one of Father's magic posters."

"Yes. No. Where's my phone?"

I texted Brixton: ONCE YOU'RE AWAKE, WE NEED TO TALK.

~

An hour later, Brixton pulled up on his bike.

"I'm not going to get mad at you," I said, "so I need you to tell me the truth."

"About what?"

"I know you didn't want to worry me, which is why you didn't tell me. But you didn't only follow Lucien from afar, did you?"

Dorian gasped. "You cannot mean the boy killed him!"

Brixton and I both rolled our eyes.

"Of course not," I said. "But I think Brixton got closer to Lucien than he wanted to admit, when Lucien was spying on Ivan at his house. He didn't want to admit his mistake."

"Is this true?" Dorian asked Brixton.

Brixton fidgeted but didn't reply.

"Your wrist," I said. "I didn't think there was anything sharp on the table. It's not a scrape from when you hit my table, is it?" Brixton shook his head but didn't look at me.

"Did Lucien grab you?" I asked. "Is that why you were extra careful to hang back when you saw him again?"

Brixton stared at us. "You mean it's *my* DNA they'll find under his fingernails?"

The air felt heavy and stifling. Brixton had a juvenile record. "Did they save your DNA in juvenile court?"

"I don't think so. That's why they had to ask my mom for DNA for that family match thing."

"At least your mom didn't give her DNA to the police. They won't have any way to match it to you."

"Actually," Brixton said slowly, "she decided to do it. It was killing her, not knowing for sure if it was her dad. When it seemed less likely it was him, that's when she realized how much she cared."

I stared at Brixton. "This is bad," I said. "Very bad."

"What happened?" Dorian asked.

"It wasn't a big deal," Brixton insisted. "He didn't think I was spying on him on purpose or anything. He just thought I was being nosy. I followed him around the side of the house, and he grabbed my arm and told me to get lost."

"It doesn't matter that the event itself wasn't a big deal," I said. "Nobody was there to see it, so nobody can back you up."

Brixton bit his lip and looked at me with fear in his eyes. I knew he was thinking the same thing: he already had a record. Even if a jury wouldn't be told, the police knew.

"They won't believe me, will they?" he said. "Even if I leave out the part that I was spying on Ivan because Dorian wanted to know if he was a trustworthy new alchemist."

"If they're looking at you as a suspect," I said, thinking it through as tendrils of worry spread over my body, "they'll be sure to notice you're lying about *something*. And even if you tell them the complete truth—*especially* if you tell them the complete truth—they'll think you're lying." I didn't add that they might even suspect he was crazy and lock him up somewhere worse than a juvenile detention facility.

"Why are you scaring the boy?"

"He's not a boy," I said.

Brixton was now nearly fifteen, older than my brother had been when he helped me escape from Salem Village. In the modern world, it was easy to dismiss a fourteen-year-old as a kid, and Brixton was indeed immature in many ways, but in important matters like this, I needed to treat him as an adult. He had to understand the full consequences of what was happening.

"What do I do?" Brixton whispered.

"You forget we had this conversation. Concentrate on supporting your mom, and leave it to me and Dorian to figure out what really happened to Lucien in that shed in the woods. Don't say a word about this to anyone, Brixton. Not to anyone."

CHAPTER 36

Dorian paced the length of the attic, past the shelves filled with antique books on herbal remedies, around the articulated skeleton of a pelican, steering clear of my set of Victorian swords once owned by a famous English physician. With his chin jutting out, left arm hanging limply at his side, and right arm tucked behind his back, he looked like a Victorian caricature. I sat on the old wooden trunk, my knees tucked up under my chin.

"We must assume that the police have not yet figured out Lucien's identity," Dorian said. "He must have left his identification papers elsewhere, since he was working undercover while he was sneaking around Ivan's home. Yet he was not staying in the shed as his lodgings, so his hotel will soon notice his absence. They will report this to the authorities."

"That's a good point," I said.

"I have many good points." He tapped his gray forehead beneath his horns. His *little grey cells.*

"We might not have much time until his identity is discovered," I said, "but we already knew that. Who knows how quickly the police labs will finish the DNA testing—that's the more important problem. Even if they learn who Lucien is, it doesn't necessarily connect him to Brixton. Lucien was a bookseller from Paris. If anything, that will connect him to me."

Dorian stopped pacing. He nodded his head only once, and the solemnity of his expression made me shiver.

"If it would help," I said, "I would take the blame." If it came down to it, I had no doubt in my mind that I would sacrifice my freedom for Brixton's. But the connection between me and Lucien was based on alchemy. Would anyone believe I was telling the truth, not simply trying to help a young man I cared about?

"I know you would," Dorian said. "Yet you could not do so even if you wished to."

"I might be able to convince them about alchemy. My old photographs. If I could prove my true identity, I'd do it to save Brixton, regardless of what it meant for us."

"I do not speak only of alchemy."

"Then what?"

"You do not know what it was that killed him. A 'head injury' is meaningless. And they are unlikely to tell you the specific method of death. Thus, the police would never believe your confession. No, we must figure out who killed Lucien."

"Maybe I was wrong about Percy. Could he be that good an actor? Maybe he doesn't actually believe the superstition that one alchemist can't kill another."

"Perhaps, though I doubt it. He does not appear to be a very intelligent man."

I steadied myself, pushing away the raw memory. "Who besides me would have a reason to harm Lucien?"

"You could return to Paris and examine his life. While you are there, you could also visit my brother again."

"I *can't* go back to France. The French authorities must have flagged my passport by now."

Dorian frowned. "Ask Brixton's young friend Veronique to hack into his personal life."

"Her name is Veronica. But she's fourteen. And she's a coder, not a hacker."

"It is the same, no?"

"No. Plus, hacking into someone's life isn't nearly as easy as it looks on television."

"Unless one can guess their passwords." Dorian drummed his claws against the side of a shelf containing Chinese puzzle boxes and apothecary jars. "A French alchemist would most likely select passwords in French or Latin, but this does not help us narrow things down."

"Ivan," I said.

"Ivan does not know how to hack into personal records."

"No. Lucien was spying on Ivan. I dismissed him as a suspect because he's too ill to hurt anyone. But unlike Percy, he doesn't believe the alchemy super-stition that you can't kill another without killing yourself. Therefore Ivan could have *hired* someone."

"We suffer the same problem as we did with Brixton's mother. *Why* kill Lucien? Even supposing you are wrong about Ivan's quest for true alchemy, and he indeed turned to the dark side of backward alchemy, it makes no sense that he would kill the man who could teach it to him."

"We're missing something," I said. "I should talk with Ivan."

Dorian picked up a hefty glass paper weight from the shelf and handed it to me.

"What's this for?" I asked, turning over the heavy piece of practical art. The glass-blown piece was filled with flower petals, giving it the illusion of being lighter than it was.

"Protection. In case Ivan is a killer."

CHAPTER 37

I brought Ivan a picnic basket filled with lunch sandwiches, potato salad, and multiple desserts; a thermos full of homemade ginger- turmeric tea; and a garlic tincture.

Yeah, I may have been overcompensating because I felt guilty for suspecting my friend. And also, assuming he was innocent, for ignoring his quest to discover the Philosopher's Stone and the Elixir of Life. But I'd taken the paper weight. It weighed down my purse.

"*Dobrý den*," Ivan said in greeting as he let me in and ushered me through to the kitchen.

"Sorry I haven't been around much," I said, setting the food on the counter.

"Young love." He winked at me. "I completely understand." He shuffled around his library, tidying up.

I would have told him not to bother with tidying, but at the moment I didn't mind that he was turned away from me. His comment had made my cheeks flush. Was I blushing? Not very dignified for a 340-year-old.

"I'm glad you didn't forget about me for too long," Ivan said. "I have a question for you about how I've set up my laboratory."

We stepped into his garage.

Ivan had done his homework. He'd followed the descriptions in historical accounts of alchemists exquisitely. My little basement lab looked pathetic by comparison.

I hadn't had a true laboratory in more than a century. My goal for buying the dilapidated Craftsman house was to ease myself back into alchemy, one step at a time. Since life never seems to turn out quite as we expect it to, I hadn't had time to build my Portland laboratory, at least not properly. I'd been thrust into solving a much more urgent problem than purifying my own alchemical practice.

As I walked through Ivan's lab, I dismissed my concerns that he might be taking backward alchemy seriously. Since the last time I'd been at his house, Ivan had done a lot more to build his laboratory. He wasn't cutting corners.

I felt like I had stepped into a workshop on Golden Lane from Rudolph II's court in Prague. I wouldn't have been surprised if John Dee or Edward Kelley stopped by for tea. In addition to having alembics, matrix vases, and a pelican vessel, Ivan had a spirit holder. Glass jars were filled with ingredients. As much as I wanted to touch them, I knew I couldn't invade his space with my own touch.

One wall bore instructional posters—the torn pages from the books he'd destroyed. Only here, the destruction made sense. From their placement on the wall, the torn pages were close at hand, looking over him as he worked. A page on the steps of the Emerald Tablet, a map of the solar system with planetary metals, and an enlarged woodcut illustration of the *tria prima*: mercury, sulfur, and salt. The only thing missing was an athanor furnace, needed for cooking the philosophical egg.

"It's perfect, Ivan," I said.

The main thing that had led me to be suspicious of Ivan was that he was becoming obsessed, but was that so bad? Many a true alchemist had focused their obsession into a discovery.

"Not quite complete, I'm afraid. My furnace is being installed in the backyard next week."

"The athanor," I said.

"I won't tell you how difficult it was finding a vendor that had something similar to what's described in these alchemy books."

"A brick pizza kiln wouldn't do it?"

Ivan groaned. "You could have saved me time if you'd simply told me that. That's exactly what I settled on."

"Sorry. I didn't think you were at that stage. But truly, it looks like you don't need my help at all. I told you I never finished my training. At this point, I'd probably only hold you back or lead you astray."

"If I didn't know you to be a terrible liar, Zoe, I would think you were simply being polite."

"Shall we go back into the house?" I asked. "That way we can keep your laboratory strictly for you."

"In one moment," he said. He tapped on his cell phone before returning it to his pocket. "I've hung this Emerald Tablet poster on the wall here. It is my favorite so far, so I'm using it as my guiding model as I create my own."

Every alchemist must create their own fourteen steps of a personal Emerald Tablet to guide their work.

"Isaac Newton's?" I asked, looking over the yellowed page Ivan had taken from an antique book.

"I knew you were good, Zoe."

Working on Ivan's ideas in his library, I lost track of time. I pointed out that Ivan was trying to be too literal, as opposed to letting his intent guide him.

"I used to think these coded woodcuts were charming," Ivan said. "But now I wish to strangle the king and the queen here in these illustrations, and even their child. Look at the smug expressions on their faces. They hold more secrets than Mona Lisa."

I couldn't blame him for the sentiment. The king and queen, representing sulfur and mercury, come together in a marriage that results many months or years later in a philosophical child: salt. The two were sometimes shown as royalty, sometimes lovers, and sometimes as the sun and moon. Regardless of how they were represented in ink, they always hid their secrets.

Frustrated, Ivan declared he needed a break. Wincing as he rose from his seat, he led us to the kitchen. He'd cleaned up much of the mess of books I'd seen the last time I was there. The house was much more orderly, but the hard work had taken a toll on Ivan. He was thinner than he had been just days before.

"I could bring you some groceries," I offered.

"Brixton brought me a big bag of groceries yesterday."

"That was good of him."

"So many people grumble about 'kids these days,' but Brixton and my neighbor Sara are two of the most considerate people I know. Brixton's shopping choices contain more desserts than I'd have chosen for myself, but with all this work I have to do, a little sugar will do me good. Energy to complete the process." The flicker of obsession in his eyes had returned.

Only that's not what it was, I realized as Ivan collapsed into a chair. I rushed to his side, wondering if I had an appropriate tincture I could fix for him. I hadn't been making many lately, in proportion to how many I'd given out, so my supplies were low.

"It's nothing." He waved me off and glanced at the antique clock on the wall. "It's later than I thought. We've been working and talking for longer than my body can handle these days."

"Do you need any—"

"No." His hands shook as he spoke. "Leave me."

"Are you sure you—"

"Go."

CHAPTER 38

Human dignity is a complex thing. Ivan didn't want me to see his body's failings any more than Dorian wanted me to see his. I wished I could do more for Ivan, but my primary goal was helping Dorian— and now, Brixton.

After visiting Ivan, I was no closer to figuring out who killed Lucien. If I didn't make progress soon, the police would connect him with Brixton. And if I didn't get back to focusing on Dorian's life force reversal soon, his whole body would return to stone.

I could think of only one person who might have been able to help me. Why had I acted so impulsively and sent Percy away? I didn't even know his cell phone number! I'd reacted emotionally, but it was a stupid decision.

Berating myself, I shuffled up my stairs to the attic. The private and cozy space with a rooftop escape hatch was where Dorian and I had set up our research center. Dorian was using my laptop, since his clawed fingers didn't work well on the touch screen of a phone, leaving me to use my phone to go online.

Was Dorian right that I'd made unfounded assumptions? I wasn't so sure. All of the mysteries surrounding me were related to alchemy, so I couldn't help thinking they were connected. Occam's Razor: the simplest explanation was most likely the right one.

While I tried to put together the pieces of the puzzle, was Madame Leblanc working on a plan to get her nephew or a private investigator to find me and expose the fact that I was an alchemist? What would they find when they looked into the murder of my old acquaintance Jasper Dubois?

Because of more pressing matters, I hadn't spent enough time either worrying about Madame Leblanc's vendetta or researching Jasper's death. Dorian hadn't found anything, but I needed to try anyway. I again searched online library archives. As I narrowed my search, so many newspaper articles involved the police that I found myself distracted by thoughts of Max. If only I hadn't been encumbered by the secrets of alchemy, he and I could have had a normal life together.

Normal life...

Damn. There was something else I'd been ignoring. I hadn't checked my business orders in days.

I only listed high-end alchemical artifacts on my website, so I didn't do a brisk pace of business. But when a customer bought an expensive matrix vase crafted in Prague or a set of apothecary jars once owned by a famous Bohemian painter in Paris, they expected good service.

I checked my orders through Elixir and found I'd made a sale two days before. I took a break to pack the item—a handwritten speech by Sylvester Graham. I added a small puzzle box as a gift to thank the customer for the delay in my acknowledging the purchase. Since the activities that had transpired earlier this spring, I hadn't been too keen on having puzzle boxes around me anyway.

There was one more parcel I wanted to send. It was Rosa's heart that ailed her, so I packaged a healing Hawthorn tincture for Tobias. Before sealing the padded brown paper envelope, I stepped outside and clipped a sprig of ivy growing wild along the side fence. Tobias would understand I meant it as a symbol of friendship.

After bringing the packages to the post office, I felt myself compelled to stay outdoors in nature. My sanctuary. I took a long walk. Too many ideas were flitting through my mind, and being outside with the early summer flowers of Portland would help me focus. Dozens of varieties of roses were beginning to bloom in the Rose City. Across time and cultures, roses have symbolized many things. Today, I let myself believe the fragrant new petals represented rebirth and life.

When I came home, I was much calmer. And hungry. I called upstairs to Dorian, but he didn't answer. Since he hated it when I interrupted his reading these days, I let him be.

I ate leftovers for dinner. A small hearty scoop of Dorian's secret garlic tomato sauce remained in the fridge in a glass mason jar, so I slathered it on crusty French bread and sprinkled arugula on top. A perfect combination of spicy and mellow flavors, and sharp and velvety textures, danced on my tongue. I had to remember to ask Dorian how he got the sauce so creamy.

There was enough food in the fridge to feed us ten times over, so I thought it would be nice to bring Ivan something else. I took out a nut loaf and a wild rice salad from the fridge and headed off. If I was honest with myself, it also served as another excuse to go for a walk outside.

Ivan wasn't home. At least I hoped that was the case, and not that he was too sick to come to the door. Our alchemical discussion that afternoon had taken a lot out of him. Had it been too much for him?

I peeked in the window of his library, much like Lucien must have done. I didn't see Ivan, but I saw something else I recognized. Percy's leather jacket. My throat clenched and I staggered away from the window. The bag of food in my hand dropped to the ground.

Percy was staying with Ivan.

That's why Ivan had glanced at the clock. He wasn't feeling as ill as he pretended; he was expecting Percy to return.

This connection couldn't be good. Using tricks I'd learned from watching Dorian use his claws to pick locks, I tried to pick the lock to Ivan's back door, shielded from view. I failed miserably.

I checked all the windows and found one that wasn't locked. It was a high one, but I was glad to find that slipping into a narrow high window was a skill one didn't forget. Either that or I had enough adrenaline pumping through my veins that I could do anything at that moment.

On Ivan's desk I found a copy of a flight itinerary. Ivan was going to Paris. Was he going with Percy? Why?

I rushed home and up to the attic to share these latest developments with Dorian.

I found my gargoyle friend tied up. His wrists were bound behind his back, rope had been wound around his body to prevent him from flapping his wings, and a handkerchief stuffed in his mouth.

His precious *Non Degenera Alchemia* was nowhere in sight.

CHAPTER 39

I shook myself and pulled the handkerchief from Dorian's mouth.

"*J'en ai ras le bol*," Dorian spat. "I have had enough, Zoe! This is too much."

"Who did this to you?" I asked, even though I already knew.

"I knew Ivan was not to be trusted!" Dorian screamed, fidgeting as I worked to untie the rope. "Hurry! We must go after them."

"We're too late."

His shoulder's fell. "*Non*. I suppose you are correct. They were here hours ago. I heard you come home, yet you did not come up when I did not answer you."

"You've hated to be interrupted lately."

Dorian sniffed. "Is a small modicum of privacy a bad thing?"

"No. Not under normal circumstances. I'm sorry. With everything going on around us, I should have checked on you. Ivan tied you up and took your book?"

"*Oui*." Dorian shook out his wings and rotated his one working arm. "Ivan and Percival."

"They're taking it to Paris."

"You know?"

"I saw the flight itinerary at Ivan's house. The plane already left, we're too late. What happened?"

Dorian chuckled.

"It's *funny*?"

"At least when I spend eternity trapped in stone, I will always have the memory of Percival's terrified face when I came to life and refused to let go of *Non Degenera Alchemia*. He is a most annoying man, Zoe. You have the worst taste in men."

"It was his father I was in love with, not Percy. And what's the matter with Max?"

"He wishes to cook in my kitchen! He leaves things in the wrong place."

"Because he's nice enough to clean up—" I stopped myself and shook my head. "How did we get off track? You're *not* going to be trapped in stone for all eternity, Dorian. You're going to tell me what happened, and we're going to fix it."

"*D'accord*. The two men, Ivan and Percival, forced the lock to the attic. They must have had a key to the front door, because I did not hear them until they opened this one. By then it was too late for me to flee. I could only turn to stone and hold my book tightly. Yet with only one working arm…"

"You couldn't hold on tightly enough."

"Nor put up a fight. If I was at full strength, they would not have been able to tie me up. That Percival wished to chip me into little stone pieces. He is a very bad man, Zoe."

"You're all right?" I looked him over, terrified I'd see pieces missing beyond his two toes that had chipped off earlier that year.

"Ivan stopped him from hurting me."

Dorian looked at me thoughtfully. "Ivan was less surprised than Percival when I began to move. It is as if nothing else in this world can surprise him."

"He's dying. He has nothing left to lose."

"Yet he did not wish to kill me. He is the weak link. It is Ivan who has not yet gone too far."

"I need to figure out why they're headed to Paris."

Dorian blinked at me. "You said you knew."

"I knew they'd booked tickets to Paris. But what are they going to do there?"

"*Merde.*"

"What is it?"

"I wish you already knew. Then I would not have to tell you."

My heart thudded. "It's bad?"

"They spoke of a backward alchemy lab in Paris. A powerful one used by all the backward alchemists throughout the ages. It is where they perform their sacrifices. Ivan and Percival plan to use the book to bring back backward alchemy."

"Percy didn't tell me there was an alchemy lab like that."

"Of course he would not. He left out many things when he brought you into his confidence. He has done the same thing with Ivan. Percival is leading Ivan to his doom."

"And you to yours," I said, "unless I stop them."

CHAPTER 40

I was too late. The next flight to Paris wasn't until the next day. But even if I could have purchased a ticket and boarded a flight, what would happen when I entered France on my own passport? Would there be a flag on my passport that I was a criminal? The man who'd helped me with IDs for decades was dead, so I needed to find someone to forge me a new passport.

It was shortly after seven p.m. and the teashop was closed, but Blue was still there cleaning up. She opened the door for me. Her gray curls gave the impression she'd been struck by lightning. With the smile on her face, it was a magical lightning bolt of happiness.

"Have you heard if Heather is all right?" she asked.

"I haven't heard anything."

"I'll put on some tea."

I shook my head. "I'm afraid this isn't a social visit. I need to ask you for help."

Blue gave me a crooked smile. "Trying to help me feel at home since Brix is at an age where he's too cool to ask for help?"

"I need a fake passport," I blurted out.

Blue choked. "Honey, we definitely need to put on a pot of tea. A relaxing blend." She locked the front door and led me to the area behind the counter.

"I wouldn't ask if it wasn't an emergency."

"I figured that part out."

"Do you still know the people who helped you change your identity?"

"Tea first, criminal activities later."

Blue brewed dandelion tea that was both calming and invigorating.

"I've always said you were an old soul, Zoe," Blue said as I sipped the tea out of a solid curved mug like the kind found in 1950s diners. "But you're taking it too far. You look like you haven't slept since I left. And if I'm eating and sleeping better in a jail cell than you are here at home, I know something's wrong."

The tea warmed my hands and belly, but with Brixton and Dorian in danger, the comforting sensation didn't reach my soul. I pushed the mug away. "When you faked your death and started a new life, you knew people who helped you set up that fake identity."

The blank look on Blue's face made me wonder if I'd misunderstood how she started over here in Portland. But then she smiled and took my hands in hers. They were calloused but full of vitality. "Whatever you're running from, doing what I did isn't the answer. Trust me, I know."

"Then you do know people. People who can work quickly."

"I'm not going to ask what's going on. It's up to you to decide whether you're ready to tell me. But I will say that however desperate you feel, it *can* get worse."

Not the reassuring words I wished to hear. "I thought you'd tell me it'll get better."

"Ha. That too. But it won't get better if you go this route."

"You don't understand what I have to do."

"I would if you'd tell me. No?" She let go of my hands and ran her fingers through her curly gray hair that was as untamable as a ferocious storm. "All right, Zoe. If you're sure."

"I'm sure. I know what I'm doing."

"I hope you're right, sugar. I do hope you're right."

I stared at the number for Blue's contact, wondering if I should call. It was so late at night that it was difficult for me to think clearly. Dorian had gone on a nocturnal walk to work out his own tension, along with living up to his nightly responsibilities at Julian Lake's house and at Blue Sky Teas. I'd made too many mistakes. I needed to get some sleep to make the right decision.

When I woke up at sunrise, I saw that I'd missed several calls from Max from the middle of the night. Because I'd wasted precious energy staying awake longer than I should have, I'd slept through the phone calls.

I called Max back. It took several rings for him to answer. He must have been sleeping. Understandable, since his calls had come in only hours before.

"Is Brixton staying with you?" Max asked.

"No. Why would he be with me?"

Max swore. "He missed dinner with his parents last night. They thought he was out with his friends, but when Abel checked Brixton's room before going to bed at around midnight, he found some of Brix's clothes missing, along with the passport they just took out of their safety deposit box so he could go on a summer trip with his friends. Abel and Heather called Ethan and Veronica and woke them up, but Brixton isn't with them. Last I heard, he still wasn't home."

No, it couldn't be...

"I'd better check with his parents again," Max was saying. "He's run off for the night before. It's the missing clothes and passport that make this case different. Zoe, are you there?"

I couldn't speak. This was far worse than I had imagined. Brixton wasn't only implicated in a murder—he might become a murder victim himself.

Brixton knew about alchemy. He trusted Ivan, and he'd been bringing him food to help the dying man. Ivan likely didn't know that an alchemy apprentice would give his life when he performed backward alchemy's death rotation.

Brixton had gone to Paris with Ivan and Percy to be the latest unknowing victim of backward alchemy.

CHAPTER 41

If only I'd heard my phone during the night, I would have known Brixton had gone with Ivan and Percy. We could have alerted the authorities in Paris that they should meet the flight on the other end to find a kidnapped child. Max put me on hold while he looked into the flight.

We were too late. The flight had already landed. Brixton was gone. In Paris.

Max said he'd be right over to my house to talk in person, after he told the authorities what he knew. I hung up the phone and ran to the attic. The door was locked.

I pounded on the door. "Dorian, let me in. I know you need your own space, but this is an emergency. Brixton has been kidnapped."

The door flew open. "Kidnapped?"

"Yes. No. Sort of. Effectively, yes."

Dorian cocked his head and wriggled his horns. "You are delirious, *mon amie.* Come inside and sit down." He took my hand and led me to a steamer trunk we used as a bench.

I breathed deeply as Dorian hopped up onto the trunk to sit next to me. A drop of a dark red substance clung to his bottom lip.

"Oh, God," I said. "You're bleeding. I didn't think you could bleed."

"I'm bleeding?" Dorian whipped his head around and flapped his wings. One of them hit my shoulder and knocked me off the trunk. "*Pardon.*" He scrambled off the seat and helped me up.

685

"Your lip," I said. "It's your lip." I held my breath. His health was worse than I thought, with a new symptom.

"Ah. Only tomato sauce."

It didn't look like tomato sauce. Was he lying to shield me from how close he was to death? But as awful as it was, Dorian's unnatural death wasn't this morning's priority. "Brixton left for Paris with Percy and Ivan."

"Along with *mon livre*. Perhaps he wishes to be a superhero and is attempting to retrieve my book."

I shook my head. "Brix doesn't know it was stolen. I've been trying to keep him out of this."

"Then why would he go with them? They are very bad men."

"He doesn't know that! He's friends with Ivan. Ivan now believes in alchemy, and if he's working with Percy, he believes what Percy has told him."

"Backward alchemy," Dorian whispered.

"Which requires a sacrifice."

"*Mais non!* Why would the boy agree to such a thing?"

"I'm sure Percy lied to Ivan and Brixton, like Lucien lied to Percy to trick him into the lazy route of becoming a backward alchemist. Ivan doesn't realize what Brix would be doing to help him."

The doorbell rang, and I moved toward the door. Dorian put his one good arm on his hip. "Max Liu?"

"I'll talk to him in the kitchen so you can hear us, okay?"

In the kitchen, I explained to Max that Ivan had grown delusional as his health deteriorated, and that I thought he'd stolen a valuable alchemy book of mine because he thought alchemy was real. I theorized that Ivan had convinced Brixton to go to Paris with him, because that's where a certain type of alchemy supposedly draws its power from.

"Why didn't you report the theft?" Max asked.

"I didn't want to get Ivan in trouble. I thought I could get it back once he came to his senses. I didn't realize he'd go so far."

Max checked with passport control and found that I was right. Brixton had arrived in Paris earlier that day. He'd used his passport to visit his stepdad before; a well-traveled teenager accompanied by two respectable-looking adults hadn't been questioned.

Max wanted to go through the proper channels, but I knew there wasn't time. Besides, it would be impossible to explain to the authorities where they should look for Brixton, especially since I wasn't sure myself.

There wasn't time for me to get a fake passport, either. If I wanted to save Dorian and Brixton, I had to get to France today.

CHAPTER 42

I had no trouble clearing customs in Paris with my own passport. Madame Leblanc's nephew must not have moved forward with the cold case.

With my adrenaline pumping, I set out to search Paris for the trio. I tied a white scarf over my hair and put on sunglasses, hoping to deter the eagle-eyed Madame Leblanc if she happened to cross my path.

I started with Notre Dame, the center of backward alchemy. I waited impatiently in the line of tourists that snaked across the courtyard. Many of the visitors carried umbrellas to shield themselves not from rain but from the spring sun. It made it difficult to identify individual people in the crowd. I listened for voices instead. Chinese, Spanish, Italian, and English with accents ranging from Australian to the American South. Nothing that sounded like Brixton, Ivan, or Percy.

Inside the cathedral's sanctuary walls, I showed a photograph of Brixton to every guide and worker in the cathedral. With the heavenly stained glass above casting a glowing light throughout the stone church above us, they all shook their heads.

Unlike many cathedrals, Notre Dame didn't contain a large crypt beneath its floors. The "official" crypt was a tourist attraction located across the court-yard from Notre Dame. Through miniature displays and audio recordings, it told the story of Paris. When construction of Notre Dame had begun in the 1200s, Paris wasn't yet known as Paris. The bishops had wished to build a monument to God in a spot where people from across Europe had gathered, and the cathedral quickly became a pilgrimage site.

As for the crypt that contained bones of bishops and other important Frenchmen, many were entombed on the street level inside the cathedral, leaving only a small crypt—and it was off limits. I gave a generous "donation" to the same security guard who had given me access to the crypt the previous week.

Brixton wasn't there.

Before leaving the Île de la Cité, I stopped inside the tourist crypt. Just for good measure. Again, nothing.

What was I missing?

I was run-down both physically and emotionally. I stopped in a café in the shadow of Notre Dame for a glass of Perrier for hydration, *pain au chocolate* for energy, and a cup of tea for my spirits.

A siren sounded, but I couldn't see where the sound was coming from.

A crowd of people rushed to the edge of the Seine, and I realized why I couldn't see the vehicle with a siren—it was in the water.

I tossed coins on the table and rushed through the crowd. From the edge of Pont Neuf bridge, I watched helplessly as the emergency boat came to a splashing halt in the river. The text on the side read SUCCURS AUX VICTIMES: SAPEURS-PUMERS DE PARIS.

Divers jumped from the boat and swam toward a still figure.

A shiver like shards of glass covered my body. I couldn't breathe. Was I too late? I imagined Brixton dumped unceremoniously into the Seine once he was no longer of use.

The first diver reached the body. And there was no question that it was a dead body, not a living person. The diver turned over the body. It was a young man, but it wasn't Brixton. I looked on in horror.

It was the police officer who had interviewed me the previous week. Madame Leblanc's grandnephew.

I was sure I was going to vomit over the side of the bridge. I felt claustrophobic in the crowd of people surging forward to catch a glimpse of the dead body. I held my head and pushed my way through the throng, also trying to push away the thought barreling through my mind: *Death follows you everywhere you go, Zoe Faust.*

Who had killed Madame Leblanc's police officer nephew?

I raced down the stone steps that led to the riverbed, but Gendarme Gilbert's body had already been pulled onto the boat. Its engine revved. From the edge of the river, I called out in my most authoritative French for them to stop.

To my surprise, it worked. Sort of. They didn't change course, but they paused for long enough for me to call out a few words to them.

I told them how sorry I was for the loss of one of their own, and asked what had happened.

"You are mistaken, mademoiselle," the officer answered, then motioned to his colleague to continue onward. The boat stirred up a froth of dark water and disappeared down the Seine.

I was mistaken? What did that mean? Did he differentiate between the branches of the police and not feel bad when a man from another division was killed? Or was I mistaken that Gilbert was dead? No, that wasn't right. I'd seen enough death to know what I was looking at. Was it possible it wasn't Gilbert? Could my mind be playing tricks on me?

I jumped as a hand pressed against my elbow. I was standing too close to the Seine. The strong hand pulled me back.

"*Je suis desolé, mademoiselle,*" he said. "I did not mean to frighten you. You seemed so distressed, I did not wish you to fall. Yet I have made things worse."

I studied the newcomer. His eyes were sharp and he spoke in polished French, but he wasn't dressed with the effortlessly put- together fashion sense one imagined such a man to have. In spite of the warmth of the day, he wore layers of ragged clothing and carried a dirty backpack over his shoulders. Two newspapers, *Le Monde Diplomatique* and *La Tribune Internationale*, poked out of his torn coat pocket, and a beaten-up book of Victor Hugo's poetry rested in the side pocket of the backpack.

"No harm was done," I said. "Thank you for your concern, monseiur."

"You knew poor Gilbert as well?"

I hadn't been imagining things. The body floating in the river was indeed the police officer who'd driven me from France.

"Please," he said, "There is a bench just here. You must sit."

"How did you know Gilbert?" I asked, letting him lead me to the bench.

"I am in between residences." He chuckled. "Being outdoors much of the time, I meet many people. Gilbert was one of the better ones. He often brought me a croissant when he took walks here."

"On his rounds as a police officer?"

The man cocked his head and laughed again. "Gilbert? He was not police."

"Not the National Police. A *gendarme.*"

He shook his head. "Gilbert was an actor."

"An actor?"

Madame Leblanc's nephew who had told me about Jasper Dubois's murder all those years ago wasn't a police officer at all.

Everything I thought I knew was a lie.

CHAPTER 43

With this new piece of information, reality snapped into focus on a different plane. A slight shift in the lens I was using to examine all the facts gave every-thing a new perspective.

Gendarme Gilbert wasn't affiliated with the police.

Had Madame Leblanc hired an actor to impersonate a police officer to scare a confession out of me? I thought that through. It was a weak plan. If she truly believed I was an immortal Zoe Faust, surely she wouldn't think I'd so easily confess. There also hadn't been time for her to coach an actor with so many facts. He did consult a notebook, though. Even if I granted he was a good improvisational actor, why had he been killed?

"Are you all right, mademoiselle?" the homeless poetry connoisseur asked.

"His death is a shock. I'll be fine. I just need a moment."

I tugged at the ends of my hair and watched the ripples of the Seine. Gendarme Gilbert hadn't been the only person acting.

I hadn't stopped to think about how implausible it was for Madame Leblanc to have such vivid memories of her childhood. Finding a dead body would leave an impression and be hard to forget. But the rest? She could very well be acting.

That meant an unknown person had hired two actors—an old woman to impersonate someone who knew me in the 1940s, and a young man who could play a rookie police officer. Why? The only answer that made sense was to convince me that I should leave France.

So not Lucien. He'd wanted me to stay so he could steal Dorian's book, and it had inconvenienced him that he'd had to follow me to Portland. Who else was there? It had to be an alchemist.

That only left one person: Ambrose's son Percy.

But why kill the actor? Was he a loose end? Was the woman who played Madame Leblanc next? Was there any way I could find the actress to warn her?

"Monsieur, did you see where exactly the police found Gilbert's body?" I spoke before realizing how odd the question must have sounded. "I mean, I'd hate to think about the indignity of him floating in the river for a long time. I hope he was found quickly."

"A woman walking her terrier saw him floating in the river right here, under the shadow of Notre Dame. I cannot imagine he was in the river long. Between the tourists and the locals, it would be impossible to miss him. Rest assured, mademoiselle. I will not be so philosophical as to assert he is now in a better place, but his dignity is intact and he will be adequately mourned by his friends."

"*Under the shadow of Notre Dame*," I whispered. "Beneath the city."

I now had an idea what I was looking for. The actor's body had washed up not only next to Notre Dame, the very place connected to alchemy and Dorian's book, but *beneath* it.

I looked around but didn't see any obvious entry points. But although I didn't know how to find it, I had an answer for how backward alchemists could have a space connected to Notre Dame without being observed as being part of it. The perfect place to hide a backward alchemy lab that needed to be close to Notre Dame. Not only a basement, but truly underground. A secret space where a backward alchemist could perform a transformation.

But where? Invisible to the city above were an assortment of catacomb passageways, bunkers that had been built during World War II, metro tunnels, shafts for water and sewage, and quarries that had been mined for limestone and gypsum for centuries, causing many a cave-in. Those cave-ins were much more common when I'd lived in Paris decades before, causing me to be wary of climbing beneath the surface of Paris.

"I hope, mademoiselle, that you are not looking to venture beneath the city to avenge Gilbert's death. People have died down there, after they've gotten lost and not been able to find their way out."

"I have a young friend," I said. "Just a boy. I think he might be with the same people who did this to Gilbert."

"Even if this is true, your death would not help him."

"There are people who know the city's underground well," I said, thinking of how it was now a trendy thing for artists to stage art shows or dance parties underground.

"You'll never find them."

"Who?"

"The Urban eXperimenters. That's who you're going to try to find, yes?"

"That's what they call themselves?"

"One of the groups. And I've tried. Believe me, I've tried. They don't like to reveal their identities. I once thought the underground might be a good place to stay during winter, but it is not what one would expect. I wish you good luck finding your young friend. But heed the words of an old man who has seen where such folly can lead. Following your heart is beautiful in the pages of a book, but in life, remember to think before you descend."

I thanked my new friend with a handshake while surreptitiously tucking a few Euros into his Victor Hugo book with the sleight-of-hand skills I'd learned from Dorian, then ran down the riverbank.

He was right: I couldn't find Brixton alone, but I now knew how to get the help I needed. I ducked into a quiet square filled with Honey Locust trees to make a phone call to my secret weapon: a fourteen-year-old.

"Hi, Ms. Faust," Brixton's friend Veronica said.

I'd never get used to the fact that people could see your name when you called them.

"I need your help finding Brix," I said.

"Mr. Liu and Brix's mom already asked me. I don't know where he went. My dad even searched my room. Like he'd be hiding in the closet! Can you believe that? I really don't know where he is."

"I think I do. But I need your help."

"You do?"

"I need to get a message to the Cataphiles of Paris."

"Paris? Brixton is in *Paris*? How did he get to Paris? I mean, I knew he had a passport cuz he went to visit his stepdad somewhere a couple of years ago."

"Veron—"

"But I always thought the two of us would go together, you know? Backpacking before college. He knows how much I wanted to go. The City of Lights. The—"

"Veronica. Please listen. He's not here on vacation."

"*Here?* You mean you're in Paris, too?"

"He's in trouble."

A pause. "Really? It's not just a crazy idea to get to Europe before Ethan?"

"I promise I'll explain everything as soon as I can. But first, I need your help."

"Okay. Um, what's a Cataphile?"

"People who like to explore underground. Sort of like what you, Brixton, and Ethan did when you explored Portland's Shanghai Tunnels."

"That was different. There aren't *graveyards* underneath Portland, Ms. Faust. That's who you mean, right? The explorers who sneak into creepy old tombs underneath Paris to walk through old bones and things? I saw the creepiest photos online from an art show and pop-up kitchen set to candle-light in Paris."

"That's them—"

"Oh, you should totally do something like that in the Shanghai Tunnels, where it's cool without being weird with all the skulls and things, you know? Is that what Brixton is in Paris for?"

"Sort of. But because what these groups do is illegal, they don't like to be found by people who aren't part of their group."

"You want me to post a message to this online group?"

"I know it's a lot to ask," I said, "but I think it'll help me find Brixton. I don't know how else to find them, but I thought if you tried you might—"

"Sure."

"What?"

"While we've been talking, I found them. Um, I've only had one year of French, though. Can you tell me whatever your message is *en français?*"

CHAPTER 44

An hour later, I sat at a crooked wooden table scarred with key carvings in the back room of a Left Bank café with Constantine and Emma, who insisted they would only use their first names. That was fine with me, since I wasn't going to reveal more than my first name to them. Yet we huddled together like old friends, speaking in low voices as we constructed our plan.

Veronica had posted a message that a boy had been kidnapped and taken to the tunnels, and that the police hadn't followed up on the tip. Anyone who wanted to help me could meet outside a café near the entrance to the catacombs. I knew the tourist attraction wouldn't be where we descended, but with urban explorers hiding their discoveries almost as well as alchemists, I couldn't think of a better place for a group of people to meet.

The eight others who'd shown up had departed as soon as they realized this wasn't a piece of performance art. They had wanted to be part of a murder mystery-themed game like a similar one staged in a newly discovered section of the catacombs the previous month. Constantine and Emma were different. They were hardcore Cataphiles who'd taken Veronica's note seriously and come prepared. They arrived in thigh-high rubber boots and carried small backpacks filled with maps, lights, and other items they didn't reveal to me. I guessed they were brother and sister, for they both had tiny bodies, ginger hair, and a familiarity that I remembered from long ago.

The first words out of Constantine's mouth, after listening to my plea and extinguishing his cigarette, were, "You were right to contact us."

"Below ground," Emma added, "we will be of far greater help than the police."

I'm not a perfect judge of character—as my misjudgment of Percy and Ivan reminded me—but in spite of their youthful arrogance, the thing that told me I could trust Emma and Constantine in this situation was their healthy skepticism of the authorities. They hadn't once asked me why I didn't try again to convince the police. Instead, they followed me to a private corner and quizzed me for details of Brixton's disappearance so we could construct the best plan of attack.

"This is our best way in," Constantine said, using his index finger to circle a hand-drawn mark on a wrinkled photocopy of official blueprints.

Emma clicked her tongue. "*Non.* That passageway is always muddy."

"But it gets us close to Notre Dame," I said. "That's what matters."

Emma's pale cheeks turned scarlet.

"Emma brings up a good point," Constantine said, his eyes not leaving the map.

"I'll pay your laundry bill," I said, not caring about the naked desperation in my voice. "I'll pay whatever you want. You know the life of a child is at stake here. *Please.*"

"You misunderstand," he said.

"The *reason* for the mud in that tunnel is the problem. I forgot there's a blockage there, after another section collapsed. We might not get through."

"Can't we climb down in a big tunnel you know isn't blocked, and go from there?" I asked. This was taking too long. What had become of Brixton?

"This attitude is why people have died down there," Emma said derisively. "It is not as easy as looking at a map. There are not only side tunnels, but different levels and many underground landslides we don't know about. There's a whole world beneath Paris."

"She exaggerates," Constantine said, "but not by much. Here." He jabbed his finger onto another spot, not far from the first. At least I thought it was close by. I wouldn't have been able to read the map without them.

"*Oui,*" Emma said. "That will work."

Constantine gave a single curt nod. "*Bon.*"

"Are you ready?" Emma asked me. Without waiting for a reply, she stood and tucked the tightly folded map underneath her shirt.

I tossed coins onto the table and chased after them.

～

When we reached the rusty metal grate that was to be our entrance, Emma handed me a hat with built-in flashlight and an extra set of gloves. I looked down at my own green ankle boots, gray cotton slacks, and black cardigan. Even with my guides, I was far from prepared for this. All that mattered was that I reach Brixton in time.

Willing myself to forget about the people who'd died during tunnel cave-ins of previous centuries, I took a deep breath or five and climbed into the darkness below.

We walked for what felt like an eternity, passing through limestone and gypsum corridors that had been mined in the Middle Ages, and passing near the more modern Metro, sewer, and water tunnels. In many of the tunnels, empty plastic water bottles and other trash was strewn about. I stepped on more than one long-dead glow stick from the parties that must have taken place here. The trash gave me hope, though. It meant we were traversing where others had recently come. We weren't going to end up as a statistic, another stupid explorer who starved to death underneath Paris.

At a crossroads, they stopped and consulted a map. After only a few seconds, they pointed to the left path.

"Why that way?" I asked. "It's going away from Notre Dame. It looked like we were almost there."

"You will not find them there," Emma said.

"But that's where I think he's been taken. That's why we're here."

Constantine exchanged a look with Emma before speaking. "Nobody goes there."

"Why not?"

"Perhaps it would be best to call the police now," Emma said softly.

I put my hand on her grimy shoulder. "They can't help," I said. "I need to go."

"You don't," Emma said, gripping my hand. "If this is where your young friend has been taken, you won't find him."

"Why?"

Emma didn't answer.

"Death," Constantine said. "Only death awaits down that corridor."

A mixture of panic and hope welled inside me. That had to be the right way.

"I'll pay you for a map and headlamp," I said, hoping they could hear the desperation in my voice. I didn't care if they asked me for all the money I possessed. "I need to find him."

The two communicated wordlessly for a few moments. I think I held my breath for every second.

"No money," Emma said finally. "But you must be safe. Take these breadcrumbs." She pressed a map and what looked like a bag of plastic sticks into my hands. No breadcrumbs in sight.

"Glow sticks," Constantine explained. "At every turn you take, break one and leave it there. You'll be able to find your way back."

Breadcrumbs to find my way out of the dark forest.

My solitary route took me through catacombs and crypts of bones as I continued the search for Brixton. It was a disheartening image that reminded me too much of the very real possibility that I could be too late to save his life.

I remembered to leave a glow stick at each turn, though in these tunnels the curves were deceptive rather than clear cut. I hoped I'd used enough.

The sound of a man's voice speaking made me stop in my tracks. A moment later, I breathed in a familiar scent that blended metallic and sweet. I ran forward, slowing only as a sliver of light cast its glow in front of me. I forced myself to slow down and approach with caution.

I found myself in an alchemy lab like no other I'd ever seen before. Instead of the complicated assortment of dozens of glass vessels, hundreds of ingredients, and countless books, a cozy armchair took up more space than the single table of alchemical apparatuses and ingredients. Candles illuminated the 50-square-meter space that looked more like a child's playroom than a serious alchemy lab.

And a child *was* there. Brixton's body was sprawled on the cold stone floor. He wasn't moving.

A lone man stood next to Brixton. He clutched Dorian's book in muscular hands. The man turned, and I saw his face. Ivan.

CHAPTER 45

Only... Was I mistaken? The hands that gripped *Not Untrue Alchemy* were too strong to be Ivan's. His face and his body looked different as well.

"You don't have to do this, Ivan," I said.

"Zoe? How—"

"Why don't you come over here?"

"What? Oh, Brixton isn't hurt. He's sleeping."

"He's not sleeping, Ivan." A ferocious anger welled up inside me. "He's dying."

Ivan looked hesitantly at Brixton, then shook his head furiously. The motion startled me. Ivan normally moved slowly. Not any longer. That's why he looked different. A vigorous middle-aged man stood before me. There was no way I could take on this new Ivan physically. If it had only been me, I would have risked fighting him. But with Brixton unconscious beneath him, I had to be smart. I had to reason with Ivan.

"The apprentice sacrifices their life," I said. "I know Percy kept the truth from you. That's how backward alchemy works. That's how it begins."

"No. That's not how it works. You're lying."

"It's Lucien and Percy who lied to you."

"Lucien? Did he find you? Where is he?"

"You don't know?"

"I now know of backward alchemy's true potential. You lied to me, Zoe.

You said it was dangerous, you said *he* was dangerous. That's why I didn't embrace backward alchemy sooner. If only—"

"Lucien is *dead*, Ivan. He's the man who was found in the shed in the woods last week."

"You're trying to confuse me. That man was Heather's father."

"No, it wasn't. Backward alchemy changes how quickly a body deteriorates. It misled the police. It was Lucien. And if Brixton survives—" I swallowed hard and looked at his unmoving form on the cold floor. *Don't look, Zoe.* I couldn't let myself break down. "If Brixton survives, he's going to be implicated as a murderer unless we find out who killed Lucien."

"This is madness. The boy is simply exhausted from the Death Rotation. And there's no reason for the police to suspect him."

"Lucien caught Brixton following him and grabbed him. Brixton's skin cells ended up under Lucien's fingernails."

"You're trying to distract and confuse me. Nothing you're saying makes any sense. Can't you see backward alchemy's potential? Look at what I've become. When Brixton wakes up, he'll be stronger too."

"You don't understand—"

"You weren't honest with me, Zoe. How can I believe you now?"

"You're right. I'm sorry. It's hard for me to open up. But I'm ready to talk now. To share everything I know. Why don't you come over here and we can talk about it?"

A pained expression crossed Ivan's face. "I see what you're doing. You think I wish to hurt Brixton. How little you know of me. I would never do that."

"I don't think you would do so intentionally." I spoke as calmly as I could manage. "It won't hurt to get him medical attention, will it? Now that you're done with the transformation, we could—"

"We're not done. Not yet."

I said a silent prayer. There was hope for Brixton. "This isn't you, Ivan. I know you're a good man. You don't know what you're doing. You've been lied to."

"Only by you. You twisted the facts so I didn't believe what Lucien had to tell me."

"You spoke with him?"

"He wanted my help. He saw that I had a vast library of books on alchemy and wanted to know if I had *Non Degenera Alchemia*—the book that you've so desperately wanted to understand. You've been lying to me since we met. You never wanted to understand that book for the sake of knowledge. Percival told me the truth. It was to save that creature who lives in your attic." His eyes were pleading. "You could have trusted me, Zoe."

"Because you're showing yourself to be so trustworthy," I snapped before I could stop myself.

"This is your fault," Ivan boomed. "Not mine. If only you'd been honest with me, I could have had the Elixir of Life so much sooner."

I looked at Ivan from head to toe. Was he as strong as he now looked? "How do you feel, Ivan?" I asked quietly.

He frowned and smoothed his wild hair. "Percy said I would feel decades younger immediately, but—" He shrugged. "It must be because there's more to the process."

I thought back on my own true alchemy transformation. I had discovered the Elixir of Life while searching for a cure for my brother, who was dying of the plague. I was so grief-stricken that I didn't realize what I had become until I saw that I wasn't aging.

But true alchemy was different from backward alchemy. The shift in true alchemy was more subtle, because it wasn't a quick fix. From what I'd seen of backward alchemy, the effects were visible and immediate. Ivan did look much healthier than I'd ever seen him, but the full power of backward alchemy was being diminished by the shift that had taken place six months ago. No matter what Percy claimed, Ivan wouldn't be able to experience the full effects of backward alchemy until that fissure was fixed.

"There's indeed more," I said, "but not in the way Percy told you. Did he tell you that a shift occurred six months ago and that everyone who'd been granted an extended life through backward alchemy began to die?"

"It was because you were hoarding that book! That's why he and the others had to make and smoke Alchemical Ashes, to fight for their lives. He had run out of his supply."

"It's not the book, Ivan. The book contains the secrets of backward alchemy and is tied to Notre Dame, but it has nothing to do with why the power is fading."

"You're still lying. I should have believed Lucien when I had the chance."

"What happened when he came to you?"

"Seeing that I was a scholar of alchemy, he confessed to me that he was a backward alchemist who had been alive for centuries. He suspected you had stolen a book that was his. But I trusted you. I foolishly trusted you, Zoe. He wanted me to steal the book from you, as he said you had done from him. He became angry when I refused. I shoved him out the door."

"You shoved him?"

Ivan snorted. "You have always thought me a weak old man, but Lucien was weaker. It was not difficult to push him out of my house.

He fell down the front steps."

I gasped.

"It doesn't take much strength to hurt a frail man," Ivan continued, "as I know all too well."

"It was you. It was you who killed him."

"No, he was not dead. I told you—"

"Did he hit his head when he fell?"

Ivan narrowed his eyes that were no longer tired and blood-shot. "He might have, but he got up and left."

"To go back to his makeshift alchemy lab to try to make more Alchemical Ashes. He died before he succeeded."

On the floor, Brixton groaned. Ivan jerked back, startled.

"Brix?" I said, rushing to his side. "Can you hear me?"

His eyes were still closed, but he moaned again. Sweat coated his body.

"Ivan, please," I pleaded. "We've got to get Brixton help."

"He's not supposed to be hurt," Ivan whispered. "He must be faking it. Yes, that's what's happening. He's an attention-seeking kid."

"He's not faking it. And he's going to be arrested for murder."

"I would never let that happen," Ivan said. "You think so little of me? If it comes to that, I'll tell the police what happened."

I recoiled when Ivan's shoulder touched mine as he knelt over Brixton.

Ivan cried out. "This isn't right." He shook Brixton's still shoulders.

"He's not pretending."

"He's cold," Ivan murmured. "Too cold. We must help him."

"Let me call an ambulance."

"No."

I squeezed my eyes shut. I'd been so sure I'd gotten through to Ivan.

"We can't call an ambulance," Ivan said. "They'll be back soon. We have to get Brixton out of here ourselves."

I opened my eyes and saw the good man I'd thought of as my friend.

Ivan handed *Not Untrue Alchemy* to me. With his newfound strength, he lifted Brixton into his arms and carried him out of the backward alchemy lab beneath Notre Dame.

In the darkness of the tunnel, Ivan swore. "I don't know if I can find my way out without them."

"That," I said, "I can help with." I turned him towards a faintly glowing light. The glow sticks Constantine and Emma had brought were the perfect breadcrumbs to make our way out.

As I watched Ivan carry Brixton's limp form from the subterranean gloom out into the summer sunlight, I was filled with two of the most conflicting emotions I'd ever experienced together. The all-encompassing relief of having found Brixton in time was weighed down with the realization that the only remaining hope I had of saving Dorian's life was the backward alchemy transformation I'd been denying: a sacrifice.

I now knew, with all certainty, that I would have to sacrifice my own life to save Dorian's. And I knew that I would do it.

CHAPTER 46

The hospital called Brixton's family, explaining that he'd been found unconscious and dehydrated, but was stable.

I hated hospitals, with their overbearing astringent scents that assaulted my senses and my memories of the horrors of medicine of past centuries, but I didn't want to be far from Brixton. Ivan stayed with me. We hadn't yet talked about what had transpired, but he'd been the one who carried Brixton's body from subterranean Paris, and he spoke to the hospital staff so I could keep my name out of it.

There was another reason it was difficult for me to talk with the staff. I was so thankful Brixton hadn't died like the actor who played the policeman that it was difficult for me to speak. My eyes kept welling with tears of relief.

Ivan and I sat together in an outdoor courtyard waiting room. People had recently been smoking here, but the scent was far better than the sterilizing chemicals and strong medicines inside. Neither of us could sit still. I paced the length of the courtyard, and Ivan prodded the newly regenerated muscles of his arms. How long would it last? I couldn't let myself begin to feel sorry for Ivan. His blind selfishness had nearly killed Brixton.

"Would you sit with me for a minute?" Ivan asked. "I see your hesitation to be near this monster, but I wish to apologize. And to understand."

I joined him on a wooden bench, not wanting to hear his apologies, but wanting even less for the other visitors to hear what he had to say.

"If I'd performed the Death Rotation experiment properly," Ivan began, then faltered. "If I—" He cleared his throat and looked up at the wispy clouds above. "If I'd done it right, the boy would be dead?"

"If you'd finished the transformation," I said. "Brixton only survived for as long as he did because of his own strength."

Brixton had survived for the same reason that my own backward alchemy transformation *hadn't* worked well the last time I'd tried it to make Dorian's Tea of Ashes. He'd lived for the flip-side of the reason I'd been sickened.

"Brix was tending to my garden," I explained. "He has a green thumb, and the garden flourished. His energy gave strength to the plants he tended, and that energy flowed back into him, giving him strength and protecting him."

"Alchemy doesn't create something out of nothing," Ivan said. "You tried to teach me that, but I wouldn't listen."

"Alchemy transforms, and the power of the transformations is tied to the practitioner and their materials."

"You can tell them the truth," he said. "Max and the beast. I can see on your face that you want to call them."

"He's not a beast," I said. The man sitting next to me was much more of a beast than Dorian would ever be. "And what could I possibly tell Max?"

"The truth. I was blinded by my desire to live, so I believed a hoax. I put Brixton's life in danger with a desperate plan."

"You're owning up to this?"

"Of course. I'm mortified by my actions, and thankful alchemy isn't real so I didn't harm Brixton."

I nodded. He understood we couldn't explain alchemy to the world. I stepped to the quietest corner of the courtyard and called Max. I kept an eye on Ivan, who wasn't interested in me. He flexed his fingers and stood on his tiptoes. It must have been a strange sensation to have one's body transform within hours.

My call to Max went to voicemail, which I was thankful for since it would be easier to stick to the somewhat truthful lies if I kept to the script I'd rehearsed in my mind. Next I called Dorian. Even with the coded timing of rings he insisted we use, he didn't answer. Where was he? With me gone, he knew he shouldn't be baking at Blue Sky Teas.

Frustrated, I hung up the phone and looked up at the sky for a few seconds. When I turned my attention back to the courtyard, Ivan was gone.

In his place on the bench was a torn piece of paper. Caught in the gentle breeze, it fluttered to the ground. I ran to it and snatched it in a tense hand. The handwritten scrawl read *I'm sorry.*

I crumpled the note in my hand and rushed inside but caught no sight of him. I asked everyone I saw, down every hall I could find, but nobody had seen him. The hospital appeared to be more labyrinthine than the catacombs.

I wasn't giving up. I looked from room to room. As I finished searching a hall of patient rooms, a news story on the television in the waiting room caused me to stop my search. On the screen was a face I recognized, one that still bore the marks of bee stings. Professor Chevalier, the scholar studying the gargoyle statue, was being interviewed by a reporter. I turned up the volume.

Professor Chevalier was explaining the mystery of the curiously posed gargoyle statue thought to be stolen from Notre Dame in the 1860s. There had been a break-in at the university, and thieves had ransacked the whole Architecture Department. The reporter asked the professor how he first noticed the theft.

"No," Professor Chevalier protested. "It was not thieves who stole the chimera. The stone creature came to life."

The reporter abruptly ended the interview and the camera switched back to a reporter sitting at a desk with a plastic smile frozen on her face. But she wasn't able to hide the flush filling her cheeks.

Was it possible? The Death Rotation Ivan and Brixton performed must have also enlivened the gargoyle. Perhaps because I'd left the Alchemical Ashes in his mouth, the nearby alchemy had woken him enough that he could swallow the ashes and escape.

If I were a gargoyle who once stood atop Europe's most famous cathedral, where would I go? I left the hospital and headed for Notre Dame.

People see what they expect to see. They believe what already makes sense to their understanding of the world. Therefore it didn't surprise me when the tourists I spoke to said they'd seen a disfigured man. They assumed him to be homeless because he wore only a sheet and carried a bottle of liquor. They pointed in the direction they had seen him go.

I thought I was going to lose my mind as I waited in line to climb to the top of Notre Dame, but it was the only way to gain access to the stairs. I used the time to look up a few things on my cell phone. Now that Brixton was safe, I felt guilty that I hadn't found the actress who played Madame Leblanc, to warn her that her colleague was dead and she might be next. I found the *gendarme* actor's website. He didn't have any affiliation with an actress who looked like Madame Leblanc.

A tap on my shoulder alerted me to the fact that the line was moving. It was time to climb the winding steps of Notre Dame once more. I hadn't heard any screams from above, so I wasn't entirely certain my theory was correct. But I had to try.

The first place I looked—near the famous Gallery of Gargoyles— was a bust. But while the guard was dealing with two people blocking the way with banned selfie sticks, I slipped into an off-limits area near the bell tower.

A scuffling sound startled me.

"*Allo?*" I said softly, hoping it wasn't a cathedral worker.

A burp broke the silence. I stepped forward and saw a lumpy sheet in the corner. The sheet moved.

"Do you remember me?" I said. "I tried to help you last week."

"*Va t'en!*"

"I'm not leaving. I can help you."

The gargoyle poked his head out from underneath the sheet and glared at me. "*T'es conne.*"

Great. That was all I needed. A drunk gargoyle telling me to get lost and calling me dumb.

"Are you drunk?

"'It is the hour to be drunken! On wine, on poetry, or on virtue, as you wish.'"

"You've only been *awake* for an hour... But if you've already found liquor, I suppose you don't need this." I held up a bottle of absinthe, the same brand that had been found in his frozen hand in Prague.

He lunged for it. I put the bottle behind my back, hoping he wouldn't tackle me. This gargoyle was more than a foot taller than Dorian, almost five feet tall.

"Only if you talk to me," I continued. "What's your name?"

He chuckled. "Leopold. *Je m'appelle* Leopold."

Now that he was standing before me, I got a better look at him. Leopold did look like he could be an older brother to Dorian. Since he'd once stood with the other stone creatures on the Gallery of Gargoyles, he was larger than Dorian in both height and girth. His body was a similar gray color, but his eyes were gray, not black like Dorian's. His horns were larger than Dorian's, yet he had no wings.

"I'm a friend," I said. "An alchemist."

Leopold blinked at me. "Your name is Alchemist?"

"No. My name is Zoe. I'm an alchemist."

He shrugged. "*D'accord.*" Did he not realize alchemy had brought him to life? This was too big a conversation to have a few meters away from the tourists atop Notre Dame.

"Myself," he continued, "I am a *poète.*"

A gargoyle poet? I supposed it was no stranger than a gargoyle chef.

"You have another friend, too," I said. "Another gargoyle, like you."

He drew his horns together. "You mock me, mademoiselle."

"Let me call him, so you can see." I dialed Dorian for a video call. "I think you'll feel more comfortable talking to him."

A moment later, Dorian's beaming face appeared on the screen. An amazed Leopold grabbed my phone.

The two gargoyles spoke rapid Latin to each other, so I wasn't able to follow most of what they said. But when they switched back to French, they told me they'd agreed Leopold would accompany me back to Portland. I hadn't thought that far ahead, but who was I to stop two living gargoyles on a mission? We quickly constructed a plan where Leopold would turn to stone in a completely different shape than he'd been found in on the Prague bridge, so nobody would suspect he was the gargoyle "stolen" from the university.

"Now we need to get you out of here," I said.

Using his sheet to disguise himself and his drunken state as an excuse to keep his head down and lean on me, Leopold and I wound down the Notre Dame stairs and away from the cathedral as quickly and quietly as possible.

Leopold spent the evening in our small rented room alternately drinking the bottle of absinthe I'd offered him and reciting poetry to it.

I flew back to Portland the next day with two special deliveries. Heather had authorized me to accompany Brixton home after I went to the hospital first thing in the morning. The doctors had determined he was suffering from dehydration and severe jet lag but was otherwise healthy, so they wanted to discharge him as soon as possible.

Brixton and I traveled with a special piece of luggage: a storage crate containing a statue I claimed to have found at a flea market. Also in the crate was a case of absinthe. It was meant to last our new friend a month, or at the very least a week. When we arrived at PDX, the bottles were empty.

CHAPTER 47

Back at home in Portland, Brixton was safe; that was the most important thing. But I couldn't rest easy. Brixton was still recovering and not yet back to his usual self. Ivan and Percy's whereabouts were unknown. And I hadn't figured out how to cure the deterioration of backward alchemy with anything short of the ultimate sacrifice: giving my own life.

Further down the line, I worried what would happen with the police investigation into Lucien's murder. They hadn't yet discovered his identity, but it was only a matter of time before they connected him to Brixton via the boy's DNA under his fingernails.

In spite of his partial backward alchemy transformation, Ivan hadn't lost his humanity. At least not yet. It was a small silver lining, but I was willing to take it. Even though he hadn't yet come forward to confess that he was responsible for Lucien's death, he'd helped Brixton escape the tunnels in Paris and had accepted that he'd been misled by Percy. I hoped he'd come through before the police got their DNA results back.

In the meantime, I had my hands full dealing with two gargoyle roommates.

I came home from visiting a subdued Brixton to find a smoky scent permeating the house.

"It is his fault," Dorian said as soon as I came through the door. "He distracted me and the bread burned in the oven."

"It's all right, Dorian. So... where's Leopold?"

Dorian frowned. "Taking a nap in the attic. I do not understand, Zoe. He does not need to sleep."

"Maybe he's just lazy."

Dorian and I climbed the stairs to the attic and found Leopold curled up on a stack of pillows on the steamer trunk. The pillows looked suspiciously like the ones from my bed.

"He's not asleep," I said, sniffing the air. "He's drunk."

Dorian gaped at Leopold. Our gargoyle guest stretched luxuriantly and sat up.

"Where is the art in this mansion?" Leopold asked. "Your walls are quite barren. Monsieur Robert-Houdin informed me this is a new abode for you. Have you not yet finished unpacking?"

"I collect books and other alchemical items, not art."

Leopold's gray eyes grew wide. "*C'est vrai?*"

"It is true," Dorian answered. "I have already explained to you that Zoe is an alchemist. This is how she understands how you and I were brought to life. We have not yet discussed the intricacies—"

"No art?" Leopold said, again completely ignoring the reference to alchemy. "*Quelle horreur!* I may as well return to stone."

I wouldn't have believed a gargoyle could be more dramatic than Dorian if I hadn't seen it with my own eyes.

"Without art, what do you do for amusement?" Leopold asked Dorian.

"Before you stated your strong desire to take a siesta," Dorian said, "I was showing you my kitchen—"

"Cooking? This is your idea of fun? I believed you to be joking. This is women's work, no?"

Dorian puffed up his chest. "I am a chef of great distinction."

Leopold giggled. Then burped. "*Pardon.*"

"Perhaps," Dorian said in his most diplomatic voice, "if you have now recovered from your journey, you will tell us of your life."

The gargoyle rolled off the steamer trunk and clasped his talons together. "'How little remains of the man I once was,'" he said softly, "'save the memory of him! But remembering is only a new form of suffering.'"

"Baudelaire," I said. "You're quoting Baudelaire. You quoted his poetry when I first met you too. You said you were a poet. So you enjoy Baudelaire's poetry?"

"*Enjoy?* Is this the right word to describe the influence of the great man? To handle language so skillfully is to practice evocative sorcery!"

"You knew him," I said. Dorian remained speechless.

"*Oui.* Monsieur Charles Baudelaire brought me from the shadows."

"*Bon!*" Dorian chimed in. "I, too, had a great man teach me. Jean Eugène Robert-Houdin. Surely you have heard of—"

"The stage magician? *Pfft.* A common entertainer."

Dorian sputtered several words, none of them intelligible.

"You have more wine?" Leopold asked. "Or hashish?"

❧

Dinner that night was a tense affair. We learned that Leopold had been taken in by a group of Bohemian artists and writers who were loosely affiliated with Victor Hugo's romantic army. Critic and poet Charles Baudelaire was the man Leopold was closest to, and upon his death, Leopold mourned him tremendously. Much poetry was written during those dark days. Leopold claimed that some of Baudelaire's last works were ghostwritten by Leopold himself. I was disinclined to believe him. Then again, Baudelaire had been drunk when he wrote many of his famous poems.

Dorian cooked a classical French feast in honor of his newfound brother, sending me to buy expensive wine in addition to a short shopping list to supplement what we already had at the house. The menu consisted of marinated olives, spinach and walnut terrine, and lentil pate for appetizers; Breton onion soup for a starter; cider casserole for a main dish; and apricot tarts for dessert.

Leopold drank nearly all of the wine himself but barely touched his food. "A man can go without food for two days," he declared, "but not without poetry."

❧

After dinner, Leopold didn't offer to help with the dishes. I began to help Dorian, but he said it would be easiest in the small kitchen for him to take care of the dishes himself, even with only one good arm. I didn't argue. It was difficult for me to talk with him alone, knowing the sacrifice I was getting ready to make. He would never agree to it, so I had to keep it to myself until the preparations were ready.

Once it was late enough, Dorian left for Julian Lake's house to prepare food for the following day, after which he'd go to the teashop kitchen to bake pastries before dawn. It felt strange to follow such a simple daily routine after

711

the crazy events of the past few days and weeks, but there was really nothing else to be done.

I made my rounds through the house, making sure it was tightly secured. As I passed back through the first floor, I found Leopold passed out. In the middle of the dining room table.

CHAPTER 48

The next day the Portland police declared Brixton well enough to talk with them about what had happened with Ivan. He told the police that Ivan had gone crazy and started to believe all the historical alchemy books he was studying. Brixton also said that Ivan had convinced him he needed his help to save his life. Of course he'd wanted to help. But Brixton swore he didn't know what Ivan had in mind. Max knew him well enough that he might have picked up on the fact that Brixton wasn't telling the whole story, but with the detectives on the case, Brix played the role of an innocent, gullible, and slightly selfish kid to perfection.

The police thankfully hadn't yet gotten the results of the full DNA testing, so they hadn't connected Brixton to Lucien's dead body. As soon as I was sure Brixton was truly safe, then I'd be ready to make my sacrifice for Dorian.

I visited Brixton after he returned home from the police station. His mom was sitting on one side of his bed.

"I'm never letting this one out of my sight again," she said. She pulled him close and planted a kiss on the top of his head. "He's grounded for the rest of the summer."

Brixton rolled his eyes. "Very funny, Mom."

Heather's breezy smile turned almost as grim as the day I'd seen her at the morgue. "I'm dead serious, Brix."

"But I—but you—I mean, I nearly *died*."

"Exactly," Heather said. "You're too old to get away with acting so stupidly.

Running off to a foreign country with a delusional neighbor? I liked Ivan, too, but you can't do things like that, honey."

Brixton leaned back on the assortment of pillows his mom had propped up. I had a feeling his summer of being "grounded" would consist of a fair amount of TLC from his parents and probably visits from his friends Ethan and Veronica.

"At least I haven't been keeping a secret," Brixton said, making a face at his mom. "You want to know why Mom has been disappearing lately, Zoe?"

"Brix!" Heather said, "I'm not telling people yet!"

"You said it wasn't a secret anymore."

"Not a secret to *you*, silly."

"Zoe is family, Mom."

I felt a lump form in my throat.

"You're right," she said. "I'm sorry for the secrecy. I didn't want to tell anyone, especially Brixton, before I knew if I'd succeed."

"You'll succeed," a deep voice said. Abel leaned against the bedroom door. "She's studying for her GED."

"That's wonderful," I said.

"You know I dropped out when I had Brix," Heather said. "In a year, he'll have more education then I do. That's not a great example."

"You're a great mom," Abel said. He strode across the room and gave them both a hug. "Stay for dinner?" he asked me.

"I wish I could," I said.

Heather pulled Abel to the bedroom door. "We'll let you two visit a few more minutes while Abel starts dinner."

I'd never been inside Brixton's room before, yet it felt to me like something was missing. "Your mom took away your guitar?" I asked.

He shook his head. "I sorta… sacrificed it."

"Why would you—"

"Ivan said I had to make a sacrifice for the alchemy to work. That's what we thought the sacrifice was. Giving up something I loved."

"Oh, Brix. I'm so sorry. Your heart was in the right place. Where did you toss it? The Willamette?"

"Pawn shop. I used the money for my ticket to Paris. Ivan talked about *intent* being important in alchemy. My sacrifice used my intent and got me to Paris. Wicked city, by the way." He smiled mischievously for a few seconds before growing serious again. "I'd do it again, you know. To help him not die. I mean, as long as it didn't mean dying myself. Which is totally messed up."

A happy tear slid down my cheek as I walked back to my truck. I'd leave my truck and trailer to Tobias, I thought to myself. Since Rosa was dying, he'd soon need a change. He liked my truck when he visited a few months ago. Maybe he'd like the Airstream too.

～

At home, Leopold was still passed out, although now his hefty gray body was sprawled on my green velvet couch. I poked the bottom of his foot. He twitched but didn't open his eyes. I poked his foot again.

"'I have felt the wind of the wing of madness,'" he mumbled, then rolled over.

I felt myself roll my eyes like my young friend would have done. Leopold wouldn't be disturbing me anytime soon. I unlocked the door to my basement alchemy lab and began the preparations for my sacrifice.

I lit a kerosene lamp and walked to my main work table. A prickle made its way up my spine. Someone had been inside my lab. *Recently.* My gold leaf was gone, as were all of my salts.

But Percy was the one who'd searched my lab before, and he was long gone. Wasn't he?

Where *was* Percy?

CHAPTER 49

"This is one of my favorites," Leopold said. "*Un moment.*" He rubbed his jaw and opened his mouth terrifyingly wide, revealing rows of pointy teeth. Squaring his shoulders, he took a stance that made it look like he was howling at the moon.

"Or this one," he added. He moved out of the werewolf position, shaking his body as if stretching after a workout. Next he crossed his arms, held his head high, and looked down his nose at us.

"That pose does not look scary," Dorian said. He tried to make a frightening pose himself, spreading his wings wide, but he nearly lost his balance. The speed of his deterioration was quickening.

"You miss the point, *mon amie.* In this simple posture, I inch closer... and closer.... It instills fear in the hearts of men!" He guffawed.

"Er, yes," Dorian said.

"Or how about this one?" Leopold thrust out his chin, baring his bottom row of teeth, and hunched his shoulders.

Dorian circled him. "Too humorous."

"*Oui,* I suspect you are right." Leopold shook out the pose.

At least the two gargoyles were getting along better.

For the last half hour, Leopold had been showing Dorian the various ways he'd stayed hidden since being brought to life. His family of drunken artists and writers had known of his existence (though I suspected half of them thought he was a figment of their collective imaginations), but nobody else did.

Like Dorian, Leopold had learned how to live in the shadows. As we were coming to realize, though, he pushed the boundaries. He went where he wanted then simply turned to stone on the spot if he was in danger of being seen. Often in a bizarre pose, to keep people off balance.

"And nobody ever saw you?" I asked. "Truly?"

Leopold shrugged. "In the music halls and museums, the people think with their hearts, not with their minds."

We all gave a start when my phone buzzed. It was Brixton texting me that he was at the front door.

"You really need a doorbell," he said after I let him inside and we were walking up the stairs. "I've been knocking for five minutes. You're always in the attic."

"Leopold Baudelaire, meet Brixton Taylor."

"Wicked," Brixton whispered, staring at the gargoyle.

"Your servant?" Leopold asked me.

"Our friend," Dorian corrected.

Leopold rubbed his chin and nodded. Dorian prodded him to shake Brixton's hand.

"I thought you were spending time with your family," I said. "And grounded."

"Yeah, Mom is studying for her GED in the open now, but then she and Abel..." He cleared this throat. "I think they wanted to do things no mom should do. Ever."

"'From love there will be born poetry,'" Leopold recited, "'which will spring up toward God like a rare flower.'"

"My life is too weird," Brixton mumbled. "Anyway, I snuck out."

"Now that we have made introductions," Leopold said, "we have important matters to discuss. A council of war, if you will."

Finally. He'd put me off every time I tried to address the problem of backward alchemy turning the gargoyles back into stone.

"It has been brought to my attention," Leopold continued, "that you are cavorting with *un flic*. This will not do. The police are not to be trusted."

I groaned. "My love life isn't your concern. I thought we were going to talk about—"

"If you think this is unimportant, you are *assez stupide!*"

"Not cool," Brixton said. "That's so not cool."

"Why don't you play some music for us, Brixton," Dorian said diplomatically. "I see you have brought your banjo."

Skeptically eyeing Leopold, Brixton picked up the banjo he carried slung over his back. He strummed a 1960s folk song.

"This is not music," Leopold said. "This is—"

He broke off when two phones began to ring at once. Grateful to head off that argument, I picked up mine and smiled.

"Max," I said into the phone. "It's wonderful to hear your voice, but this isn't really a good time."

"I won't take long. This isn't a social call—but I hope it's a good one. Is Brixton there with you?"

"Yeah, he is." How could this be good? Brixton had answered his own phone and stood in the corner, his back to us.

"Good," Max said. "Ivan gave a confession."

"Ivan," I whispered, closing my eyes as I let out a sigh of relief.

"Not what I expected either," he said, misinterpreting my surprise. "He emailed a confession, and we know he's not lying to protect anyone, because he gave us details that led to blood evidence. The man was apparently an aggressive salesman who came to the house while Brixton was there. Grabbed Brixton's arm, which is why Ivan threw him out. I'm betting it'll be Brixton's DNA the lab finds under his fingernails when they conclude their analysis. It was an accident, so I wish Brixton had just told us what happened, but I understand that he's scared. This has been such a strange case—but now life can go back to normal."

Normal. I bit back my true reaction. Everything would be all right without me now. It was time to make my sacrifice.

CHAPTER 50

Brixton used the interruption of the phone calls as an opportunity to escape the rude gargoyle. I walked him downstairs.

"I can let myself out," he said.

"I need a break from those two too," I said. "You hungry? Before you go, you can grab something from the kitchen."

He turned to me, and I saw in his face the caring man he was growing into. "You're different today, Zoe. I don't know what it is. I don't think it's your frustration with Leo—even though you're gonna have to watch that dude."

I gave him a hug. I hadn't meant to, but I was overcome with emotion realizing that I wasn't going to live to see Brixton grow up. "I'm so proud of you," I said, blinking back tears.

Once I was sure I wasn't going to cry, I pulled back from the hug. Brixton was rolling his eyes. "Okay, Zoe. Whatever."

I watched Brixton ride his bike down the driveway with his banjo slung over his back. When he reached the street, he briefly glanced both ways. Catching a glimpse of his profile, I was struck by the handsome man he would soon be.

Instead of going back upstairs, I grabbed my silver raincoat. I scribbled a note to Dorian so he wouldn't worry, then set off on foot.

For the next three hours, I walked around my Hawthorne neighborhood of Portland, stopping to speak to the locals walking their dogs, browse the wares of the quirky stores, pick up a cup of tea at Blue Sky Teas, and literally stop and smell the roses.

Without realizing the route I was taking, I found myself in front of Max's house. The sun hung low in the sky. The day was coming to a close. As was my life.

I was here to say goodbye.

I stood in front of the red door with a gold dragon knocker but paused before I raised my hand to lift it.

The door swung open and a very wet Max grinned at me. In jeans and a white t-shirt, his feet were bare and he held a towel to sopping wet hair. "I thought I saw someone out here. Sorry, I didn't hear the door."

Inside, I walked through the uncluttered living room, filled with a white couch, pewter coffee table, and paintings of forests that were taller than either of us. I came to a stop in front of the sliding glass door that led to the back-yard garden. Max laced his fingers through mine as I looked out at the wooden bench where we'd spent so many happy hours together.

When I'd been in a reckless mood, I'd allowed myself to fantasize about spending years with Max, sitting on that bench watching the night-blooming jasmine unfurl and the morning-blooming California poppies awaken with the day.

"You want to go outside?" Max whispered. "Let me grab my—"

I stopped his words with my lips. He didn't object. And it was a good thing he didn't have many things in the house to bump into. Only that plastic skeleton in the hallway.

～

An hour later, Max fixed us a pot of lemon balm tea using his grandmother's iron tea kettle.

"Sorry about that skeleton," I said. "I can put it back together. I'm good with my hands."

"I know." He kissed my shoulder. "But don't worry about it. It's time I got rid of it. Time I moved on." He added a sprig of fresh mint to the tea, then handed me a white porcelain cup with deep blue Chinese characters. The minty steam made it the perfect choice.

It hit me that it had been selfish of me to come here. While I was here to say goodbye, Max was ready to take the next step with me.

"I'm not entirely convinced the stories about the skeleton are true anyway," Max said.

"You didn't tell me the story. Only that Chadna wanted to draw it out so you'd learn more about it each year as you grew old together."

"Supposedly this skeleton originally contained some *real* human bones."

"That's how med schools used to train their students, you know."

"Apparently some of them still do. My guess was that it was a secret society type of thing. Creepy, huh?"

"Oh my God," I whispered.

"It's not *that* great a story."

"Max, I'm so sorry, but I have to go. I lost track of time."

"You're not staying?"

I kissed him hard and fast. "No, but I'll be back."

Maybe this wasn't goodbye after all.

I ran home, my silver raincoat flapping behind me and hope surging within me. I might not have to sacrifice myself. I now knew what had changed. As a true alchemist, I was looking at it the wrong way around. I was in control of my own life force, but backward alchemists weren't. They relied on the remains of other willing sacrifices.

In spite of the late hour, I was energized with hope. Too energized. I failed to notice the front door of the house wasn't as securely locked as it should have been.

Only as I bounded up the attic stairs, calling for Dorian and Leopold, did I notice something was off. The house was quiet. Yet it was too early in the night for the gargoyles to be on the prowl.

I thought to myself that I'd have to lecture Dorian about not following Leopold's lead of trying be cool. Did gargoyles even care about being cool? Never mind. I'd have years to find out. Since I now knew a better way to save the gargoyles. A way that didn't involve sacrificing my life. I knew that—

I stepped into the attic and froze. I saw not two gargoyles, but two *people*: Percy and Madame Leblanc.

Only Madame Leblanc wasn't quite herself. This woman was decades younger. Her daughter? Granddaughter?

No, it couldn't be...

The woman in my attic looked almost identical to the woman with movie-star good looks in the black-and-white photograph Percy carried in his wallet.

Madame Leblanc wasn't an innocent actor like the man who played the part of her nephew. She was the backward alchemist who'd killed him. This whole time, she was the mysterious mastermind.

CHAPTER 51

All the pieces fell into place. Madame Leblanc—or whatever her real name was—was the true charismatic leader of the backward alchemists. Not Lucien. Not Percy.

I should have seen it sooner. In Paris, Madame Leblanc played her role with me so lyrically it was almost theatrical, and she'd believed in my immortality all too readily. She knew I worked with Jasper Dubois, who was an aspiring alchemist, so she was able to create a believable lie. The actor who played her grandnephew policeman had looked young from afar but up close he looked tired— because he was a backward alchemy apprentice. Back in Portland, Percy had said "only three of us left" while telling me about backward alchemy. The woman in the photo in Percy's wallet had looked familiar. And when Ivan had said *"they'll* be returning soon" to the alchemy lab, as opposed to *"Percy* will be returning soon," it was Madame Leblanc he was referring to.

"Cat got your tongue, Zoe?" she said. The accent was English. "Don't look so surprised. I'm sure you've figured everything out."

"I was so gullible," I hissed, barely able to control my anger at having been so close to the truth but also so far off.

"Don't be too hard on yourself, dear. I really am an actress. Made quite a splash in the West End for a while. That's where Percy found me." I could believe it. Though her skin was pinched, her large eyes and lips were stunning. Her hair was a rich, lush black, and it flowed past her shoulders.

"You killed the actor playing your nephew," I said. "He was your apprentice. That's how you look so young again."

"Oh, do catch up, my dear. And hand over the book. *My* book."

I smiled. Now *I* had the upper hand. If she didn't already have Dorian's book, that meant Dorian and Leopold had gotten away through the hole in the roof. It also meant Madame Leblanc hadn't figured out the book was, as Dorian would have put it, a McGuffin. Everyone was searching for the damn book, but it *wasn't* the key. It was only the clue that pointed to Notre Dame.

"Why are you smiling? Percy, restrain her."

So strong was Madame Leblanc's presence that Percy had faded into the background. He now stepped forward, though the movement was half-hearted. His eyes darted between the two of us. His hair was flecked with gray, and his jowls sagged. While Madame Leblanc had grown younger, he'd grown older.

"Don't touch me, Percival," I said.

He stopped.

Madame Leblanc sighed. Theatrically. "Do I have to do everything myself?"

"You have me at a loss," I said. "I don't even know your real name."

She smiled wickedly. "I wondered if I'd gone too far there. Blanche Leblanc: White White. The embodiment of a Ms. Goody Two-Shoes."

Mentally kicking myself, I edged my way toward the attic door.

"I see you moving, Zoe. Stop right there. Don't you want to know my true name?" The look in her black eyes told me I wasn't sure I wanted to. "The name I've used since my transformation is Raven. And you don't want to mess with the Raven."

The skin on her forearm had firmed enough for me to realize that what I'd mistaken for faded numbers from a concentration camp was actually a tattoo of a raven. My subconscious had noticed it and turned it into a dream.

"You will give me that book," she said. She didn't yell. Her words were so soft that I barely heard them. Yet there was a cold forcefulness to the directive that made me shiver. "I will be restored to my former beauty for eternity."

"I don't have it," I said, matching her strong, stoic intonation.

"Wrong answer." She drew a sword from behind her back.

CHAPTER 52

It was one of *my* swords from my collection of antiques that Raven held in her hand.

"Percy," I said, "you don't have to go along with—"

"Enough!" Raven thrust the sword into the creaking floorboards, showing its might.

"I swear I don't have the book here," I said. I knew I was convincing, because it wasn't a lie.

"I know. We've searched the house. But I have very persuasive ways of making people talk."

I nodded. Not too quickly. I couldn't let her think I was eager. I couldn't let her know I now knew more than she did. "I'll tell you where it is," I said, "if you let me understand what's happened. I need to know."

"Why?"

"I have a friend who's dying, like you."

"The gargoyle," Percy said, raising his hand in earnest like a sycophantic schoolboy. "The gargoyle I told you about."

Raven and I both ignored him.

"I don't care what happens to me," I said, "but I want you to help Dorian."

I knew she wouldn't, but there was still a chance I could, if I could think of a way out of this.

"All right," Raven said cautiously. She motioned for Percy to close the attic door. He rushed to oblige.

"I thought you would find our secret alchemy lab," Raven continued once the door was bolted. "That would have ruined our plans to sacrifice the actor. I couldn't kill you without hurting myself, so I devised a plan to get you to leave Paris of your own accord."

"Because an alchemist can't kill a person without hurting themselves."

She smirked. "Nice try. Percy convinced me it was true, long ago. But now, thanks to you, I know the truth. It's only a superstition."

Me and my big mouth...

"I never suspected that you had Lucien and Olav's backward alchemy book," she continued, "or that you could help us. It was Lucien who realized you had the book and could help solve what the rest of us could not. You aroused his suspicions, and when he asked Percy about a woman called Zoe Faust, Percy told us who you were. That's why Lucien followed you to Portland."

"I made it so easy for him. I even gave him my address."

"Most backward alchemists aren't 'friends,' so we don't keep each other's confidences. Stupid Lucien didn't tell us his suspicions that you could help us. And I didn't tell Lucien of my plan to get rid of you."

"That's why Lucien was truly shocked when I said I was leaving Paris. He was upset that you'd messed up his plans, so he followed me to steal *Non Degenera Alchemia*—which he originally planned on doing more easily in Paris, before you ruined his scheme."

"Lucien was almost out of Alchemical Ashes. He was smoking them frequently to stay young until we could permanently stop our life forces reversing. Lucien was arrogant, and thought he could get the book without much effort."

"That's why he lost his temper so quickly at my friend Ivan's house," I said, using the word *friend* automatically before I could think better of it. "Lucien was upset that Ivan refused to help him."

"I've never trusted Lucien, so I sent Percy to follow him. Can you believe Lucien once said theater was for the mindless masses? Yet it was my acting skills that fooled you. I'm the one who has outlived them all—"

Percy cleared his throat.

"Oh, yes, my love," Raven said. "Of course I meant *we* are the ones who have outlived them all. And now we are going to retrieve our long-lost book and live on forever as the beautiful specimens we once were."

Raven had to come to Portland to do her own dirty work. And she still mistakenly believed Dorian's book contained the secret to the "change" that had reversed the transformations of backward alchemy.

"You're forgetting the most important part of the story," I said. "*What was the shift that occurred six months ago?*"

She blinked at me. "What do you mean?"

"What happened six months ago?"

"We began to age and die."

"Percy already told me that much," I said. "I need to know what *triggered* the change."

"You're trying to confuse me. Percy warned me that you were overly intellectual. Half of your antiques are books. What good are books? Scripts for the theater are different, of course. The only book I need is the one Olav and Lucien created."

Was my theory right? "Who was the first to die?" I asked.

"Why does it matter?"

"Humor me."

"Olav," she said, a look of suspicion creeping onto her face.

"Percy said he wasn't very intelligent. Is that right?"

"He was a stupid, stupid, man," she agreed.

"How did he die?"

"The same as the rest of us. He began aging rapidly."

"You saw his transformation take place?"

She hesitated. "We weren't friends. Who wants to associate with a man less interesting than a rock?"

"How did you know he died, then?"

"I found him," Percy spoke up. "Inside the underground tunnels not far from the alchemy lab. The smell... I went to investigate."

"What was he doing in there?"

Percy shrugged. "It's trendy for people to go down into the catacombs and tunnels these days, so I assumed he was making sure our laboratory entrance remained hidden, as I was."

"People get lost down there," I said. "Especially people—"

"The idiot!" Raven shrieked. She grasped the hilt of the sword and paced back and forth on the creaky attic floor, her silky black hair snarling around her face. "You mean he got lost in the tunnels and starved or froze to death, like other stupid explorers have done. We're not immortal, we just don't age."

"Exactly," I said.

"Hang on," Percy said, "I don't get it."

"Olav didn't die because of a shift," I said. "His death *was* the shift. Because backward alchemy is a shortcut *tied to another person*, Olav's death broke the link. That's why you're all dying."

"The sacrifices," Raven said, comprehension sinking in. "The sacrifices aren't enough?"

"What happened to Olav's bones, Percy?" I asked. "What happened after you found him?"

"When I touched him," Percy said, "he turned to ash."

I nodded. "And the ashes?"

"I sprinkled them in the Seine."

"So it's over," I said softly. "The link is broken."

Bones and ash are our core essence. That's why relics have significance. And that's why Max's skeleton helped me see the possibility that a person's physical body was tied to the shift.

Raven's eyes locked on mine. "No. There's got to be another answer in that book."

I shook my head sadly. I didn't think there was.

I understood the truth about *Non Degenera Alchemia*. Backward alchemy was a quick fix for lazy people who were willing to sacrifice the life of another for their own unnatural immortality. To get around the core tenet of alchemy —using guided intent to transform the impure into the pure—backward alchemists had to sacrifice an innocent.

An alchemist's lab is their sanctuary and thus inexorably linked to their work. The pure intent of Notre Dame Cathedral balanced the impure intent of the two men who recorded their backward alchemy steps in *Not Untrue Alchemy*, allowing for some sort of stability. Because Dorian and Leopold were *innocents* from the cathedral, the book itself was able to bring them to life without an external sacrifice. Yet when the original intent was broken, everyone given life through backward alchemy faced the consequences.

Steps sounded beneath us. Had Dorian gone to Max to get help?

The attic door opened. Ivan stepped inside and relief washed over me. He'd had a change of heart after all.

Ivan wasn't quite as young and vigorous as he'd been when I saw him at the alchemy laboratory in Paris, but he was strong enough to help.

"The book?" Raven asked him.

Ivan shook his head. "I searched again. It's not here."

My relief turned to cold terror. Ivan was still working with the backward alchemists?

But it didn't matter. The quick deterioration of Ivan's body showed me that backward alchemy was over. And Dorian's life along with it.

CHAPTER 53

"It's over, Ivan," I said. "We've figured out that backward alchemy is done for."

"She's lying," Raven said. "She's trying to trick us into thinking there's no solution. But her beastly friend is hiding the book that will save us."

"I'm telling you the truth," I said, wondering where my decidedly non-beastly gargoyle friend had gone. "She and Percy misled you—"

"It's because of *us* that you're healthy again, Ivan," Raven said.

"Zoe would have had you die."

"And *you* would have had him kill Brixton," I said.

Ivan winced.

"I forgive you, Ivan," I said. "I know you didn't know—"

"Enough with the sentimentality," Raven said. "Do you want to survive or not, Ivan?"

He nodded silently, his jaw clenched. He refused to look me in the eye.

"How many more sacrifices will you make?" I asked. "With the link broken, it will never stop."

"Men will always willingly give me this gift," Raven said. "Jasper jumped at the chance."

I gasped. "It *wasn't* a lie that Jasper Dubois was murdered. Only it was *you* who did it."

"I'll let you in on a secret, my dear: if you want to tell a convincing lie, stick to the truth as closely as possible."

I glared at her. That was *my* secret. And she'd killed *my* shopkeeper assistant. Not that I'd been all that fond of the misogynistic Jasper, but still, he didn't deserve to be murdered.

"Didn't you wonder how I knew you wouldn't be able to trace Jasper's movements?" she continued.

"Because you knew he was already dead." I should have thought of it, but she'd thrown me off balance by appearing in my attic today.

"I can practically feel my face sagging," Raven said, feeling her neck with the hand that wasn't clutching the sword. "Percy, Ivan, stop standing there like useless lumps."

Now I was *really* angry. Not only had she manipulated me, but she'd turned Ambrose's son Percy and my friend Ivan against me. I lunged for the second sword that was part of the pair. I'd been so calm until now that she didn't anticipate the movement.

"Stay out of my way, Percy. Ivan." My voice didn't sound like my own, but I was fairly certain it was me speaking. "This is between me and Raven."

Decades ago, I'd taken some fencing lessons with a lovely German man named Anton. I hoped I'd remember what he taught me.

The men stepped back as Raven and I lunged at each other. In our rage, we weren't going for proper form. We were trying to kill each other.

Raven was already aging, so she wasn't as strong as she thought she was. She was the first to draw blood, a shallow wound to my hip. While she regained her balance, I slashed a long cut across her shoulder. She cried out, more in shock than pain, I expect. Her sword dropped from her hand and she gripped her arm.

I immediately thought of Tobias, who carried cayenne pepper with him in his role as an EMT, as an unconventional herbal remedy to stop blood loss. I kept a glass jar of cayenne on an antique spice rack there in the attic and wondered if it would help staunch the flow of blood from the wound I'd inflicted.

I knew then that I couldn't kill Raven. It wasn't in my nature.

But there was something else I could do. I grabbed the jar of cayenne, tore the lid off, and threw the spice into her eyes.

Raven screamed in pain, blinded and writhing on the floor. Since she was no longer a threat, I pressed a towel to her bleeding shoulder and looked for something with which I could tie her arms.

A piece of rope secured a curtain in the corner of the attic that Dorian kept for his private reading room. I yanked off the rope and turned back to Raven. But she was no longer sprawled on the floor. She stood in front of me, red-faced and wielding her sword.

Then the look on her face morphed into surprise. A spot of deep red formed in the middle of her chest. The tip of a sword burst through her chest. A metallic scent filled the air. She looked down at her chest for a brief moment before her eyelids closed and she crumpled to the floor.

Behind her stood Ivan, a blood-drenched sword clutched in his hands.

CHAPTER 54

"On my God!" Percy screamed. He repeated the words again and again until I slapped him.

Unlike Percy, Ivan stood as still as a nonliving gargoyle statue.

"Ivan?" I said quietly.

"She was going to kill you," he whispered. "I couldn't let her. I couldn't."

As we stood there, the three of us in shock, Raven's body shriveled from a woman into a skeleton, then before our eyes changed from bone to ash.

A siren sounded in the distance.

I swore. "Dorian and Leopold must have sent for help."

"Nobody will believe what has happened," Ivan said.

"Oh my God!" Percy started repeating again. Goodness, that man was tiresome. And he hadn't lifted a finger to help me.

"Percy," I said, shaking him by the shoulder. "You're not doing anyone any good. You're going to give me your cell phone number and then get out of here. All right?"

He nodded, wide-eyed.

"Ivan," I said. "Pick up Raven's ashes and then leave. The cut on my leg will explain the mess. I'll tell the police there was an intruder." The sirens grew louder. "Hurry."

I scooped Raven's ashes into a set of glass apothecary jars. After a quicker cleanup of Raven's remains than I thought was possible, I collapsed onto the attic floor. I hadn't attended to the cut on my hip. There wasn't enough blood loss for me to pass out, but it was the middle of the night. I didn't have the natural energy from the sun to draw upon.

I closed my eyes and felt the cool hardwood floor on my cheek. I'd rest for a few moments...

"Zoe?" a distant voice called. "Zoe?"

"Mmm?"

"You're awake," a familiar voice said, followed by a sigh of relief.

"No, I'm not," I mumbled.

Max's lips found mine. "I hope you're awake now."

I opened my eyes. I was still sitting on the attic floor, but now Max had wrapped an arm around my shoulder. His other hand pressed a cloth to the wound on my leg.

"EMTs are on their way up," he said. "Hang on."

"I could hang on better if you put both of your arms around me."

He laughed. "You scared me, Zoe. You said you'd come back, but you didn't. Instead I got a call from that French friend of yours—the guy I've never met. He said you were in danger. He wouldn't give me details, but insisted I rescue you. He's a strange guy. I don't know how he knew, if he wasn't involved—"

"He didn't do this to me."

"I know. We saw Ivan Danko leaving your house." "You have him?" What would Ivan tell them?

"No, he got away. I can see that you rescued yourself, so I'll have to play hero another day, but what exactly happened here, Zoe?"

"That question can wait, Detective Liu," a woman said. She and a man rushed over to me and examined my hip. "We're having a hell of a time getting a stretcher up here. These old houses aren't up to code. Let me check out this wound and get you downstairs."

My wound was deemed superficial, so I was treated by the paramedics but I wasn't forced to go to the hospital. Max, however, wasn't happy about my decision to stay home.

"If you won't go to the hospital," he said, "you could at least stay with me. Or I'd be happy to..."

I swept an errant lock of hair from his forehead. "I appreciate the offer, but I won't get any rest if you stay. I need to sleep."

He took my hand and kissed it. "I promise I'll let you get some sleep."

With how much my insides melted with that gentle brush of his lips against my hand, I gave him a truthful answer. "I don't trust myself to make you keep that promise."

That seemed to appease him. I sent him home and awaited Dorian's return, which was the more important reason I couldn't have Max stay.

I wasn't sure what I was going to tell Dorian, now that all hope was lost. There was no cure for the backward alchemists and those who'd been brought to life by backward alchemy's power. I could continue making the Tea of Ashes frequently enough to keep Dorian alive temporarily, but I'd be killing myself while he'd continue to slowly die. I should have accepted the truth earlier, but I hadn't been open to the possibility that I wouldn't be able to save Dorian.

I wished Dorian would return home. Everyone had left over an hour ago. A detective had taken my statement. I told him that Ivan Danko had returned to seek revenge on me after I thwarted his crazy attempt to kill Brixton. I hated that it was the lie closest to the truth. I really had wanted to save Ivan.

I fixed myself a chocolate elixir in the blender in an attempt to stay awake, but I fell asleep on the couch waiting for a gargoyle who never came.

At dawn, I awoke to the sound of singing and the scents of cinnamon and smoke.

Dorian stood at the kitchen counter, whisking batter in a stainless steel bowl. Turning at the sound of the swinging kitchen door, he hopped down from the stool and grinned at me. "*Bon*, you are awake, *mon amie*. I have only just returned from Monsieur Lake's home."

"I have so much to tell you, Dorian."

"And I you. Why do you look so sad?"

"Why didn't you come home sooner?"

"I was confident you could defeat the insane woman who was after my book, as you have. I also knew you would not be alone. I was certain Max would come to your aid. He is a good man, and he cares very much for you. I decided it was best to remain hidden and attend to pressing matters."

I sat morosely. "I have news. It's bad. I don't know how to tell you this, so I'm going to come right out and say it."

Dorian rocked back and forth on the linoleum floor and looked at me expectantly.

"There's no cure, Dorian. There's no cure for a backward alchemy trans-formation."

"Ah. Is that all?"

"Is that *all*?"

"I will share my news." He gave a little hop and clapped his hands.

Hopping and clapping...

"You're moving your left arm. And your ankle. It bends again."

"*Oui*. And all the rest of me. He wriggled his horns and flapped his wings gracefully. "You see, my friend, I have discovered true alchemy. I have found the Elixir of Life!"

"But how?"

"Through cooking."

CHAPTER 55

"Like alchemy," Dorian said, "cooking, at its core, is about transformation."

"You truly found the Elixir?" I asked. "You're not joking? Trying to make me feel better about failing?" I'd had so much false hope that I was scared to hope again.

"*Il est trop vrai.* It is as true as true can be. This is why I returned to Julian Lake's house last night instead of coming to check on you. I knew you were safe, so I wanted to complete the transformation."

"At his house rather than your own? I'm sorry if I haven't made you feel like you belong—"

"Not *inside* his house. His backyard, you may recall, has an outdoor brick kiln. It is meant for pizza, but it is the same heat—"

"As an athanor." The fire to cook the philosophical egg.

Dorian grinned. "I cooked many foods in that oven, each of which represented a step to create the Philosopher's Stone."

"You're the one who was moving things around in my laboratory! I worried that was Lucien or Percy. I had the locks changed for nothing."

"*Oui.* I apologize for the deception. But it was necessary."

"And you weren't even bleeding the other day, were you? I knew it wasn't tomato sauce."

He shook his head. "Cinnabar."

"I *knew* someone had taken my dragon's blood."

"I am sorry, my friend. But as you know, alchemy is a personal process. That is why I roped off my own meditative space in the attic."

"Your reading space."

"Yes, only it was not a reading space. I was meditating on alchemy. Did you not wonder why I had not asked you to obtain more library books lately?" He smiled sheepishly.

"What was your philosophical egg?"

"Can you not guess?"

I smiled. "A food?"

"An avocado." He beamed at me. "It was the perfect ingredient for the first step to my Emerald Tablet: Gourmet Food Version."

I burst out laughing.

"It is perfect, no? The avocado is the shape of an egg, and it represents life and fertility. The tree lives hundreds of years. It is even green, like an emerald."

"And your last step must have been salt."

"But of course. Salt purifies and protects foods from being corrupted, as alchemy's transformations purify the impure. Salt is the truest, most natural, and most essential of all foods."

"The product of mercury and sulfur. The child of the spirit and the soul."

"You alchemists are more clever than I gave you credit for. I knew there was a reason I sought you out, Alchemist. We are a perfect balance, you and I. You claim you are not prepared to train others in the art of alchemy, yet it was your guidance that enabled me to find the Elixir."

"But I didn't—"

"You are too humble, Zoe. You are the one who showed me that a meal need not be complicated to reach perfection. You are the one who taught me that salt is the child of the alchemical king and queen. And you are the one who sacrificed yourself for me by creating the Tea of Ashes, showing me that backward alchemy was not the way I wished to live."

I hugged my friend, and he wrapped his wings around me. His wings were no longer the stiff-yet-malleable stone they once were. Now they felt like I imagined the wings of an angel would feel.

I squeezed Dorian's strong, feather-like wings, then pulled back to look at his transformation. He looked much the same as when I'd met him six months before, but his gray skin held a radiance that hadn't previously been there.

"Where's Leopold?" I asked.

Dorian blinked. "Is he not in the attic?"

"I don't think so."

Dorian ran up the stairs. I tried to keep up, but now that he was healthy again, it was all I could do to keep him in sight.

"*Merde,*" Dorian said from the attic doorway. "He promised he was coming back here. I had to leave him so I could finish my transformation alone."

"It's not your fault. I'm sure he'll turn up."

"Zoe, you do not understand. He has *my book.*"

"You don't need it anymore. And what could he do with it on his own?"

Dorian rubbed his chin. "I wonder."

We tromped down the stairs, me pestering Dorian about the fourteen food steps he used to create the Elixir of Life.

"To the kitchen," he said. But as soon as he opened the pantry door, he flapped his wings in earnest. He turned around, clutching a mangled note in his clawed hand. "From Leopold," he sputtered. "He has taken the last of my wine from the pantry. And look, that is the least of the affront."

I eased the wrinkled note from his hand.

It is by universal misunderstanding that we agree with each other, it read. *You have convinced me, my friend, that I must come to understand this foul alchemy that has given us this malady of life. This is why I must borrow your book, say farewell, and accompany my new friend Ivan to the land of alchemists.*

Adieu. L.B.

Leopold and Ivan together, with Dorian's book? That couldn't be good.

I quickly looked up the local Portland news on my phone to make sure there hadn't been any gargoyle sightings. Thank goodness for small favors.

"Zoe," Dorian interrupted. "I hate to alarm you, but your leg is bleeding."

I put my phone down and looked at my healthy friend once more. "I wasn't kidding when I said I had a lot to tell you about what happened last night."

"Let me cook us breakfast. We have much time to talk, and much grand food to eat."

THE END

∼

Zoe and Dorian's adventures aren't over! Read the first chapter of Book 4, The Alchemist's Illusion, *after the recipes, or buy it now!*

Get a free novelette and more recipes when you sign up for Gigi's newsletter. Scan the code below, or go to www.gigipandian.com.

Scan to subscribe to Gigi's newsletter!

RECIPES

Each of these recipes is an easy dish that Dorian was able to make with only one good arm. Using simple ingredients doesn't mean sacrificing flavor.

CREAMY GARLIC TOMATO SAUCE (VEGAN)

Total cooking time: 1 hour
Makes 4 servings
Ingredients:

- 2 tbsp plus ¼ cup olive oil, divided
- 10 medium-size cloves garlic
- 24 oz. jar tomato puree or strained tomatoes
- 1 tsp salt (or to taste)
- ¼ tsp red chili pepper flakes (or to taste)

Directions:

Smash the garlic cloves, and let them rest for 10 minutes. Heat a medium saucepan on low heat while peeling and mincing the smashed garlic. Add 2 tbsp olive oil and garlic. Cook garlic and oil slowly on low heat for 20 minutes. Add tomato puree and simmer for another 20 minutes, minimum.

Remove from heat and cool for a few minutes, then stir in ¼ cup olive oil. Use an immersion blender or transfer to a blender. Watch the color of the red sauce transform to a lighter shade of pink before your eyes, as if you'd added cream.

Once blended, stir in salt and red chili pepper flakes.

Add to 4 servings of a grain (e.g., pasta or freekeh) or use as a dipping sauce for bread.

Note:

You can skip the step of letting the garlic rest for 10 minutes, but the most health benefits will be released by letting it rest for at least 10 minutes once smashed or chopped before heating.

Note:

The trick of transforming these simple ingredients into more than the sum of their parts is *time*. For the best results, don't skip the step of letting the garlic and sauce simmer.

CHOCOLATE MOUSSE (VEGAN, RAW)

Total cooking time: 10 minutes
Makes 2 servings
Ingredients:

- 1 large ripe avocado
- ¼ cup cacao powder
- ¼ cup maple syrup (or ⅓ cup for a sweeter mousse)
- ¼ cup cashew milk (or other nut milk of choice)
- ½ tsp vanilla
- dash sea salt

Directions:

Add all ingredients to a food processor. Puree for at least 1–2 minutes, until smooth and creamy. If lumps persist, stop the food processor and stir the mixture before resuming blending.

Divide into two dessert serving bowls. Optional: garnish with fresh berries on top.

Note:

Skeptical that avocado is the main ingredient? Tasters were surprised to learn the mousse even contained avocado.

FROZEN LEMON CHEESECAKE DROPS (VEGAN, RAW)

Total cooking time: 15 minutes hands on (plus overnight soaking time, and time to set in freezer)
Makes 6 servings (approx. 24 drops)
Ingredients for the topping:

- ¼ cup dates (or up to ½ cup, if you prefer a sweeter crust)
- ½ cup walnuts (or substitute almonds)

Ingredients for the cheesecake:

- 1½ cup raw cashews
- ⅓ cup maple syrup
- ⅓ cup coconut oil
- 3 tbsp lemon juice (add an additional tbsp lemon juice for a tarter tart)
- dash of salt
- dash of turmeric (optional)

Directions:

Soak the cashews in water overnight. Or, if in a rush, boil water and soak in hot water for 4 hours.

To make the topping, chop the dates and walnuts in a food processor. Set aside in a small bowl.

To make the cheesecake drops, drain and rinse the cashews. Melt the coconut oil. Puree all cheesecake ingredients in a blender or food processor until smooth, around 1 or 2 minutes. Line a baking pan with parchment paper. Scoop heaping tablespoons of batter onto the parchment. Sprinkle with the date and nut topping. Let set in the freezer for at least 2 hours.

AUTHOR'S NOTE

As with the other books in the Accidental Alchemist mystery series, *The Elusive Elixir* is a work of fiction, but the historical backdrop is real.

The façade of Notre Dame Cathedral in Paris includes several alchemical carvings, including a person carrying a shield with a salamander in flames. My addition of Dorian's alchemy book to the carving is fictional, and there aren't currently any alchemists using Notre Dame as described in the book—as far as I know.

Dorian Robert-Houdin is based on the famous *Le Penseur* gargoyle that sits high on Notre Dame. If you're ever in Paris, he's worth the long line and stairs to visit.

Nicolas Flamel's house still stands in Paris at 51 *rue de* Montmorency, and is now a restaurant. *Rue Nicolas Flamel,* a street in the 4th Arrondissement in Paris, is also named after the famous alchemist. Le Cabaret de L'Enfer was a real Hell-themed café that opened in the 1800s in Paris's Pigalle neighborhood, the red-light district famous for the Moulin Rouge.

The Death Rotation is a real concept in alchemy, but backward alchemy as portrayed in this book is fictional. I enjoyed developing this idea because alchemy is so shrouded in secrecy that it's easy to imagine what some of the codes and concepts might have meant. Alchemy is an example of a subject where the Internet doesn't reveal all. In my research I came across many old books that have not been digitized, filled with fascinating historical facts about alchemy and old alchemical drawings.

Alchemy, in reality, is both a figurative concept and a precursor to modern chemistry. As Zoe explains, alchemy is about transformation. Alchemists of previous centuries wanted to transform their bodies (seeking the Elixir of Life for immortality) or the elements (transmuting lead or other metals into gold). Their experiments resulted in many discoveries that led to chemistry as we know it today. Zoe is a spagyric alchemist, someone who uses alchemical processes to extract healing properties from plants. Spiritual alchemy is the practice of inner transformation.

I'm not an alchemist (nor am I a French gargoyle chef), but my life transformed five years ago when I was diagnosed with breast cancer in my thirties. I began writing this series steeped in alchemy and cooking transformations while I was undergoing chemotherapy. I took cooking classes and learned how to cook healing vegan foods that nourished both my body and soul. As I write this, I'm four years cancer-free and working on the next Accidental Alchemist mystery.

Read the next Accidental Alchemist Mystery, *The Alchemist's Illusion* (Book 4)

Winner of the Anthony Award for Best Paperback Original! Nominated for the G.P. Putnam's Sons Sue Grafton Memorial Award

"Surprising plot twists, several cliffhangers, and vivid magical imagery will keep fans of paranormal cozies turning the pages." —Publishers Weekly

Centuries-old alchemist Zoe Faust is tired of running from her past. She's finally got her life on track in Portland, Oregon, gardening and cooking in her fixer-upper house with her mischievous best friend, Dorian the gargoyle chef. It seems like the perfect life for Zoe, until she discovers that her old mentor Nicolas Flamel, who she thought had abandoned her, has been imprisoned.

Available now!

~

THE ALCHEMIST'S ILLUSION: CHAPTER 1

The last rays of daylight were descending over the Willamette River when I looked into the eyes of a man who'd been buried six hundred years ago.

I grasped the chain I wore around my neck, now bearing both my gold locket and the pewter carving of a phoenix that my friend Dorian had given me as a good luck charm. The commingling metals were cool against my chest.

"Are you okay?" A young man with flecks of dried red and orange paint on his hands startled me as he touched my elbow. "You look like you've seen a ghost."

He wasn't wrong. Not exactly.

"I'm all right," I said.

He looked unconvinced as his gaze fell to my tightly clenched fist, but he nodded politely and pulled open the glass door leading into the art gallery. The narrow space along the river was wedged in between larger warehouses. I hadn't noticed it on my last waterfront walk the day before. Which wasn't surprising. The Portland art scene was thriving, with new spaces popping up all the time. But that didn't explain the painting visible through the glass front window.

The man who'd shaken me to the core wasn't flesh and blood. But his presence shone as resolutely in pigments as it had in life. Nicolas had never let a living soul capture his image. It was impossible for this painting to exist. Yet here it was.

How had an artist painted such an accurate likeness of my mentor, Nicolas Flamel?

I hadn't seen Nicolas in over three hundred years, and he'd officially been dead for many more. The Paris grave in which he'd supposedly been buried in 1418 was discovered to be empty when it was exhumed years later. The graves of both Nicolas and his wife, Perenelle, had been a ruse so that no curious Parisians would believe they were alive and look for them. They hadn't wanted to risk being burned as witches. Which was fair enough, considering they weren't. But if people knew the truth—that they practiced alchemy—they would have been condemned for practicing witchcraft anyway, just as I had been. So they'd fled and reinvented themselves.

I stepped closer to the portrait. The deep charcoal blacks in the background were at first glance merely shadows, but within those shadows were lush reds and indigos that hinted at the materials in a workshop that lay beyond the subject. With rows of oddly shaped glass jars filled with indistinguishable contents, this could have been an apothecary's home. Normally I would have been more interested in those ingredients hidden in the shadows, but I couldn't take my eyes off the man in the center of the painting.

Many artists had come up with their own imaginings of Nicolas Flamel, once he'd become famous a century after his supposed death. Those sketches looked nothing like the man. Yet in front of me was the real Nicolas, with his sunken cheeks and wild hair the color of sulfurous ashes tossed in a haystack. The painter had even captured the haunted look in his piercing silver-blue eyes.

Nicolas had never agreed to sit for a portrait. *Never.* Just as I never let myself be photographed. If I did, people would see that I'd been twenty-eight years old for much longer than they believed natural.

I'm Zoe Faust. At least that's what I've called myself for over three hundred years. Aside from every hair on my body having turned white, I stopped aging the year I turned twenty-eight, in 1704. I was born with the name Zoe, but I christened myself Faust because I felt like I'd made a deal with the devil when I accidentally discovered the Elixir of Life. If only I'd listened to Nicolas... But that was a long time ago.

I touched my hand to the glass between me and the painting. The artwork bore no signature, nor was there an explanatory placard nearby. The eyes in the portrait were unnerving. Whoever painted it must have known Nicolas personally. I was certain of it.

I shifted my position as a gust of cool wind blew my hair into my eyes. From a new angle, I noticed a strange detail in the painting. The walking stick resting against the cabinet of glass jars took on a different appearance. The ornate carvings now looked like calligraphic letters. I moved closer. The walking stick was also a book. *Alchemia.*

I smiled. The painting was using anamorphosis perspective— meaning it altered the viewer's perception when observed at different angles. Together with the rich colors applied with thick dabs of paint that stood out on the canvas and gave it its personality, it reminded me of the work of the famous Renaissance artist Philippe Hayden. Nicolas and Perenelle had appreciated the alchemical subject matter of Hayden's paintings. They'd owned several of his works of art. Unlike me, the Flamels were good at turning lead into gold.

My silver raincoat blew in the wind as I stepped backwards, away from the window, looking for the name of the new gallery. My breath caught when I saw the distressed wooden plank hanging above the entrance. Two chains squeaked as the sign swung gently in the wind. Painted script as thick and black as tar spelled out the purpose of the place: *Logan Magnus Memorial Gallery.*

Logan Magnus. A man who had killed himself two weeks prior in a most distressing way—poisoning himself by swallowing container after container of the toxic paints and binders he used in his artwork. Had he discovered an unknown work of art by Hayden? Or could Logan Magnus have been the one to paint this portrait? I would never be able to ask the artist how he had possessed the only true likeness I'd ever seen of the man I was desperately trying to find.

Buy the book to keep reading!

BOOKS BY GIGI PANDIAN

The Accidental Alchemist Mysteries

The Accidental Alchemist (Book 1)
The Masquerading Magician (Book 2)
The Elusive Elixir (Book 3)
The Alchemist's Illusion (Book 4)
The Lost Gargoyle of Paris (Book 4.5, a novella)
The Alchemist of Fire and Fortune (Book 5)
The Alchemist of Riddle and Ruin (Book 6) - coming in 2022

Jaya Jones Treasure Hunt Mysteries

Artifact (Book 1)
Pirate Vishnu (Book 2)
Quicksand (Book 3)
Michelangelo's Ghost (Book 4)
The Ninja's Illusion (Book 5)
The Glass Thief (Book 6)
The Cambodian Curse & Other Stories (Locked Room Mystery Short Story Collection)

The Secret Staircase Mysteries

Under Lock & Skeleton Key (Book 1)
The Raven Thief (Book 2) - coming in March 2023

ACKNOWLEDGMENTS

The Accidental Alchemist

The following people were instrumental in making this new series come together:

My early critique readers, whose feedback helped me turn this book from a mess with promise into something I'm proud of: Brian Selfon, Nancy Adams, Sue Parman, Emberly Nesbitt, Daryl Wood Gerber, Ramona DeFelice Long, Amber Foxx, and Patricia Winton. My local writer pals, who keep me sane and make this the most fun job in the world: Emberly Nesbitt, Juliet Blackwell, Sophie Littlefield, Rachael Herron, Mysti Berry, Lynn Coddington, Martha White, Lisa Hughey, Adrienne Miller, Jon-David Settell, Michelle Gonzalez, and the Sisters in Crime Northern California Chapter. And my writer pals from afar, who make modern technology worth it! I don't know what I'd do without the Sisters in Crime Guppies, especially my partners in crime Kendel Lynn and Diane Vallere.

My publishing team, who made this book come to fruition: My amazing agent, Jill Marsal, for never settling for "good enough"; Terri Bischoff at Midnight Ink, for believing in this new series and being awesome all around; Nicole Nugent, for stellar editorial feedback; and the rest of the Midnight Ink team for all the work that went into producing this book.

The independent bookstores that have supported me, especially A Great Good Place for Books and Murder By The Book. The city of Portland, Oregon, which gave me the heart of this series, and my Portland writer pals, who've made me feel like I have a second home in Portland. My coworkers, who inspire me daily and send me out into the world ready for anything, especially Catrina Roallos, the best office-mate ever. Victoria Laurie, for writing an amazing set of books I discovered while undergoing chemotherapy; those books gave me hours of enjoyment during a dark time and inspired me to try my hand at writing in this mystery subgenre.

As for my family, there are way too many thanks to list here! The short version: My mother and father, for giving me the world; Leslie Bacon, as true a sister as there ever was; and James, without whom none of this would be possible—or at least it wouldn't be nearly as fun.

And last, but definitely not least, my wonderful readers. All of you have made the last few years more amazing than I ever dreamed.

— January 2015

Huge thanks to my amazing publishing team: At Midnight Ink, my editors Terri Bischoff, Amy Glaser, and Nicole Nugent; publicist Beth Hanson; cover designer Kevin Brown; and cover illustrator Hugh D'Andrade. At the Marsal Lyon Literary Agency, my agent Jill Marsal, who pushed me to turn an amorphous idea into the Accidental Alchemist mysteries.

This book also wouldn't exist without the insights of readers Emberly Nesbit, Nancy Adams, Adrienne Bell, Ramona DeFelice Long, and Susan Parman, or the moral support from my local writers group, the Pens Fatales.

And as always, I count my blessings for James and my parents, who have always believed in me, and who only occasionally grumble about the long hours I spend absorbed in my writing.

— *January 2016*

What would I do without my critique readers? Huge thanks go to the ever-insightful and supportive Emberly Nesbitt, Nancy Adams, Brian Selfon, Stephen Buehler, Juliet Blackwell, Susan Parman, my agent Jill Marsal, and my editorial team at Midnight Ink: Terri Bischoff, Amy Glaser, and Nicole Nugent.

I'd go crazy without the support from the writers in my life. Local pals Emberly Nesbitt, Mysti Berry, Juliet Blackwell, Lisa Hughey, and Michelle Gonzales make sure I make it to the café and keep writing. Sisters in Crime, especially the Guppies, provide endless online support. And Diane Vallere, my kindred spirit on this path, is always there to bounce around ideas.

My parents always told me I could be anything I wanted to be. Without their early encouragement, there's no way I would have conceived of this series. And my amazing husband James encourages my dreams in every way.

— January 2017

Available now from Minotaur Books: *Under Lock & Skeleton Key*, **the first book in the new Secret Staircase Mysteries.**

An impossible crime. A family legacy. The intrigue of hidden rooms and secret staircases.

Multiple award-winning author Gigi Pandian introduces her newest heroine in this heartfelt series debut. *Under Lock & Skeleton Key* layers stunning architecture with mouthwatering food in an ode to classic locked-room mysteries that will leave readers enchanted.

Praise for *Under Lock & Skeleton Key*

"**Wildly entertaining.**" —*The New York Times Book Review*

"An enchanting new series . . . **a must-read.**" —Deanna Raybourn

"Pandian is **this generation's queen of the locked-room mystery!** A whimsical confection." —Naomi Hirahara

"**Excellent... a fresh and magical locked-room mystery** filled with fascinating and likable characters, incredible settings, and Tempest's grandfather's home-cooked Indian meals." —*Library Journal*

"**Pandian is in top form** in this thoroughly enjoyable series launch. . . Lovers of traditional mysteries with quirky characters will be well rewarded." —*Publishers Weekly* (starred review)

"**An absolute sparkling gem of a book!**" —Jenn McKinlay

Learn more about Gigi's next novel, *Under Lock & Skeleton Key*, at www.gigipandian.com. Available now at bookstores everywhere!

ABOUT THE AUTHOR

 Gigi Pandian is a *USA Today* bestselling and award-winning mystery author, breast cancer survivor, and accidental almost-vegan. The child of cultural anthropologists from New Mexico and the southern tip of India, she spent her childhood traveling around the world on their research trips. She now lives in the San Francisco Bay Area with her husband and a gargoyle who watches over the backyard vegetable garden. A cancer diagnosis in her thirties taught her that life's too short to waste a single moment, so she's having fun writing quirky novels and cooking recipes from around the world. Her debut novel, *Artifact*, was awarded the Malice Domestic Grant, and she's won Anthony, Agatha, Lefty, and Derringer awards. Her books include the Accidental Alchemist Mysteries, the Jaya Jones Treasure Hunt Mysteries, and the Secret Staircase Mysteries. Read more and sign up for Gigi's email newsletter at www.gigipandian.com.

BB bookbub.com/profile/gigi-pandian
facebook.com/GigiPandian
instagram.com/GigiPandian

Made in the USA
Las Vegas, NV
07 November 2022

58991664R00420